THE BASTARD KING

THE BASTARD KING

BOOK ONE OF THE SCEPTER OF MERCY

DAN CHERNENKO

A ROC BOOK

ROC
Published by New American Library, a division of
Penguin Putnam Inc., 375 Hudson Street,
New York, New York, 10014, U.S.A.
Penguin Books Ltd, 80 Strand,
London WC2R 0RL, England
Penguin Books Australia Ltd, 250 Camberwell Road,
Camberwell, Victoria 3124, Australia
Penguin Books Canada Ltd, 10 Alcorn Avenue,
Toronto, Ontario, Canada M4V 3B2
Penguin Books (N.Z.) Ltd, Cnr Rosedale and Airborne Roads,
Albany, Auckland 1310, New Zealand

Penguin Books Ltd, Registered Offices:
Harmondsworth, Middlesex, England

First published by Roc, an imprint of New American Library,
a division of Penguin Putnam Inc.

First Printing, March 2003
10 9 8 7 6 5 4 3 2 1

ROC REGISTERED TRADEMARK—MARCA REGISTRADA

LIBRARY OF CONGRESS CATALOGING IN PUBLICATION DATA:
Chernenko, Dan.
The bastard king / Dan Chernenko.
p. cm.—(The scepter of mercy ; bk. 1)
ISBN 0-451-45914-8 (alk. paper)
1. Illegitimate children of royalty—Fiction.   I. Title.   II. Series.
PS3603.H48 B3 2003
813'.6—dc21   2002031531

Printed in the United States of America
Set in Adobe Garamond
Designed by Ginger Legato

PUBLISHER'S NOTE
This is a work of fiction. Names, characters, places, and incidents either are the product of the
author's imagination or are used fictitiously, and any resemblance to actual persons, living or dead,
business establishments, events, or locales is entirely coincidental.

BOOKS ARE AVAILABLE AT QUANTITY DISCOUNTS WHEN USED TO PROMOTE
PRODUCTS OR SERVICES. FOR INFORMATION PLEASE WRITE TO PREMIUM
MARKETING DIVISION, PENGUIN PUTNAM INC., 375 HUDSON STREET, NEW
YORK, NEW YORK 10014.

To Lisa, Joshua, and Christine

THE
BASTARD
KING

PROLOGUE

Once upon a time, a long time ago, the Kingdom of Avornis had two kings at the same time. King Lanius was the son of a king, the grandson of a king, the great-grandson of a king, and so on for a dozen generations. King Grus was the son of Crex the Unbearable. Between them, they brought the Scepter of Mercy back to the city of Avornis in triumph, and did many other deeds of which the bards will sing for ages yet to come. One of them, pretty plainly, was a great king. The other, just as plainly, was not. The only trouble is, it's not always obvious which was which. . . .

CHAPTER ONE

T his tale begins a little less than nine months before King Lanius was born. That was when Certhia, King Mergus' concubine, went to Mergus and told him she thought she was with child.

Mergus, by then, had been King of Avornis for almost thirty years. He was a big, rawboned man with a long white beard and a scar on his cheek above it that proved he'd been a warrior in his younger days. His eyes were a dusty, faded blue—a hopeless blue, you might say, for he had no sons.

Waiting to succeed him was his younger brother, Prince Scolopax. Mergus hated Scolopax. The hatred was mutual. Scolopax waited . . . impatiently.

Hearing Certhia's news, Mergus put his big, knobby-knuckled hands on the concubine's soft shoulders and rumbled, "Are you sure?" The rumble ended in a harsh, wheezing cough—several harsh, wheezing coughs, in fact. Mergus had been coughing more and more the past couple of years. Prince Scolopax might not have to be impatient too much longer.

On the other hand, after this, he might.

Certhia looked up into the king's lean, haggard face. Her eyes were blue, too, the deep, striking sapphire blue for which so many women gave so many wizards so much gold. For her, the color was natural. Mergus thought so, anyway.

"Not yet, Your Majesty," she answered. "In another month, though, I'll know for certain."

"If it's a boy—" Mergus paused to cough again. He had trouble stopping. When he finally did, a tiny fleck of pink-stained spittle rested on his lower lip. He flicked out his tongue and it was gone. He gathered strength. "If it's a boy, Certhia, I'll wed you."

Those sapphire blue eyes widened. "Oh, Your Majesty," Certhia whispered.

"I mean it," Mergus declared. "If it's a boy, he'll be my heir. To be my heir, he has to be legitimate. For him to be legitimate, you have to be my wife."

"But—" Certhia said, and then said no more.

But indeed. Commoners in Avornis were allowed three wives, nobles four, and the king six. Even Olor, king of the gods, had no more than six wives. Mergus had long since gone through his allotted half dozen seeking a son. He'd lost one wife in childbirth, one to a fever. One he'd sent away for barrenness. The remaining three had given him five daughters, two of whom still lived.

"I don't care," he said now. "I'll find a way."

"The priesthood won't like it," Certhia predicted.

Mergus scowled. "The priesthood never likes anything," he said, which wasn't far wrong, either. "But if I have a son, he *will* sit on the Diamond Throne after me. If I can't get a priest to listen to me any other way, I can buy one, or more than one. I can—and I will."

Certhia cast down those blue, blue eyes. "Yes, Your Majesty," she murmured. More than anything else, she wanted Mergus to marry her. To be Queen of Avornis . . . But she was shrewd enough to know that letting him see that would hurt her chances.

Mergus reached out and caressed her breasts through the thin linen of her smock. Instead of stepping forward into his arms, she flinched away. "They're tender?" he demanded.

"Yes," she said. "I'm sorry, Your Majesty."

"Don't be," Mergus told her. "You're pregnant, all right. If it's a boy . . ." He had the face of a man who'd forgotten how to dream but suddenly remembers.

Grus commanded a river galley on the Stura, southernmost of the Nine Rivers cutting across the plain that made up the heart—and the breadbasket—of the Kingdom of Avornis. He was almost thirty—he'd been born in the year Mergus took the Diamond Throne. Slightly above middle height, he was lean and dark-eyed, with a thick black beard he trimmed very close. He'd taken a sword cut on one side of his chin a couple of years earlier, and the hair in the scar, when it began to grow again, grew in silver.

Like the rest of the Nine, the Stura flowed east, out from the foothills of the Bantian Mountains toward the Sea of Azania. The *Tigerfish* fought her way upstream on oar power. An officer with a kettledrum beat out the stroke for the rowers (free men, every one of them, not dead-souled slaves or chained captives who pulled oars for the Banished One).

Grus swigged from a wineskin and wiped his mouth on the sleeve of his linen tunic. He kept a wary eye on the southern bank of the Stura. The river belonged to Avornis; the land beyond it to Prince Ulash—and thus to the Banished One. Ulash's grandfather had once ruled on this side of the Stura, as well; the Prince made no secret of wanting to do the same. But Grus saw only a few thralls laboring in the fields—no signs of trouble.

He turned to his first lieutenant, a leathery veteran named Nicator, and remarked, "The latest truce seems to be holding."

Nicator's teeth were startlingly white against his sun-cured hide when he grinned. "Oh, yes—for now. And it'll keep right on holding for as long as Ulash wants it to, or until the Banished One tells him different. After that? Ha!" He shook his head.

"I know." Grus went on watching the thralls. They went on working without even looking up at the *Tigerfish*. In a very real sense, the river galley wasn't there for them. Grus shivered, though the sun blazed down from a cloudless sky. The thralls' ancestors had been Avornans. They were . . . something else, something less. He shivered again, and took another pull at the wine. "Poor buggers."

"Who? The thralls?" Nicator asked. At Grus' nod, his lieutenant spat into the Stura. "They don't know the difference—or care, either."

"I know," Grus said again. "That makes it worse, not better."

Nicator thought it over. "Well, maybe," he said.

As Grus passed the wineskin to Nicator, the ship's wizard bustled up to him. "Excuse me, Captain—" he began.

"What is it, Turnix?" Grus broke in.

"Seeing shadows that aren't there again, Turnix?" Nicator added scornfully.

The tubby little wizard turned red. "I do my best to keep this vessel safe," he said with dignity.

His "best" had sent sailors scrambling and marines grabbing for their weapons three times in the past two days. He spied danger whether it was there or not. "What is it—what do you think it is—this time?" Grus asked with such patience as he could muster.

"May it please you, sir, it's danger—great danger," Turnix quavered.

Grus laughed in his face. "Oh, yes, fool, danger pleases me. But what pleases me about it is that it'll be no more dangerous than these last three times. For that, I thank Olor and all the other gods."

"All but one," Turnix said, and Grus nodded. No Avornan would thank the Banished One. He was less than a god these days for his banishment, but more dangerous to mere men than all the heavenly hierarchy put together. For, being banished from the heavens, he manifested himself on the suffering earth and meddled directly in the affairs of men.

"Well, what is this danger, then?" Grus asked gruffly. "Have Ulash's men crossed over to the north bank of the river? Have they set some sort of ambush for the *Tigerfish?* Has he put galleys of his own in the Stura?"

"None of those, sir. Worse than those, sir," the wizard answered.

The sailors muttered, some in fear, some in derision. Nicator said, "Fling him over the rail and let him swim home, the useless, shivering son of a yellow dog."

"I know what I know," Turnix declared.

"I know what you know, too," Grus said. "Less than you think you know, that's what you know. And until you know you know less than you think you know, I think you'd better know enough to get out of my sight."

That wasn't easy to do on a river galley, which measured only about eighty feet from ram to dragon, forepost to rudder. Turnix did make himself scarce, though, and that served well enough. "Too bad he doesn't make himself disappear," Nicator muttered darkly.

As the sun sank behind the *Tigerfish,* her anchors splashed into the river at bow and stern. Grus ate hard bread and salty sausage with his men, and washed supper down with wine. He made sure the night watch was strong—the Banished One claimed the darkness as his own. After everything seemed as safe as Grus could make it, he lay down on the deck planking, wrapped himself in a thick wool blanket, and fell asleep.

And he discovered that Turnix wasn't such a bumbler after all. For when Grus fell asleep that night, he dreamt, and when he dreamt, he saw the Banished One face-to-face. He fought to wake up, of course. He fought, and lost, and wished the wizard had been wrong instead of all too right.

"I see you, Grus," the Banished One said. His voice and his face held the same terrifying, unearthly beauty. He was not a thing of this world. He belonged in the heavens—or he had.

Which would be worse, answering him or not? "I see you," Grus heard some inner part of him say.

"You will fail. You will fall," the Banished One told him. Those terrible eyes looked into his soul, and Grus quailed. Men were not meant to be measured so. Vast contempt blazed forth from the Banished One. "And even if you think you triumph, you fail regardless." He laughed. That was harder to bear than the gaze. Grus hadn't thought anything could be.

"Go away," his inner voice croaked. His spirit made a sign he would have used in the flesh.

And he was awake, staring up at the innocent, cheerfully twinkling stars. Except for a few mosquitoes buzzing overhead, everything was calm and peaceful as could be. The sailors on watch strode along the deck, bows in their hands, swords on their belts. But sweat soaked Grus, and he smelled the sour reek of his own fear.

He looked around for Turnix. The wizard lay snoring, not ten feet away. Grus silently begged his pardon. Facing the Banished One was a more deadly danger than any on the river. This time, Turnix had known more than even he'd thought he'd known.

"Come on," Mergus said testily as he led Certhia down a seldom used corridor somewhere in the bowels of the royal palace. Torches burned fitfully in sconces on the wall. The air had a dead, unbreathed feel to it. The king was impatient. "Do you know how hard this was to arrange?"

Certhia was getting impatient, too. "You're the king. You can do whatever you want."

Mergus laughed. "That only proves you've never been a king." His laughter and his words echoed oddly from the rough-hewn stone. The stone might have been unused to having sounds bounce off it.

His guards waited at the top of the stairway. They were probably sniggering and poking one another in the ribs with their elbows. They thought he'd brought his concubine down here so he could make love to her in this strange, uncomfortable, but private place. Mergus had let them think so. Mergus the proud, Mergus the arrogant, submitted to embarrassment— even courted embarrassment—without a murmur, without a whimper.

Certhia giggled. Mergus hadn't told her why he'd brought her down here, either. She drew her own conclusions. Mergus looked around. He wouldn't have chosen this for a trysting ground, but . . .

The witch appeared in the corridor in front of him and Certhia. One instant, she wasn't there; the next, she was. Certhia squeaked in surprise.

The witch ignored her and dropped King Mergus a curtsy. "You summoned me, Your Majesty?"

"Yes." Mergus had summoned *someone,* at any rate. The witch was younger than he, older than Certhia, her brown hair lightly streaked with gray. She had a broken nose that somehow made her look interesting, not homely. By her plain linen smock and long black wool skirt, she wasn't rich. By the silver rings in her ears and on one finger, she wasn't poor, either. Mergus asked, "What do I call you?"

"Rissa will do," she answered. "It may be my name, it may not. But it will do."

His answering nod was quick and harsh. "All right, Rissa. You know what I want of you?"

"Would I be here if I didn't?" Without more ado, Rissa turned to the king's concubine. "Take off your smock, dear. I need to feel of you."

Certhia squeaked again, this time in outrage. *"What?"*

"Do it," the king said, the iron clang of command in his voice no less than if he'd been ordering soldiers into battle against the Thervings.

She bridled. She was no soldier, and the iron clang of command only put her back up. "What for?" she demanded.

Mergus visibly started to say *Because I told you to.* A moment later, he visibly thought better of it. "Because I'm going to find out if you're carrying a boy," he replied after that tiny pause.

"Any court wizard could tell you," Certhia said.

"No court wizard could keep his mouth shut afterward," the king said. "Rissa here will. Rissa here had better, anyhow. Now come on. We haven't got all day down in this miserable hole."

Certhia started to argue more. Then *she* thought better of it. With a sigh that said she was still unhappy—and that she expected King Mergus to know it—she pulled her smock off over her head.

A heavy gold chain supporting an amulet hung in the shadowed valley between her breasts. They were larger and sagged a bit more than they had before she conceived.

Rissa paid no attention. She set her hands lower, on Certhia's belly. The king's concubine hadn't shown her pregnancy for long. Clothed, she hardly showed it even now. But the witch nodded as soon as she touched Certhia's flesh. "Yes," she breathed.

"Yes, what?" King Mergus' voice was hard and urgent.

"Yes, it will be a boy," Rissa answered matter-of-factly. Then, the palms of her hands still on Certhia, she stiffened. When she spoke again, she sounded nothing like herself. "I hate him. I shall punish him. Though he have a son, let him be impotent. Let his hope die before him. Let all laugh at what he has become. As I have ordained, so let it be." The brass of a slightly sour trumpet rang in her words.

Certhia gasped in terror. "That is the Banished One, cursing your son!" Her hand flashed to the amulet she wore. In danger, she forgot she was naked from the waist up. "King Olor, protect him! Queen Quelea, protect *me!*"

Mergus' fingers twisted in a protective gesture every Avornan learned by the age of three. He murmured prayers, too. After his heart's first frightened lurch steadied, he also murmured defiance. "He'll not have him!" Now his hands folded into fists. "He'll *not!*" He'd been without an heir of his flesh too long. He would have defied worse than the Banished One to keep that heir . . . he would have, *were* there worse than the Banished One.

Rissa's hands fell away from Certhia. The witch blinked a couple of times, as though coming back to herself. She did not seem to remember what she'd said—what had been said through her—or Certhia and Mergus' replies. Only when she saw their faces did she ask, "Is something wrong?"

Words tumbled from the king and his concubine. The witch stared from one of them to the other, horror filling her face. Her fingers writhed in the same gesture as Mergus had used.

"I am unclean," she gasped when she could speak at all. "I am violated!" She pressed both hands against her crotch, as though the Banished One had used her body, not her mind. A moment later, Certhia put on her smock again. But she let the amulet hang outside the crimson silk now, where she could quickly seize it at need.

Mergus asked, "Can the taint be taken away?"

"I know not," the witch told him. "I shall speak to those set over me." The king's hand fell to the hilt of his sword. It was no ceremonial weapon, but a blade that had seen much use in war. Rissa's eyes followed the motion. She nodded. "If you doubt I will abide by their verdict, Your Majesty, strike now."

A couple of inches of the blade came out of the jeweled scabbard. But then Mergus shook his head. "No. I believe you. You will do what needs doing. Can you go to them by the way you came here?"

Rissa nodded again. "I can. I will. And I will say one last thing to you, if you give me leave."

"Go on." King Mergus' voice was rough as sandstone.

"Hear me, then: If the Banished One hates your son, if he curses your son, surely he also fears him."

Back and forth along the Stura, from the last cataract in the foothills of the mountains to the Sea of Azania and then upstream once more. This was the life the *Tigerfish* and the rest of the Avornan river galleys led when on patrol.

Grus had duly written up his dream of the Banished One and submitted it as part of his report to his superiors. For a while, he wondered if he would be summoned to the city of Avornis and questioned further. When no summons came, he began to wonder if it had been only a meaningless dream.

But part of him knew better.

Not many men, even aboard the *Tigerfish*, knew what had chanced that night. Grus had never been one to make much of himself or of what happened to him. He had told Turnix, though; he wanted the strongest protective amulets the wizard could make. And he'd told Nicator. If anything happened to him, his lieutenant needed to know why it might have happened.

They were drinking in a riverside tavern one day—on the north bank of the Stura, of course; the south was not for the likes of them—when Nicator asked, "You never heard a word about that, did you?"

Grus shook his head. "Sometimes you wonder if anybody back in the city of Avornis remembers how to read."

"Wouldn't surprise me if nobody did," Nicator agreed. "Wouldn't surprise me one bloody bit." He slammed his fist down on the tabletop for emphasis. He'd taken a lot of wine on board.

So had Grus, come to that. He said, "What do they care about the border? The king's going to have a baby—or maybe he's had it by now. That's *important,* if you live in the capital."

"I didn't know the king *could* have a baby. They must do things different in the big city," Nicator said. They both laughed, which proved they were drunk. He went on, "I don't care who's king. Our job stays the same any which way."

"Of course it does," Grus said. "We take care of what's real so they can worry about shadows back there."

Next morning, when the *Tigerfish* raised sail and glided on down toward the sea, his own headache seemed the realest thing in the world. He sipped at the rough red wine the river galley carried, trying to ease his pain. Nicator also looked wan. Grus tried to remember what they'd been talking about in the tavern. They'd been complaining about the way the world worked; he knew that much. But what else would you do in a tavern?

Turnix came up to him. Sweat poured down the wizard's chubby cheeks. This far south, summer was a special torment for a round man. "A quiet cruise we've had," Turnix remarked.

"Yes." Grus wished the wizard would keep quiet.

No such luck. Turnix went on, "Somehow, I don't think it'll stay that way." His eyes were on the southern shore; the shore that didn't belong to Avornis, the shore the Banished One claimed for his own.

"No," Grus said. Maybe, if he kept answering in monosyllables, Turnix would take the hint and go away.

But Turnix had never been good at taking hints. He said, "Something's stirring."

That got Grus' attention, however much he wished it wouldn't have. Like a miser coughing up a copper penny, he spent yet another syllable. "Where?"

"I don't know," the fat little wizard admitted. "I wish I did. So much that's closed to me would be open if only I were a little more than I am." He sighed and looked very sad. "Such is life."

Grus didn't answer that at all. He stood there letting the breeze blow through him. And then, of course, he too looked to the south.

Oh, trouble *might* come from any direction. He knew that. The Thervings dreamt of putting a king of their own in the city of Avornis. They always had. They always would. Maybe the Banished One worked through them, too. Maybe they would have been nuisances just as great if he'd never been banished. Grus wouldn't have been surprised.

And off in the north, the Chernagors plotted among themselves and with Avornis and against Avornis. Some of them wanted Avornan lands. Some of them wanted their neighbors' lands. Some of them, from some of the things Grus had heard, plotted for the sake of plotting, plotted for the sport of plotting.

So, yes, trouble might come from anywhere. But the south was the direction to look first. The Banished One was there. The principalities of the Menteshe who followed him were there. And, of course, the *Tigerfish* was there, too. Just their luck.

"What *do* you know?" Grus asked Turnix.

"Something's stirring," Turnix repeated helplessly.

"If I were foolish enough to put my faith in wizards, you'd teach me not to," Grus growled. He never could tell what would offend Turnix. That did the job. The wizard strode away, his little bump of a nose in the air.

But however vague he was, he wasn't wrong today. Trouble found the *Tigerfish* that very afternoon. It came out of the south, too. Had Grus wanted to, he could have patted himself on the back for expecting that much.

He didn't. He was too busy worrying.

When trouble came, it didn't look like much: A lone thrall ran up to the southern bank of the Stura and shouted out to the river galley, crying, "Help me! Save me!" The thrall didn't look like trouble. He looked like any thrall—or, for that matter, like the Avornan peasant his ancestors had surely been. His hair and beard were long and dirty. He wore a linen shirt and baggy wool breeches and boots that were out at the toes.

No matter how he looked, he was trouble. In lands where the Banished One ruled, most thralls—almost all thralls—forgot Avornis, forgot everything but getting in the crops for their Menteshe masters and for the One who was the master of the Menteshe. When the Kingdom of Avornis pushed back the nomads, her wizards sometimes needed years to lift the magic from everyone in a reconquered district. But every so often, a thrall would come awake and try to escape. Every so often, too, the Banished One would pretend to let a thrall come awake, and would use him for eyes and ears in Avornis. Much harm had come to the kingdom before the Avornans realized that.

"Help me!" the thrall called to the *Tigerfish*. "Save me!"

Nicator looked at Grus. "What do we do, Captain?"

Grus didn't hesitate. He wasn't sure he was right, but he didn't hesitate. "Lower the sail," he commanded. "Drop the anchors. Send out the boat. But remember—not a man is to set foot on the southern bank of the river. We aren't at war, and we don't want to give the Menteshe an excuse for starting one when we're not ready."

"What if the thrall can't get out to the boat?" Nicator asked. Grus shrugged. He intended to play the game by the rules. Nicator nodded.

"Help me! Save me!" the thrall cried. The boat glided toward him. Peering south past him, Grus spied a cloud of dust that meant horses—horses approaching fast. The Menteshe had realized a thrall was slipping from their power—or they were making a spy seem convincing.

Which? Grus didn't know. *Let me get the fellow aboard my ship, and then I'll worry about it,* he thought.

As the boat drew near him, the thrall waved for the sailors to come closer still. When they wouldn't, he threw up his hands in what looked like despair. Grus' suspicions flared. But then, as the horsemen galloped toward the riverbank, the fellow splashed out into the Stura. The sailors hauled him into the boat and rowed back toward the *Tigerfish* as fast as they could go.

The nomads reined in. Pointing toward the boat, they shouted something in their harsh, guttural language. When the boat didn't stop, they strung their bows and started shooting. Arrows splashed into the river around it. One slammed home and stood thrilling in the stern. And one struck a rower, who dropped his oar with a howl of pain. Another man took his place.

"That thrall had better be worth it," Nicator remarked.

"I know," Grus said. By then, the boat had almost reached the *Tigerfish*. The arrows of the Menteshe began to fall short. The nomads shook their fists at the river galley and rode away.

Turnix, who was a healer of sorts, bound up the wounded sailor's arm. It didn't look too bad. Grus eyed the thrall, who stood on the pitching deck with a lifelong landlubber's uncertainty and awkwardness. The fellow stared as Grus came up to him. "How do you move so smooth?" he asked.

"I manage," Grus answered. "What are you?"

"My name is—"

Grus shook his head. "Not *Who* are you. *What* are you? Are you a trap for me? Are you a trap for Avornis? If you are, I'll cut your throat and throw you over the side."

"I do not understand," the thrall said. "Something died in me. A deadness died in me. When I came alive"—he tapped his head with a forefinger—"I knew I had to get away. Everyone else in the village was dead like that, even my woman. I had to run. How could I be the only one who heard himself thinking?"

He said the right things. A thrall who somehow came out from under the Banished One's spells would have sounded the way he did. But so would a spy.

"Turnix!" Grus yelled. The wizard hurried up to him, still scrubbing the wounded sailor's blood from his hands. Grus pointed to the thrall. "Find out if the Banished One still lurks in his heart."

"I'll try, Captain." Turnix sounded doubtful. "I'll do my best, but magic is his by nature, mine only by art."

And you haven't got enough art, either, Grus thought, but he kept quiet. Turnix pointed at the thrall as though his finger were a weapon. He chanted. He made passes, some sharp, some slow and subtle. He muttered to himself and gnawed his lower lip. At last, he turned to Grus. "As far as I can tell, he is what he claims to be, what he seems to be."

"As far as you can tell," Grus repeated. Turnix nodded. Grus sighed. "All right. I hadn't planned to put in at Anxa, but I will now. They have a strong fortress there, and several strong wizards. I'll put him in their hands. If they find he's clean, they'll make much of him. If they don't . . ." He shrugged.

"You think I still have—that—inside me," the thrall said accusingly.

"You may. Or you may not. For Avornis' sake, I have to be as sure as I can," Grus replied. Even letting the fellow see Anxa was a certain small risk. No, Avornis wasn't at war with the Menteshe, not now—but she was not at peace, either. With the Banished One loose in the world, there was no true peace.

Mergus felt helpless. He'd never had to get used to the feeling, as ordinary men did. But not even the King of Avornis could do anything while his concubine lay groaning in the birthing chamber and he had to wait outside.

How long have I been out here? he wondered, and shook his head. A steward came in with a silver carafe and cup on a golden tray. "Some wine, Your Majesty?"

"Yes!" Mergus exclaimed. The man poured the cup full and handed it to him. As he raised it to his lips, Certhia cried out again. Mergus' hand jumped. Some of the wine slopped out of the cup and onto the polished marble floor. The king cursed softly. He didn't want to show how worried he was. Rissa had said Certhia would bear a boy. She hadn't said that the baby would live—or that his concubine would.

The steward tried on a smile. "Call the spilled wine an offering, Your Majesty."

"I'd sooner call you an idiot," Mergus growled. "Get out—but leave that pitcher." The servant fled.

By the time the birthing-chamber door opened, the king was well on the way to getting drunk. He glowered at the midwife. "Well, Livia?"

"Very well, Your Majesty," she answered briskly. Her wrinkles and the soft, sagging flesh under her chin said she was almost as old as Mergus, but her hair, piled high in curls, defied time by remaining black, surely with the help of a bottle. "I congratulate you. You have a son. A little on the small side, a little on the scrawny side, but he'll do."

"A son," King Mergus breathed. He'd wanted to say those words ever since he became a man. When he was young, he'd never dreamt he would have to wait so long. When he got older and hope faded, as hope has a way of doing, he'd almost stopped dreaming he would be able to say them at all. That only made them sweeter now.

He looked into the carafe. It was empty. His cup was about half full. He thrust it at Livia. "Here. Drink."

She would not take it, but shook her head. Those piled curls never stirred. Tapping her foot impatiently, she said, "Won't you ask after your lady?"

"Oh." Mergus had never had to get used to feeling embarrassed, either. "How is she?"

"Well enough," the midwife said. She paused, tasting her words, and seemed to find them good, for she repeated them. "Yes, well enough. She did well, especially for a first birth. If the fever holds off"—her fingers twisted in a protective gesture—"she should do fine."

Mergus offered her the wine again. This time, she took it. He asked, "Can I see the boy—and Certhia?"

"Go ahead," Livia told him. "I don't know how glad she'll be to see you, but go ahead. Remember, she's been through a lot. No matter how well things go, it's never easy for a woman."

Mergus hardly heard her. He strode past her and into the birthing chamber. The room smelled of sweat and dung and, faintly, of blood—a smell not so far removed from that of the battlefield. Certhia had managed to prop herself up against the back of her couch. She held the newborn baby to her breast. The stab of jealousy Mergus felt at seeing the baby sucking there astonished him.

Certhia managed a wan smile that turned into a yawn. "Here he is, Your Majesty. Ten fingers, ten toes, a prick—a big prick, for such a little thing."

The king had already seen that for himself. It made him as absurdly proud as he'd been jealous a moment before. "Good," he said. "Give him to me, will you?"

Awkwardly, Certhia pulled the baby free. His face screwed up. He began to cry. His high, thin wail echoed from the walls of the birthing chamber. Certhia held him out to Mergus.

"A son," the king murmured. "At last, after all these years, a son." He held his newborn heir much more easily than Certhia had. He'd never had a son before, no, but he'd had plenty of practice with daughters. Putting the baby up on his shoulder, he patted it on the back.

"That's too hard. You'll hurt him," Certhia said.

"I know what I'm doing," Mergus told her. And he proved it—a moment later, the baby rewarded him with a surprisingly loud belch. The baby stopped crying then, as though he'd surprised himself.

"We'll call him—"

"Lanius," King Mergus broke in. He wanted to say the name before anyone else could, even his concubine. "Prince Lanius. King Lanius, when his time comes." The prince—the king to come—had, at the moment, an oddly shaped head much too big for his body, and an unfocused stare. Mergus' daughters had outgrown such things. He knew Lanius would, too.

Livia the midwife stuck her head into the chamber. "There's a priest here," she said.

"Good," Mergus said. "Tell him to come in." As the man in the green robe did, Certhia squeaked and tried to set her robe to rights. Ignoring that, King Mergus nodded to the priest. "Get with it, Hallow Perdix. I need a proper queen."

CHAPTER TWO

Captain Grus was drinking wine in a riverside tavern in the town of Cumanus when the news got to him. The fellow who brought it to the tavern stood in the doorway and bawled it out at the top of his lungs. The place—it was called the Nixie—had been noisy and friendly, with rivermen and merchants chattering; with a dice game in one corner; with about every other man trying to get one of the barmaids to go upstairs with him. But silence slammed down like a blow from a morningstar.

Nicator broke it. "He *married* her? He took a seventh wife? Go peddle it somewhere else, pal. Nobody'd do anything like that. It's against nature, is what it is."

All over the Nixie, heads solemnly bobbed up and down, Grus' among them. The very idea of a seventh wife was absurd. (His own wife, Estrilda, would have found the very idea of a second wife for him absurd—but that was a different story, and a different sort of story, too, since it had nothing to do with the gods—but if Olor had only six wives . . .

The news bringer held out both hands before him, palms up, as though taking an oath. "May the Banished One make me into a thrall if I lie," he said, and the silence he got this time was of a different sort. Nobody, especially here on the border, would say such a thing lightly. Into that silence, he went on, "He *did* marry her, I tell you. Said he wanted to make sure his heir—Lanius, the brat's name is—wasn't a bastard. Hallow Perdix said the words over him and his concubine—I mean, over Queen Certhia."

"How'd he find a priest who'd say such filthy words?" somebody asked belligerently.

"How? I'll tell you how," answered the man in the doorway. "The priest who married them was Hallow Perdix. Now he's High Hallow Perdix. He was no fool, not him. He knew which side his bread was buttered on."

"That's terrible!" two or three people said at once. Whether it was terrible or not, Grus was convinced it was true. The man with the news had too many details at his fingertips for it to be something he was making up.

"What does the arch-hallow have to say about the whole business?" he asked.

"Good question!" the news bringer said. "Nobody knows the answer yet, I don't think. If he says Prince Lanius is a bastard, he's a bastard, all right, and he isn't a prince, not anymore."

"If he says that, I know what King Mergus says: 'Out!' " Nicator jerked a thumb at the door, as though dismissing a rowdy drunk.

"*Can* the king sack the arch-hallow?" Grus asked.

"*I* don't know," Nicator said. "*Can* the arch-hallow tell the king the son he's waited for his whole life long is nothing but a little bastard who'll never, ever, plop his backside down on the Diamond Throne?"

That was another good question. Grus had no idea what sort of answer it had. He was sure of one thing, though—Avornis would find out. No, he was suddenly sure of two things. He wished he weren't, and gulped his wine cup dry to try to chase the second thing from his head.

No such luck. Nicator knew that had to mean something, and asked, "What is it, Skipper?"

"I'll tell you what," Grus answered. "I can almost hear the Banished One laughing from here, that's what." He held up his cup to show the nearest barmaid it was empty, then proceeded to get very drunk.

King Mergus strode through the royal palace in the city of Avornis in the center of a bubble of silence. Whenever servants or courtiers or soldiers saw him coming, they jerked apart from one another, bowed with all the respect they were supposed to show, and stayed frozen as statues till he'd passed. Then they started up again, talking behind his back.

He'd tried catching them at it a couple of times. He could, but the sport soon palled. They didn't even have the grace to look embarrassed.

The real trouble began a few days after Hallow Perdix made the king's concubine queen. Mergus came up a corridor at the same instant that his brother, Prince Scolopax, started down it from the other end.

They both stopped for half a heartbeat when they saw each other, and then both kept walking. Mergus braced himself, as though heading into battle—and so he was.

For close to thirty years, Mergus had ruled Avornis. For close to thirty years, his younger brother had been a spare wheel—and a mistrusted spare wheel, at that. With nothing useful to do, Scolopax had thrown himself into drink and dissipation. These days, he looked ten years older than the king.

With a grim nod, Mergus started to walk past Scolopax. "You bastard," his brother said, breathing wine fumes into his face. "You and your bastard."

A couple of servants had been walking along the passageway, too. They froze and turned back toward the king and his brother, staring as they might have stared after the first warning rumble of an avalanche. King Mergus hardly noticed them. If his look could have killed, Scolopax would have lain dead on the floor. "Call me what you choose—" Mergus began.

Prince Scolopax glared back with loathing all the greater for being, unlike Mergus', impotent. "If I did, your bones would catch fire inside your stinking carcass."

Mergus went on as though his brother hadn't spoken: "—but Lanius is my legitimate son and heir, being the child of my lawfully wedded wife."

Scolopax's scornful snort sounded as though he were breaking wind. "Throw seven and you'll win at dice. At marriage?" He made that rude, rude noise again. "How much did you pay Perdix the pimp, besides promotion?"

"He won promotion on his merits, and I paid him not a copper halfpenny." Mergus lied without hesitation.

Scolopax's laugh was more a howl of pain. He shook a long, bony finger under the king's nose. "All right. All right, gods curse you. Olor has six, but you think you're entitled to more. But I tell you this, my *dear* brother." A viper could have given the word no more venom. Shaking his finger again, Scolopax went on, "I tell you this: Whether you have that bastard or not, I know who's going to rule Avornis when you're stinking in your grave. Me, that's who!" He jabbed his thumb at his own chest.

"Do you hear that sound?" King Mergus cupped a hand behind his ear. Scolopax frowned. But for their two angry voices, the corridor was silent.

Mergus answered his own question anyhow. "That's the Banished One, licking his chops."

The prince went death pale. "You dare," he whispered. "You dare, when the Banished One whispered in your ear, telling you to wed your whore in spite of all that's right and prop—"

He ducked then, just in time. Mergus' right fist whistled past his ear. But Mergus' left caught him in the belly and doubled him up. Scolopax hit the king in the face. The two old men—the two brothers—stood toe to toe, hammering away at each other with every bit of strength that was in them.

Their quarrel had drawn more servants to the corridor. "Your Majesty!" cried some of those men, while others said, "Your Highness!" They all rushed toward the king and the prince and got between them so they couldn't reach each other anymore.

"I'll have your head for this!" Mergus shouted at Scolopax.

"It's better than the one you've got now!" Scolopax shouted back.

And Mergus knew his threat was idle, empty. However much he wanted to be rid of his brother forever, he knew he couldn't kill him, not unless Scolopax did something far worse than giving him a black eye (he'd bloodied his brother's nose, he saw with no small satisfaction). He didn't have many years left himself. With Scolopax gone and his son a child, who would rule Avornis after him? A regency council—and the only thing Mergus feared more was the Banished One in all his awful majesty. If there was a better recipe for paralyzing the kingdom than a squabbling regency council, no one had found it yet.

Scolopax dabbed blood from his upper lip with a silken kerchief. "You maniac," he panted. "If you had the Scepter of Mercy, you'd bash people's brains in with it."

"If I had the Scepter of Mercy—" Mergus stood there panting, trying to get enough air. He scowled at Scolopax, feeling all the bruises his brother had given him. He tried again. "If I had it—" That was no good, either; he had to stop for a second time. "Get out of my sight," he said thickly, rage almost choking him.

He was closer to taking his brother's head for that remark than for all the bruises he'd had from the prince. And Scolopax had to know as much, too. He shook himself free of servants and courtiers and left Mergus without another word.

"Your Majesty—" one of the servants began.

"Go away," Mergus said. "Leave me." One advantage of being king was that, when he said such things, people obeyed him. The corridor emptied as though by magic.

But that proved less helpful than Mergus had hoped. It left him alone with his thoughts—and with his brother's final mocking words.

If I had the Scepter of Mercy . . . His shoulders slumped. He sighed. No King of Avornis had looked on, let alone held, the great talisman for four hundred years. It had been on procession in the south, to hearten the people against the Banished One and against the fierce Menteshe who did his bidding (and who, then, were newly come to the borders of Avornis), when a band of nomads, riding faster than the wind, swooped down on its guardsmen and raped it away. These days, it stayed in Yozgat, the capital of the strongest Menteshe principality.

The Banished One couldn't do anything with the Scepter. If he could have, he surely would have by now. And if ever the Banished One found the power to wield it, he wouldn't merely storm the city of Avornis. He would storm back into the heavens themselves. So the priests said, and King Mergus knew no reason to disbelieve them.

But even if the Banished One couldn't hold the Scepter in his fist, he kept the kings of Avornis from using it for the good of the kingdom. Mergus thought his distant predecessors had taken its power for granted. People often did, when they'd had something marvelous for a long time.

I wouldn't. If the Scepter of Mercy came to me, I'd do right by it. He laughed a sad and bitter laugh. Surely every king of Avornis for the past four centuries had had that same thought. And how much good had it done any of them? Exactly none, as Mergus knew all too well.

"Fire beacon!" Turnix called. The wizard pointed to a hilltop north of the Stura atop which, sure enough, a big bonfire had flared into life.

"I see it," Grus answered. "The Menteshe are loose, gods curse them."

Nicator also peered toward the north. "Now—let's see exactly where-abouts and how bad it is."

Three more, smaller, signal fires sprang to life to the west of the first one. "That way—a medium-sized raid," Grus said. Five would have meant a major invasion—a war. Grus pointed west. "We'll see what the next beacon tells us." He set a hand on Nicator's shoulder. "Pass out weapons to the rowers. Who knows what sort of fighting we'll be doing?"

"Right you are, Skipper," Nicator answered, and saw to it.

Propelled by sails and oars, the *Tigerfish* sped down the river toward the trouble. The next flaring fire beacon still urged it toward the west. "We're on the way to Anxa," Grus murmured, disquieted.

"And so?" his lieutenant said. Then, perhaps a moment slower than he should have, he caught on. "Oh. That thrall we handed over to the wizards there. Don't you think they should have figured out whether he was dangerous or not?"

"Yes, I think they should have," Grus told him. "Trouble is, I don't know whether they *did*."

"Well, even if they didn't, how much trouble could one thrall cause?" Nicator asked.

"I don't know that, either. I hope nobody's finding out."

He watched anxiously for the smoke rising from the next beacon, which stood on a hill north of the riverside town. The smoke didn't always predict what the fires themselves would say, but he'd gotten good at gauging it. Even before he saw the flames showing that trouble lay due north hereabouts, the way the smoke rose made him think they would tell him that. He also spied smoke rising from places that did not hold fire beacons. The Menteshe burned for the sport of it.

Just before he came in to the town of Anxa (which, thanks to its wall, remained in Avornan hands), a young officer on horseback waved to him from the northern bank of the Stura. The sun glinted off the fellow's chain-mail shirt and conical helm. "Ahoy, the river galley!" he shouted.

Grus waved back to show he'd heard. "What can I do for you, Lieutenant?" he yelled back—the plumes of the officer's crest were dyed blue.

"We'll be driving the wild men back this way before long," the young officer answered. "Driving 'em out of Avornis is one thing. Making sure they don't do this again . . . that's something else, something a lot better."

"I like the way he thinks," Nicator said in a voice too low for the lieutenant to hear.

"So do I." Grus nodded, then cupped his hands to his mouth once more to shout over to the riverbank. "We'll do our best, Lieutenant. What's your name?"

"Hirundo. Who're you?"

"I'm Grus," Grus answered, adding, "Now we both know where to lay the blame if things go wrong."

Hirundo laughed. "Here's hoping we don't have to," he said. "Stay there, if you can. I'll do my best to push the Menteshe your way." Before Grus could reply, Hirundo wheeled his horse and rode away from the river, up toward the fighting.

"Think he can do it?" Nicator asked.

"You never can tell. A million things might go wrong," Grus said. "He might get an arrow in his face half an hour from now. But if he doesn't, I think he's got a pretty fair chance."

Nicator nodded. "I was thinking the same thing. Hirundo, eh? He's still wet behind the ears, but that might be a name worth remembering."

"Let's see how he does. That'll tell us more," Grus said. His lieutenant nodded again.

Before they found out what to make of the lieutenant, two more river galleys came rowing up the Stura toward the *Tigerfish*. Since Grus was on the scene first, they followed his lead. He spaced them out along the river to wait for the Menteshe, too. "How long are we going to wait?" one of their captains called.

"As long as we have to," Grus answered, which probably didn't make the other officer very happy. He had no better answer to give the fellow, though, for Hirundo had given him none.

They ended up dealing with their first Menteshe before Hirundo could have done anything at all about them. This little band of nomads had had enough looting and raping and killing in Avornis to satisfy them. They were ready to cross back over the Stura into their own country. They expected no trouble. Why should they have expected any? They'd had none coming into Avornis.

Grus saw them before they spotted the river galleys. He ordered the *Tigerfish* to pull back, in fact, so they'd be less likely to spot her. To his relief, the other captains did the same. The Menteshe and their horses boarded the rafts the nomads had hidden among riverside rushes and reeds and started paddling across the Stura.

"Forward!" Grus shouted when those rafts were well out into the stream. Forward the *Tigerfish* went, and the other galleys, too. How the Menteshe howled! They'd had it all their own way on land. They'd done just as they pleased. No more.

The *Tigerfish*'s ram smashed up three rafts in quick succession. Menteshe and horses splashed into the water. Avornan sailors plied the nomads with arrows. The rest of the river galleys treated the other rafts just as rudely. Grus didn't think any Menteshe in that band made it to the far side of the river.

But the real herding of the nomads began the next afternoon. Avornan soldiers began pushing them back toward the Stura. By then, too, more than three galleys had arrived to dispute their passage. Now, with plenty of sailors on hand, Grus and his fellow captains handled things differently. The Menteshe couldn't get past their ships, which cruised close to the shore so their archers could hit the nomads on land. The Menteshe couldn't gallop out of range, either, for Avornan cavalry kept pushing more of them toward the riverbank.

Maybe they called on the Banished One to come to their aid. If they did, he failed to hearken to them. Caught between the hammer of the Avornan cavalry and the anvil of the river galleys, they were crushed. Not many got away.

When the fighting ebbed, Hirundo rode down to the riverbank and waved to Grus. "Good job!" he called.

"Same to you," Grus replied. "They didn't buy anything cheap on this raid."

"No, indeed." Hirundo sketched a salute. "I'd work with you again anytime, Captain."

Grus returned that salute. "And I with you, Lieutenant—and I'm afraid the Menteshe will give us the chance, too." He realized he hadn't had the chance to find out whether the escaped thrall he'd brought to Anxa had had anything to do with this raid. *Well, it's not that you weren't busy,* he told himself. *And even if he did, we hurt the Menteshe more than they hurt us.*

This time.

Lanius' first memory was of humiliation. He couldn't have been more than three years old. He and his mother and father, all splendidly robed, left the palace in a gilded carriage to go to the great cathedral.

He hadn't been out of the palace very often. Riding in the carriage was a treat. He squealed with glee as the wheels bounced over cobblestones. "Whee!" he shouted. "Fun!"

He sat between his mother and father. They smiled at each other above his head. "I wish I thought this was fun," his father said.

"Why don't you, Papa?" Lanius asked in surprise. He couldn't imagine anything more delightful. Another jounce made him whoop again.

"My back," his father said.

His mother's smile faded. "It's the cobbles," she said quickly. "Shall I tell the driver to slow down?"

"No, don't bother," his father answered. He coughed wetly. "It's not the road. It's . . . my back. I'm not a young man anymore."

His father had a white beard. Lanius had never thought anything about it. He didn't now, either. His father was simply his father, as much a fixture of the world as his favorite blanket or the sunshine that came through his window in the morning.

The carriage stopped. A soldier opened the door. His mother got down. "Come on, Lanius," she said. He slithered across the velvet. She caught him, swung him up in the air, and set him down on the bumpy stones of the street.

"Do it again, Mama!"

"Maybe later. We have to go to the cathedral first." His mother peered into the carriage, from which his father hadn't yet emerged. "Are you all right, dear?"

"I'm coming." His father sounded angry. Lanius knew the tone, and shrank from it. But his mother hadn't done anything to make King Mergus angry. Lanius didn't think he had, either. What did that leave? Could his father be angry at himself? Grunting a little, the king finally descended.

"Are you all right?" Lanius' mother asked again.

"I'll do," his father said testily. "It's just . . . my back. And my gods-cursed cough. Come on. Let's find out what Arch-Hallow Bucco does this time."

Lanius' mother steered him forward, her hand on his shoulder. He took a couple of steps. Then, all at once, the grandiose immensity of the cathedral ahead filled his sight, and he stopped and stared and stared and stared. Every single line leaped to the sky—pointed windows; tall, narrow arches; buttresses that seemed to fly; and spires, the highest of all crowned by a silver statue of Olor.

His mother let him gape for a moment or two, then urged him on again. That was when he noticed the man in the red silk robe standing in the gateway, backed by several others in robes of the same cut but of saffron yellow silk. The man in red carried a staff topped by a little silver statue just like the big one on the highest spire. Lanius liked that.

The man held the staff in front of him, across his body, now. "You may not pass, Your Majesty," he said—everybody but Lanius and his mother called his father that. "You know you may not pass. We have done this before. Neither you, nor your concubine, nor your bastard."

"Have a care, Bucco," Lanius' father growled. He was angry now; Lanius was sure of it. "If you insult my wife and my heir, I'll make you sorry for it."

"You have gone against the gods themselves," the arch-hallow said. "Where Olor contents himself with six, you have taken a seventh. It is sin. It is wickedness. It shall not stand. I have told you this each year when you brought the boy and the woman here." Behind him, the men in the yellow robes solemnly nodded.

"One of your priests thought different," King Mergus said. "He knew what would happen to Avornis without a proper successor to the throne.

You'd know it, too, if you'd think a little." He coughed once more, and turned as red as Arch-Hallow Bucco's robe.

"No." Bucco sounded very certain. "Where you break a rule for the sake of convenience, there the Banished One shows his face." The priests in saffron silk nodded again, all in unison.

"They're funny, Father!" Lanius exclaimed.

"They're fools, Son," his father answered. "But, whether they're fools or not, this time we *are* going to worship here." He started forward, pushing Lanius and his mother along with him.

Clang! Iron gates slammed shut, pushed to by more priests, these in blue robes. *Thud!* A bar slammed into place to make sure they stayed shut. From behind them, Bucco called, "You may not enter. The cathedral is closed to you. Begone, in the name of the gods!"

"Begone!" the other priests chorused, which made Lanius laugh.

His mother was not laughing. "They dare," she said.

"Fools dare all sorts of things," his father said grimly. He wasn't red anymore. He was white—with fury, or with pain? "It's what makes them fools."

Chain mail clanking, one of his guardsmen strode up to the king. "Your Majesty, we'd need about two companies' worth of men to storm the gates," he said. "Half an hour's work, no more."

King Mergus shook his head. "No. We'll go back to the palace. Let Arch-Hallow Bucco think he's won—for now. This time, though, he will pay."

Lanius started to cry when his father steered him back toward the carriage. "I want to go in there!" He pointed to the cathedral. "It's pretty in there!"

"They won't let us go in there," his mother told him. That made him cry harder than ever. He was used to getting what he wanted.

"Be quiet, Son," his father said, and his tone was such that Lanius *was* quiet. The king went on, "Bucco has had his day. He's truly a fool if he thinks I won't have mine." Lanius didn't understand that. He didn't understand anything except that they had to go back to the palace. It didn't seem fair at all.

Three days later, a palace servant bowed low to King Mergus. "Someone here to see you, Your Majesty."

"Ah?" Mergus' shaggy eyebrows rose. "Someone I'm expecting?" The servant nodded. Mergus' grin showed teeth yellow but still sharp. "Well, send him in, send him in."

In came Arch-Hallow Bucco, escorted—none too politely—by several palace guards. He did not wear his red silk robes now, only an ordinary shirt and pair of breeches. He looked more like a retired schoolmaster, say, than a man who dared thunder at kings. He also looked frightened, which was nothing less than Mergus had expected.

"Will you speak to me of bastards now, Bucco?" the king demanded.

One of the guards prodded the arch-hallow. Before speaking at all, Bucco bowed very low. "What—what is the meaning of this, Your Majesty?" he quavered.

"I am going to explain something to you, something that has to do with which of us is stronger in the kingdom," Mergus answered. "When you shut the gates in my face, you thought you were. I am here to tell you, you are wrong."

Arch-Hallow Bucco gathered himself, looking sternly at Mergus. "I did what I did because I had to do it, Your Majesty, not from hatred of you. I have told you that before, when you tried to flaunt your sin. If I did otherwise, I would not be worthy of the rank I hold."

"I take a different view," King Mergus said. "I say that, because you did what you did, you are not worthy of the rank you hold. And, as I am king, what I say in these matters carries weight. As of now, this instant, Bucco, you are no longer Arch-Hallow of Avornis."

"What will you do with me?" Bucco knew fear again, but did his best not to show it.

"For your insolence, I ought to take your head," Mergus said, and the newly deposed arch-hallow quailed. "I ought to," the king repeated, "but I won't. Instead, I'll send you to the Maze, where you can pray for wisdom. You'll have plenty of leisure to do it in, that's certain, and company, too, for a good—no, a bad—dozen of your followers will go with you."

Bucco looked hardly more happy than if King Mergus had ordered his immediate beheading. Not far to the west of the city of Avornis, several of the Nine Rivers came together and split apart in a bewildering group of marshes and islands—the Maze. No one knew all the secrets of navigating there, and those secrets changed from year to year, from day to day, sometimes from hour to hour. Kings of Avornis had stashed inconvenient people on insignificant islands there for hundreds of years. Few thus disposed of ever came back.

"And who do you think will make a better arch-hallow than I do?" Bucco asked.

"Almost anyone," Mergus said brutally. "The man I am naming to the post, if that's what you mean, is Grand Hallow Megadyptes."

Now Bucco stared. "He would accept it? From you? He is a very holy man."

"Yes, he is." King Mergus smiled a nasty smile. "He actually believes in peace among us, which is more than you can say. For the sake of peace, he *will* become arch-hallow."

"You may send away those who condemn your sin, Your Majesty, but you cannot send away the sin itself," Bucco said. "It remains here in the palace. It will not be forgotten. Neither will what you do to me today."

King Mergus yawned in his face. "That's what you think. I told you, I take a different view. And when the king takes a different view, the king is right." He nodded to the guardsmen who'd brought Bucco into his presence. "Be off with him. Let him lie in the bed he's made."

Without giving Bucco a chance for the last word, the guards hauled him away.

Captain Grus had a pleasant home in one of the better—although not one of the best—parts of the city of Avornis. His home would have been even more pleasant, in his view, if he saw it more often. His river-galley cruises sometimes kept him away for months at a time.

He happened to be at home, however, when Mergus cast down Bucco and raised Megadyptes in his place. His father brought the news back to the house from the tavern where he spent his afternoons soaking up wine, rolling dice, and telling lies with other retired soldiers. Crex was a big man, stooped and white-bearded, with enormous hands—far and away the largest Grus had ever seen on any man. Grus never knew why his father was called Crex the Unbearable; everyone but Crex who knew was dead, and his father was not the sort to encourage such questions.

"Aye, he sacked him," Crex said in the peasant accents of the central plains from which he'd come. "Threw him out on his ear, like he was a servant who dropped a soup bowl once too often."

"There will be trouble," Grus predicted.

"There's always trouble," Estrilda said. His wife was a couple of years younger than he. She had light brown hair and green eyes. At the moment, she looked tired. Their son, Ortalis, was four, and playing with a toy cart in the garden, while their two-year-old daughter, Sosia, slept on Estrilda's lap. With them to look after, she'd earned the right to be tired. She went on, "There's been trouble ever since the king married Queen Certhia. That's hard to stomach."

"He wants a proper heir," Crex said. "He wants a better heir than Scolopax, and how can you blame him?"

"Shhh, Father," Grus said. Crex *would* speak his mind, and he wouldn't keep quiet while he did it. Estrilda said the servants were trustworthy, but that wasn't something you wanted to find out you were wrong about the hard way.

"I can blame him for a seventh wife," Estrilda said now. "It's not natural. And plenty of people will say he got rid of Bucco to keep the archhallow from telling him the truth about that."

"Megadyptes is a holy man," Crex said. "He's a holier man than Bucco ever dreamt of being, matter of fact."

"Well, so he is," Estrilda admitted. She suddenly raised her voice: "Ortalis! Don't throw rocks at the cat!"

"I didn't, Mama," Ortalis said, revising history more than a little.

"You'd better not," his mother told him, rolling her eyes. She looked back to Crex. "You're right. Megadyptes is holy. I don't understand how he can stomach any of this."

"It's simple," Crex said. "He knows Avornis needs a proper king once Mergus is gone, that's how."

With some amusement, Grus listened to his wife and his father going back and forth. Because he was away from the city of Avornis so much, he didn't bother keeping track of which priests here were holy men and which weren't. But Estrilda and Crex hashed them over endlessly.

"Ortalis!" Crex yelled. "Your mother told you not to do that. D'you want your backside heated up?"

"No, Grandpa." When Ortalis said that, he was, no doubt, telling the truth.

"Hasn't Bucco been dickering with the Thervings?" Grus said. "What's King Dagipert going to do when he has to talk to somebody else?"

"If he doesn't like it, Mergus can give him a good kick in the ribs, too," Crex said.

"It's not that simple," Grus said. When it came to the Thervings, he knew what he was talking about. "The way things are nowadays, Dagipert's about as likely to give us a kick in the ribs as the other way round. And he wants to give us one, too."

"He spent some time here in the city of Avornis when he was a youth, didn't he?" Estrilda asked.

Crex nodded. "That's right. Mergus' father thought it would make him admire us too much to want to bother us. We were stronger in those days, too, and Thervingia weaker. *Ortalis!*"

"He admires us, all right—just enough to want what we've got," Grus said. "And you never can quite tell. Is that his greed . . . or is the Banished One looking out through his eyes, too?" They all made a sign against the coming of evil, but Grus wondered how much good it would do.

Something was wrong in the palace. Lanius was only five, but he knew that. People bustled back and forth, all of them with worried looks on their faces. No one had any time for him. He noticed that, most of all. He had been everyone's darling. He'd gotten used to being everyone's darling, too, and he'd liked it. Now nobody paid any attention to him. He might as well not have been there.

"Mama—" he said one day.

But not even his mother had any time for him. "Not now," Certhia said, impatience and anger in her voice.

He tried again. "But, Mama—"

"Not now!" his mother said again, and swatted him on the bottom. He burst into tears. She didn't pat him and comfort him, the way she usually did. She just went off and left him to cry till he stopped.

And he couldn't see his father. They wouldn't let him. All sorts of strange people got to see his father—priests and wizards and men wearing green gowns, like the fellow who took his pulse and looked at his teeth and gave him nasty potions when he didn't feel good. But Lanius couldn't.

"It's not fair!" he wailed. That didn't get him what he wanted, either. Nothing did. Nothing could.

Once, his father's chamber lit up as bright as noon in the middle of the night. Loud voices spoke from the ceiling, or so it seemed to Lanius, whose own room was nearby. The light and the voices woke him up. They didn't frighten him—they sounded like nice voices—but they did annoy him, because he wanted to sleep. Before long, though, the chamber went dark and the voices fell silent.

Lanius' mother and a man walked down the corridor in front of his room. "Nothing more to do, if *that* failed," the man said. Lanius' mother began to weep, quietly and without hope. "I'm sorry, Your Highness," the man told her, "but it's only a matter of time now."

Two days later, everybody in the royal palace began to weep and wail. Nobody would tell Lanius why, which made him start crying, too. No one even bothered to wipe his nose for him. Wet, slimy snot dribbled down his chin.

And then Uncle Scolopax strode into his room. Lanius didn't like

Scolopax. He never had. Scolopax didn't like him, either, and hardly bothered hiding it. He didn't hide it now. "Shut up, you little bastard," he snarled. "Your old man's dead, so *I'm* the king now. You're too young, no one will support you. And if I'm the king, you'd best believe you *are* a bastard."

CHAPTER THREE

"Wine!" King Scolopax shouted. Servants rushed to obey. When the wine cup was in his hands, Scolopax threw back his head and roared laughter. It echoed from the ceiling of the throne room. He gulped down the wine, then thrust the cup at the closest servant. A moment later, it was full again. Scolopax drank it dry once more.

He'd never imagined life could be so sweet. It wasn't that he hadn't drunk before. It wasn't that he hadn't *been* drunk before. As the younger brother of the king—as the despised, distrusted younger brother of the king—what else did he have to do? But now what he did wasn't what a despised, distrusted younger brother did. Now what he did was what the king did. And that made all the difference in the world.

"Avornis is mine!" he chortled. "Mine, I tell you!"

If he'd ever said anything like that before, the servants would have made sure Mergus knew about it. Scolopax was in many ways a fool, but he knew what his brother would have done to him. That had been especially true after Lanius was born. If the brat hadn't been on the sickly side, Mergus might have done it anyway. Scolopax had therefore never even let himself think such thoughts, for fear they would come out when he was drunk. Now he didn't have to run away from them. He didn't have to hide them. He could come right out and say them. And they were true.

All the servants in the throne room bowed very low. "Yes, Your Majesty," they chorused. Scolopax laughed again. Only a couple of weeks before, they'd hardly bothered hiding their scorn for him. These days, they had to be hoping he'd been too sodden to remember. Oh, life was sweet!

He sat on the Diamond Throne, drinking, looking out across the chamber at the heart of the palace. It seemed bigger, grander, even brighter from here than it had before. He hated Mergus all the more for holding him away from this delight for so long.

Presently, one of Mergus' ministers—Scolopax, in his cheerful drunkenness, couldn't be bothered recalling the man's name—approached the throne and bowed even lower than the servants had. "Your Majesty, how shall we deal with the Thervings?" he asked.

"Give 'em a good swift kick in the ass and send 'em to bed without supper," Scolopax answered—the first words that popped into his head. He laughed again, loudly and raucously. So did the nearby servants.

Mergus' minister—*my minister now,* Scolopax thought—did not laugh. He said, "King Dagipert will be looking to see what kind of example you set, Your Majesty. So will all the princes of the Menteshe, down in the south." He lowered his voice. "And so will the Banished One, behind them."

Scolopax didn't want to think about the Banished One. He didn't want to think about anything except being *King* Scolopax. "So will the Chernagors, on their islands in the Northern Sea, and the barbarians beyond the mountains," he said.

Mergus' minister looked pleased. "That's true, Your Majesty. They will. Everyone will. What sort of example *do* you intend to set?"

"Wine!" King Scolopax shouted. "Some for me, some for him." He pointed to the minister.

"No, thank you, Your Majesty," the fellow said. "The healers forbid it. My liver . . ."

"You won't drink with me?" Scolopax said ominously. "I ask no man twice. I need ask no man twice. You are dismissed. Get out of my sight. Get out of the palace. Get out of the city of Avornis."

With immense dignity, Mergus' minister bowed before departing. Scolopax wondered for a moment with whom he should replace him. Then he shrugged and laughed. The fellow was plainly useless. Why bother replacing him at all?

"And speaking of useless . . ." The new king snapped his fingers. The palace servants all looked attentive and eager. Scolopax laughed again. So this was the world Mergus had known for so long, was it? No wonder he'd kept it all to himself. It was too fine to share. The king pointed to the closest servant. "You! Fetch me Certhia, miscalled the queen. Hop to it, now."

"Yes, Your Majesty," the man said, and off he went. King Scolopax marveled. No insolence, no back talk, no delay. Ah, to be the king!

In due course, Certhia entered the throne room. Still in mourning for dead Mergus, she wore black, but her gown was of glistening silk, and worth a not so small fortune. *Sour-faced bitch,* Scolopax thought as she curtsied. And when she murmured "Your Majesty," she might have been saying, *You swine.*

But she was only Lanius' mother. Scolopax was—king. "Your marriage to my brother will not stand," he said.

"Hallow Perdix wed us," Certhia answered. "Arch-Hallow Megadyptes has declared the marriage fitting and proper."

"*This* for Arch-Hallow Megadyptes." Scolopax snapped his fingers. "And *this* for that pimp of a Perdix." He made a much cruder gesture.

Certhia's eyes widened. "May I be excused, Your Majesty?"

"You are not excused. You are dismissed, just like what's-his-name was," King Scolopax declared. "Get out of the palace. At once. If you show your nose around here again, I'll make you sorry for it."

"But—my son," Certhia said.

"*I* shall tend to my nephew, that little bastard." Scolopax turned to the wonderfully pliant servants. "Throw her out. Don't let her come back. Do it right this minute."

"Yes, Your Majesty," they chorused, and they did it. Watching them obey was almost more fun than drinking wine. Almost.

Scolopax pointed to yet another servant—he seemed to have an unending supply of them. "You! Go tell the so-called Arch-Hallow Megadyptes he is to come before me at once. And you!"—this to another man—"Draft a letter for delivery to the Maze, summoning that wise, holy, and pious fellow, Arch-Hallow Bucco, back here to the capital as fast as he can get here. Go!" They both bowed. They both went.

Megadyptes was gaunt and frail, a man with more strength of character than strength of body. When he came before Scolopax, the palpable aura of holiness that shone from him gave the king pause. Bowing, he said, "How may I serve Your Majesty?"—and not even Scolopax could find the faintest hint of reproach in his voice.

But that didn't matter. Scolopax knew what he knew. "You made my brother's marriage legitimate. You made his brat legitimate."

"Why, so I did, Your Majesty," Megadyptes agreed, showing the king nothing but calm. "King Mergus had, till then, no heir but you. The gods gave him no son till the autumn of his years. They have given you no son at all, I am sorry to say."

He *did* sound sorry. That didn't keep King Scolopax's wrath from rising, though the arch-hallow had spoken nothing but truth. Scolopax's wife was a sour harridan named Gavia. But she could have been the sweetest woman in the world, and it wouldn't have mattered much. Scolopax had married her because his father made him marry her. He'd always spent more time with his favorites among the guardsmen than with Gavia or any other woman. His current favorites were two stalwart mercenaries from the Therving country, Waccho and Aistulf.

"You never mind me," Scolopax growled. "You mind the gods." That wasn't quite what he'd meant to say. At least, it wasn't quite how he'd meant to say it. But he was the king. He didn't have to take anything back. He didn't have to, and he didn't.

Megadyptes looked at him with sorrowful eyes. "I do mind the gods, as best I can," he said. "And I mind the kingdom, as best I can. I did what I did for Avornis' sake."

"Avornis is mine!" Scolopax shouted.

"For now, Your Majesty," Arch-Hallow Megadyptes said calmly. "For now."

"Mine!" Scolopax yelled again, even louder than before—loud enough to bring those echoes from the ceiling. But even that wasn't enough for him. He sprang down from the throne, seized Megadyptes' long white beard with both hands, and yanked with all his strength. The Arch-Hallow of Avornis let out a piteous wail of pain. Scolopax yanked again. "You are deposed!" he cried. "Get out, you wretch, before I give you worse!"

Tufts of Megadyptes' beard, like bits of wool, fluttered out from between the king's fingers and down to the floor. The arch-hallow's cheeks and chin began to bleed. "I will pray for you, Your Majesty," he said.

Courtiers and servants looked this way and that—every way but at King Scolopax. The king was too furious to notice, or to care. *"Get out!"* he screamed. Megadyptes bowed once more, and departed. An enormous silence settled over the throne room once he had gone.

Later that day, Aistulf told Scolopax, "Don't worry about it, Your Majesty. You did the right thing. Whatever you want to do, it is the right thing." The guardsman was tall and blond and muscular and handsome, with a bristling mustache and a chin shaved naked. Scolopax found that most exciting.

"Of course I did," the king answered. "How could I do anything else?"

And when Scolopax slept that night, he saw in his dreams a supremely handsome face studying him. The face was splendid enough to make even Aistulf (even Waccho, who was handsomer still) seem insipid—but cold, cold. Scolopax stirred and muttered. Something in those eyes . . . Then the watcher murmured, "Well done," and smiled. That should have made the king feel better. Somehow, it only made things worse.

Lanius recited the alphabet perfectly. His tutor beamed. "That's very fine," the man said. "Now, can you write it for me, too?"

"Of course I can." Lanius hardly bothered hiding his scorn.

"*Can* you?" The tutor was brand new in the palace. He'd spent the last several years trying to educate the sons of the nobility, most of whom were as resistant to learning as a cesspit cleaner's children were to disease. To find a pupil not only willing but eager felt like something close to a miracle. He pulled pen and ink and parchment from his wallet. "Show me."

"I will." And Lanius did. As soon as he took hold of the pen, the tutor knew he told the truth. His letters staggered and limped as much as any five-year-old's, but they were all properly shaped. "There!"

"That's . . . very good indeed," the tutor said.

No one had praised Lanius since his father died and his mother went away. It went straight to his head, as wine would have in a grown man. "I can do more than that," he said. "I can write words, too."

"Oh, you can, can you?" Again, the tutor had trouble believing him. He was a solemn child, small for his age, with eyes as big in his face as a kitten's. When he nodded, he showed disconcerting wisdom. The tutor said, "Well, why don't you let me see that, too?"

I want my mother to come back to the palace. I miss her, Lanius wrote. Again, the letters were of a child. The thought behind them was simple, but how many children his age could have put it forth so accurately? Not many, and the tutor knew it full well.

"You really can write!" he exclaimed. "That's wonderful!"

Again, Lanius blossomed with the praise. But then he looked at the tutor once more with those eyes wise beyond his years. "If I already know these things," he asked, "why do I need *you?*"

The tutor coughed. However arrogant the question, he thought he'd better give it a serious answer. "Well, for one thing, you know a lot—an amazing lot—but I still know more."

Lanius wasn't at all sure he believed that. He asked, "What else?"

Now the tutor laughed. "For another, Your Highness, if I go away, who will tell you how clever you are?"

"You're right," Lanius said at once. "You must stay." The tutor had praised him. If he could get praise for being clever, he would show the man he was very clever indeed. "Teach me!"

"I . . . will." No one had ever spoken to the tutor with such urgency. "What would you like to learn?"

"Anything. Everything! Teach me. I'll learn it. Where do we start?"

Lanius seemed desperate, like a drowning man grabbing for a spar. The tutor could no more help responding to such eagerness to learn than he could have helped responding to a pretty girl's different eagerness in bed. "Your Highness," he said, "I'll do everything I can for you."

"Just teach me," Lanius told him.

Grus was glad to get out of the city of Avornis. He wished he could have gotten his family out of the capital, too. He didn't like the way people were choosing between Arch-Hallow Bucco and former arch-hallow Megadyptes. That also meant they were choosing sides about whether Lanius was a bastard or King Mergus' legitimate son—and so the likely heir and possible rival to King Scolapox. No matter how it ended, it would be messy.

Thanks to his victories over the Menteshe, Grus had been promoted to commodore—a captain commanding a whole flotilla. Nicator, his lieutenant aboard the *Tigerfish* in days gone by, now commanded Grus' flagship. "That last one will take care of itself," Nicator told him when he grumbled as the flotilla stopped in the town of Veteres one evening.

"How?" Grus asked. "Either you're for one of 'em or the other. You can't very well be for both, and nobody's about to change sides."

"I know, I know," Nicator said patiently. "But Megadyptes is such a holy old geezer, he's got to fall over dead one day soon. Then everybody will be for Bucco, on account of what choice will they have?"

"The people who follow Megadyptes will make a party, that's what. They'll say Scolopax never should have thrown him out, the way people were saying Mergus never should have thrown Bucco out. They'll riot—you wait and see if they don't."

"And Scolopax'll turn soldiers loose on 'em, and that'll be the end of that." Nicator saw the world in very simple terms.

"Well . . . maybe." Grus didn't think things were so simple, but he didn't feel like arguing with his friend, either. He set a silver groat on the tavern table in front of him and rose to his feet. "Come on. Let's get back to the ships."

"Right," Nicator said. "I'm with you."

Veteres lay on the upper reaches of the Tuola River, heading up toward the foothills of the Bantian Mountains. River galleys couldn't go much farther west. Some of the hill country beyond the Tuola belonged to Avornis. As in the south, the kingdom had once held more land. Over the past few years, though, King Dagipert and the Thervings ruled what had been western provinces of Avornis.

A couple of Thervings led a string of hill ponies through the streets of Veteres toward the market square. They were big, broad-shouldered men, bigger than most Avornans. They wore their fair hair down to their shoulders, but shaved their chins. Grus thought that looked silly. Foreigners had all kinds of odd notions. There was nothing silly about the sword on one Therving's hip, though, or about the battle-ax the other one carried. Grus kept his mouth shut. Avornis and Thervingia weren't at war—now.

Nicator muttered, "Miserable bastards." But he made sure the Thervings didn't hear him.

Down by the riverside, three or four more Thervings strode along the bank from one pier to the next. Their eyes were on Grus' flotilla, so much so that they didn't even notice Nicator and him coming up behind them. Pleasantly, Grus asked, "Help you with something?"

The big men jumped. One of them spoke in slow, accented Avornan. "We are just—how you say?—taking the air. Yes." He nodded. "Taking the air."

"That's nice," Commodore Grus said, still pleasantly. "Why don't you take it somewhere else?"

He didn't put his hand anywhere near his own sword. The Thervings could have given him and Nicator a hard time before more Avornans came to help. They didn't. They went and took the air somewhere else. "Spies," Nicator said.

"What else would you expect?" Grus said blandly.

Nicator pointed to a warehouse roof pole that stuck out from the building for some little distance. "We ought to hang them right there," he said.

"Why?" Grus asked.

Nicator stared at him. "Olor's throne, man!" he said. "We hang them *because* they're spies."

"But they're very bad spies," Grus said. "If we do hang them, King Dagipert will only send more, and the new ones may know what they're doing."

After chewing on that for close to a minute, Nicator finally decided to laugh. He said, "You're a funny fellow, Skipper."

Now it was Grus' turn to be puzzled. "But I wasn't joking," he said.

With another man, or another pair of men, that might have started an argument, even a fight. Grus and Nicator ended up laughing about it. They got along even when they disagreed.

No bridges spanned the Tuola. A long time ago, when Avornis was stronger, there had been some. After the Thervings came, the Avornans wrecked them—why make invasion easier? The Thervings found it easy enough even without bridges. It was still the custom, though, for Therving embassies to come down to the Tuola where the ruined end of a bridge still projected six or eight feet into the water. In the old days, embassies had crossed by that bridge. The custom had outlived the span.

A flag of truce flew above the embassy. Grus studied the Thervings from the deck of his river galley—an ambassador with a gold chain of office around his neck, a wizard, half a dozen guards. An Avornan embassy would have included a secretary, too, but not many Thervings knew how to write.

"Who are you? What do you want? Why do you come into Avornis?" Grus called. As the highest-ranking Avornan present, he asked the formal questions.

"I am Zangrulf," the ambassador answered in good Avornan. "I come from King Dagipert, the mighty, the terrible, to King Scolopax to talk about renewing the tribute Avornis pays to Thervingia."

Grus sighed. Most of him wished his kingdom didn't pay tribute to the Thervings, even if it was cheaper than fighting. But, from what he'd heard and seen of Scolopax, he didn't like the idea of his going to war against a sly old fox like Dagipert. "I will send a boat," he said. "Then I will take you to Veteres, and you can go to the city of Avornis on the royal highway."

Zangrulf and the wizard put their heads together. The ambassador waved out to the river galley. "I agree. Make it so."

He had no business giving Grus orders, but Grus kept quiet. Thervings always acted as though they owned the world. The boat went to the riverbank. It wasn't a big boat, and needed two trips to bring the whole embassy back to the galley. Zangrulf's wizard came in the second trip.

Except for two rings in the shape of snakes—one silver, one gold—he wore on his little fingers, he looked like any other Therving: big, fair, long-haired, smooth-chinned. But his eyes—clever eyes—narrowed when he looked at Grus. Then he looked a little longer, and those clever eyes went wide. He spoke in Thervingian to Zangrulf.

The ambassador looked at Grus, too. He said, "Aldo says you are a great man."

"Tell him thank you," Grus answered, smiling. "Except for my wife, he's the only one who seems to think so."

He also evidently followed Avornan, though he chose not to use it with Zangrulf. King Dagipert's envoy spoke for him once more. "He also says you will be an even greater man, if you live."

"Does he?" Grus wondered exactly what that was supposed to mean. "Well, I'm likelier to be a greater man if I live than if I don't."

Zangrulf chuckled. Aldo didn't. Again, he spoke in Thervingian. Again, the ambassador translated. "He says yes, that is true. But he also says there are men, and more than men, who will not want you to live. He says, beware."

Grus started to answer that with another joke. The words stuck in his throat. It had been years since the Banished One appeared in his dreams, but he'd never forgotten—however much he wished he could.

Prince Lanius bowed to his tutor as a peasant might have bowed to the King of Avornis. "Please!" the prince said. "I'll work twice as hard tomorrow if you let me see the Thervings today!"

He'd had to learn flattery. Some of his lessons said that people flattered princes, not the other way round. Maybe that was true for other princes. It wasn't true for Lanius.

His tutor didn't answer right away. The man plucked at his beard, thinking things over. At last, he said, "Let me ask His Majesty's chamberlains. It's not really up to me. It's up to the king."

Hope died in Lanius. "He won't let me. He never lets me do anything I want. He won't even let me see my mama." He'd just lost his first tooth. His tongue kept exploring the hole where it had been. Once there, now gone. Having Queen Certhia banished from the palace left the same sort of hole in his life. He would grow a new tooth. How could he grow a new mother?

"Let me ask," the tutor said again. "You *are* King Scolopax's heir, after all." That meant little to Lanius. From everything he'd seen, it also meant little to Scolopax. But when the tutor came back, he was smiling. "It's all arranged. You can do it. You have to put on your fancy robe and your coronet, but you can do it."

"Oh, thank you!" Lanius cried. The robe, heavy with gold thread, made his skinny shoulders sag and hurt from its weight. The coronet was too small for him, and most uncomfortable. He didn't care. Getting something he really wanted didn't happen very often. He intended to enjoy it as much as he could.

He had a place not far from the throne, across the aisle from Arch-

Hallow Bucco. Even that couldn't ruin his day, although the arch-hallow kept glaring at him as though he had no right to exist.

King Scolopax sat impassive on the sparkling Diamond Throne. His robes, of cloth-of-gold, put Lanius' to shame. His golden crown, set with rubies and sapphires and emeralds, was far heavier than Lanius' coronet. His expression might have been regal calm. On the other hand, he might have been slightly sozzled.

But then Lanius forgot all about his uncle, the king. Here came the Thervings. Their ambassador wore a fur jacket, leather trousers, and boots that clomped on the marble throne-room floor. Avornan soldiers in gilded chain-mail shirts surrounded him and his companions. Lanius wished they would go away. They made it hard for him to see the Thervings.

A herald bawled out the ambassador's name—Zangrulf. He bowed very low to King Scolopax. The other Thervings, the ones who served the ambassador, bowed lower still. Lanius wanted to imitate them. Only the thought that he would probably get a spanking if he did made him hold still.

"Avornis has paid tribute to Thervingia for many years," the ambassador said in fluent if accented Avornan. "The last treaty for the tribute is going to expire. King Dagipert expects you to renew it at the same rate."

Behind Lanius, his tutor, dressed in a robe so fine it was surely borrowed, let out a soft hiss of anger. "He bargains over kingdoms the way an old woman in the vegetable market bargains over beets."

Lanius hardly heard him. He was watching his uncle, up there on the Diamond Throne. Scolopax looked every inch a king. He sat hardly moving, staring down at the Therving ambassador like a god looking down on creatures some other, clumsier, deity had made. When Zangrulf finished, Scolopax deigned to speak one word: "No."

At that one word, whispers almost too soft to hear raced through the throne room. Lanius felt the surprise and excitement, though he didn't know what they meant. Zangrulf spelled that out for him like his tutor spelling out a new, hard word. "If you refuse, Your Majesty, King Dagipert will be within his rights to go to war against you, to go to war against Avornis."

Those whispers raced through the throne room again. This time, they had a little more weight to them. This time, too, that one word was loud even in the quiet. *War.*

"No," King Scolopax repeated. "That's what I said, and that's what I meant. You can tell it to your precious king, or to anyone else you please."

"Think twice, Your Majesty," Zangrulf said. "Think three times. King Dagipert is fierce, and dangerous to anger. The armies of Thervingia are brave, and ready for battle. King Mergus did not refuse us. He—"

Lanius could have told the Therving that mentioning his father was not the way to get his uncle to go in a direction he wanted. He could have told that to Zangrulf, but he never got the chance. King Scolopax did it for him. When Scolopax said "No!" this time, he shouted the word out at the top of his lungs. Then he pointed to the door. "Get out!" he yelled. "Get out, and be happy you still keep your head on your shoulders. *Get out!*"

As though the embassy had gone just the way he'd hoped, Zangrulf bowed again. So did his retainers. They turned and trooped out of the throne room. The Avornan guards surrounded them, as they had before. Lanius wanted to clap his hands. All through his life, he would love a parade.

"He did what?" Commodore Grus said when news of the fiasco in the throne room got to Veteres.

"He turned down Dagipert's ambassador," said the man with the news. "Turned him down flat, by the gods."

Grus gulped his wine. "Now what? Is it war with the Thervings?"

"It had better not be war," Nicator exclaimed. "If it is, how do we fight it? We haven't got enough soldiers, and we haven't got enough river galleys, either."

"You know that," Grus said. "I know that. Why doesn't King Scolopax know that?"

"Beats me." Nicator drained his mug and waved to the barmaid for another. "He's king, after all. He's supposed to know things like that. He's supposed to know everything that's going on in Avornis."

"I should say so," Grus exclaimed. "I know everything that's going on in my flotilla—that's my job. The whole kingdom is his job."

"There's a certain kind of captain who doesn't think that way," Nicator said. "You know the kind I mean. He'll say 'Do this. Do that. Do the other thing,' but he won't bother to find out if you've got the men or the gear or the money or the time to carry out his orders. That's not his worry—it's yours. But then *you* get the blame if what he says turns out to be impossible."

Grus nodded. "Oh, yes. I know officers like that. I run them out of my service just as fast as I can."

"I know you do, skipper," Captain Nicator said. "A lot of buggers like that, though—they're nobles, and they're not so easy to get rid of."

"Don't remind me," Grus said. He'd come as far as he had because he'd proved he was good at what he did. Nobles who'd gotten their posts because of who their grandfathers were had to obey his orders. That didn't keep them from looking down their noses at him.

The barmaid came over to the table with a pitcher of wine. She filled Nicator's mug. Grus shoved his across the table toward her. She poured it full, too.

"Thank you, sweetheart," Nicator said, and patted her on the bottom.

She drew back. "You can buy the wine," she said, "and I'll be glad to see your silver. But you can cursed well keep your hands to yourself. *That's* not for sale. If I could line up all the bastards who make filthy jokes about barmaids so I could swing a sword once and take off all their empty heads, I'd do it." She stomped away.

"Whew!" Nicator said, and took a long pull at his mug. "She had steam coming out of her ears, didn't she?"

"Just a little," Grus answered. "I think I'm going to keep my mouth shut for about the next ten years." He'd been known to make jokes about barmaids. He'd been known to do more than joke. He had a bastard boy down in Anxa. Every quarter, he sent gold to the boy's mother. Estrilda knew about that. She'd given him her detailed opinion of it when she found out, but she'd eventually forgiven him. Grus shook his head. That wasn't true. She hadn't forgiven him, but she had decided to stop beating him over the head.

Three days passed before Zangrulf the Therving arrived on his return journey to King Dagipert. Escorting his party was an Avornan officer named Corvus, a fellow whose gilded armor, fancy horse, and supercilious expression said he had more land and more money than he knew what to do with. "Take these nasty fellows over the river," he told Grus, an aristocratic sneer in his voice. "We're well rid of them, believe me."

Zangrulf wasn't supposed to hear that, but he did. He looked down his nose at Corvus. "We'll be back one day soon," he said. "See how you like us then."

The Avornan nobleman turned red. "I'm not afraid of you," he said. "I'm not afraid of anything."

"Stupid twit," Captain Nicator said in a low voice. Grus nodded.

Aldo the wizard came up to Zangrulf and muttered something in the

Thervings' tongue. Zangrulf laughed out loud. Pointing at Corvus, he said, "He tells me you'll get just what you deserve."

"Oh, he does, does he?" Corvus' hand fell to the hilt of his sword. "Tell him to keep his stinking mouth shut, or I'll give him just what he deserves."

"I'll take you and your men across the river," Grus said to Zangrulf, before a war broke out on the spot. King Dagipert's ambassador nodded. All the way back to the ruined bridge, though, Aldo kept looking first at Grus, then back toward Corvus. He kept laughing, too.

King Scolopax celebrated his third year on the throne with a party that lasted for eight days. He hated Mergus more than ever, for depriving him of this pleasure for so long. He'd spent too much of his life doing what Mergus told him to do. Now he was king, and everyone—everyone!—had to do as *he* said.

In fact, only one thing still troubled him a little. "I wish I had a proper heir, an heir of my own body," he complained to Aistulf one day. "That horrid wart Lanius gives me the shivers. His pointed little nose is always in one book or another, *and* he's Mergus', not mine."

"An heir of your own body?" the king's favorite murmured. "Well, there is a way to arrange that, you know, or at least to try."

Stroking him, Scolopax shook his head. "Not for me, or so it seems. I do try every now and again—by the gods, every wench in the palace throws herself at me these days—but I don't rise to the occasion."

"Too bad, Your Majesty," Aistulf said. "Women can be fun, too."

"I've got you, and I've got Waccho," King Scolopax said. "If I had any more fun, I'd fall over." Aistulf laughed. These days, everyone laughed when Scolopax made a joke. The king went on, "Besides, that wart won't put his scrawny little backside on the throne till after I'm dead, and I don't expect I'll care about it then."

"That's so," Aistulf agreed. Everyone agreed with Scolopax these days. He liked that, too.

He said, "Shall we go out to the meadow and knock the ball around?" He was an avid polo player. Considering his years and thick belly, he was a pretty good one, too.

"Whatever you like, Your Majesty," Aistulf said. Polo wasn't high on his list, or on Waccho's. But keeping Scolopax happy was.

"Yes," the king said—happily. "Whatever I like."

Before long, he was galloping across the meadow, wild as a Menteshe nomad. The cavalrymen who rode with him and his favorites played hard.

Scolopax couldn't be bothered with running Avornis—the Thervings had been ravaging the west for a year now, and he had yet to send much of a force against them; that was what he had generals for, after all—but polo was different. Polo was important. No one who thought otherwise got to play with the king twice.

His horse thundered past his last opponent. He swung his mallet with the power of a man half his age. The mallet caught the ball exactly as he'd wanted. He couldn't have aimed it any better if he'd rolled it into the net. "Goal!" he shouted joyously, and threw his arms up in triumph.

"Well shot, Your Majesty," said the defender he'd beaten.

"A perfect shot, Your Majesty," said Aistulf, who didn't want anyone but himself—and perhaps Waccho—flattering the king.

And then, quite without his bidding it, Scolopax's mallet slipped from his fingers and fell to the trampled meadow. He swayed in the saddle. He tried to bring up his right hand to rub at his forehead, but it didn't want to obey him. He used his left instead. He swayed again, and almost fell.

"Are you all right, Your Majesty?" Aistulf asked.

"I have a terrific headache," Scolopax answered. His whole right side seemed numb—no, not numb, but as though he had no right side at all. He couldn't keep his balance. Slowly, he slid off the horse. He gazed up at the sky in mild surprise, the smell of dirt and grass in his nostrils.

"Your Majesty!" Aistulf shouted, and then, "Quick! Go fetch a healer!"

Scolopax heard someone galloping away. He hardly noticed, for he saw, or thought he saw, a face full of cold, cold beauty staring down at him. "Too bad," the Banished One said. "Oh, too bad. And I had such hopes for you." Scolopax tried to answer, but couldn't. Though it was noontime, the sky grew dark. Very, very soon, it grew black.

CHAPTER FOUR

Lanius jumped into the air, as high as he could. "Mama!" he cried, and ran to her. He hadn't seen her since his father died. In the life of a child, three years are an age. He'd sometimes wondered if he would even recognize her. But he did. Oh, he did!

"Darling!" Queen Certhia squeezed the breath out of him. "You've gotten so big and tall," she said. "But you're too skinny. You need to eat more. You look like a boy made out of sticks."

"I'll eat more," Lanius promised. He would have promised his mother almost anything. "I'll even eat—" He shook his head. He wouldn't promise to eat his vegetables. That would be going too far.

"You're the king now, after all," Certhia said. "The king has to be strong, so Avornis will be strong."

"All right." It didn't seem real to Lanius. He was only eight years old. The one change he'd been able to notice was that palace servants called him *Your Majesty* now instead of *Your Highness*. Even his tutor called him *Your Majesty*. But he still had to go to lessons every day—not that he minded them. He said, "I'm sorry Uncle Scolopax died."

His mother's face went hard and cold. "I'm not," she said. "He was a stupid, nasty man, Lanius. You'll make a much better king when you grow up. I'm sure you will."

"How are you sure, Mama?" Lanius asked, genuinely curious.

"Because you couldn't possibly be a worse one," Queen Certhia snapped.

"That isn't logical," Lanius said. "If I tried, I'm sure I could—"

"But you wouldn't try any such thing—that's the point," his mother answered. "All Scolopax wanted to do was throw down everything your father ever did, just because he did it. You wouldn't do anything like that. You're still a little boy, but you know better."

"No, I don't suppose I *would*," Lanius said. "But I *could*."

Certhia gave him an odd look. "Never mind," she said. "I—"

"Good day, madam." Arch-Hallow Bucco stood in the doorway. He looked at Lanius' mother as though he'd found her on the bottom of his sandal. "What are you doing inside the palace? Who gave you leave to come here?" His voice was chilly as winter in the mountains of Thervingia.

"She's my mama. I'm King of Avornis!" Lanius exclaimed.

Bucco bowed. "Indeed you are, Your Majesty. But I am the head of the Council of Regents your uncle appointed to rule until you become a man. My word has weight here."

Certhia laughed scornfully. "And a fine Council of Regents it is, too. You and Waccho and Aistulf—"

"And Torgos," Bucco broke in. "Torgos is a wise and learned man."

"How did he put up with Scolopax, then?" Lanius' mother demanded. She pointed a finger at Bucco. "It's *your* council, and everyone knows it. You're the one who will get blamed when things go wrong."

"I do not intend that things should go wrong," the arch-hallow said, even more frigidly than before. "When your son becomes a man, Avornis will be strong for him. He is, after all, the only one left of our ancient dynasty."

"Yes, and you've called him a bastard, too," Certhia said. "What do you propose to do about that?"

"I'm not a bastard," Lanius said. "You were Father's queen. I was only little then, but I remember."

"It is not so simple as that, Your Majesty," Arch-Hallow Bucco said. "Your mother was King Mergus' wife, yes, but she was the king's seventh wife."

Even Lanius, young as he was, knew what that meant. He stared at his mother. She scowled at Bucco. "Arch-Hallow Megadyptes declared he was legitimate."

Bucco coughed. He'd been ousted so Megadyptes could say that. He could hardly be expected to like it. "Arch-Hallow Megadyptes' opinions were his own, not mine," he said, and coughed again.

Lanius saw the logical flaw there. "If I'm not legitimate, if I am a bastard, how can I be king?"

Certhia pointed at the arch-hallow again. "And if he's not king, how can *you* head the Council of Regents for him?"

Bucco did some more coughing. "The entire situation is most irregular," he said.

"It certainly is," Queen Certhia said. "And since it is, how dare you try to keep me from seeing my son?"

"I head the regency council," Bucco said stiffly. "I decide whom King Lanius should see."

"I'm the king, and I want to see my mama!" Lanius said.

His mother said, "Who made a better arch-hallow for Avornis, Bucco? You or Megadyptes? Plenty of people would say he did, especially after the way Scolopax abused him. Do you want those people howling for your blood in the streets of the city? They will, especially if you keep calling Lanius a bastard."

"Don't you threaten me!" Bucco said.

"Don't you think you can keep me away from my son!" Queen Certhia retorted. "You're not the king. He is."

They glared at each other over Lanius' head. The new king of Avornis felt as though they had hold of him by the arms and were trying to pull him in two.

Commodore Grus didn't like riding a horse. Some people got seasick. This animal's endless rocking gait left *him* queasy. "I wish we could sail down to the south," he told Nicator.

"So do I," Nicator answered. "My legs feel like they've been stretched on the rack. I'll walk bowlegged the next week, see if I don't." He had his own reasons for disliking horses.

Sighing, Grus said, "The gods chose to give us rivers that run from west to east. If we want to go north, we can either let the horses do the work or we can do it ourselves. Those are the only choices we've got."

"Who says I *want* to go from north to south?" Nicator asked. "I've got to, but I don't much want to. As soon as the Thervings are quiet for a little while, the Menteshe start tormenting us again. Feels like the two sets of bastards have got Avornis by the arms, and they're trying to pull us in two."

That comparison was too apt for comfort. Grus said, "It could be worse. If they both jumped on us at the same time, we'd have real trouble."

Captain Nicator spat. "You ask me, Skipper, this *is* real trouble. If it wasn't real trouble, why would they send us to take command down south again, eh? Answer me that, if you please."

Since Grus couldn't, he didn't. He did reach down and make sure his sword was loose in its scabbard. Smoke darkened the southern horizon. The Menteshe were burning fields and farmhouses and villages. If they got lucky enough to break into walled towns, they'd burn those, too. And, if they came across a couple of mounted Avornans, they would try to kill them.

Seeing the motion, Nicator laughed. "Oh, you'll make a fine cavalryman, Skipper, same like me. You're likelier to whack me with that sword than you are to hit one of the Banished One's bastards."

"Thanks so much, *friend*," Grus said. "I'll stay away from you, too. You see if I don't." He pointed. "Is that an inn up ahead?"

"Sure looks like one to me," Nicator answered. "Shall we stop for the night? We won't get a whole lot further even if we do go on."

"Suits me," Grus said. Once he and Nicator came into the common room, though, it didn't suit him so well. The merchants eating and drinking in there were loudly arguing about whether Bucco's faction or Megadyptes' had a better right to the arch-hallowdom. Some of the men had drunk enough to seem ready to argue with fists and knives, not words.

"This is foolishness," Nicator said. "Haven't we got more important things to worry about?"

He'd pitched his words to Grus, who nodded. But a young merchant at the next table turned toward them and said, "The Banished One will seize us if we make the wrong choice." His fingers writhed in a preventive sign.

Grus made the same gesture, but he asked, "Don't you think the Banished One is more likely to seize us if we quarrel among ourselves?"

By the way the merchant stared at him, he might as well have started speaking the language of the far northern Chernagors. Unlike most of the men in the dining hall, Grus didn't feel like arguing. He and Nicator finished their suppers—not so good—and their wine—worse—and went off to the cramped little room the innkeeper had given the two of them. Grus barred the door.

"That may not help," Nicator said.

"I know," Grus answered. "I don't see how it can hurt, though."

Somehow, the merchants didn't come to blows. When Grus and Nicator rode south the next morning, they were both scratching themselves. Grus almost decided the Banished One was welcome to have the inn-keeper. Almost. Like anyone who'd seen what life was like on the far bank of the Stura, he didn't care to wish it on anybody else.

If the Menteshe won here—if their raids forced Avornan soldiers and wizards and priests off this land—the Banished One would bring his spells that much closer to the city of Avornis. *We'd better not let that happen,* Grus thought gloomily.

"I hope Anxa hasn't fallen," he said.

"It better not have!" Nicator said.

"I know," Grus answered. "But there's a lot of smoke down in the south. That means a lot of Menteshe running around loose."

How right he was, he and his companion found out a couple of hours later. They'd just passed a burnt-out farm when a couple of horsemen came up the road toward them. Those weren't Avornans in mail shirts—they were Menteshe, tough little men on tough little ponies. Seeing Grus and Nicator, they yanked sabers from scabbards and spurred their ponies forward.

Grus wished he were wearing chain mail. He had a helmet on his head, but no other armor. His own sword came out. So did Nicator's. He booted his horse toward the enemy. With horses as with river galleys, you didn't want to be standing still while the other fellow charged.

"King, uh, Lanius!" Grus shouted—a feeble war cry if ever there was one. What would the king have done if he'd been there? He was a little boy. He would have gotten killed, and in short order, too.

One of the nomads chose Grus; the other, Nicator. *How do I keep from getting killed in short order?* he wondered. He wasn't so bad on horseback as Nicator had said, but he wasn't good, either. This wasn't his chosen way to fight. By the way his foe rode, the nomad might have been born in the saddle. Up came his saber.

Iron belled on iron as Grus parried the Menteshe's cut. Sparks flew. The nomad cut again, backhand this time. Again, Grus parried. He tried a cut of his own. The Menteshe beat it aside and slashed at his horse. Grus kept the foeman's blade away from the beast. He couldn't stop the next cut, not altogether, but he deflected it enough to make it slide off his hel-met instead of laying his face open.

The longer he fought, the more the lessons his father and a couple of implacable swordmasters had given him came back. The Menteshe howled a curse at him. The nomad must have expected sport, not work.

A moment later, the Menteshe howled again, in pain. Blood ran down his leather sleeve—a cut of Grus' had gotten home. The nomad wheeled his pony and booted the animal up into a gallop toward the south.

Instead of going after him, Grus turned to see how Nicator was doing. The other river-galley captain traded sword strokes with his enemy. Neither seemed to have much of an edge. Nicator bled from a cut on his cheek. The very tip of the Menteshe's left little finger also poured blood. That had to hurt, but it would do the nomad no great harm.

Grus rode up to the fight. The nomad was so hotly engaged with Nicator, he didn't realize he had a new foe till too late. Grus' sword slammed into the side of his neck. Blood sprayed, then rivered out of him. He gave a gurgling cry of pain. His sword flew from his hand. He tried to ride south, as his comrade had. But he stayed in the saddle only a furlong or so. After he slid to the ground, his horse slowed to a walk.

"Thank you kindly, Skipper," Nicator said, dabbing at his cut with a scrap of rag. "That was a pretty bit of work."

"Only goes to show I'm good for something on land," Grus answered. "I wouldn't have bet on it, if you want to know the truth."

"Let's round up that pony. We can sell it," Nicator said. "And who knows what that Menteshe bastard's got on him?"

"All right," Grus said. "We're just lucky we didn't run into archers. They would have filled us full of holes, and we couldn't have done much about it."

"That's what the nomads say when we catch their rafts on the water in our galleys." Nicator grinned fiercely. "Here's hoping they say it plenty."

The Menteshe's sword would bring something, too. Grus got off his horse to pick it up and stow it in a saddlebag. Then he mounted once more and went after his friend. When Nicator dismounted, he squatted beside the dead Menteshe. He cut the nomad's pouch from his belt. Hefting it, he whistled. "Nice and heavy." He opened it and looked inside. "Silver, with a little gold."

"Make two piles," Grus told him. "If there's an odd coin, you take it. I've got his saber."

"Sounds fair," Nicator agreed, and did it. "Only thing I feel bad about is knowing he probably stole it from Avornans."

"He paid a bigger price than money," Grus answered. "What's that he's got around his neck?"

"One of their amulets, I expect, on a cord." Nicator drew it out and scowled. "A nasty one."

Grus nodded. "I'll say it is." The main ingredient of the amulet was the skull of some small animal with sharp teeth—a weasel, perhaps. What bothered him most was that the eye sockets, though empty, kept giving him the feeling they were looking at him. "Take it off the bastard. Let's get rid of it."

"Right." Nicator cut the rawhide loop that held the amulet in place. When he reached for the skull, he jerked back his hand with a startled curse. "Shit! It *bit* me!" Sure enough, blood dripped from his thumb.

"I'll take care of it." Grus used his sword to flick the amulet away from the dead Menteshe. Its teeth clicked on the blade, too, but uselessly. He stomped on it, hard. It shattered under his boot heel. Even then, he felt a tingling jolt of power. The hair on his legs and arms and at the back of his neck stood up for a moment. Then the sensation ebbed. "There. That's done it."

Nicator bandaged his thumb. "Hurrah," he said sourly.

"Come on. Let's get down to the river," Grus said. "As long as we meet them on land, we're playing their game. But once their miserable little boats start trying to sneak back over the Stura, they're playing ours." His smile showed teeth almost as sharp as the amulet's as he went on, "And their river galleys aren't worth much. They can make thralls row, but they're even worse on the water than people like us are on land."

"Right," Nicator said again. He held up his hand. The bandage was turning red. "I want to have a wizard look at this anyway. It's liable to fester."

"Don't worry about it, Your Majesty," Arch-Hallow Bucco said, reaching out to pat Lanius on the head. "The other regents and I have everything well in hand."

The King of Avornis was only nine, but Bucco couldn't have taken a worse tack with him if he'd tried for a year. "Really?" Lanius said. "Then why are the Menteshe tormenting the south while the Thervings arm for war? Do you not think you made some bad choices there?"

Bucco stared at him. Lanius had said such things before, but they never failed to surprise the grown-up on the receiving end. "Your Majesty, you are, ah, misinformed," the arch-hallow said slowly.

That was also a mistake. Lanius knew what he knew. And, as he had since he was a baby, he cherished facts. He could rely on them, unlike people, not to desert him. "Oh? How?" he said now. "Do you mean the Menteshe didn't raid us? Or do you mean the Thervings aren't arming for war? What exactly *do* you mean?"

"Isn't it . . . time for your lessons?" Bucco asked. He ran a finger around the neck opening of the silk shirt he wore under his red robe. It hadn't grown too tight, but it felt as though it had.

"Yes. I will go to them," Lanius answered. "Don't you have some lessons *you* could go to, so you could do a better job of running this kingdom?"

Arch-Hallow Bucco muttered to himself as he went away. Lanius didn't understand why. He'd told the man the truth. He had no trouble seeing it. Why was it so hard for the arch-hallow?

His lessons should have been boring. Grammar and arithmetic and history horrified students in Avornis no less than anywhere else. Like any other tutor, Lanius' carried a switch to make sure the lessons took hold. But he hadn't had to use it for a long time. Lanius loved lessons—loved them enough to alarm the man who taught him, though the tutor never let on.

Some time later, Lanius looked up from his exercises to find his mother standing there in place of the tutor. Queen Certhia smiled at him. "You've been working hard, sweetheart," she said.

"I hope so," Lanius answered seriously. "I need to work hard. Someone has to be able to rule Avornis the way it should be ruled, and Arch-Hallow Bucco doesn't seem to be the man."

Certhia's mouth tightened. "No, he doesn't," she agreed. "I could do it better than he can."

"Why, so you could, Mama!" Lanius exclaimed. "I was reading about Queen Astrild just the other day. She ruled Avornis all by herself for a while. I'm sure you could do the same thing. You ought to."

"It's not quite so simple, I'm afraid," his mother said.

"Why not? You're the queen, and Bucco's only the arch-hallow." Lanius was a learned child, a precociously learned child, but he was only a child. What lay under his words was, *You're my mother. You can do anything.*

"But he's the head of the Council of Regents, and I'm not," Certhia said. "And the soldiers will follow him, and they won't follow me. I'm only a woman, after all." She didn't try to hide her bitterness.

"You could make them follow you. Queen Astrild did," Lanius said.

"I wish they were here to listen to you," his mother told him. She sounded amused and proud at the same time.

"Here are some soldiers." Lanius pointed to the doorway. Sure enough, in tramped four grim-faced troopers. Lanius raised his voice. "You men! Since the arch-hallow plainly has no idea what he's doing, your duty to Avornis is to obey someone else. Here is the queen, who—"

"That will be quite enough of that." Arch-Hallow Bucco followed the armed men into the room. He went on, "You see how Certhia seeks to corrupt the child. She can no longer be trusted around him. Seize her."

"Yes, sir," the soldiers chorused. They advanced on Queen Certhia.

"You stop that! You leave her alone!" Lanius cried, and sprang at them. It did him no good. One of them caught him and held him in spite of all his thrashing.

His mother kicked and cursed the soldiers. That did her no good. She cursed Arch-Hallow Bucco, too, at the top of her lungs. That did her no good, either. "Take her away," Bucco told them.

"Don't you do that! She's my mother!" Lanius shouted.

"She is leading you in the ways of the Banished One," Bucco said.

"She's not doing any such thing," Lanius said indignantly.

"She certainly is," the arch-hallow replied. "Otherwise, you wouldn't be so disrespectful to your elders."

"You're making a mess of the kingdom," Lanius said. "Is it disrespectful to tell you the truth?"

"I don't need to argue with you. You're only a little boy," Bucco said. He nodded to the soldiers. "Away with the slut. I wish we could be rid of her bastard as easily."

"I'm no bastard!" Lanius' voice went high and shrill. "Don't you call me one, either, or you'll be sorry."

"The whole kingdom is sorry because you're the king," Arch-Hallow Bucco said. "And your mother was a seventh wife. What else would you call yourself, *Your Majesty?*" He turned the royal title into one of scorn.

Yes, Lanius knew what being the son of a seventh wife meant, or what it ordinarily would have meant. But he said, "A priest married my mother and father, so that was all right. And Arch-Hallow Megadyptes said the priest didn't do anything wrong when he made the marriage, so *that* was all right, too. So there." He stuck out his tongue. He might have been educated beyond his years, but he had only nine of them, and sometimes it showed.

Bucco gave him a look full of loathing. "I don't care what Megadyptes said. He shouldn't have been arch-hallow then, and he isn't arch-hallow anymore." He didn't say, *So there,* and stick out his tongue—he was, after all, a grown-up—but he looked as though he wanted to.

"He isn't arch-hallow *now,*" Lanius said, "but he could be again, when I come of age."

The look Bucco gave him this time didn't hold just loathing. It held fear, too. "If you weren't the last of your dynasty—" he began, but then broke off, shaking his head. He gave Lanius a bow much sharper and shorter than the King of Avornis deserved, and went off, shaking his head.

Not long after that, the meadows around the walls of the city of Avornis began filling up with soldiers. When Lanius went up to one of the taller towers in the royal palace, he could see tents stretching out across the grasslands. Tiny as ants in the distance, men marched and countermarched in lines and squares. "Now we'll beat the Thervings," he told his tutor. He'd read of the Avornan army suffering defeats, but that didn't seem real to him.

His tutor, though, looked worried. "May you prove right, Your Majesty," the man said, "but I'm not sure that army is even there to fight King Dagipert and his savages."

"What do you mean?" Lanius asked.

"Well . . ." The tutor didn't want to go on but finally did. "Duke Regulus is a very bold man; a very brave man. He's also a man of very high blood, and a man who's good friends with Arch-Hallow Bucco."

Lanius hadn't read lots of chronicles for nothing. "You think he means to steal the throne from me!"

"I don't know whether he means to do it, or whether Bucco means for him to do it," the tutor answered. "Regulus is very bold and very brave, but no one ever said he was very bright. Bucco could lead him the way you would lead an ox."

Fear filled Lanius. "What do I do?" he whispered. He wasn't asking his tutor. He might have been asking himself, or he might have been asking the world. Whatever he asked, he got an answer. He snapped his fingers. He'd just learned how to do that, and liked the noise it made. "I know!" he said.

"What?" his tutor asked.

"I won't tell you," Lanius said. "I won't tell anybody."

Grus was a mightily puzzled man. Any man who loves a woman—and, especially, any man who has children—will find himself puzzled now and again. But this was a different sort of puzzlement. The *Osprey,* flagship of his present flotilla, made her way upstream along the Stura. The rowers had to work hard; both current and wind were against them.

He stared south, into the lands the Menteshe held. All seemed quiet there. Avornis had handled the latest raid from Prince Ulash roughly enough to make Ulash—and, Grus supposed, the Banished One, too—thoughtful. That left the commodore only more puzzled than ever at being ordered to stay on the Stura.

"Do you think the Menteshe are likely to try anything any time soon?" he asked Captain Nicator.

"Never can tell what those gods-cursed bastards are up to, not for sure," Nicator answered. "Anytime you think you know, that's when they'll up and kick you in the balls."

"Well, yes," Grus agreed. "But what are the odds?"

"Slim," Nicator said. "That I grant you. They *are* slim. We put the fear of Olor into the nomads."

Now if only we could put it into the Banished One. Grus shook his head. That was neither here nor there. He made himself stick to what had been uppermost in his mind: "Arch-Hallow Bucco is arming for war against the Thervings, isn't he?"

"He says he is," Nicator allowed. "Duke Regulus thinks he is. An awful lot of soldiers think he is."

"Just so." Grus nodded. "Duke Regulus. An awful lot of soldiers. Has he done anything about getting river galleys or sailors ready for the fight?"

"He hasn't called us. That's all I know for sure. We wouldn't be down here on the Stura if he had, now would we?" Nicator chuckled, then spat into the river.

"He hasn't called anybody. We'd know if he had," Grus said. Nicator nodded. Sailors knew what other sailors were up to. Grus went on, "So how does Bucco aim to fight the Thervings without river galleys? He won't be able to attack, and he won't be able to defend, either."

"Looks that way to me, too," Nicator said. "But Bucco, he's not a general, you know. He's a holy man."

"Then why is he trying to fight?" Grus burst out. "I'm not a holy man. If you gave me a red robe and put me in the cathedral, I'd make an ass of myself. Doesn't he see it works the other way round, too? Aren't there any generals trying to talk sense into him? If I had to pretend I was an arch-hallow, I'd listen to the priests who knew what they were doing."

"Ah, but you've already got your head on straight, Skipper."

"Thanks." Grus tugged at his beard, as though making sure his head wasn't at some strange angle. "By the gods, though, Bucco's no fool."

"Then why is he acting like one?"

"That's the question, all right," Grus said. "Why?"

"Maybe he's not aiming at fighting the Thervings," Nicator said. "Maybe he's got something else in mind."

"Like what?" Grus asked.

Nicator looked this way and that. Nobody stood particularly close to Grus and him. The sailors aboard the *Osprey* had learned Grus and his longtime comrade liked to have room to talk. Even so, Nicator didn't answer, not in words. He just looked up at the sky and whistled a tune peasants sang when they trampled grapes in the fall.

"What's that supposed to mean?" Grus asked irritably. Nicator went on whistling. Grus felt like hitting him. "Are you playing the fool or making me out to be one?"

Nicator still didn't answer. Grus started to get really angry. Then he stopped and stared. "You don't suppose—?"

"Me, Skipper?" Nicator was the very picture of innocence. "I'm just a dumb old sailorman. I don't suppose anything."

Grus ignored that. "D'you think Bucco can get away with it?"

"Who's going to stop him?"

A dour soldier named Lepturus commanded the royal bodyguard. King Lanius, by the nature of things, saw him every day. That made Lepturus one of the most important men in the kingdom. Lanius didn't usually pay much attention to him, maybe because he saw him so often. He might have been part of the furniture. You didn't pay attention to a chair—till you needed to stand on it to climb out a window in a fire.

"I know my father always thought you were a wonderful officer," Lanius said.

In a way, that was a lie. So far as Lanius could remember (which, since he was only nine, wasn't very far), King Mergus had never said a word about Lepturus. But it also held a truth. Mergus wouldn't have put Lepturus in such an important post if he hadn't thought the man could handle the job.

It worked. Lepturus' face softened more than Lanius would have guessed it could. The soldier said, "Your old man—uh, His Majesty—was one of a kind. Too bad he's not here now. We could use him."

"Yes." Lanius nodded. "We could. But he wasn't one of a kind. He was part of the dynasty. I'm part of the dynasty, too."

"That's true." Somber once more, Lepturus nodded. "King Mergus, he went to a lot of trouble to make sure you'd be part of it, too. Seven wives!" He rolled his eyes. "If that's not trouble, curse me if I know what is."

"Er—yes." Lanius wasn't sure what that meant. But, since he had no other good hopes, no other choice, he plunged ahead. "I don't want to be the *last* part of the dynasty."

"What?" Lepturus had black, bushy eyebrows that reminded Lanius of caterpillars. They wiggled like caterpillars now. "What are you saying, boy?" That was no way to address the King of Avornis, but Lanius didn't mind. He told Lepturus what he meant. Lepturus' eyebrows did some more wiggling. "You figured this out all by your lonesome?"

"Well, with some help from my tutor," Lanius answered.

"And what do you suppose *I* can do about it?" Lepturus asked.

Again, Lanius told him. *Now, will he take me seriously?* he wondered. On the one hand, he was King of Avornis. On the other hand, he was nine years old. He'd seen—as what child has not?—that grown-ups often treated children like fools just because they were children.

But Lepturus thought for a little while and then said, "Do you know, Your Majesty, I think we can do something like that."

"I hope you can." Lanius had never been more sincere.

A couple of days later, Duke Regulus rode from his encampment outside the city of Avornis to have supper with Lepturus at the royal palace. Only a few soldiers rode with Regulus. He plainly expected no trouble. Lanius' tutor had said he wasn't very smart. If that didn't prove it, nothing ever would.

Smart or not, though, Regulus looked splendid as he rode up to the palace. Lanius watched him from a window where he wouldn't be seen. Regulus looked more like a king, a warrior king, than he ever would.

But did looks make the King of Avornis? Lanius hoped not. If they did, he would never sit on the Diamond Throne when it really mattered.

Down below, big, bluff Regulus dismounted. So did his companions. Royal guardsmen took charge of their horses. Lepturus came out and embraced Regulus. They went into the bodyguards' dining hall arm in arm. The door closed behind them, and Lanius couldn't see any more.

After a while, a serving woman told him to go to bed. In such matters, he was a child, not the king. They could make him go to bed. They couldn't make him fall asleep. He lay awake a long, long time, listening. But he didn't hear anything out of the ordinary. At last, sleep sneaked up on him.

Next thing he knew, the morning sun shone in his face. He needed a moment to remember something important should have happened. Had it? He didn't know. The serving women at breakfast chattered among themselves in voices too low for him to make out what they were saying, but they always did that. One of the bodyguards winked at him, but *they* were always doing things like that. Lanius didn't know whether he felt like shouting or crying.

"Time for your lessons, Your Majesty," one of the maidservants said.

"All right," Lanius answered, so eagerly that she blinked. People had trouble understanding he really liked to study. They didn't, so they thought he shouldn't. And he especially wanted to go to his lessons today.

"Good morning, Your Majesty," his tutor said. "We'll be reading the chronicles this morning, for style and for grammar and for history."

"Yes, yes." Lanius was monstrously impatient. "Speaking of history, what happened last night? Tell me!"

His tutor gave him a sidelong look. "What happened last night? Well, that *great* general, Duke Regulus, didn't go back to his army. Lepturus arrested him and sent him to the Maze instead. And if you go into the Maze, you don't come out again. Now, Your Majesty, to your lessons, if you please."

"Yes. My lessons," Lanius said. Regulus deposed and imprisoned didn't solve all his problems. Nothing but growing up would. But he'd just bought himself a better chance *to* grow up.

CHAPTER FIVE

A nomad paced the *Osprey.* He had a good horse. He had several good horses, in fact; he frequently changed them. That was what let him keep up with the river galley. Grus looked over at him every so often as the ship made its way along the Stura. The rider might have been waiting for a moment of inattention to start shooting. Or he might have been a wizard, with some darker, deadlier purpose in mind.

"Me, I don't miss Regulus," Nicator remarked.

"No, I don't miss him, either," Grus answered. "He wanted to be King of Avornis, and we've already got one."

"He wouldn't have made a good one, either," Nicator said. "Bastard thought he knew everything when he didn't know enough to stay out of a trap that shouldn't have fooled a half-witted dog. The Thervings would have served him up for supper—with garlic bread, by the gods."

Grus nodded. His own opinion of Regulus was no higher. On the other hand . . . "Now our army in front of the city of Avornis has no general at all, not to speak of."

"It didn't before," Nicator said scornfully. "Just a sorry bastard with more ambition than brains. And speaking of sorry bastards—" He jerked a thumb toward the Menteshe. "What do you suppose he's up to?"

"Just keeping an eye on us, I hope," Grus replied. "They haven't got many river galleys of their own, so they use horsemen instead. We've seen it before."

"Haven't seen one of the buggers dog us quite like this." Nicator scowled. "He's up to something."

"Maybe. If he is, we can't do much about it," Grus said. "We can't give the Menteshe any excuse to go to war with Avornis, not when King Dagipert's ready to throw every Therving in the world across our western border."

"If we had the Scepter of Mercy, we'd make 'em all think twice," Nicator muttered. He sighed. "And if pigs had wings, everybody'd need to stay under shelter."

"Shelter," Grus said. Involuntarily, he looked up into the sky. No fat porkers overhead—only a few swifts and swallows after the insects buzzing above the river. Somehow, the sight of them helped him make up his mind. He raised his voice to call, "Turnix!"

"Yes, Commodore?" the wizard answered, hurrying back from the *Osprey*'s bow. The gray in his beard reminded Grus how long they'd been together. Not as long as with Nicator, but still quite a while. Turnix went on, "What can I do for you?"

Grus pointed to the Menteshe rider. "Can you tell me what he's up to?"

"I can try. If a Menteshe wizard has warded him, I may not succeed. If the Banished One has warded him"—his fingers twisted in a sign to turn aside evil, which Grus imitated—"I *won't* succeed."

"Try," Grus urged. "And why would the Banished One care about one river galley in particular? Avornis has a fine, big fleet."

"Yes, Commodore," Turnix said, "but Avornis has only one Grus."

"What's that supposed to mean?" Grus shook his head. "Never mind. I don't want to know. Just tend to your wizardry, all right?"

"Of course, Commodore." But Turnix's eyes gleamed. He might obey, but he would go on thinking his own thoughts. He took from his belt pouch a stone of sparkling, shifting color. Holding it up to Grus, he said, "This is the famous amandinus, from out of the distant east. It's an antidote to poison; it makes a man overcome his adversaries; it lets him prophesy and interpret dreams; and it makes him understand dark questions, questions hard to solve."

"That all sounds splendid," Grus said agreeably. "So long as it does what I want, too." Before Turnix could reply, Grus went on, "One thing I've always wondered—if a wizard has a stone like that, why doesn't he quickly become very powerful?"

"Well, for one thing, sir, this isn't the only bit of amandinus in the world, you know," Turnix said. "And, for another, there are other magics besides the one inherent in the stone. But it does have its uses even so."

"All right. I'm answered. I'll let you tend to your business."

"I think I can manage, sir." Turnix aimed the amandinus stone at the Menteshe. He began a chant of which Grus understood not a word. He did understand that, had the wizard aimed an arrow, instead, he would have been drawing back a bow. The chant grew higher and sharper. Turnix called out one last word.

The nomad cried out as though he *had* been pierced by an arrow. He spurred south as fast as he could ride. "Nicely done," Grus said. "I don't think we'll see him again anytime soon."

"No." But Turnix's voice was troubled. "He *was* well warded, sir. But one thing I noted beyond any doubt."

"What's that?" Grus asked, as he was meant to do.

"He wasn't riding along to keep an eye on the *Osprey*, sir," Turnix replied. "He was keeping an eye on *you*—on you in particular, I mean."

"Well, what of it?" Grus tried not to take that too seriously. "I'm not unknown down here in the south. I've been commanding river galleys and flotillas of river galleys in these parts for a good many years now. If the Menteshe *didn't* know who I was and worry about me, I'd be disappointed."

Turnix shook his head. "That's not why he was following this ship." He sounded very sure of himself. "If he's not heading straight back to a wizard with connections to the Banished One—or maybe to the Banished One himself—I'd be amazed."

"Why would the Banished One care so much about me? I'm not *that* important in the scheme of things," Grus said. The wizard only shrugged. Grus muttered something under his breath. Now he wished he hadn't summoned Turnix.

As the *Osprey* approached the little riverside town of Tharrus, a dispatch boat shot out from the waterfront. The rowers pulled as though demons were right behind them. Grus had intended to pass Tharrus by, but slowed down to let the dispatch boat come alongside. "Permission to come aboard?" one of the men on her called.

"Granted," Grus replied.

"Here you are, Commodore Grus," the fellow said when he stood on the planks of the *Osprey*'s deck. He thrust a rolled-up scroll at Grus.

"I expect you want me to read this now, don't you?" Grus asked. That was wasted irony—the other man just nodded. Sighing, Grus broke the seal. He read and sighed again. After that, he rolled up the parchment and stood there without a word.

"Well?" Nicator asked at last.

Grus shook his head. "Not very well. Not very well at all, I'm afraid. The Thervings are over the border in the northwest, and there's not a single, solitary thing between them and the city of Avornis."

A few weeks before, Lanius had been able to look out from the royal palace and see the encampment of the Avornan army beyond the walls of the capital. He saw an army encamped there once more, but it wasn't an Avornan army—the Thervings had come to the city of Avornis. If they broke in, he wouldn't be King of Avornis anymore. If they broke in, Avornis wouldn't be a kingdom anymore, only a conquered part of Thervingia.

Arch-Hallow Bucco stood on the tower with him. "How do you explain this?" Lanius asked him.

"How do I explain it?" Bucco echoed, as though wondering whether he'd heard right. "What do you mean?"

Is he really so thick? Lanius wondered. He doubted it. "You head the Council of Regents, don't you? That means you do now what I'll do when I'm older, doesn't it? You rule Avornis, don't you? That means *that*"—Lanius pointed out toward Dagipert's host—"is your fault. And if it's your fault, you'd better explain it, hadn't you?"

Bucco looked as though he hated him. Bucco undoubtedly did hate him. The arch-hallow opened his mouth, closed it, and then tried again. "Our army would have been better off with a general at its head."

"Why?" Lanius asked. "Would he have helped it run away even faster than it did? Do you think it *could* have run away any faster than it did?"

"If you weren't the king, I'd turn you over my knee," Bucco snarled.

If I were really *the king, if I could give orders here and have them obeyed, I'd do worse than that to you,* Lanius thought. Aloud, he said, "What exactly *can* you do? By the gods, you had better do *something*, don't you think?"

"Our army would have had a general who *could* do something if your mother hadn't somehow managed to spirit Duke Regulus off to the Maze," the arch-hallow said. "You ought to blame her, not me."

Lanius almost laughed in Bucco's face. His mother hadn't had a thing to do with that. He'd managed it all by himself. But maybe it was better that the arch-hallow didn't grasp that. Lanius said, "If Regulus hadn't disappeared, would I still be king?"

"Of course you would, Your Majesty!" Bucco exclaimed, too quickly to be quite convincing.

"If I'm not king anymore, if a grown-up is, there won't need to be a Council of Regents anymore, either," Lanius pointed out. Bucco drummed his fingers on the stone of the battlement. He'd probably thought he could ride Regulus as a man rode a horse. Seeing how readily Regulus had stumbled into a trap, Lanius figured that Bucco had probably been right, too. But another man might not prove so easy to ride. *I have to make him worry about such things,* Lanius thought. He pointed east once more, toward the Thervings' tents. "What will you do about them?" he asked again.

"I have a plan," Arch-Hallow Bucco said in his loftiest tones.

"I'm *so* glad to hear it," Lanius replied. "Will it work as well as your last plan—the one that brought the Thervings here to our door?"

Bucco took a step toward him. Lanius flinched. He hated himself for it, but couldn't keep from drawing back. For all his wit, he was only a boy—and on the skinny side, and not very tall. Arch-Hallow Bucco nodded grimly. "You would do well to remember, Your Majesty, that if you provoke me far enough I *will* have you given a common, everyday whipping."

"You wouldn't dare!" Lanius' voice went high and shrill.

Arch-Hallow Bucco didn't answer. But he looked as though he would enjoy, enormously enjoy, having Lanius whipped. He wouldn't do it himself, perhaps; make his holy palms sting from walloping a boy's, even a royal boy's, backside? No. He'd give the order to a servant or a bodyguard. It would be his, though, and he and Lanius would both know it.

"I *will* come of age, you know," Lanius remarked. "And when I do, I *will* remember. I promise you that."

"Good. Remember, then, that I try to make a man of you, not a spoiled, whining puppy," Bucco said. "When you have a man's judgment, you will see that."

Will I? Lanius had his doubts. He'd never read of anyone who grew up grateful for whippings. If he hadn't read of such things, they weren't real to him. But he put this one aside for now. Real or not, it could wait. "Can the Thervings take the city of Avornis?" he asked nervously. He'd never read of that happening, either, but what he'd read seemed somehow less reassuring when measured against the swarm of enemy tents out beyond the city wall.

And he felt uncommonly relieved when Arch-Hallow Bucco shook his head, smiled, and gave him not a whipping, but a patronizing pat on the shoulder. "No, Your Majesty," the arch-hallow said. "Not without treason, and probably not with it, either. King Dagipert's not out there to take the city."

"Then why didn't he stay home?" Lanius burst out.

Bucco laughed—also patronizingly. "He is trying to make us do what he wants."

"He's doing a good job of it, too!" Lanius said.

"In the end, it will come out right. You'll see," Bucco said. "We will give him money and presents, and he will go back to Thervingia. He wants our gifts, and believes he can force us into giving them to him. Unfortunately, he is, for the moment, liable to be right."

King Dagipert did mount one attack on the walls of the capital. Maybe he thought the Avornans too demoralized to fight back, even with the advantage the fortifications gave them. If Dagipert did think that, he soon found out he was wrong. Once he saw the attack had no chance, he called it off.

Then he sent an envoy up to the main gate of the city with a flag of truce. Bucco went to the gate to treat with the Therving. When he came back to the royal palace, he looked pleased with himself. "Just as I thought—King Dagipert wants money," he told Lanius. "If we give it to him, he will go away. The only question now is, how much? Oh, and the Therving wants to send his son here to the palace to meet you."

"I'll meet him," Lanius said. "Of course I will." He was always eager to meet anyone new. He saw the same faces day after day inside the palace. Some of them, like Bucco's, he would have been happier *not* seeing.

The arch-hallow nodded. "I will make the necessary arrangements, then." He would have made the same arrangements even if Lanius had said he didn't want to meet Dagipert's son. Lanius was sure of that. And Bucco might as well have admitted as much, saying, "We are hardly in a position to refuse."

"I suppose not," Lanius said. "Which son of Dagipert's is coming here? Is it Berto, his heir, or is it one of his younger sons?"

"It's Prince Berto." Bucco gave Lanius a thoughtful look. "You do soak up all sorts of things, don't you, Your Majesty?"

"Of course. The more I know, the better off I am." Lanius spoke as though that were an article of faith. So he'd taken it, from his earliest days. *But now I know lots of strange things, and I'm still not very well off,* he thought. *Would I be worse off still if I knew less? Could I be worse off?*

He sighed. *I probably could.* Being a king, even a king who was a powerless boy, wasn't so bad. *I could be a starving peasant who was also a pow-erless boy. Or, if I hadn't figured out what to do about Duke Regulus, I could have ended up in the Maze—or dead.*

Prince Berto came to the royal palace the next afternoon, after wor-shiping at Olor's cathedral. That touch made Arch-Hallow Bucco happy. So did the news Berto brought. Presenting the prince to King Lanius, Bucco said, "I am invited to the Thervings' encampment tomorrow, to talk with King Dagipert face-to-face. Prince Berto has given me his fa-ther's safe-conduct."

"Good." Lanius hoped Dagipert would ignore it, as he'd ignored so many agreements. He spoke to Berto with the formality that had been drilled into him. "I am pleased to meet you, Your Highness."

"And I am pleased to meet you, Your Majesty." Berto spoke good Avor-nan, with only a slight guttural Therving accent. Like most of his coun-trymen, he was big and fair. He wore his hair long. That, with his wolfskin jacket and cowhide boots with the hair out, made him seem extraordinar-ily shaggy to Lanius. But his smooth-chinned face was open and friendly as he went on, "When I come here, I feel . . . closer to the gods than I do in Thervingia."

"But Thervingia is full of mountains," Lanius said. "You're closer to the heavens there, closer to the gods." *Closer to all of them but the Banished One, anyhow,* he thought uneasily.

Berto shook his head. "When I walked into the cathedral, I didn't know if I was still on earth or up in the heavens myself. You're so lucky, Your Majesty, to be able to worship there whenever you please."

Lanius shot Arch-Hallow Bucco a hooded look. One of his earliest memories was of Bucco turning his mother and father and him away from the cathedral. Did Bucco remember? Did Bucco know Lanius remem-bered? Lanius made himself hide his thoughts—one more thing he'd learned. He said, "As long as there is peace between Thervingia and Avor-nis, Your Highness, you are welcome to come here and worship at the cathedral whenever you like."

Prince Berto bowed very low. "This is a great boon you have given me, Your Majesty. I had heard you were wise beyond your years. Now I see with my own eyes it is true."

"Do people talk about me in Thervingia, then?" Lanius asked. He might almost have said, *Do people talk about me on the dark side of the moon?* He'd read of many distant lands. For all his reading, though, the only place he really knew was the city of Avornis, and especially the royal palace.

But fierce King Dagipert's son nodded. "Oh, yes," he said, his eyes wide. "People talk about the King of Avornis everywhere. How could it be otherwise? Whoever rules Avornis is the great shield against the Banished One. That makes him very important, all by himself."

"Prince Berto is a pious and wise young man," Arch-Hallow Bucco said in his own most holy tones.

Lanius had no idea how wise Berto was. But the Therving prince did strike him as pious. And what did King Dagipert think of that? Dagipert said he worshiped Olor, but the only things he really loved were himself and power. *He* wanted to be the one who ruled Avornis, the one people talked about. So Lanius' tutor said, at any rate. Lanius knew Arch-Hallow Bucco had a different opinion of the King of Thervingia. From what Lanius had seen, his tutor seemed more likely to be right.

"We all fear the Banished One, and slay his spies whenever they reveal themselves," Berto said.

"As all good men should do," Bucco said.

Did King Dagipert really do that? Or did he bargain with them and try to get the most for himself, as he did with Avornis? Some said one thing, some another. Lanius wanted to ask Berto. If anyone would know, Dagipert's heir would. But the question might not be what people called "polite." Lanius' tutor went on and on about politeness. Even Lanius himself could see the point of not offending King Dagipert when he stood with an army under the walls of the city of Avornis.

Besides, if Dagipert really did treat with the Banished One, he might want to lie about it afterward. He might lie even to his own son. If his own son was truly pious, like Berto, he might have special reason to lie.

After a while, Berto said, "Again, Your Majesty, it is a pleasure to meet you." He bowed to Lanius. "Now I am bidden by my father to bring Arch-Hallow Bucco back to his tent so they can speak of peace."

"I hope they find it, Your Highness," Lanius said.

"I hope so, too." Berto sounded as though he meant it.

Off Bucco went, riding on a white mule alongside Berto's horse and those of the prince's Therving bodyguards. The arch-hallow's crimson robe made a bright spot of color that let Lanius see him for a long way. Lanius even thought he spied Bucco outside the walls as the arch-hallow went off to confer with Dagipert.

Maybe he won't come back, Lanius thought. *Maybe Dagipert does love the Banished One, and will do something dreadful to Bucco.* At first, that brought Lanius a small stab of fear. But then he thought, *If Dagipert hurts Bucco, my mother will come back to the palace.* After that, he stopped worrying about what the king of the Thervings might do to the arch-hallow.

Night had fallen before Bucco returned. When he did, he was grinning from ear to ear. By then, Lanius was getting sleepy and cross. But he did want to hear what the arch-hallow had to say. "I have pledged presents to the king of the Thervings," Bucco told him. "Men are taking them from the treasury even now, and he will withdraw his army back into his own country."

"All right. We don't seem able to fight him right now, so all right," Lanius said. "How long did he promise to keep his soldiers in Thervingia and out of Avornis?"

Some of Bucco's grin slipped. "Ah . . . he did not name any set period of time, Your Majesty."

"That's not so good," Lanius said. "Now he can invade again whenever he pleases, and we can't even say he's breaking a treaty."

"True. Or it would be true." Bucco patted Lanius on the shoulder. Lanius glanced down at his own hand, to make sure the arch-hallow hadn't stolen it. Bucco went on, "It would be true, but I gave him excellent good reason to stay his bloody hand and remain at peace with us."

"What sort of reason?" Lanius asked, as he was plainly meant to do.

"Why, the best sort, Your Majesty." Bucco's smile got broad again. "The Therving has a daughter of not far from your years. Her name is Romilda. When the two of you come of age, a union between the royal house of Avornis and that of Thervingia will make the two kingdoms one and ensure eternal peace between them."

"But I don't want to marry any little Therving princess!" Lanius exclaimed in horror. He had no more use for girls than any other boy his age, and if the girl in question was a Therving princess . . .

Arch-Hallow Bucco's smile became indulgent. "By the time you marry, you will be a young man, and Princess Romilda will be a young woman. You'll feel differently about such things then, I promise you."

"No, I won't," Lanius said. He believed Bucco no more than any boy his age would have. "I'll hate her. And I hate you for making the bargain with the Therving. Get out!"

"Really, Your Majesty! I was simply—"

Lanius wouldn't let him finish. "Get out!" he shouted, and then, "Guards! Guards! The arch-hallow is bothering me!"

Bucco left before the bodyguards could come. He might command the army as a whole, but the royal bodyguard was loyal to the person of the king. Still grumbling, Lanius went to bed. After what seemed a very long time, he went to sleep.

"Here we are on horses again," Nicator said. "By the gods, I wish we'd get back on a ship."

"Oh, we will," Grus said. "We'll go on patrol against the Thervings— now that the Thervings have gone back to Thervingia. Isn't it grand?"

"It would've been even grander if we were patrolling against 'em before they invaded," Nicator said.

"You expect the arch-hallow to think of something like that? Perish the thought," Grus said. "Regulus might have—if he had any brains, and if he hadn't been angling for the throne. And once he fell, nobody paid any attention to the Thervings."

"Why are people such idiots?" Nicator asked.

"Good question," Grus told him. "Awfully good question. You'd be better off asking somebody like Turnix, though, or else a priest. I haven't got any answers for you."

"I wouldn't ask a priest," Nicator said scornfully. "Why should a priest know anything about why people are idiots? It's the arch-hallow who got us into this mess in the first place. Far as I can see, that makes him the biggest idiot of all. He's just lucky Dagipert didn't pull the walls of the capital down around his ears. Then we wouldn't have anyplace to come back to, and wouldn't that be a fine kettle of trout?"

"Trout," Grus echoed. He opened and closed his mouth several times, suggesting a fish out of water. Nicator laughed. So did Grus, though he didn't think it was really funny. He doubted Nicator did, either.

He and the veteran captain rode round a bend in the road, then they had to rein in. Several peasant families clogged the dirt track. A couple of the men pushed handcarts in front of them; the others had great packs strapped to their backs, as though they were beasts of burden. Some women wore packs; some carried bundles in their arms; some carried babies, instead. All the children bore burdens that fit their size, down to those just past being toddlers.

Slowly, awkwardly, wearily, the peasants made way for the men on horseback. "Where are you bound?" Grus asked them.

"City of Avornis," answered one of the men hauling a handcart.

Crex, Grus' father, had come off a farm and headed for the capital. He'd managed to land a place in the royal guards, and had done well enough for himself. But most peasants weren't so lucky. Grus said, "Why don't you stay on your own plots of land?"

A few minutes before, Nicator had called Arch-Hallow Bucco the biggest idiot in the world. Now all the peasants—men, women, and children—looked at Grus as though the title belonged to him. "Haven't got 'em anymore," said the fellow with the handcart.

"Why not?" Grus asked. They all looked tired, but otherwise hale enough. "You don't seem too lazy to keep them up."

That got him more than he'd bargained for. All the peasants shouted indignantly. The man who seemed more willing to talk than the others said, "Count Corvus pitched us off our land so he can raise cows and sheep on it. And what can we do about that? Not a gods-cursed thing, that's what we can do."

"Oh." Grus kicked his horse up into a trot. However little he liked the motion, he wanted to get away from those irate peasants. Nicator stuck by his side like a burr. At last, Grus said, "How are we going to stay strong if we throw all the peasants off the land? Where will we get our soldiers?"

"Beats me," Nicator answered. "How can anybody keep nobles from grabbing up land? That's half of what being a nobleman's all about." He sighed wistfully. "I always thought it sounded pretty good—buying land out to the horizon, I mean."

"It may be good if you're doing the grabbing." Grus jerked a thumb back toward the dispossessed peasants. "What about them? They're Avornans, too."

"If I'm a noble, I just give 'em the back of my hand," Nicator said. Grus laughed again, though that wasn't so funny, either.

Before he got to the royal capital, Grus heard a rumor so strange, he refused to believe it. But when he repeated it after coming into the city of Avornis, his wife only nodded. "Yes, that's true," Estrilda said.

"They've betrothed King Lanius to a Therving princess?" Grus said. Estrilda nodded again. "That's right."

"But that's madness," Grus said. "Once they're wed, who's the real power in Avornis? Dagipert of Thervingia, that's who."

"That's right." This time, his father spoke before his wife could. Crex sounded revoltingly cheerful about it, too.

"Who arranged it? Arch-Hallow Bucco?" Grus asked. Estrilda and Crex both nodded. After a moment, so did Grus. "Yes, in a way it must make sense for him," he said. "It keeps the Thervings quiet for the time being, and I don't think Bucco sees or cares about anything past that."

"Stupid bastard doesn't need to," Crex said. "Stupid bastard isn't king. He just gets to play at the job till he's buggered it up for everybody else." A long string of such cracks might have been what helped him get called Crex the Unbearable.

Before Grus could answer, a dog yelped in pain in the next room. A moment later, so did a boy. "Ortalis!" Grus called. His son came in, an apprehensive look on his face. He was holding one hand in the other. "Let me see," Grus said. His son plainly didn't want to, but had no choice. Grus nodded to himself, then asked, "Why did Rusty bite you?"

"I don't know," Ortalis mumbled, looking down at the floor. "Because he's mean."

"Because you hurt him?" Grus suggested. Ortalis didn't say anything. Grus pointed to the doorway. "Go to your room. No supper for you tonight."

"You ought to give him a good walloping," Crex said as Ortalis suddenly departed. "I gave you a good walloping whenever I thought you needed it, and you didn't turn out too bad."

Grus didn't argue with his father. What point? But he didn't agree, either. The way he remembered it, Crex had walloped him whether he needed it or not. Before his beard began to grow, he'd promised himself he wouldn't treat his own son the same way if he ever had one. He wondered whether it would have made any difference if he had decided to whack Ortalis at the first sign of misbehavior. He doubted it. Nothing except help from the gods could have turned Ortalis into a good-natured boy.

To keep from thinking about that, he went back to what they'd been talking about before. "How can Bucco stay head of the Council of Regents when he's gone and sold us to Dagipert and the Thervings?" *Sold us to the Banished One,* he almost said. But no one had ever proved that about the King of Thervingia, and the Avornan peasants who now lived under Thervingian rule weren't the soulless thralls the Menteshe treated like cattle.

Crex said, "Pack of spineless swine in the palace, that's how."

Estrilda added, "Lanius isn't old enough to rule on his own, and won't be for years. Who else can do the job? Queen Certhia?"

"How could she do it worse than Bucco has?" Grus demanded.

Crex loosed a long, loud, sour laugh. "If she gets the chance, sonny, maybe she'll show you how."

"Good day, Your Majesty." Lepturus bowed to King Lanius.

"And a good day to you." Lanius gave back the bow to the commander of his bodyguards.

To his surprise, Lepturus pulled out a sheet of parchment from the gold-embroidered pouch he wore on his belt. "Read this," he said, his lips hardly moving. "Read it, then get rid of it."

No less than any other boy, Lanius delighted in intrigue for its own sake. He unrolled the parchment. The note was short and to the point. *Do you want to see your mother back in the palace?* it asked. *If you do, help Lepturus.*

"Well, Your Majesty?" the dour guards commander asked gruffly.

Before answering, Lanius tore the parchment into tiny scraps, then went to a window and scattered the scraps to the wind. As he came back, Lepturus nodded approval. The young King of Avornis whispered, "You know I want her back. How can we do it?"

"That depends," Lepturus said quietly. "Do you really want to marry this Therving princess?"

Lanius made a horrible face. "I don't want to marry *anybody*. Who'd want to have anything to do with *girls?*" A world of scorn filled his voice.

Lepturus' furry eyebrows twitched. So did his mouth—about as close as he could come to a smile. "Oh, they have their moments," he observed. Lanius, who would argue about anything, was more than ready to quarrel over that. Lepturus didn't give him a chance. He held up a hand and said, "Never mind. Call Bucco to the palace and tell him you won't marry Princess What's-her-name no matter what."

"Will he pay any attention?" Lanius asked. "He's head of the Council of Regents, after all. He runs Avornis. I don't. He won't let me."

"He may run Avornis," Lepturus answered. "He doesn't run *you*. If you say you *won't* marry this girl, what can he do except try to talk you into it?"

"I don't know." Lanius wasn't so sure he wanted to find out, either. But he decided he would, if that meant Bucco left and his mother came back.

When he nodded, Lepturus clapped him on the shoulder, hard enough to stagger him. "Good lad," he said. "Do you want someone to write the words for you, or would you sooner do it yourself?"

"*I'd* sooner do it." Lanius drew himself up, though he still reached only the middle of Lepturus' chest.

The guards commander nodded. "All right. By all the signs, you'll do a better job than a secretary's liable to. Tell him to come tomorrow, in the middle of the morning. The rest will be taken care of. Easier and neater here than at the cathedral."

"Taken care of how?" Lanius asked. Lepturus just looked at him, and Lanius realized he wouldn't get any more answer than that. He started to get angry, but checked himself. "Never mind. I'll write the letter."

He did, and sent it off by a servant he trusted more than most of the others. The man brought back a reply from Bucco. *I shall be there, Your Majesty. You may rely on it,* the arch-hallow wrote. *I trust I shall be able to persuade you to reconsider.*

"Ha!" Lanius said. "*I* trust you won't."

Bucco came at the appointed hour. Lanius received him in as much state as he could. He had no formal power in Avornis, but he had rank, and rank could look like power. Arch-Hallow Bucco wore his most ornate crimson robe, shot through with gold thread and encrusted with pearls and rubies and sapphires. He played the same game as Lanius, but he had power to go with his rank.

He'd just launched into his speech to Lanius when Queen Certhia strode into the audience chamber, backed by Lepturus and two squads of royal bodyguards. "Mother!" Lanius exclaimed, and ran to her.

"Halt!" Bucco commanded. Lanius, to his own astonished dismay, halted just beyond the reach of his mother's arms. Bucco stabbed a forefinger at Certhia. Had he worn a sword on his belt, he might have stabbed with that, instead. The arch-hallow said, "You were banned from the palace, madam."

"And now you are, *sir*." Certhia laced the title with cold contempt. She beckoned to Lanius. He realized he didn't have to obey the arch-hallow, and threw his arms around his mother.

"On what authority?" Bucco demanded.

"Mine," Queen Certhia said.

"And mine," Lepturus added. The guards commander had a sword on *his* belt, and didn't seem likely to be shy about using it.

Certhia went on, "And the other regents have voted you off the council for daring to propose this marriage alliance. They agree with me that it would do nothing but deliver Avornis into Dagipert's bloodstained hands. Here is the notice of their vote." She handed Bucco a sheet of parchment. "They have also voted me, as King Mergus' widow, its head until King Lanius comes of age."

Bucco read the parchment, then crumpled it and threw it down. "This is outrageous! This is illegal!"

"After the fiasco you've caused, you'd better be grateful you're getting off with a whole skin," Lepturus said. "If you let your jaw flap, maybe you won't." Bucco gave him a terrible look, but found it better to say nothing. His stiff back radiating fury, he stalked away.

"Does this mean I won't have to marry King Dagipert's daughter?" Lanius asked.

"Let's see him *try* to marry her to you," his mother answered. Lanius clapped his hands.

CHAPTER SIX

The *Otter* glided along the Tuola River, on patrol against the Therv-ings. Now that Arch-Hallow Bucco no longer headed the regency, now that Queen Certhia had taken his place, King Lanius would *not* be betrothed to Princess Romilda of Thervingia. Grus approved of that. He didn't expect King Dagipert would, though. No one in Avornis expected Dagipert would. War was coming now. The only question was when.

"We never should have landed in this mess in the first place," Nicator grumbled. "Bucco never should have made that bargain."

"Of course he shouldn't," Grus said. "I just think it's a gods-cursed shame he's still in the cathedral. They should have thrown him out of there when they flung him out of the palace."

"I hear old Megadyptes didn't want the arch-hallow's job back," Nica-tor answered. "He's too holy for his own good, you ask me."

"Me, I'd sooner have an arch-hallow who spends his time praying than one who tries to run the kingdom."

Nicator grunted. "I don't mind Bucco trying so much as I mind him botching the job. And he cursed well did. And we'll have to pay for it."

"Don't remind me," Grus said. The *Otter* and the rest of his flotilla could give the Thervings a hard time if they tried to cross the Tuola. But the river galleys could go only so far up the stream. Past that, Avornis' horsemen and foot soldiers and wizards had to hold back Dagipert's army. Could they? *We'll find out,* Grus told himself, trying to smother his own doubts. Wistfully, he added, "It would be nice if *somebody* could run the kingdom, wouldn't it?"

"Well, you just might say so, yes," Nicator answered. He looked northwest, toward the rapids that kept the river galleys from moving any farther up the Tuola. Water boomed and thundered over black jagged rocks. Rainbows came and went in the flying spray. "What do we do when the Thervings try to go around us? They will, you know."

"Of course they will," Grus said. "We'll just have to work with the soldiers as best we can, that's all."

"Happy day." Nicator sounded unimpressed—but then, Nicator made a habit of sounding unimpressed. "If those bastards had any brains, they wouldn't have been soldiers in the first place."

Plump and fussy, Turnix bustled up to Grus and waited to be noticed. The commodore nodded to him now. "What's up?"

"Something's stirring, sir," Turnix answered.

"What do you mean, stirring?" Grus demanded. "And where?"

Turnix pointed toward Thervingia. "Something there. Something magical. Something big, or I wouldn't know anything about it. I do believe they're trying to mask it, but it's too big for that. I know it's there even through their spells."

"Ax is going to fall," Nicator said grimly.

"I think you're right," Grus said. "Turnix, can you tell exactly where this spell's coming from?"

"I haven't tried, not up till now," the wizard said. "I will if you like. The Thervings' masking makes it harder."

"Do your best," Grus said. "It's important."

"Well, it may be important," Nicator said. "Their wizards may be trying to bluff us about whatever they're keeping under wraps."

Grus didn't want to think about that. By Turnix's pained expression, the wizard didn't, either. It wasn't that Nicator was wrong. It was only that knowing he was right made everyone's life more complicated. Grus spoke to Turnix. "See if you can find it. Maybe that will tell you whether it's real or not."

"Good enough." Turnix turned toward Thervingia. He took an amulet set with a translucent green stone out from under his shirt and held it up so that the sun sparkled off it. Then he began to chant. He made one pass after another with his left hand. A couple of minutes into the spell, he staggered and muttered to himself.

"Are you all right?" Grus asked.

"I think so," Turnix said. "They've got wizards looking for people who try to sneak through their masking spells, too. Whatever they're doing, they don't want anybody knowing about it."

"All the more reason for us to find out," Grus said.

Turnix nodded. He started chanting again, and swung the amulet back and forth, back and forth. Suddenly, he let out a sharp exclamation of triumph. The stone in the amulet turned clear as glass on part of the arc. Turnix pointed. "There!"

"Toward the northwest, where we'd expect to have trouble," Grus noted.

"But do the Thervings mean it, Skipper, or are they trying to trick us?" Nicator persisted.

"I don't know." Grus turned to Turnix. "You're the wizard. What do *you* think?"

Turnix looked troubled. "I still can't be certain."

"I won't let anyone beat you if you're wrong," Grus said. "I want your best guess."

The wizard nervously plucked at his beard. "I don't think the Thervings know I got through their sorcerous screen. I do think they're hiding something real, not running a bluff. You asked . . . sir."

"You gave me what I asked for." *Now—what to do with it?* Grus went into the tiny cabin at the stern that let him and Nicator and Turnix sleep out of the rain. He found a scrap of parchment, a quill pen, and a bottle of ink. He wrote rapidly, then brought the note to Turnix. "Here. Send this to one of the wizards with the cavalry and foot soldiers and back to the city of Avornis."

Turnix read the note, then nodded. "You've summed things up here very well."

Grus shrugged. "Never mind that. As long as they know."

By the nervous way people went through the halls of the royal palace in the city of Avornis, one might think that one of the gods had stirred the place with a stick for sport. King Lanius felt the trouble without knowing what had caused it. When he asked his mother, Queen Certhia patted him on the head and told him, "It's nothing for you to worry about, sweetheart."

She could have done no better job of making him angry if she'd tried for a month. Glaring at her, he said, "Arch-Hallow Bucco would have told me just the same thing, Mother."

Certhia mouthed something silent about Bucco. Then she said, "It's nothing you can do anything about, and that's the truth."

"I don't care whether I can do anything about it or not," Lanius said. Like any child, he'd had to get used to the idea that things happened regardless of his opinion about them. "But I do want to know. I'm only a few years from coming of age. Then I'll be King of Avornis in my own right. I should know as much as I can before then, don't you think?"

His mother sighed and ruffled his hair. "I remember when I could hold you in the crook of my elbow. You were such a tiny thing then."

Lanius hated when his mother told him things like that. "I'm not a tiny thing anymore."

She had to nod. "No, that's true. You're not."

"Tell me, then," he said.

"All right. Let's see what you make of it," his mother said. "We have word from Commodore Grus and his wizard on the Tuola that the Thervings are planning something sorcerous farther up the river than his galleys can go." She waited to hear what he would say next.

He frowned in thought. "Is this Grus a good officer?"

"Lepturus keeps track of such people. He says Grus is very clever," Queen Certhia answered. "Lepturus says he may be too clever for his own good, but no doubt he's able."

"Would *you* have known that if Lepturus hadn't told you?" Lanius asked.

His mother looked impatient. "Really, Lanius, you can't expect me to keep track of all the officers who serve you."

"Why not?" Lanius asked in genuine surprise. "You're the head of the Council of Regents now. That means you might as well be King of Avornis. You should know these men."

"Never mind that," Certhia said. "I do know Grus now, thanks to Lepturus. What do you think we ought to do, supposing this report is true?"

"That's the place everyone expects Dagipert to attack anyhow, just because our ships can't help stop the Thervings there," Lanius replied. "We ought to do everything we can to hold him back."

Certhia gave him an odd look. "Did someone tell you to say that? One of your bodyguards, maybe? Or your tutor?"

"No, Mother," Lanius replied. "I figured it out for myself. It looks pretty obvious, doesn't it?"

For some reason he couldn't fathom, that only made his mother's expression odder. "How old are you?" she asked, and held up her hand before he could answer. "No, never mind—I know you're eleven. But you don't talk like you're eleven. You talk like a man who's my age, or maybe twice my age."

"I just talk the way I talk," Lanius said.

"I know," Queen Certhia said. It didn't sound like praise, or not altogether like praise. After a moment, she went on, "Lepturus gave me the same advice you did—that we go out and face the Thervings there in the foothills with everything we have."

"Will you take it?" Lanius asked.

She nodded. "Yes. Lepturus will lead the army out of the city of Avornis. As head of the regency, I'm going with them."

"I should come, too," Lanius exclaimed. "I'm the king, after all." *Even if I can't do anything much,* he added to himself.

"Your coming along is fine if we win," his mother said. "But what if we lose? What if King Dagipert gets his hands on you?"

"I suppose I'd have to marry his silly daughter," Lanius said, which struck him as all too close to a fate worse than death. Other than that, though, falling into Dagipert's hands didn't worry him all that much. He'd been in someone else's hands—one someone's or another's—ever since his father died. He didn't like it, but he was used to it. And besides . . . "With me there, the soldiers will know they'd better not lose."

"I want you to stay here safe in the city of Avornis," Queen Certhia answered, and nothing Lanius could say to her would make her change her mind.

Nothing Lanius could say to her . . . After his mother left—stalked out of his bedchamber, really—the King of Avornis sent a servant to Lepturus, asking if the commander of the royal bodyguard would come and see him. Lepturus came at once. "You don't ask me to come see you, Your Majesty," he said after making his bows. "You *tell* me to come see you. That's what being king is all about, you know."

"No, I don't know anything of the sort," Lanius answered. "How should I?"

Lepturus grunted laughter. "Well, you'll find out, Your Majesty. By the gods, you will. When you say 'Hop,' you'll never see so many hop toads as go up in the air for you. Won't be so very long, either."

Lanius remembered that for the rest of his days, even though his coming of age seemed much further away to him than it did to Lepturus.

The guards commander asked, "What can I do for you, Your Majesty? You just name it. If it's in my power, it's yours."

That was what Lanius wanted to hear. He said, "When you march against King Dagipert and the Thervings, take me along with you."

"What?" Lepturus rumbled, his eyes widening. Lanius repeated himself. Grown-ups, he'd noticed, had trouble hearing, or at least trouble listening. Lepturus heard him out for the second time, and then asked, "Why do you want to do a thing like that?"

"Because I'm the King of Avornis, and that's what the King of Avornis is supposed to do." Lanius sounded very sure. He explained why. "I've read it in books, you see."

"But the books don't say anything about what happens when the King of Avornis is only eleven years old," Lepturus said.

"Well, if I were bigger, I could fight better, but I don't think one soldier more or less would make a lot of difference about whether we win or lose," Lanius said. "Do you, Lepturus?"

With a chuckle, Lepturus shook his head. "No, I don't suppose so. Tell me, though, Your Majesty, what's your mother got to say about all this?"

"She says, 'No!' She says, 'Heavens, no!'" King Lanius answered. "That's why I called you—to see if I could get you to change her mind."

"She heads the regency council now. She doesn't have to change her mind for anybody," Lepturus said, and Lanius nodded unhappily. Lepturus went on, "I don't know that she ought to change her mind here, either, meaning no disrespect to you."

"Wouldn't the soldiers fight better if they knew the king shared danger with them?" Lanius asked. The books said things worked that way.

And Lepturus didn't laugh, or chuckle, or even smile. He just rubbed his bearded chin and looked thoughtful. "They might," he admitted. "They just might."

Lanius leaned forward. "Will you talk to my mother, then?" His heart thudded in excitement.

Lepturus rubbed his chin some more. At last, slowly, he nodded. "I might," he said. "I just might."

Aboard the *Otter,* Grus waited for trouble. It hadn't come yet. What had come was a message from the city of Avornis that astounded everyone aboard, from him down to the juniormost sailor.

"King Lanius is leading the army against the Thervings." Nicator still sounded disbelieving.

"Maybe there's more to him than meets the eye," Grus said.

"He's a boy. There could hardly be less to him than meets the eye, now could there?" Nicator answered.

"He's a boy, but he's the King of Avornis," Grus said.

"He's the King of Avornis, but he's a boy," Nicator retorted.

"If he carried the Scepter of Mercy, how old he is wouldn't matter," Grus said.

Nicator scowled. "There weren't any Thervings in the mountains the last time a King of Avornis wielded the Scepter of Mercy. The Banished One stole it before they filtered off the plains to the east."

"I know that. Everybody knows that, the same way everybody knows the Banished One can't use the Scepter of Mercy."

"Sending a little boy into the field isn't the way to make up for not having it," Nicator said.

"How do you know he was sent?" Grus said. "Maybe he wanted to go."

"Not likely," Nicator disagreed. "I wouldn't want to go face the Thervings when King Dagipert's feeling testy. Neither would anybody else in his right mind—and if Lanius does, he likely isn't in his right mind."

"Well, if you put what you're trying to show into what you claim, that does make arguing easier," Grus said, more annoyed at Nicator than he usually let himself get.

Before the veteran could answer back, a watchman called out and pointed to the bank of the Tuola, where a ragged-looking fellow who might have been either an Avornan or a Therving stood waving by a horse on its last legs. *At least he's not a soul-dead thrall,* Grus thought, and ordered the *Otter* to a halt. He hailed the stranger. "Who are you, and what do you want with us?"

"I'm Count Corax, by the gods," the ragged man replied, as though Grus were supposed to know who he was. And, in case Grus didn't, he went on, "I'm just back from a mission to the Heruls, on the far side of the Bantian Mountains."

"Ah," Grus said, and called an urgent order to his sailors. "Man the boat and bring him aboard."

As they hurried to obey, one of them asked, "What about the horse, Skipper?"

"If you can get it onto the boat without any trouble, fine," Grus answered. "If you can't, too bad. I don't think Corax there will miss it."

Sure enough, the horse stayed behind. Corax scrambled up from the boat onto the river galley. No matter how ragged he looked, he carried himself like an Avornan noble, sure enough—one of the arrogant type. He looked at the *Otter* as though it were as much his to command as the horse had been. "Take me to the city of Avornis, so I may speak to the regents at once," he said.

Grus shook his head. "Sorry, Your Excellency, but I can't do it."

Count Corax turned red. Grus got the idea he wasn't used to hearing people say no. "Why not?" he demanded.

"For one thing, I'm on war patrol," Grus answered. "I can take you to the nearest town and put you on a better horse than the one you had, but that's it. And, for another, the regents aren't—or at least Queen Certhia isn't—at the city of Avornis."

"Well, where are they?" Corax asked. "Wherever it is, you have to take me there right away." He looked set to add, *Now hop to it, gods curse you,* but somehow held back.

"I can't do that, either," Grus said.

"Well, what in creation *can* you do?" Count Corax barked.

"I can tell you that Queen Certhia has taken the field against the Thervings," Grus replied. "I can tell you that King Lanius is in the field, too. And I can do what I said I'd do before that—I can take you to the next town and put you on a horse. The army is covering territory river galleys can't reach."

Corax swore. He kept on swearing for the next several minutes, hardly seeming to draw breath and not repeating himself once. At last, he calmed down enough for a coherent sentence. "I need to see the queen this instant."

"I do understand that it's important, Your Excellency," Grus said. "I'm doing the best I can for you."

"It isn't good enough," Corax snarled.

"Tell me, Your Excellency, are you by any chance related to Count Corvus?" Grus asked.

Corax blinked. "He's my brother. Why do you ask? Do you know him? I don't recall hearing that he knows you." Suspicion filled his voice.

"We met once, a long time ago," Grus said. "And I've heard a lot about him." None of what he'd heard was good. And Corax sounded as hard and unpleasant as his brother.

One thing Corax couldn't do was take a hint. "I should hope you've heard about him," he said. "All of Avornis should know about us." The *Otter*'s bow dipped. He grabbed for the rail.

"I'm sure all of Avornis will." Grus didn't mean it as a compliment, but Corax didn't need to know that.

Nicator asked, "What about the Heruls?"

"What business of yours are they?" The nobleman looked down his nose at the river-galley officer.

"Well, if I'm going to fight me a war, I'd sort of like to know how big a war I'm fighting," Nicator answered. "If the Heruls will pitch into

Thervingia, King Dagipert can't hit us near as hard as he can if they sit on their hands."

Corax weighed a sardonic reply. Grus reluctantly gave him credit for deciding against it. The envoy did say, "You need to worry less than you may have thought you did."

"Oh, I always worry," Nicator said. "But you're right—the thing is, how much?"

Grus always worried, too. He was more imaginative than Nicator, and so found more things to worry about. A kingdom full of bad-tempered, haughty nobles like Corax and Corvus came to mind. They could do whatever they pleased, especially when the King of Avornis was weak. How many men, all through the realm, were busy lining their pockets because nobody was keeping an eye on them? The answer was, *too many.*

When he let Corax off the *Otter* at the town of Veteres the next day, the noble started screaming at the people there to get him a horse and get out of his way. Grus looked at Nicator. "You see?" he said. "He's like that with everybody."

Even before Count Corax galloped off to the northwest, Grus had the *Otter* heading back out toward midstream to resume his patrol. He took war patrol duties seriously. And he needed to. That very afternoon, another horseman came galloping down to the riverbank. This fellow had a bloody bandage on one arm and an arrow sticking out of the saddle behind him. "The Thervings!" he cried. "The Thervings are over the border!"

"Really?" Grus murmured. "I never would have guessed."

King Lanius hadn't known what to expect from life in the field. It was, he realized, much less of a hardship for him than for the Avornan soldiers. His tent could have held a couple of squads of them. He didn't suppose they got the same food he did, either.

On the other hand, none of them had a tutor accompanying him to war. Lanius wouldn't have minded, or didn't think he would have minded, trading books for a sword. But the tutor wasn't so harsh a taskmaster as usual. He kept looking around, eyes wide and frightened. At last, Lanius asked, "What's wrong?"

"Nothing's wrong *now*, Your Majesty," the man answered. "But many more things can go wrong here than they can back at the royal palace."

For a while, Lanius enjoyed looking at the countryside. He rarely left the palace, and up till now he'd never gone outside the city of Avornis. But after a few days, the landscape began to pall. It was, after all, just a landscape—little villages and farmhouses and fields and meadows, some with sheep or cattle or horses in them, and groves and patches of forest and streams and ponds and, rising in the distance, the Bantian Mountains. Lanius began to wish he were home, especially as the terrain grew more rugged and the going slowed.

He made the mistake of saying as much to his mother. "Shall I send you back to the city, then?" Queen Certhia asked eagerly.

He shook his head. "No, thank you. I still want to see what happens."

"People kill each other," Certhia said. "Do you think you'll learn something, watching all the different ways they can die?"

"Yes, Mother, I do," he answered. Certhia gave him an annoyed look and waved him out of her pavilion, which was even larger and fancier than his.

The rough country from which Avornis' famous Nine Rivers sprang was interesting, but only for a little while. As the flatlands had, hills and gorse and heather and bushes for which he had no names soon lost their appeal. Then a rider came galloping out of the southeast as though he had demons on his tail. He shouted for Queen Certhia and for Lepturus, and closeted himself away with them when they met him.

Again, Lanius' mother wouldn't tell him what was going on. Again, the commander of the royal bodyguards proved more willing to talk. "That's Count Corax who just came into camp," he said when he emerged. "He's back from a trip to the other side of the mountains. Bet you can't guess why."

"To incite the Heruls against the Thervings?" Lanius asked.

Lepturus jerked in surprise. "Well, I guess I should have known better than to say something like that to you, Your Majesty. Still, if you don't mind my asking, how *did* you know?"

"It's the kind of thing Avornis does, whenever we have someone who thinks of it," Lanius answered. "Sometimes it works, sometimes it doesn't. That's what I've read, anyhow."

"Oh," Lepturus said, and then, "Me, I don't have a whole lot of book learning."

"It's all I have," Lanius said. "How could I have anything else, when I've never been out of the city of Avornis before?"

"Now that you are out, what do you think of the countryside?" the guards commander asked.

"Not much," Lanius answered. "I like the royal palace a lot better."

Lepturus threw back his head and laughed. "Well, you're honest about it, anyway."

"Why shouldn't I be?" Lanius asked.

"No reason, Your Majesty. No reason at—" Before Lepturus could finish, horns blared and men started shouting his name. He hurried out of the royal pavilion. Over his shoulder, he said, "Sorry to go like this, but sounds like somebody just dropped a pot. I get to pick up the pieces." The tent flap fell behind him. He was gone.

With his mother still talking things over with Count Corax, there was no one to tell Lanius he couldn't step outside his pavilion and see what was going on. Horsemen and foot soldiers hurried north and west in a steady stream. The guards by his tent, though, didn't leave. If they had, it would have been treason. Lanius asked one of them, "Where are all the soldiers going?"

"Off to fight, Your Majesty. Off to fight," the guardsman answered.

"Are the Thervings over there, then?"

"That's right," the fellow said. "But we'll lick 'em. You can count on that."

Lanius didn't just want to count on it. He wanted to see it for himself. If he hadn't come here to see a battle, what was the point to this long, dull, uncomfortable journey? He pointed in the direction the soldiers were going. "Fetch my pony," he told the guards. "I'm heading that way myself."

Queen Certhia would have said no. (Actually, Lanius was sure his mother would have had hysterics before saying no.) Lepturus would have said no, too. But Certhia was busy with Corax, and Lepturus was busy with the army. That left it up to the bodyguards. They were young men themselves. When they grinned at one another, Lanius knew he had a chance. When one of them hurried off to get the pony, he knew he'd won his gamble.

He was on the pony's back and riding in the direction everyone else was going in less time than it takes to tell about it. The guardsmen clustered round him. They hadn't forgotten their duty, even if they'd interpreted it in a way that would have made his mother blanch.

"The king! The king! Look, it's the king! He's come to fight along with us!" Soldiers stared at Lanius and pointed his way. Then they began to cheer. The cheers spread through the whole army, getting louder and deeper as they did.

By then, Lanius was only a little way behind the battle line that was taking shape on what looked to have been a field of barley. "I think this here's just about far enough," one of his bodyguards said. The others nodded. It was high ground. Beyond the Avornan soldiers, Lanius watched another line of battle forming. The sun glinted from the Thervings' helmets and spearpoints. Their horn signals, thin in the distance, sounded not much different from those Avornan trumpeters used.

"What are you doing here?" someone behind Lanius demanded: Lepturus.

"That's, 'What are you doing here, Your Majesty?'" Lanius replied in his haughtiest tones.

Those tones didn't work. "Don't get smart with me, sonny, or you'll find you're not too big to get your bottom warmed," Lepturus said. "Now answer me—what are you doing here?"

"I came to see the battle," Lanius said, much more quietly.

The guard commander's gaze raked the men who'd let Lanius come so far from the pavilion. They all looked as though they wished they could disappear. "I'll deal with you later," Lepturus said, and they looked unhappier yet. Lepturus turned back to King Lanius. "This isn't a game, Your Majesty. The men who die will stay dead when it's over. The men who hurt will go on hurting. The same goes for the horses. It's worse for them, I think—they have no idea why these things happen to them, and all the loot they can hope for is a few mouthfuls of grass."

"I understand that," Lanius said, though he wasn't sure he did. "I want to see it."

As he had back at the pavilion, Lepturus got interrupted, this time by roars first from the Thervings and then from the Avornans. The two armies started moving toward each other. Lepturus looked very unhappy indeed. "Well, you're going to get your wish, Your Majesty, on account of I haven't got time to deal with you right now. But I'll tell you something— if you get killed, I'm going to be very annoyed at you." He hurried away, leaving Lanius to chew on that.

"Don't you worry none, Your Majesty," said one of the guardsmen who'd brought him forward. "Nothing's going to happen to you. We'll make sure of that."

His comrades nodded. Lanius wondered what would happen to a bodyguard who let something happen to him. Nothing pretty, he suspected.

Less than a quarter of a mile ahead, the Avornan army collided with King Dagipert's Thervings. Lanius hadn't expected the noise to be so dreadful. It sounded as though a hundred palace servants had dropped trays full of bowls and goblets and all started screaming about it at once. But it didn't end in a matter of moments, as dropped trays would have done. It went on and on and on.

An Avornan came staggering back out of the fighting. Blood splashed his coat of mail and his breeches. More blood dribbled out through his left hand, which was clenched around his right. In eerily conversational tones, he said, "Two fingers gone. Just like that, two fingers gone."

Lanius gulped. His belly churned. He'd come out to see the Avornan army triumph. Watching a mutilated man, standing close enough to smell the hot, metallic odor of the blood the fellow was losing, wasn't what he'd had in mind. *I will not be sick,* he told himself sternly. *By Olor's beard, I won't.* One of his guards pointed toward the surgeons. The wounded soldier stumbled away. He still sounded as though he couldn't believe what had happened to him. Lanius wished he couldn't believe it, either.

The fighting came closer. The Thervings were pushing the royal army back. An arrow thudded into the ground about twenty feet in front of Lanius. A guard said, "Beg your pardon, Your Majesty, but if them bastards—uh, beg your pardon again—get any nearer, we're going to have to move you back."

"All right," Lanius said, and all the guards looked relieved. He didn't want to fall into Dagipert's hands. The idea of marrying Romilda terrified him. He was much more afraid of that than of getting hurt or killed. Death wasn't real to him. Injury hadn't been—not till he saw the man with the ruined hand. But having to spend the rest of his life with a *girl*— if that wasn't horror, he didn't know what was.

More bloodied Avornans came back past him, some under their own power, others helped by friends. A few of them, seeing who he was, saluted or called out his name. Most, lost in a private wilderness of pain, paid him no attention.

Lightning struck from a clear sky, right in the middle of the Thervings' line. The thunderclap staggered Lanius. Lurid purple afterimages danced in front of his eyes when he blinked. A guardsman said, "Oh, good! Our wizards aren't asleep after all."

Another bolt struck, and another. The Thervings staggered back. The Avornans surged forward after them. "King Lanius!" they shouted. "King Lanius and victory!"

"How's that, Your Majesty?" a bodyguard asked.

It was heady, sure enough. Queen Certhia kept an eye on what Lanius ate and drank, but every once in a while he got enough wine to feel a little drunk. This reminded him of that, but even better. Still, he couldn't help asking a question of his own. "What will the Thervings' wizards do?"

He didn't have to wait long to find out. Flames shot up from the ground. As Lanius had heard soldiers calling out his name, so he also heard them scream as the fire engulfed them. To his relief, they didn't scream long.

"That's a foul magic," one of the guardsmen said. "If lightning hits you, you're gone, just like that." He snapped his fingers. "But fire? Fire makes you suffer."

All at once, the flames died. Another bodyguard said, "Our wizards *are* awake today." Still shouting Lanius' name, Avornan soldiers forced their way forward again.

The Thervings fought stubbornly. From everything Lanius had read about them, they usually did. No matter how stubbornly they fought, they had to give ground. At last, with the sun halfway down the sky in the west, they withdrew from the field. A fierce rear guard kept the Avornans from turning a victory into a rout.

But it was a victory. Soldiers gathered around King Lanius, cheering till they were hoarse. Lepturus came up and asked him, "What do you think of that? Plenty of grown men, they'd give their left nut to have people shout for 'em this way."

Lanius beckoned to the commander of his bodyguards. Lepturus obediently leaned close. In a low voice, Lanius said, "I think I'd sooner be back at the palace."

Lepturus laughed. "Well, Your Majesty, can't say I'm too surprised. But we won, so it was worthwhile."

Ravens and vultures had already started squabbling over the corpses lying on the field. Wounded men's groans rose into the air. Dejected Therving prisoners, hands bound, stood under guard. Relatives might ransom a few nobles. The others faced hard labor the rest of their lives. "Was it?" Lanius asked.

"Yes, Your Majesty," Lepturus answered. "Bad as this is, it'd be four times worse if we'd done our best and the Thervings licked us anyway."

After some thought, Lanius sighed. "Maybe," he said, and then, "What did Count Corax tell my mother? Will the Heruls bother King Dagipert, too?"

"I think so." Lepturus looked up. "But here she comes. You can ask her yourself."

Queen Certhia didn't give Lanius the chance. She came up to him and hugged him. Under cover of that hug, she whispered, "You don't know how foolish you were, or how much danger you were in there."

"It worked out all right, Mother," Lanius answered. "We won."

"You didn't know we were going to," his mother said. "You should never have come on this campaign in the first place."

"But I did," Lanius said. "I did, and we won."

CHAPTER SEVEN

Oars rose and fell in smooth unison as the *Otter* fought her way upstream on the Tuola. Commodore Grus had several lookouts posted. A few Therving raiders had crossed the river under cover of darkness. Now, hunted by Avornan soldiers, their main army turned back two weeks earlier, they were desperate to escape.

"Been a while since we won a battle against Dagipert," Grus remarked.

"So it has," Nicator agreed. "I wonder how long it'll be till we win another one, too."

"Who knows?" Grus said. "Maybe he'll be so surprised we won this one, he'll keel over and die of shock."

"Too much to hope for," Nicator said. "When have you known a Therving to be so considerate to his neighbors?"

"Funny," Grus said. "A year ago, Dagipert must have thought he was on top of the world. He was sitting right outside the city of Avornis with his whole army. Arch-Hallow Bucco'd just pledged King Lanius to his daughter. He would've been the King of Avornis' father-in-law, and grandfather to Lanius' heir. Now—" He snapped his fingers. "That's all he's got left."

"Don't count him out," Nicator answered. "Like I say, when's the last time you saw a Therving make things easy for Avornis?"

Grus had no good reply to that. Even had he had one, he wouldn't have gotten to use it. The *Otter* rounded a bend in the river, and two lookouts started yelling at the same time. "Thervings!" one shouted. "Dead ahead!" the other one added.

There they were, only a couple of hundred yards in front of the river galley, more than a dozen men crammed into a rowboat that should have held half as many. They saw the *Otter*, too—saw it and knew how much trouble they were in. Their cries of dismay came clearly across the water. They tried to row harder, to get across the Tuola before the *Otter* could reach them. They weren't rivermen by training; all they succeeded in doing was fouling one another. A couple of them drew bows and started shooting at the *Otter*, a gesture both brave and futile.

"Up the stroke!" Grus commanded. The professionals aboard the river galley followed the rhythm the drummer beat out. The *Otter* seemed to leap ahead. Grus hurried to the stern and seized the rudder from the steersman. He wanted to make the kill himself.

As though aiming an arrow at a running stag, he pointed the *Otter*'s bow at the place where the rowboat would be when the river galley met it. An arrow, once shot, was gone. Here, he could and did correct his aim all the way up to the instant of impact.

Before then, archers on the *Otter* were shooting at the luckless Thervings. "Brace yourselves!" Grus cried just before the ram struck home.

The *Otter* hit the rowboat amidships, exactly as he'd hoped. He staggered at the collision. One archer fell into the Tuola. The fellow grabbed at an oar and held on. The river galley rode up and over the boat full of Thervings.

"That'll be the end of that," Nicator said with no small satisfaction.

"We'll stop to make sure—and to pick up the poor bastard who went over the side," Grus answered. He raised his voice. "Rowers, rest on your oars."

As the *Otter* glided to a stop, Grus felt a tug on the rudder. He wondered if it had caught on a snag. But it wasn't a snag, as he discovered when he looked down. A Therving clung to the rudder. Grus yanked out his sword. "Come up," he called. "Come up and we'll spare your life." He added gestures in case the Therving spoke no Avornan.

He was strong enough, that was certain. Hanging on to the rudder with one hand, he got the other one on the rail. Then he hauled himself up into the *Otter* and stood there for a moment. With his soaked clothes and long hair, with water dripping from his stubbly chin, he looked as much like a river god as a man.

"Take his blade," Grus told a couple of soldiers who'd hurried back to the stern. "I don't want him doing anything stupid."

"Right you are, sir," one of them said. They advanced on the Therving together.

Maybe he thought they were coming to kill him. Maybe he'd been one of the men who'd shot hopeless arrows at the *Otter* as the river galley bore down on the rowboat, and still didn't feel like giving up. Maybe he'd intended to sell his life dear from the moment he grabbed the rudder. Whatever the reason, his blade leaped free with a wet hiss of metal. He sprang past the startled sailors and straight at Grus.

Only because Grus had half expected the Therving to do something foolish did he keep from getting cut down in the first moments of the fight. The enemy warrior was bigger, stronger, and younger than he was, and fought as though he didn't care whether he lived or died. Had a half-mindless thrall from the southern lands under the Banished One's sway been able to fight at all, he might have fought like that. But thralls mostly lacked the wit to fight at all.

Grus gave ground. It was that or be hacked down where he stood. The Therving was utterly without fear. Killing seemed the only thing that mattered to him.

Thunk! An arrow sprouted in his side, as though it had grown there. He grimaced when it struck home, but kept right on trying to slay Grus. *Thunk! Thunk!*—one in the side, one in the chest. The Therving grunted. Blood began to run from his nostrils and from the corner of his mouth, but he fought on.

Thunk! Another arrow, this one right in the middle of his chest. Swaying, he nodded to Grus as though to an old friend. "He still remembers you," he said in excellent Avornan. Only then did he topple.

"Tough bugger," a sailor remarked, more in praise than otherwise. "You all right, Skipper?"

"Yes, I think so," Grus answered, panting. "Tough bugger is right. I had all I could do to keep him from carving me."

Sailors picked up the Therving's body and flung it over the rail into the Tuola. As it splashed into the river, one of them asked, "What was that he meant, sir, about somebody remembering you?"

"I don't know. He was dying. And he didn't have any idea who I was, anyhow," Grus said. "How could he?"

The sailor shrugged and went about his business. Grus wished he could do the same. For him, though, it wasn't so easy. He had a pretty good idea whom the Therving might have meant. There was only one being who had ever taken note of him. And, just for a moment, he'd thought the Banished One stared out through the dying warrior's eyes.

He tried to tell himself he'd been imagining things. He tried and tried, but couldn't make himself believe it.

Winter in the city of Avornis was a slow time, a time to spend with friends and family. Rain and snow made travel outside the city difficult, sometimes impossible. Even travel inside the city often wasn't easy. Without the rivers that came together at or near it, the place never could have grown bigger than an average provincial town. But in a hard winter, the rivers froze, and could stay frozen for weeks at a time. Poor people went hungry then, and the poorest starved. In a very hard winter, the kind that came once or twice in a hundred years, even people not so very poor starved.

At first, King Lanius didn't worry about the snow that fell day after dreary day. He enjoyed playing in it and throwing snowballs as much as any other boy his age. Servants' children could throw snowballs at him without fear of arrest for treason.

Lepturus was the one who began worrying out loud a couple of weeks before the winter solstice. "We've had a lot of snow already this year, Your Majesty," he said.

"I know that," Lanius answered. He knew it quite well. He'd had some of that snow delivered, with considerable force, just in front of his left ear, not long before coming back into the palace.

But Lepturus persisted. "If it keeps up like this, it's going to be a nasty one. I think the rivers *will* freeze, and I think they'll stay frozen too cursed long."

Lanius frowned. He'd come across accounts of such hard times in his reading. "That could be very bad."

"You're right. It could." Lepturus drummed his fingers on his thigh. "When I was your age, or maybe even smaller, my granddad used to tell me stories about a hard, hard winter that had happened when he was small. He said it got so bad, some people had to turn cannibal to get by. It was as though the Banished One prowled through the streets of the city. We don't want times like those coming back."

"Gods forbid!" Lanius exclaimed. But then, wistfully, he asked, "What was it like—having a grandfather, I mean? I hardly knew my own father, and both my grandfathers died years before I was born."

"My granddad was an old man who liked wine a bit too much and talked and talked when he got tiddly," the commander of his bodyguards said with a reminiscent smile. "But you need to think about the city of Avornis now, and—"

"Bring in as much grain as we can while the rivers are still passable?" Lanius broke in.

Lepturus looked at him and clicked his tongue between his teeth. "You're getting ahead of me, Your Majesty," he said, almost reproachfully. "Yes, I think that's what we ought to do, and the sooner the better."

"Go tell my mother, then," Lanius said. "Tell her I think it's a good idea, too." His mouth twisted. "Or maybe you'd better not. She doesn't seem to want to heed anything I say these days."

"You're not that far from coming of age, Your Majesty," Lepturus said. "Your mother . . . likes heading the regency."

"And so she doesn't like it when I show I know what I'm doing?" Lanius asked. The guards commander nodded. Lanius sighed. "That's silly. I'd come of age even if I didn't know what I was doing. Would she like that better?"

"*You'd* have to ask her that," Lepturus said. "Me, I'll take her what you said, and I hope she pays attention."

He strode out of King Lanius' chamber. Not too many days passed before palace servants reported to Lanius that a lot more barges and boats than usual were stopping at the docks. All were full of wheat and barley and rye. He nodded, pleased with himself. *Nobody out there in the city is likely to know it, but I've done something right,* he thought.

And not long after that, an embassy from the south came up into the city of Avornis. The princes of the Menteshe treated with Avornis as did King Dagipert and the lords of the cities of the Chernagors. This embassy was different. It wasn't a mission from the Menteshe, but from their overlord—from the Banished One himself.

His envoy was a Menteshe, of course, a round, swarthy man named Karajuk. The Banished One hadn't spoken this directly with Avornis in almost a century. Queen Certhia kept Karajuk and his henchmen outside the walls of the city for a couple of days while secretaries pawed through musty scrolls to make sure they received him as their forefathers had received the Banished One's last embassy. More than any mere mortal, the Banished One had a long memory. He would not overlook a slight, even an inadvertent one.

Because the reigning King of Avornis had received his last embassy, Lanius had to sit on the Diamond Throne to receive this one. Loremasters worried that having Karajuk come before Queen Certhia would be reckoned an insult, even if she did head the regency council. Certhia fretted. "What if he does something to you?"

"I'll have wizards warding me," Lanius answered patiently. "It will be all right. If he wanted to kill me, he'd use an assassin, not an ambassador."

"Is there a difference to the Banished One?" his mother asked bleakly.

Lanius had no good answer for that. The Banished One was a law—or rather, no law—unto himself. But one of the protocol experts said, "We dare not offend him, Your Royal Highness," and Certhia had to yield to his advice.

Thus Lanius sat enthroned in his heaviest, most gorgeous robe, the spiked crown of Avornis heavy on his head, as Karajuk and four followers—there had been four a hundred years ago, so there were four now—approached. The envoy wore a wolfskin hat, a snow-leopard jacket, and deerskin trousers. His supporters had a similar style with less rich garments.

Karajuk bowed low to Lanius. "I greet you, Your Majesty, in the name of my Master." He spoke excellent, unaccented Avornan. Something glittered in his dark eyes as he added, "One day soon, maybe, he will come forth to greet you in person."

Not for nothing had Lanius looked through the old documents the loremasters had unearthed. He said, "The Banished One's last emissary said the same thing on his visit. He himself has not come yet."

Karajuk studied him. "Yesss," the Menteshe murmured, drawing the word out into a long hiss. "Your Majesty, my Master bids me say, you are not so clever as you think you are."

"Neither is he," Lanius replied. "If he were, he would still live with the other gods."

Behind Karajuk, his henchmen muttered in their own language. If the gibe sank deep, the ambassador did not show it. He looked at Lanius once more. Were those his own eyes boring into the King of Avornis, or did the Banished One look out through them? Lanius didn't know. He wondered if Karajuk did.

"You had better listen to me, Your Majesty," Karajuk said. "You had better hear the words of my Master."

Queen Certhia, who sat below and to the right of the throne, and Lepturus, who stood below and to the left, both stirred angrily. Lanius just looked down at the Menteshe, as though he'd found him on the bottom of his sandal. "Say on," he said.

"Good. Maybe you have good sense after all," Karajuk said. "My Master asks, how bad will this winter be? How long will this winter last?"

"The gods know that," Lanius answered. "No one else does."

Karajuk smiled a singularly nasty smile. Since being cast forth from the heavens, the Banished One wasn't exactly a god. On the other hand, he wasn't exactly *not* a god, either. Could he know things like that? Lanius wasn't sure. Another question occurred to him, one he wished he hadn't thought of. Could the Banished One *influence* things like that? Lanius wasn't sure there, either, and wished he were.

By his smile, Karajuk suggested an answer. Of course, he would have suggested that answer regardless of whether it was true. He said, "Do you really want to find out, Your Majesty? You will. Oh, indeed you will. And when ice grips your rivers in the cold fingers of death, how will you feed your people?"

Certhia stirred again. She looked up to Lanius. Ever so slightly, he shook his head. He didn't want the Banished One's envoy hearing he'd already started bringing extra provisions into the city of Avornis. If Karajuk—if his Master—learned that, a different threat might come next— one he wasn't so well able to meet.

He said, "You tell me the Banished One will ease the winter if I do what he wants? What is his price?"

"Yes, my Master will do that," the Menteshe answered. He didn't call the Banished One by that name. As far as the Banished One was concerned, he'd done nothing to deserve being ousted from the heavens. *Master* pleased him much better. Karajuk went on, "What do you have to do? You have to yield up the province of Perusia, north of the Stura. Set Perusia in my Master's hands and you will pass through this winter untroubled by his wrath."

"Yes—this winter. But what of next winter, or the winter after that?" Lanius shook his head. "You may tell the Banished One no. I will take my chances. My city will take its chances."

"On your head shall it be," Karajuk said. "I tell you—I tell you in my Master's mighty name—you will regret your foolishness."

"I will take my chances. The city of Avornis will take its chances," Lanius replied. "You are dismissed. Go back to him with my words."

"I will," the Menteshe said. "You have already heard his words. Soon you will see how he keeps his promise." He bowed and left the throne room. His henchmen glared back over their shoulders at Lanius as they followed him.

After the Menteshe had departed, Lepturus turned and nodded up at Lanius. The King of Avornis only shrugged by way of reply. He had no idea whether he'd done the right thing. *I'll find out,* he thought, and then shook his head. Come what might, *he* would have plenty to eat. The city of Avornis would find out.

An icy storm whipped the waters of the Stura up into whitecaps. Sleet and flurries of snow blew almost horizontally. Icicles hung from the *Pike's* rigging and from the river galley's yard. Little icicles also clung to Grus' beard and mustache. "Isn't this a bastard?" he shouted to Nicator.

"Never seen anything like it in all my born days," the veteran captain answered. "Never once. And down here, where the weather's supposed to be good. Gods only know what it's like up by the city of Avornis, places like that. Got to be pretty foul, though. Only stands to reason."

"Yes, it does," Grus agreed, and shivered. "Somebody ashore told me the Banished One's embassy to the king came back with one unhappy envoy."

"Oh, too bad." Nicator's voice dripped false distress. "That breaks my heart, that does. Tears me all in two, yes indeed."

"I can tell," Grus said dryly. "But do you think the one has got anything to do with the other?"

"Don't know." Now Nicator sounded thoughtful. "Who can say for sure what the Banished One's full powers are? Curse me if I'm certain he knows himself."

"Something to that, I shouldn't wonder," Grus agreed. He'd spent a lot of time in the south. Taken all in all, the Menteshe were the most dangerous foes Avornis had. That would have been true even without the Banished One's patronage, for only the Stura held them away from the rich farmlands in the wide, friendly valleys of the Nine Rivers. With the Banished One urging them on, aiding them . . .

A line carrying too much ice parted just then. The *Pike's* mast swayed alarmingly. If it went over, the river galley might turn turtle—and who could last long with the Stura so cold and fierce?

Sailors hauled on other lines to keep the mast upright. A couple of men went to the length of mountain fir and hung on to it, literally for their lives. Still others, with Grus shouting orders, seized the wildly blowing length of line that had snapped, spliced it to a replacement for what had carried away, and made it fast to a belaying pin once more.

Only then did the mast stop groaning in its socket. Only then did Grus let out a sigh of relief the savage wind promptly blew away. "Never a dull moment," he said at last. "I wonder if we ought to take the mast down, but I don't want to try it in this weather. Too easy for something to carry away—"

"Like that line did," Nicator broke in.

"Like that line, yes." Grus nodded. "And if it happened at just the wrong time, the way those things usually happen, we'd be worse off than if we left it up."

Nicator nodded, too. "Makes sense to me."

Turnix came bustling up to them. With his robes blowing like wash on a line, the wizard looked about to blow away himself, but he'd proved tolerably surefooted. "Have you ever had an arrow go past your head, close enough to feel the wind of it?" he asked.

Grus and Nicator both nodded this time. Grus said, "Wish I hadn't, but I have. Why? What's the point?"

"I think . . . something just went past the *Pike* the same way, Commodore," Turnix answered. "It was there and gone before I could even think to ward it. But it missed."

"You may be right," Grus said slowly. "I think you are, but I couldn't prove it."

"I'm not sure I could prove it, either," Turnix said. "I'll tell you this, though—if it was real, the way I think it was, I'm awfully glad it missed." His laugh was shaky. "I wish I could claim credit for turning it aside— you'd like me better if I did. But the shooter missed. I didn't block it."

Grus nodded yet again. He had a brief vision of the Banished One's beautiful yet terrible face, eyes narrowed and nostrils flared with frustration. When the vision faded, he was even gladder it had been brief than that the spell, if spell it was, had missed the *Pike*. A man wasn't meant to look into those eyes for long—not if he hoped to stay sane afterward.

"Well, Your Majesty, when you're an old man with a long white beard, you can tell your grandchildren you came through this winter," Lepturus said. "Their eyes will get all big, and they'll go, 'Tell us some more, Granddad Your Majesty.' "

However clever Lanius was, he couldn't imagine himself old and bent and with a long white beard. At twelve, he eagerly imagined himself with any sort of beard at all; as yet, his cheeks were bare even of what people called peach fuzz. More impatient than ever to become a man, he remained a boy in the eyes of the world.

But the commander of his bodyguards was right in general, if not in particular. He'd never seen a winter like this one before, and he didn't expect to see another like this one even if he did become a bent old man with a long white beard. "Some people say the rivers are frozen clean to the bottom," he remarked.

"I don't know about that," Lepturus said. "And I don't think they can know anything about that, either. Have they been down to the river bottoms to see for themselves?"

"I don't suppose so," Lanius admitted. He filed that one away, as he did with thoughts every now and then. It boiled down to three words—*what's the evidence?* But not even an interesting idea could keep him from going on, "There's an awful lot of snow and ice, though, even if it doesn't go clear to the bottom."

"That there is. I said so myself, as a matter of fact," Lepturus answered. "And the ice is mighty thick. I won't argue about that, either. I'd bet you could stampede a herd of elephants across the rivers, and they wouldn't come close to cracking it."

"I wish we had a herd of elephants in the city of Avornis," Lanius said. "That would be fun to try, if they didn't freeze."

"Yes—if," Lepturus said. "But everything that stays out in the cold freezes this winter. If the weather were only a little better, I'd worry about King Dagipert laying siege to us, what with the rivers and the marshes frozen hard as iron. But I don't think even Dagipert can get the Therving army from the mountains to here without losing most of his men, maybe all of 'em, on the way."

"*Even* Dagipert?" Lanius said. "Does that mean Dagipert's a good king?"

"A strong one, anyhow, and a cursed fine general," Lepturus said. "That makes him a lot more dangerous to Avornis, to us, than he would be otherwise."

Lanius hadn't thought being a good king and being a strong king might differ. Everyone said King Mergus, his father, had been a strong King of Avornis. He'd assumed that made Mergus a good king, too.

He started to ask Lepturus, then changed his mind. Instead, he found a different question. "Does the city have enough in the way of supplies?"

"For now, Your Majesty," the officer answered. "If you hadn't said we ought to start laying in more when you did, we might not've, but you did and we did and we do. I think we'll be all right no matter how long this cold weather lasts."

"Even if it goes right on into summer?" Lanius' eyes widened.

"Well, no," Lepturus said. "Not if it does that. But I don't see how it could do that, do you? Not even the Banished One could make it do that . . . I don't think."

"I don't think he can, either," Lanius said. "He's never done anything like that, not in all the years since Olor cast him out of the heavens." He sighed. "I've never thought it was fair for the gods to get rid of the Banished One and to inflict him on us poor mortals."

"You don't want to talk to me about that," Lepturus said. "You want to talk to Arch-Hallow Bucco."

"No, I don't. I never want to talk to Arch-Hallow Bucco." Lanius made a nasty face. "If Megadyptes wanted the job back, Bucco wouldn't *be* arch-hallow anymore. But Megadyptes would rather spend his time praying than riding herd on unruly priests, and so . . ." He sighed again.

"Can't say as I blame him," Lepturus remarked. "You could ask some other priest, then, Your Majesty. It doesn't have to be Bucco."

"I've tried that, as a matter of fact." Lanius screwed up his face again. "Do you know what they say when I do?"

The guards commander thought, but not for long. Then he intoned, " 'It's a mystery,' " exactly as a priest would have—exactly as a couple of priests had when Lanius asked the question.

"That's it! That's the answer!" Lanius said. "It's the answer, but it doesn't help."

"One thing you find out as you get older, Your Majesty," Lepturus said. "Getting answers is easy. Getting answers that help is a whole different business."

Winter went on and on. The Banished One might not have been able to make it stretch into summer, but he seemed to be doing his best. Blizzards kept roaring through the city of Avornis all the way through what should have been the beginning of spring. Right about what should have been the beginning of spring, Karajuk returned to the city.

As before, Lanius ascended to the Diamond Throne. As before, Queen Certhia sat at his right hand. As before, Lepturus stood at his left. "How now?" he asked when Karajuk and what looked like the same four henchmen made their bows before him.

"My Master asks if you are ready to do his bidding now that you have had a taste of winter and hunger," Karajuk said.

"It has been a cold winter, hasn't it?" Lanius said, as though he hadn't particularly noticed till the Menteshe reminded him. "But there is no special hunger here—no worse than any other winter, anyhow."

Karajuk's narrow eyes widened. In that moment, Lanius was sure he saw the Banished One looking out through his envoy. "You lie," the Menteshe hissed.

"You mind your tongue, wretch," Lepturus rumbled, "or we'll send you back to your vile Master with it in your pocket."

Lanius raised his hand. "It's all right, Lepturus. He's a barbarian, and knows no better." As he'd been sure it would, that angered Karajuk all over again. "But what I said is true. No one starves here in the city of Avornis. By all the gods, I swear it."

That was also calculated to infuriate Karajuk, who served one no longer, or not quite, a god. "With this winter?" the Menteshe growled. "I don't believe you."

"Believe what you please," Lanius said politely. "If you like, after you leave the palace our soldiers will escort you through the city so you can see for yourself whether I am telling the truth."

"Do you take *me* for a little boy?" Karajuk could be insulting, too. "Your soldiers will show me what Avornis wants me to see."

"No." When Lanius shook his head, he felt the weight of the crown. "Go where you will in the city of Avornis. The guards will protect you. Folk do not love the Banished One here. You need protection in the city."

Karajuk and his henchmen put their heads together. When he turned back to Lanius, he said, "I will take you up on your generous offer." Irony dripped from his words. "I think you are bluffing. I think you are lying."

Not only Lepturus but several of the bodyguards growled at that. Lanius said, "I think you are rude and serve a bad Master. After you go through the city, we can see who is right. For now, you are dismissed."

"You had better be careful, bastard boy who calls himself king," Karajuk said. "If my Master—"

"You are dismissed," Lanius said again. Karajuk, scowling blacker than the storm clouds outside, had to withdraw. Lanius might not rule on his own yet, but he had discovered that the king got the last word.

Karajuk and the Banished One's lesser servants took their tour the next day. Along with ordinary guardsmen, Lepturus sent a couple of wizards with them. Lanius didn't know what the ambassador and his henchmen might do in the way of magic, but he agreed with the commander of the bodyguard—better not to have to find out the hard way.

When Karajuk and his followers returned to the throne room after going through the city, the Menteshe looked less happy than ever. "I still say it's some sort of a trick," he ground out.

"You may think what you like, of course," Lanius said. "We here in Avornis have a word in our language for someone who will not believe what his eyes tell him." He'd pulled that gibe from an ancient book of japes. He'd hoped he would get the chance to use it. He didn't smile at Karajuk, but he felt like it.

The Banished One's ambassador said, "You will regret this." He turned and stalked out of the throne room without waiting to be dismissed. The other Menteshe, as always, followed him. They might have been puppies trailing after their mother.

"Nicely done, Your Majesty," Lepturus said when they were gone.

"Maybe," Lanius answered. "We'll have trouble once good weather finally comes again."

His guards commander only shrugged. "Name a year when we haven't had trouble." Try as he might, Lanius couldn't.

Resentfully, sullenly, six weeks after it should have, winter finally left Avornis. "Now we'll have floods, on account of all the melting snow," Nicator predicted.

"I hope not," Grus said, fearing his friend was right.

"As soon as things thaw out and dry out, we're going to have the Menteshe on our backs, too," Nicator said. "*And* the Thervings—you mark my words. Dagipert's still got to be steaming because we held him last summer."

"Well, in that case we ought to get a call to come back to the north before too long," Grus said. "We've gone back and forth between the Stura and the city of Avornis so often, I'm actually starting to know what to do on horseback."

"Me, I don't fall off so much anymore," Nicator said. "That'll do."

"What worries me is what we'll do if the Thervings come down out of the mountains and the Menteshe boil up from the south at the same time."

"Yes, that'd be bad, all right," Nicator agreed.

"Here's hoping it doesn't happen." Grus made the finger sign to repel bad luck. He went on, "You know, there's one good argument that King Dagipert *isn't* the Banished One's creature."

"What's that, Skipper?"

"Well, if he were, the Thervings and the Menteshe would move against us together more often than they do," Grus answered. "Since they don't, odds are Dagipert's his own man."

"His own miserable old dragon, you mean," Nicator said. Grus laughed. Nicator went on, "He couldn't have caused Avornis any more grief if he were the Banished One's mother-in-law."

That probably wasn't true. Peasants on lands the Menteshe conquered were lost to true humanity forever. Peasants on lands the Thervings overran just started working for them instead of for their own kingdom. In one way, the difference was profound. In another, though, it wasn't. No matter who took them away or what happened to them, they were still lost to Avornis.

Before very long, the message the two river-galley officers had expected proved to be waiting for them in a little town alongside the Stura. Grus read the parchment a watch officer handed him, then nodded to Nicator: "We're ordered to return to the city of Avornis as fast as we can get there. That means by horseback."

"Of course it does," Nicator said gloomily. "If they could stick us in a catapult and shoot us from hither to yon, they'd do that instead."

"And you'd like it better, too, wouldn't you?" Grus asked with a sly smile.

"Who, me? I might, by the gods. I don't know for sure. I wouldn't get saddle sore, anyhow, I'll tell you that."

"No, but you'd like coming down from getting flung a lot less than you like dismounting from a horse."

"I might," Nicator said. "But then again, I might not, too. You never can tell." Grus snorted. Nicator let out a rumbling chuckle.

They rode north on a couple of horses the royal post lent them. The royal post of Avornis was supposed to be able to get anywhere in the Kingdom of Avornis in a hurry. If it relied on horses like those first two it furnished Grus and Nicator, Grus had trouble seeing how it did its job. He'd never ridden a more lethargic beast, and Nicator's was no livelier. "They've got two gaits," Grus said after another vain try at coaxing a canter, let alone a gallop, from his mount. "One's a walk—"

"And so's the other," Nicator said.

Grus made a face at him. "If stepping on your commander's jokes isn't mutiny, it ought to be."

"If you call that a joke, Skipper, it deserves stepping on," Nicator replied. They both laughed, and rode on at the best speed the sorry horses would give them.

When they came to the next relay station, they changed mounts. The horses they got there were a little livelier than the ones they'd had before, but not much. They kept heading north, changing horses every station or two. Sometimes they got bad horses, sometimes indifferent ones. If the royal post owned any good horses, it hid them very well.

And then, as they were drawing near the city of Avornis, the relay stations abruptly stopped. A peasant working in a muddy field laughed when Grus asked him where the next one was. "I'll tell you where, pal," he answered. "The other side of Count Corvus' lands, that's where. We ain't had nothing like that hereabouts since my granddad's day—and Corvus' granddad's, too."

"Why not?" Grus asked. "The kingdom needs them."

"Take it up with Corvus, if you care to," the peasant said. "It's none of my business, and it'll go right on being none of my business, on account of I want to keep my head attached to my neck." He went back to grubbing in the mud.

Grus and Nicator rode their sad, weary mounts across Count Corvus' lands. They rode past the great, frowning castle in which Corvus dwelt. Grus decided to ask the Count no questions after all. He didn't forget, though. To Nicator, he said, "Some of these nobles need reminding they aren't kings themselves."

"Only way you'd make 'em remember is by dropping a rock on their heads," Nicator answered.

"I know." Grus looked around. "Where can I get my hands on a rock?" Nicator laughed. Grus didn't.

CHAPTER EIGHT

Arch-Hallow Bucco lifted up his hands in prayer. "From cold, from hunger, from flood, and from the wrath of our foes, deliver us, O ye gods!" he prayed.

Not even Lanius could quarrel with that. When the ice finally melted, the capital's drainage channels had faced a challenge as dangerous as any Therving siege. They'd guided away the floodwaters, and Lanius was glad to thank the gods that they had.

Standing next to him, though, his mother sniffed scornfully. "If Bucco said the day was sunny, I'd carry an umbrella," Queen Certhia remarked, not bothering to hold her voice down.

Lanius laughed. So did several other people who heard her. Bucco peered toward the noise. When he saw it centered on Certhia, his mouth tightened, but he went on with the service. He'd had his time in the sun, had it and not succeeded. Now Lanius' mother had her chance.

"We need to beat the Thervings again," she told Lanius after they returned to the palace. "We need to, and we will. And you"—she pointed at him—"you will stay in the city of Avornis while our armies go do it."

Sometimes even a king couldn't escape the hand of fate. Lanius recognized this as one of those times. "Yes, Mother," he said. If he'd been anxious to watch another battle, he might have made a bigger fuss—or he might not have, and quietly tried to arrange something with Lepturus instead. As things were, one introduction to the iron world of warfare would last him a lifetime.

"Everything should go well," Certhia said. Lanius wondered whether she was trying to convince him or herself. But she went on, "Corax is leading a band of Heruls across the mountains, and Corvus will command our army."

"And the Menteshe have been very quiet this spring," Lanius added. "We made the Banished One thoughtful when we came through his dreadful winter so well. He thinks we're strong, and so he doesn't want anything to do with us for a while."

Queen Certhia nodded. "Just so. I'm glad I thought to make sure the city was so well provisioned. Otherwise, who knows what might have happened?"

"Who knows?" Lanius echoed tonelessly. He raised an eyebrow as he eyed his mother. She looked back, smiling and candid. As far as he could tell, she really believed supplying the city of Avornis had been her idea. If she ever wrote her memoirs—something Lanius found unlikely, but even so—she would undoubtedly write that she'd had the idea to bring extra grain into the capital to ward against the harsh winter she'd seen coming. Later historians and chroniclers, believing her, would write the same thing. She might be remembered as Queen Certhia the Forethoughtful, or something of the sort.

Contemplating that made Lanius distrust every work of history he'd ever read. Were they all full of such foolishness? He would have to do more judging for himself. Plainly, he couldn't believe everything that was written down.

He saw no point in arguing with his mother about it. He wouldn't change her mind. He did ask, "Is it wise to have so much power resting in the hands of two brothers?"

"Corvus and Corax, you mean?" Certhia asked. Lanius nodded. His mother shrugged. "They're both good officers, and they both have splendid blood."

She waited for him to tell her, *Yes, Mother,* again. He didn't. He said, "Isn't that more likely to make them rebel, not less? Half the nobles in the kingdom think they deserve to be King of Avornis."

"But without nobles, we'd have hardly any officers," Queen Certhia pointed out—which, unfortunately, was also true. Certhia ruffled Lanius' hair. He hated that. She went on, "If you're looking for an officer who isn't a noble, Commodore Grus is in charge of the river galleys that will bring the Heruls into the Thervings' rear." She sniffed, as she had in the cathedral. "*His* father's called Crex the Unbearable, and I'm not sure even Crex himself knows who *his* father was."

"Grus has done well," Lanius said.

"Well, maybe he has, but even so . . ." His mother sniffed yet again. "It's not as though he were a man to take seriously."

A serving girl came up to them with a tray of cakes and wine. Lanius took a cake—they were glazed with honey and full of raisins—and a cup of wine. The girl smiled at him. He smiled back. He didn't quite know how it had happened, but girls, lately, didn't revolt him nearly as much as they had when he was younger.

His mother had noticed that, too. Frost filled her voice as she said, "You may go now, Prinia."

"Yes, Your Royal Highness," the girl said, and hurried away.

"Why did you snap at her like that?" Lanius asked. "She didn't do anything wrong."

"Not yet," Queen Certhia said dryly.

"I don't understand," Lanius said.

"I know," his mother answered. "But you will. Very soon now, you will. And then life will get more complicated—though you may be having too much fun to think so."

Lanius scratched his head. Sometimes his mother made no sense at all.

"Another ship, another stretch of the Tuola River," Grus said with a sigh as he boarded the *Bream*. One river galley was much like another, but they weren't all identical. The *Bream* had seen better days. Her planking was pale with age. She seemed sound enough, but somehow didn't feel lucky. Grus eyed the sailors. They looked back at him and Nicator.

"We'll do our job here, and then they'll send us south to the Stura again," Nicator said. He muttered something under his breath that had to do with horses, then, "Thervings or Menteshe. Thervings or Menteshe . . ."

"Gods grant we have an easy time for a change," Grus said.

"That would be nice," Nicator agreed. "What they've set us to *sounds* easy enough, anyhow. All we have to do is get Corax's band of Heruls down the river and onto our bank of it so they can go on and pitch into the Thervings from behind. Should be simple as you please, so long as everything goes like it's supposed to."

"If everything went the way it was supposed to, the King of Avornis wouldn't need to keep moving us around like pieces on the board," Grus said. "And remember, this is Count Corax, dear Count Corvus' brother."

Nicator walked over to the rail and spat into the swift-running, cold water of the Tuola. "*That* for dear Count Corvus, the cheap, power-grabbing bastard." He spat again. "And *that* for his gods-cursed, arrogant brother."

"As long as you're there, spit once for the Heruls, too," Grus said.

"Sure." Nicator did. "Now tell me why."

"Because I wouldn't give better than about even money that they go kick King Dagipert in the ass once they're on this side of the river," Grus answered. "They're liable to decide they'd have more fun murdering farmers and raping their wives and stealing their sheep."

"Or maybe stealing their wives and raping their sheep," Nicator suggested.

Grus rolled his eyes. "I don't know anything about that, and I'm cursed glad I don't. If you really want to find out, ask Count Corax."

The *Bream* served as flagship for a good-sized flotilla of river galleys, smaller boats, scows, and barges—not a flotilla that could do too much fighting on its own, but more than good enough for taking an army along the Tuola and moving it to the other side. When the *Bream*'s oarmaster shouted out the command for them to leave the port where they were tied up, they all obeyed promptly enough to give Grus no reason to complain.

Their rendezvous with Count Corax lay downstream, and they would deliver the army farther downstream still. That showed good planning by those who'd put the flotilla together. Grus doubted whether a good many of the scows and barges could have gone upstream at anything faster than a crawl, if indeed they could have made headway against the current at all.

"What do you want to bet Count Corax and these savages aren't even there when we get where we're supposed to be?" Nicator said. "It'd be just like him to leave us stuck with nothing to do. He's a noble, after all. Why should he care if ordinary people have to sit around twiddling their thumbs, waiting for him?"

But when the flotilla rounded the last bend in the river, there on the northwestern bank sat the Heruls' encampment, large, messy, and unlovely. The wind wafted the stink of it to Grus' nostrils. He coughed and wrinkled his nose. He knew what camps were supposed to smell like. This was even worse.

"Oh, by the gods!" Nicator pointed. "Look at 'em! They're pissing upstream from where they drink."

"Well, so they are," Grus said. "Corax didn't fetch them here because they were neat and tidy. He fetched them here because they could fight."

"They won't do much fighting if they all come down with the galloping shits," Nicator retorted. "And if they keep doing that, they bloody well will. Don't they know any better?" He answered his own question. "No, by the gods, of course they don't know any better. That's what being a barbarian's all about, isn't it?"

"I suppose so." Grus did some pointing of his own now. "There's the mighty Count Corax's banner, see? I suppose we ought to pick him up. Then we can ferry the Heruls downstream and across, and *then* we can hope they do some good."

He sent the *Bream*'s boat to the far bank of the Tuola. Count Corax, now, wasn't grubby in furs and leather. He wore a golden circlet that wasn't quite a crown on his head and a cloth-of-gold robe more splendid than any Grus had ever seen adorning a King of Avornis. Nicator muttered something under his breath.

"What was that?" Grus asked.

"I said, now we know where all the money goes that Corvus and, looks like, Corax save by not keeping postal stations open on their lands."

"Oh," Grus said, and then, "Yes. He's got his own army there, and he's got his own raiment. When does he start stamping his own gold pieces and calling himself a king?"

"Pretty gods-cursed soon, by the look of him," Nicator replied.

"Or here's another question for you," Grus said. "When does he take these Heruls, move on the city of Avornis with them, and start calling himself *our* king?"

The boat pulled up to the *Bream*. "Let's see what Corax has to say for himself." From their brief acquaintance, and from Count Corax's being Corvus' brother, Grus was ready to dislike him for any reason or none.

Corax scrambled up onto the deck of the *Bream*. "Hello, Commodore," he said, striding back to greet Grus. "We meet again. Remind me of your name, if you'd be so kind."

"Grus, Your Excellency," Grus said tightly. He couldn't order Corax flung into the Tuola no matter how much he wanted to. But, aboard his own river galley, he didn't have to take that lying down—didn't have to, and didn't intend to. "Remind me of yours, if *you'd* be so kind."

"What?" Corax turned red. "If that's a joke, it's not funny, friend. Everybody knows who *I* am." The nobleman struck a pose.

"Not on the rivers," Grus told him. "The rivers have buried men more famous than you'll ever be."

That might have been true, but it wasn't calculated to endear Grus to Count Corax. From red, the Avornan nobleman went a dusky purple.

"You had better hold your tongue, you insolent puppy, or I'll paddle your backside for piddling on my shoes. I am in command of that army yonder, and I ought to turn them loose on you."

"You're welcome to try, Your Excellency," Grus answered.

"I'm not used to having some jumped-up skipper from a fishing scow telling me what I can do and what I can't. By Olor's beard, I don't intend to stand for it, either." Corax set a hand on the hilt of his sword.

Nicator whistled shrilly. Several marines aboard the *Bream* nocked arrows and drew their bows back to the ear. The iron points on the arrowheads, all aimed at Corax, shone in the sun. "You want to think about where you are and what you're doing, don't you, Your Excellency?" Nicator said.

The nobleman had nerve. He didn't let go of the sword right away. Grus had rarely seen an Avornan noble he would have called a coward. A lot of them, though, sadly lacked sense. Corax proved not to belong to that school.

"Oh, good," Grus said when Corax's hand did at last fall to his side. "I wouldn't want to see you all quilled like a hedgehog, Your Excellency, and blood's hard to scrub out of the timbers. It *will* stain."

"You are a funny man, aren't you?" Corax growled. "Let's see how funny you are when the King of Avornis sacks you."

"I'm not losing any sleep over that," Grus answered. "You're the one who's been robbing the king for years, not me."

"Why, you lying sack of turds!" Corax shouted.

"You're the liar, Your Excellency—you and your brigand of a brother." Grus made Corax's title of respect one of reproach. Corax gobbled and turned purple again. With savage relish, Grus went on, "I know the two of you don't keep up the royal post on your lands. When was the last time you sent any taxes to the capital?"

"Taxes?" Corax's gesture of contempt was, in its own way, magnificent. "You gods-cursed fool, taxes are for peasants!"

"Do you suppose the king would say the same?" By *the king*, Grus meant *Queen Certhia and the rest of the regents*, as Corax no doubt had before.

"You swine!" Corax yelled. "You rustic oaf! You—you enema syringe! You brawling, disobedient lump of guts! You pus-filled, poxy villain! You hairy-assed son of a whore! I piss on you!" He started to undo his fly.

"If he comes out, you'll sing soprano the rest of his days," Grus said through clenched teeth. Again, Corax stopped with the motion half complete. Grus gestured to the sailors and marines. "Take this foul-mouthed fool back to the barbarians. They seem to suit him well. May he have joy of them."

"Yes, Commodore," the men chorused. Heedless of Corax's bellows, they bundled him back into the boat. When they got back to the north-western bank of the Tuola, they showed what they thought by dumping him into the middle of a mudflat and letting him make his filthy, dripping way back to the Heruls.

"What do we do now, Skipper?" Nicator asked.

"I'll stay here for a few days," Grus answered, still seething. "If he shows any sign—any sign at all—of acting like a civilized human being, I'll ferry him and the Heruls across the river."

"And if he doesn't?"

"If he doesn't? A pox on him and a plague on the barbarians, that's what."

"What about the fight with the Thervings?"

"Well, what about it?" Grus returned. "Do you think I should be the only one worrying about it? Let's see if Corax cares about the kingdom, or if the only thing in the whole world Corax cares about is Corax."

"Something's gone wrong somewhere," Lepturus said.

"What do you propose to do about it?" Queen Certhia demanded, blue eyes flashing fire.

The guards commander sent King Lanius an annoyed glance. He might have been saying, *Pretty soon you'll be old enough to rule on your own, and I won't have to put up with this nonsense from your mother.* That often worked well for him—often, but not always. And not today, for Lanius wanted to know exactly what was going on, too. "What *do* you propose to do about it?" he asked.

Lepturus sighed. "I don't know just what I *can* do about it, Your Majesty," he said. "All I know is, the Heruls didn't cross the Tuola the way they were supposed to. You know what that means as well as I do. It means our army's going to have to fight the Thervings without any help. Count Corvus keeps telling everybody what a great general he is. Pretty soon we find out if he's right."

He didn't sound as though he believed Corvus were such a great general. He sounded as though he doubted whether the nobleman could find the fingers at the ends of his hands without a map. And he managed that without a word of open reproach for Count Corvus. Lanius admired him; he was used to more direct insults.

"But Corax is Corvus' brother," Queen Certhia said. "He'd come to his aid if he possibly could."

"Maybe." Lepturus didn't sound as though he had much use for Corax, either.

"I think it's Commodore Grus' fault," Certhia said. "I think he should come to the city of Avornis at once, and explain his disgraceful conduct."

"For one thing, we don't know it's disgraceful, Your Majesty," the guards commander said patiently. "Why don't we wait and see how the campaign goes before we start throwing blame around like it was mud?"

Certhia fumed. "I am going to give orders that Grus come to the city of Avornis at once. At once, do you hear me?"

"I hear you, Your Royal Highness," Lepturus answered wearily.

"Well, I am," Certhia said, and hurried out of the chamber where the three of them were meeting.

"You don't think that's a good idea?" Lanius asked.

Lepturus shook his head. "No, I don't. Too soon to start blaming. You ought to wait till a campaign's over before you do that. Try doing it in the middle and you're liable to end up looking like a first-class fool—meaning no disrespect to the lady your mother, of course."

"Ah, of course," Lanius said. Lepturus was better than anyone he knew at getting his point across by denying he had any point to get across. Lanius asked, "How do *you* think the campaign will turn out, Lepturus?"

"If you want to know ahead of time how things'll turn out, Your Majesty, you talk to wizards or witches, not to soldiers," the commander of his bodyguards replied. "They'll be glad to tell you. Sometimes they'll even be right."

"I'm talking to you right now, Lepturus." Lanius put an edge in his voice. "Do you think it will turn out well?"

Lepturus looked at him for a long time, then said, "No."

"Well, Skipper, what are you going to do with *that?*" Nicator pointed to the parchment Grus held.

Grus read the parchment one more time. Then he crumpled it and tossed it into the Tuola. "There. That takes care of that. They never sent it. I never got it."

"Commodore, that's mutiny!" Turnix exclaimed.

"No." Grus shook his head. "If I ordered every river galley on all the Nine Rivers to make for the city of Avornis and throw little King Lanius out of the royal palace on his backside, *that* would be mutiny. I don't intend to do any such thing."

"But you're disobeying an order." The wizard, at times—the most in-convenient times, generally—showed a remorselessly literal mind.

"How can I disobey an order I never got?" Grus asked.

"But they'll find out you did, and then you'll be in even more trouble," Turnix said.

"That won't be for a while. I'll worry about it later," Grus said. Turnix threw his hands in the air and walked up the deck of the *Bream* toward the bow.

Nicator said, "Skipper, if you *did* order all the river galleys to make for the capital, do you suppose their captains would do it?"

"I don't know," Grus answered. "I don't want to find out. I don't want to have to find out."

"Well, no," his captain admitted. "But if you did, I think they might. You've won victories, and the blue-blooded generals mostly haven't. It'd make all those blue bloods who look down their pointy snoots at the navy think twice, eh? You just bet it would."

He was right, Gus knew. The Avornan navy was and always had been a stepchild. It was there. It was sometimes useful. But it wasn't where ca-reers were made. It wasn't where heroes were made. The cavalry came first, then the foot. River galleys? A long way after either. A man with a father called Crex the Unbearable could never have risen to high rank on land, as Grus had in the lesser service.

"I hope it never comes to that," Grus said. "And I hope they hang Corax from the tallest tree they can find. But he's the one who wants to be King of Avornis, not me."

"All right, Skipper. All right." Nicator nodded. "I know why you have to talk like that. But like I said, if you ever did give the order, I bet the other captains *would* follow it."

"Who knows? I'm not going to give it, so what's the point of wonder-ing?" He had to say that, too.

But river galleys had one advantage over foot soldiers and even horse-men. They were swift, swift, swift. If he ever chose to move against the capital—and if his captains chose to move with him—he could move fast. He rubbed his chin. He could . . .

He'd never wanted to strike for the royal power. Only in the past cou-ple of years had he realized he *might* strike for it, it might be within his grasp. Yes, he was the son of Crex the Unbearable. Yes, he was only a com-modore, not a general—not even an admiral, since the Avornan navy rarely gave out such an exalted rank. But if he seized the capital, if he seized the palace, who could stop him from putting the crown on his own head? Nobody, not so far as he could see.

"What happens if you get another letter that says you have to go to the city of Avornis?" Nicator asked.

"I don't know," Grus said. "Maybe I'll lose that one, too. I won't worry unless they try to take my command away."

"What do you think will happen to Corvus' army without Corax and the Heruls coming along to give it a hand?"

"I don't know that, either." Grus shrugged. "You're just full of inconvenient questions today, aren't you?"

"I don't think Commodore Grus is coming to the palace," Lanius remarked to Lepturus.

"I don't think he is, either," the commander of the royal bodyguards replied. "If I were him, I don't think I would have."

"But doesn't that turn him into a traitor?" Lanius asked. "Mother heads the regency council, after all. Till I come of age, she rules Avornis."

Lepturus coughed. "If your mother goes and pushes things, she can probably *make* Commodore Grus into a traitor, make him a rebel. If she doesn't, he's just an officer who had a quarrel with another officer and fears the other fellow has more clout than he does."

"What's the difference?" Lanius asked.

"I'll tell you what the difference is, Your Majesty. If he's somebody who's had a quarrel with another officer, he'll go on obeying any orders he gets that don't put him straight into danger from his own side. If he's a traitor, he won't. He'll rebel. What with King Dagipert and the Thervings marching on us, we don't really want to have to fight a rebel, too."

"Oh." Lanius pondered that, and then reluctantly nodded. "Yes, I suppose you make sense there."

"Thank you, Your Majesty," Lepturus said. "I'm not good for much—especially these days, on account of I'm getting old." His eyebrows waggled. Sure enough, those hairy caterpillars had gray in them that hadn't been there a couple of years earlier. "But I've always had pretty fair luck at making sense, and I'm glad you think I do even yet."

King Lanius eyed him. "That's the oddest sort of modesty I think I've ever heard." Lepturus snorted and spluttered. The king went on, "How well will Count Corvus do—how well *can* Count Corvus do—fighting the Thervings without Corax and this army of Heruls that was supposed to attack them from the rear?"

"We drove them back last summer, you know," Lepturus said.

"Yes, but Corvus wasn't commanding our army then. You were," Lanius said.

"Count Corvus has his connections with the Heruls, and he makes a pretty fair soldier, when he pays attention to what's going on around him," the guards commander said. "And now, Your Majesty, if you'll excuse me—" He left before King Lanius could ask him how often Corvus paid attention and how often he didn't.

With a sigh, Lanius got to his feet and walked through the hallways of the palace. He wasn't going anywhere in particular. He should have been doing his lessons, but writing verses wasn't his favorite part of them. He would sooner have poked around in the archives. He would have gotten his shirt and breeches dusty, which would have annoyed his mother, but so what? But his tutor was a conscientious man, and would insist that he do the verses.

Later, Lanius thought, and kept on wandering.

When he went by, servants bowed if they were men, curtsied if they were women. "Your Majesty," they would murmur. It was almost as though he really ruled Avornis—almost, but not quite.

"Good morning, Your Majesty," a serving girl said. She smiled at him.

"Oh. Good morning, Marila," Lanius answered. He smiled, too. Marila was a couple of years older than Lanius. But she didn't smile at him as though he were just a little boy, as so many of the servants did.

"Where were you going, Your Majesty?" she asked. "What were you doing?"

"Nowhere much," he said. "Nothing in particular." He took a deep breath. "Would you . . . ?" he began, and then stopped. His ears felt as though they were on fire. Try as he would, he couldn't go on.

Marila curtsied. "Would I what, Your Majesty?" she said, and gave him another smile.

That encouraged Lanius to try again. "Would you . . . like to come with me?" The last few words came out in a rush.

Her eyes got big. They were very blue—not as blue as his mother's, which would have alarmed him, but very blue even so. "All right, Your Majesty," she said. "Where will we go?"

Panic rolled over him. "I—I—I don't know," he whispered.

Marila laughed. Had she laughed *at* him, he would have run away. But she didn't—or he didn't think she did. She asked, "Well, where would you go if I wasn't coming along?"

That, he could answer. "To the archives," he said at once.

The serving girl blinked. Whatever she'd expected, that wasn't it. She nodded, though, and then brushed back a lock of hair—somewhere between brown and auburn—that had fallen down in front of her face. "All right, Your Majesty, we'll go to the archives."

They weren't far. Lanius' feet might have been leading him there even when the rest of him had no idea that was where he planned to go. He opened the door, then stood aside to let Marila go in ahead of him.

She looked at him as though he were utterly mad. "You're the *king!*" she exclaimed.

"Well," he said. Feeling foolish, he walked in. She followed. He closed the door.

They were the only ones in there. He would have been surprised had it been otherwise. The room was surprisingly large. Halfhearted sunshine filtered in through a skylight and a couple of windows high up on the southern wall that hadn't been washed for a long time. Books and ledgers and scrolls and maps—some a few months old, some a few years old, some a few centuries old, and a few even older than that—were piled, stacked, or sometimes just thrown on or into tables and chests and trunks and cases. The air smelled of leather and parchment and ink and dust. Motes danced in pale sunbeams.

"What a funny place!" Marila said. "What do you *do* here? Uh, Your Majesty?"

"I come here to look through things," Lanius answered. "When I go through these parchments, I never know what'll be on them. Sometimes it's interesting—things nobody's seen for years and years. Sometimes it's boring."

"What do you do then?" the serving girl asked.

Lanius shrugged. "Then I look at another one."

"How funny," Marila said. If she'd laughed then, he would have taken her out of the room and that would have been that. But she didn't. In the dim light, her eyes seemed enormous. Her voice dropped. "It's so *quiet* here."

"I know. That's one of the reasons I like this place," Lanius answered. "It's just me and . . . whatever I can find. I've seen parchments in here that go back to the days before the Banished One was banished. I could show you." He ought to do *something* with the girl besides stand there and gab at her.

"If you want to." Now Marila shrugged—a motion more complex and interesting to look at than Lanius' simple gesture had been. She giggled. "I thought you brought me in here for something else."

"You did?" he said. "What?"

"I could show you." More than half to herself, Marila added, "You'll need some showing, won't you?" She giggled again.

"What are you talking ab—?" Lanius began. That changed to a sudden, startled bleat. "What are you *doing?*"

Marila pulled her tunic off over her head. She slid out of her long wool skirt, then eased off her breastband and let her drawers fall to the floor. She stood before Lanius, naked and smiling. "I could show you, if you like," she said again.

Lanius stared. He'd started to notice girls, yes, but hardly more than theoretically. In that same theoretical way, he knew what went on between men and women. But it was all theory. "Are—are—are you sure?" he quavered.

"You're the king. You can do whatever you want," Marila answered. "Besides, I think you'll like it."

"All right," he said warily. "I'll . . . try."

Years later, he realized Marila must have done a lot of acting in the next few minutes. He also realized how clumsy and puppyish he must have been himself. At the time, every moment brought a new discovery, a new astonishment, a new pleasure: a first kiss, the softness of Marila's skin, the funny way the tips of her breasts crinkled up when he put his mouth on them, and then . . . He'd never imagined his body could feel like *that*.

"Let me up, Your Majesty," Marila said from beneath him.

"Oh! I'm sorry!" If she hadn't said something, Lanius would gladly have stayed there forever.

The serving girl dressed. More slowly, Lanius followed suit. She smiled at him again. "Everything's fine," she said. "You were sweet."

She didn't say he'd been good, or that she'd enjoyed it. He was too amazed to notice. "So this is why people sing about love," he said.

"Of course it is. Didn't you know?" Marila answered her own question before the king could. "No, you didn't." Lanius could never remember that without a blush, either.

At the time, he just answered, "No." Then, slower than it should have, something else occurred to him. "When can we do that again?" he asked.

"Why, whenever you want to, Your Majesty." Marila batted her eyelashes. "How could I say no to the king?"

"Nobody else in the palace seems to have any trouble," Lanius answered.

This time, she definitely blinked. It wasn't coquettish, only surprised. "But you're the king!" she exclaimed.

"Sort of. After a fashion. In a manner of speaking," Lanius said. "I can do whatever I want, all right, as long as it's someone else's idea." Too late, he realized that lying down with Marila had been her idea, not his. He didn't want her to think he hadn't liked it. Oh, no—he didn't want her to think that at all! He tried to make amends. "That's the best idea anybody's ever had."

"I'm glad, Your Majesty. Maybe you'll . . . think of me again, a little later." Marila kissed him on the cheek, then slipped out of the archives.

"Now what did she mean by *that?*" Lanius asked himself. He was tempted to shuffle through parchments till he found the answer. A sated laziness he'd never known before fought against his wits but he didn't need long before he found his answer. "She wants a present," he murmured. Half the treasury seemed about right. But that would cause talk. A trinket of silver or gold would probably do the job.

He left the archives, too. As he closed the door behind him, he stopped as though frozen. If Marila had given herself to him, might other serving women—Prinia, say—do the same? "I'll have to find out," he whispered. "I really will."

And then he suddenly started laughing again. A few years earlier, Arch-Hallow Bucco had said that when he became a man, he might find Princess Romilda of Thervingia more interesting and attractive than he thought. He'd mocked the notion. The marriage wouldn't happen now. Even so, Lanius shook his head in slow, understanding wonder. "Gods curse you, Bucco," he said. "Gods curse you, but you were right."

CHAPTER NINE

The green-robed priest held out the torch to Grus. "As the flames and smoke rise to the sky, so may his soul ascend to the heavens," he said as Grus took the torch and walked toward the pyre.

"So may it be." Grus blinked back tears. Atop the pyre lay his father. Crex, to look at him, might have been asleep. An embalming spell had kept his body fresh while Grus came up from the south. From what Turnix had said while they watched the Thervings, such spells differed little from those the well-to-do used to keep their meat fresh longer than nature usually allowed. That was a bit of lore Grus could have done without.

Crex had been dead for almost a month. Grus had known his father was dead for half that time. He'd have to leave the fleet on the Tuola to come home. He should have been hardened to the knowledge by now—or so he kept telling himself. But his hand shook as he thrust the torch at the pyre.

He died easy, he told himself. *You should be so lucky. He was sitting in that tavern with his disreputable friends, and he slumped over, and that was the end of it.* Some of Crex's disreputable friends—retired royal bodyguards, most of them—stood with his family to do Grus' father honor.

"Have a drink up there for me, you old bastard," one of them called to Crex. "And pinch the barmaid's bottom after she fetches it for you."

"You have to pinch 'em afterward," another graybeard added. "Otherwise, they're liable to spill the wine in your lap—accidentally on purpose, you know."

In spite of himself, Grus smiled at that. He touched the torch to the oil-soaked wood. It caught at once, with a blast of heat that made him step back in a hurry. He held a hand up in front of his face. When he took it down, he couldn't see his father's body anymore. The flames had swallowed it.

He and his family had given the old man the best send-off they could afford. The pyre was of cedar and cypress and sandalwood, the oil scented with cinnamon, so even the smoke was sweet. "Good-bye, Father," Grus whispered. "Gods keep you joyous forever—and I hope you do pinch that heavenly barmaid's bottom."

Estrilda came up to him. He put his arm around his wife. "He was a good man," she said, and a tear slid down her cheek. "He was like my own father to me—he was nicer to me than my own father, if you want to know the truth. I'll miss him."

Sosia came up, too, and put her arms around Grus. His daughter was taller than his wife now, and starting to be shaped like a woman. That astonished him. Neither had been true the last time he saw her, half a year earlier. Sosia was a sweet-natured girl. She had to take after Estrilda there, he thought, for she surely didn't take after him.

He glanced over at Ortalis. His son was well on the way to becoming a man, and a handsome man at that. At the moment, he was avidly watching the pyre. Grus' mouth tightened. *If I know him, he's trying to see the body burn,* he thought unhappily. That he'd gotten a vicious son surprised him as much as having a sweet daughter, and distressed him far more.

"If you will excuse me, Commodore, I must return to my sanctuary," the priest said. "I shall pray to the gods to sustain you in the wake of your loss, and also to guard and honor your father's spirit."

Grus bowed. "Thank you for all you've done, Your Reverence. I'm grateful, and so is my family. . . . Yes?" That last was aimed at a pair of newcomers. They were both solidly made men, with hard, watchful eyes, and a weathered look that came from spending a lot of time outdoors. Swords hung from their belts. *Soldiers,* Grus thought.

"You're Commodore Grus?" one of them asked.

"That's right."

"You need to come with us right away," the fellow said.

"Come with you where?" Grus asked in more than a little irritation. "I've just burned my father's body. I'm off to his memorial feast. It isn't something that can wait."

The two soldiers looked at each other. The one who hadn't spoken before said, "To the royal palace. Queen Certhia's orders." The other one nodded, relieved that his companion had come up with an answer.

He looked so relieved, in fact, he made Grus' suspicions flare. "I'll come as soon as the feast is done," he said, as mildly as he could. *He* wasn't carrying a sword. He hadn't thought he would need one at his father's farewell. How bad a mistake would that turn out to be?

"That's not so good, Commodore," one of the strangers said. "That's not so good at all. Her Royal Highness won't be happy with you, not even a little she won't. Why don't you just come along now, like you're supposed to?"

"I'll apologize when I get to the palace," Grus said. "It'll be on my head, not yours." He wanted to keep wearing his head awhile longer. *What do I do if they draw sword on me?* One knife against two longer blades made fearful odds.

And then, from behind him, someone said, "These lugs bothering you?" Grus cautiously looked over his shoulder. Four or five of Crex's old soldier friends had drifted up to stand at his back. *They* wore swords; he would have bet they wore them everywhere except to bed. As Crex had been, they were nearer seventy than sixty, but they weren't soft and they weren't feeble. Two of them against the pair of ruffians wouldn't have made an even fight. The lot of them together? That was a different story.

Ortalis came up behind Grus, too. He didn't have a sword and he wasn't quite a man yet, but he did have a look on his face that said he'd jump right into a fight and do something nasty to the losers if he won.

The men who'd asked Grus to come with them looked to be weighing their chances. One of them made shooing motions at the retired soldiers. "Shove off, old-timers," he said. "This here is none of your business."

Grus could have told him that was a mistake. The graybeard who'd spoken before said, "It is if we make it our business. And if you don't like it, you can bend over and stick it right there." The other veterans nodded. A couple of them had already let their hands fall to the hilts of their swords.

"I'll go to the palace right after the feast," Grus said. "We can sort everything out then. I'll see you there, won't I?"

He didn't think he would ever see these fellows again. He just hoped they wouldn't try to murder him now that they hadn't managed to spirit him away. When one of them said, "Queen Certhia won't like this," and started to walk off, he allowed himself the luxury of a sigh of relief—they hadn't been paid to risk their lives, then. More reluctantly, the second soldier followed the first. They argued as they went.

"Who *are* those men?" Estrilda asked quietly.

"My first guess would be, Count Corax's soldiers," Grus answered. "He owes me one—or thinks he does."

"I'm glad you don't believe they came from Queen Certhia," his wife said. "What would they have done with you?"

"Nothing good. He must have tried this on the spur of the moment, when he found out I was in the city. Otherwise, he would have managed something better." *Queen Certhia would have managed something better, too, if she'd really wanted my head,* Grus thought uneasily. He remembered tossing that letter summoning him to the city of Avornis into the Tuola. Sometimes things like that came home to roost, though he hadn't worried about it then.

One of Crex's friends tapped him on the shoulder. "You want us to go home with you, Commodore? Never can tell where you'll find more buggers like that pair prowling around."

"Thanks, but—" Grus stopped. The graybeard was right. Being polite here might get him killed. Grus shook his head. "No buts. Thanks. I'll take you up on that."

"Smart lad," the veteran said, just as Grus' father might have. "Let's go, then."

"Yes." Grus turned away from the pyre. "Let's."

King Lanius' tutor clucked reproachfully. "Your Majesty, you're not paying attention," he said. "I don't even bother bringing my switch with me anymore, but maybe I should start again. What *has* been the matter with you lately?"

"I'm sorry." Lanius knew exactly why he'd had trouble thinking about geometry. He'd been thinking about Prinia instead. She'd taught him a couple of things the day before that he hadn't learned from Marila. He wondered what the archives had to say about things a man did with a woman. He'd never tried to find out, not till now. The archives said something about almost everything. What they had to say about *that* might prove very interesting.

"'Sorry' is not enough," his tutor declared. "You'll need to show more effort—and more success—or I'm going to have to speak to your mother." He sighed. "I haven't had to warn you like that for a long time, either."

Before Lanius could answer, a bodyguard stuck his head into the little room where he had his lessons. "What's this, Rallus?" Lanius asked in surprise. No one bothered him during lessons. He'd decreed that a long time ago, and in that his word was law—not least because the decree was so inconsequential.

But Rallus said, "Marshal Lepturus wants to see you right away, Your Majesty. It's important."

"What is it?" Lanius asked. Rallus just stood there. With a sigh of his own, Lanius told his tutor, "I'd better go. I'll be back soon."

He wasn't wrong very often. This turned out to be one of those times.

Rallus led him to a chamber off the throne room. Lepturus sat there. So did Lanius' mother. Lepturus always looked gloomy. Now he looked as though he never expected to see day dawn again. Queen Certhia might have aged five years since the morning. Her face was pale. It showed more lines than Lanius had ever seen there. Her eyes were wide and staring.

"What is it?" Lanius said in shock. Then his mind made one of its swift leaps. "Oh, by the gods," he whispered. "Count Corvus has finally fought the Thervings, hasn't he?"

Jerkily, Lepturus nodded. "Yes, Your Majesty, he did. A little the other side of the Tuola, it was—he got sick of waiting for Dagipert to come to him, and went out after the Thervings instead. The first fugitives just got back here with word of what happened. The short answer is, Corvus picked the wrong time to get bold."

"The first fugitives?" Lanius didn't like the sound of that.

Lepturus gave him another jerky nod. "Dagipert met him on a meadow with a glade of trees off to one side. Corvus, like I said, was feeling bold. He sent his men—our men—charging ahead, and the Thervings gave ground before him."

Three sentences were plenty to give Lanius the bad feeling that he knew what was coming next. Hoping against hope, he asked, "Did Count Corvus send scouts into that—glade, you called it?"

This time, the commander of the royal bodyguards shook his head. "We were advancing. Why did he need to worry about anything like that? I'm guessing what went through his mind, understand. I don't know for sure."

"Nobody knows for sure whether *anything* went through his mind," Queen Certhia said bitterly.

"Nobody—nobody here, anyhow—knows for sure whether he's alive or dead," Lepturus went on. "He pushed on, happy as—"

"Happy as any man pushing it in," Certhia interrupted again. "Just that happy, and just that stupid."

Lanius looked at the floor, at the walls, at the ceiling—anywhere but at his mother. He hadn't thought she knew what he'd been doing with the serving girls. But she was unlikely to have chosen that particular comparison by accident. Next to this news, though, even that was small. "And there were Thervings in amongst those trees?"

"Oh, yes. Oh, by the gods, yes," Lepturus answered. "They stayed hidden there till our battle line had pushed past 'em, then they all came swarming out, and they rolled us up like a pair of socks. The soldiers who've gotten here are the ones who ran first and fastest, so things may not be quite as bad as they say, but they're pretty gods-cursed bad—no two ways about it."

"What do we do?" Lanius asked. "What can we do?"

"I see two things," the guards commander told him. "Number one is, we ready the city here to stand siege, on account of it'll draw Dagipert the way candied apricots draw ants. And number two is, we bring up all the river galleys we can to help hold him back and help defend this place."

Queen Certhia looked as though she'd bitten into an unripe persimmon. Lanius needed only a moment to realize why. "That means calling on Commodore Grus for help," he said. Lepturus nodded. Certhia's face puckered up even more. Lanius said, "Mother, *you've* got to write that order."

"Me?" his mother burst out. "If Grus hadn't left Corax and the Heruls behind—"

"Who knows what would have happened?" Lanius broke in. "Corvus might have walked into an ambush anyhow—he seems rash enough. But we need Grus now, and he knows you're angry at him. That means you need to be the one who softens him up."

Certhia shook her head. Lepturus said, "He's right, Your Royal Highness."

"Are you betraying me, too?" Lanius' mother demanded.

"No one's betraying you, Mother," Lanius said. "We're trying to help the kingdom. Grus will do whatever you order. He seems a clever man, and he's done a lot of good for Avornis. Don't let *your* pride get in the way."

"Oh, gods help me! I'll write the letter," Certhia said. But before Lanius could get too happy about that, she added, "Anything—anything at all—to keep from being lectured by my own son." Lanius started to get indignant about that. Then Lepturus couldn't quite smother a chuckle. Lanius deflated in a hurry.

*   *   *

Some Thervings were watering their horses at the bank of the Asopus, not far from the city of Avornis, when Commodore Grus spotted them. "Let's make them pay!" he shouted to the men aboard the *Crocodile*. "Oarmaster, up the stroke! Marines, stand to starboard with your bows!"

The drumbeat picked up. The river galley glided along the Asopus toward the invaders. The Thervings hadn't even bothered posting sentries. After smashing Count Corvus' army to bloody rags, they'd pushed east all the way to the walls of the capital, and no one had come forth to challenge them. Why should they have worried?

"I'll show them why," Grus muttered.

He'd gotten almost within arrow range when King Dagipert's men noticed the *Crocodile*. Even then, the Thervings kept right on tending to their animals. A couple of them shook fists at the river galley, but that was all. The *Crocodile*, after all, was in the Asopus, and they were on the riverbank. What could the ship do to them? She might look like a centipede, with her oars rhythmically rising and falling, but she couldn't run after them on land.

"Ready!" the marines' lieutenant shouted, and the men drew their bows back to the ear. He raised his hand and let it fall. "Shoot!"

The volley tore into the Thervings and their horses. The big blond men shouted and shrieked. The animals screamed. The Avornan marines reached into their quivers for more arrows and shot again. The second volley wasn't quite as smooth as the first had been, but more Thervings fell. A few of Dagipert's men started shooting back, while others either mounted horses or led them back out of range. That took a while, and the Avornans punished them till they escaped.

"Well, that was fun," Nicator remarked. Two marines had taken arrows—one in the shoulder, the other in the hand. Neither wound looked serious, and they were the only hurts aboard the *Crocodile*. Eight or ten Thervings sprawled and writhed by the riverbank—some dead, others injured. Several horses were down, too.

"So it was," Grus said. "One more fleabite for Avornis. They got careless, and we nipped 'em."

"They won't bring their horses to the Asopus again anytime soon, or to any other stream with enough water in it to float a river galley," Nicator said.

"No, so they won't," Grus agreed. "But they don't have to, either. They can still besiege the capital."

"What are *we* doing here?" Nicator grumbled. "Shooting up a few fools is fine, but we should be doing more."

"Well, if we had some soldiers aboard, we could put them and our marines ashore where they might do the Thervings some harm," Grus said.

"Oh, happy day." Nicator spat. "Just like Corax and his gods-cursed Heruls, you mean."

That made Grus spit, too. "Gods curse Corax, and gods curse Corvus, too. Between the two of them, they've done Avornis more harm than Dagipert ever dreamt of. Corvus threw away all the soldiers we might be carrying."

"I hear he made it back to the city of Avornis," Nicator said.

"Why am I not surprised?" Grus said. "You can't kill fleas, however much you want to. Or maybe Dagipert told his men to let the bastard go on purpose, figuring he might want to beat him again someday."

"Wouldn't surprise me a bit," Nicator said. "Dagipert is smart, and Corvus—"

"Thinks he is," Grus broke in.

"Right," Nicator said.

"Until we raise more men down in the south, I don't know what we can do except pray the walls hold," Grus said. "They should. They really should." He hoped he wasn't just trying to convince himself. He also hoped the Menteshe wouldn't swarm north over the Stura with Avornis so busy here by the capital. And he kicked at the deck of the *Crocodile,* for he could do so very little to make either hope come true.

Lanius wore an iron helmet shaped like a pot, a plain linen surcoat over an equally plain shirt of mail, and baggy wool trousers that itched. If he'd had a beard, he would have looked like a soldier on the walls of the capital. Since he didn't, he looked like one of the youths who brought the men food and arrows and whatever else they might need.

What he didn't look like was the King of Avornis. The Thervings weren't likely to shoot at one nondescript youngster on the walls. Lanius enjoyed the disguise. He also liked the taste of freedom it gave him. Count Corvus and Lepturus, who accompanied him, hid their rank the same way. He wondered if they enjoyed it, too.

Thervings out beyond the ditch in front of the wall did shoot arrows at the defenders. More Thervings threw bundles of sticks and brush into the ditch, trying to work their way close enough to the wall to set scaling ladders against it. The Avornans concentrated their arrows on those men, and also shot fire arrows at the fascines. Lanius thought the curved trails of smoke from the fire arrows were fascinating.

Then one of the bundles caught. Dagipert's men poured water on it, but it kept burning. The fire quickly spread to other fascines thrown into that part of the ditch. Cheering, the Avornans pincushioned the Thervings who were trying to put out the blaze.

Count Corvus said, "We ought to sally against them, Your Majesty, while they're in this pickle."

"I don't think so," Lepturus answered. "We're not trying to beat them. We're only trying to make them give up and go away." He had good sense. Protecting the king and the capital was usually more important than commanding in the field. Comparing Lepturus' performance and Corvus', Lanius regretted that.

"That is a coward's way to fight," Corvus declared.

"You had your chance in command, Your Excellency," Lanius said coolly. "You had it, and look what you did with it. Lepturus leads in the city of Avornis."

"I was stabbed in the back." Corvus reddened with anger. "That baseborn turd Grus betrayed me. He betrayed my brother. He betrayed the whole kingdom. Do you blame me for what he did?"

"No, I blame you for what you did. Grus didn't command against King Dagipert," Lanius said; as always, illogic oppressed him. "Had Grus commanded, he might not have fallen into Dagipert's ambush. *You* fell into it."

Corvus' hands folded into fists. "Nobody talks to me that way," he said.

In a voice like ice, Lepturus said, "You're speaking to the King of Avornis. You had better remember it if you ever want to see your estates again. He's earned the right to be angry at you, considering how much you threw away."

"I was stabbed in the back," Count Corvus repeated.

"By your own stupidity, maybe—no one else's," Lepturus said.

"Enough," Lanius said. "If we fight among ourselves, who wins? King Dagipert." *Not that he hasn't won already,* he thought. But he added, "And who laughs? The Banished One."

Lepturus bowed. "That's so, Your Majesty, every word of it. You've got good sense."

Lanius thought he had tolerably good sense, too. *And what has it gotten me?* he wondered. *I could be a drooling idiot, and I'd still wear the Avornan crown. More than a few people might like it better if I were a drooling idiot. Then they wouldn't have to worry about what I thought, because I wouldn't think anything at all.*

"The Banished One laughed when Grus betrayed Corax," Corvus said furiously. Neither Lanius nor Lepturus said a word. They both just looked at him for a long time. Lanius wasn't sure what his own expression seemed like. He was sure he wouldn't have wanted anyone with Lepturus' scowl glaring at him. And Corvus, most reluctantly, yielded. "All right," he muttered. "Let it go."

A stone-thrower hurled a rock as big as a man's head—Lanius glanced at Corvus to make the comparison—out toward the Thervings. They had no weapons to match the catapult. But it did less good than it might have. It skipped—as a smaller, flatter stone might have skipped on water—and landed harmlessly, well beyond the clump of men at whom it was aimed.

The soldiers serving the siege engine cursed furiously. "They've got a wizard out there working for them," one of the men said. "By the gods, why haven't we got wizards here to put their bastard down?"

"That's a good question," Lanius said. "Why haven't we, Lepturus?"

"Because somebody's gone and botched things, that's why," the commander of his bodyguards answered. Wizardry was a rare talent; reliable wizardy even rarer. Still, a sorcerer should have been on the wall. Corvus brayed laughter. "Oh, shut up," Lepturus told him, "or we'll shoot that boulder on top of your neck at the Thervings next." Lanius snickered. He couldn't help himself. He wasn't the only one who'd had that thought, then.

Scowling, Corvus stalked away. If he could have raised fur on his back like an offended cat, he would have done it. Lanius sighed. "I suppose we shouldn't bait him."

"Why not?" Lepturus said. "He shouldn't just be baited—he should be bait. You could catch plenty of fish with bits of him on the hook."

"Heh," Lanius said, though he didn't think the guards commander was joking.

The Thervings held their ring around the city of Avornis. Out beyond that ring, they did as they pleased. Pillars of smoke marked the funeral pyres of farmhouses, villages, towns. Lanius began to wonder if any of the northwestern part of the kingdom would remain unravaged by the time Dagipert finally decided to go home for the harvest.

Instead of going home, the King of Thervingia launched a furious, full-scale assault on the capital three days later. His wizards did their best to hide his preparations, and then, when the attack was launched, they hurled fireballs and lightning bolts and sudden storms of rain at the Avornans on the walls.

More than a few of the first messengers who brought word of the attack back to the palace sounded panicky. Like most people inside the city, Lanius had thought Dagipert would know he couldn't take it, and so wouldn't try very hard. To find out he was wrong alarmed him, as it always did. Might he also have been wrong about the city's invulnerability?

He couldn't ask Lepturus. The guards commander was on the walls himself, seeing to the defense. Lanius tried to go out there, but palace servants stopped him. "Sorry, Your Majesty," said a steward who sounded not sorry in the least. "Your mother has forbidden you to go to the fighting."

Lanius fumed and pouted. Later, he realized he might have done better to bribe the man. That might have worked. His show of temper didn't. He had to stay and wait and wonder if the next soldiers he saw rushing toward the palace would be Avornans or ax-wielding Thervings.

Only as the sun set behind the Bantian Mountains did the din abate. A last messenger came to the palace. "Olor be praised," he said simply. "We've thrown 'em back."

Even then, though, King Dagipert refused to withdraw. Instead, he went back to ruining the Avornan countryside. Trapped within the capital, all Lanius could do was watch the smoke rise. After a week, Dagipert sent a messenger up to the walls under flag of truce. "Hear my master's terms," the Therving shouted in good Avornan.

Lepturus let him enter through a postern gate and sent him to the palace. There he bowed to Queen Certhia and, a little less deeply, to Lanius himself. "King Dagipert must see he can't break into the city of Avornis," Certhia said. "What do we have to give him to make him go away?"

"You Avornans must see you cannot drive King Dagipert from your land," said the envoy, whose name was Claffo. "He says, Thervingia and Avornis should not have to fight anymore. He says, we should make them one, to keep it from happening again. He says, let King Lanius wed Princess Romilda, as was agreed once before."

Lanius no longer looked at the idea with automatic horror, as he had a few years earlier. If Romilda had a pretty face and a nice shape, he was willing to think about it. But his mother spoke only one word, and that was "No."

"King Dagipert says he will make you sorry if you refuse," Claffo warned.

"No," Certhia repeated. "Tell Dagipert he cannot make me as sorry as I would be if that wedding went forward."

"I will tell him," Claffo said mournfully. "But you will regret this."

After he'd gone, Lanius said, "Mother, maybe I could—"

"No," Queen Certhia said yet again. "Bedding serving girls is one thing." Lanius looked all around again, his face heating with embarrassment. His mother went on, "Taking a queen is something else again, and I will not have the Therving as your father-in-law. I've made mistakes, but I won't sell Avornis to Thervingia. Do you understand me?"

"Yes, Mother." Lanius didn't always think his mother ran Avornis wisely—which meant she didn't always do things the way he would have, had he been of age. Here, though, he couldn't quarrel with Certhia's choice. Marrying him to Romilda meant marrying Avornis to Thervingia, and he knew which partner would rule the roost.

"All right, then," his mother said. "Dagipert can't break in here. We've seen that—and if he does, everything's over anyway, so there's no point worrying about what to do next. Sooner or later, his men have to run short of food. The way they're tearing up the countryside, it'll probably be sooner. Once they start getting hungry, what can they do but go home?"

"Nothing, I suppose," Lanius said. "Still, I wish they'd go home sooner than that."

"So do I," Certhia said. "But I don't know how to make them do it. Do you? If you think you do, I'll be glad to listen."

She sounded as though she meant it. Lanius pondered. At last, scowling because he couldn't come up with a right answer when he needed one most, he shook his head. "No, Mother. I'm sorry. I wish I did."

"Well, well. What have we here?" Grus said.

"What have we here?" Nicator repeated, his voice rising in excitement. "We have us a chance to grab Dagipert's balls and give 'em a good squeeze, that's what."

"So we do," Grus agreed. "But that's what it is—a chance, nothing more. We've got to make the most of it."

He turned and looked back over the *Crocodile*'s stern. River galleys and small boats coming up the Asopus from the south had finally brought enough soldiers so that, added in with the flotilla's marines, they might be able to give Dagipert and the Thervings a hard time. He hoped so. Up till now, the invaders had had everything go their way since breaking into Avornis.

Nicator said, "The Thervings'll still have more men all told than we do."

"I know." Grus nodded. "But we can put ours right where we want them, and we can pick them up and take them somewhere else if they get in trouble." He scuffed his foot across the decking. "When we're fighting foes who haven't got any ships of their own, this is a floating fortress—nothing else but."

"It had better be," Nicator said. "After the knife that stinking Corvus stuck in our hopes, it's not like we've got a lot of room for mistakes."

Grus wished he could have argued with that, but it was plainly true. He called out to the oarmaster: "Quicken the stroke. We're going up toward the capital." And to the boatswain: "Run up the *Follow me* pennant."

The Thervings had learned part of their lesson. They didn't camp right alongside the Asopus anymore, or next to any other navigable stream. But Thervingia was landlocked and mountainous. Its rivers weren't navigable. They didn't realize just what a flotilla could do. Grus was determined to show them.

He spotted a band of Thervings—about a regiment's worth of men—marching back toward their main encampment under the walls of the city of Avornis. They trudged along in loose order. Why not? Who would challenge their right to rule this country? No one they'd met lately.

Boats took some Avornans ashore. River galleys scraped keels on mud and gravel close to the bank so more men could scramble down and rush toward the invaders.

Shouts of surprise rose from the Thervings. They weren't shouts of alarm; Dagipert's warriors had often beaten Avornans in the open field, and no doubt thought they could go right on doing it. Grus hoped they were wrong. He wasn't sure, but he hoped so. One thing he knew—he was about to find out.

Slower than they should have, the Thervings formed a battle line perhaps a quarter of a mile from the Asopus. At that range, soldiers and marines might fight them, but the river galleys themselves couldn't.

"Don't you want to be a hero?" Nicator made cut-and-thrust motions. "Charge the Thervings and chop them into steaks?"

"I'll fight as much as I have to," Grus answered. "But I'm a sailor first, not a soldier. If I don't have to, I won't mix it up that much myself." He pointed to Nicator. "I don't see you charging the Thervings, either."

"Me? I'm an old man," Nicator said, which was on the way to being true but hadn't gotten there yet. He was also good enough with a sword in his hands. Even so, he added, "I don't care about being a hero. That's your job, Skipper—you're the commodore."

"If the soldiers and marines beat the Thervings, I'm a hero, all right," Grus answered. "If they don't, I'm just another gods-cursed fool."

The Avornans formed their own line of battle. They advanced on King Dagipert's men. They outnumbered the Thervings, and their lines overlapped the foe to both left and right. The enemy soldiers spread themselves thinner to keep from getting outflanked. That did them little good; many of them found themselves attacked by two or more Avornans at the same time.

When their line unraveled, it came undone all at once. They stopped trying to hold back the Avornans, and ran for whatever shelter and safety they could find. They found very little. Howling like wolves, the men from the flotilla gave chase, cutting them down from behind. Few Thervings outran their pursuers or got to the shelter of the woods farther from the river.

"Blow *Recall*," Grus told the trumpeter. "I don't want them running into a Therving ambush."

As the notes rang out, horns from the other ships of the flotilla echoing them, Grus hoped the Avornans would heed the call. If their blood was up, they might keep going, and run headlong into trouble. More than once, armies had thrown away victories doing that.

Not here, though. Grus made a fist and pounded it against his thigh in silent celebration as the Avornan sailors and marines started back toward the Asopus. "Well done!" he shouted to them when they got close enough for his voice to carry. "Now we go on up the river and hit them again."

The Avornans raised a cheer coming back. They hadn't had much to cheer about lately. They boarded boats and river galleys with more spirit than Grus had seen for a long time. He waved to the oarmaster, who bawled, "Back oars!" The *Crocodile* freed herself and started up the Asopus once more. Grus scanned the riverbank for Thervings.

Later that afternoon, he ordered the soldiers and marines ashore again. Again, they rushed at a startled band of Thervings who'd been tramping through the Avornan countryside without the slightest notion they might have to fight. Again, they punished the Thervings and then returned to Grus' flotilla.

"This is fun," Nicator said. "We can do it as often as we want."

"Yes, for a while we can," Grus agreed. "Sooner or later, though, they'll figure out what's going on."

That took longer than he'd expected. He sent the Avornans forth against King Dagipert's men twice more the next day, and won another couple of quick, easy victories. The morning after that, he spotted yet another band of Thervings out in the open close by the river, apparently going about their business without a care in the world.

"Shall we hit 'em again, Skipper?" Nicator asked.

Grus shook his head. Nicator blinked in surprise. But Grus pointed to the trees on either side of the clearing where those Thervings displayed themselves. "What do you want to bet those woods are full of archers?" he said. "That's how Dagipert ruined Corvus. If it worked once, why wouldn't it work again?"

Nicator plucked at his beard as he thought that over. "You may have something there," he said at last. "We leave 'em alone, then?"

"I intend to," Grus answered. "Maybe we waste a chance. But we're just here to harass the Thervings, anyhow. We can't conquer them, not with what we've got—and we can't afford to waste more men in an ambush, either. Better safe." Nicator thought some more, then nodded.

CHAPTER TEN

King Lanius looked out from one of the towers of the royal palace. "They really are pulling back this time," he remarked.

"Yes, Your Majesty, I do believe they are," Lepturus agreed. "And about time, too."

"They couldn't take the city," Lanius said with a certain amount of pride.

The guards commander nodded, but his eyes, as usual, were somber. "No, that's true—they couldn't," he said. "But they've taken just about everything else—taken it or wrecked it or burned it. The northwest is going to be a long time getting over this—and so will the army."

"That's Corvus' fault," Lanius said, "his and Corax's."

"And Grus'," Lepturus added.

"Yes, and Grus', I suppose." Lanius nodded. "If he hadn't quarreled with Corax—" He kicked at the gray stone under his sandals. "From everything I've seen and heard, Corax is pretty easy to quarrel with."

"Something to that," the head of the bodyguards said. "And Grus did hurt the Thervings once they'd besieged us."

"That's more than you can say Corvus did after he got back to the city of Avornis," Lanius remarked. "All he did was grumble and make stupid suggestions."

Lepturus spoke in meditative tones. "As long as he's here in the city of

Avornis, it might not be the worst thing in the world if he stayed here awhile."

"Hmm," Lanius said. "You're right—it might not be. He's caused the kingdom a lot of trouble. Not much point to giving him the chance to make more, is there? See to it, Lepturus."

"I'll take care of it right now, Your Majesty." Lepturus vanished down into the palace. Lanius watched him go, nodding approval at his broad back. From what he'd seen in his not very many years, most people promised to do something, then forgot all about it as they went off to do what they wanted to do instead. Not Lepturus. When he said he'd take care of something, he took care of it.

Except, this time, he didn't. He sent a guardsman who found Lanius a couple of hours later, after the young king had come down from the tower and was working his way through some interesting—well, interesting to him—parchments he'd found in the archives. "Marshal Lepturus humbly begs your pardon, Your Majesty—" the bodyguard began.

That was plenty to get Lanius' nose out of the old tax documents. "What's gone wrong now?" he asked.

"We can't arrest Count Corvus, on account of he isn't in the city of Avornis anymore," the bodyguard said. "Seems he went south as soon as the Thervings went west and left him a way home. Lepturus says it'd mean civil war to try to seize him there. Is it worth it to you?"

"No," Lanius said. "Let him go." At the time, he thought the decision made good sense. Corvus hadn't actually moved against the Kingdom of Avornis. All he'd done—all!—was lose a battle he might not have fought, or might have won if he'd paid closer attention. That was bad, but it wasn't really treasonous.

So Lanius calculated then. Lepturus didn't try to change his mind. Later, they both had plenty of chances to wonder if they'd chosen rightly.

A few days afterward, Lanius rode out of the city of Avornis to look at the devastation the Thervings had caused and to promise people he and the royal government would do everything they could to make losses good. The promises made peasants look happier. Lanius knew too well they weren't intended to do anything else. The royal government paid the soldiers who protected peasants from invaders—or, sometimes, didn't protect them—but couldn't do much more than that.

"It'll be good when you come of age, Your Majesty," Lanius heard at least a dozen times. "High time we had a man's hand on things again."

Like Arch-Hallow Bucco's? Lanius wanted to ask. The cleric had made a worse hash of things than Queen Certhia, by far. Lanius was impatient to come of age, too, but not because he thought his mother had done a particularly bad job of ruling Avornis.

When he returned to the capital, he mentioned to Certhia what he'd heard. His mother's mouth tightened. "Yes, I've heard the same," she said, no small bitterness in her voice. "And it's not from farmers who haven't bathed since spring before last, either. It's from people whose opinions carry weight and whose frowns are like a wasting sickness to my hopes. Corvus was a prop, but he knocked himself out from under me when he failed."

"What will you do now?" Lanius asked.

"Find another prop, I suppose," Queen Certhia answered. "But who?"

"Why not Commodore Grus?" Lanius said. "Out of all our leading officers, he's the only one who didn't end up looking like a fool or a knave."

"Not if you hear Corvus or Corax tell it," his mother said. "And besides, I tried to arrest him after he wouldn't take the Heruls across the river. Do you think he would forget?"

"To prop up the government?" Lanius said. "I think he'd forget a lot for a chance like that."

Certhia sniffed, but thoughtfully. "He's not a noble. He can't have any nasty, ambitious ideas, the way Corvus or Corax would. He'd be leaning on me as much as I'd be leaning on him." She smiled. "The more I think about it, the better I like it."

"Let's hope it works well," Lanius said.

His mother's smile faded. "It had better," she said. "I hate needing to lean on soldiers and sailors—it's the drawback to being a woman. But you're likely right—he's the only real choice we've got."

As Commodore Grus walked down the gangplank from the *Crocodile* to one of the quays of the city of Avornis, marines formed up around him. Trumpets and drums began to play, blaring out a fierce and martial music. Anyone listening to it would have thought he was entering the city in triumph. And so, in a manner of speaking, he was. The Thervings had gone back to their own kingdom, and he'd had something to do with that. In a war where most Avornan soldiers had fallen or fled, anyone who'd gained any success looked like a hero by comparison.

That was one reason Grus chose marines as his bodyguards. The other was that they came from the flotilla he'd commanded, and so were likelier to be loyal to him than men who didn't know him.

The music got louder. Nicator looked at the scarlet silk tunics shot through with sparkling golden threads that the trumpeters and drummers were wearing. "How'd you like to have a shirt like that?" he asked.

"A little gaudy for my taste." Grus pointed ahead. "And, speaking of gaudy, here come the royal bodyguards."

They wore tunics—surcoats, really—even fancier than those of the musicians. They left them unbuttoned, too, to show off the gilded mail-shirts that matched their gilded, crested helms. But despite those gorgeous uniforms, the men who wore them looked tough and capable. At their head marched Marshal Lepturus. Having dealt with him before, Grus knew *he* was tough and capable. The two men eyed each other, sizing each other up. Lepturus spoke first. "Welcome to the city."

"Thanks," Grus said. "Let's see what we can do about getting things shipshape again, shall we?"

"Sounds good to me," Lepturus answered. He turned and gestured to his men, who opened a lane up which two sedan chairs advanced. Queen Certhia got out of one, King Lanius out of the other. The bodyguards moved to form a protective screen between them and Grus' marines.

Grus bowed low to the head of the regency council, then even lower to the king. "I'm proud to serve Avornis any way I can," he declared.

Queen Certhia replied—not Lanius. "I'm pleased that you have come to help me restore good order in the kingdom."

"We can use it, Your Royal Highness, after everything that's happened this year," Grus said.

King Lanius nodded. So did his mother. But, by the glance she shot Grus, she still judged some of what had happened this year—maybe more than some—was his fault and no one else's. Even so, she said the right things. "I am delighted you will support the king and protect the land he rules." If she looked as though the words tasted bad, how much did that matter?

I'll find out, Grus thought. Aloud, he said, "Anyone who doesn't sup-port King Lanius is a traitor to Avornis. Anyone at all." Corvus and Corax wouldn't like that when they heard about it. Grus didn't care. As far as he was concerned, they were already traitors, even if they hadn't openly de-clared themselves.

Lepturus said, "When you get to the palace, Commodore, the royal bodyguards will be pleased to take over the job of protecting you and your family."

Beside Grus, Nicator coughed. Grus needed no signal to recognize the danger that lurked—or might lurk—in that proposal. What he did need was a moment to figure out how to evade it without offending. After that moment, he said, "Thank you, Marshal, but the royal bodyguards should watch over His Majesty here, and over nobody else. My marines are plenty good enough for me. I think I'll just keep them on, if nobody minds too much."

"I would be happy to share my guardsmen with you, Commodore," King Lanius said. "As you guard the kingdom, so they should guard you."

"That's very kind of you, Your Majesty," Grus said, eyeing the young king with curiosity. Lanius was supposed to be clever. Was he clever enough to go along with Lepturus' scheme for separating Grus from the men most loyal to him, or was he just naive and trying to be helpful? Grus couldn't decide. He went on, "Any which way, though, the honor's too much for the likes of me. I'll stick with marines, the way I said before."

"Are you sure we can't change your mind?" Queen Certhia asked.

"Your Royal Highness, I'm positive," Grus answered, and waited to see what would happen next. Certhia's question convinced him that she and Lepturus and Lanius were all part of this ploy. Grus eyed the king again. He wasn't anything special to look at—for his age, he was small and skinny. But he did look alert, and anything but naive. Sure as sure, he'd tried to get Grus away from the marines.

How desperate are they? Grus wondered. *How much power have I really got?* Better to find out here and now. If they kept on trying to thwart him . . . *I'll have to figure out what to do if they try that.*

But they didn't. Before either Certhia or Lepturus could speak, King Lanius said, "Let it be as you wish. You know best what you require." His mother and the commander of the royal bodyguards both looked as though they wanted to say something more—Certhia bit her lip—but neither one did. They nodded at about the same time.

Well, well. Isn't that interesting? Grus thought. Lanius wasn't of age, but his word carried weight. That was worth knowing. Grus bowed to him once more. "Thank you, Your Majesty. I appreciate it. These boys here" — he gestured to the marines— "have been through a lot with me."

"A commander should have loyal men," Lanius said. "So should a king."

His cheeks were still smooth, though the down on them was starting to turn dark. His voice remained a boy's treble. Even so, Grus got the feeling that this child-king was very clever indeed. *I'm going to have to watch myself.* But all he asked was, "Have my wife and son and daughter moved to the palace yet?"

"Oh, yes," Lepturus replied with a bland nod. "Royal bodyguards took care of that earlier this morning." He smiled. His words meant, *Your marines may watch you, but they can't be everywhere at once.*

"Thank you so much," Grus said, as blandly. *If anything happens to them, you pay.*

"I'm sure they'll be very comfortable there," Queen Certhia said. *For as long as we need you to do these things we can't do for ourselves,* she didn't add. Again, Grus had no trouble hearing it even so. *As soon as that's taken care of, we'll throw you out—if we decide to let you live, that is—and we'll throw them out, too.*

"I'm looking forward to doing everything I can," Grus said.

For a wonder, King Lanius asked him a serious question. "How will you hold back Dagipert and the Thervings when Count Corvus couldn't?"

"I'd be a liar if I said I knew all the answers yet, Your Majesty," Grus replied. "The only thing I can promise is, I'll do my best not to let Dagipert or anybody else catch me napping."

"Good," Lanius said. His mother and Lepturus didn't seem to think it sounded quite so good. When Grus said he wouldn't let *anybody* catch him napping, he'd included them along with everyone else. Plainly, they'd understood that.

Lanius had wondered whether having a protector in the palace would be like having his father back again. He didn't remember King Mergus well; the older he got, the more he realized just how young he'd been when Mergus died. Grus didn't remind him of the dead king, or try to fill Mergus'—or even Lepturus'—place. He simply went about the business of trying to put Avornis back together again. Any kingdom that owed its survival only to the strong walls of its capital and to paying tribute needed rebuilding.

He wasted no time in summoning counts Corax and Corvus to the royal palace to account for themselves. He also summoned several other nobles close to the brothers. They all wasted no time in refusing him. Grus sent for them again, this time in King Lanius' name.

As Lanius signed the orders, he asked Grus, "Why didn't you summon them in my name in the first place?"

"Well, Your Majesty, if I'm the legal protector, my orders should be good on their own, shouldn't they?" the naval officer replied. "The other side of the coin is, if they refuse me, it's not quite treason. Now they've had that chance, and they've taken it when I wish they wouldn't have. So we give it another try, this time with your signature. Maybe it won't drive them into real rebellion. I hope it doesn't."

"Do you?" Lanius eyed him. "If you did, wouldn't you not summon them at all? Wouldn't you pretend nothing bad had happened?"

"Yes, I suppose I could do that, Your Majesty," Grus said. "But if I did, who'd be running Avornis? Would you? Would I? Or would Corvus and Corax be calling the shots? If I'm going to play this part, I'll play it to the hilt."

"All right," Lanius said. "That does make some sense. You're not doing it just because you don't get along with them." He raised an ironic eyebrow.

"Why, Your Majesty!" Grus said, eyes widening. "Would I do such a thing?"

"Probably," Lanius answered. "If people get to the top, one of the things they do is pay back their enemies."

He watched Grus watching him. Grus' mouth twitched. Anger? A suppressed smile? Lanius couldn't tell. At last, the commodore said, "No, you're no fool, are you?"

"I try not to be," Lanius answered. "I'm never going to be a big, strong man. If I don't use my head, what have I got going for me?"

"What? I'll tell you what. You're the king, that's what," Grus said.

"How long will I *stay* the king if I don't know what I'm doing?" Lanius returned. He felt himself flushing, and hoped Grus wouldn't see. "And even if I do stay king, what does it matter?"

Again, Grus thought before he spoke. When he did, he said, "The first part of that is a real question. As for the second, though, Your Majesty, being king matters a lot. Never doubt it. If it didn't, why would so many people want the job?"

Lanius considered that. It was his turn not to answer for a while. He finally said, "There's more to you than meets the eye, I believe. You think about these things."

"Who, me?" Grus shook his head. "Not a chance. I'm just a tool your mother picked up on account of it was handy. She'll use it till it does what she needs or till it breaks, whichever happens first. Then she'll get herself another tool, and use that instead. If you don't believe me, just ask her."

Lepturus presumed to be sardonic in Lanius' presence. So did his tutor. They both enjoyed an immunity based on long acquaintance. Grus didn't. He spoke his mind anyhow. He spoke it as though he didn't care what Lanius thought of him. Maybe he truly didn't. Maybe he wanted Lanius to think he didn't. The more Lanius saw of him, the deeper he seemed.

"What are you planning to do about the Thervings?" Lanius asked him. "That's why you're here, after all."

"Can't go fight 'em in their country, not the way things are," Grus answered, and the king couldn't disagree. "I can—I hope I can—pick generals who're able to see past the end of their noses. And I can hold the city of Avornis, and King Dagipert knows I can, too. That means he can't conquer the kingdom, no matter how much trouble he makes. It's an edge for us."

"Yes." Lanius nodded. "You're no fool, either."

Grus only shrugged. "Like you said, I try not to be. If *you* don't think I am, Your Majesty, I take that for a compliment. And now, if you'll forgive me . . ." He bowed and left Lanius' presence.

Before long, Queen Certhia came into Lanius' room. "Well, you suggested him," she said. "Now that he's here, what do you think of him?"

"There's more to him than meets the eye, isn't there?" Lanius said after some thought.

"Yes, and I don't know that I like it," his mother answered. "He's got a lot of his marines here inside the city of Avornis. They're behaving most correctly, but they're *here,* and that's a worry."

"Why?" Lanius said, and then, feeling the fool Grus had said he wasn't, "Oh." The walls of the capital could hold out Dagipert and the Thervings, yes. But they could also hold out anyone else who wanted—or needed— to get into the city of Avornis. That included soldiers who might need to come to the king's rescue. "Can Lepturus do anything about it?"

Certhia shook her head. "I don't think so. Grus' men outnumber the royal guards. This is Grus' city right now." Her mouth tightened. "I didn't intend for it to work out like that. He talks like a bumpkin, but he doesn't act like one. That makes him more dangerous than I thought he was."

"What are you going to do about it? What *can* you do about it?" Lanius asked.

His mother's lips got even thinner and paler than they had been. "I don't know, Son," she said. "I don't know that I can do anything, not when he has so many men here. Trying something and failing would be worse than not doing anything."

"Yes, I think you're right about that," Lanius agreed. "Best you don't try anything, then."

"Best I don't fail," Queen Certhia said.

Grus drummed his fingers on the table in front of him. He glared across the table at his son. Ortalis glared back. That meant nothing. Ortalis always seemed to glare. Grus said, "Son, I don't mind you bedding a serving girl. Boys do that, when they can. When I was your age, I got it wherever I could, too."

"Then what are you bothering me for?" Ortalis asked sullenly.

"I'm bothering you because you had no business bruising her like that," Grus snapped. "It wasn't even that she said no, and you hurt her then. She said yes, and you hurt her just for the fun of it. Your fun, not hers."

"So what?" Ortalis said. "She's only a serving girl."

"No. That's not how it works," Grus said. "For one thing, I got called here to protect Avornis from the Thervings. If you think I won't protect Avornans from my own son if I have to, you're wrong. And there's something more. If you hurt your women, people start talking about you. They start laughing at you behind your back. They start doing the same about me, because I'm your father. Or they would. This is *not* going to happen again. Do you understand me?"

"She just wants money, the little whore. Give her some silver. That'll shut her up," Ortalis said.

"I've already given her some," Grus said. "But she won't keep quiet. She'll say why she got it. People do things like that. They aren't toys. You can't put one here or move another one there and expect them to stay where you leave them. You can't hurt them for the sport of it, either."

He might have been speaking Chernagor for all the sense he made to Ortalis—he could see as much. His son's eyes were opaque as jet, hard as glass. *You do see people that way, don't you?* Grus thought sadly. *As your toys, as your puppets. But they aren't, and you'll be sorry if you try to make them so.*

"Are you done?" Ortalis asked at last.

"No." Grus shook his head. "The next time you hurt a girl like that, I'll hurt you worse. I promise you, I will. Do you believe me?"

Ortalis' eyes weren't opaque enough to hide fear. His father had the strength to check his viciousness. If Grus promised he'd suffer for doing something, he knew he might suffer. Looking away, he muttered, "I believe you."

"Good. You'd better, because I mean it. Now get out of my sight," Grus said.

Ortalis stormed from the room. Grus let out a long, sad sigh. *Hard when I can't trust my son at my back—gods-cursed hard.* But he couldn't, and he knew it. Ortalis could be more dangerous to him than King Dagipert ever dreamt of being. Grus drummed his fingers some more. *What went wrong with him?* He shrugged. He doubted he'd ever know.

After a moment, he shook his head. One of the things that had gone wrong with Ortalis was that Grus himself had done so little to raise him. *How could I?* he thought. *I was keeping the Menteshe and the Thervings out of Avornis.* That was true. He knew it was true. Also true was that the job had desperately needed doing. *But still, had I been there more, would Ortalis have turned out better?* Grus shrugged. He could think that likely, and he did, but he knew it wasn't something he could be sure of.

Sosia's fine, he reminded himself. But it wasn't the same. Estrilda had always been there for their daughter. She'd been there for Ortalis, too, but that wasn't quite the same, either. A mother and a grandfather couldn't make up for a father who wasn't there. Maybe Crex hadn't tried enough to make Ortalis behave. On the other hand, maybe he'd tried too hard. Either way, he was with the gods now.

And how many people with you *were with the gods now?* Grus asked himself. The list seemed depressingly long. King Dagipert, perhaps some folk here in the palace, Count Corvus, Count Corax, the Avornan nobles who leaned their way, Prince Ulash and the other Menteshe lords down in the south, perhaps the Banished One behind the Menteshe . . . The Banished One, of course, wasn't a person, or wasn't merely a person.

As Kings of Avornis and others who'd held or longed for power in the kingdom for the past four hundred years had done, Grus thought, *I wish I held the Scepter of Mercy. They would have to take me seriously then.* He closed his eyes, to make the wish seem more real.

When he opened them again, his first thought was that someone had blown out the lamps in his chamber, leaving it in darkness. Fear slammed down a couple of heartbeats later, when he remembered it was the middle of the afternoon and no lamps were lit. Someone had stolen the light from the room—or rather, from his eyes—even so.

Small, soft, hungry noises came from the clotted darkness. Grus didn't know what the creatures that made those noises were hungry for. He didn't know, but he could guess. If they were hungry for anything but him, he would have been astonished. And what would be left of him once they'd fed? He didn't want to think about that. No, he didn't want to think about that at all.

As quietly as he could, he got to his feet. The small, soft noises were getting louder, as though whatever made them was getting closer. Grus blinked and blinked, however little it helped. But even though he couldn't see the things making the noises, that didn't mean they weren't there. Oh, no. It didn't mean anything of the sort.

When Grus looked toward the doorway, he couldn't see it. That left him unsurprised and also, somehow, unafraid. Plainly, he wasn't meant to come out of this room alive. But just because he couldn't see the door didn't mean he didn't know where it was. He started toward it, wondering if he would get there before the other things he couldn't see tore him to pieces.

His hand scraped against the planks of the door. The latch was— where? He almost wept with relief when he found it and opened it. He could see no more out in the corridor than he could in his room. But his hearing, like his fingers, still worked. He'd put those small, hungry noises behind him, at least for a little while. Soon, though, they would come after him.

He blundered along the hallway, feeling for the wall like a blind man—which, at the moment, he was. "Commodore Grus!" someone exclaimed. "Is something wrong? Do you need a healer?"

"I need a wizard," Grus answered hoarsely. "Someone's . . . something's . . . ensorcelled me. Quick!" He didn't think he was hearing those noises with ears alone, but they were getting closer again.

The servant or soldier or whoever it was took off at a dead run. Grus did hear his sandals slapping against stone in the ordinary way. Grus went on down the corridor, too, still feeling his way along. Now, though, he was pursued. Whatever was after him had a good notion of where he was and in which direction he was moving. The noises still weren't very loud, but they sounded hungrier than ever.

They're going to catch me, Grus thought. *Gods curse me if I'll let them pull me down from behind. I'll give them the best fight I can.* He turned at bay. His right hand found the hilt of the knife he wore on his belt. Could it do any harm to these things? He didn't know, but he intended to find out.

His left hand went to his throat. That was as much to protect a vulnerable place as for any other reason, but his fingers brushed against the amulet he wore under his shirt. Something close to hope caught fire in him. He'd worn that amulet for a long time, and it had warded him before. Turnix had said it was strong when he gave it to him. How strong was it? Grus knew he was about to learn.

He yanked out the amulet and clutched it tight. "Protect me, King Olor! Protect me, Queen Quelea! Protect me, all ye gods!" he gasped, hoping with every fiber of his being that Turnix hadn't botched the spell. Turnix, unfortunately, had been known to do exactly that.

But not this time. The amulet didn't completely return Grus' sight— return Grus' self—to what was known in the ordinary world. It gave him a glimpse of that world, though, as well as giving him a glimpse of the other world, the world into which the wizardry had cast him. It also gave him a glimpse of the creatures pursuing him in that world. The glimpse was blurry and shifting, as though through running water. He was glad it was no more distinct; most of him wished he hadn't had it at all.

Those horrid creatures seemed to sense he could see them. They drew back in what might have been alarm. Was he as revolting to them as they were to him? He didn't know. He didn't much care, either. As long as they stayed away, what did *why* matter?

More running footsteps, these coming toward him. Some small part of him noted that the servant and the wizard—no, he realized after a moment; she was a witch—looked as fuzzy and indistinct as the creatures from the other plane of reality, and almost as appalling. But Grus had to rely on them, and especially on the witch. "Help me!" he cried. "I'm beset!"

The witch began a spell. Grus had no idea whether the woman could actually see the creatures or just sense them in some sorcerous way. That was one more thing he didn't care about. He wished he couldn't see them himself.

Whether the witch could see them or not, she knew which charm to use. In that curious half-vision of Grus', he watched the creatures turn tail—though they didn't exactly have tails to turn—and run away. As they did, the last of the darkness lifted from his sight. With an almost audible snap, he returned completely to the real world he'd taken for granted up till a few minutes before.

"Well!" The witch sounded pleased and surprised. "I didn't think that would work so nicely. Someone put a nasty sending on you, sir, a very nasty sending indeed. You're lucky you lasted long enough to cry for help, let alone till it got to you."

Grus stood there shaking. Sweat dripped from him. He'd never felt so drained in all his life. "I have—a good—amulet." He had to force the words out one or two at a time.

"You must, sir. Truly, you must." The witch liked to repeat herself.

"My thanks," Grus told her, a little slower than he should have. And then, again a beat late, he asked, "What's your name?"

"Me, sir? I'm Alca." The woman was a few years younger than Grus, her brown hair getting its first streaks of silver. Her face wore a look of intense concentration. Grus wondered whether that meant she was wise or simply shortsighted.

Alca was wise enough to have done the job. What else counted? Nothing Grus could see. He said, "Well, my friend, I can't pay you back for what you did—who can give back fair payment for his life? But what I can give, believe me, I will."

"Thank you, sir, but I didn't do it for money," Alca replied. "As I said, a very nasty sending. It deserved to be stopped, and I'm glad I could."

"So am I, believe me!" Grus said. "Now the next question is, who would want me out of the way enough to try to get rid of me like that?"

"I . . . wouldn't know, sir," Alca said uncomfortably.

Grus needed a moment to realize why she sounded uncomfortable. When he did, he said, "Oh," softly to himself. Then he asked Alca, "Whoever did this—the wizard, I mean, not the person who arranged for it—is here in the palace, isn't he?"

Picking her words with care, Alca said, "I don't know that for a fact, sir. But it does seem reasonable, doesn't it?"

"Yes, doesn't it?" Grus agreed. "And whoever wanted me dead is likely to be here, too, eh?"

He had good reasons for hoping it wasn't the king. As the upstart son of Crex the Unbearable, he felt no small respect for a ruler who was about the dozenth member of his dynasty to come to the throne. He knew the people of Avornis felt the same way, too.

"Indeed, sir. May the gods forbid it," Alca said. "His Majesty and . . . all those who work to make Avornis a better, safer place should fight our foreign foes, not one another." She'd chosen her words with great care there, too, and had managed to sound loyal to King Lanius without sounding as though she opposed Grus. That couldn't have been easy, and Grus admired her for it.

Since Alca had, after all, saved him from the sending, Grus thought he could ask, "Will you help me find out who did it?"

Alca licked her lips. "That depends. What will you do when you know?"

"That depends, too," Grus answered. "Whatever I have to do. I didn't come to the city of Avornis to let myself get killed, you know. I can't very well worry about the Thervings if I'm dead." He didn't mention the Banished One. If a fallen god hated him enough to try to get rid of him, it wouldn't be with anything so trivial as a sending. He eyed Alca, waiting to hear what the witch would say. If Alca said no, they wouldn't stay friends even though she'd saved him.

But, after a long, long pause, she nodded. "Yes, I will do that. As I say, there are means, and then there are means. No one should use a black sending like that; it would sicken a Menteshe."

That wasn't quite how Grus had thought of it, but maybe it wasn't so far removed, either. He said, "I'll talk to each of them in turn, with you behind an arras. Will you be able to tell if I'm talking to a liar?"

"I believe so, sir," Alca replied. "There are wards against truth spells, but those are also likely to reveal themselves."

"All right, then," Grus said. "Let's get on with it." He wanted to find out as soon as he could, before whoever'd come so close to killing him tried again.

When Lepturus came at a servant's request, the guards commander asked, "You all right? Some funny stories are going through the palace."

"And well they might." Grus briefly explained what had happened, finishing, "I am . . . interested in getting to the bottom of this, you understand."

"I should hope so," Lepturus said. "I'll tell you straight out, Commodore—I didn't do it, and I don't know who did. I don't love you, but you haven't done anything to make me want you dead." He scowled. "I don't like a lot of the thoughts I'm thinking."

"I'm thinking them, too, and I don't like them, either." Grus nodded to the marshal. Face full of thunderclouds, Lepturus left. Alca emerged from behind the arras. "Well?" Grus demanded.

"He spoke the truth," the witch answered. Grus nodded. He'd thought so, too. He sent out another servant to ask Queen Certhia to see him.

One look at her face when she saw him hale told him everything he needed to know, even without Alca's help. He asked a short, sad question—"Why?"

"To keep you from stealing the throne from my son," she said. "Your men are everywhere in the city. Even a blind beggar could tell what you were up to, and I'm not blind. I'm not sorry I did it. I'm only sorry it didn't work."

Maybe she didn't know what sort of sending her wizard had used. Maybe. Grus said, "You're wrong. I meant no such thing." Maybe he was telling the truth. Maybe. He went on, "But now, I'm afraid, you've forced my hand."

CHAPTER ELEVEN

L anius had seen his mother exiled from the palace before. She'd come back in triumph after Arch-Hallow Bucco sent her away. Somehow, he didn't think the same thing would happen this time. He glared at Grus. "You have your nerve, Commodore, asking me to come talk with you after what you've done."

"Your Majesty, I know you're going to be angry at me," Grus said.

"Do you?" Lanius was just learning how to use sarcasm, which made him enjoy it all the more.

He might have been shooting arrows at a boulder, though, for all the effect he had on the naval officer. "Your Majesty, I'm sorry I sent your mother to the Maze," Grus said. "By the gods, I am. My life would've been easier if we'd managed to get along. But she tried to kill me, and she came too close to doing it. What was I supposed to do, leave her here to take another stab at it?"

He sounded reasonable. He sounded sincere. And Lanius knew perfectly well that his mother *had* tried to kill Commodore Grus. That didn't make him like Grus any better, even if it did mean he understood why Grus had done what he'd done. Lanius said, "Will you get rid of *me* now, for fear of what I might do to you one day?"

Grus' face froze. Something in Lanius froze, too. He hadn't imagined Grus would really dare do any such thing. Slowly, the commodore said, "I don't want to do that, Your Majesty. I don't want to do that at all. Everybody in Avornis cares about the dynasty."

"But if you think I'm dangerous enough, you will." Lanius had to force the words out through lips stiff with fear.

And Grus nodded. "If I have to, I will, yes. I don't want your blood on my hands, but I don't want my blood on your hands, either. I think you can understand that."

The worst of it was, Lanius *could* understand it. Had he stood in Grus' sandals, he would have thought about how best to get rid of himself. How could he have done otherwise? The King of Avornis—even if not of age, even if not trusted with the reins of government—was and always would be a menace to any mere protector simply by virtue of his office and the tradition and power that went with it.

"I think I may have found a way around the problem, though," Grus said. "I just might have." He eyed Lanius with what looked to the king like wry amusement; Lepturus had sent him more than a few such glances. "It keeps you breathing, too, which I hope you'll appreciate."

"I've heard ideas I like less," Lanius answered, which made Grus chuckle. Lanius went on, "What *is* this way of yours?"

"I'm going to have myself crowned King of Avornis," Grus said.

Rage ripped through Lanius. He'd never imagined he could be so furious. Having his mother exiled had frightened him as well as angered him. This was pure, raw fury. "You would dare?" he whispered in a deadly voice. "You dare speak of the dynasty in one breath, and then use the next to cast me down?"

"Who said anything about casting you down?" Grus said. "I don't intend to do anything of the sort. You've got all those ancestors who wore the crown. The people are used to having somebody from your family on the throne. That's fine with me. You'll keep on being King of Avornis. But I'll be King of Avornis, too."

"That's . . . very strange," Lanius said. "I've never heard of anything like it. I don't think anyone else has, either."

"So what?" Grus said cheerfully. "The other choice is leaving you shorter by a head. If that's what you want, I can arrange it." He folded his arms across his chest and waited.

Lanius almost told him to do his worst—almost, but not quite. Just in time, he realized Grus was neither joking nor bluffing. If he said something like, *I can't live with the humiliation,* he would, very shortly after that, stop living. He didn't want to, and so shook his head.

"Good," Grus said. "I don't want to kill you, Your Majesty. I didn't want to send your mother away, either, but she didn't leave me with a whole lot of choice."

Can I believe that? Lanius wondered. He had to believe it. Grus was letting him live. If the commodore—the commodore who was promoting himself to wear a crown—wanted him dead, dead he would be. He asked, "If we're both going to be King of Avornis, who will rule the kingdom?"

Grus jabbed a thumb at his own chest. "I will. You can wear the crown and the fancy robes. But I'll say who does what. I've heard you like to read old books and play around in the archives. Is that so?"

"Yes," Lanius answered. "That is so." He remembered playing with Marila in the archives, and how much he'd enjoyed that. But it wasn't what Grus meant, and he also loved going through old documents.

"Good," the commodore—the usurper—said again. "You can do that to your heart's content. If you find anything interesting, you can write a book of your own. As long as you don't jog my elbow, you can do whatever you please. If you do—but I already talked about that."

"So you did," Lanius said. "I suppose I ought to count myself lucky." He'd intended that for sarcasm, too, but it came out sounding different. He knew a good deal about Avornan history. The kingdom had known its share of usurpers, including the founder of his own dynasty. They hadn't gone out of their way to try to mollify the kings they overthrew. On the contrary—they'd gotten rid of them as fast as they could, and often as bloodily as they could.

Grus nodded now, to show he knew that, too. "Yes, Your Majesty, I suppose you should," he replied.

Lanius had never felt the lure of great power—he didn't want to take the throne so he could tell people what to do. He'd thought that, as King of Avornis, he was more likely to be able to do the things he wanted—like reading old books and playing around in the archives. Once he came of age, who would presume to tell him he couldn't?

And now here was Grus, telling him he not only could but had better do that. Oh, yes, there were worse usurpations, which didn't mean Lanius liked this one. He didn't. But what could he do about it? He could fume quietly, or he could die. Past that, nothing he could see. And there were worse fates than losing himself in the archives.

Arch-Hallow Bucco's beard was white as snow. Age bent his back and made him walk with the help of a cane. A cataract clouded one eye. He had to cup a hand behind his ear when someone spoke to him.

But his wits still worked. Once Grus made him understand what he wanted, the arch-hallow grinned a wide and eager grin. Grus didn't care that that grin showed several missing teeth. He cared much more that it was there.

"A pleasure!" Bucco said. "Yes, sir, it will be a great pleasure. I'd like it even better if you kicked the miserable little gods-despised bastard off the throne altogether. I'd truly like that, I would. Thinks he's three times as smart as everybody else, too."

Grus wondered exactly what had passed between King Lanius and Arch-Hallow Bucco. He didn't ask Bucco; he wanted the prelate's help. *One day, I might ask Lanius,* he thought, *though that would only give me his side of it.* He said, "I can't afford to get rid of him. The people like the dynasty. If I killed the boy, I'd be 'that bloody-handed murderer' the rest of my days."

"Well, you may be right," the arch-hallow admitted. "Yes, you may be right. But I don't have to like it, and I don't." He leaned forward. "What did you do with that miserable whore Certhia?"

What went through Grus' mind was, *Not* everybody *loves the dynasty.* He answered, "She's in the Maze. Deep in the Maze. She won't come out again, either, not unless there's worse treason than I can imagine."

"In Avornis, there's always worse treason than anyone can imagine," Bucco said. "I marvel that the Banished One tries so hard to overthrow us, I truly do. If he left us to our own devices, some of us would sell him Avornis soon enough, so long as they saw even half a chance to pay back their enemies that way."

Grus wanted to tell Bucco he was full of nonsense and bile. He wanted to, but he didn't. He feared the arch-hallow all too likely knew what he was talking about. Instead, Grus said, "You *will* crown me, then?"

"I won't just crown you, Commodore. I'll enjoy doing it," Bucco replied. "Let's pick a day, and I'll set the crown on your head. Do you want me to do it in the palace or in the cathedral?"

"I've been thinking about that," Grus said. "I'd like you to do it in the square in front of the palace. The more people who can crowd in, the better."

"You're right," Arch-Hallow Bucco answered. "You'll make a pretty good King of Avornis. You see how the pieces fit."

"Let's spread the news through the city and then hold the ceremony."

"You *do* know how the pieces fit," the arch-hallow said approvingly. "We'll do it exactly like that. You ought to have Lanius come and be a witness, too."

"He hates the idea," Grus said.

"Too bad," Bucco answered. "That isn't what anyone will see."

"Oh, no," Grus agreed. "Lanius knows what he's supposed to do, and what will happen if he doesn't. He's not stupid."

"No, he's not." By the sour expression on Bucco's face, he would have liked Lanius better had the young king been stupid. That would have made him easier to lead by the nose. The arch-hallow eyed Grus. "And since he isn't stupid, and since you say he doesn't like your stepping in front of him, he's going to spend a good deal of his time from now on plotting against you. How do you propose to get around that?"

He does want me to get rid of Lanius. He wants it very much, Grus thought. Now he eyed Bucco. "You like twisting people this way and that so they do what you want, don't you?" he said.

"Me, Commodore? I don't know what you're talking about," Bucco answered. Maybe he meant it; some men were curiously blind about their own character. More likely, though, he donned innocence as readily as his red ecclesiastical robes. "You may insult me if you please. It is your privilege, as the man who will be King of Avornis. But do remember, you have not answered my question."

"How will I stop Lanius from plotting against me?" Grus echoed, and Bucco nodded. With a shrug, Grus went on, "I have some ideas about that. I'm not going to tell you what they are, because I will tell you they're none of your concern."

"All right. It's your worry, not mine. The little bastard and his slutty mother discovered they couldn't do without me," Arch-Hallow Bucco said. "Now—when do you want the coronation?"

"As soon as you can arrange it and spread word through the city of Avornis that it's going to happen," Grus replied. "We do want a good-sized crowd there."

"There's the anniversary of the consecration of the cathedral—that's coming up six days from now," the arch-hallow said. "It's not one of the major festivals on the calendar, but a lot of people do take the day off from work. They'd come to the square, or a good many of them would."

"Perfect," Grus said. "We'll do it two hours after sunrise, to make sure everyone's out of bed."

"You may rely on me . . . Your Majesty," Bucco said.

"Your . . . Majesty." Grus tasted the words. After a moment, he nodded. "I'll just have to get used to that, won't I?"

Not being of age, King Lanius had never had true power in Avornis. He'd had influence with his mother and with Lepturus, though. With Grus he had none. The protector—the man who would make himself king—did listen to him; Grus was unfailingly polite. But Grus was also plainly a man who trusted his own judgment and no one else's. The next suggestion of Lanius' he took would be the first.

Grus did nothing to rob Lanius of his ceremonial role as king. Two days before the commodore was to steal a share of the title that by rights should have belonged to Lanius alone, the young king sat on the Diamond Throne to receive a party of merchants and ambassadors—with the Chernagors, the titles went hand in hand—from the folk who dwelt along the northern coast and on some few of the nearer islands in the Northern Sea.

The head of the embassy was a big, broad-shouldered man with a black beard—just beginning to be streaked with gray—that tumbled halfway down his chest. He wore his hair tied back in a neat bun at the nape of his neck. Fancy embroidery in vivid colors decorated his shirt. In place of trousers, he wore a wool kilt that showed off his knobby knees and hairy calves. His name was Yaropolk.

"Greetings to you, Your Majesty," he said in fluent if gutturally accented Avornan. "Greetings from my sovereign, Prince Vsevolod of Nishevatz, and from all the princes of the Chernagors."

"I greet you in return, and your prince through you," Lanius answered. He said nothing about the other princes of the Chernagors. Yaropolk probably would have been astonished if he had. The Chernagors lived in independent city-states, and fought among themselves over trade or, sometimes, over what seemed to an outsider like nothing at all. The only time they pulled together was when outsiders threatened. Sometimes they didn't do it then, either; several of those city-states had passed part of their history in Avornan hands.

Bowing, Yaropolk said, "You are very kind, Your Majesty, too kind to a stranger."

"By no means," Lanius said—this was all part of the ritual of dealing with Chernagors. "Behold—I have gifts for you and your companions." He nodded to a servant, who came forward with a silver tray on which sat a plump leather sack for each of the men who'd come to the throne room. Yaropolk's sack was a little plumper than the others.

"You are truly too kind, Your Majesty!" Prince Vsevolod's ambassador cried. He hefted his sack. Lanius was sure he knew to the farthing how much was due him, and that he could tell by the weight of the sack in his hand whether he'd gotten what he was supposed to. He seemed satisfied, as well he might have. Once he'd stowed away the sack, he went on, "We are also privileged to give you a gift, Your Majesty."

"Thank you," Lanius said, as impassively as he could. But he couldn't help leaning forward a little. The gifts Avornis gave to Chernagors followed strict and ancient custom. The gifts the Chernagors brought to the city of Avornis could be anything at all, by equally strict and ancient custom. Master traders and master mariners, the Chernagors traveled widely over the world's oceans. They came across things no one else—no one else from lands Avornis knew, anyhow—had ever seen, and sent some of those strangenesses down to the city of Avornis to amaze and delight her kings.

Bitterness surged through Lanius. *I won't be King of Avornis much longer.* But stubborn honesty made him shake his head. *I won't be* sole *King of Avornis much longer.* Grus could easily have slain him or sent him to the Maze with his mother. The commodore hadn't. That was something. Still, Lanius found resentment easier to cultivate than acceptance.

But resentment, too, was forgotten as a pair of Yaropolk's henchmen carried something large and bulky—but, apparently, not too heavy—and covered by a sheet of silk up to the base of the throne. Two or three royal guardsmen started to interpose themselves between the Chernagors and Lanius. He waved them back, saying, "It's all right." They didn't look as though they thought it was all right, but Lepturus, who as always stood to the left of the Diamond Throne, did not contradict the king. Muttering, the guardsmen returned to their stations.

"Behold, Your Majesty," one of the Chernagors said, and whisked away the silk to reveal a cage with gilded bars. And in the cage were . . .

"You're giving me two *cats*?" Lanius asked in surprise of a sort altogether different from what he'd expected.

But he realized his mistake even before Yaropolk shook his head and said, "Your Majesty, these are no ordinary cats."

"I see," Lanius breathed. "By the gods, Your Excellency, I see."

At first glance, they did look like plain tabbies, one grayish brown, the other reddish. Only at first glance, though; Lanius' error had come from speaking too soon. He stared and stared. The beasts had cat faces—indeed, cat heads—but those heads were set on their necks at an angle different from that of any cats he'd ever seen. They were more upright, more erect, not quite manlike but perhaps halfway between man and beast. And their arms—and legs, too, he noted—ended not in paws but in hands with real thumbs.

Some tiny motion in the throne room made the grayish one start. It sprang off the cage floor and swung from bar to bar and from perch to perch as nimbly as a monkey. "Have you Chernagors found some wizardly way to make cats and apes breed?" Lanius asked.

Yaropolk shook his head once more. The tip of his beard whipped back and forth. "A good question, Your Majesty, but not so," he answered. "Our traders found 'em. There's an island chain out in the Northern Sea—just where, you'll understand, I'd sooner not say—where they live. They aren't as tame as your ordinary cat, but they're not quite wild, either. The folk who live there use 'em as hunting animals, but most don't make real friends of 'em, the way we do with cats and dogs. Still, they won't be dangerous to anybody if you left 'em out of the cage after a bit."

"What do you call them?" Lanius asked, entranced by the gymnastic show the gray one was putting on. The reddish one stayed on the floor of the cage. It was, he realized, a female, and its belly bulged.

"We can't pronounce the name the natives use," the Chernagor said. "They speak a strange language in those islands, one that . . . oh, never mind. In our tongue, we say *obezyanakoshka.*"

"That seems strange enough to me," Lanius remarked.

"In Avornan, it would mean *monkey-cat,*" Yaropolk said. "Sometimes we just say *koshkobez.* That would be more like"—he frowned in thought— "like *moncat,* maybe, though I know moncat isn't a real word."

"Moncat." Lanius tasted the sound of it. "It *wasn't* a real word," he said. "I think it is now, because there's the thing it names."

"We've given you a mated pair, Your Majesty, and the female's carrying a litter. If you're lucky and you take care of them, you'll be able to keep the line going," Yaropolk told him. "You can make a pretty penny, I'd bet, selling 'em to folk who have to have the latest thing." As an ambassador, he should have been more polite, but as a merchant, he could speak freely— and practically. "They aren't hard to care for, not really. They eat kitchen scraps and anything they can catch. There aren't a whole lot of squirrels on those islands, I'll tell you that."

"I believe it." Lanius stared at the male beast—*the male moncat,* he reminded himself. It stared back out of slit-pupiled eyes yellow and shiny as a gold piece. "How soon can I let them out of their cage?" he asked.

"Why, whenever you please, Your Majesty," Yaropolk answered. "But you'll maybe want to be careful about where you do it. You have no idea how nimble they can be. If you want to make sure you'll see them again once you let them out, you'll do it in a room with narrow, narrow bars across all the windows, and with no holes in the walls." He paused, seeming to remember something else. "Oh. And once the female has her kittens, you'll want to find another room like that for the male. Otherwise, he'll try to kill them."

"I understand. Thank you for the warning." Lanius got down from the Diamond Throne and came up to the cage for a closer look at the moncats. Again, royal bodyguards started to shield him from the Chernagors. Again, he waved them back. Again, Lepturus let him get away with it.

He held his hand just outside the bars of the cage, to give the male a chance to smell him. He would have done the same when greeting an ordinary cat he hadn't met before. The moncat stuck the tip of its nose out through the bars, till it brushed the back of his fingers. He felt the animal's breath stir the tiny hairs growing there. The moncat sniffed interestedly; his was a smell it hadn't known before. And it looked at him with, he thought, more attention than a common cat would have paid. After a moment's thought, he decided that made sense. An animal that spent most of its time in trees would have to be able to see where it was going as well as sniff out prey.

Reaching into the cage with a forefinger, Lanius cautiously scratched the moncat behind the ears. "Careful, Your Majesty," Yaropolk warned. "It may bite. Like I said, it's not as tame as your everyday cat."

"I know," Lanius answered. "Even an everyday cat *may* bite. I don't think the moncat's going to, though."

Sure enough, the animal's eyes slid half shut—it enjoyed the attention. After a moment, it started to purr. The sound wasn't quite the same as an ordinary cat's purr; it was a little deeper, a little raspier. But a purr it unmistakably was. Lanius smiled. Yaropolk grinned. So did a couple of the guardsmen close enough to hear the contented buzz.

But then the moncat did something no common cat would have—something no common cat *could* have—done. It reached up with its left front foot—no, its left hand—and wrapped its fingers and thumb around Lanius' forefinger. The grip was gentle; the moncat's flesh was just a tiny bit warmer than his own. Its claws weren't the curved needles an ordinary cat would have had. They were still sharp at the tips, but broader than a regular cat's claws—halfway between claws and nails, in fact. The beast didn't try to scratch with them; they were simply there.

From behind Lanius, Lepturus said, "Looks like it likes you, Your Majesty."

"Yes, it does seem so," Yaropolk agreed. "Good. I am glad." He bowed.

Even with that small, warm, furry hand wrapped around his index finger, Lanius went on stroking the moncat. Its purr, if anything, got louder. "It *does* like me," he said, wonder in his voice. He wasn't used to being liked. He especially wasn't used to being liked for himself, for his own sake, and not for the sake of whatever he might do for whoever was talking to him at the moment. That sort of liking was the curse of kings. But the moncat couldn't know anything about it. It was only a beast, but it was sincere.

Grus won't mind if I breed moncats, Lanius thought. *He won't mind at all. He'll think it'll keep me out of mischief.* He tried to summon up scorn for the commodore who was promoting himself to a higher rank than any naval officer had ever enjoyed in all the history of Avornis. He also tried to summon up scorn for the idea of spending a lot of time breeding moncats. With the moncat's hand on his, he had more trouble finding that scorn than he'd expected he would.

When the time came to be crowned King of Avornis, Grus had expected to be nervous. He'd expected to be, but found he wasn't. He'd been nervous going into fights against the Menteshe and the Thervings. He'd had reason to be nervous, too. If anything went wrong in a fight, he wouldn't have the chance to make amends—he'd be dead or maimed.

If anything went wrong at his coronation . . . He shook his head. The most that was likely to happen was that some people might laugh at him. He knew he could live through that. His nerves stayed calm.

Estrilda, on the other hand, did get nervous. "What if Lanius betrays us?" she said a few minutes before the ceremony was set to begin. "What if Bucco betrays us? What if—"

"If Lanius betrays us, we make him sorry for it, and Bucco still puts the crown on my head," Grus told his wife. "The arch-hallow won't betray us, because he's hated Lanius since before the little know-it-all was born, and I haven't done anything to make him angry."

"What will you do if he gives you trouble?" Estrilda asked.

"When Bucco gave Mergus trouble, Avornis had itself a new arch-hallow the very next day," Grus answered. "I can do the same thing Mergus did, and Bucco has to know it. Everything will be fine. You look beautiful."

"Oh, foosh." Estrilda did her best to wave away the praise. Grus had distracted her, though, as he'd hoped he would. He hadn't even been lying. The glittering royal robes the palace servants had found for Estrilda played up her coloring and, with their jewels and thread of precious metal, made her look like a noblewoman born.

What struck Grus about the royal robes was how heavy they were. He might almost have had on a shirt of mail, instead. He wondered if they made him look like a king. He suspected it would have taken more than robes to pull off that trick. On the other hand, *anyone* who wore royal robes would likely find himself obeyed, at least for a while. And Grus did have practice at giving orders.

He glanced over to his son, whose robe was almost as gaudy as his own. Ortalis looked handsome as a prince—which suited Grus fine, for Ortalis was about to become one. Maybe rank and being able to get whatever he wanted as soon as he wanted it would cure the nasty streak in him. Grus hoped something would.

He wished his own father could have seen this ceremony. Crex's father had been a peasant. Crex's son was about to become King of Avornis. Grus smiled. You couldn't come up in the world much more than that, or much faster, either.

Grus smiled again, this time at his daughter. Sosia looked like a princess from a fairy tale. Grus thought she would have even without her robes, but knew he was prejudiced. Still, no one could deny she'd done a lot of growing up the past couple of years.

"Are we ready? Is it time?" Estrilda asked.

A glance at the hourglass told Grus they still had a quarter of an hour to wait. A glance at his wife told him he would get in trouble if he told her to look at the glass. Even if he was about to be crowned, that didn't make him sole ruler in his own family. All he said was, "Not quite yet, dear."

As the sand in the glass ran toward the end, a servant came through the door and said, "This way, please, everyone." Though he said *please,* he assumed he would be obeyed—and he was right. Grus and his wife and children followed the servant as meekly as though *he* ruled Avornis.

For the past several days, the sounds of hammering had filled the square in front of the royal palace. Now Avornans filled the square—men and women, some children beside them, others on their shoulders to see better. Marines and royal bodyguards kept the throng away from the platform and away from the roll of carpet that led to it from the palace gate. Grus and his family strode along the carpet and up the hastily knocked-together stairs that took them up onto the platform.

Arch-Hallow Bucco and King Lanius already waited there. When the crowd saw Grus, they went from buzzing interestedly to cheering. Grus waved to them. As he waved, he stole a glance at Lanius. The young king looked disappointed to hear those cheers. He'd probably hoped people would shout "Robber!" and "Usurper!" at Grus and ruin the coronation.

If he had a few more years and a little more craft, he would have made sure there were people out there shouting "Robber!" and "Usurper!" Grus thought. *Not quite yet, though, and gods be praised for that.*

Bucco raised his hands in a gesture that both offered the crowd a blessing and asked for silence. Little by little, people quieted down. "Avornis finds itself in danger," the arch-hallow said. "The barbarous Thervings have ravaged our land. They have even dared to lay siege to the city of Avornis itself. In the south, the Menteshe are an ever-present danger, and the shadow of the Banished One hangs over their every move. In times like these, we need a man of courage and might to lead the kingdom, and King Lanius is only a child."

Lanius stirred angrily at that. He had some reason to stir; he wasn't far from coming into his majority. But Bucco was putting the best face on things he could. He went on, "No one did more to make King Dagipert leave the city of Avornis and go back to Thervingia than Commodore Grus, commander of our river-galley fleet. Who, then, is better suited to lead Avornis in years to come than he?"

More cheers rose. Grus had made sure the audience held people who would applaud at the right time. Lanius wouldn't have thought of that. Arch-Hallow Bucco gestured to the young king. Lanius stepped forward, almost to the edge of the platform. "People of Avornis!" he called. "People of Avornis, hear me!"

Grus tensed. If Lanius had the nerve, this was the moment when he might try to incite the mob against Grus. If he called for folk to rise against the man stealing his throne . . . Grus' hand went to the hilt of his sword. *He may pull me down if he tries that, but he won't live to enjoy it.*

"People of Avornis," Lanius continued, "this is a time when we truly do need a strong king, a king who is tried in war. I am willing—I am pleased—to share my crown with Commodore Grus."

That was, word for word, what he was supposed to say. Grus let out a sigh of relief. Lanius gave him a cold nod as he came forward. The young king might have said he was pleased to share the crown, but he didn't mean it. Grus shrugged. What Lanius had meant didn't matter. The crowd out there was cheering—cheering loud enough to make Grus want to raise his hands to his ears. That mattered.

I suppose I ought to thank the Chernagors for bringing him those funny cats, too, Grus thought. *He's just young enough to think they're as interesting as girls. Another couple of years, and nothing but a really beautiful concubine would have distracted him so well.*

A servant walked up to Arch-Hallow Bucco. The man carried on a velvet cushion a crown identical to the one Lanius wore. The arch-hallow lifted the crown from the cushion and held it high so the people packing the square could see it. As though on cue, the sun came out from behind a cloud and sparkled from the gold and rubies and emeralds and sapphires. "Ahhh!" said the men and women who'd come to see Grus made a king.

Bucco quickly lowered the crown. He motioned for Grus to bend his head. Grus obeyed. *This is the last time I have to obey anyone,* went through his mind. If that wasn't a heady notion, he didn't know what would be. The arch-hallow put the crown on his head. As Bucco set it there, he called out, "It is accomplished!" in a great voice.

Grus straightened. In straightening, he discovered why Arch-Hallow Bucco had wasted no time lowering the crown. It was even heavier than he'd thought it would be—far heavier than the iron helmets he'd worn when he fought. All they'd had to do was keep some savage from smashing in his head. The crown had to look impressive instead. It had to, and it did.

"Hurrah for King Grus!" "Long live King Grus!" "King Grus! King Grus! King Grus!" The shouts washed over Grus like the tide. He didn't have to worry much about the tide, not serving on river galleys as he'd always done. He didn't have to worry about it, but he knew what it did.

He raised his hands above his head, asking for quiet in the same way as Arch-Hallow Bucco had. He needed longer to get quiet than Bucco had. He hoped that was a good sign.

"People of Avornis!" he called, pitching his voice to carry, as he would have on the deck of a river galley during a storm. "People of Avornis, I never expected—I never intended—to be set above you." That was true, or had been true till he'd been summoned to defend the capital from Dagipert and the Thervings. By the way people applauded when he said it, they believed him, too.

He went on, "We have many enemies. I'll do everything I can to hold back the ones outside the kingdom. And the nobles inside the kingdom who want to take what isn't theirs also had better look out. They are no friends of Avornis."

The cheers he got then almost knocked him off the platform. He smiled a little. He'd hoped and thought ordinary people resented greedy nobles like Corvus and Corax. It was good to see he'd been right.

To his surprise, he saw King Lanius clapping his hands, too. *Isn't that interesting?* Grus thought. *I wonder what Lanius has against the nobility.*

Meanwhile, though, he had to finish talking to the crowd. "With your help—with the help of the gods—Avornis will be a great kingdom again," he told them. "We can be. We aren't far from it, and you must know that. As long as we pull together and don't fight among ourselves, we have a chance. The Banished One wouldn't try so hard to lay us low if he weren't afraid of us."

Of course, the Banished One might have wanted to lay Avornis low for no more reason than that it stood in the way of his Menteshe. Having been cast down from the heavens, he thought the material world was his by right—*by divine right,* Grus thought, and shivered a little. The Banished One had never stopped being offended that any mere mortals wanted to keep on ruling themselves instead of letting him take them in his hands and do with them what he would. Grus looked toward the south. *Too bad,* was what went through his mind.

"At this time, I'd like to recognize Alca the witch, and to reward her with the post of chief sorcerous aide to the throne," Grus said. "Alca, step forward!" Alca ascended to the platform, waved, and went down again. Her husband put his arm around her. Pride filled his face. Grus continued, "Alca saved me from a wizardly attack, and deserves promotion. All those who serve me well will get what they earn. Those who don't will get what *they* earn, too."

Again, applause filled the square. Grus had left the impression the Banished One, not Queen Certhia, had launched that attack against him. He didn't want to humiliate Lanius in public, not unless he had to. Lanius nodded to him, ever so slightly. He recognized what Grus had said, and what he hadn't. Unless Grus mistook his expression, he was grateful for what hadn't been said. *Maybe we can work together,* Grus thought. *Maybe.*

CHAPTER TWELVE

Lanius gave the moncats the chamber next to his bedroom. He'd named the male Iron and the reddish female Bronze. Then, two weeks later, he'd had to find another chamber for the male. When Bronze had her kittens—twins—Iron wanted to kill them, just as Yaropolk had warned he might.

The kittens each clung to Bronze's fur with all four hands, and wrapped their tiny tails as far around her as they would go, too. For their first couple of weeks of life, clinging and sucking were about all they could do. Bronze was almost as suspicious of Lanius as she had been of Iron before the king gave him a new home. Little by little, feeding her bits of pork and poultry, Lanius won her trust.

When the kittens' eyes opened, they came to take Lanius as much for granted as they did their mother. One was a male, the other a female. He wondered whether that was happenstance or the way moncats always did things. By then, though, Yaropolk had left the city of Avornis, and none of the Chernagors in the capital admitted to knowing the answer.

He called the male kitten Spider and the female Snitch—she had a way of reaching for anything she could get her tiny hands on and popping it into her mouth. With Grus running the kingdom, Lanius did enjoy having time to spend on the moncats.

He made sure he kept visiting Iron, too, to keep him tame. After sending him away from Bronze and the kittens, Lanius thought about renaming him the Banished One. He thought about it, but then put the idea aside. In Avornis, that was not a name of good omen, even in whimsy.

He was picking fleas off Spider when someone knocked on the door to the moncats' room. "Who's there?" he asked. With a little moncat purring on his lap, he didn't want merely human company just then.

But the answer was, "Grus."

Grus didn't throw the title he'd stolen in Lanius' face. He was doing what he could to get along with Lanius and work with him wherever he could. Lanius couldn't decide whether that made him dislike his fellow king more or less. Whichever the answer was, he couldn't ignore Grus. "Come in," he said.

When Grus did, his gaze traveled from Spider to Snitch to Bronze. He quickly closed the door behind him so the moncats couldn't get out. Yaropolk had been right about that, too—once loose, they were very hard to recapture. "Fascinating creatures, Your Majesty," Grus remarked. "Really fascinating. I see why you're so taken with them."

"Yes, they are," Lanius agreed. "Your Majesty," he added, a bit slower than he should have. He didn't like yielding Grus the title, but saw no way around it. "Did you come here just to tell me that?"

Grus shook his head. "Not at all. I came to ask you a question."

"Go on," Lanius said. Spider squirmed. He let the moncat go. It scrambled over to its mother. Bronze scooped up the kitten and held it in an amazingly humanlike embrace.

"You've met my daughter, Sosia," Grus said. Lanius nodded, puzzled—that wasn't a question. When Lanius did no more than nod, Grus *did* ask a question. "What do you think of her?"

In truth, Lanius hadn't thought much of Sosia, for good or ill. He'd noticed she wasn't far from his own age, and that was about all. He didn't much care for her brother, but he got the notion Grus didn't much care for Ortalis, either. "What do I think of your daughter?" he echoed now. "She's . . . very nice." That seemed as safe an answer as he could give.

But it turned out not to be safe enough. Grus beamed at him. "I'm glad to hear you say so, Your Majesty. By the gods, I'm very glad. I'll announce the betrothal tomorrow."

"Betrothal?" Lanius squeaked. He hadn't even seen the trap till it flipped him up into the air and left him dangling upside down.

Grus nodded vigorously. "Certainly, a betrothal. What better way to tie our two houses together than a wedding between them?"

"King Dagipert wanted to marry me to his daughter, too," Lanius said.

Had Grus wanted to take that the wrong way, he could have made La-nius sorry—very sorry—he'd ever said it. As things were, the other king answered mildly, saying, "Dagipert is a foreigner, a barbarian, an enemy to Avornis. I hope you'll agree I'm none of those things."

You'd better agree I'm none of those things, his tone warned. And he was an Avornan, no doubt of that. Still . . . "I'm not sure I want to marry at all," Lanius said, trying to escape the snare.

"Oh, of course you do," Grus said. "You've found out about women, haven't you?" He was gentle. He was genial. He was also implacable. La-nius hadn't imagined how formidable he could be.

I can't even lie. He knows better. "Yes," he said unhappily.

"Well, then." Grus smiled a wide, cheerful smile. Lanius supposed it was a father-in-lawish kind of smile. He didn't have standards of compar-ison there, though. He'd never seen Dagipert smile, although he supposed Arch-Hallow Bucco had. Grus went on, "Don't you think it would be bet-ter to get yourself a wife and not have to worry about chasing after serving girls when you're in the mood?"

"I don't know," Lanius answered honestly. Then he asked a question of his own. "Didn't you do some chasing of your own even after you got yourself a wife?"

By the look Grus gave him, the other King of Avornis hadn't expected that. But Grus soon steadied himself. "Yes, as a matter of fact, I did. As you'll probably have heard—you seem to have heard all sorts of things—I have a bastard boy in the south. He's not far from your age, as a matter of fact. I spent a lot of time away from home, you know."

Lanius didn't know. Except for his one brief campaigning foray, he'd never spent *any* time away from home. "What's his name?" he asked. That wasn't just his usual curiosity. Grus' illegitimate son might soon become a sort of relative by marriage.

"He's called Anser," Grus replied. "He seems a likely lad, or reasonably so. I've been giving his mother money to raise him for years. Now that I've . . . come up in the world a bit, I'll have to do more than that."

Lanius didn't say anything. If this Anser *was* a likely lad, he could fill one of any number of posts, and perhaps fill it well. If he turned out not to be so likely, would that stop Grus from appointing him to a position where what he did mattered? Lanius filed that away. He'd have to see what Grus did, and what Anser did after Grus decided where to put him.

Meanwhile, Grus wasn't about to ease the pressure on Lanius himself. "What do you say?" he asked. "I want to announce the betrothal as soon as I can."

I'm sure you do, Lanius thought. The more tightly Grus grafted his family to the longtime reigning dynasty, the harder he'd be to pry loose. Lanius considered simply telling him no. Then he looked at Grus' face. On second thought, that didn't seem so wise. *What kind of accident or illness would you arrange for me?* he wondered. Bucco had tried it. Lanius had managed to foil him. He didn't think he could foil Grus, who seemed alarmingly capable. *Maybe I'd better become his son-in-law. He might not want to arrange any misfortune for me if I'm married to his daughter.*

But despite that thought, Lanius asked, "What does Sosia think about marrying me?"

"She thinks you're very nice," Grus answered, which might have meant his daughter thought Lanius was very nice, or might have meant Grus hadn't bothered getting his daughter's opinion. But then Grus added, "And I believe she also thinks joining our two houses would be a good idea."

That, if true, interested Lanius. Unlike the other, it wasn't something Grus had had to say. "*Does* she?" Lanius asked.

His fellow king nodded. "Yes. Sosia's a clever girl. She'll do what needs doing."

Had he said she was beautiful, Lanius would have known he was lying. He'd seen her himself. She was pleasant, but far from gorgeous. Cleverness, though . . . Cleverness did pique Lanius' curiosity. He didn't know much about what he wanted in a wife, but he didn't think he could put up with a stupid woman.

"Well," he said, "let's see what happens."

"Do we really have to do this?" Estrilda asked.

Grus stared at his wife. "Where do you think we'll get a better match for Sosia? How *can* you get a higher match than the King of Avornis?"

"I don't say you can get a higher match. Of course you can't. But better?" Estrilda shrugged. "How can you know? I wouldn't have wanted to marry anybody like Lanius when I was a girl. He thinks too much."

"Well, you never said I did anything like that," Grus answered, trying to tease a smile from Estrilda. It didn't work. Frowning himself, Grus went on, "It's the best thing we can do for the family."

"How often do men 'help' the family by making their women miserable?" his wife returned. "You didn't even ask Sosia if this was what she wanted to do. You just went and told Lanius he'd wed her. That's no way to do things."

"All right, then—we'll ask her," Grus said. "If she tells us yes, we'll go ahead. If she says no . . ." His voice trailed away. He didn't know what he'd do if Sosia said she didn't want to marry Lanius. Probably see if he could talk her into changing her mind. He'd have to do that when Estrilda wasn't listening.

When he and Estrilda walked into Sosia's chamber, he found his daughter embroidering a unicorn on a square of linen. He thought unicorns were imaginary beasts, but wasn't quite sure. After the Chernagors had brought those moncats to the city of Avornis, he wasn't so positive what could be real and what couldn't.

He wasted no time on preliminaries, but asked Sosia, "What do you think of being betrothed to Lanius?"

Sosia only shrugged; she seemed less worried about it than her mother. *That's something, anyhow,* Grus thought. Then his daughter answered, "I think it will be all right. He's not ugly, and I don't think he's mean."

She looked around after she said that. So, automatically, did Grus and Estrilda. But Ortalis, wherever he was, wasn't in earshot. Grus said, "I'm sorry I didn't talk more with you about the match before I went and made it." He was willing to throw Estrilda a sop if he could. Why not? Sosia seemed willing to marry Lanius, if not bursting with enthusiasm at the prospect.

And then she answered, "It really is all right, Father. I expected you to do something like this. How else are we going to make sure Lanius stays loyal to us?"

Grus' mouth fell open. What he'd told Lanius proved true after all. He didn't bother looking over at his wife. Estrilda couldn't have been more surprised than he was. "Are you sure, dear?" she asked.

"I'm pretty sure, Mother," Sosia said. "I'm going to marry *someone,* and better Lanius than some count three times my age who gets drunk all the time and sings songs about sheep when he's feeling jolly."

Now Grus did catch Estrilda's eye. She wouldn't meet his, not for long. Throwing her hands in the air, she said, "All right. I give up. Let the match go forward. I only wanted what was best for you, sweetheart, and to be sure you knew your own mind."

"I usually do," Sosia said.

"Well." Even Grus sounded a little dazed. He tried to make the best of it. "As long as that's settled."

"Yes, Father. Yes, Mother. Is there anything else?" Sosia waited while Grus and Estrilda both shook their heads. Estrilda looked as dazed as Grus felt. Not Sosia. Sosia knew her own mind perfectly well. Grus wondered if she'd decided she was going to marry Lanius before Grus came to the same conclusion. As he retreated in what he hoped was well-concealed disorder, he decided he wouldn't have been a bit surprised.

Lanius found himself looking forward to his wedding day. That surprised him. No matter what Grus said, Lanius remained convinced he could have more fun with a string of compliant, pretty serving girls than with a single, solitary wife. A wife—especially a wife who was also the daughter of the man who'd usurped his power, if not all of his throne—seemed more likely to prove an encumbrance than an advantage.

And yet . . . However much Lanius resented Grus, he had trouble resenting Sosia. Whenever he saw her in the palace, she was unfailingly polite and pleasant. She never had a great deal to say, but what she did say proved she had a head on her shoulders. Things could, he decided, have been worse.

And wedding Sosia would settle his life. Up till then, he'd known nothing but disruption since his father died. King Scolopax had despised him. Arch-Hallow Bucco had reckoned him—still did reckon him—a bastard. His own mother had coddled and patronized him. And then Queen Certhia, too, was whisked from the palace, and Grus took her place. Lanius didn't know exactly what Grus thought of him. He suspected Grus wanted to think of him as little as possible.

He minded less than he'd thought he would. At fifteen, he was content—even eager—to be left alone. He had his books. Now he had the moncats. If he had a wife, too, he wouldn't need to worry about chasing the maidservants—not that some of them required much chasing.

Besides, he couldn't do anything about getting married. However little Grus had to do with him, the former commodore who'd promoted himself to king made that very clear. Lanius decided to make the best of it.

His wedding day—appointed by King Lanius—dawned cool and rainy. Servants decked him in the snow-white shirt and midnight breeches bridegrooms wore. He being king, his wedding shirt was of silk, and shot through with silver threads. His breeches were spun from the finest, softest wool in Avornis. A grinning young man fastened to them a codpiece whose extravagance was likelier to frighten a new bride than intrigue her.

"Too much," Lanius said. "Take out some of the padding."

But the servant shook his head. In some matters, not even kings were masters of their fate. The man said, "Not today, Your Majesty. Today you've got to show yourself off."

"That's not me," Lanius said. "By the gods, the stallions who go out to stud would have trouble matching what you've put in there."

"It's custom," the servant declared. Against custom, the gods themselves protested in vain.

Sosia was dressed all in red, to symbolize the loss of her maidenhead that would follow the wedding ceremony—would, in fact, for all practical purposes be a part of it. Lanius got a glimpse of her as she climbed into one carriage and he into another for the short journey to the cathedral.

One of Lanius' earliest memories was of priests lined up shoulder to shoulder behind Arch-Hallow Bucco to keep his father and mother and him from worshiping at the cathedral. Now soldiers—or were they Grus' marines?—surrounded the place to make sure nothing happened to him. Lanius would have been happier about that had the men been there to obey his orders and not his fellow king's.

He couldn't do anything about it, though. He got out of the carriage in the square in front of the cathedral. The square was the second largest in the city of Avornis, smaller only than the one in front of the royal palace. He'd come through it more times than he could count, once Bucco finally condescended to let him pay his respects to the gods. It seemed different now. He needed a moment to figure out why—no ordinary worshipers streaming into the cathedral. The wedding party would have the place to itself.

Even so, royal bodyguards formed up around Lanius. At their head marched Lepturus. "Congratulations, Your Majesty," he said in tones likelier to be used for condolences.

"It won't be so bad," Lanius said. They walked on for a few paces before he added, "And it could be a lot worse." He laid a hand on the back of his neck to show what he meant. To Lepturus, if to no one else left in the palace these days, he could say what he meant.

"Yes, Your Majesty, that's so," Lepturus allowed. "You could have gone to the block. For that matter, so could I. I'm still a little surprised I haven't."

"If you suggest it to Grus, I'm sure he could make the necessary arrangements," Lanius murmured.

"Heh," Lepturus said. But Lanius noticed that he didn't disagree.

When they came to the entrance into the cathedral, one of Grus' henchmen—a river-galley captain named Nicator—strode up with enough marines to outnumber Lanius' bodyguards about two to one. He nodded to Grus and said, "We'll take care of him from here on out."

Lepturus bristled. "Who says? Nobody told me about that."

"Not my worry," Nicator replied with a shrug. "Your boys can clear out now." The warning behind his words was, *If they don't clear out, we'll clear them.*

No less than Lepturus himself, the bodyguards looked furious. More than a few of them had served not just Lanius but his father, King Mergus. By their expressions, they feared Nicator's men were getting them out of the way as a first step toward putting Lanius out of the way. Lanius didn't believe that. Grus had too many other simpler, less public ways of disposing of him; he didn't need to do it in a setting like this. "It's all right, boys," Lanius said.

Lepturus' scowl said he didn't think it was all right. He glared at Nicator and said, "I'm coming with His Majesty." *And you'll have to kill me to stop me,* the forward thrust of his body warned.

"I want Lepturus with me," Lanius said.

He waited for Nicator to argue. But the naval officer only nodded and said, "That's fine, Your Majesty. He's on my list. Even if he wasn't, we'd fix things. I know he's been guarding you since you were tiny." Nicator nodded again, this time to Lepturus. "Come right ahead, Marshal."

Anticlimax. Maybe Lepturus really had been worrying over nothing. Maybe. Any which way, he and Lanius went forward, escorted by Grus' marines and by this fellow who'd been at Grus' side longer than Lanius had been alive.

Incense filled the inside of the cathedral. The sweet smoke made Lanius' eyes water even as it tickled his nose. Olor, king of the gods, peered down from the dome at the King of Avornis. Quelea, Olor's Queen, stood behind her husband in the vast fresco that must have taken years to paint.

Neither the divine king nor his queen looked directly at their puny human worshipers in the cedarwood seats below. Instead, their gaze was on the Banished One, whom the painters had shown at the edge of the dome, tumbling endlessly down from the heavens after the other gods cast him out. By the satisfied, almost smug look on Olor's face, he was pleased with himself at solving a problem.

Olor had solved his own problem. The Banished One would trouble him and his domain no more. But the king of the gods had given mortal men an altogether different problem. Maybe Olor had thought the Banished One would smash to pieces when he struck the surface of the material world. If he had, he'd been wrong. More likely, he simply hadn't cared one way or the other. Ever since that fateful day, the Banished One had been mankind's worry, not the gods'.

Lanius, at the moment, had more immediate worries than the Banished One. King Grus came up the aisle toward him. Grus bowed. "Welcome, Your Majesty," he said. "You do my family great honor."

Returning the bow, Lanius answered, "I am glad we join our families together." He wasn't sure he was glad of any such thing, but those words had to be spoken. His father couldn't say them—King Mergus was dead. His mother couldn't say them, either—Queen Certhia was exiled to the Maze. With no one else to speak the required words, Lanius had to say them himself.

Grus held out his hand. Lanius clasped it. That too needed doing. "Come with me, then, Your Majesty," Grus said. "Your bride awaits."

Sure enough, Sosia stood in front of Olor's golden altar, between Arch-Hallow Bucco and Queen Estrilda. Lanius gathered himself, almost as though he were going into combat. Licking his lips, he said, "Thank you, my father-in-law to be. I go to her with all my heart."

What a liar I am.

Sosia's brother, Ortalis, sat in the very first row of seats. He was part of the bride's family, yes, but had no role to play in the ceremony, as her father and mother did. *He's been shoved into the background,* Lanius thought, *just like me.* That gave him a sudden burst of sympathy for Sosia's brother.

Ortalis promptly made him regret it. As though by accident, he stuck his leg out into the aisle just as Lanius went by. If Lanius hadn't seen it, he would have tripped and fallen on his face. As things were, he sidestepped. Ortalis sent him a horrible look. Grus sent Ortalis a horrible look. Nobody said a word. *And so I join my new family,* Lanius thought.

But he hadn't joined it yet, not officially. There stood Arch-Hallow Bucco, robed in a shade of red different from Sosia's, waiting to bind Lanius to Grus' daughter and, through her, to Grus himself. *And to Ortalis.* Lanius wished that hadn't crossed his mind.

Sosia smiled at Lanius as he approached. Bucco bowed as low as his old bones would let him. "Your Majesty," he murmured.

Lanius dipped his head to the arch-hallow, thinking, *You miserable hypocrite. You never thought I should be King of Avornis, and you're tying me to Sosia to make sure I don't get the chance to do anything on my own.*

Bucco raised his hands in a gesture of benediction. The nobles and courtiers in the cedarwood seats fell silent . . . more or less. "A wedding is always a new hope," Bucco said. His voice was twenty, maybe thirty, years younger than the rest of him, a subtle, supple instrument that remained his greatest tool—and his greatest weapon. He went on, "That being so, a wedding between king and princess is a new hope not just for the groom and bride but also for the Kingdom of Avornis."

He was a man who thought of himself first, Avornis distinctly afterward, and King Lanius last of all, but that didn't make him wrong. Up till then, Lanius hadn't been nervous. Now the magnitude of what he was doing pressed down on his shoulders like a great weight.

"To the great and ancient dynasty of which King Lanius is the scion, we add now the vigor and courage that come from King Grus' line," Bucco intoned. *Does that mean I've got no vigor or courage of my own?* Lanius wondered. Bucco probably thought it did. *Well, a pestilence on Bucco and what he thinks.* But then the arch-hallow said, "Your Majesty, be so kind as to take Her Highness' hand."

Lanius had been king since he was a little boy. Sosia had been a princess for only a few weeks. She needed a moment to remember that "Her Highness" meant her. Then she held out her hand. Lanius took it. It was the first time he'd ever touched her. Her flesh was warm and smooth. He suspected fear made his own grip cold and clammy.

"Before the eyes of the gods, Your Majesty, do you take Princess Sosia for your wife, to have her bear your legitimate children?" Bucco said. "Do you pledge not to exceed great Olor's example?"

The arch-hallow looked pointedly at him. He himself sprang from his father's exceeding of Olor's example and taking his mother as seventh wife rather than concubine. But all he could say was, "I do." The marriage oath, as his work in the archives had proved, was as old as Avornis.

"Do you reject, now and forever, all blandishments of the Banished One? Do you swear to do all you can to return the Scepter of Mercy to the city of Avornis, its one true and proper home?"

"I do," Lanius repeated. The last question was reserved for Kings of Avornis alone, and had been added to the oath after the Menteshe carried the Scepter into captivity. Lanius made the pledge, but wondered how much all he could do would be. The Scepter of Mercy, after all, had lain captive in Yozgat for four hundred years. Every one of his predecessors had sworn he'd do all he could to redeem it. Every one of them hadn't done enough.

If I fail, too, I won't be disgraced, he thought. *Nor will Grus, if he also fails.* Lanius didn't like that second thought so well, but he couldn't do anything about it.

Arch-Hallow Bucco turned to Sosia. "Before the eyes of the gods, Your Highness, do you take King Lanius for your husband, to bear his legitimate children? Do you pledge not to allow him to exceed great Olor's example?"

"I do," Sosia answered, so quietly that Lanius didn't think anyone but he or Bucco could hear her. Maybe she was nervous, too.

"Do you reject, now and forever, all blandishments of the Banished

One?" the arch-hallow asked. He didn't say anything to her about recovering the Scepter of Mercy.

"I do," Sosia repeated, a little louder this time.

Bucco bowed creakily, first to Lanius, then to Sosia. "I say to the two of you, then, that you are married. Treat each other kindly. Be patient with each other. If you do, you will be happy together. The gods grant it be so."

"The gods grant it be so," Lanius and Sosia said together. Greatly daring, he squeezed her hand a little. She jerked in surprise, ever so slightly, then smiled at him and squeezed back.

"It is accomplished." Bucco nodded to Lanius. "You may kiss your bride."

Till then, that had hardly occurred to Lanius. He leaned toward Sosia. The kiss he gave her was a sedate peck on the lips. Even that was plenty to set off cheers and shouts of bawdy advice from the assembled courtiers and nobles. Lanius' ears got hot. Sosia turned pink.

"Now we feast! Now we drink!" Grus called in a great voice he might have used on the foredeck of a river galley. "And then . . ." He paused. More shouts rose. So did whistles and cheers. Sosia turned pink again.

Lanius leaned toward her once more and whispered, "It will be all right." He was glad he'd had lessons from some of the serving maids. He wouldn't have wanted to go into a marriage where neither he nor his bride had any notion of what they were supposed to do when they were alone together.

They went back to the palace for the feast. Meat and drink were magnificent. *And why not?* Lanius thought. *Grus can spend whatever he likes.* If Grus spent this way very often, of course, he'd bankrupt the kingdom. But, to be fair, he probably didn't plan to marry off his only daughter again anytime soon. *He'd better not plan to marry her off again soon,* went through Lanius' mind.

Somewhat elevated from fine red wine, Grus came over and put a hand on Lanius' shoulder. "Take good care of her," he said, as though it were a wedding of artisans rather than that of a king to another king's daughter.

"I will," Lanius said.

"Take good care of her," his fellow sovereign and new father-in-law repeated, "and she'll take good care of you."

"I'm sure of it," Lanius answered, sure of nothing of the sort. Wasn't Sosia likely to be her father's creature first, last, and always? But then Lanius looked over at her. She smiled back and fluttered her fingers. *She wants to like me, I think. I have to give her reason to like me, then. She's always going to be Grus' daughter, but she* is *my wife, too.*

As the feast went on, more and more people started looking expectantly from Lanius to Sosia and back again. Lanius knew what that meant. He wondered whether Sosia did. He also wondered how much she knew of what went on between men and women. Whatever she didn't know, he would have to teach her. *What a strange burden to lay on a bridegroom's shoulders, and what a heavy one.*

Sosia went over and started talking with her mother. Lanius wondered what Queen Estrilda was saying. That could make a difference, too. Sosia didn't look appalled or terrified, so maybe it wouldn't be too bad. Lanius dared hope.

Then Grus came up to him. "Are you ready?" he asked. Lanius took a deep breath and nodded. "Good, good," Grus said. "Best to have the whole business over and done with, eh?" Lanius nodded again. Grus clapped him on the back. "Besides, you'll enjoy it."

"Er—yes," Lanius said.

Grus wasn't looking for anything but agreement. By then, he'd taken on quite a lot of wine himself. But, sober or drunk, he got things done. Before long, Lanius and Sosia went through the corridors of the palace to the chamber where they'd pass their first wedded night. Everyone followed them—nobles, courtiers, bodyguards, palace servants. Everyone yelled advice, too. By the time Lanius closed the bedroom door and barred it after himself and his new bride, his ears were burning. He wondered what she thought.

She managed a smile, even though the lewd chorus went right on and pierced the door as though it weren't there. "My mother told me it would hurt the first time, but that it would get better once things stopped being sore," she said.

"From what I've heard, that's right," Lanius answered. "I don't know for sure. The only virginity I've ever taken is my own, I'm afraid."

"I'm glad you know something about it, anyhow," she said. "We'd probably make a real mess of it if we both had to find out at the same time."

"I was thinking the very same thing not long ago," Lanius said. "If we think alike, maybe that's a sign we'll get along. I hope so, anyhow."

"Me, too," Sosia said. "We're stuck with each other regardless of whether we do or not. We ought to try our best. My father and mother seem to manage pretty well."

"Yes, I've seen that," Lanius agreed. "I hope we can, too. You will have seen more about that side of things than I have, though, because my father died while I was still little."

He wondered if she'd say anything about his coming from a seventh marriage. He'd heard too much about that, all through his life. It wasn't *his* fault. But Sosia said not a word. Her silence made him like her better.

Whoever had set up the room had obligingly turned back the covers on the bed. Lanius nodded to it. "Shall we . . . ?"

"We'd better, hadn't we?" Sosia said. "We should get it over with."

That sounded more businesslike than wanton, but if she was frightened she didn't show it. Lanius took off his shirt and breeches—and that miserable codpiece—and stood there waiting in his drawers. He was suddenly shy about stripping himself naked before her.

She reached over her head. Her mouth twisted in annoyance. "This gown has clasps in the back, and I can't undo them without seeing what I'm up to. Can you help me?"

"I hope so." Lanius came over and stood behind her. He had no trouble undoing the clasps. Then he leaned forward to kiss her on the back of the neck. She flinched. "I'm sorry," he said.

"It's all right. You startled me, that's all." Sosia managed a shaky smile. "I'd better get used to things like that, hadn't I?"

"Well, I hope so." Lanius hoped he would still want to kiss her on the back of her neck after they'd been married for a while.

She pulled the gown off over her head. Under it, she wore a thin shift and her own drawers. Something like reckless defiance on her face, she took off everything. After that, Lanius could only do the same.

"You're beautiful," he whispered.

Sosia looked embarrassed. "How do I know you're not just saying that?"

"It would be easy for me to lie. Not for *him,* though." Part of him was unmistakably enthusiastic. He hadn't been around unclothed girls so often as to keep from rising to the occasion whenever he was. If Sosia in fact wasn't quite beautiful, she came close enough to let him be gallant with no trouble at all.

"Him?" she echoed as she examined the evidence. "You talk as though there were two of you, not just one."

It sometimes seemed that way to Lanius, too. He himself was fussier about who interested him than was his sometimes unruly part. He didn't try to explain that to Sosia; he wasn't sure he understood it himself. He only shrugged and nodded and answered, "Sometimes, that's how it feels."

"That must be . . . strange." Sosia sounded as though she was giving him the benefit of the doubt.

He took a step toward her. She didn't draw back. After a moment, she took a step toward him. More than a little cautiously, he took her in his arms. Again, she hesitated a moment before her arms went around him. She started to pull back when he pressed against her, but she didn't. He kissed her. She responded clumsily. He was, no doubt, pretty clumsy himself, but that didn't occur to him till years later.

He led her over to the bed. They lay down together. He kissed her again, and caressed her. When his mouth went to the tip of one breast, she let out a small surprised sound. "That's . . . nice," she said. He kept at it. A little later, his hand strayed to the joining of her legs. She made as though to twist away, but she didn't. After a bit, she made that small surprised noise again. Then his kisses strayed down from her breasts.

"What are you doing?" Sosia said, and then, "Oh," and then, "Oh!"

"Do you like that?" he asked a couple of minutes later. She didn't answer, not with words, but he thought he knew anyhow. "This is the part that may hurt," he warned as he poised himself between her legs and thrust home. His journey briefly stopped halfway. He pushed on. Sosia's face twisted, and then he was sheathed to the hilt.

"It's done," she said.

"Not quite," he answered. Before very long, though, it was. "All right?" he asked; he was always one to worry.

"All right," she said, "except you're heavy."

"Sorry." He took more of his weight on his elbows and knees. He hadn't known what to expect about marriage. So far, it didn't seem bad at all.

CHAPTER THIRTEEN

Grus found the Avornan crown annoyingly heavy; it made his neck ache. The royal robes were thick and hot. Beneath them, sweat trickled down his sides from under his arms and slid along the small of his back. On the deck of a river galley, he could have dressed as he pleased. Servants and courtiers gave him no such choice when he sat down on the Diamond Throne.

Before that heavy crown went on his head, he had fondly imagined the King of Avornis was the one man in the whole kingdom who could do what he wanted all the time. Now he found out how wrong he'd been. Ceremony and tradition hemmed in the king on all sides. He'd given up asking why. *Because this is how we've always done it* irked him more each time he heard it, but he had no good comeback for it. Precedent ruled. Grus hoped he could.

On a steamy summer's day three weeks after Lanius' wedding, he had his doubts about that. The crown seemed particularly heavy, the robes particularly oppressive. He wondered what would have happened had he insisted on sitting on the Diamond Throne bareheaded and wearing a light linen shirt and trousers. He didn't try it. He feared it was likelier to cause an uprising against him than acts of out-and-out tyranny.

And he had enough worries without making more for himself. A herald called, "Behold Zangrulf, ambassador from King Dagipert of Thervingia!"

Accompanied by a small retinue, the Therving approached the throne. He gave Grus an impeccable bow. Then, in a low voice, he murmured, "Well, Your Majesty, you've got a fancier rank than when I saw you last."

"So I have," Grus answered. "I wondered if you'd remember me ferrying you across the Tuola."

"Oh, yes," Zangrulf said. "You were too good an officer to forget in a hurry. You proved that again the last time King Dagipert found it necessary to invade Avornis."

"The last time?" Grus raised an eyebrow. "I tell you straight out, Your Excellency, I don't care for the sound of that."

Zangrulf shrugged. He drew himself up and raised his voice till it filled the whole throne room. "Hear the words of my master, the mighty King Dagipert of Thervingia." He looked and sounded the very picture of arrogance. Unfortunately, considering what the Thervings had done to Avornis during their last invasion, he'd earned the right. He went on, "My master demands that you forthwith divorce from King Lanius your daughter, Sosia, since Lanius has long had a valid wedding contract with his daughter, Princess Romilda."

"No," Grus said. "Your master knows that contract is *not* valid. He extorted it from Arch-Hallow Bucco by force, but King Lanius' own mother, Queen Certhia, repudiated it as soon as she heard of it."

Zangrulf coughed. "Odd to hear you praise Queen Certhia, all things considered."

That made Grus cough, too. He had, after all, exiled Lanius' mother to the Maze. And, just as Dagipert had hoped to force Lanius to wed Romilda, he *had* forced Lanius to marry Sosia. What, then, was the difference between him and Dagipert?

Simple, Grus thought. *For one thing, I'm an Avornan and Dagipert isn't. For another, I got away with it.*

Dagipert had aimed to bind Avornis to Thervingia, with himself as master of both. He wouldn't get away with that, either, not as long as Grus had a word to say about it. "King Dagipert has no business meddling in Avornis' internal affairs," Grus declared.

"It is easy to tell a man he has no business doing this or that," Zangrulf said. "If the man is strong, though, and you are weak, you are a fool to speak too boldly. Here is what my master says." He raised his voice again. "Dissolve the marriage between Lanius and your daughter, restore the marriage vowed between Lanius and Princess Romilda, or my master will invade Avornis again and punish you for your usurpation. Do this or there will be war."

The word seemed to echo from the high ceiling. Courtiers whispered it and carried it back to the farthest reaches of the chamber. Zangrulf stood there, tall and haughty and savage and fierce, as though he were the very personification of the terrible, terrifying word. No one could forget what the Thervings had done in Avornis only the year before.

Grus sighed. He'd hoped for better news than Zangrulf had brought, but he hadn't really expected it. "Here is what I say to your master," he told the Therving envoy. "I say no. I say he can do his worst, and it will not make me change my mind. Take my words to him, and let him do what he wants with them."

Zangrulf bowed. "You will be sorry you have defied him."

No, I would be sorrier if I yielded to him, and so would the kingdom. "We will fight you," he said. "You will not have such an easy time of it. Tell that to King Dagipert, too."

With another bow, one that put Grus in mind of an offended cat, Zangrulf walked out of the throne room. Courtiers buzzed and fussed as they left the chamber in the wake of the ambassador. Grus didn't like their frightened voices, but didn't know what he could do about them.

"You did the right thing," Lepturus said to him. The guards commander sounded very much his normal self, for which Grus was duly grateful.

"Dagipert can ravage lands he's already ravaged," Grus said. "What else can he do? Nothing I can see. We'll ride that out, he'll get tired of it, and life will go on again. Most of the people have fled from that country by now."

"Sounds right to me," Lepturus agreed.

Grus was starting to like the veteran officer. Lepturus was fiercely loyal to Lanius; that had been plain from the beginning. *If I'd gotten rid of Lanius, he'd've found some way to make me pay,* Grus thought. *Since I didn't, he'll work with me. And, since I didn't, I think I can work with him. He's a good soldier, too.*

The two of them stayed in the throne room, talking about ways they might throw Dagipert back. A few of Grus' marines lingered, too, to make sure Lepturus had nothing evil in mind. One of the marines yawned. Another one leaned toward a pal and whispered what was probably a joke. The other marine snorted, then did his best to pretend he hadn't.

And then a messenger rushed into the chamber, crying, "Your Majesty! Your Majesty!"

"I don't like the sound of *that*," Grus remarked to Lepturus. He nodded to the messenger. "What's gone wrong now? It can't be Zangrulf. He only just left."

"No, Your Majesty, it's Count Corvus." When Grus heard that, his heart sank. The messenger, oblivious, confirmed his worst nightmare. "Except he's not calling himself Count Corvus anymore. He's just declared that he's king!"

Lanius got much less upset about Corvus' rebellion than Grus did. In a sour sort of way, he even found it funny. "He's done to you what you did to me," he remarked to the man who'd taken most of his place.

But Grus shook his head. "If he wins, I'm a dead man. Did I kill you, Your Majesty? I wed you to my own flesh and blood, is what I did. And if Corvus wins, what happens to *you?*"

Lanius started to say something like, *No one can rule Avornis without me.* But he didn't know that was true, and he didn't want to get Grus any angrier than he was already. And so he asked, in a smaller voice than he'd thought he would use, "What will you do?"

"What will I do?" Grus echoed. Lanius expected the ex-commodore's fury to burst into flame. Instead, it came out cold as ice. "I am going to beat that bastard. I am going to beat him like a drum. And by the time I'm done, no other miserable noble will dare raise his hand against a King of Avornis for the next fifty years." He stalked away like a tiger on the prowl.

Up till then, Lanius hadn't quite taken Grus seriously. But Grus' display of chilly, purposeful rage—that, Lanius couldn't ignore. He had no trouble at all imagining Grus turning it against him if he displeased his father-in-law. He did have trouble imagining what would happen after that, but only because he knew he wouldn't be there to see it.

For the next several days, he spent most of his time either with his new bride (would Sosia prove any sort of shield against her father?), holed up deep in the royal archives, or with the moncats. Grus was unlikely to come after him in any of those places. In spite of his fears, Grus didn't come after him.

The moncats fascinated Sosia as much as they did Lanius. She went to see them and play with them whenever she could. They soon became as used to her as they were to him. For one brief moment, that made him jealous—after all, Yaropolk had given Iron and Bronze to *him.* Then he thought about it and laughed at himself. He could imagine a lot of worse reasons to be jealous of his wife than that his pets also liked her.

He'd taken her into the archives, too, not long after they were wed.

The great chamber full of books and scrolls and sheets of parchment proved to interest her not at all. She could read and write. She wasn't stupid; Lanius had seen that almost at once. But Avornis' past was a closed door to her, and she didn't care to open it. He was disappointed, but, he knew things could have been much worse.

Spider and Snitch grew by leaps and bounds—literally. When they first came into the world, they clung to Bronze's fur and to her limbs all the time. They had to. Like any kittens, they were born with their eyes closed. Once they began to see, once their arms and legs and tiny almost-clawed hands began to gain some cunning . . .

Spider, in particular, seemed determined to kill himself before he grew up. Nothing fazed him, not even things that should have. He took dizzying leaps. Every so often, one of them proved too dizzying, and he would land on the carpeted floor of his room with a splat. He seemed to think that was funny. Up till then, Lanius had never imagined an animal with a sense of humor, but he was convinced Spider had one. The moncat would scramble up to the same perch and fall down in the same way two or three times in a row. Sometimes he would miss leaps he should have made, and miss seemingly on purpose, just for the fun of it.

He would beg for treats, as solemnly as any beggar on the streets of the city of Avornis. He would sit there and stare up at Lanius or Sosia with solemn eyes—bluer than Bronze's—and hold out his little hands, palms up. Or he would stand on his head and hold out his little gripping feet, soles up. Upside down and right side up were all one to him.

Snitch was more direct. She didn't beg very often—she stole. That was how she'd gotten her name. She was good at it, too. She soon learned in which pocket Lanius carried the treats he gave the moncats. After that, those treats weren't safe anymore. She would reach in with any of four hands, filch what she wanted, and then scramble up high where Lanius couldn't catch her and take back the bits of dried meat. At least half the time, she picked Lanius' pocket without his being any the wiser. The first he would know that she'd struck again would be the sight of her streaking to one of those high perches to enjoy what she'd won.

She could easily outclimb Lanius. Staying away from Spider—and from Bronze—wasn't so simple. Unlike a mere human, her brother and her mother were as spry as she was. She had to eat fast or risk losing her gains and getting bitten.

Once Sosia watched her scamper away with a treat—this one given, not stolen—only to have Spider jump on her, thrash her, and take it away. To Lanius' amazement, his wife left the moncats' room in tears. He didn't dare ask her what was wrong. That night, as they lay down and began to drift toward sleep, she said, out of the blue, "That reminded me too much of the way my brother and I were when we were little."

"What did?" Then Lanius realized what she had to be talking about. "Oh!" he exclaimed.

Sosia nodded. "Yes. Ortalis could be . . . a handful."

As far as Lanius was concerned, Ortalis remained a handful. He had taken Ortalis' measure early on, and had as little to do with Grus' son as he could. To his relief, that seemed to suit Ortalis, too. The prince showed no interest in affairs of the kingdom—only in his own affairs with an endless stream of serving women. Some he dropped when they began to bore him, which didn't usually take long. Some abandoned him. A couple abandoned the palace and disappeared into the city or left for the provinces. Lanius wondered what Ortalis could have done to make them leave a situation they could hardly hope to improve upon. He never asked Ortalis—and the maidservants, of course, were no longer there to be asked.

King Dagipert, predictably, roared over the border. Grus' response struck Lanius as tepid. His co-ruler sent horsemen out to harass the invading Thervings, but ordered his commanders not to try to bring on a general battle.

"Why don't you want to fight them?" Lanius asked. "Didn't you get summoned here as Avornis' protector?"

"Yes, and I need to keep an army to be able to do any protecting," Grus answered irritably. "Trying to deal with Dagipert and Corvus together is more than twice as hard as dealing with either one of the bastards by himself. Some of the soldiers I could use to fight the Thervings have gone over to Corvus, and they won't follow my orders. And I can't use all the men who *are* loyal to me to fight against that rebel bastard, or else Dagipert will ride roughshod over us again. Do you see what I'm saying, Your Majesty?"

In his mouth, Lanius' royal title somehow became one of reproach. And, regretfully, Lanius had to nod, for he *did* see. "Corvus wouldn't have rebelled against *me*," he said.

"Maybe you're right. On the other hand, maybe you're not. Corvus wants to do what Corvus wants to do, first, last, and always. And Corax is just as bad." Grus gave Lanius a sour stare. "I do hate to remind you, Your Majesty, but I never would have reached for the throne in the first place if your mother hadn't come much too close to murdering me."

Maybe he was right about whether he would have reached for the throne. On the other hand, maybe he wasn't.

Grus went on, "I'm sure you don't care about what happened to me." Before Lanius could even try to deny it, the other king added, "Think about this, though—if your mother *had* slain me by sorcery, what do you suppose would have happened to Sosia right afterward?"

Lanius hadn't contemplated that. Now he did. What would his mother have done to the kinsfolk of someone she'd toppled? He didn't *know,* not for certain, but the histories he'd read offered several possibilities—none of them pretty. He thought about some of those things happening to his wife. He wasn't head over heels in love with her, but he was fond of her. Imagining a couple of those things . . . His stomach flip-flopped. He turned away.

Grus' voice pursued him. "You see what I mean. This isn't a game, Your Majesty, or if it is, I'm playing for my life. And do bear one other thing in mind, if you please."

"What's that?" Lanius asked.

"I'm playing for yours, too," Grus answered.

"Well, well," Grus said to the smiling cavalry officer who stood before him. "I remember you, Colonel Hirundo. You've come up in the world a bit since we played hammer and anvil with the Menteshe." Zangrulf had said the same thing to him.

Hirundo's smile became a saucy, sassy grin. "I was thinking the same thing about you, Your Majesty, if you want to know the truth."

"I always want to know the truth," Grus answered. "Life's hard enough to deal with even when you do. When you don't—" He shook his head. "Forget it. So tell me the truth about what we can do to Dagipert and the Thervings."

That grin faded back into a smile. Even the smile had trouble staying on Hirundo's handsome face. "The truth? We can't do much. We can do what you've been doing—nip at him, pick off a few men who stray too far from his main line of march. Past that . . ." He shrugged. "If we try to slug it out with him with the army we've got, he'll stomp us."

"I was hoping you might tell me something different," Grus said glumly. "I'm a river-galley man, so I thought I might be missing something when it comes to fighting on dry land."

"I'm afraid not," Hirundo answered. "Or if you are, I'm missing something, too."

"All right, then," Grus said. "Do what you can. Meanwhile, I have to do what I can to keep Corvus from walking in the back door while Dagipert's trying to get in at the front."

"Yes, that might be a problem," Hirundo agreed airily. "Aren't you glad, Your Majesty, that you decided you wanted to be king?"

"I didn't particularly decide I *wanted* to be king," Grus answered. "I decided that was the best way to keep from getting murdered. And now that I'm on the throne, I'll be gods-cursed if I let that arrogant bastard of a Count Corvus throw me off of it."

"Ah, dear, dear Corvus," Hirundo said. "He always did endear himself to everyone around him, didn't he?"

"If that's the word you want to use," Grus said. "Go on now. Keep the Thervings in play, and I'll see what I can do about making sure our own nobles don't cost us too much."

"Good luck," Hirundo told him. "At least when I go forth, I'll be sure all my foes are in front of me. You'd better worry about your back, too." He sketched a salute, bowed, and hurried away. Grus had given him something clear-cut to do, and he would do it. Grus was sure he would do it well, too.

Grus' own fight, as Hirundo had said, was less simple. The King of Avornis wished his officer hadn't spelled that out *quite* so plainly. How many men who said they were loyal to him really spent their time praying to Olor and Quelea—or to the Banished One—that he would fall and Corvus ascend to the Diamond Throne? He didn't know. He hadn't the faintest idea. Hirundo could see Thervings and Avornans and know which side was which. No, things weren't so easy in a civil war.

I can't know who's loyal to me and who's a traitor behind a smiling mask, Grus thought. *No, I can't. But I know someone who can, or who may be able to.*

He summoned Alca the witch. She bowed very low before him. "How may I serve you, Your Majesty?" she asked.

"You can stop that, to start with," Grus said roughly. "You saved me from something so nasty, I'd rather not think about it. If that didn't earn you the right to treat me like a human being and not something made out of gold and ivory, I don't know what would."

She cocked her head to one side, studying him. It was an unnerving sort of scrutiny; he had the feeling she was looking not just at his face but deep inside him. He didn't think he was ready for such an examination. He didn't think anyone could be.

It lasted no more than three heartbeats, four at the outside. It only seemed to go on forever. After that uncomfortably long little stretch of time, Alca nodded. "I am your servant, Your Majesty. Say what you require, and I will give it to you if I can."

"My servant?" Grus doubted that. He doubted it very much. He didn't think the witch served anyone but herself, any more than Lanius' mon-cats—or ordinary cats, for that matter—did. But he didn't care to argue with her, either. Her politeness, like a cat's, deserved to be respected. So, as she'd suggested, he said what he required. "I want to know how many folk here who say they're loyal to me really back Count Corvus."

Alca frowned. "I can try, Your Majesty, but that's not an easy sorcery to bring off. And I could make mistakes. Sometimes someone can be un-happy with you without being a traitor. The spell I'd use would—or could, anyhow—find both kinds of people."

"I see." Grus nodded, less happily than he might have. "How about this? Can your magic find someone who really hates me and is hiding that, and tell him from someone who's just unhappy with me, from somebody who might or might not be disloyal?"

"Maybe." Alca sounded dubious. "I can try."

"I'll tell you what," Grus said. "Run the test on King Lanius first. He hides it pretty well for someone so young, but I know he doesn't love me and he never will."

"All right." Alca looked startled. "You're taking a certain chance, you know, depending on how *I* feel about you."

"You saved me once," Grus said.

"Ah, but you weren't a usurper then," the witch answered. "You were an officer the kingdom needed. Now you're someone who's put the an-cient dynasty in the shade."

Grus studied her. If she'd been startled, he was astonished. "If you think I did that to the dynasty, what am I liable to do to someone who has the nerve to call me on it?"

Alca didn't flinch. "For one thing, I did save you, no matter why. I think you have honor enough to spare me on account of that. And if you don't . . . well, even kings ought to think twice before they strike at witches. Witches have ways of taking vengeance ordinary mortals don't."

"That might do me harm," Grus said, "but it wouldn't do you any good."

"True." Alca surprised him again, this time by smiling. "I am not an ordinary mortal, but I am a mortal. Witches are. Wizards are. So are kings."

"Test your spell on Lanius, as I said," Grus told her. "I don't punish people for speaking their minds to me, but I do want to know if they know what they're doing."

"If I didn't know what I was doing, why would you want me working any sort of magic for you?" Alca asked.

Grus laughed. "You don't know Turnix, the wizard who served with me when I was a river-galley skipper."

"Oh, but I do!" Alca said. "He isn't that bad a wizard." She stopped short of suggesting he was a good one. She was better, and they both knew it. Grus waved his hands, yielding the point. Alca asked, "Does it matter to you whether Lanius knows I'm testing him?"

"Go ahead and tell him," Grus answered. "I think he knows I know what he thinks of me." He listened to what he'd just said. "Did that come out right?"

"I think so," Alca said. "All right, Your Majesty. I'll attend to it."

Lanius stared at the bright-eyed witch. "You want to work *what* kind of magic on me?" he said.

"One that will measure the strength of a spell to detect dislike and disloyalty toward King Grus," Alca said again.

One that would give Grus an excuse for getting rid of me, Lanius thought. "You wouldn't find anything," he said. "How can I dislike King Grus when I'm married to his daughter?" He was sure his life was at stake here. *If Grus can claim I'm plotting against him, he'll dispose of me as fast as he can.*

"You misunderstand, Your Majesty," Alca told him. "King Grus told me he already has an idea of your feelings, and won't worry about what they are. All he cares about is using them to measure the way the spell works."

"He told you that, did he?" Lanius said suspiciously.

Alca nodded. "He did."

"Well, regardless of whether he told you that or not, why should I believe it?" Lanius demanded.

"May I speak frankly, Your Majesty?"

"Why not?" Lanius didn't bother trying to hide his bitterness. "It's not as though I can do anything to you any which way." He eyed the witch. She wasn't far from his mother's age, and seemed nice enough. A few years before, that would have made him want to trust her. Now it made him more suspicious than ever; he wondered whether Grus had chosen her to lull him into a false sense of safety.

But then she said, "Even so, Your Majesty. And Grus would need no special excuse to get rid of you . . . if he wanted to do that. He could do it, and then give out whatever reason he chose after he had. Am I right or am I wrong?"

No one, not even Grus, had ever spelled out Lanius' helplessness quite that way before. Now, all at once, Lanius began to think he would hear truth from this woman. He said, "You tell me he will only use what you learn here to go after enemies he doesn't already know about?"

Alca nodded once more. "That is exactly what I tell you. Ask King Grus, if you like, and he will tell you the same."

"Never mind," Lanius said. "The point is, I believe you. Go ahead. Make your magic."

"Thank you, Your Majesty," Alca said. "I'll be back directly, then. I need to bring a few things here."

The spell proved much more formidable than Lanius had expected. The witch peered at him through peacock feathers, and through what looked like picture frames first of horn and then of ivory, while she chanted and made passes. She had a couple of retorts bubbling over braziers during the spell. One of them sent up yellowish smoke, the other reddish. Lanius expected to smell the sweetness of incense, but the odors that reached his nose were harsher, more acrid. He coughed once or twice.

Alca's chant rose and fell, rose and fell. The spell took longer than Lanius had thought it would, too. Suddenly, he snapped his fingers and said, "It doesn't *have* to be this showy, does it?"

"I don't know what you mean, Your Majesty," Alca said when she found a moment to pause in her enchanting.

"I think you do," he said. "I think you're making this magic fancy on purpose, to overawe the people you aim it at."

She paused. Her eyes gleamed as she peered at him in a new and thoughtful way. He wasn't sure he wanted anybody looking at him like that, but realized he'd invited it. After that long, thoughtful silence, she said, "You see through things, don't you?"

"You mean, the way a wizard sees through things?" Lanius shook his head. "I have no gift along those lines. I wish I did."

Alca shook her head. "No, that isn't what I meant, Your Majesty," she answered. "I can tell you will never make a wizard, yes. But what of that? A man who is learned and wise sees through things in his own way, too."

"Do you think so?" Lanius won praise so seldom, he wanted to blossom like a flower in sunlight when he did. But praise also made him suspicious. He was King of Avornis, after all. What did someone who flattered him want?

If the witch wanted anything from him, she hid it very well. "I do, Your Majesty," she answered, and then said, "And now, if you'll excuse me . . ." When Lanius didn't say no, she packed up her sorcerous apparatus and left without another word.

* * *

King Grus stood before his assembled captains and couriers in the square in front of the palace, Alca the witch at his side. He bowed to her as to an intimate friend. She dropped him a fine curtsy in return. He spoke with unusual formality to the men through whom he ran Avornis. "Alca is an extraordinary woman, and has served me extraordinarily well. Not only did she save my life when foul wizardry beset me, but, through her own rare magical talent, she has found a perfect way for me to test the hearts of those in my command, and to know exactly who is in the pay of the Thervings, or of Corvus and Corax the traitors . . . or of the Banished One."

Alca stirred beside him when he said that. "Your Majesty, when a mortal pits his sorceries against those of the Banished One, he usually loses," she whispered. "You shouldn't tell them that I—"

"Hush," he said, also quietly. "You may know I'm not telling the whole truth, but they don't, do they?"

"Ah." Ever so slightly, the witch's eyes widened. Still speaking in that tiny whisper, she went on, "You're sneakier than I thought."

With a bland smile, Grus answered, "Me? Sneaky? I haven't got the faintest idea what you're talking about." Alca rewarded him with a noise halfway between a snort and a snicker. She knew him well enough not to take that too seriously.

His officers and ministers, on the other hand . . . Looking as regal as he could, Grus stared out at them. His face might have been carved from marble, like the relief portraits of long-dead Kings of Avornis set into the palace walls as decoration—and perhaps to intimidate the kings who came after them.

The men's faces were livelier and more interesting. Some of them, like Nicator, looked delighted that he could sniff out enemies with the witch's help. Others, like Lepturus, showed little—but then, Lepturus never showed much. Three or four tried to look delighted and ended up looking bilious instead. A couple seemed angry. *Angry that I presume to spy on their thoughts, or angry that I might discover their treason?* Grus wondered. And one or two looked terrified. The king knew that didn't necessarily prove anything, but noted who they were even so.

"Before long, Alca will call in each of you and work her magic," he said. "And we will go on and beat our foes. For now, my friends, you're dismissed." He waved, as though shooing them out of the square.

In a low voice, Alca said, "You know, Your Majesty, you might be able to get the same result if I knew no magic at all. So long as those people think I know what's in their hearts, they'll behave as though I really do."

"Yes, that occurred to me," Grus answered. "We'll go on from here, and we'll see what happens next."

What happened next was that two ministers and three officers slipped out of the city of Avornis. Grus wasn't surprised to hear they'd surfaced with Corvus. He was a little surprised when one of Arch-Hallow Bucco's aides disappeared from the capital. So, by all appearances, was Bucco. "I never thought the man anything but a hard-working, holy priest," the arch-hallow said.

"I believe you," Grus told him. "Just to be on the safe side, though, I'd like you to let Alca test you with her spell."

"You cannot doubt *me,* Your Majesty!" Bucco exclaimed. "After all, I put the crown on your head."

"And you would have put it on Corvus', if he hadn't made a hash of his chance," Grus answered. "We both know that's true, don't we? So I had better find out what's in your heart."

He didn't say what he would do if Bucco refused to let the witch use her wizardry. He didn't have to say anything. Letting Bucco draw his own pictures worked much better. Several men had fled before Alca could see their secrets. The arch-hallow didn't. He went to his sorcerous appointment with the air of a cat going into a washtub, but he went. When he and the witch emerged, Alca said, "He is tolerably loyal to Your Majesty."

"Good," Grus said heartily. "I expected nothing else."

That made Bucco bristle. "If you expected nothing else, why did you put me through that humiliating ordeal?"

Grus' smile seemed to show as many teeth as a moncat's. "Because what you don't expect can hurt you worse than what you do." Bucco bowed stiffly and left the palace as fast as his old legs would carry him.

"Whom shall I examine next, Your Majesty?" Alca asked.

The smile Grus gave her was of a different sort. "For the time being, I think you can let your spell rest. If you use it too often, you're liable to cause more disloyalty than you root out."

She nodded. "I knew that. I wasn't sure you did."

"Oh, yes," Grus said. "Oh, yes, indeed."

"Do you mind if I ask you something?" Lanius said to Sosia.

"Mind? Why should I mind?" she answered. "You're my husband."

Things weren't quite so simple. Lanius knew as much. He was sure she did, too. Even so, he asked, "Do you know why your brother"—he didn't want to call Ortalis *Prince Ortalis,* but didn't dare leave off the title when speaking of him by name, either—"has that bandage on his right hand?"

"I don't *know,* no," Sosia said. "But I don't think he had it before he went into the room where you keep Iron these days."

Ice walked up Lanius' back. "That's what I thought, too. But Iron's still all right. I bet it bit him or scratched him before he could hurt it. What am I going to do?"

"Talk to my father," she said at once. "If anyone can put a stop to it for a while, he can."

It wasn't a long answer. Still, Lanius had seldom heard one that gave him more to chew on. That *for a while* was truly frightening. But so was the prospect of talking to King Grus. "Why should he do anything at all?" Lanius asked bitterly. "Ortalis . . . Prince Ortalis is his son. I'm just . . . me."

"Oh, he knows about Ortalis," Sosia said. "He's known about Ortalis and animals for a long time. He can make Ortalis fear the gods . . . for a while. I don't think anyone can make Ortalis do any more than that. It's like he has a demon inside, and every so often it comes out—or maybe more like he has a hole inside himself, and every so often he falls into it. If you want to keep the moncats safe, you'd better talk to my father."

Where nothing else would have, that did it. More than anything else, Lanius did want to make sure the moncats stayed safe. And so, nervously, he spoke to Grus. To his surprise, the man who'd stolen part of his throne and all of his power heard him out. The more Grus heard, the colder and harder his face got. When Lanius finished, Grus said, "Thanks for telling me. Don't worry about the beasts. He won't bother them again."

"How will you stop him?" Lanius asked. "What will you do?"

"Whatever I have to," Grus said grimly. For the first time, Lanius began to believe Sosia had known what she was talking about.

The next time he saw Prince Ortalis, his brother-in-law scuttled out of his way. Ortalis moved as though in some little pain, or perhaps some not so little. And he stayed away from the rooms where the moncats lived for a long time afterward. There, at least, Grus kept his promise.

CHAPTER FOURTEEN

Colonel Hirundo watched King Grus with more than a little amusement. Grus' mount was a bay gelding calm as a pond on a breezeless day, but the king clutched the reins and gripped the horse with his knees as though afraid of falling at any moment—which he was. "Meaning no offense, Your Majesty, but you'll never make a horseman," Hirundo remarked.

"Really? Why on earth would you say such a thing? Because I'm as graceful as a sack of beans on horseback?"

"Well, now that you mention it, yes."

"So what?" Grus said. "I give the men something to laugh at. Better they could laugh than quiver in their boots for fear of bumping into Dagipert and the Thervings."

"When you put it that way, maybe," Hirundo said.

"Whether I'm a horseman or not, Colonel, I have my reasons for coming along, believe you me I do," Grus said. "I don't want to stay in the capital the rest of my days. I want to see more of Avornis than that. How can I deal with what goes on in the kingdom if I don't keep an eye on it?"

"Plenty of Kings of Avornis have tried," Hirundo observed. Like Grus, he had risen in the world since their wars against the Menteshe in the south.

"I don't intend to be one of them," Grus said.

He was glad to escape the capital, even if escaping it meant going into battle against the Thervings. An army on the march, he was discovering, was different from a fleet of river galleys on the move. In one way, the army had the advantage—it could go anywhere, while available waterways limited the fleet. But the army carried its own stink with it, a heavy odor compounded of the smells of horses and unwashed men. It stayed in Grus' nostrils and would not go away. Even after his conscious mind forgot about it, it lingered. He smelled it in his dreams.

He led the soldiers west, toward Thervingia, toward danger. No one could doubt the Thervings had used this route to come through Avornis and approach the capital in the recent past. The signs were all too clear— torched villages, empty farmsteads, fields that should have been full of ripening grain going to weeds, instead. Once, Grus' army came upon what was left of a detachment of Avornan soldiers King Dagipert's men had met and overwhelmed. Not much remained of the Avornans—only a few scattered bones still recognizable as human, and fragments of clothing enough to identify them as Grus' countrymen. The Thervings had stolen everything they found worth taking.

"This could happen to us, too," Grus told the men he led. "It could— if we aren't careful. If we are, though, nothing can beat us. We just have to watch ourselves, don't we?"

"Yes," the soldiers chorused dutifully. He also watched them, sometimes in ways they didn't expect. He posted extra sentries that evening on the roads leading east, for instance. Those sentries captured six or eight men trying to slip away from the danger they'd seen. Grus didn't make examples of them, as he might have. But he didn't let them desert, either. Back to the encampment they went.

Whenever the army passed woods on its way west, Grus sent scouts into them. He didn't want to give Dagipert the chance to ambush him, as the King of Thervingia had ambushed other Avornan armies. Three days after the army found what was left of that Avornan detachment, the scouts Grus sent to examine a frowning pine forest burst out of it much faster than they'd gone in. They came galloping back toward the main mass of men.

"Thervings!" they shouted. "The Thervings are in the woods!"

"Good!" Grus exclaimed, though he was anything but sure how good it was. "Now we can make them pay for what they've done to Avornis." He raised his voice to a shout like the one he might have used aboard a river galley. *"Revenge!"*

"Revenge!" the soldiers echoed.

Grus had never led a battle on land before. He didn't try to lead this one now, either, not really. He'd brought Colonel Hirundo here for just that reason. Hirundo handled the job with unruffled competence. At his orders, horns bellowed from metal throats and signal flags waved. The Avornan soldiers shook themselves out, moving from column to line of battle as smoothly as Grus could have hoped. As they were deploying, Hirundo turned to Grus and asked, "What now, Your Majesty? Do we await the enemy on open ground here, or do we go into the woods after them?"

"Into the woods," Grus replied at once. "They won't surprise us now."

Hirundo nodded. "All right. I hoped you'd say that. If you'd care to do the honors . . . ?"

"What do you—? Oh." Grus raised his voice again, this time shouting, *"Forward!"*

The Avornans cheered as they began to advance. Grus and Hirundo both weighed those cheers, trying to gauge the army's spirit from them. At almost the same instant, they both nodded. Despite the attempted desertions a few nights before, the soldiers seemed ready enough to fight.

Well before the Avornans could push in among the pines, Thervings began emerging from them. They formed their own line of battle, which looked more rugged than the Avornans', then surged toward Grus' men, roaring like beasts.

"Come on, boys!" Colonel Hirundo called gaily. "Now we get to pay these bastards back for everything they've done to Avornis lately. *King Grus!*" When he used it, he had a pretty good battlefield roar himself.

"King Grus!" The shout rose from the Avornans. Men also yelled, "King Lanius!" Grus knew he couldn't complain about that. Lanius was, after all, still king, and they were cheering the dynasty as much as the young man.

To show he didn't mind, he shouted, "King Lanius!" himself, and then, "Avornis and victory!" He hoped it would be victory.

Dagipert's men, though, had other things in mind. They cried out their king's name, as well as guttural bits of Thervingian. Grus didn't know any of the mountain men's language, but doubted they were complimenting either Avornis or him.

Most of the Thervings were on foot. The Avornan army had more horsemen than foot soldiers. Hirundo led them to the wings, to try to outflank the Thervings and soften them up with arrows. The Thervings' riders stayed in the center of their line, in a tight knot around a wolfhide standard. *That's Dagipert's emblem,* Grus realized. He spurred toward it, brandishing his sword.

"Come on, Dagipert!" he yelled. "Fight me, or show yourself a coward!"

The King of Thervingia was at least twenty years older than he was. But if he could cut Dagipert down, he would cut the heart out of the Thervings. *And what if you fall yourself, instead? You're still a long way from the best horseman the gods ever made.* Once upon a time, a King of Thervingia had beaten a King of Avornis in single combat and made a drinking cup from his skull.

Grus wished he hadn't chosen that moment to remember that bit of lore. Lanius, no doubt, could have told him the names of both kings and whatever else he wanted to know about them—except that he didn't want to know anything. And he hadn't answered his own question. He tried now. *What if I fall, instead? Well, Avornis can get along better without me than Thervingia can without Dagipert. I'm pretty sure of that.*

Forth from the Thervings' ranks came a rider with gilded chain mail and a long gray beard. "You pimp!" Dagipert roared at Grus. "Prostitute your daughter with my daughter's betrothed, will you?" If the King of Thervingia felt his years or anything but raw fury toward Grus, he didn't show it.

"I'll give your daughter to my hangman's son," Grus yelled back. Dagipert bellowed with fury. *Maybe he'll have a fit and fall over dead,* Grus thought hopefully. That would make his own life easier.

No such luck. Grus hadn't really expected it. The two kings traded sword strokes between their armies. Dagipert might have been old, but he knew how to handle a blade. And rage seemed to lend him strength. Before long, Grus knew he would be lucky to beat down his foe—would be lucky, in fact, to live.

But their private duel lasted only moments. Avornans rushed forward to help Grus rid the world of Dagipert. Thervings ran up to protect their king and assail Grus. In the battle that developed around them, Grus and Dagipert were swept apart. Grus was anything but sorry. He hoped he'd managed to put some fear into King Dagipert, too, but wouldn't have bet on it.

Meanwhile, of course, ordinary Thervings could kill him as readily as King Dagipert might have—more readily, in fact, for most of the Thervings were younger and better trained than their king. Grus thrust and parried and slashed. Before long, his sword had blood on it. The blood wasn't his, though he couldn't remember wounding any of the enemy.

"Grus!" his men shouted, and, "Avornis!" and, "Lanius!"

Hirundo's horsemen kept nipping in behind Dagipert's men, trying to cut them off from the woods and surround them. The Thervings detached men from their main line to hold off such flanking moves, which let the Avornans put more pressure on their front. Little by little, that front began to crumble.

Had it happened all at once, Dagipert's army would have fallen to pieces, and Grus might have won a famous victory, one that would have let him be talked about in the same breath with storied Kings of Avornis from far-off days. It didn't. The Thervings kept enough order to withdraw into the forest under good discipline, and he had no great inclination to go after them once they'd drawn back.

"Congratulations, Your Majesty!" said Colonel Hirundo, coming up to him after the fighting ended. "We beat them!"

"Yes." Wearily, Grus nodded. "And do you know what, Colonel? I'll take that. Considering everything that could have happened, I'll take it, and gladly."

Lanius had always loved the archives. They never argued with him. They never told him no. Not only had he learned a great deal going through them, he'd learned a great deal about how to learn. No one, not even his tutor, ever seemed to have thought about that. The more he did, though, the more important it seemed.

If he wanted to find out what had happened in ancient days, he went through chronicles, and through the reports generals and other officials had left behind—those were often the raw material from which the chroniclers shaped their stories. If he wanted to find out about money, he started pawing through tax rolls. If he found himself interested in sorcery, a separate part of the archives concerned itself with that. Knowing where and how to start looking was often as important as anything else when he was trying to find out something.

He breathed in the smells of old parchments and ink and dust as a lover breathed in his lover's perfume. And, when he decided to find out what the archives had to say about moncats, he went with confidence to the records of old-time Avornan sailing expeditions. In days gone by, Avornis had ruled the northern coast. That was before the Chernagors settled there and began squabbling with Avornis, amongst themselves, and against the Thervings.

Yaropolk hadn't told him the name of the island chain Iron and Bronze had come from. That would have made things easier, but he managed well enough without it. And poking through parchments, never quite sure what the next one would show, had a pleasure of its own. Some of those Avornan explorers had sailed a long way. Going through the records they'd left behind, Lanius felt like an explorer himself.

None of the records used the word *moncat*; that was just his translation of the name the Chernagors had given the creatures. Of course the old Avornan explorers, if they'd ever come across the animals, would have called them something else.

When he figured that out, he realized he would have to go back through several parchments he'd already set aside. That left him imperfectly delighted with the world, but he saw no help for it. By then, he was bound and determined to get to the bottom of the mystery. His father had been a stubborn man, too. Had Mergus not been, he never would have taken a seventh wife when Certhia found herself with child.

Lanius was in no position to defy the world. All he could do was try to learn something he wanted to know. King Grus was making sure nothing more important or glamorous would come his way.

One of the reports he came across for a second time had nothing to do with ships sailing out across the seas to the north. Just the opposite, in fact—it was an account by some intrepid Avornan who'd pushed far into the south not long after the Menteshe swept the Avornans out of that part of the world.

He started to put that book aside yet again. But the Avornan explorer, despite his old-fashioned language, wrote in an entertaining style. And so Lanius kept reading.

"Oh, by the gods!" he said in a low voice. Things down in the south had been a lot more chaotic in the old days than they were now. When Avornis and the Menteshe weren't fighting these days, they traded across the border. The Menteshe princes, though, made sure Avornans didn't go too far south of the frontier, while Avornans, fearing each nomad as the Banished One's eyes and ears, refused to let any Menteshe come very far north.

Once upon a time, it hadn't been like that. The fellow whose report Lanius was reading had gotten all the way down to Yozgat, where the Menteshe stowed away the Scepter of Mercy after capturing it from Avornis. That truly amazed Lanius. He hadn't had the faintest idea any Avornan had set eyes on it from the day the Menteshe took it till now. Yet here was a detailed description of the building where the nomads kept the Scepter. The explorer wrote:

Were it within the bounds of our own realm, I should without hesitation style it a cathedral. Yet that were false and misleading, the Menteshe now hallowing no other gods save only the false, vile, and wicked spirit cast from the heavens for that he was a sinner, the spirit known as the Banished One. Him do they worship. Him do they reverence, and give no tiniest portion of respect unto King Olor and Queen Quelea, the which thereof are truly deserving.

He went on for some little while, spewing forth one platitude after another. That tempted Lanius to put aside the old parchment after all. He didn't, though, and ended up glad he didn't, for the explorer went on,

At length, they suffered me to gaze upon this grand and holy relic, now no more than a spoil of war. Yet, like a slave woman once the beautiful and famous wife of some grand noble, it doth retain even in its lowly state a certain haggard loveliness. Indeed, I believe the building wherein it is enshrined was peradventure once a house for the proper gods, though now sadly changed into a hall in which the Banished One receives his undeserved praises of those he hath seduced away from truth and piety.

That *was* interesting. Lanius hadn't believed any shrine to Olor and Quelea had existed so far south. He read on, doing his best to ignore the old-fashioned language. The merchant had been lucky to get out of Yozgat in one piece, for he'd left just before the Banished One himself came to view the Scepter.

Had I been there then, the Menteshe do assure me, nothing less than death or thralldom had been my portion. The Menteshe have no love for us Avornans, but the Banished One, being filled with a cold and bitter hate against us, is here even harsher than these his people. In his jealousy, he minds him that we were privileged to wield the Scepter of Mercy, whose touch he to this day may not abide. Thus he stole it, for to keep it from being turned against him.

Lanius slowly nodded. That all fit in with what other sources told him, but was more definite and emphatic than anything else he'd seen. He wished the merchant had gotten a glimpse of the Banished One. *That* might have told him things worth knowing. Or, on the other hand, more likely it wouldn't have. Had the Banished One sensed an Avornan close by, the intrepid explorer would have paid the price for his zeal.

Carefully, Lanius returned the ancient parchment to its pigeonhole. If ever an Avornan army went down to Yozgat, it might prove useful to the commander. Lanius had never seen a better description of the city's walls and defenses. On the other hand, it was also more than three hundred years old. No telling what the Menteshe had done since to make sure the Scepter of Mercy stayed exactly where it was.

He laughed a little, sadly, as he left the archives. No telling, either, when an Avornan army might push south past the Stura River, let alone all the way down to Yozgat. These days, the fight was to keep the Menteshe on their side of the river, and to keep the Banished One from making yet more Avornan farmers into soul-dead thralls.

The tide may turn again, Lanius thought, and tried very hard to believe it.

Colonel Hirundo beamed at King Grus. "The tide has turned, Your Majesty!" he exclaimed. "We drive the barbarians."

"Yes." Grus sounded less delighted than his officer. "We've given Dagipert something to think about, anyhow."

"Something to think about? I should say so," Hirundo answered. "Three weeks, and we've driven his army all the way out of Avornis. There ahead, across that stream, that's Thervingia. We're heading into Thervingia." By the way he said it, he might have been talking about exploring the dark side of the moon. Up till now, the Thervings had had all the better of the fighting between the two kingdoms during Dagipert's long reign.

"Send your cavalry across," Grus told him. "Find a good farm, a prosperous farm, close by the border. Burn it. Run off the livestock. If the farmer puts up a fight, deal with him or capture him and bring him back for the mines. If he flees, let him go. Once you've done that, bring your horsemen back."

"Bring them *back*?" Hirundo gaped. "Olor's beard, *why?* Uh, Your Majesty?"

"Because we've still got to worry about Corvus and Corax, that's why," Grus answered. "Dagipert's never going to take the city of Avornis, not if he sits outside it for a thousand years." He'd been more worried than that when Dagipert besieged the royal capital not so very long before, but he wasn't about to admit it now, not even to himself. He went on, "The rebels just might, though, if we stay away from home too long. Bound to be traitors in the city that Alca's witchery didn't find, and who knows how much trouble they can cause if we give 'em the chance?"

Would Lanius sooner have Corvus for a protector than me? Grus wondered. He'd done everything he could to make his usurpation as painless as possible. He couldn't very well have gone further than marrying his own daughter to the young king. From all the signs Grus could read, Sosia and Lanius were getting on as well as a couple of newlyweds could. But would Lanius think he could be king in his own right if Corvus overthrew Grus? Grus was convinced he'd be wrong, but that might not have anything to do with what Lanius believed.

With a sigh, Grus waved Hirundo on. "Go do as I tell you. We'll let Dagipert know what we might have done. Next time, if we have to, we *will* do it. This time, he gets off easy, and let him thank the gods for it."

Grus hoped Dagipert would take his moderation as a warning and not as a confession of weakness. He knew that was only a hope, though, not a guarantee. Dagipert might think the Avornan civil war was a pot he could stir to his own advantage. He might think that—and he might be right.

Hirundo saluted. "One burnt-out farmhouse coming up, Your Majesty."

He called orders to his horsemen. They rode along the stream, looking for a ford. Before long, the whole band splashed across, then raced on into Thervingia. Grus waited on the Avornan side of the border, worrying. If the Thervings had an army waiting in ambush among those trees over there, as they were fond of doing . . .

But no roaring horde of Thervings burst from the woods. No more than a quarter of an hour after Hirundo's men crossed the border, a column of smoke rose into the air. The soldiers who remained in Avornis with King Grus pointed to it and nudged one another. The vengeance the horsemen were taking might be small and symbolic, but vengeance it was.

Then Hirundo led his column back from the west. This time, they made for the ford without hesitation. Water dripping from his mount's belly and from his own boots, Hirundo rode up to Grus. "It's taken care of, Your Majesty," he said. "The farmer and his kin tried putting up a fight from inside the house. Brave—but stupid. One of their arrows hurt a horse. I hope it makes 'em feel better in the next world, but I wouldn't bet on it."

"All right," Grus said. "We've done what we came to do." *We've done enough of what we came to do, anyhow.* "Now we go back to the city of Avornis and take care of something else." *We'll take care of a piece of something else, anyway. I hope we'll be able to take care of a piece of it.* He wished he could worry about one trouble at a time, instead of having them land on him in clumps.

At Hirundo's orders, the army turned about. Grus watched the men, liking the way they kept looking back toward the border. They weren't worrying about the Thervings falling on them. They were wishing they could have done more in the enemy's land. That was all to the good.

Hirundo seemed to be thinking along with him. "These men have the Thervings' measure," he said.

Grus nodded. "I think you're right. We've spent a while running away from them—running away or getting trapped. The sooner Dagipert decides he can't get away with bullying us, the better off we'll be."

"Well, we made a fair start here," Hirundo said.

"It also helps that we had an officer here who did such a good job against the enemy. Congratulations, General Hirundo."

Hirundo's eyes glowed. "Thank you very much, Your Majesty! This is a lot better than chasing the Menteshe all over the landscape."

Grus looked south. "One of these days, maybe, we'll see if we can do a proper job of chasing the Menteshe." He sighed. "It won't be anytime soon, though, I'm afraid. We have a few other things to worry about first." A laugh without mirth. "Oh, yes, just a few."

But, as the long column of horsemen and foot soldiers and wagons made its way back toward the city of Avornis, Grus kept looking southward. He knew where the kingdom's greatest enemy dwelt. He would have been a fool if he didn't. He laughed that unhappy laugh again. *I may be a fool. I've been a fool before—the gods know that's true. But there are fools, and then there are fools. I'm not the kind of fool who forgets about the Banished One. I hope I'm not. I'd better not be.*

Part of King Lanius was disappointed to have King Grus come back in what looked very much like triumph. Part of Lanius, in fact, was disappointed to see Grus come back to the capital at all. Had the Thervings overwhelmed the usurper, Lanius would have been King of Avornis in fact as well as in name.

Unfortunately, though, becoming king in fact as well as in name wouldn't have magically turned him into a general. And, if Dagipert's men had slaughtered Grus, they would have slaughtered his army, too—which would have left exactly nothing between them and another siege of the city of Avornis. They'd come too close to taking the capital the last time. This time, they might actually bring it off. *And then where would you be?* Lanius asked himself. He liked none of the answers he came up with.

Grus, meanwhile, had other things on his mind. "Well, Corvus has proved he's just as bad a general when he's fighting against Avornis as he was when he claimed he was fighting for the kingdom," he said.

"I don't understand," Lanius told him. "How can you say that? You haven't fought Corvus at all, not yet."

"That's exactly how I can say it—because I haven't fought Corvus yet, I mean." Grus grinned at Lanius.

Lanius didn't grin back. He knew he was being teased, and he'd always been sensitive of his dignity. "Stop joking and tell me what you mean," he said severely.

To his annoyance, Grus' grin only got wider. His unwelcome colleague on the throne bowed low and said, "Yes, Your Majesty," as though Lanius held it all by himself—*the way I'm supposed to,* Lanius thought. Grus went on, "If Corvus were any kind of a soldier, he would have come up here and tried to take the city of Avornis away from me while I was busy with the Thervings. Since he didn't, I get to move against him instead of the other way around—and I intend to."

"Oh." Lanius' irritation evaporated. He nodded to King Grus. "Yes, you're right. I understand now. Thank you."

" 'Thank you'?" Grus echoed. "For what?"

"For showing me something I hadn't seen myself, of course," Lanius answered. "It hadn't occurred to me that you could judge a general by whether he fought at all as well as by how well he fought."

"Well, you can. And you're welcome, for whatever it's worth to you." Grus' expression remained quizzical. "You're a funny one, aren't you?"

"So I'm told, now and again. I don't see the joke myself—but then, that may be what makes me funny to other people." Lanius shrugged.

"You *are* a funny one," Grus said positively. "If you're willing to give it, I'm going to want your help against Corvus and Corax."

"What kind of help?" Lanius asked. "I just proved I'm no soldier myself." He remembered his own recent reflections on what he might have done if Grus hadn't come back from his campaign against King Dagipert. And, eyeing his fellow sovereign, he added, "Besides, didn't your pet witch show you I'm not to be trusted?"

"Alca's not my pet. Alca's not anybody's pet, and you'd be smart not to call her that to her face," Grus replied. Lanius decided he was probably right. Grus continued, "And she didn't show me I couldn't trust you. She only showed me you didn't like me. I already knew that."

He didn't sound angry. He didn't sound amused, which would have made Lanius angry. He might have been talking about the weather. On that dispassionate note, Lanius had no trouble dealing with him. "What do you want me to do?" he asked.

"Come along with me when I move against Corvus and Corax," Grus told him. "When the time comes, show you're with me and want me to win. That will make the men fighting for the gods-cursed nobles know they've picked the wrong side."

But the right side is mine, not yours, Lanius thought. Grus waited. Lanius made himself ask another question. *Is Grus' side better or worse than Corvus'?* He sighed. However much he wished he did, he didn't need to think very long before finding an answer there. "I'll come with you," he said.

Back in the city of Avornis, people spoke of the Maze as though it were impassable, as though a man who once set foot in it were certain never to come out again. No doubt the Kings of Avornis had encouraged that view of the marshes and swamps behind the capital. When they exiled foes to the Maze, they didn't want them emerging again. They didn't want people thinking they could help exiles emerge again, either.

The truth was less simple, as truth had a way of being.

Grus had no qualms about moving an army through the Maze. There were streams that traversed the entire region. He'd learned about some of them while still commodore of Avornis' river galleys. Others were known to the folk who dwelt in the Maze without being exiles—fishermen, hunters, trappers. River galleys couldn't make the whole journey. They drew too much water. Flat-bottomed barges, on the other hand . . .

Despite that, he hadn't been in the Maze very long before he started to wonder whether he'd made a ghastly mistake. That had nothing to do with the barges. A breeze even meant they could move by sail. The men who poled and rowed them along rested easy for the time being. Everything was going as well as it could. Grus still worried. The more he looked at Lanius, the more he worried, too.

Lanius kept looking now this way, now that. It wasn't curiosity, of which Grus had seen he owned an uncommon share. The more he stared around the Maze, the paler and quieter he got. His lips thinned. His jaw set. He kept sneaking glances at Grus. Grus didn't like those glances. He knew looks couldn't kill. If he hadn't known that, he would have feared falling over dead.

Here, at least, he thought he knew what the trouble was. When King Lanius looked out into the Maze and then glowered at him yet again, he decided to strike first, before things got even worse. "Are you looking for your mother's convent?" he asked.

Lanius started. Grus hid a smile. Lanius hadn't thought he was so obvious. Grus didn't think he had. After a moment, the young king nodded. "Yes, I am," he said with as much defiance as he could muster.

"It's over that way, I believe," Grus told him, pointing southeast. "I'm sorry she's there. You can believe that or not, just as you please, but it happens to be true. If she hadn't tried to kill me, she'd still be in the city of Avornis. I'd like to hope you believe that's true."

He waited. Lanius said nothing for a long, long time. At last, though, he nodded. "I suppose it may be. But it doesn't make things any easier for me." He shook his head. "No, that's not true. It doesn't make things *much* easier for me."

"All right, Your Majesty," Grus replied. "I don't ask that you love me, even if one of the other things I hope is that you'll come to love my daughter one of these days. But I do wish you'd try to be fair to me."

He waited again. Lanius looked like a man doing his best to hate him. After another pause, the youth said, "I suppose even the Banished One deserves that much. I'll give it to you, if I can."

"Thank you so much." Grus didn't try to hide the sarcasm. Lanius turned red. Grus went on, "The gods gave the Banished One what they thought he deserved. Now they're rid of him, and they don't have to worry about him anymore. We still do. Kings of Avornis have tried to be fair to him, or what they reckoned fair to him, before. You'd know more about that than I do, wouldn't you?"

"Probably." Lanius didn't notice how arrogant he sounded.

"Fine," Grus said. Odds were Lanius *did* know much more about it. But Grus knew what counted. "It's never worked, has it? The only thing the Banished One calls fair is everything for him and nothing for us—not even all of our souls. Am I right about that, or am I wrong?"

"Oh, you're right." Lanius was willing—more than willing, even eager—to talk seriously about something abstract and intellectual. He went on, "The best explanation for it that I've read is that he reckons the gods his equals, and might deal fairly with them if they would deal with him at all. But we're only people. He doesn't see much more point to fair dealings with us than we would to fair dealings with so many sheep."

He wasn't stupid. He was, in fact, anything but stupid. "That's interesting—makes a lot of sense, too, I think." Grus sighed. "But it doesn't make dealing with the Banished One any easier."

"No," Lanius agreed. "I don't think anything will ever make dealing with the Banished One much easier. Even if we could get the Scepter of Mercy back, that wouldn't make him want to deal with us. It would just make him worry about us more."

"The way we'd worry about a sheep that could shoot a bow," Grus suggested. Lanius nodded. Then he snickered. He didn't laugh very often, and Grus felt a prick of pleasure at teasing mirth out of him.

Then he felt a prick of a different sort, and another, and another. The marshes and puddles and swamps and tussocks of the Maze bred mosquitoes and flies and midges and gnats in swarming, buzzing profusion. Lanius was slapping and muttering, too. On a nearby barge, horses' tails switched back and forth, back and forth. The animals' ears twitched. On yet another barge, a sailor fell into the water because he kept on swatting bugs without noticing he was walking off the stern. The air smelled wet and stagnant.

Here and there in the Maze, willows and elms and swamp oaks and other water-loving trees created little forests amidst the grasses and bushes and reeds and cattails and water lilies that covered most of the region. Kingfishers shrieked. Dippers chirped. Sun-dappled shadows danced. The trees marked higher ground—not high ground, for there was none hereabouts, but higher, and drier. People lived on that higher ground, those who made their living from what the Maze gave them and those who got sent there for what they'd done in the wider world.

Grus knew just where Queen Certhia's convent lay. He said not a word as the barge passed within half a mile of it. Instead, he listened to the chirping frogs, pointed out a swimming water snake to Lanius, laughed when half a dozen turtles leaped off a floating log into the stream, and thought about fair dealing with the Banished One. "Baaa!" he said softly. *I may be a sheep to him. One day, I'd like to be a sheep with a bow.*

CHAPTER FIFTEEN

The last time Lanius had been so far from home was on Lepturus' campaign against the Thervings. He'd still been a boy then. He'd told himself then that he never wanted to become a general. Moving against Corvus and Corax did nothing to change his mind. In fact, that they were no less Avornan than he only made the fight harder to bear.

He kept an eye on Grus. If the former commodore worried about fighting his countrymen, he didn't let it show. He went after the two rebel counts as ferociously as he might have attacked the Menteshe if they'd irrupted into Avornis.

Seeing that finally made Lanius remark on it. Grus gave him a long, slow, thoughtful look and said, "Your Majesty, if you think I like fighting a civil war, you're wrong. But there's only one thing worse than fighting a civil war—fighting it and losing it."

That gave Lanius something to look thoughtful about. Having thought, he found he couldn't criticize Grus on the grounds of how hard he fought. *I'll have to look for something else,* went through his mind. When his fellow king at last led them from the Maze—where no one could move fast even if he wanted to—they swarmed south, toward Corvus' crag-mounted castle. "Do you plan to get there before Corvus knows you're coming?" Lanius asked him.

"Too much to hope for, even though it'd be very nice," Grus answered. "Getting between his army and his castle would be all right, though."

"How do you propose to manage that?" Lanius inquired. As he put the question to Grus, their horses trampled swaths through a field of ripening barley. Corvus' men wouldn't harvest it this year. Neither would any other Avornans.

"Well, Your Majesty, you may nave noticed that I didn't bring my whole strength through the Maze," Grus said mildly.

As a matter of fact, Lanius hadn't noticed that. How could he have, when Grus' army was split up among so many barges? But he nodded wisely, as though he had. "Yes, of course," he said, even if it wasn't *of course* at all. And then, because Grus seemed to expect something more, he asked, "Where's the rest of it?"

By the way Grus beamed, that was the right question. "Very good, Your Majesty," Grus said. "That's what you need to know, sure enough. The rest of it's with Hirundo. He marched out on dry land, just as openly as you please. Corvus and Corax didn't have any doubts at all that he was coming."

"No, eh?" Lanius said, and Grus solemnly shook his head. He waited to see what Lanius would make of that. Lanius didn't need long. "Then the rebels went forth to fight Hirundo!" he exclaimed. "No wonder no one's come out to try to stop us!"

"No wonder at all, and I hope so," Grus answered. "Hard to pay attention to the Maze, anyhow. Nobody ever expects anything to come out of it. And if you happen to be looking the other way when something does—well, too bad for you."

He didn't get very excited. He didn't brag or boast. That, Lanius had seen, was not his style. But he had ways of doing the job. In all the history of Avornis, had anyone just settled down and done the job so well? Lanius had read a lot of that history. He had his doubts. Grus might have been the best.

Corvus was also trying to do his job. Only a couple of days after Grus' army burst out of the Maze, horsemen began shadowing it. They weren't there in any numbers; they couldn't have hoped to beat back the army or even slow it down. They simply hung off its flank and kept an eye on it. Lanius presumed they reported to Corvus or to Corax or to both of the brothers together.

Grus presumed the same thing. He asked Lanius, "Are you ready to do what I asked of you, Your Majesty?"

Lanius sighed. "I suppose so," he answered.

Grus laughed at his hesitation. That was, Lanius supposed, better than having Grus get angry. Grus said, "Do try to conceal your enthusiasm. Otherwise it might sweep me off my feet altogether."

"Er—yes," Lanius said, not sure what to make of Grus in a sportive mood.

To his relief, Grus didn't stick around. He just went on tending to his business. Riders loyal to him went out and skirmished with Corvus' scouts. They drove the scouts back, killed a few of them, and captured two or three. The captives they brought before Lanius.

Those captives looked scared to death. That was almost literally true. They had to expect their heads to go up on pikes as soon as Lanius finished gloating over them. He did take a certain amount of pleasure in letting them know that wouldn't happen. "Hear me, and you'll be free to go," he told them. Their eyes widened. They didn't trust him or believe him. He went on, "All you have to do is take word back to everyone who follows Corvus and Corax that King Grus is my legitimate co-ruler, and that Corvus and Corax are enemies to Avornis and deserve whatever happens to them. No matter what they say, they aren't for me. They're against me. Their rebellion is bound to fail."

Calling Grus a legitimate king left a bad taste in his mouth. The rest of it? To his own surprise, he discovered he meant the rest of it. One of Corvus' riders said, "Grus is making you say that. Tell us the truth."

"I am telling you the truth," Lanius said—and, on the whole, he meant that, too. When he added, "The nobles you follow are the ones who've lied to you," he thought that was the truth. He repeated, "Go back to your friends. Tell them what I told you. Tell them there's safe-conduct and amnesty for anyone who leaves the rebels' army. And tell them whoever doesn't leave it will be very sorry."

The riders seemed surprised when they got their horses back. They seemed amazed when they got their sabers and bows back. Escorted by Grus' troopers, the rebels rode out of the camp. They kicked up a small cloud of dust as they trotted off after their fellows who'd escaped.

Now, who will believe them? Lanius wondered. Then he wondered how much of human affairs everywhere turned on that question.

Scouts came galloping back toward King Grus. "Your Majesty! Your Majesty!" they cried, and pointed westward. "The rebels' army is over there, less than a day's ride away."

"Ah," Grus said, a sound full of eagerness, and then, "Do they know you've been shadowing them?"

"Probably," one of the riders answered, while two or three more shrugged and nodded. The fellow who'd spoken added, "You know how it is."

"Oh, yes." Grus nodded, too. "I know how it is. Now we're going to show Corvus and Corax how it is, eh?" The scouts grinned. Grus asked, "Any sign of Hirundo's army?"

"No, Your Majesty," the men chorused.

"Too bad," Grus said. "If I knew what he was doing—if I could get hold of him—we'd smash the rebels between us. Well, maybe scouts from the band he leads will show up here before too long." He made himself sound hopeful.

A rider said, "If you like, Your Majesty, we could go out to the west again, ride around the rebels, and see if we could join up with him."

Grus shook his head. "Not you boys personally. You've already been working hard. Take a rest. You've earned it. I'll send some other men out to the fellows who'll be shadowing the rebels. Some of them can try riding around Corvus' army to see if they can find Hirundo."

A couple of the horsemen looked disappointed. A couple of others looked relieved at not having to gallop straight out again. Grus had expected both reactions. He sent the scouts away. None of them looked sorry at the prospect of dismounting, getting some food, and maybe even grabbing a little rest.

"Trumpeters!" Grus called. When the men with the long brass horns looked his way, he added, "Blow *Column left*. We're going straight after the rebels." The soldiers who heard him raised a cheer.

He rode over to King Lanius. To his younger colleague, he said, "Well, Your Majesty, we've found them."

"A good thing, too, seeing that they'd already found us," Lanius remarked.

"Uh, yes," Grus said. Sometimes Lanius, though still a youth, could make him feel he was running in circles. He tried again. "Before we go into battle with the rebels, I'll want you to ride out in front of the army and tell the lot of them what you told those scouts."

"Oh, you will, will you?" Lanius said tonelessly. His head pointed toward Grus, but, whatever he was looking at, it wasn't his fellow king. After half a moment, he seemed to remember where he was. He deigned to give Grus one word. "No."

"But, Your Majesty, this *is* why I asked you to come along," Grus reminded him. "Or do you want the rebels to win?" *How good was Alca's wizardry?* he wondered. *What is lurking in Lanius' heart?*

"No, I don't," Lanius said. "But no, I won't go up in front of the army before a battle, either." He sounded very determined.

"By the gods, why not?" Grus exclaimed.

"I've seen one battle up close. That was enough to last me a lifetime. I never want to see another one like that."

So many young men were pantingly eager to blood themselves in the field. Grus almost asked Lanius if he were a coward, but something in the young king's eyes made him hold back. Whatever troubled him, Grus didn't think cowardice was it. He sighed and said, "Tell me more."

"There's nothing more to tell. If you want to bring enemy prisoners before me and then turn them loose, I'll tell them I'd sooner have you as my protector than Corvus. That's the truth. It would be the truth even if I weren't married to your daughter. But maybe you can make me go out in front of your army. Once you've made me do what I truly don't want to do, though, can you be sure what I'll say?"

Grus eyed him. Yes, Lanius looked very determined. Did he mean what he said, or was he bluffing? *Can you afford to take the chance?* Grus asked himself. He'd expected the young king to be a puppet, not a bargainer. *He's growing up.* That realization startled him almost as much as it had about his own children.

"All right, Your Majesty." This one time, he let irony seep into his use of Lanius' title. "Have it your way, since that's what you're bound to do."

"I . . . will." Lanius was relieved, and still young enough to show it.

"Have it your way," Grus repeated. "Just remember, having it your way means giving Corvus a better chance to beat me."

Lanius grimaced. But after a moment's pause, he said, "If I weren't confident in you as a general, would I want you for my protector?"

If that didn't make a deadlock, Grus didn't know what could. He sketched a salute to Lanius, then rode off. He didn't look back at his son-in-law, not even once.

"Come on," he snapped at the captains who served him. "The sooner we close with the rebels and smash them up, the better off we'll be, and the better off Avornis will be, too."

The army trampled fields as it advanced. Whatever livestock it got its hands on, it devoured. Grus had known those sorts of things would happen. Part of him exulted; they would make it harder for Corvus and Corax to keep on fighting against him. But part of him mourned, for everything that hurt his foes also hurt Avornis. That was the curse of civil war. No help for it, though.

Thinking of curses made him order a couple of wizards to stick close by Lanius. The rebels might try to steal a victory the same way Queen Certhia had tried against him. Sorcerously killing the king from the ancient dynasty was one obvious way to go about it. Sorcerously killing Grus was another obvious way. He didn't go too far from wizards himself, either.

Things would have been easier had Corvus and Corax quietly stayed in the trap and let themselves be ground to bits between Grus' army and Hirundo's. But, like Grus, they had swarms of scouts out and about.

"They're falling back to the south, Your Majesty," one of Grus' riders reported. "Sure as anything, they've figured out how close we are."

"Too bad," Grus growled. "We'll just have to press them hard, then." He turned to the trumpeters and shouted orders. Once again, they blew *Advance*. His men cheered as they went forward. They thought they had the rebels on the run.

And what would the soldiers whom Corvus and Corax commanded think? With any luck, they would think they were in trouble. Thinking that could help turn it true. Only the very greatest generals could take a retreating army and make it fight hard once it stopped retreating. From everything Grus had seen, Corvus and Corax weren't generals of that stripe. He didn't want them suddenly proving him wrong now.

Not much later, another rider came in to report to him—not one who'd traveled with him through the Maze, but an unfamiliar fellow. Grus' guards and the wizards with the army all kept a wary eye on the newcomer—another quick way for Corvus and Corax to win their fight would be by sending out an assassin.

But the rider said, "General Hirundo's compliments, Your Majesty, and he's ready to work with you any way you like."

"That's good news," Grus answered, thinking, *That's good news if it's true.* He went on, "How am I to know you come from Hirundo and not from the rebels?"

"You could just keep me prisoner and take my head if the general doesn't vouch for me when he joins you," the scout said. "Or you could let me tell you that Hirundo says the two of you first met down in the south, where he drove the Menteshe to the Stura River and your galleys kept them from crossing back to the land they hold."

"We did meet that way," Grus said, nodding. "But even so, I am going to keep you here till he vouches for you—just to be sure. I don't think Corvus and Corax know that story, but they could."

The scout nodded. "The general told me you'd probably say that. He said you didn't like to take chances unless you had to."

"Did he?" Grus murmured. One corner of his mouth quirked up in a wry smile. "Well, I suppose he's right." He turned to the guards. "Treat this fellow well, but don't let him go anywhere till we find out exactly who he is."

"Yes, Your Majesty," they chorused.

"Sounds to me like General Hirundo was right," the rider said as Grus' soldiers led him off.

When the sun was setting that day, Hirundo himself rode into Grus' camp. He rode in with no ceremony at all. In fact, Grus' guards greeted him with as much suspicion as they had the rider he'd sent before him. He'd shed all trappings of rank, and wore plain, grimy clothes and a broad-brimmed hat as disreputable as any Grus had ever seen.

Grus greeted him with, "I'd say *you* don't mind taking chances for the fun of it."

"Ah." Hirundo grinned. "Dromas got here ahead of me, did he? And you probably went and clapped him in irons because you weren't sure I'd sent him."

"I did not," Grus said indignantly. "But I didn't let him go, either. Now that you're here, I will."

"That'll make him happy," Hirundo said. "And as for me, I figured I'd take fewer chances gallivanting over the landscape like this than I would in gilded mail and helmet. Nobody takes scouts seriously. Even if the rebels caught me, they wouldn't do anything much to me. But if they'd captured me while I was dressed as the famous and ferocious General Hirundo, they'd either kill me or hold me for ransom."

"Famous and ferocious?" Grus said.

"At the very least, Your Majesty." Hirundo's grin got wider. "And very much at your service, I might add."

"Glad to hear it," Grus said, meaning every word. "Pity we couldn't quite catch Corax and Corvus between us."

"When children play at war, or when poets write about it, they make it easy," Hirundo answered. "We know better, or we're supposed to. The gods-cursed bastards on the other side have plans of their own, and they're rude enough to think *we're* the gods-cursed bastards. We just have to keep after 'em, that's all, and show 'em they're wrong."

"Anyone would guess you've been doing this for a little while," Grus observed.

"Who, me, Your Majesty? I started day before yesterday. Next battle I see will be my first."

"If I had the Scepter of Mercy in my hands right this minute, I do believe I'd clout you in the head with it," Grus said, and Hirundo laughed out loud. After a bit of thought, Grus shook his head. "No, I'd save it, and clout Corvus and Corax in the head with it instead."

"Clout them in the head with what?" asked King Lanius, who, unlike anyone else in the encampment, had no trouble getting through Grus' guards.

"Oh, hello, Your Majesty. Allow me to present General Hirundo to you," Grus said. "Hirundo, here is my colleague, King Lanius." Lanius and Hirundo said all the right things. Hirundo was much more polite with Lanius than with Grus, whom he knew well. After the formalities, Grus went on, "I'd like to clout the rebels in the head with the Scepter of Mercy."

"Would you?" Lanius sounded prim and disapproving; rough soldiers' jokes were not usually for him. But then he surprised Grus by saying, "Well, if that's what you have in mind, I can tell you how to go about it."

"I know how to go about it," Grus answered. "All I have to do is march halfway down from the Stura River to the southern hills, beat all the Menteshe who try to stop me, lay siege to Yozgat, beat the Banished One in person if *he* tries to stop me, take up the Scepter, and start clouting." He snapped his fingers. "What could be simpler?"

Lanius' face froze. "Since you already have all the answers, I won't trouble you any further." He nodded to Hirundo. "A pleasure to make your acquaintance, General." Turning on his heel, he stalked away.

"Oh, dear," Grus said. "I put his back up, didn't I? He looks like a cat after you've rubbed its fur the wrong way."

"I wonder what he was going to tell you about the Scepter of Mercy," Hirundo remarked.

Grus shrugged. "Could have been almost anything. He knows . . . a lot, is all I can tell you. But he doesn't always know which parts of what he knows are worth knowing, if you know what I mean." He paused. That had confused even him. After a moment, he resumed. "Whatever he knows, though, it doesn't matter, because every word *I* said was true, too. I can talk about the Scepter of Mercy till I'm blue in the face, but I can't get my hands on it, no matter how much I'd like to. Corvus and Corax, now, they're a different story. Them, I can reach. Since we didn't manage to trap them this time around, the next thing we need to try is . . ."

Lanius had never been so angry—not even, he thought, when Arch-Hallow Bucco sent his mother away for the first time. That had been a boy's burst of temper. This was a man's rage—the rage any man grown might feel at being condescended to, talked down to.

What made the rage worse yet was that Lanius knew how completely impotent it was. If he summoned soldiers to seize his fellow king, what would they do? He knew all too well. They would laugh, seize him, instead, and haul him before Grus.

What if I flee the camp? he thought. *What if I go over to Corvus and Corax myself?*

He stopped and rubbed his chin. His beard was still thin and scraggly, but it was a beard; that it might make Grus think him still a boy never crossed his mind. If he went over to the rebels, he would strike his father-in-law a heavy blow. Some of the soldiers who fought for Grus might follow him to Corvus and Corax. Others would surely waver in their loyalty to the new king.

A lot of youths would have thought so far and no further—except how to sneak out of camp and head south. But second thoughts, for Lanius, were as natural and automatic as first ones. King Mergus, his father, had been a man of headlong action. King Grus was cut from the same cloth. Lanius wished *he* were. Whatever he wished, he knew he wasn't.

As things were, he stood rubbing his chin for some little while, thinking things through. The question he asked himself that most youths wouldn't have was, *If I go over to Corvus and Corax, and if Grus doesn't catch me trying it, what happens next?*

The more he thought about that, the less he liked the answers he got. Corvus had already declared himself king. Would he drop that claim because the legitimate king came into his camp? Lanius' lips quirked in a bitter, mocking smile. Not likely. From everything Lanius could see, nobody ever dropped a claim like that as long as his head stayed on his shoulders.

What then? Lanius saw only one answer—Corvus would treat him the same way Grus was treating him, would use him as a puppet, as a mask. He himself would stay king in name, and Corvus would be king in fact. He had no particular illusions about Count Corvus' character. If Corvus ever decided he wasn't useful or wasn't necessary anymore, he would suffer an unfortunate accident or illness in short order.

Grus could have slain him. Instead, Grus had married him to Sosia. Lanius had come to be fond of Grus' daughter, no matter how furious he was at Grus himself. Would he stay—would he be allowed to stay—wed to her if he went over to Count Corvus and Corvus won? He shook his head. That answer was painfully obvious. *You might not stay wed to her if you go over to Corvus and Corvus loses,* he told himself.

Lanius started to laugh, though it wasn't really funny. Here in half a minute, he'd talked himself out of running off to the rebels. *I'll have to avenge myself some other way.*

Scowling, Grus peered across the Enipeus River. On the far side stood Count Corvus' keep and, somewhat farther away, Count Corax's. More to the point, drawn up on the far side of the river stood the rebels' army, plainly determined to keep Grus and his men from crossing.

He turned to General Hirundo. "What do we do about this?" he asked.

"I presume we can get the boats and such we need to force our way across?" Hirundo asked in return.

Directed at the man who had been commodore, that was the next thing to an insult. "We can get them, yes," Grus said shortly.

"All right, Your Majesty." As usual, Hirundo sounded cheerful. "Once we do, we use them to run the rebels ragged. We get part of our army over the river someplace where they're not patrolling very hard, and we make that part out to be bigger than it is, so they come pelting up with all their men to squash it. Then we put the rest of the army on the southern bank somewhere else and go after them hard from behind."

"The risk being that they beat the one part and then come back and beat the other," Grus remarked.

"Your Majesty, there is some risk of that, yes, but not a lot. The way I look at things, Corvus couldn't beat a rug if you handed him a paddle."

Grus snorted. "You're probably right." He grew a little more serious. "Don't take too many chances, though. Remember—even though you're probably right, you may be wrong, and you may make yourself wrong by being too sure you're right."

Hirundo contemplated that. At last, he said, "There are times when I think you're wasted as King of Avornis, Your Majesty. You might have done better as arch-hallow instead."

"No, thanks," Grus said at once. "Let's make the arrangements."

He summoned Captain Nicator and told him what he wanted. Nicator's beard had grown white as new snow, and Grus' longtime comrade now had to cup a hand behind his ear to make out the king's words. Once he did, though, he nodded. "I'll take care of it, boss," he said. "Don't you worry about a thing."

"I always worry," Grus answered.

"Well, don't—not this time," Nicator told him. "When I say I'll take care of things, don't I do it?"

He proved as good as his word. He always had, for as long as Grus had known him. Along with river galleys, smaller boats started showing up on the Enipeus within a few days. Grus didn't know where Nicator came up with them; by all he could tell, the captain might have pulled them out of his back pocket. They raced up and down the river. That was a game Nicator's and Grus' ships had played against the Menteshe down in the far south. The rebels' horsemen galloped after the ships, now this way, now that. Some of Hirundo's men started moving up and down the river, too.

"By the time we're done, Corvus and Corax won't dare sit down, for fear we'll be standing behind their chairs with a knife." Nicator sounded as though he was enjoying himself.

Grus grinned. "That's what I want. That's exactly what I want."

Nicator proved as good as his word, or even a little better. He started landing little bands of soldiers on the southern bank of the river, some here, some there, some somewhere else. They would shoot a few arrows at the rebel scouts who came up to spy out how many of them there were, start a few fires, run off a few sheep and pigs, and then get back onto the boats and river galleys and recross the Enipeus. Corvus and Corax had nothing to speak of on the river. Some soldiers had gone over to them, and they'd raised more from the farmers on their estates. But sailors remained overwhelmingly loyal to Grus.

"Think they're ripe yet?" Nicator asked one afternoon.

After weighing things, Grus nodded. "Yes. Let's get this over with—if we can."

When the sun rose the next day, Nicator ferried Hirundo's force over the Enipeus. Corvus and Corax's men needed longer than they should have to realize this wasn't another pinprick raid. The first few scout companies that went up against the attackers vanished without trace. Then the whole rebel army began to move, in sudden, desperate haste. From the north bank of the river, Grus watched the pillar of dust that signaled where every force moving on land in summertime was.

As soon as he was sure Corvus and Corax had committed themselves, he ordered the rest of his own force onto Nicator's fleet. Horns blared. Sergeants shouted and cursed. Horses neighed or simply snorted in resignation. And the fleet did what Grus had wanted from it—it put his men right in the rebels' rear.

Sergeants shouted louder than ever as soldiers streamed off the barges and boats and river galleys. "Move!" they bellowed. "Move fast! Help your friends! We do this the right way, we all get to go home afterward!" If anything would make the men fight like fiends, that was it.

As soon as he was on the south side of the Enipeus, Grus mounted his horse. As a rider, he remained a good sailor. King Lanius, not far away from him, had a much better seat. But Grus stayed on, and he stayed out in front of his men. "Come on!" he shouted. He waved his sword, and didn't quite cut off the horse's ears with it. "We've got 'em where we want 'em now! This time, we finish 'em!"

The men cheered. Lanius said nothing at all, and didn't try to keep up with the van of the onrushing army. Grus knew his fellow king was unhappy with him. He also knew Lanius wasn't, and never would be, a warrior.

Grus had more urgent things to worry about, anyhow. Before long, his soldiers started scooping up men who'd fought for Corvus and Corax. "What are you bastards doing here?" one of them snarled as he went off into captivity. "You're supposed to be up there." He pointed upstream, where Hirundo's men unquestionably were.

"Life is full of surprises," Grus answered. The rebel only gaped at him.

Others who fought for Corvus and Corax must have galloped ahead to let the brothers know they were under attack from front and rear at once. Before long, Grus found rebels drawn up in a ragged line across a field of barley. He pointed his sword at them. "Can *they* stop *us?*" he yelled. His men roared in response, and he led the charge at a gallop, hoping all the while he wouldn't fall off his horse.

Some of the rebel horsemen and foot soldiers had bows. Grus watched a rider take aim at him. He hoped the fellow wasn't taking dead aim. The archer let fly. The arrow hissed past Grus' head. Then he and his men were on the soldiers who followed Corax and Corvus.

Battle, as always, seemed a blur. Grus struck and turned blows and shouted and cursed and urged his followers on. Sometimes he missed; sometimes his sword bit on flesh. Even when the blade did strike home, more often than not he had no idea how much damage he did. Everyone on the field was shouting and groaning and screaming. What was one more cry of pain among the rest?

"We've broken them!" someone yelled. It was, Grus realized, someone on his side. Sure enough, the rebels—those of them still on their feet— streamed off in flight.

"This is only the beginning," Grus called. "This was just a rear guard. They wanted to slow us up. We didn't even let them do that. We've got to keep moving now, come to grips with the rest of the army, and break it, too." He pointed west. "Forward!"

His men cheered. Why not? They'd won a fight, and hadn't suffered much doing it. That made them ready for more.

They got it, too. A scout came galloping back with news: "Corax and

Corvus are mixing it up with Hirundo's men. If we pitch into their rear now—"

"That's what we're here for," Grus agreed. He shouted, "Forward!" again at the top of his lungs.

As his scouts told him what the rebels were doing, so their outriders warned them his army was on the way. His men couldn't simply pitch into their rear, taking them by surprise. But Corvus and Corax didn't have enough soldiers to withstand Hirundo and Grus at the same time. When the rebel leaders pulled men out of the fight against Hirundo to confront Grus' advancing army, Hirundo pressed them harder. And Grus could see how the line they'd quickly turned about and formed against him wavered.

He spied Corax, who was crying, "Kill the king! Kill the false king!"

"Come and try it!" Grus yelled. He spurred toward Corvus' brother. The rebel count, seeing him, booted his own horse up into a gallop. Grus wondered if he'd made a mistake, and if he would live through it. Unlike him, Corax really knew what he was doing on horseback. The noble's sword sparkled in the sun.

No matter what Corax knew, it didn't help him. An arrow caught him in the face. That bright blade flew from his hand. He slid off his horse and thudded down into the dust. He might have died even before he hit the ground. Grus, clutching the hilt of his own sword, allowed himself the luxury of a sigh of relief.

And seeing him fall broke the rebels' spirit. Some of them ran off in all directions, thinking of nothing but saving themselves. More threw down swords and spears and bows and flung up their hands in surrender. Only a stubborn handful around Corvus fought their way free of the disaster and headed south in any kind of order.

By then, the sun was almost down. Grus let that last knot of rebels get away, not least because he doubted any pursuit could catch up with them. He was, for the moment, content to see what he and his men had won.

He turned to Hirundo, who had a bloody rag tied around a cut on his forehead just below the brim of his helmet. "Let's camp here for the night. We'll care for the wounded and go on from there in the morning."

"That seems fine, Your Majesty." Hirundo sounded as weary as Grus felt. He had a dent in his helm that hadn't been there the day before; maybe the wound to his forehead had come when the brim got forced into his flesh. He waved. "The men are camping here whether we want them to or not."

Sure enough, tents sprouted like toadstools at one edge of the battle-field. Soldiers prowled the field, plundering the dead and looking for missing friends who might have been hurt. Grus tried not to listen to the moans of the wounded. He always tried. He always failed. To take his mind off them, he pointed to an especially large tent and said, "There's King Lanius' pavilion."

Hirundo nodded and pointed in a different direction. "And here comes Lanius himself."

"Good." Grus waved to his fellow king. He'd hardly seen King Lanius since the fighting started. He was glad Lanius had come to him now. He didn't want them quarreling. Lanius waved back, and Grus' bodyguards stepped aside to let the young king join the older one.

And then, altogether without warning, Lanius jerked out a dagger and stabbed Grus in the chest. He let out a horrid, wordless cry of dismay when the point snapped off—King Grus still wore a light shirt of mail un-der his tunic.

Grus' response was altogether automatic. His sword sprang from its scabbard. He struck once, with all his strength. *His* blade bit deep into La-nius' neck. Blood fountained. It smelled like hot iron. With a groan, head half severed, the young King of Avornis fell dead at his feet.

CHAPTER SIXTEEN

C haos in the camp. The racket a little while before had been bad enough. Anyone who hoped to sleep would have had a hard time of it. Now the endless moans of the wounded—and their shrieks when surgeons set about trying to repair their wounds—were joined by a sudden chorus of outraged shouts. And those shouts didn't ebb. They spread over the whole encampment like wildfire, getting louder and more furious at every moment. Running feet were everywhere, too. All at once, no one in Grus' army or Hirundo's seemed content to walk anywhere.

At first, the shouts had been wordless—expressions of raw, red rage and horror. Little by little, though, men started yelling one king's name or the other's. And they started using a word that, when connected to any king's name, meant nothing but trouble and worry and sorrow ahead for the realm the man had ruled. They started yelling, "Dead!"

Up till then, it had been possible to ignore the racket, especially for someone who wanted nothing but food and rest. But hearing the word *dead* connected with the name of Grus and with the name of Lanius proved impossible to ignore, even for the most detached, scholarly individual in the whole encampment.

With a sigh, and with a look of regret aimed at the bread and dried meat he wouldn't be able to eat, at the cup of wine he wouldn't be able to finish, and at the inviting cot he wouldn't be able to fall into any time soon, King Lanius got to his feet and ducked his way out through the tent flap and into the night.

"What on earth is going on around here?" he demanded of the first soldier he saw.

He expected an answer. He might have gotten an excited answer, an angry answer, even an incoherent answer, but he thought he would acquire something in the way of information. Instead, the soldier gaped at him, mouth falling open. The man's eyes bugged out of his head. "A ghost!" he cried. "Sweet Queen Quelea guard me, a ghost!" He fled.

Lanius said something nasty under his breath. He drummed his fingers on the outside of his thigh. *Why me?* he wondered. *Why do I find the maniacs when all I'm looking for is the answer to a simple question?*

The frightened soldier's wails made other men stare his way. He walked toward them, repeating, "What on earth is going on?"

"Oh, by the gods," one of them said fearfully. "It *is* him. I know his look, and I know his voice, too."

Then they all cried out, "A ghost!" and fled every which way.

King Lanius pinched himself. It hurt. He was, emphatically, still flesh and blood. He hadn't really needed to do any pinching, either; all the time he'd spent on a horse that day had left him saddlesore. Avornan lore said a great many things about ghosts. Some he'd heard from servants, some he'd found poking through the royal archives. Never in all his days had he heard of a saddlesore spook.

He strode forward. If things had been confused before—and they had—the addition of eight or ten fleeing men screaming, "A ghost!" at the top of their lungs did nothing to calm the situation. He heard more soldiers—men who couldn't possibly have seen him—also start shouting, "Ghost! Ghost! Gods preserve us, a ghost!"

"Idiots," Lanius snarled. "Fools. Morons. Imbeciles. Lackwits. Dolts. Clods. Chowderheads. Buffoons. *Soldiers.*"

One of them, trying to run away from him, almost trampled him instead. Lanius grabbed the fellow and refused to let him go. "Oh, Queen Quelea save me, it's got its claws in me now!" the man moaned, plainly believing his last moments on earth had arrived.

"Shut up, you . . . you soldier, you," Lanius told the trooper. He shook him, which only terrified the fellow worse. "Now, gods curse you, tell me why you think I'm dead."

"Because . . . Because . . . Because . . . King Grus killed you." The soldier got it out at last. Then his eyes rolled up in his head. He went limp in

Lanius' arms. Lanius had heard of people fainting from fright. Up till that moment, he'd never seen it.

And he'd finally gotten an answer. He didn't think he'd gotten any information, though. "King Grus did what?" he said. The soldier, of course, didn't answer. Lanius let go of him in disgust. The man slumped to the ground and hit his head on a rock. As far as Lanius could tell, that was more likely to hurt the rock than the man's obviously empty head.

Resisting the impulse to kick the fellow while he was down, Lanius looked around for Grus' pavilion. He didn't see it, and growled something he'd heard a bodyguard say after banging his thumb with a hammer.

If he couldn't find the pavilion, maybe he could find his fellow king. No sooner had that thought crossed his mind than another soldier caromed off him. He grabbed this one, too, and snarled, "Where's Grus?"

The man goggled at him, but didn't faint. Lanius *would* have kicked him if he had. Instead, still gaping, the soldier said, "He's over that way." A moment later, he blurted, "Why aren't you dead?"

"I don't know," Lanius snapped, exasperated past endurance. "Why aren't *you,* you simple son of a whore?"

"You're the bastard," the soldier retorted, at which Lanius, in a perfect transport of fury, *did* kick him. He howled. He also managed to break free, which was lucky for him—Lanius was reaching for the dagger he wore on his belt. Up till then, he'd used the fancy weapon only as an eating knife. Now he wanted to kill with it. "Nobody cut me down," the soldier added. "That's why I'm not dead." Lanius would gladly have taken care of it, but the man ran off into the night.

Since the soldier had escaped, Lanius went on in the direction in which he'd pointed. A couple of minutes later, he came upon Grus and General Hirundo. Bodyguards surrounded them. And, sure enough, a corpse dressed in royal robes much like those Lanius was wearing lay only a few paces away.

"What happened here?" Lanius asked loudly.

Everyone stared at him. The guards, after a moment's astonishment, started forward to lay hold of him. "Stop!" Grus said, and they did. Lanius knew a momentary stab of jealousy. Nobody ever obeyed him like that. With what Lanius later realized was commendable calm, Grus went on, "I just killed somebody who looked and sounded exactly like you. Are you the real Lanius, or are you somebody else who looks like him and wants to do me in?"

"By Olor's beard, I'm beginning to wonder myself," Lanius answered. "You realize I'd say I was myself regardless of whether that were so?"

"Oh, yes." Grus nodded. "The other fellow had your voice, but you sound more like you even so, if you know what I mean." He wore not a dagger but a sword on his hip. His hand had closed on the hilt, but he didn't draw the blade. Instead, he asked, "What was the name of that Therving trader who gave you your first pair of moncats?"

"He wasn't a Therving. He was a Chernagor," Lanius said. At first, he thought Grus a fool for not remembering. Then he realized his father-in-law was testing him, and felt a fool himself. "His name was Yaropolk."

"Relax, boys," Grus told his bodyguards. "This is the real King Lanius. Hello, Your Majesty. That fellow there"—he pointed to the corpse—"has your face and your voice. Or he did, till I let the air out of him."

"Looking like me let him get close to you," Lanius said slowly.

"I'd say you're right," Grus answered. "I'd say Corvus and Corax have a pretty good wizard working for them, too. Or Corvus does; Corax is dead. I came as close to being dead myself as makes no difference. But here I am, and I still aim to have my reckoning with *dear* Count Corvus." He sounded thoroughly grim.

"All right. Better than all right, in fact—good," Lanius said. "I don't like having my image stolen."

"Your Majesty, I didn't like it, either, not even a little bit," Grus said. "And remember, it could have gone—it could still go—the other way, too. Wouldn't you have let someone who looked like me get close?"

"Yesss." Lanius stretched the word out into a long, slow hiss. "Yes, I think I might have."

"We'll both be careful, then," Grus said. "But I'll tell you one thing more." He waited till Lanius raised a questioning eyebrow, then continued, "Corvus had better be more careful than either one of us."

"Yes," King Lanius said once more. Just for a moment, he too sounded fierce as a soldier. "Oh, yes, indeed."

General Hirundo pointed up the steep slope toward the castle perched at the top of the crag. "There it is. There *he* is," Hirundo said. "That's what Corvus is king of these days. The rest of Avornis is yours."

"True." Grus nodded. "That makes us better off than we were when Corvus decided to start calling himself king, and half the countryside hereabouts decided it would sooner have him with a crown on his head than Lanius."

That stretched the truth a bit, and Grus knew it. Corvus had proclaimed he wouldn't do anything to Lanius. The countryside in the south had risen against Grus himself, not against his colleague on the throne. He intended to go right on telling his version of the story, though. People would feel better about his crushing Corvus if they thought Corvus threatened the old dynasty. Grus was every bit as much a usurper as the nobleman who'd rebelled against him. The only difference between them was that Grus was more successful than Corvus.

That's the difference that matters, Grus thought, and then, *One of these years, some dusty chronicler pawing through the archives Lanius loves so much is liable to realize Corvus' revolt was aimed at me, not at Lanius at all. He'll write it all down, and everybody will call me a liar.* Grus considered that, then shrugged. *People will call me a King of Avornis who was a liar. That's what counts.*

Hirundo brought him back to the here-and-now by asking, "You don't intend to try storming that place, do you?"

"By the gods, no!" Grus exclaimed. "I'd have about as much chance as the Banished One would of storming his way back into the heavens."

Hirundo's expressive features showed his relief. He accepted the figure of speech as meaning Grus knew he had no chance of storming Corvus' keep. Grus had meant it that way, too. But he realized he didn't *know* what kind of chance of storming back into the heavens the Banished One had. All he knew was that the Banished One hadn't done it yet, not in all the time he'd spent here in the material world. By human standards, he'd been banished a very long time. By his own? Who could say, except for him?

Contemplating how to take Corvus' stronghold was more comforting than thinking about the Banished One's return to the heavens. What would he do, if he ever forced his way back? Nothing pretty—Grus was sure of that.

Up on the walls of the grim gray stone keep, men moved. Grus could barely make out the distant motion, like that of ants on the ground as seen by a man standing upright. Hirundo look toward the castle, shielding his eyes from the sun with his hand. He stared so fixedly, Grus wondered if he could make out more than someone with ordinary eyesight might have done. But before Grus could ask, Hirundo turned to him with a question of his own. "If Corvus yields himself to you, will you let him live?"

Grus scratched at the corner of his jaw. "I *would* have, if he hadn't sent that sorcerously disguised fellow to try to murder me." He sighed. "I suppose I would even now, for the sake of having the civil war over and done with. We don't have time for it, you know—not with Dagipert still in arms against us and with the Menteshe ready to come to the boil whenever they choose." Another, longer, sigh. "Yes, if Corvus wants to live out his days somewhere in the very heart of the Maze, in a place he'll never come out of, I'll let him do it."

"All right, then," Hirundo said. "You should send a messenger and let him know as much, in that case. His keep will take a lot of besieging, and who knows what may go wrong while we're waiting down here to starve him out?"

Grus said one more time, "You make more sense than I wish you did. I'll do it."

He sent a young officer up the slope, a white banner in hand to show he had no hostile intent. The youngster went up to the wall of the keep. Grus made out his progress by keeping an eye on the white moving against the dark background. After a while, his officer trudged down the slope once more. Little by little, he grew from moving white speck to man once more.

"Well?" Grus asked him when he came back into the encampment.

"Sorry, Your Majesty, but he says no." By the indignation on the young man's face, Count Corvus had not only said no but embellished upon it. "He says he can't trust you."

"I like that!" Grus exclaimed. "He rebelled when I was crowned, he just sent a sorcerously disguised assassin against me, and now *I'm* the one who can't be trusted! Some people would call that funny."

"I said as much," the young officer answered. "And when I said it, Count Corvus called *me* a traitor."

"He can say whatever he likes." Grus' smile was predatory. "That's what he's got left—nasty talk from a mewed-up castle. I hope he enjoys it."

"I wonder how much grain he has in there, and how many men," Hirundo said.

"Yes, those are the questions," Grus agreed. "I'm sure he's wondering the same thing. The answer will tell him how long he can hold out. He doesn't have enough men to sally against us. I'm sure of that, or he wouldn't have let himself be locked away in his lair."

"Does he think we'll go away before he starves?" Hirundo said. "Not likely!"

"No," Grus said. But it was perhaps more likely than his general thought. If the Thervings or the Menteshe started moving, Grus knew he might have to break off the siege to deal with them. Corvus was playing a desperate game, yes, but not quite a hopeless one.

These days, Lanius needed approval from a wizard or witch before he could come into Grus' presence. That would have offended him more had not Grus required sorcerous approval of himself before he saw Lanius. He was equitable in small things. Maybe he thought that made his usurpation of all large things more tolerable to Lanius. Sometimes, it even did.

Having proved he was himself, Lanius told Grus, "I know how we can solve all these questions of who's who."

"Oh?" Grus said. "Well, tell me, Your Majesty."

"Send me back to the city of Avornis," Lanius answered. "I'm of no use to you here, and of no use to myself here, either. I'd like to go home to my wife. I'd like to go home to the moncats. I'd like to go home to the archives."

Grus eyed him. "And when *I* go home, Your Majesty, would I find the city of Avornis closed up tight against me? The question I'm asking is, How do I trust you?"

That he'd made Lanius his son-in-law apparently counted for nothing. And, perhaps, with reason. Had Lanius thought he could get away with revolt, he might have tried it. But this journey with Grus warned him he would only lose if he rebelled. And so he said, "Send enough soldiers back to keep an eye on me, if you feel the need. But send me home."

"I'll think about it," Grus said, and no more.

King Lanius thought that would prove nothing more than a polite dismissal. He wondered if he ought to be glad to get a polite one. Whenever Grus thwarted him, his first reaction was usually to get angry. His second reaction was usually to think, *Well, that could have been worse.* So it was here.

And, a couple of days later, Grus came to him. Alca the witch meticulously made sure Grus was himself before the other King of Avornis strode up to Lanius. "I've made up my mind," Grus said.

"Yes?" Lanius braced himself for the rejection he was sure would follow.

But Grus said, "All right, Your Majesty. Back to the city of Avornis you may go, if that makes you happy."

"Really? Thank you very much!" Only afterward did Lanius pause to wonder if he should have been so grateful. At the moment itself, glad surprise filled him too full to worry about such trifles.

"Yes, really." Grus seemed amused. "But you'll do it my way. I'm sending Nicator back with you to command in the city till I get back."

"Ah?" Lanius said cautiously. If he had been thinking about rebellion, that would have made him think twice. Nicator was not only altogether loyal to Grus, he was popular with the men he would lead.

"Yes," Grus said. "I trust you don't mind going back aboard a river galley full of marines?"

Lanius said what he had to say. "No, I don't mind in the least, as long as you haven't told them to pitch me into the Enipeus as soon as we get out of sight of camp here."

"Sosia would have something to say if I did," Grus remarked.

Lanius wondered how true that was. Even more than most in Avornis, his had been a marriage made for reasons having nothing to do with any initial attraction between the two parties most intimately involved. But he'd done his best to please Grus' daughter once they were joined. Thinking about it, he supposed she'd done the same for him. Maybe he'd succeeded better than he knew. He hoped so.

When he didn't answer, Grus asked, "Does it suit you, Your Majesty?"

"Yes—very much so." Lanius considered, and then added, "Thank you." He said that seldom; as best he could recall, he hadn't said it to Grus since the older man put the crown on his own head.

Grus noticed that, too. "You're welcome," he answered, the same note of formality in his voice as Lanius had used. He hesitated, made a small pushing gesture, as though urging Lanius to be on his way, and then held up a hand to stop him from leaving. When he spoke again, he sounded uncommonly serious. "We *can* work in harness together, can't we, Your Majesty?"

"Maybe we can," Lanius said. "Yes, maybe we can." Now he did turn to go. A moment later, he turned back again. "I'll see you in the city of Avornis . . . Your Majesty."

Grus had always been scrupulous about using Lanius' royal title. Lanius had always been grudging about using Grus', which he hadn't reckoned—and still didn't reckon—altogether legitimate. Grus had noticed. By the nature of things, Grus would have had to be a far duller, far blinder man than he was to keep from noticing. Now a broad smile spread over his face. "So you will, Your Majesty—and, with luck, sooner than you think."

"Really?" Lanius pointed an accusing finger at him. "You have some sort of plot in mind."

"Who? Me?" Grus' smile turned into an out-and-out grin. For a moment, gray streaks in his beard or not, he looked hardly older than Lanius was. He asked, "Do you want to stay around awhile longer and see what it is?"

Lanius thought it over. He hadn't expected to be tempted, but he was. Tempted or not, he shook his head. His answer needed only one word. "No."

*   *   *

Grus and Alca walked along together at the base of the crag. The witch nodded. "Yes, I can do that, Your Majesty, or I think I can. You do understand that even if I manage it, it may not do everything you want? They may have other ways of solving the problem."

"Not from what the prisoners say," Grus answered. He looked up at the sky, which was fine and blue and fair. Motion on the battlements caught his eye. Someone up there in the castle, implausibly tiny in the distance, was looking down at him. Was it Corvus? No way to tell, of course, any more than Corvus—if that was he—could recognize Grus down here at the base of the mountain whose peak was all the kingdom he had left. "With any luck at all, we can do this quickly and get back to the city of Avornis."

Alca gave him a sidelong look. "Are you really so worried about Lanius?" she asked.

"Among other things, yes," Grus told her. "Some more than others, I grant." He sighed. "Now that I'm King of Avornis, I worry about everything. The only way I have of taking care of the worries is deciding which one to fret about first."

That made Alca smile, though he hadn't been joking. She said, "Well, Your Majesty, I will do what I can to make sure you need not worry about Corvus anymore. I think I can find everything I need."

"If it turns out that you can't, say the word," Grus replied. "Whatever it is, I'll get it for you."

"I thank you, Your Majesty," the witch said.

"Believe me, you're welcome," Grus said. "This is for my advantage, after all. And for the kingdom's advantage," he added, but he didn't think he was dishonest in putting his own first.

Alca began her magic the next day at noon, when the sun stood highest in the sky. She took from a silk sack a curious red and white stone, all branched like a tree. "This is coral," she told Grus. "It washes up on seaside beaches."

"I've heard of it," he answered. "Up till now, though, I haven't seen it more than once or twice in all my days."

"Coming out of the sea, it naturally has power over water," the witch said. Grus nodded. From everything he knew about sorcery—admittedly, not much—what she said made good sense.

Alca held the coral up high over her head and began to chant in an ancient dialect of Avornan. Grus recognized a word here and there in what she said, but no more than that. *Lanius would probably follow every bit of it,* he thought. After a moment's resentment, he shrugged. Yes, Lanius had more education than he, but so what? *I'm the one who makes things happen.*

Just then, after a sharp word of command, Alca took her hands off the coral. It kept on floating in midair, above the level of her head. The shadow it cast on the ground was of a hue different from ordinary shadows—it was reddish, like the coral stone itself. Grus muttered to himself when he saw that. Power might command knowledge, but a powerful man didn't necessarily know things himself.

In that scarlet shadow, Alca set a basin of water. Then, moving swiftly, she mixed lime and olive oil and wax and some strong-smelling substance—"Naphtha," she said, seeing the question on Grus' face—and shaped them into the form of a man. On the image's chest, she placed a pinch of earth from beside the basin. "This is the land Corvus claims as his own. With it, I will make the image stand for him."

Grus nodded again. Even he recognized such correspondences, such links, between the everyday world and that in which magic worked.

Alca held up the image as she'd held up the coral stone. Her chant, though, was different this time, harsh and angry and insistent. When she finished, she cast the image into the basin of water instead of letting it float in the air.

It burst into flames. Grus exclaimed and took a quick step back. Whatever he'd expected, he hadn't expected *that*. The image burned and burned, with a sputtering blue-white flame painful to the eyes. A great cloud of steam rose from the basin.

Alca smiled at his surprise. "Sometimes, sorcery should be interesting, don't you think?" she remarked.

"Interesting? By King Olor's beard, that almost made *my* beard turn white," Grus answered. "I wouldn't mind seeing Corvus go up in flames the same way."

Now the witch frowned. "That is not the purpose of this wizardry," she said severely.

"No, I suppose not," Grus admitted. "Magic's almost killed me twice. I don't really have any business wishing that sort of death on anybody else, do I?"

"I would think not, Your Majesty." Alca still sounded offended. As one skilled in sorcery should have, she took its limits seriously, and expected everybody else to do the same.

Respecting that, Grus changed the subject by asking, "The magic you worked did what it should have done?"

"Oh, yes." Alca nodded. "The spell is accomplished."

"Will Corvus' wizards be able to reverse it?"

"They will try. I have no doubt of that," the witch answered. "But some things are easier to do than to undo once done. This is one of those, or so I believe."

"May I ask one last question?"

Amusement glinted in Alca's eyes. "You are the King of Avornis. You may do whatever you please."

"Ha!" Grus said. "That only goes to show you've never been king. Here's my question, then: How long before we know what we've done up there?"

"I can't tell you—not exactly," Alca said. "That depends on several things—just how many men are shut up in the fortress, what all they can broach, and so on. But I don't think it will be long—not unless Corvus' wizards manage to surprise me. By the nature of things, I don't see how it could be. Do you?"

"No. I don't." Grus sighed. "On the other hand, I've been wrong before. Maybe Corvus' wizards will work something out, or maybe he'll find some other way to hang on up there. I have to stay ready, don't I?"

"If you stay ready for all the uncertain things, the things that may happen but may not, you will make a better king than if you let them take you by surprise," Alca said.

Grus shrugged. "I don't know about that. What I do know is, I'm likely to stay on the throne longer if I'm ready for anything. Maybe that amounts to the same thing."

The witch nodded. "Yes. Maybe it does."

For several days, nothing happened up in the castle on the crag—nothing the army surrounding it could see, at any rate. Grus wondered whether Alca's wizardry had worked as well as she thought. He said nothing about that. If his worries turned out to be right, the time to talk about them would come later. If he turned out to be wrong, he would have made a fool of himself by needlessly showing them.

Eight days after Alca worked her magic, a soldier came down from the castle carrying a flag of truce. "In the names of the gods, Your Majesty," he said when Grus' men disarmed him and brought him before the king, "give me something to drink, I beg you!"

"So I'm 'Your Majesty' now, am I?" Grus asked, hiding the exultation that leaped in him. Corvus' soldier nodded, as eagerly as he could. With a smile, Grus said, "Well, that's earned you a little something, anyhow." He nodded to one of his own troopers, who ceremoniously poured a cup of wine and handed it to the man just down from the stronghold.

Corvus' soldier gulped it down so fast, a little spilled out of his mouth, trickled through his beard, and dripped down onto the dry, dusty ground on which he stood. He wiped his lips and chin on his sleeve, saying, "Ahhh! That's sweeter than Queen Quelea's milk, Banished One bite me if it isn't!"

"I'm glad my wine makes you happy," Grus said dryly. "I do have to ask, though, if you came down just to guzzle it, or for some other reason, too."

That seemed to remind the fellow of the white flag he still carried in his left hand. "Oh." He grimaced. "Count Corvus would yield himself and his garrison and his keep to you, and begs you to spare their—our—lives."

"Would he? Does he?" King Grus whispered. His own soldiers grinned and murmured and nudged one another. Alca, who stood not far away, smiled a small, weary smile. Grus asked, "Why did he suddenly decide to give up?"

"Why?" Corvus' man echoed. "I'll tell you why, Your Majesty. On account of our stinking spring failed, that's why. You can fight a long time without food, even without hope. But you can't go on without water."

"Why shouldn't I let the lot of you parch to death up there?" Grus demanded. "Why shouldn't I take Corvus' head the instant I've got him?"

"Here's why: Because if you tell me no, we'll sally from the keep and fight as hard as we can as long as we can," the soldier answered. "You'll be rid of us, but we'll hurt you, maybe hurt you bad, going down. What have we got to lose?"

Why shouldn't I promise Corvus his life and then *take his head?* Grus wondered. But that had its own obvious answer. If he swore an oath here and then broke it, who would ever trust him the next time he swore one? He scowled but nodded. "Agreed. Come forth with no weapons, with only the clothes on your backs. Tell Corvus he'll tend a shrine in the heart of the Maze till they lay him on his pyre. Tell him he *will* die if he ever sets a toe outside that shrine. Make sure he understands, for I'd sooner kill him than look at him."

"He . . . thought you might say something like that, Your Majesty," Corvus' man replied. Grus gestured—*away*. The soldier started back up the crag.

Going uphill took longer than coming down. Before too very long, though, a long column of soldiers came out of the main gate and marched into captivity. Grus' men hurried up to make sure they were obeying the terms the king had set them. Waves and whoops and joyful shouts announced they were.

Grus had Corvus brought before him. The count looked disgusted. "If you hadn't struck at our spring, we'd've held out a lot longer," he snarled. Then, remembering where he was and who held the power, he grudgingly added, "Uh, Your Majesty." The title seemed to taste bad to him.

"I did, though," Grus answered. "And you would be wise, very wise, to give me no tiniest excuse to slay you."

"You swore you wouldn't," Corvus exclaimed.

"Maybe I lied," Grus said. The defeated rebel looked as appalled as he'd hoped. He went on, "Or maybe, if you push me, you'll make me lose my temper, and I'll forget about what I promised. I'd be sorry afterward."

"That wouldn't do me much good," Corvus muttered.

"No, it wouldn't, would it?" Grus agreed with a smile.

Corvus kept very quiet after that. He gave Grus no excuse for anything at all. Grus gestured, and his men took Corvus away.

He put a garrison of his own in the keep from which Corvus had dominated the countryside for so long. Then he turned back toward the city of Avornis. He still had to worry about the Menteshe and the Thervings, but he wouldn't have to fear civil war as well as his foreign foes—not for a while, anyhow.

But for how long? he wondered. *When will some other nobleman decide he ought to be King of Avornis? Half the counts in the kingdom turn the peasants on their lands into their own private armies. Have to do something about that one of these days.* He wondered what he *could* do. He wondered if he could do anything but beat the rebels one by one as they arose. *There has to be a better way than that. There has to be, if only I can find it.*

When the army encamped that night, he asked Alca to supper with him. She raised an eyebrow when she found she was the only one he'd invited. "Your Majesty, is this proper?" she asked.

"You just helped me put down a civil war," Grus answered. "What's improper about celebrating that?"

"Nothing," Alca admitted, and stayed in the pavilion. Over supper, he asked whether she had any ideas about keeping other nobles with wide estates from imitating Corvus and Corax. She didn't, not on the spur of the moment. He swallowed a sigh.

Over the course of the meal, he also swallowed a good deal of wine. So did Alca. Before long, he tried to kiss her. She twisted away. "Your Majesty, I'm married," she reminded him.

"So what? So am I," he said grandly—yes, he'd had a lot of wine.

"And what would Queen Estrilda say if she found out about this?" Alca asked.

"She'd say it was how I fathered my bastard boy," Grus answered. She would also say quite a few other things, most of them at the top of her lungs. Grus was sure of that. He didn't mention it to Alca.

The witch got to her feet. "I did not come here for that, Your Majesty. I'm not angry—not yet. Being noticed is always flattering, up to a point. If someone goes past that point when you don't want him to . . ."

She didn't say what might happen then. But Grus, wine or no wine, abruptly remembered she *was* a witch. Unpleasant things might follow if he pushed too hard. "All right," he said grumpily. "Go on, then."

"Thank you, Your Majesty." Alca hesitated, then added, "If neither of us were wed, that might be different. But as things are?" Shaking her head, she slipped out of the tent. Grus poured his goblet full again and finished the job of getting drunk.

CHAPTER SEVENTEEN

For the most part, Lanius was glad to get back to the royal palace. He had, after all, lived there his whole life. Coming back to the moncats and the forays into the archives meant returning to comfortable routine. Coming back to Sosia was pleasant, too. But, as day followed day and routine submerged him, he did wonder if he'd lost a chance he might not see again.

Even finding an answer was far from easy. When Lanius asked the question in the privacy of his own mind, that was one thing. But when he asked it out in the world, that was something else—something more dangerous. Asking the wrong person could prove deadly dangerous. Who was the right person? Was *anyone* the right person?

After some thought, he arranged to see Lepturus. The commander of the royal bodyguards had always been loyal to the dynasty of which Lanius was the last survivor. Even if Lepturus gave an answer he didn't like, he doubted the older man would pass his words on to Grus.

Lepturus heard him out in thoughtful silence. The officer plucked at his beard. It was white these days. It had been iron gray when Lanius first knew him. How had Lepturus gotten so old without his noticing? At last, the guards commander said, "Me, I think you did just the right thing by sitting tight and not starting a fight here when you got back from the field, Your Majesty. If you'd risen against Grus, you would have lost."

In a way, that was what Lanius wanted to hear. It was what he'd told himself. And yet . . . "Don't you think the soldiers would have risen for me, for the dynasty, against the upstart?"

"Some of them would have," Lepturus replied at once. "Some of the bodyguards would have, too."

"But not all of them?" Lanius asked, and the guards commander shook his head. Lanius grimaced. That hurt. If not all the men who'd protected him since he was a baby would have risen for him, he *would* have lost, without a doubt. "Why wouldn't they?"

"On account of Grus looks to be a pretty good fighting man, and we need that," Lepturus answered. "It's not the only thing we need, but it's the one soldiers think about. You can't expect anything different. And Grus was smart when he sent Nicator back here with you. Everybody likes Nicator. Olor's beard, I like the old pirate myself. And *he* likes Grus—always has, always will."

King Lanius sighed. No, that wasn't what he'd wanted to hear. But he'd called Lepturus to tell him the truth, or as much of it as the guards commander saw. He asked, "What do *you* think of Grus?"

"Me?" That question seemed to startle Lepturus, where the others hadn't. "Me?" he said again. "He could have done a lot worse, I will say that."

"If he had, I'd be dead," Lanius said.

"That's part of what I mean," Lepturus replied. "He's held back King Dagipert for one more year, he beat Corvus and Corax, he married you to Sosia instead of putting you in the grave. . . . He could have done a lot worse. Plenty of other people would have—Corvus springs to mind."

That wasn't what Lanius wanted to hear, either. "But what about Grus?" he demanded. "Do you think anybody needs him? Do you think the kingdom needs him?"

"Probably," Lepturus answered. Lanius threw his hands in the air and walked off. The commander of the bodyguards called, "Don't do anything foolish, now," after him.

"I won't," Lanius answered. He had a pretty good idea of what Lepturus meant by the words—*don't start plotting against Grus.* He hadn't intended to do that even if Lepturus had shown interest in the idea. Grus had already proved he was good at sniffing out conspiracies about as fast as they were born.

Lanius went in to watch Bronze and the young moncats and to stroke them. They didn't give him any trouble, except when he scratched their furry bellies and they snapped at his hand for no particular reason. They were more skittish than ordinary cats, but ordinary cats sometimes nipped for no particular reason, too.

As far as Lanius' pets knew, he remained sole and all-powerful King of Avornis. He fed them and cared for them and petted them. Past that, what else mattered? Nothing—not as far as the moncats were concerned. Lanius' laugh made the beasts turn their slit-pupiled eyes his way. They wouldn't have understood that he didn't really think anything was funny, or why he didn't.

The door opened behind him. He turned with the same sort of surprise the moncats had given him when he laughed. When he came in here, people usually left him alone. That was exactly how he wanted it, too.

"Oh," he said. He couldn't even snarl like a moncat, the way he wanted to. "Hello, Sosia."

"Hello," his wife answered. "Am I bothering you?"

That was a poser. If he said no, he'd be telling a lie; if he said yes, he'd offend her. Silence stretched. Too late, he realized that was as bad as "Yes" would have been.

Sosia sighed. "Well, I'm sorry," she said, "but I do think we'd better talk."

"Do you?" Lanius didn't feel like talking to anybody, not then.

But Sosia nodded, though she had to know something was bothering him. She owned some of Grus' stubbornness in going straight at whatever troubled her. "Yes, as a matter of fact, I do," she told him. "It has to do with my father, doesn't it?"

"How can you imagine that?" Lanius said.

Sarcasm didn't deflect her. He'd hoped it might, but hadn't really expected it would. "Everything has to do with my father. He's the king who gives the orders, and I know how much you hate that."

"I'm sorry," Lanius answered. "I didn't mean for you to know."

"Well, I do," Sosia said. "I don't know what I can do about it, though."

"Not much," he said.

She nodded again. "No, I suppose not. But the one thing I can tell you is, he's not your enemy. He likes you."

That jerked more bitter laughter from Lanius. "He has an odd way of showing it, wouldn't you say? Stealing my power—"

"Marrying you to me," Sosia broke in. "He wouldn't do that with someone he hated. I hope he wouldn't, anyhow. He and I have always gotten on well, so I don't think he would do anything like that to me, either."

"I should hope not. You're his daughter. People are supposed to treat their children right." Lanius spoke with great conviction. He believed with all his heart that he would have been treated better if King Mergus had lived longer. "When we have children, by the gods, I'm going to spoil them rotten."

Now, though, Sosia shook her head. "That isn't the way to do it, either. My father thought my grandfather was too rough on him, so he decided to spoil Ortalis rotten. Look how well my brother turned out."

With his mind's eye, Lanius looked—and then quickly looked away. Ortalis frightened him too much for long contemplation. "Maybe you're right," he said. "But maybe Ortalis would have turned out like that any which way. How can you tell?"

"I don't suppose you can," Sosia admitted. One reason they got along was that they both respected reasoned argument. But she added, "Still, do you think he'd have turned out *worse* if Father had tried harder to teach him he had no business doing things like that?"

Unhappily, Lanius, who had to respect reasoned argument himself, shook his head. "No, that doesn't seem likely, does it?"

Unhappily, Grus eyed Ortalis, who had never shown any sign of respecting any argument whatsoever. "A serving woman is not a toy," he growled, loud enough for his words to echo from the walls of the small audience chamber.

His son's expression, and every line of the younger man's body, said he didn't believe that, not even for a minute. "We were only having fun," the prince said sulkily.

Grus shook his head. "*You* were having fun. What *she* was having . . . I'd rather not think about some of that. The healers say she *will* get better, though."

"Well, there you are, then." Ortalis seemed convinced Grus was getting upset over nothing.

"I made a promise to you a while ago," Grus said. "Do you remember?"

Ortalis plainly didn't. Grus hit his son, hard, in the face. Ortalis fell back with a cry of pain and, especially, of shock. When he straightened, murder was in his eyes. Grus could see it all too clearly. He set his hand on the hilt of his sword. Ortalis checked the forward lunge he'd been about to make.

"That's better," Grus snapped. "And I only gave you a piece there, a little piece, of what I promised you the first time you did something like this. Count yourself lucky, by the gods."

Again, Ortalis plainly didn't. "You can't do that to me," he whispered in a deadly voice.

"I can. I did. And I'll do more. I'm sending the girl back to her home village." Grus wondered if walloping his son whenever he'd stepped out of line as a boy would have done any good. Too late to worry about that now, worse luck. "I'm taking the indemnity that I'm giving her straight out of your allowance, too."

"That's not fair!" Ortalis exclaimed. Whenever something touched him, he was quick enough to talk about what was fair and what wasn't. Whenever something touched someone else, he might as well have been a blind man.

"Suppose I mark you just the same way you marked her?" Grus asked. "Would you think *that* was fair?" It was what he'd promised to do, but he didn't have the stomach for it now. He wished he did.

In any case, it didn't get through. Grus could see that it didn't. His only son's eyes remained shiny as glass, opaque as stone. *If I die tomorrow, he'll try to claim the throne. What happens to Avornis if he does?* Grus didn't care to think about that, so he shoved it to the back of his mind. He didn't want to think about Ortalis in control of *anything. I just have to make sure I don't die tomorrow, that's all—and make sure he doesn't help me.*

"That's my silver, and you've got no business touching it."

"I ought to touch *you,* and with a horsewhip, too," Grus growled. "Get out of my sight—and if you abuse another girl like that one, by the gods, I think I *will* horsewhip you. You don't blacken only your name when you do such things—you blacken mine, too, and I won't stand for it."

Without another word, Ortalis stormed off. Grus turned to a jar of wine sitting on a table close by. He poured a mug from it and gulped thirstily, wishing he could rinse the taste of his son out of his mouth. *He's what I've got,* Grus thought, and took another swig from the wine. *I have to make the best of him.*

His fist slammed down on the table. The wine jug jumped. He had to grab it to keep it from falling over. *What if there's no best to make of Ortalis?* That had occurred to him more than a few times. Whenever it did, he told himself his son just needed a few more years to finish growing up, and that everything would be fine once Ortalis did. Telling himself the same hopeful story over and over again got harder as the years went by. Lanius, on the other hand . . . But Lanius wasn't of his own blood.

Estrilda walked into the room. "Well?" she asked.

Grus shook his head. "No, not very well," he answered. "But we do the best we can—all of us do. I don't know what else there is."

Estrilda sighed deeply. "No, not all of us do the best we can," she said. "Things would be easier if we did."

That made Grus pour his mug full again. "Want one?" he asked his wife. When she nodded, he grabbed another mug and filled it for her. He stared toward the door through which Ortalis had left. "I suppose it could have been worse," he said at last.

"Yes. He could have killed her. It wouldn't have taken much more."

"I know." Grus moodily started on that second cup of wine. Thinking about Ortalis—dealing with Ortalis—was going to turn him into a drunk. "What are we going to do about him?"

"I don't know." Estrilda sounded as gloomy as Grus felt. "We've been trying to do anything at all since he was little, and we haven't had much luck. He's got a streak of blood lust this wide in him." She held her hands far enough apart to make Grus wince.

"Maybe I can get him interested in the chase," Grus said suddenly. "If he's killing stags and boar and tigers, maybe . . ." He didn't quite know how to go on from there. "Maybe that will be enough to keep him happy," he finished at last.

His wife raised her mug to her lips. She looked at him over the rim. Little by little, her expression went from dubious to thoughtful. "Maybe," she said. "It has a chance, anyhow—as long as he thinks going hunting is his idea, not yours."

"Oh, yes, I know that," Grus said. "If it's my idea, something must be wrong with it. I have to say, though, I was the same way with my father."

Estrilda snorted. "With your father's ideas, a lot of the time something *was* wrong."

"You never said that when he was alive," Grus said.

"I know I didn't. What would the point have been? But are you going to tell me I'm wrong?"

Grus considered. Crex had started out with nothing. He'd been one more farm boy come to the city of Avornis trying to make something of himself. Unlike most, he'd actually done it. He deserved credit for that. Even so . . . "No, you're not wrong," Grus admitted. "He was a hardhead, first, last, and always. Maybe that's where Ortalis comes by it."

He sounded hopeful. If he could blame blood for the way his son behaved, he wouldn't have to blame himself. He wouldn't even have to blame his son so much. If it was in the blood, how could Ortalis help acting the way he did?

"Your father was stubborn, and he had bad ideas sometimes—well, more than sometimes—but he wasn't . . . like that," Estrilda said. "He never enjoyed . . . hurting things." Even she shied away from saying *hurting people.*

She was probably right. No, she was certainly right. Grus sighed. He didn't like to think of himself as a man who had a vicious son. That he didn't like it, unfortunately, didn't mean it wasn't so.

Lanius was trying to coax Iron from a high perch near the door to the older male moncat's room. Iron still lived by himself. He showed a regrettable tendency toward infanticide.

When living by himself, though, Iron wasn't a bad-natured beast. People were too big for him to try to kill. Besides, they fed him and stroked him. For that, he was willing to tolerate their not being moncats.

"Come here," Lanius urged. Talking to a moncat was as useless as talking to an ordinary cat. He could have talked sweetly to Iron till he was blue in the face, and the male would have kept on staring at him out of those amber eyes. It wouldn't have come down to within arm's length.

The chunk of raw meat Lanius held in his hand was a lot more persuasive. Iron made an eager little keening noise. Lanius knew what it meant—*I want that. Give it to me!*

Lanius didn't give it to the moncat. He held it just beyond the reach of Iron's little, almost-clawed hands. The moncat swiped at it, but missed. Those amber eyes sent Lanius a baleful stare.

He'd seen that before. The glare had more force than an ordinary cat's pique; Lanius still wasn't impressed. Iron was going to do what Lanius wanted, not the other way around.

So he thought, anyhow. Then, as Iron was coming down to take the tidbit, the door to the moncat's room opened. A servant said, "Excuse me, Your Majesty, but—"

Quick as a wink, Iron streaked past the startled servitor and out into the hallway.

"You idiot!" Lanius shouted.

"Your Majesty!" the servant said reproachfully. Lanius was almost always polite to the servants, more as though they were equals than subjects.

Not here. Not now. "You idiot!" the king said again, even louder. "By the gods, Bubulcus, don't just stand there! Help me catch him!"

"Which way did he go?" Bubulcus asked. "I wasn't paying any attention to the stupid—" He broke off.

"He could be anywhere by now!" Lanius groaned. "Come on!" He pushed by Bubulcus and looked up and down the hallway. Iron had already turned at least one corner, for Lanius couldn't see the beast. Down on the ground, the moncat was about as quick and nimble as an ordinary cat. And once Iron found somewhere to climb . . . Lanius groaned again. "If he gets away, you'll be sorry," he told the servant.

Bubulcus turned pale. Lanius had always been mild, but he'd read in histories and chronicles about things some of his predecessors had done to serving men and women who'd displeased them. He doubted Bubulcus had read any of those things. He had no idea whether Bubulcus could read at all. But stories of what kings in a temper might do had probably passed from one generation of palace cooks and sweepers and tailors to the next.

"Come on!" Lanius said. "Let's go after him." He started up the hall-way. He wasn't sure he was going in the right direction. All he knew was that he had no chance at all of catching Iron if he just stayed where he was. If he went *somewhere,* he had an even-money chance of proving right.

And he did prove right. A startled squawk from a serving woman up ahead told him he'd picked the proper direction. When he rounded the corner, he almost ran over her—she was a laundress, bending to pick up linens she'd dropped. "That horrible, gods-cursed thing nipped my ankle when it ran by," she said, "and everything went flying. If I got a shoe into its ribs, *it'd* go flying, let me tell you it would."

"A good thing you didn't, then," Lanius said. "Come on, Bubulcus. You, too, girl. Worry about the laundry later. Iron is more important."

"I can't imagine why," the laundress said, but she came.

Before long, Lanius led a procession of seven or eight servants through the corridors of the royal palace, all of them shouting and pointing and tripping over one another. The moncat darted and dodged and scurried and, once, ran back through all the pursuers.

Iron swarmed up a tapestry toward the ceiling. Lanius cursed as Iron sprang out from the wall, seized the stem of a candelabra, swung up to a cornice—and then discovered he had nowhere else to go.

The king murmured a silent prayer of thanks that Iron hadn't knocked down the candelabra. All those burning candles falling . . . Lanius shivered. The whole palace might have gone up.

Iron, meanwhile, snarled and bared needle-sharp teeth at the panting king and the servants who'd brought it to bay. "Easy, there," Lanius said soothingly. Then he remembered the scrap of meat he'd been about to feed the moncat. He looked down. Sure enough, he'd never dropped it. He held it out to Iron. "Here, boy."

"Which it doesn't deserve, not after all the trouble it's caused," Bubulcus said.

"Who helped him?" Lanius retorted. "What wouldn't wait?"

"I just wanted to know what you intended to wear to the reception tonight," Bubulcus answered.

"And for that you turned the whole palace upside down?" Lanius wanted to hit the servant over the head with a rock. "You *are* an idiot."

"Well, how was I supposed to know the miserable moncat would run wild?" Bubulcus sounded indignant.

So did Lanius. "Why do you suppose there's a rule against bothering me when I'm in with any of the moncats, not just Iron?"

"I don't know why you have the stupid creatures in the first place. What are they good for?"

"Thank the gods I don't ask the same question about you," Lanius replied. He held out the strip of meat to Iron. The moncat reached for it with little sharp-nailed hands. Lanius pulled it back out of reach. Iron's eyes flashed. Lanius took no notice. He let Iron see the meat and smell it.

"Rowr?" the moncat said.

Lanius took another step back. Iron jumped down to his shoulder. The moncat's hands and thumbed feet gripped Lanius' tunic. Its nails weren't out. One hand reached for the piece of meat.

This time, Lanius let the moncat have it. He got a firm grip on Iron. The moncat, intent on tearing at the meat, didn't notice till too late and wasn't too upset when it did notice.

"I think that's that," Lanius told the servants. "I *hope* that's that. Thank you all for your help. Well, almost all." He sent Bubulcus a last sour look.

"*I* didn't do anything, I'm sure," Bubulcus protested.

"Yes, you did—you opened that miserable door," Lanius answered. He looked down at Iron. "It's a good thing I managed to lure you down, or Bubulcus would have found out what trouble really is."

The moncat purred.

Grus drummed his fingers on the top of the table behind which he sat. "One of these days," he said, "I have to do something about the nobles. If another count takes it into his head to raise a rebellion like Corvus and Corax's, he'll probably have the men to do it. They all want to hang on to their peasants and keep the tax money that should come in to the city of Avornis."

Nicator and Hirundo both nodded. "That's true. Every word of it's true, by the gods," Nicator said. "Those bastards all think they're little kings. They don't care what happens to Avornis, as long as they get to do what they want."

"True enough," Hirundo said. "But what can the man who really *is* King of Avornis do about it?"

"There ought to be laws against letting nobles buy up small farmers' land and turning the farmers into their own private armies," Grus said.

Even Nicator, normally the most tractable of men, gave him an odd look then. "Who ever heard of a law like that?"

"I don't think anybody's ever heard of anything like that," Hirundo added.

"I suppose not." But Grus kept right on drumming his fingers. "Maybe somebody *ought* to hear of a law like that."

Nicator looked unhappy. "I can't think of any faster way to get nobles up in arms with you. If you sent out a law like that, you might touch off the uprisings you were hoping you'd stop."

"He's right, Your Majesty," General Hirundo said.

"Maybe he is," Grus said. "But maybe he isn't, too. What we have now *is* a problem, no doubt about it. Maybe we'd have another problem with a law like that—"

"By the gods, you'd have a problem getting the nobles to pay any attention to a law like that," Nicator said.

No doubt he was right there. Still, Grus said, "We ought to do *something,* or try to do something, anyhow. Leaving the farmers at the mercy of the nobles isn't doing Avornis any favors. And if we're going to put in that kind of law, when better than now? After we've beaten Corvus and Corax, the rest of the big boys out in the provinces will be on their best behavior for a while."

"Till one of them decides he can win in spite of everything," Hirundo said. "How long will that take?"

"If we start hitting them with new laws, maybe it'll take longer," Grus said.

"Or maybe it'll set 'em off," Nicator said. "That's the chance you take."

Grus sighed. "I don't think I've done anything but take chances since I ended up with a crown on my head. If I hadn't taken chances, I'd probably be dead now. I'm going to take some more."

He didn't try to draft laws on his own. He wanted no room for doubt in them, which meant he needed to deal with Avornis' chief lawmaster, a gray-bearded man named Sturnus. The lawmaster had big, bushy eyebrows. They both jumped when Grus spelled out what he wanted. "You aim to keep the nobles in check through *laws?*" he said. "How unusual. How . . . creative."

"Cheaper than fighting another civil war," Grus observed. "I hope it'll be cheaper, anyhow."

"That is what the law is for," Sturnus said. "Letting people do this, that, and the other thing instead of fighting, I mean."

"Let's hope it works that way," Grus said. "I think it's worth a try. If we make a few nobles hurt, maybe the rest will remember the local farmers owe allegiance to me first—and so do they."

"I'm sure stranger things have happened," Sturnus said. "I trust you will forgive me, though, if I can't remember where or when."

"You don't think the law will do what I want, then?" Grus asked.

The lawmaster shrugged. "I don't think it will do all of what you want. Laws rarely work exactly the way the people who frame them intend. This one may well do *some* of what you want. The question is, Will that be enough to satisfy you?"

"We'll find out," Grus replied. "If it doesn't work—and if I win against whatever rebellions it causes—I'll tinker with it."

"That strikes me as a wholesome attitude," Sturnus said. "How soon would you like to see a draft of your proposed law?"

"Tomorrow will do," Grus answered. Sturnus laughed. Grus didn't. "I wasn't joking, Your Excellency. Did I say something funny?"

"You said—tomorrow," Sturnus replied. "I didn't think you were serious."

"I'd intended to ask for this afternoon, but I thought that might be too soon," Grus said. "Why? When did you have in mind giving me the new law?"

"In a couple of months, as I got around to drafting it," Sturnus answered. "After all, winter is coming on. Nothing much will happen out in the provinces till spring at the earliest." By the way he spoke, nothing that happened out in the provinces was likely to matter much anyhow.

"What are you working on that's more important?" Grus held up a hand before Sturnus could say anything. "Let me ask you that a different way. What are you working on that's more important than something the King of Avornis tells you to do?"

Sturnus started to give a flip reply. Grus could see as much. But the lawmaster wasn't stupid. As Grus asked it, the question had teeth—sharp ones. Sturnus saw them before they closed on him. He said, "When you put it like that, Your Majesty, you'll have it before the sun sets tomorrow."

Grus smiled. "Good. I knew I could count on you."

*　　　*　　　*

Lanius wished he could be angrier at Grus. The only thing he found wrong with the law protecting the peasantry from the nobles of Avornis was that he hadn't thought of it himself—and hadn't had any share in drafting it. He went to Grus to complain. "Am I of age, or not?" he asked.

"You certainly are, Your Majesty," Grus answered, polite as usual.

"Am I not King of Avornis?" Lanius persisted.

"You wear the crown. You have the title. What else would you be?" Grus said.

"A statue?" Lanius said. "A clothier's mannequin? Something of that sort, surely. Being King of Avornis means more than crown and title. The King of Avornis rules the kingdom. Do I rule Avornis?"

Grus—King Grus—had the grace to look faintly embarrassed. "Well, Your Majesty, you do need to remember, you're not the only King of Avornis right now."

"Yes, I'd noticed that," Lanius said dryly. "Do I rule half of Avornis? The north, maybe, with you ruling in the south? Or the east, with you in the west? No? Do I rule *any* of Avornis? Any at all?"

"You reign over the whole kingdom," Grus said. "You get all the respect you deserve—every bit of it."

"I point out to you, there is a difference between reigning and ruling," Lanius said, his voice under tight control. "Who *rules* the Kingdom of Avornis?"

Grus had never been a man to back away from saying what he thought. Today proved no exception, for he replied, "Who rules Avornis? I do, Your Majesty. We've had this talk before, you know, though you likely didn't understand what it meant quite so well back then. But I'd say I've earned the right. I was the one who drove the Thervings back into their own land—"

"Till they come over the border again," King Lanius broke in.

"Yes, till they do." Grus, to Lanius, sounded maddeningly calm. "I was the one who put down Corvus and Corax. You helped some there, and I thank you for it, but I was the one who did most of the work. If the Menteshe turn troublesome down in the south—and there's always the chance they will—who's going to lead the fighting there? I will. Of the two of us, I'm the one with the experience. Are you going to tell me I'm wrong?"

However much Lanius wished he could, he knew he couldn't. But he didn't try to hide his bitterness as he answered, "How am I supposed to get experience if you hold everything in your own hands? The more you do that, the less chance I have to win any experience, and the more you'll be able to blame me for not having it."

"I don't blame you," Grus said. "You can't help being young, any more than my son can." He sucked in an unhappy-sounding breath; he wasn't blind to what Prince Ortalis was, though he didn't seem able to change him. "No, I don't blame you a bit. But that doesn't mean I'm going to climb down off the horse and hand you the reins. Avornis, right now, is mine, and I intend to keep it."

"You *are* blunt, aren't you?" Lanius said.

"It saves time," Grus answered. "In the end, time is all we really have. Suppose you tell me what you think of this whole business, and then we'll go on from there."

If I told you what I thought, I'd end up in the Maze, probably in whatever sanctuary's housing Corvus these days, Lanius thought. On the other hand, how could Grus not already know what he thought? He said, "I don't like it a bit. Would you, in my place?"

"Probably not," Grus said. "If our places were flip-flopped, I'm sure you'd keep as close an eye on me as I do on you."

Sometimes Grus could deliver a message without coming right out and saying it. He'd just done that now, or so Lanius thought. And this message was something like, *Don't try overthrowing me, because I'll know what you're up to before you get well started.* Lanius wondered how true that was. He decided he didn't want to find out—not right now. "I think we're done here," he said coldly.

"Yes, I expect we are." Grus sounded cheerful. Why not? He had the power Lanius thought should be his by right of birth. "Any time you've got troubles or worries, Your Majesty, don't be shy. Bring 'em to me. I'll help you if I can."

"I'm sure of it," Lanius said. "You certainly helped me here."

" 'If I can,' I told you," Grus replied. "For some things, there's no answer that makes everybody happy. That's where we are right now, I'm afraid."

"Yes. That's where we are. Your Majesty." Lanius stalked away. He listened hard, wondering if Grus would laugh out loud as he left. Grus didn't. As far as he could be, he was sensitive to Lanius' pride. Sometimes, that stung worse than outright contempt.

What can I do to Grus? Lanius wondered. *How can I pay him back? Can I pay him back at all?* When Grus first took his share of the throne—and took over the whole job of running Avornis—he'd warned against trying to unseat him. He'd just done it again. And he'd shown himself a man whose warnings deserved to be taken seriously. Most of the time, Lanius kept that in mind.

Now . . . Now he was too furious to care. He stormed into his own living quarters and glared at Sosia for no more reason than that she was her father's daughter. She, fortunately, had enough on her mind not to get angry at him. "I'm glad to see you," she told him. "I've got news."

"What is it?" he growled.

Even his tone didn't faze her. He wondered if he were altogether too mild-mannered for his own good. Then she said, "I'm going to have a baby."

"Oh," he said, and no doubt looked very foolish as he said it. "That's—wonderful," he managed, and then, "Are—are you sure?"

"Of course I am," Sosia answered, as indulgently as she could. "There are ways to tell, you know. Now—what were you all upset about a minute ago?"

"Oh, nothing," Lanius said, and discovered he meant it. How could he stay furious at the other king when he'd just gotten Grus' daughter pregnant? He supposed some men could have managed it, but he wasn't one of them. He hugged Sosia. "That *is* wonderful news—especially if it turns out to be a boy."

She nodded. "What if it's a girl?" she asked, worry in her voice.

"In that case, we just have to try again," he replied, and grabbed her as though he intended to do that there and then. Sosia laughed. Maybe that was happiness, maybe just relief.

CHAPTER EIGHTEEN

The yellow-robed cleric named Daption bowed low before King Grus. "Your Majesty, I'm sorry to have to tell you that Arch-Hallow Bucco met the common fate of all mankind last night. The end must have come easily—he went to bed in the evening, and no one could wake him come morning."

"That *is* an easy passing," Grus agreed. "My father was lucky in his going, too. I wonder if I will be." He sighed. The gods knew the answer to that, but he wouldn't, not till the day.

"May it be so, Your Majesty," the cleric said, and then, quickly, "May you not need to learn for many years to come. I meant no offense, no ill-wish, no—"

Grus raised a hand. "You didn't offend me. I understood what you meant."

"Your Majesty is gracious," Daption said, relief in his voice. "Uh, have you yet thought about who will follow Bucco as Arch-Hallow of Avornis? There are, of course, several good candidates from among the senior clerics of the capital, and no doubt others in the provinces, as well. Do you know when you will announce Bucco's replacement, or will you ask for advice from the hierarchy before making your choice?"

"Arch-Hallow Bucco was a bold and powerful man," Grus observed. "He always had his own notion of what should be done."

"Indeed he did." The yellow-robed priest sounded proud to have served under such a man. But Grus hadn't meant it for praise. As far as he was concerned, Bucco had stuck his nose where an arch-hallow had no business putting it. Daption coughed a couple of times before continuing, "As I say, Your Majesty, there are several excellent candidates for the position. If you like, we would be pleased to submit to you a list of the possibilities, from whom you may, of course, choose."

"I'm sure you'd be pleased," Grus said. Like the nobility, the priesthood wanted more power for itself and less of what it saw as interference from the Kings of Avornis. Of course, what it saw as interference looked like necessary oversight to Grus, as it had to the kings who came before him. "I won't need a list, though. I know the man I want as arch-hallow."

"Do you?" Daption raised an eyebrow in polite disappointment. "And he is—?"

"His name is Anser," Grus replied.

Daption thought for a moment, then frowned. "I'm very sorry, Your Majesty, but I must confess I do not know the name. From what city does he come?"

"From Anxa, down in the south," Grus said.

"I . . . see," Daption said. "How interesting. Since the Menteshe came, we haven't had so many arch-hallows from that part of the kingdom. Not a few kings have feared to choose southern men because of the possible taint from the Banished One."

"I'm not worried about that here," Grus said firmly.

"I do admire your intrepid spirit, Your Majesty." The yellow-robed cleric made his praise sound like, *I think you're out of your mind, Your Majesty.* His frown hadn't gone away, either. "What is this Anser's rank, if I may make so bold as to ask? Surely he cannot now wear the yellow robe; I believe I know all the clerics of my own rank throughout Avornis. Would you elevate to the arch-hallowdom a man from the green, or even from the black?" He closed his eyes for a moment in well-bred horror at the thought.

Grus sighed. He'd hoped Daption wouldn't make him give all the details so soon, but the other man had, and now there was no help for it. "Anser will be a red-robed priest—which is to say, the Arch-Hallow of Avornis—as soon as he is consecrated," the King of Avornis said.

Daption's eyes grew wide. "Do you mean to say he is . . . a secular man?" the priest whispered. "You would place a secular man on the arch-hallow's throne? That is—highly irregular, Your Majesty."

"Maybe so," Grus said, "but he has one virtue that, to me, outweighs all the rest."

"And that is?" The priest sounded as though it couldn't possibly be anything important enough to counterbalance his secularity.

"He's my son," Grus answered. To him, that counted for more than anything else.

"Your son?" Daption echoed. "But I thought Prince Ortalis was your only son."

"Prince Ortalis is my only legitimate son," Grus said. "Anser was . . . just one of those things that sometimes happens. He's part of my family, though, and I intend to take care of him."

"Is that what you call it, Your Majesty?" the cleric demanded. "But what of our holy faith?"

"I think our holy faith will do quite well, thanks," Grus said. "The gods have children. I don't expect King Olor and Queen Quelea will be too upset because I had one out of wedlock. Queen Estrilda has forgiven me." *Mostly,* he added to himself.

"But . . . Your Majesty!" Daption seemed to be struggling to put his protest into terms that wouldn't infuriate the King of Avornis. "Appointing a . . . a boy who has lived a . . . a secular life to the post of arch-hallow offends the dignity of all holy clerics who have held the post since the beginning of time."

"After Anser's been arch-hallow for a while, he'll be as holy as any other cleric, don't you think?" Grus asked mildly.

"But—" Daption tried again.

This time, Grus cut him off with a sharp question. "Are you telling me I haven't got the right to appoint the man I want as Arch-Hallow of Avornis? Is that what you're saying?"

"I'm not, Your Majesty." The yellow-robed priest did have the sense to see he was treading on dangerous ground. But he went on, "Appointing such a person to such a position, though, is . . . is unprecedented."

Grus gave him a cheerful smile. "Maybe it was. It isn't anymore, is it? I've just created a precedent for it, haven't I?"

As King of Avornis since he was a little boy—as the descendant of a dozen generations of Kings of Avornis—Lanius naturally had a strong sense of dignity. The idea that his bastard half-brother-in-law should be named Arch-Hallow of Avornis offended that sense.

"Have you ever met this Anser?" he asked Sosia.

His wife shook her head. Before she answered, she yawned. Early in her pregnancy, she was sleepy all the time. "No," she said. "Are you surprised? I know *of* him, but that's all."

"Has your father—his father—ever met him?"

Sosia shrugged. "I don't know for certain. I don't think so, but I couldn't take oath on it."

"Well, who on earth would appoint someone he doesn't even know to such an important job?"

"No one appoints kings at all. They just happen," Sosia said pointedly. As Lanius was a king who had just happened, that struck home. His wife went on, "The kingdom seems to get through with good kings and bad ones and indifferent ones. Do you think it can't survive with Anser as arch-hallow?"

"No," Lanius admitted. "But couldn't your father have picked a better man for the spot, since he does get to choose?"

"Better how?" Sosia asked.

"Wiser. More holy. Older. Anser can't even be as old as I am, can he?"

"I don't think so, not quite," Sosia said. "Maybe that wasn't what Father meant by 'better,' though. Maybe he cared more that Anser would stay loyal to him. Family counts for the world with Father. If you don't know that, you don't know anything about him."

Lanius started to make a sarcastic remark about Ortalis, but changed his mind at the last minute. Sosia had a point. Bucco, loyal only to himself, had menaced the crown and Lanius' grip on it as long as he lived. What Lanius *did* say was, "Well, maybe you're right. But what am I supposed to tell this Anser when he comes to the city of Avornis?"

"How about, 'Welcome to the capital'?" his wife suggested. "How about, 'I hope you do a good job as arch-hallow'?"

Since Lanius had no better ideas, those were the first two things he did tell Anser when, not quite a month later, Grus' bastard son arrived from the south. "Thank you so very much, uh, Your Majesty," Anser replied. His eyes were enormous with wonder at where he found himself. But for that, he looked much like a younger version of Grus—looked more like him, probably, than either Sosia or Ortalis, both of whom had a good deal of Estrilda in their features.

"What do you know about the priestly hierarchy?" Lanius asked him, coming up with a question of his own.

"Not much," Anser said frankly. "I would worship down in Anxa. Everybody down in the south worships hard. With the Menteshe and the

Banished One so close, we know the gods are our hope. But I never thought of being a priest, let alone arch-hallow, till . . . till Father sent word for me to come here."

He seemed open and friendly and easy to like, none of which Lanius had expected. The king asked, "What did you want to do, then?"

"I was apprenticed to my uncle—my mother's brother. He's a miller, with the biggest mill in Anxa. He has four daughters and no son, so I suppose it might have been mine one day. And I like to hunt—I really like to hunt, and I'm a dead shot with a bow—and I'd love to breed horses if I had the money."

Lanius tried very hard not to smile. He didn't think he'd ever met such an . . . ordinary person in all his life. "If the Arch-Hallow of Avornis doesn't have the money to do whatever he wants, I don't know who would," he remarked.

Anser's eyes got wider yet. Lanius hadn't thought they could. "Really?" the young bastard breathed. "That never occurred to me. Do you suppose I'd have the time to go out hunting, too?"

"If you want to, I think you might," Lanius answered. "Except for a king"—he couldn't say *except for the King*, not when Avornis had two—"who could tell the arch-hallow no?"

"Really?" Anser said again. "You have to understand, Your Majesty, I never thought about any of this till Father told me to come here. I've thought about it since, of course, but I don't know enough about what I'll be doing to have my thoughts make a whole lot of sense, if you know what I mean."

"What do you *think* you'll be doing?" Lanius asked.

"Whatever Father wants me to, I expect," Anser said. His grin made that disarming. "That's why he chose me for the job, isn't it?"

"Probably," Lanius said. "What do *you* think about it?"

"It's all right with me," Anser said. "Father always took the best care of me he could. He didn't pretend I wasn't there, the way a lot of men do with their bastards. What else can I do—what else should I do—but pay him back for that as well as I know how?"

Loyalty, Lanius thought. Grus expected to get it. And, evidently, Anser expected to give it. The whole family put a large weight on it. Lanius shook his head. *Ortalis? I don't think so. I don't think Grus thinks so, either.*

He wondered for a moment why Grus hadn't named his legitimate son Arch-Hallow of Avornis. He wondered for a moment, yes, but no longer. *Grus is liable to want Ortalis to be King of Avornis after him. He probably wishes Ortalis were better than he is, but I'm afraid he wants him to be king any which way.*

Lanius couldn't remember the last time he'd had a more frightening thought.

Not even Grus could make the clerics anoint Anser as arch-hallow in one fell swoop—not when his bastard boy wasn't a priest at the start of the process. If the men who consecrated Anser and appointed him to the priesthood wore sour expressions, they were wise enough to keep their mouths shut except for the necessary prayers. And Grus was wise enough to keep his mouth shut about their expressions.

Having been hallowed, Anser wore a black robe for one day, a green robe on the next, and a yellow one the day after that. Then the clerics could give him a red robe with clear consciences. Grus didn't see that the quick parade through the ecclesiastical ranks mattered very much, but he was wise enough to keep his mouth shut about that, too. He was not a man who ran from trouble, but he wasn't a man who stirred it up for no good reason, either.

Anser's wide-eyed, openmouthed awe at the royal palace, the great cathedral in the city of Avornis, and, in fact, everything about the capital made Grus smile. He didn't quite know what to do about discovering his bastard was a much more likable youngster than his legitimate son.

One thing he didn't do was mention it to Estrilda. One day, though, his wife asked, "Did you think about inviting Anser's mother up here to see him made arch-hallow?"

"No," Grus replied at once—he knew a question with more prickles than a porcupine when he heard one.

"Why not?" Estrilda asked.

"Because I didn't think you'd like it."

"Ah." Estrilda considered that, then nodded. "Well, you were right." He'd thought he'd gotten away as clean as a married man who'd fathered a bastard could hope to with his wife, but then Estrilda asked, "What was she like? Anser's mother, I mean."

Grus could have told her in great detail. Before he started to—*just* before he started to—he realized that question had plenty of prickles, too, even if they were better hidden. As casually as he could, he answered, "Do you know, it was so long ago I hardly remember. I was drunk when it happened, anyhow."

Estrilda didn't find any more porcupinish questions for him, so he supposed he'd given the right answer to that one. He also supposed she didn't know he'd tried to take Alca to bed with him after her magic had helped him end Count Corvus' rebellion. Had she known, she would have expressed her detailed opinion about it—Grus was sure of that. Estrilda had never been shy.

A couple of days later, still wearing his red robes, Anser came to the palace and asked, "Now that I'm arch-hallow, what do you want me to *do?*"

"See that things run on an even keel," Grus told him. "Don't let clerics meddle in politics—they don't belong there. Past that, whatever you please, as long as you don't make a scandal of yourself."

"I'll try," Anser said. "But I don't know anything more about the gods than what the priests down in Anxa taught me when I was little."

"That should be plenty," Grus answered. "Be good yourself, and expect the priests to be good, too. If you find some who aren't—and I'm sure you will—then talk to me, and we'll figure out what to do about them."

His bastard son nodded. "All right. I'll do that. Thanks, uh, Your Majesty."

"Go on," Grus said, liking him very much. "Just do the best you can, and everything will be fine."

Not even Estrilda had an easy time disliking Anser. "He's . . . sweet," she admitted grudgingly.

"He is, isn't he?" Grus said. "And the other thing is, with any luck at all, I won't have to worry about who's arch-hallow and whether he'll give me trouble for the next twenty or thirty years." He liked fixing things so they stayed fixed.

He wished he could fix things with the Thervings as readily as he'd fixed the arch-hallowdom. But Anser was cooperative. Fierce old King Dagipert wasn't. With the coming of spring came another invasion from the west.

Lanius said, "Last year, you told me you couldn't fight Dagipert with all your strength because of Corvus' rebellion. There's no rebellion now. Will you fight him with everything we have?"

Grus didn't want to fight Dagipert with everything he had. He feared the Thervings would thrash the Avornan army, as they'd already thrashed it too many times. He needed a force that could stand up against them. He was building it, yes, but he knew the job was far from over.

But he didn't want to look like a coward before his fellow king—or before all of Avornis, either. So he answered, "I'll do everything I can, Your Majesty, to keep the Thervings from ravaging us the way they've done before."

Lanius was harder to satisfy with a bland generality than he might have been. He asked, "What exactly does that mean?"

Since Grus didn't know exactly what it meant, he answered, "You'll see. Part of what we do—part of what we're able to do—will depend on what King Dagipert does, you know."

He didn't think that completely satisfied the younger man, either. But Lanius held his peace. *He's seeing how much rope I've given myself,* Grus judged. For the kingdom's sake as well as his own, he hoped he could make good on what he'd promised.

To General Hirundo, he said, "When you move against the Thervings, do your best to keep them on land where they've already gone pillaging two years in a row. The sooner they get hungry, the sooner they'll start thinking about going home."

"I'll try," Hirundo said. "They don't have much in the way of a supply train, and that's a fact."

"No, they don't," Grus agreed. "They keep themselves going by eating the countryside bare, like any locusts."

Hirundo laughed. "That's funny."

Grus shook his head. "Maybe it would be, if the Thervings weren't so dangerous. But they are, worse luck."

"We beat 'em last year." The general sounded confident enough. "I don't see any reason why we can't do it again."

"I see one," Grus said, "and that is that we *did* beat them last year."

"I don't follow you." Hirundo frowned, perhaps to show how much he didn't follow. "Now that we have beaten them, the men will know they can do it. They should have an easier time, not a harder one."

"Maybe you're right. I hope you're right," Grus said. "But the other thing you have to remember is, Dagipert's trouble. He knows we beat his Thervings last year, too, and you can bet he's had steam coming out of his ears ever since. He's smart and he's tricky and he's nasty. If he hasn't spent all winter trying to come up with some sneaky way of making us pay for what we did to him last year, I'd be amazed."

"Ah." Now Hirundo nodded. He seemed to decide nodding wasn't enough, so he bowed, too. "You're pretty smart and tricky and nasty yourself, Your Majesty. Trying to figure out what the other bastard's going to do before he does it is always a good idea, but how often do people really sit down and think that through?"

"They ought to," Grus said. There, he was sure, Lanius would agree with him. He wished he and the young king could find more things to agree about.

Hirundo, meanwhile, let out a scornful snort. "How often do people do what they ought to do? If they did, what would clerics use for sermons?"

"A point. A distinct point," Grus admitted.

"Maybe you ought to take the field again, Your Majesty," Hirundo said. "If anybody can outthink Dagipert, you're the one."

Grus hadn't intended to. At the suggestion, though, he stroked his beard in thought. "Maybe I will," he said at last. "I hadn't planned on it, but maybe I will."

Sosia beside him, King Lanius watched King Grus ride out of the city of Avornis at the head of his army, hurrying off to fight the Thervings. "I hope he'll be all right," Sosia said anxiously.

"So do I," Lanius said. His wife hoped Grus would be all right because Grus was her father and she loved him. Lanius hoped Grus would be all right because, if he weren't, some disaster would have come down on the army he led, and on the Kingdom of Avornis. Lanius didn't love Grus. He didn't think he ever would. He'd acquired some—well, more than some—reluctant respect for his father-in-law's brains and nerve, but love? He shook his head. Not likely.

He glanced over toward Sosia. Her arms were folded across her belly. They lay there more easily than they would have not long before. She had more belly than she'd had not long before. The more she bulged, the more the reality that she was going to have a baby sank in for Lanius. *Let it be a son,* he thought. *Let the dynasty go on. I'll worry about Ortalis after my son is born.*

Soldiers closed the great gates of the city after Grus' army passed out of it. A carriage took Lanius and Sosia back to the palace. Another one took Estrilda and Ortalis. Lanius got on well enough with his mother-in-law, but he was glad not to travel in the same carriage as Ortalis.

At the palace, Sosia and Estrilda started chattering. Ortalis went off to do whatever he did. Whatever it was, Lanius didn't want to know. He himself went looking for Marshal Lepturus.

"Hello, Your Majesty," the commander of the royal bodyguards said when Lanius found him just coming out of the palace steam bath. "Trying to warm up my old bones, see if they'll move a little smoother."

Lanius started to say, *You're not old.* The words died unspoken. They wouldn't do, even for a polite compliment. Lepturus had commanded the bodyguards when Lanius' father ruled Avornis, and he'd been commanding them for some time before King Mergus died. He remained sturdy, but his wrinkled, age-blotched skin, bald head, and snowy beard told him their own tale. Lanius wondered uncomfortably if the same thing would happen to *him* one day. He shivered, as though winter had suddenly run an icy finger along the ridge of his spine.

"Here." Marshal Lepturus' joints creaked and crackled as he sat down on a marble bench outside the door to the steam bath. "What can I do for you?"

Lanius sat down beside him. He looked around before he answered. No servants were in sight. He spoke in a low voice—fortunately, Lepturus' ears, unlike Nicator's, still worked fine. "Now that Grus has left the city, I want your help with something."

The guards commander leaned toward him. "What have you got in mind? I'm listening." He too spoke so quietly, no one but Lanius could possibly have heard him.

"I want to bring my mother back from the Maze," Lanius said.

Marshal Lepturus looked at him for a long time before answering, softly and sadly but very definitely, "No."

"What?" Lanius couldn't remember the last time Lepturus had said that to him, certainly not on anything this important. "In the name of the gods, why not?"

"Do you aim to fight your own civil war against King Grus, Your Majesty?" Lepturus asked. "We've been over that ground before, you know."

"Civil war? No, of course not," Lanius said. "All I want to do is set my mother free."

"That may be all you want, but that's not all you'd get." Lepturus spoke with mournful certainty. "What's Grus going to do when he hears Queen Certhia's back in the royal palace, eh? She *did* try to kill him, you know. He's bound to figure she'll try it again, first chance she gets. Wouldn't you, in his boots?"

"It could be all right," Lanius said. "It really could. He's King Grus now. Nobody would try to take that away from him. Things aren't the same as they were before."

He was trying to convince himself as well as Lepturus. He believed what he was saying. Lepturus, plainly, didn't. "If you bring your mother back, one of two things happens. Either she ends up dead—and maybe you along with her, depending on how it all works out—or Grus ends up dead. Those are your choices. I know which way I'd bet, too."

"Wouldn't *you* back me?" Lanius yelped. Lepturus' saying no shook him to the core.

"I shouldn't, not if you go ahead and try anything that stupid," Lepturus said. "I won't help you get your mother. I'll tell you that right now, straight out. If you do somehow get her here without my help . . . you'd be a gods-cursed fool. My help wouldn't do you any good, anyhow. You'd still lose. Certhia'd end up dead, you'd likely end up dead, and I'd likely end up dead, too. Happy day."

"Is this the thanks I give her for giving me life?" Lanius asked bitterly. "Do I let her get old in a convent in the Maze?"

He'd meant it for a rhetorical question. But, to his surprise, Lepturus nodded. "I'm afraid it is, Your Majesty. It's the *best* thanks you can give her. If you bring her out of the Maze, she *won't* get old. That's what I was telling you."

"Yes." Lanius tried a different tack. "Don't you think *she'd* want to take the chance?"

Marshal Lepturus surprised him again, this time by smiling. "Yes, I think she would. I'd bet money on it, matter of fact. She's got nerve—and to spare, your mother does." He sounded very fond—and very knowing. Lanius suddenly wondered if the two of them had been lovers after King Mergus died. He'd never wondered anything like that about his mother before. If they had been lovers, they'd kept quiet about it; there'd never been the faintest whisper of scandal, and people had always been ready to do more than whisper—they'd been ready to shout.

Before Lanius could wonder how to ask or even whether to ask, Lepturus went on, "But that's why you've got to have the sense to leave her where she is. If you bring her out of the Maze—if you bring her back to the city of Avornis—odds are you'll just get her killed. Is that what you want?"

"Of course not. Don't you think I could win? Don't you think *we* could win?"

"You watched Grus against Corvus and Corax. What do you think?"

Lanius winced. While he'd watched Grus against the rebels, he'd been convinced he would lose if he tried to rise up against his father-in-law. When Grus had let him go back to the city of Avornis while besieging Corvus, he hadn't tried to hold the capital against Sosia's father. For one thing, Nicator and a good-sized host of marines had come back to the city of Avornis with him. But, for another, he simply hadn't dared. He'd been too sure he would lose.

Why did he think differently now? Only one answer occurred to him—he would have his mother at his side. Would having Queen Certhia with him make enough difference to let him beat Grus? When he looked at that with his heart, he felt it would. When he looked at it with his head, he knew it wouldn't.

And when he looked at Lepturus . . . The guards commander hadn't quite answered his question before. He asked it again. "You wouldn't help, would you?"

Regretfully, Lepturus shook his head. "I want you to stay alive, and I want Certhia to stay alive, and I've got this low, sneaking yen to stay alive a while longer myself."

"Curse you, Lepturus," King Lanius said wearily. Lepturus bowed his head, as though Lanius had praised him. Maybe, in the end, Lanius had, though he would never have admitted that even to himself. He made a fist and slammed it down on his thigh, again and again. "All right. All right. I'll leave it alone."

"Thank you, Your Majesty. Thank you from the bottom of my heart. You won't be sorry."

"No? I'm sorry already." Lanius rose from the marble bench and hurried away. No one, not even a man who'd known him his whole life long, should have to see a king cry.

"We beat the Thervings last year," Grus told his men. "We beat them when we had a civil war simmering, too. This year, our back is safe. When we meet them again, let's beat them again."

The soldiers raised a cheer. Grus nodded approval. They weren't where he wanted them to be as far as fighting strength went, but they didn't quake in their boots at the prospect of facing King Dagipert's men, either. That would do.

General Hirundo said, "We're gaining, Your Majesty."

"Just what I was thinking, as a matter of fact," Grus answered. "If we can keep from getting overrun and massacred, we'll have ourselves a pretty fair army in a couple of years."

"Er . . . yes." Hirundo gave him a curious look. "That's a cheery thought you had there." He pretended to shiver to show just how cheery he thought it.

"We're going out against the Thervings. We're not staying behind the walls of the city of Avornis," Grus said. "Year before last, we'd have waited for him to quit tearing up the countryside and go away, and we'd have hoped he didn't do *too* much harm while he was tearing things up. So, yes, it is a cheery thought if you look at it the right way."

"Well, I'd rather look at it like that than think of the Thervings overrunning us, I will say," Hirundo replied. "Thinking about that for too long puts a crimp in your day."

"If we think about it, we can think about ways to keep it from happening," Grus said. "That's what I want to do. If we don't think about it . . . If we don't think about it, then we might as well bring Corvus out of the Maze and put him in charge of the army again."

"No, thanks, Your Majesty," Hirundo said. "We tried that once, and it didn't work out very well." He waved. "We can still see just how well it worked."

"I know," Grus said. Here, not far from the Tuola River, the Thervings had done a lot of burning and looting. They hadn't come so far east this year, but the land remained empty, almost barren. They'd killed a lot of the farmers who'd worked it, and carried others back to Thervingia with them. One of these days, when things were safer, Grus knew he would have to try to resettle this land. But not yet. First, he'd have to work to make things safer. And he had a lot of work ahead of him.

Riders came galloping back from the direction of the river. "Thervings!" they shouted. "A whole great swarm of Thervings!"

Grus looked at Hirundo. "Well, General," the king said, "now we have to make sure we don't get overrun and massacred, don't we?"

"That would be nice," Hirundo agreed.

Horns screamed out commands to shift from marching column into line of battle. The men obeyed the trumpets—and their officers' bellowed orders—without fuss and without worry, or at least with no outward show of it. Grus watched them closely. He liked what he saw. Turning to Hirundo, he said, "They're ready enough."

"Yes, I think so, too," the general replied. "Pretty soon, we'll find out how ready the Thervings are."

They didn't have to wait long. The Thervings came forward already in line of battle. The sun glinted from spearheads and sword blades and helmets and chain-mail shirts. The Thervings howled like wolves and roared like tigers. They actively liked to fight. That seemed very strange to Grus. He didn't know a single Avornan to whom it didn't seem strange. Liking to fight was a sure hallmark of barbarians—the Menteshe did, too.

Like it or not, the Avornans sometimes *had* to fight. This was one of those times: Fight or run away. They'd done too much running, and suffered too much for it. Not liking to fight didn't mean they couldn't. Grus hoped it didn't, anyhow. If it did, he was in a lot of trouble.

"Forward!" he shouted, and pointed to the trumpeters. Their horns blared out the same message.

And the Avornan soldiers, horse and foot, went forward. They shouted Grus' name, and Lanius', and Hirundo's, and that of Avornis itself. The first time Grus heard men shouting his name, the hair had stood up on the back of his neck with awe and pride. Now that he'd been at the game for a while, he gauged other things, such as how ready to fight they sounded. Again, he found nothing about which to complain.

King Dagipert's men always sounded ready. They sounded so very ready, no sane soldier should have wanted to face them. Grus, sword in hand, wondered what he was doing here. Then he shrugged. If he fell, Ortalis would doubtless try to rule. If Ortalis could, he would. If he couldn't, Lanius would. Who would get rid of whom? *Either way, my line goes on,* the king thought.

He wanted to go on himself. But here he was on horseback, brandishing that sword, galloping toward men who wanted nothing more than to kill him—unless, of course, it was to torture him and then kill him. A sensible man would have galloped in the other direction. Lanius was sensible. Grus, or some large part of him, wished he were.

A big, burly, bearded, braided Therving stood in front of him, holding his ax in both hands. The Therving swung up the ax at the same time as Grus drew back his sword. They both tried to kill each other at the same time, too. The Therving's ax stroke missed—missed by what couldn't have been the thickness of a hair. Grus' sword bit. The Therving howled.

And then Grus was past, and hacking and slashing at more of Dagipert's soldiers. By himself, he was no great warrior, as he knew too well. But he wasn't by himself. He headed hundreds of horsemen, most of them shouting his name. At their head, he was something larger, grander, and altogether more menacing than an ordinary soldier. He and his riders drove deep into the Thervings' ranks, as though nothing in the world—certainly not the men from the Bantian Mountains—could stop them.

This time, that turned out to be true. For a while, the Thervings fought with all their usual ferocity. But they weren't used to meeting Avornans who fought at least as savagely as they did. When Grus and his men kept going forward in spite of all the Thervings could do to stop them, panic seeped through the enemy's ranks.

All at once, Grus wasn't striking at men who were trying to cut him down. All at once, there were only Therving backs before him, as Dagipert's host broke and fled.

Half an hour later, his horse stood panting at the eastern bank of the Tuola. Therving corpses lay scattered from the battlefield all the way to the riverbank. If Dagipert's men hadn't had boats in the river, none of them would have gotten away. Grus paused for a long, deep breath. "They won't cross back this year, by the gods," he said. The men with him cheered.

CHAPTER NINETEEN

Lanius had seen Prince Ortalis in a lot of different moods—sullen, sulky, angry, nasty, vicious, cruel. He couldn't ever remember seeing Ortalis with a simple smile of pleasure on his handsome face. "Great sport!" Lanius' brother-in-law exclaimed. "By King Olor's strong right hand, there's no better sport in all the world."

"What's that, Your Highness?" Normally, Lanius said as little as he could to Ortalis. Seeing Grus' son without a sneer on his face, though, made him break his own rule.

"Why, the boar I killed this morning," Ortalis answered. "Would you care to come hunting with me one of these days, Your Majesty?"

He didn't even sound as though he wanted Lanius to be his quarry. He seemed for all the world a man who'd found something he enjoyed and wanted someone he knew to enjoy it, too. To Lanius, though, it was no wonder *boar* and *bore* sounded alike. He shook his head. "No, thanks," he told Ortalis. But then he had the wit to add, "Maybe you'll tell me about the hunt you're just back from."

Ortalis did, in alarming detail. Lanius heard all about flushing the boar from the brush in which it hid, about chasing it on horseback through the woods, about the way its tushes had ripped the guts out of one hunting dog and scored a great wound in another's flank, how Ortalis' spear had gone in just behind the shoulder, how the boar had struggled and bled and finally died.

"Then the beaters and I butchered it," Ortalis finished. He laughed and held up his hands. "I've still got blood under my nails. And how does roast boar sound for supper tonight?" He smacked his lips to show what he thought.

Roast boar sounded good to Lanius, too, and he said so. Prince Ortalis went off, whistling a cheery tune.

He still likes the blood, Lanius thought. *It's in his soul, not just under his fingernails. But if he's killing beasts, maybe that will keep him happy—and keep him from wanting to do anything worse. By the gods, maybe it will.*

When he went to tell Sosia what he'd seen and what he thought of it, she nodded. "Mother and I have been trying to talk Ortalis into going hunting for a while now—Father, too, before he went out on campaign. We had to do it a little at a time, for fear of making him think we were trying to push him into it."

"That's . . . sneaky," Lanius said. "It's a good idea, though, I think. Who came up with it?"

"Father did," Sosia answered. "Mother thought it was a good notion, too, but Father was the one who had it."

"I might have known," Lanius muttered. Grus had a knack for figuring out how to get the better of people—if not one way, then another. Lanius sighed. *He's certainly gotten the better of me.*

He glanced over to Sosia. "How do *you* feel?" he asked. Her belly bulged enormously. The baby would come before long.

"I just want it to be done," she said, and then, sharply, "Stop that!" She looked up at Lanius. "He's kicking me again."

"I figured that out," he answered. Feeling the baby move—now, sometimes, *seeing* the baby move—inside his wife was one of the strangest things he'd ever known. It made everything seem inescapably real.

"Careful in there, Crex," Sosia said. "That hurt." She looked up at Lanius with a rueful smile on his face. "He doesn't know what he's doing."

As always, she called the baby by the name they would give it if it turned out to be a boy. They hadn't even talked about what they might call it if it was a girl. Lanius' answering smile was probably rueful, too, though he did his best to make it seem cheerful. He didn't have mixed feelings about getting kicked, of course. But he did have mixed feelings, and feelings worse than mixed, about naming their son—if he was a son—after

Grus' father. He'd wanted to call a baby boy Mergus, for his own father. He'd wanted to, but Sosia had gotten her way.

Oh, I make a mighty king, don't I? Lanius thought. *I'm so mighty, I can't even give my firstborn son the name I want.*

Sosia said, "When we have another boy, we'll name him Mergus."

Lanius started. "How did you know what I was thinking?"

"Whenever I call him Crex, you look . . . I don't know . . . not quite the way you should. Not quite happy. I want you to be happy, you know."

If she didn't, no one in all the world did. Lanius believed she did. But she didn't care enough to let him call a boy Mergus. He muttered to himself. That wasn't quite right. She *did* care. But she had to weigh other things against what he wanted.

Family, Lanius thought. Hers included not just him but also Grus and Estrilda and Ortalis and, the king supposed, now Arch-Hallow Anser, too. Lanius had seen how much family counted among Grus and his kin. The only exception to the rule he'd found was Ortalis—and he'd never thought of Ortalis as a good example for anyone.

With a sigh, Lanius nodded. "All right." It wasn't, but he had no choice. When he spoke again, he spoke as firmly as though he were a king issuing a decree other people really had to obey. "Our second son *will* be named Mergus."

"Come on!" Grus called to his men. "Keep after them. If we beat them on our side of the Tuola, we drive them out of Avornis altogether. Let's push them back into Thervingia where they belong."

"Campaigning right by the Tuola on our side almost feels like campaigning in Thervingia," Hirundo remarked.

"I know it does," Grus said. "It shouldn't, though. This is just as much Avornan soil as the ground the royal palace sits on. It's closer to the border, so the barbarians keep trying to take it away from us. But it's *ours.*"

"I'm not arguing, Your Majesty." Hirundo grinned. "You'd probably take my head if I tried it."

"I ought to take your head for your silly talk," Grus replied—with a laugh to make sure Hirundo and everyone else listening knew he was joking.

His army certainly seemed to feel it wasn't in Avornan territory, or maybe just that it wasn't in safe territory, when it encamped that night. Even without orders from General Hirundo, the soldiers set out swarms of sentries and chopped down trees and dragged them around the camp to make a palisade that would, at least, slow down any Therving rush out of the darkness.

A courier from the capital rode into camp not long after sunset. "What have you got for me there?" Grus asked when soldiers brought the fellow before him.

"A letter from your daughter, Queen Sosia," the man answered.

"Ah? By the gods, has she had her baby?" Grus demanded. "Tell me at once! At once, I say! Is she well? Is the baby a boy?"

But the courier was shaking his head. "I'm sorry, Your Majesty, but no," he said. "She's not given birth yet. Thinking on what the lady your daughter looks like and remembering my wife, I'd say it'll come any day now, but it hasn't happened yet."

"All right." Grus clamped down on his disappointment. "What is she writing about, then?"

"I'm sorry again, sir, but I don't know," the courier replied. "She gave me the letter sealed, just as you see it, and she didn't tell me why she'd written to you."

"Well, in that case I'll have to find out, won't I?" Grus turned to the soldiers who'd escorted the courier to his pavilion. "He's come a long way and ridden hard. Give him food and wine and a place by a fire to sleep tonight."

As they led the man from the capital away, Grus ducked into his tent. He sat down in a folding chair by a lamp on a light folding table. Breaking the green wax seal on the letter, he unrolled the parchment and began to read.

Hello, Father, Sosia wrote. *King Olor keep you and the army safe. I wish I would have this baby. I think I have been carrying it for the last five years. It feels that way, anyhow.* Grus smiled. His daughter with a pen in her hand sounded the same as she did when she was talking. Sosia didn't put up with much nonsense—her own or anyone else's. She went on, *I really did not write to complain. I wrote because I thought you might be interested to hear that Ortalis has gone out hunting again, and come back happy after the kill. I also thought you might be interested to hear that he and Arch-Hallow Anser, our half brother, went hunting together. They both seemed to have a good time.*

Grus stroked his beard. That *was* interesting. He'd known his bastard boy was a passionate hunter. When he'd started trying to get Ortalis to kill wild things instead of tormenting pets and people, he hadn't connected the one and the other. Evidently his sons had made the connection without any help from him.

Knowing Ortalis for what he was, he wondered if the connection was safe for Anser. After a moment, he decided it was. Ortalis didn't want to be Arch-Hallow of Avornis, and he had to know a bastard couldn't supplant him. That meant Anser was probably in no danger of suffering a hunting accident.

Sosia finished, *This was a fine idea of yours, Father. I wish you had thought of it years ago. I have never seen Ortalis as cheerful as he is these days. May it last. And may I have this baby soon! The next time you hear from me, I think you will be a grandfather. With love—* She signed her name.

After reading through the letter again, Grus slowly nodded. It wasn't the news he'd wanted to hear, but it was good news all the same.

Bronze had just had another pair of kittens. Again, one was male, the other female. That didn't prove moncats always did things so, but made it seem more likely to Lanius. As had Spider and Snitch, the new babies clung to their mother's fur with all four hands and wrapped their tails around her for whatever extra help those could give. He wondered what to name the new ones.

He just watched her. That she accepted, warily.

Someone knocked on the door. "Who's there?" Lanius asked, doing his best to stifle his annoyance at being disturbed here.

"Me, Your Majesty," Bubulcus replied.

Now Lanius snarled much as a moncat would have done. "*Don't* come in," he told the servant who'd let Iron get loose in the palace corridors. "Just tell me what you want."

"Believe me, Your Majesty, I wasn't going to come in," Bubulcus said with such dignity as he could muster. "Not me. Not again. But you have to know, sir—the lady your wife's been brought to her bed."

"Oh!" Lanius said. Baby moncats were one thing—important, yes, but . . . Next to his own firstborn, they were only little animals, after all. "I'm coming."

Bronze didn't seem the least bit sorry to see him go. Even so, he made sure he closed and barred the door behind him when he left. Now that she was a mother again, the female moncat wouldn't be quite so agile as usual, but he didn't want her getting away anyhow. If she escaped, she could still find places to go from which no mere human could easily retrieve her.

Lanius hurried through the palace to the birthing chamber. He'd been born there himself. Since then, the room had been used to store this, that, and the other thing . . . till Sosia realized she was going to have a baby. Then the servants quietly took away crates and barrels and sacks and got the chamber ready for its most important function.

A couple of serving women stood outside the doorway now. "You know you can't go in there, Your Majesty," one of them said. "It isn't customary." She'd never had the chance to tell the King of Avornis what he could and couldn't do before. *It isn't customary,* though, said everything that needed saying.

"Yes, I know that," Lanius said. Ever since his wife got pregnant, people had been telling him what was and wasn't customary. He raised his voice and called, "Are you all right, Sosia?"

"It's not too bad so far," Sosia answered. "My waters broke—that's what they call it—and they brought me in here to . . ." She paused. After half a minute or so, she went on, "That was a pang. It wasn't much fun, but I could stand it."

"Have you sent for the midwife?" Lanius asked the serving women.

They both nodded. The one who'd spoken before sounded a little put out as she replied, "We certainly have, Your Majesty. *And* we sent a messenger to the arch-hallow, to ask him to pray for Her Majesty."

Would the prayers of Grus' bastard sway the gods? They might, Lanius supposed—after all, Anser was praying for his half sister. Still, it was irregular.

"*Here* comes the midwife," the other maidservant said, pointing up the corridor. "Her name's Netta, Your Majesty. She's the best one in the city."

"I should hope so," Lanius said; that the Queen of Avornis should have anything but the best in any way had never crossed his mind.

Netta was somewhere in middle age, with one of those strong faces that looked little different at thirty-five and sixty. Plainly, she had no use—or, better, no time—for nonsense. "Hello, Your Majesty," she said, startling Lanius by speaking to him as one equal to another. "Before long, you'll have yourself a little boy or a little girl. I expect everything to go just fine."

"Good," Lanius said. "Why do you expect that?"

"Because it usually does. If it didn't, we'd run short on people, eh?" Netta said. "I'm ready in case things turn sour, but I don't expect them to. You understand what I'm saying? You've got nothing to worry about."

I don't want you joggling my elbow, was what she plainly meant. Lanius asked, "Can I do anything to help you?"

That did surprise Netta, just a little. She shook her head. The big gold hoops she wore in her ears flipped back and forth. "All you have to do is stay out here and wait till you hear the baby yowl." She started into the birthing chamber, then checked herself. "Oh, one other thing—don't get upset by whatever noises you hear before the baby's born. Women in labor aren't quiet—believe me they aren't. All right?"

"All right," Lanius answered—she *did* want him to keep out of her hair. But what else could he do? He felt singularly useless.

Netta eyed him, as though to make sure he meant what he said. At last, satisfied, she nodded. Into the birthing chamber she went. For good measure, she closed the door behind her. *She didn't need to do that,* Lanius thought. *I wasn't going to look in. I don't think I was, anyhow.*

She'd also shut the door on the two serving women, of course. One of them asked, "May I get you a chair, Your Majesty?"

"Please." Lanius wouldn't have thought of sitting down if the serving woman hadn't suggested it. He'd expected to pace back and forth till Sosia delivered their child, however long that took. How long *would* it take? He didn't know. This was the first birth with which he'd ever concerned himself. Some went faster than others—he did know that much.

When the servant came back with a chair, he perched nervously on the edge of it. Then he got up and started pacing again. He paced for a while, sat for a while, paced for a while. He expected to hear strange noises from the birthing chamber. For a long time, though, he heard nothing at all, except occasionally the midwife's voice or his wife's coming faintly through the closed door.

Word of Sosia's confinement spread through the palace. Estrilda came to the birthing chamber. The serving women let *her* inside, which irked Lanius. Netta didn't throw her out, either, which irked him more. *What a stupid custom,* he thought. *Just because I'm a man, that doesn't mean I'm worthless.*

A great many Avornan customs kept women from doing things they might have done. A great many customs assumed they were worthless, or else simply ignorant. Lanius had never stopped to wonder about those. Why should he have? They didn't pinch him.

After half an hour or so, Sosia's mother came out again. She nodded to Lanius. "Everything seems to be going as well as it can. Her pangs are coming closer together, the way they should. Netta knows her business, too."

"That's good." Lanius got up from the chair. "Here—sit down." To the serving women, he said, "Bring us another one, please."

"And food, and wine," Estrilda said. "We're going to be here for a while."

The serving woman curtsied to her. "Yes, Your Majesty," she said, and hurried away.

She came back leading a manservant, who carried a chair for Lanius.

The woman bore a tray with bread, a pot of honey, a jar of wine, and two cups. Lanius poured for himself and Estrilda. No indignity to a king's pouring for a queen, especially if she was also his mother-in-law.

"Thank you, Your Majesty." Queen Estrilda was always polite to Lanius. "Here, let me get you some bread. Do you want honey to go with it?"

"Yes, please. Thank you very much." Lanius took the bread, ate half of it, and then said, "You're sure everything's all right?"

"It seemed to be," Estrilda said, as she had before. "These things go on and on for a while before a woman really gets down to business." She looked down into her cup, then softly added, "I remember."

If you didn't remember, I wouldn't have a wife, Lanius thought. *And I wouldn't have Ortalis to worry about. Is that a good bargain, or a bad one?* He couldn't very well ask Estrilda. Instead, he picked a safer question, saying, "How long is a while?"

She shrugged. "Nobody can guess ahead of time. It could be a few hours, or it could be most of a day or even all day. It varies from woman to woman, and it varies from baby to baby, too. We'll just have to wait and see."

"All right." Lanius didn't know what else to say. He'd always wanted definite answers to his questions, but this question didn't seem to have one. He wished it did.

He and Queen Estrilda drank more wine. They finished the loaf of bread. The serving woman brought another, and cheese and sausage to go with it. Lanius had had what amounted to supper before he thought about eating food better suited to a farmer or a soldier than a king. Estrilda seemed to take it for granted. Surely she'd never gone into the field with Grus?

Before Lanius could ask about that, Estrilda said, "Food like this takes me back to the days when we didn't have much. Grus' father was just a guardsman, you know, and *his* father was a peasant down in the south."

"Yes, I know," said Lanius, the twelfth king of his line. He hadn't expected to wed the great-granddaughter of a peasant. Even Princess Romilda of Thervingia had fancier bloodlines than Queen Sosia did. But, while Lanius sprang from a long line of kings, Grus was the one who held the power in Avornis these days. Lanius liked that no better than he ever had, but he knew he couldn't do anything about it.

Darkness fell. Servants lit lamps outside the birthing chamber. Light seeped out from under the closed door, too, so lamps also burned in there. Lanius yawned.

"We should have cots sent down," Estrilda said. "We're liable to be here all night long."

Before Lanius could nod and send the servants to do just that, a groan came from inside the birthing chamber. Netta opened the door and stuck her head out into the corridor. "Now we're getting somewhere," she said briskly. "The opening is wide enough to let the baby out. Another hour, maybe a little more." She started to go back in, then checked herself. "Don't know if it's a boy or a girl, but it has dark hair."

"Oh!" Lanius said. That the midwife might see such a thing before the mother did hadn't crossed his mind.

Queen Estrilda laughed softly. "The midwife always finds out first. It doesn't seem fair—"

"It certainly doesn't," Lanius agreed.

"But it's true, even so," Estrilda said.

More groans came from the birthing chamber, and then something that sounded uncommonly like a shriek. Lanius jumped. "Is she all right?" he asked anxiously.

"I think so," Estrilda answered. "Netta would come out and tell us if anything bad had happened. I hope she would, anyhow." She checked herself. "Yes, I'm sure she would. Women make those noises when they have babies, that's all."

Another cry made Lanius flinch. The last time he'd heard such sounds was from wounded men on the battlefield. Men took their chances there, taking life. Women took theirs here, bringing forth new life.

When Lanius said as much to Queen Estrilda, she only nodded. "Well, of course," she replied, as though surprised that wasn't obvious to him.

He realized it should have been. But it hadn't, not till he heard his own wife cry out in pain giving birth to the child he'd seeded in her. Men took women for granted more readily than the other way round, or so it seemed to Lanius. He wondered what he could do about that. He wondered if he could do anything about it. Since he hadn't noticed something so fundamental till he got his nose rubbed in it, how likely was that? Perhaps better not to dwell on the answer there.

More shrieks came, one hard on the heels of another. Despite her air of confidence, Estrilda went pale. Her lips moved silently. Lanius had begun to read lips; he'd seen it might come in handy every now and then. He still wasn't very good, but he had no trouble recognizing Queen Quelea's name.

After those shrieks, he heard a noise he'd never heard before: half grunt, half scream. It suggested not pain but rather supreme effort. A man trying to lift twice his own weight and knowing he would die if he failed might have made a noise like that. The hair at the back of Lanius' neck prickled up.

Queen Estrilda, by contrast, looked relieved. "She's pushing the baby out," she told Lanius. "That's what that sound means. Everything else was just getting ready. This is what really matters."

Lanius tried to imagine pushing a baby out—tried and felt himself failing. He wasn't physically equipped to understand. But he was, as always, relentlessly curious. "What's it like?" he asked his mother-in-law.

Again, her lips shaped a silent word. This time, it was *Men*. The way she looked saying it made Lanius embarrassed to belong to his half of the human race. But then Estrilda said, "Imagine you've swallowed a big pumpkin—whole. Imagine it's gone all the way through your guts—whole. Now imagine you're squatting over the pot and you've got to get rid of it or burst. *That's* what it's like."

He did his best. He'd always had a vivid imagination, too. "Why on earth would any woman ever do this more than once?" he blurted.

Estrilda looked at him. "That may be the most sensible question I've ever heard a man ask about giving birth," she said. "Because you forget some of it afterward, that's why. Otherwise . . ." She shook her head. "Otherwise we wouldn't do it twice—I'm sure of that—and people would get fewer and fewer, till nobody was left. I suppose the forgetting is Queen Quelea's gift, if you want to call it that."

In the birthing chamber, Sosia made that effort-filled grunting cry one more time. A moment later, Netta shouted. And then the king's hair prickled up in awe, for he heard yet another voice from the birthing chamber—the high, thin, furious wail of a newborn baby.

Netta shouted again. This time, the shout held words. "Your Majesty, you've got yourself a son!"

"Crex!" King Lanius and Queen Estrilda said at the same time. Estrilda leaned over and kissed him on the cheek. Then she got up and dashed into the birthing chamber.

Plaintively, Lanius called, "May I come, too?"

"Wait a minute," the midwife answered. "Here comes the afterbirth now."

Lanius hadn't known what the word meant till he watched Bronze deliver her kittens. In moncats, the afterbirth, like the kittens, was small.

What it would be like in a woman . . . The king wasn't sorry Netta kept him out till she disposed of it one way or another.

In hardly more than the promised minute, she said, "All right, Your Majesty. You can come in now."

When Lanius opened the door, he smelled sweat and blood and dung—maybe Estrilda hadn't been joking about squatting over the pot. If a woman was trying to push out a baby, Lanius supposed it made sense that she would push out whatever else happened to be in there, too.

His wife lay on a low couch, covered by a blanket. She looked as though a brewery wagon had run over her. Her hair flew out in all directions in sweaty, spiky tangles. Her face was pale as whey, except for the black circles under her eyes. She panted as though she'd just finished running five miles. She managed a smile for Lanius, but she almost needed to prop up the corners of her mouth to hold it on her face.

In Netta's arms, Crex started crying again. That reminded the king of the reason all this had gone on. "Let me see him," he told the midwife.

"Here." Before she handed him to Lanius, she said, "You've got to keep a hand or an arm under his neck. You'll need to do that for months yet, till his head's not all floppy anymore. But he looks fine—he's a good-sized boy."

He didn't look good-sized to Lanius; he was no bigger than a moncat. He weighed no more than one, either. His skin was reddish purple, his head squeezed almost into a cone, and his genitals absurdly large for his size. Netta had tied off and cut the umbilical cord; the stump still remained attached to what would become his navel.

He did have five fingers on each hand and five toes on each foot. Lanius carefully counted them all. And, by the noise Crex was making, he had a fine set of lungs. "Are you sure this is how he's supposed to look?" the king asked nervously.

"I asked her the same thing," Sosia said.

"He's fine," the midwife repeated. "Almost all the mothers and fathers having their first one ask me that. He's got everything he should, just the way it ought to be." She sounded very certain. Estrilda nodded, so Lanius supposed it was true. Netta went on, "What he'll want now, I expect, is something to eat."

For a moment, Sosia didn't follow. Then she did. "Oh!" she said. "That means me, doesn't it?" She pushed down the blanket, baring her breasts. Awkwardly, Lanius set Crex on her. She didn't handle the baby much more smoothly than he did. But, though neither the king nor the queen quite knew what to do, the baby did. He rooted till he found Sosia's nipple and began to suck.

Netta smiled. "That's how it's supposed to work, all right."

"Yes," Lanius said softly. He'd done a lot of reading about magic. He'd seen some of what wizards and witches reckoned it to be. Here, though, looking down at his son, he understood the word in a way he never had before.

Some of General Hirundo's cavalrymen led a line of unhappy-looking Therving prisoners past King Grus. Grus nodded. "Send them back over the Tuola," he said. "We can get some useful work out of the ones King Dagipert doesn't bother ransoming."

"Right you are, Your Majesty," a cavalry captain replied. He added something in Thervingian. The prisoners shambled away.

Grus turned to Hirundo and said, "Somewhere else in this province, Dagipert is probably saying the same thing about some sorry Avornan captives his men have taken."

"I know," Hirundo answered. "There's no quit in that man. He's brought more and more men from Thervingia. He doesn't want us getting the notion we can beat him."

"No," Grus agreed. "Nothing comes easy against Dagipert. If he weren't so stubborn, we'd be fighting in Thervingia now—I'm sure of it."

With a sly smile, Hirundo answered, "He's bound to be saying the same kinds of things about you. He must be thinking that if it weren't for that miserable King Grus, he'd be laying siege to the city of Avornis again. Odds are he's right, too."

"Well, maybe," Grus said. "I like to think we can take care of ourselves well enough so that whoever's on top doesn't make all the difference." He liked to think that, but didn't know that it was true.

His horse's hooves thumping, a courier came into camp. "Your Majesty!" he called. "I've got news from the capital, Your Majesty!"

"What kind of news?" Grus asked. One obvious possibility was that he'd finally become a grandfather. That was the news he hoped for, the news he'd been expecting. The news he dreaded was that the Menteshe might have taken advantage of his war against the Thervings to swarm over the Stura River down in the south. It hadn't happened yet, but he knew all too well it could.

By the courier's grin, though, he bore news of the other sort. "Congratulations, Your Majesty!" he said loudly. "Queen Sosia and your grandson, Prince Crex, are both doing as well as anyone might hope."

Hirundo and all the soldiers who heard the fellow burst into cheers. They pressed forward to shake Grus' hand and pound him on the back. He said the first thing that came into his mind, which was, "But I'm too young to be a grandfather."

A grizzled sergeant said, "And it was only last week you were telling people you were too young to be a father, wasn't it?"

Amid laughter, Grus answered, "It certainly seems that way."

"Well, Your Majesty," the sergeant went on, "one of these days, I hope you get to tell everybody who'll listen to you that you're too young to be a great-grandfather." Hirundo and the grinning soldiers nodded and clapped their hands.

"I like the sound of that," Grus said. To show how much he liked it, he tossed the veteran a gold piece. As the sergeant bowed his thanks, Grus went on, "And let's whip the Thervings right out of their shoes, to make sure this province west of the Tuola belongs to little Prince Crex when he puts the crown on his head."

More cheers rang out. Grus knew how chancy things were, how many babies never lived to grow up. He didn't dwell on that thought, not now. Now he could let his hopes and dreams run free—though he didn't want to get too fanciful about ways and means of beating the Thervings. If he did, Dagipert would make him regret it in a hurry.

And Dagipert *did* make him regret it. Maybe the king of the Thervings had heard about little Prince Crex, too. As far as King Dagipert was concerned, Lanius should have been having children by Romilda, not Sosia. After all, Dagipert had spent the past couple of years ravaging northwestern Avornis because Lanius hadn't married his daughter. Before then, Grus supposed, the Thervings had ravaged northwestern Avornis just for the sport of it.

A company of Thervings assailed some of Hirundo's scouts ahead of the main force. Seeing the chance to make the enemy pay for coming out of the woods, Hirundo sent out more horsemen to cut off Dagipert's men. And so they did—till more Thervings, who'd been lurking just inside the trees, rushed out and turned the tables on them.

Some of the Avornans got away. King Dagipert's men cut down a lot of them, though, and then went back into the forest before the main body of Grus' army could come to the riders' rescue. Grus thought about throwing his men after the Thervings, but held back. For all he knew, Dagipert had another ambush waiting if he tried that.

Hirundo blamed himself, saying, "I'm sorry, Your Majesty. It's my fault, nobody else's. I thought I could make the Thervings pay, and Dagipert outsmarted me. That's what happened, no two ways about it."

"Don't get too upset," Grus told him. "Dagipert would have outsmarted me, too, because if you hadn't given those orders I was going to. Every once in a while, the other fellow gets a jump ahead of you, that's all."

"You'd better not let him stay that way, or else you're in trouble," Hirundo said.

"True enough," Grus said. "Now, Dagipert's going to expect us to try to lure him into some kind of ambush to pay him back."

"That's what I'd do," Hirundo declared.

"Then you'd let him stay a jump ahead of you," Grus pointed out. "I don't think he'd bite on any bait we threw him, so I'm not going to throw him any. I'm just going to keep on after him till we beat him and drive him back into Thervingia."

"If we can," General Hirundo said.

Grus nodded. "That's right. If we can."

He sent riders out to knock down as many of Dagipert's scouts as they could find. If the Thervings' king didn't know what was going on around him, he might make a mistake. Dagipert responded by attacking viciously wherever the Avornan horsemen showed themselves in any numbers.

"*Now* maybe we can lure him into a trap," Grus said.

They sent the whole army after a band of horsemen who went up against another of the Thervings' outposts. As Grus had expected, Dagipert struck back at the riders hard, using more of his own men to try to drive off the Avornans. Grus and Hirundo threw the rest of the army into the fight, hoping to bag all those Thervings. But Dagipert had his own reserves waiting.

"We've got a big battle on our hands," Hirundo said. "What are we going to do?"

"I think we'd better fight it, don't you?" King Grus answered. Hirundo nodded. Neither of them had much wanted a full-scale battle there, but Grus saw no way to avoid it, not with his men and the Thervings both pouring into the engagement as fast as they could. It wasn't a proper trap—or, if it was, it had closed on both sides at once.

They hammered at each other all day, neither side giving much ground. Only at sunset did they draw apart. Even then, Grus thought they would clash again the next morning. He ordered his men into line of battle before the sun came up.

But when they went forward, they found that King Dagipert's army had left its position during the night and fallen back toward the west, toward Thervingia. Only then did Grus begin to think he might have won.

CHAPTER TWENTY

As King Lanius had the summer before, he greeted King Grus when Grus' army returned from the west. This time, the army didn't return in gaudy triumph. It had fought hard, and was badly battered. But the Thervings had gone back to their own kingdom. The previous summer, Grus' soldiers had seemed astonished and delighted to have driven off the enemy. This year, Lanius thought, it was more as though they had the Thervings' measure. Maybe that counted for more than a parade through the streets of the city of Avornis.

Lanius wanted to ask Grus what he thought of that, but Grus forestalled him, saying, "Where are Sosia and little Crex?"

"Back at the palace," Lanius answered.

Grus looked unhappy, but then nodded. "Yes, I suppose they would be. Don't want to put a new mother and a little baby through too much. How are they?"

"As well as anyone could hope," Lanius said. Grus smiled, which made him look like anything but a stern soldier. Lanius went on, "I like this business of being a father better than I thought I would. I think Crex looks like me."

"I don't suppose that's anything against the rules," Grus said. "Better he should look like you than me, anyhow. I'll never be what anybody calls handsome, though Sosia's lucky enough to favor her mother's side of the family."

He was right about that. Lanius had already seen how Anser looked more like Grus than either Sosia or Ortalis did. Thinking of Anser and Ortalis, Lanius said, "Your sons are both out hunting again today."

"Are they?" Grus said. "That's good, I think. I hope. Come on. Let's go to the palace."

When they got there, Grus kissed Queen Estrilda. Then he kissed Queen Sosia. And then, at last, he all but slobbered over his grandson. Crex stared up at him with the bemused look he wore a lot of the time. That look had bothered Lanius till he thought about it. It didn't anymore. He'd decided the world had to be a very confusing place for a baby. Everything, everyone, was new. Crex had to figure out what he liked, who his parents were—everything about the world around him, the world in which he suddenly found himself. He didn't even have any words to help him make sense of things. No wonder he looked confused.

To Lanius, Grus had always seemed a hardheaded, hard-hearted man. Not here. Not now. The word that came to Lanius' mind was *sappy*. Grus looked up from Crex at last, a broad, foolish smile on his face. "He's wonderful," he said. "And you're right—I think he does look like you."

Estrilda asked him, "How does it feel, being a grandfather?"

"First thing I said was, 'I'm too young,'" Grus answered. "But, now that I see what I've got here, I take it back. I like the whole business just fine. How about you, dear?"

"Me? Oh, I hate it. I can't stand it at all," his wife said. They both laughed.

"Congratulations on driving the Thervings back again," King Lanius said.

"Oh. The Thervings." Holding Crex, Grus might never have heard of Thervingia. He had to pause and think about Dagipert and the neighboring kingdom. The process was not only visible, it was funny to watch. When it ended, he looked more like the Grus who Lanius usually saw. "Thanks," he said. "Yes, we've bought a respite till the next campaigning season, anyhow. And Dagipert's an old man. One of these days, he'll finally drop dead."

"Prince Berto is a different sort," Lanius said. "I met him when he came here once. I was still a boy then. All he cared about were cathedrals."

"I hope he's still like that," Grus said. "Cathedrals are a very good thing for a King of Thervingia to care about. If he spends his time caring about cathedrals, maybe he won't have the chance to care about invading Avornis."

"That *would* be good," Lanius said. "We could use a few years of peace."

"So we could." When Grus looked down at Crex in his arms, his face softened into a smile once more. "And he could do with growing up in a city that doesn't stand siege every so often. Couldn't you, little one?"

Crex responded to that by screwing up his face and grunting. Estrilda laughed. "I know what he's done!" she said with a laugh.

Grus laughed, too. He sniffed. "Oh, yes—so do I. But one nice thing about being grandparents—and about being king and queen—is that we don't have to clean up the mess ourselves." He handed the baby to a serving woman. She went off to give Crex fresh linen.

"That *is* nice," Estrilda said. "That's very nice indeed."

Lanius took servants for granted. How could it be otherwise? He'd had them at his beck and call ever since he'd learned to talk—and before that, too, as the woman changing Crex attested. Now he eyed Estrilda in some surprise. Had she herself—and maybe Grus, too—changed Sosia and Ortalis? By the way she spoke, perhaps she had. She hadn't been royal all her life. She hadn't, but her grandson would be.

Grus' father, for whom the baby was named, had been a man off a farm in the provinces who'd done modestly well for himself as a guardsman. *His* father had been a peasant of no distinction whatever. And yet Grus ruled Avornis, Sosia was wed to the scion of the ancient dynasty, and little Crex shared that dynasty's blood. Not for the first time, Lanius thought about how different the world was likely to look to a peasant's grandson from the way it looked to him.

Having thought about it, he eyed Grus with a good deal more respect. He himself took the kingship for granted. Why not, when he was the dozenth of his line to hold it? But to Grus, gaining the crown had to feel like climbing a mountain covered with nails and thorns and nettles. And yet he hadn't murdered his way to the throne. He hadn't slain Lanius, and he hadn't even slain Lanius' mother, who'd done her best to kill him.

"Thank you," Lanius said suddenly, out of the blue.

Grus looked back at him as though knowing exactly what he was thinking. And maybe the older man did, for he nodded, set a hand on Lanius' shoulder, and said, "You're welcome." Lanius nodded back. He still wasn't sure he would ever like his overbearing father-in-law, but the beginning of understanding brought with it the beginning of respect.

The peasant bowed low before King Grus. He looked nervous. In fact, he looked scared to death, as any peasant coming before the King of Avornis was liable to look. "It's all right, Dacelo," Grus reassured him. "By King Olor's beard, I promise nothing will happen to you, regardless of whether I decide to do anything to your baron. But I want to hear from your own lips what Fuscus is up to."

"All right," Dacelo said, his tone suggesting it was anything but. "He's buying up our plots of land on the cheap, turning us from freeholders into his tenants. Some men let him, and sell out. Some hold their land as long as they can. And some, like me, figure it's no good either way there and try to make our living somewhere else."

"That's why you came to the city of Avornis?" Grus asked.

"Sure is, sir," Dacelo answered. A secretary taking notes of the conversation coughed. Dacelo turned red. "Uh, Your Majesty," he amended.

"It's all right." Here, Grus was more interested in finding out what was going on than in standing on ceremony. "You know Baron Fuscus was breaking the law I put out after Corvus and Corax rebelled against me?"

Dacelo nodded. "Yes, sir—Your Majesty." He caught himself this time.

"Did anyone in his barony point this out to him?" Grus asked.

"One fellow did," Dacelo replied, and then, after a pregnant pause, "He's dead now."

"Is that so?" the king said, and the peasant nodded again. Grus scowled. "I don't like seeing my laws flouted. Do you suppose Baron Fuscus breaks them because he thinks I don't mean them, or just because he thinks they're wrong?"

"Sir, I think he breaks 'em because he thinks he can get away with it," Dacelo said.

"I think you're dead right, Dacelo," Grus said. "And I think I'm going to have to show Baron Fuscus he's dead wrong."

Despite his bold words, he didn't want to start another civil war on the heels of the last one. He reflected on the old saw about different ways to kill flies, and sent Fuscus an elaborately formal invitation to the royal palace "so that I might gain the benefit of your wisdom."

"Why on earth are you telling him that?" King Lanius demanded. "You don't care what he thinks. You only want to land on him with both feet."

Grus smiled. In a way, seeing his fellow king so naive was reassuring. He wondered whether explaining would be wise. In the end, he decided to, and said, "If I tell him I want to land on him with both feet, Your Majesty, he won't come. If I say nice things to him, maybe he will—and *then* I'll land on him."

Once Lanius understood, he nodded. He might be naive, but he was anything but stupid. "I see," he said. "And if he says he won't come after an invitation like that, he's put himself in the wrong and declared that he's a rebel."

"Just so." Grus nodded, too.

And Baron Fuscus not only came to the city of Avornis, he brought his whole family with him. They rented a large house near the royal palace, as though Fuscus had not the smallest doubt that Grus would want his advice for a long time to come. He had a few bodyguards with him, but only a few, and he left them behind when Grus summoned him to the palace.

"At your service, Your Majesty," Fuscus said after making his bows. He was in his early forties—not far from Grus' age—with a handsome, fleshy face and an unconscious arrogance about him. "You tell me what needs doing, and I'll tell you how to do it." By the way he made it sound, Grus had no hope of doing anything without him.

Hiding annoyance, Grus said, "Well, one problem I have is getting the nobles in the provinces to pay their taxes and to leave their farmers alone."

"Yes, they're a wicked lot, aren't they?" Fuscus said.

"Some of them are," Grus agreed. "You know, I've made laws against that sort of thing."

"Laws are no good," Fuscus told him. "Who pays attention to laws? The weak and the fearful, nobody else. A strong man ignores useless laws and does what he needs—or else what he pleases."

"You enlighten me," Grus said, and Baron Fuscus preened. The king went on, "Is that why *you've* ignored my laws, Your Excellency?"

Fuscus opened his mouth to answer before realizing just what the question was. He looked around. All of a sudden, he seemed to realize he had no guards of his own, and that Grus' men—all of them ex-marines, and thoroughly loyal to their sovereign—surrounded him. His mouth slowly closed.

"You don't say anything," Grus remarked.

"I—I don't really know what you're talking about, Your Majesty." Fuscus no longer sounded so self-assured. He sounded like someone who was lying, and not doing such a good job of it.

"What about the man who reminded you of my laws, the man who's no longer among the living?" Grus asked.

Fuscus went pale. "I still don't know what you're talking about," he said, a little more conviction—or perhaps desperation—in his voice this time.

"I'd like to believe that," Grus said. Fuscus looked relieved. Then Grus continued, "I'd like to, but I can't." He unfolded the parchment on which the secretary had written down Dacelo's charges and read them out in detail, finishing, "What do you have to say about that, Your Excellency?"

"That it's all a pack of lies, Your Majesty," Fuscus declared.

"Then you haven't bought up lands from the farmers around your estates? Then no one who tried not to sell to you suddenly lost his life in strange circumstances?"

"Of course not," the baron said.

"Then if I checked here in the city of Avornis, I wouldn't find any peasants you'd bought out for next to nothing, peasants who sold you their land and came here because they knew something nasty would happen to them if they didn't?" Grus persisted. "I wouldn't find anybody else who knew about this fellow who was murdered by ruffians?"

"That's what I'm telling you," Baron Fuscus said.

"Yes, it is, isn't it?" Grus pulled out more parchments. "But just because you say it doesn't make it so. Here is the testimony of three farmers from your barony, men you bought out in the past six months. They say you did do what you say you didn't. I've had wizards check what they say, too. The wizards say they're telling the truth. Shall I have wizards check you, too?"

He wondered whether Fuscus would have the gall to play it out to the bitter end. But the baron glared and shook his head. "No, you've got me, gods curse you," he snarled. "Who would have thought anybody could expect a nobleman to take an idiot law like that seriously? It's not a proper law—more like a bad joke."

"Stealing farmers from the kingdom is a bad joke, Your Excellency. They aren't yours—they're Avornis'," Grus said. "And Avornis is going to keep them. You, on the other hand, are going to the Maze, and so is your family. Generous of you to bring everybody along with you when you came to the city."

Fuscus invited him to do something he wasn't physically able to manage. The deposed baron added, "And see if the next nobleman you invite to the capital is dumb enough to come."

He had a point there, no doubt about it. But King Grus only shrugged. "With you as an example, maybe the rest of the nobles will think I don't issue laws for the sake of making bad jokes." He nodded to his guards. "Take him away."

Off Fuscus went, into captivity. Grus nodded to himself. He might be the son of a guardsman, the grandson of a small farmer. But he was King of Avornis now, regardless of whether the nobles with their old bloodlines and fancy pedigrees liked it or not. And if they thought they could pretend his laws didn't apply to them, he was going to teach them just how wrong they were.

The city of Avornis went through a hard winter, almost as hard as the winter where the Banished One had tried to bring the capital to its knees. The weather was bad enough to make King Lanius suspicious, bad enough to make him mention his suspicions to his father-in-law.

Grus looked thoughtful. "I was down in the south then myself," he said, "so I don't know the details of that. But maybe we ought to find out about this business, eh? I wonder what a wizard or witch would have to say."

"So do I." Lanius nodded. "I think it would be worth knowing."

"Yes, me, too." Grus also nodded. "And I have someone in mind who might be able to tell us."

"Alca the witch?" Lanius asked. When Grus nodded again, he had a startled expression on his face. Smiling to himself, Lanius went on, "She's the one who shut down the spring that kept Corvus' castle drinking, isn't she?"

"How did you know that?" his father-in-law demanded. "You were already on your way back here to the capital by then."

"I know. I found out later," Lanius answered, more than a little smugly. "I like to find out about as much as I can."

"What else did you find out about what Alca and I did there?" King Grus asked.

He sounded ominous. Lanius wondered why. When he tried to make sense of Grus' expression this time, he couldn't. "What else should I have found out?" he inquired.

"Oh, nothing." Grus sounded much too casual to be convincing. But, since Lanius couldn't figure out what he was missing, he saw nothing to do but let it go.

Alca didn't look happy when Lanius and Grus summoned her. "You want me to try to learn whether the Banished One is behind this winter weather?" she said. "I wish you'd give me something else to do. I think I've said this before"—she eyed Grus in a way Lanius couldn't quite fathom—

"but mortals who measure themselves against the Banished One's magic often end up wishing they hadn't."

Lanius said, "If he dares to use his magic and we don't dare use ours, how can we hope to stand against him?"

The witch let out a long sigh. "Your Majesty, that is the question that has led many mortals to use magic when they felt they had to. It is also the question that has led many of them to be sorry they did."

"Will you try, or won't you?" Grus asked. "I won't order it of you, but I wish you would—for Avornis' sake." Lanius would have ordered her. He wondered why Grus, usually so hard, declined to do so.

Alca sighed again, a sound more wintry than the freezing wind that moaned around the palace. "For Avornis' sake," she repeated in a gray voice. "Yes, that is a key to undo a witch's locks, isn't it?" Grus stirred, but didn't answer. At last, with another sigh, Alca nodded. "I will see what I can do."

"Thank you," Grus said soberly.

"Yes, thank you," Lanius said. "You may not know how important this is."

The witch looked at him—looked through him. "Your Majesty, you may not know how dangerous this is." She didn't raise her voice. She didn't even sound angry. Lanius' cheeks and ears heated, even so. He hadn't been dismissed like that since he was a very little boy. Turning to Grus, Alca asked, "May I be as indirect as I possibly can, Your Majesty? The less of myself I show, the better my chances of living to work some other wizardry one day."

"As you think best, of course," Grus answered. "I don't want your blood on my hands—you know that."

"Do I?" Alca said, still in those gray tones. But then she nodded once more. "Yes, I suppose that's true. If you wanted it, you've had plenty of excuses to take it."

Lanius looked from one of them to the other. They knew what they were talking about, and he didn't. They knew, and spoke obliquely so he wouldn't. He asked Alca, "How soon will you be able to cast your spell?"

"A few days," she said. "I have a lot of studying to do before I try it. And even after I cast it, how much good will knowing do you? If the Banished One *is* making the weather worse, how do you propose to stop him? I know of no spells to let a mortal wizard change the weather."

"Knowing is always better than not knowing," Lanius said.

Alca raised an eyebrow. "Always, Your Majesty?"

"Yes, of course." Lanius believed it with every fiber of his being. He was, of course, still very young.

Grus said, "I think King Lanius is right here. We may not be able to stop the Banished One, but taking his measure, finding out how much he hates us at the moment, is worth doing."

"Maybe." The witch didn't sound convinced. But she dropped them both curtsies—first to Grus, then to Lanius, who resented taking second place to his father-in-law. "You are the kings. I will give you what you think you want." Lanius didn't like the sound of that. Before he could make up his mind to say so, Alca walked out of the chamber, her back very stiff. But she paused in the doorway. "Will either of you want to watch the spell as I cast it?"

"I will." Lanius' magpie curiosity made him speak up at once.

"It may be dangerous. Anything that has to do with the Banished One is dangerous," she said. He shrugged. He wouldn't back away while she and Grus listened.

"I'll come, too," Grus said. "Lanius isn't the only one who wants to know what's going on."

"The more fools both of you," Alca said, and went her way before either one of them could answer her.

More than a week went by before she let the two kings know she was ready. That was longer than she'd said the spell would take to prepare. Lanius almost sent her a message, asking her about the delay. In the end, he didn't. As she'd said, even if they learned the Banished One lay behind the hard winter, what could they do to him? Nothing. That being so, where was the rush?

When Lanius walked into the cramped little room where she'd try her magic, he was surprised to see a large bowl full of snow sitting on top of a battered, stained, and scarred wooden table. But then he exclaimed, "Oh! The law of contagion!"

"What's that?" Grus asked, and sneezed. As he wiped his nose, he said, "I hope it doesn't have anything to do with this cold I've caught." He sneezed again.

"No, Your Majesty," Alca told him, and turned to Lanius, to whom she said, "Yes, Your Majesty, the law of contagion. If our blizzards spring from the Banished One, they were once in contact with him, so to speak. That's what I intend to try to find out. Of course, what the Banished One intends may be something very different. We'll see."

She held a chunk of rock crystal in a sunbeam that fell on the table but not on the bowl of snow. Lanius exclaimed in amazement, for a rainbow suddenly appeared on the wall nearby. "Pretty," Grus remarked. If he too was amazed, he hid it very well.

"How did you do that?" Lanius asked.

"It is a property of the crystal," Alca answered, which told him nothing. She twisted the crystal this way and that, till the rainbow fell across the bowl of snow.

Steam immediately began to rise from the snow, though the room was not nearly warm enough to make any such thing happen. Alca started chanting. The words were in an ancient dialect of Avornan, one even more archaic than that which clerics used in their prayers and hymns. Lanius understood bits and pieces of it, but no more.

"What's she saying?" Grus whispered to him; to the older king, the archaic Avornan made no sense at all.

And as soon as Lanius shifted his attention to try to explain, he found it stopped making any sense at all for him, too. "I don't know, not exactly," he whispered back, and let it go at that. "We'll find out when we see what the spell does." Grus nodded; that seemed to satisfy him well enough.

Despite what Lanius had told Grus, he did have some general idea of what Alca's spell was doing—she was trying to detect any sorcerous link between this snow on the one hand and the Banished One on the other, and trying to do it in such a sneaky, roundabout way that the exile from the heavens wouldn't notice. Whether that would work—whether, in fact, there was any link to detect . . . That was what the witch was trying to find out.

The first chant ended. Alca shrugged. "Nothing obvious," she reported, sounding not a little relieved that she *hadn't* found anything. "There's one other spell I might try, though, if you like." She looked from Lanius to Grus.

Grus looked at Lanius, as though to say, *This was your idea in the first place. You figure out what you want her to do.* Lanius said, "We've come this far. If we can find out, we ought to try all the arrows in our quiver."

"As you wish, Your Majesty," Alca said. "Give me a moment." She closed her eyes and took a couple of deep breaths, steadying herself, concentrating, before she resumed. Then, as though to be sure, she carried the bowl of snow from the chamber. Looking out the window, Lanius saw her dump what was left in it, move away a few feet, and scoop up a fresh bowlful.

When she came back, she set down the bowl and picked up the chunk of rock crystal. Again, a rainbow sprang into being on the wall. The witch began to chant once more. This spell was also in old-fashioned Avornan—if anything, more so than the first. It had a stronger, harsher rhythm; Lanius could imagine soldiers marching into battle to a chant like this.

As she had before, Alca swung the crystal this way and that, till the rainbow it engendered fell across the bowl of new snow. As it had before, the snow began to steam. There all resemblance to the previous conjuration ended. Lanius stared in mingled fascination and horror at this new rainbow. Little by little, it grew redder and redder and redder, as though the color of blood were drinking up all the other hues, the oranges and yellows and greens and blues and violets. And as it got redder, it somehow got brighter, though the sunbeam from which it had to be formed remained unchanged.

More and more steam rose from the snow. Peering down into the bowl, Lanius saw it too looked as though it were made from blood—blood now boiling, bubbling—rather than frozen water. "Enough!" he said suddenly. "We have all the answer we need!"

All at once, the question wasn't whether they would learn what they wanted to know but whether they could escape the chamber. With a whooshing roar, all the snow—the blood?—in the bowl turned to steam. Coughing, choking, his lungs half scalded, Lanius staggered out of the room.

Grus was only a couple of steps behind him, and dragged Alca along to make sure she got out, too. She had the presence of mind to slam the door behind them. For a moment, Lanius felt, or thought he felt, a power inside the room trying to pull the door open again and come after them. Then that perception faded. He breathed a sigh of relief, at last convinced they had won free.

Expressionless, Alca said, "Now you see, Your Majesties, why wizards fight shy of measuring themselves against the Banished One."

"Er—yes." That was Grus. Normally the most unflappable of men, he sounded shaken to the core. "Are we really so small when set against him?"

"As a matter of fact," Alca answered, "yes."

"Then why does he fear us?" Grus asked. "Why does he torment us? Why does he send this dreadful winter weather against us? What can we do to him that makes him even bother noticing us?"

"We hold back the Menteshe," Lanius said. "We have our own wills. We don't care to be his thralls. We fight back against him, and against his puppets. If we had the Scepter of Mercy, we might do even more."

"Do you really believe that?" Grus still sounded dazed.

"I believe the Banished One believes it," Lanius replied. "If he didn't, why would he have stolen the Scepter in the first place? Why would he keep it closed away in Yozgat? He doesn't want us to have it."

"You speak the truth there, Your Majesty." Alca seemed more like herself than she had a little while before.

Grus frowned. He started to say something. Alca raised a finger to her lips, telling him to stay quiet instead. Grus nodded. Lanius started to ask Grus what he would have said. The witch shook her head at him. He frowned. But then, after a moment's thought, he also nodded. They'd just drawn the Banished One's notice to them. If his presence somehow lingered, did they want him hearing them talking about the Scepter of Mercy? Lanius was willing to admit they didn't.

Alca asked, "Do we have enough grain to get through this winter?"

"Of course we do," Lanius declared. "The harvest was good, and we made a point of stockpiling while we could." That wasn't strictly true, but he didn't care. If the Banished One *was* listening, Lanius wanted him to hear whatever would disconcert him most.

Grus came over and set a hand on his shoulder. The older king grinned and nodded. He understood what Lanius was doing—understood and approved. Somehow, and much to Lanius' surprise, that made him feel very good.

After a couple of weeks, the grip of winter on the city of Avornis eased. Maybe the Banished One decided that keeping up his magic was more trouble than it was worth. Grus couldn't have proved that, but he strongly suspected it. When the blizzards stopped coming one after the other, he hoped the Banished One had stopped paying attention to the capital.

With that hope in mind, he sought out Lanius and asked, "Do you think it's safe to talk about the Scepter of Mercy now?"

"Why are you asking me?" Lanius replied. "Your witch would have a better idea of that than I do."

"Alca's not my witch." Grus hoped he managed to keep the stab of regret from his voice. "And you're the one who knows about the Scepter."

Lanius only shrugged. "Maybe. I wonder if any Avornan these days can *know* about the Scepter of Mercy. It's been gone so very long now. Everything we think we know about it is in the old books. But the people who wrote them really *did* know about the Scepter, because they'd seen it or sometimes even held it. I don't understand some of the things they say. How can I? I haven't done the things they did."

"Good point," Grus said. "What did you think when you realized reading something in a book wasn't the same as actually doing it?"

His son-in-law gave him an odd look. "I didn't much like the idea, to tell you the truth."

That, Grus believed. Lanius was convinced books made the sun go round the earth. At least he *had* realized they weren't a perfect reflection of and substitute for reality. That was something, anyhow. For somebody as naturally bookish as Lanius, it was probably quite a bit.

"What do you want to know?" the young king asked him.

"Suppose I was holding the Scepter of Mercy right this minute." Grus held out his arm, his hand closed as though gripping a shaft. "What could I do with it? What would the Banished One be afraid I could do with it?"

"Remember how Alca said merely human wizards are all very small and weak when they're measured against the Banished One?" Lanius asked.

"Oh, yes." Grus nodded and shivered at the same time. "I'm not likely to forget—not after that snow turned to blood and boiled."

"No. Neither am I. Neither is Alca, I expect," Lanius said. "Well, if you were holding the Scepter of Mercy, you wouldn't be small anymore. That much is pretty plain."

"So I'd be able to face him on something like even terms, would I?" Grus said, and Lanius nodded. Grus went on, "Suppose I was holding the Scepter, then, like I said. How could I use it to smash the Banished One, to give him what he deserves?"

"That's where things get tricky, or maybe just where I don't understand," Lanius answered. "The Scepter of Mercy isn't a weapon, or isn't exactly a weapon. It is what it says it is—the Scepter of *Mercy*. The way you'd use it is tied up in that—tied up tight."

"Tied up how?" Grus demanded. "This is the important stuff, you know, or would be if we had the Scepter."

"Yes. If." Lanius' tone made it plain how large an *if* that was. "It's also what's hardest to understand in the old writings. Some of the Kings of Avornis who used the Scepter of Mercy wrote down what they did and felt while they held it, but how can I know what that *means* when I haven't held it myself?"

"I don't suppose you can," Grus admitted with a sigh. "But I'll tell you something, Your Majesty—I wish you could."

King Lanius sighed, too. "You aren't the only one. But I don't suppose it's very likely, not when the Scepter's been gone so long."

"I'm sure that's what the Banished One wants us to think," Grus said. "How long has it been since anybody seriously tried to take the Scepter of Mercy away from him?"

"Two hundred and"—Lanius paused to count on his fingers—"twenty-seven years. The expedition didn't get even halfway to Yozgat. Only a few men came back. The rest either died or were made into thralls."

"Oh." Grus winced. Down in the south, he'd seen more thralls than he cared to remember. To his way of thinking, a clean death was preferable. Still . . . "Maybe, if the time ever seems ripe, we ought to think about trying again."

"Maybe." But Lanius didn't sound as though he believed it.

Despite Lanius' frowns and shrugs, the idea wouldn't leave Grus' mind. Ortalis greeted it with a shrug, too. He said, "I never have been able to understand what good the Scepter of Mercy was in the first place."

King Grus sighed once more. That sounded altogether too much like his only legitimate son. But even Estrilda had a hard time following him here. She said, "It would be nice, yes, but how can you hope to do it? You might want to leave well enough alone, don't you think? Would you like to cross the Stura and end up a thrall?"

"No, of course not," Grus answered. "What I'd like would be to cross the Stura and win."

"Well, yes," his wife said. "But how can you?"

And to that reasonable question he had no answer, none at all. He drank more wine than he might have with supper that night, and went to bed earlier than usual. He soon fell into a deep, deep sleep—and then wished he hadn't, for out of the mists and confusions of the dream world came an image neither misty nor confused nor, for that matter, a proper part of the dream world at all.

The king hadn't seen the Banished One in his sleep for many years, but the superhuman beauty of the exile from the heavens hadn't changed a bit in all that time. When the Banished One spoke, his words reverberated inside Grus' mind. "You think to trifle with me, do you? To rob me? To take what is mine by right and mine by might? Little man, you are a fool. You cannot harm me and my purposes, any more than a buzzing gnat could hamper you and yours. And if a gnat does somehow annoy you, what do you do? You crush it. Think on that. Think on it well. If you annoy me, gnat of a man, you will wish you were only crushed."

Quite suddenly, he was gone. Grus woke with a groan. Sweat drenched him. His heart pounded. He hadn't known such terror since . . . since the last time the Banished One came to him in his dreams.

Only in dreams could the Banished One reach him here. If he ever went south over the Stura, that might well not be so. *Better to die than to fall into his hands,* Grus thought. Or maybe better just to stay here safely in the city of Avornis.

But would the Banished One have delivered such dire threats if he weren't worried about what Grus and Avornis might do? *How can I know?* Grus wondered. *Is he trying to lure me south with false hopes?* He got no more sleep the rest of the night.

CHAPTER TWENTY-ONE

King Lanius saw the Banished One in his dreams, too, as he hadn't since he was a little boy. Confronted by that coldly handsome, coldly perfect visage, his first urge was to run and hide. Had he been able to, he would have, but the Banished One ruled the kingdom of his night.

"Think you to trifle with me?" he heard, the chambers of his skull suddenly a prison. "You had better think again. Son of a dozen kings, are you? Have you any idea how little that matters, how small a stretch of time that covers, what a weak and puny land Avornis truly is?"

Contempt radiated from him like light and heat from a fire. In his dream, Lanius answered, "Say what you will, but this is mine."

"No." Contempt turned to something harsher—absolute rejection. "No, and no, and no. Stupid little man, ugly little man, the world is mine. It is not much, not when I have had better stolen from me, but it is *mine*. And I will use it as my stepping-stone to return to what truly belongs to me. Rest assured, I shall step on you, too. Rest assured, the more you make your maggot wriggles against me now, the more I shall enjoy it. Rest assured, your slimy, stinking, puling brat will not enjoy even what you do. Rest—"

He might have gone on, but Lanius, who could rest no more, woke then with a gasp of horror. He sprang out of bed, waking Sosia, too, and rushed to the nursery to make sure Crex was all right. The baby slept, peaceful as could be, snoring a little around a thumb stuck in his mouth. Feeling a little foolish, or perhaps more than a little, Lanius went back to his own bedchamber.

"What was that all about?" Sosia already sounded half asleep again.

"A bad dream," Lanius replied. Sosia grunted, nodded, and started to snore herself. Lanius lay awake for a long, long time afterward. Calling the Banished One's visit a dream didn't begin to do justice to what had happened. His memory was as precise, as real, as though they'd spoken face-to-face. The visit held none of a dream's usual blurriness and ambiguity. It was *real.* He would have staked his life on that.

Maybe he slept again that night. On the other hand, maybe he didn't. Either way, he was yawning and fuzzy-headed the next morning. When he saw King Grus, he found his fellow sovereign in much the same straits. "Bad dreams?" he asked.

Grus nodded. "You might say so. Yes, you just might say so. You?"

"The same," Lanius agreed. "It might be better not to name any names."

"Yes." Grus nodded again. "It might. Do you believe your dreams?"

"Do I believe I had them? Of course I do," Lanius said. "Do I believe what I heard in them? He has reason to lie."

"I tell myself the same thing," Grus said. "I keep telling myself the same thing, over and over, doing my best to convince myself of it. I'm glad you're doing the same thing. He would be easy to believe."

"He would be easier to believe if he didn't hit so hard," Lanius observed. "But we're only mortals, after all. Why should he waste his time finding out the best ways to get us to do what he wants?"

"Not what he wants," Grus broke in. "What he requires. There's a difference."

"Well, yes," Lanius said. "Of course, you have your ways of getting me to do what you require, and—"

His father-in-law's face froze. Lanius had had that same thought many times. He hadn't spelled it out in Grus' hearing before. Part of him was glad to see he had at least struck a nerve. A good deal more of him was frightened. Every so often, he managed to get Grus angrier than he really wanted to. This looked like one of those times.

"You don't even know what a spoiled brat you are and how soft you've had it," Grus said quietly. "I ought to beat the stuffing out of you for that—it might give you a hint. But I won't dirty my hands with you. If you want to see the difference between the Banished One's methods and mine, cross over the Stura and try thralldom. That will tell you what you need to know, though I doubt you'd care for the lesson."

"I—I'm sorry," Lanius said. "I went too far."

"Yes, you did, didn't you?" Grus still steamed. "Even if I'd married you to the headsman's daughter instead of my own, you'd have gotten off easier from me than you would from the Banished One." He turned his back and walked away.

Lanius' ears burned. The worst of it was, he knew Grus was right. He'd said something cruel and stupid, and Grus had pinned his ears back. But knowing he'd gotten what he deserved didn't make getting it any more pleasant.

He muttered something he'd heard an angry guardsman say. The trouble was, his own words had held some truth, too. He couldn't do as he pleased, and the reason he couldn't was that Grus wouldn't let him. That didn't mean Grus thought the world was his by right. It just meant Grus didn't like to take chances.

No doubt that made a difference in how the gods would judge Grus when he came before them at the end of his days on earth. He did—Lanius grudgingly supposed—have hope of a happy afterlife. Where it seemed to make little difference, though, was in its effect on Lanius. *Grus can say whatever he wants. I may not be a thrall, but I'm not free, either. And if he thinks I like that, he's wrong.*

Grus made a point of not seeing Lanius for the next few days. Had he seen him, he still thought he might have punched him in the face—the temptation lingered. Only little by little did he realize Lanius was as irked with him as he was with his son-in-law. Grus didn't think Lanius had any business being so irked, but that didn't mean he wasn't.

Lanius didn't come seeking him out, either. Maybe that meant the younger king was embarrassed, too. Grus wouldn't have bet on it. More likely, Lanius was still fuming, too. Eventually, they would need to work together again. As far as Grus was concerned, it could wait.

He didn't seek out Alca. Things hadn't gone as he wanted the last time he tried that. They could undoubtedly go worse still if Estrilda found out what he wanted to do with her. But Grus didn't flee the witch when they met in a corridor, either. Instead, he asked her, "Have you had bad dreams?"

"Oh, yes." Had she answered any other way, Grus would have been sure she was lying. Her face was pale, skin drawn tight across her bones.

Dark circles shadowed her eyes. "I have had dreams. He does take his revenge."

"Did you know he would?" Grus asked.

"Not that way," she replied. "I knew I would pay for the spell somehow or other. He might have done worse. He might yet do worse."

"Do you believe what he tells you in the dreams?" Grus thought for a moment, then decided to change the way he'd said that. "When he tells it to you, you can't help but believe it. How do you make yourself stop once you wake up?"

"Because I know he lies," Alca answered. "When we're face-to-face, so to speak, I must believe him, as you say, because he is so strong. But even then I know I'm going to wake again, and when I wake I'll know he was trying to befool me."

"If I had the Scepter of Mercy, what could I do to him?" Grus asked.

Alca raised an eyebrow. "I don't know, Your Majesty. The Scepter of Mercy has lain under the Banished One's hand for a long time. I can't begin to tell you what it might do. You would be wiser to ask King Lanius. He studies times past and the things of time past, doesn't he?"

"Yes, but he's no wizard," Grus replied. "I was hoping you might be able to tell me more than he can." *I was hoping not to have to listen to another one of his lectures, too.* "After all, the Scepter of Mercy is a sorcerous tool, and—"

"No, I don't think so." Alca shook her head. "I don't think so at all, Your Majesty, not in the sense you mean. No wizard made it—no human wizard, I mean. It wouldn't have power against the Banished One if it came from the wit and will of an ordinary wizard."

"No? I always thought—" He'd never sought to learn where the Scepter came from. Maybe that was a mistake on his part. But he'd always had more important things to worry about. *And I probably still do,* he thought. He tried a different tack. "If no ordinary wizard made it, where does it come from?"

"I don't know that, either, Your Majesty. Maybe the gods gave it to us, a long, long time ago. Maybe the power was always in some part of it, and wizards recognized power and made the Scepter around that one potent part. Maybe—" The witch broke off. "I can guess for as long as you like. But I'd only be guessing, for I don't know. I don't think anyone knows, except perhaps the Banished One."

Grus' fingers twisted in a sign of rejection. "I'm not going to ask *him.*"

He'd meant it for a joke, but Alca nodded seriously. "That's wise, Your

Majesty. That's very wise. If you plan to have anything to do with the Scepter of Mercy, the less the Banished One knows of whatever you have in mind, the better."

"Yes." Grus hadn't thought of it in quite those terms. He hadn't thought hard about trying to regain the Scepter of Mercy, either—not till recently. The more he thought about it, though, the better he liked it. *If I could somehow bring it off, I'd be the greatest hero Avornis has known for hundreds of years.*

And if I fail, I'll die a thrall, knowing the Banished One is laughing at me.

Not till later did he realize that wasn't necessarily so. He could order an army—led by Hirundo, say—south across the Stura, while he stayed here safe in the city of Avornis. He could. He didn't think he ever would, though.

He wondered why not. What could he do that Hirundo couldn't? He had no answer for that. But he knew what he thought about officers who sent men into danger they feared to face themselves. And something else also applied—or he thought it did. One day not long after that, he asked Hirundo, "Have you ever dreamt of the Banished One?"

"Me?" The general shook his head. "No, and I thank all the gods I haven't. I can't imagine a worse omen. Why, Your Majesty? Have you?"

"Now and then," Grus answered. "Every now and then."

"May you stay safe," Hirundo said. "Have you got a wizard or a witch keeping watch over you? You'd better."

"I do." Grus didn't know how much Alca—or anyone else—could do if the Banished One seriously sought his life. No, that wasn't true. He did know, or at least had a pretty good idea. He preferred not to think about it, though. Instead of asking Hirundo anything more about the Banished One, he said, "What do you think the Thervings are likely to do come spring?"

"They'll be trouble, I expect. They usually are." Hirundo accepted the change of subject with obvious relief.

But the answers he'd given left Grus thoughtful. Why hadn't the Banished One shown himself to Hirundo? He *had* come to haunt the dreams of Grus himself, of Lanius, and of Alca. Why not Avornis' best general? Because they offered a real challenge, and Hirundo didn't? But how? That, Grus did not know.

How could a mere man hope to outguess, hope to outsee, the Banished One, who, if he wasn't immortal, certainly came closer than any human being? *You can't,* he thought. *You will always face—Avornis will always face—an enemy wiser than you are.*

Then how to win? Logic said he had no chance. Yet Avornis had sur-vived all these centuries despite its great foe's wisdom and strength. *The Banished One makes mistakes, too,* Grus realized. *No matter how wise he is, he can't help underestimating mankind. That costs him. Sometimes it costs him dear.*

Hope, then. Hope in spite of logic. But Grus was not greatly reassured. He played a dangerous game indeed if he relied on his opponent's making a mistake to give him any chance of winning.

These days, King Lanius was not only a father but felt like a grandfather. Not only had Bronze presented him with a new litter of moncat kittens, but Snitch, whom he'd helped raise from a tiny thing, had also bred. He worried a little about breeding family members, but his books seemed to think it was acceptable for dogs, so he put it out of his mind. He had no choice, anyhow. Both new litters consisted of a male and a female. Lanius was growing convinced moncats usually did things that way.

"Before too long," he told Sosia, "they'll be as common around the palace as ordinary cats are."

"Is that such a good thing?" his wife asked. "Ordinary cats can be a nuisance. Moncats can be even more trouble, because they've got hands."

Part of Lanius knew she was right. The rest did its best to reject the idea. "They're wonderfully interesting beasts," he said. "I could write a book about them."

"I'm sure you could," Sosia said. "That doesn't mean they aren't nui-sances, or couldn't be if they got the chance. If they started swinging through the trees here in the city, we wouldn't have any songbirds left be-fore long."

"Don't be silly. Songbirds can fly away," Lanius said.

"Grown songbirds can," Sosia replied. "But what about the ones in their nests? What about eggs? Do moncats eat eggs?"

"I don't know." Lanius felt harassed. He probably sounded harassed, too. But his stubborn honesty made him add, "When the Chernagors gave me Iron and Bronze, their leader did say the islands they came from didn't have a lot of squirrels."

Sosia nodded. "Squirrels, too. I hadn't thought about them, but that certainly makes sense. If moncats get loose in Avornis, they could be as bad as a plague."

"Plagues don't purr," Lanius said. To his relief, his wife had no quick comeback for that. Here, though, Sosia had gotten a step ahead of him. He'd thought of giving moncats as presents to favored nobles and courtiers—that had been in his mind since the day Yaropolk presented him with the first pair. What if whoever got them let them roam like ordinary cats? Birds and squirrels would be very surprised and very unhappy.

Could I give them on condition they stay indoors? No sooner had the thought crossed Lanius' mind than he shook his head. He couldn't possibly hope to enforce such a condition. Giving an order he couldn't enforce would only make him look the fool.

Then he laughed bitterly. *I can't enforce any order I give. After all, I'm only the King of Avornis. Grus now, Grus is the King of Avornis. If he gives orders, people follow them . . . or else. But even Grus knows better than to give orders nobody's likely to obey. He's shown as much by the way he's handled his laws on taking land away from the peasants.*

"What's funny?" Sosia asked him.

"Nothing, really," he answered.

She looked at him. "When you say things like that, you're usually angry at my father. Do you think I don't know?"

"I suppose not." Lanius felt a dull embarrassment, almost as though his wife had caught him looking at lewd drawings. His temper slipped. "It *is* hard, staying here in the palace and not able to do anything about anything except the moncats and the archives."

"I'm sorry," Sosia said quietly.

"Are you? Why should you be?" He lashed out at her—she was close and handy. "Your father's the *real* King of Avornis, the one who really can do things."

"Why should I be sorry?" She still didn't raise her voice. "Because I'm your wife. Because I don't want you to be unhappy."

"Whyever not?" Lanius asked, sarcastic still.

Sosia flushed. Lanius felt ashamed of himself. That didn't deserve a serious answer, and he knew it. But Sosia gave him one. "Why? Because I love you, that's why."

He stared at her. Of all the things she might have said, that was the last one he'd expected. They were married, of course. That hadn't been love, though; that had been Grus' orders, as much to Sosia as to Lanius. They'd tried to please each other in bed, yes. He didn't think that was necessarily love, either—more on the order of two polite people making the best of the situation in which they found themselves. And they had a son. When they lay with each other so regularly, that wasn't surprising. Lanius loved Crex. He knew Sosia did, too. But that she loved *him* . . .

He started to answer, *I don't know what to say.* Just before he did, he realized that would be a mistake. There was only one thing he could possibly say, and he did. "I love you, too, Sosia. I have for a long time. I just didn't know if I ought to say so."

Did he mean it? He didn't know. But the way her face lit up made him glad he'd said it. "Why *wouldn't* you say so?" she asked.

Lanius hoped his resentment didn't show on his face. Now he had to come up with another answer! But, to his relief, he did, and he decided it was at least half true. "I was afraid to," he told her. "If I'd said something like that and then found out you didn't love me back—I don't think I could have stood that."

She set her hand on his. "That's funny," she said, her voice hardly above a whisper. "I was afraid of the same thing. That's why I stayed quiet so long, even after Crex was born. But I knew I had to say something now, or else we might never be able to trust each other again."

He took her in his arms. "Thank you," he said. Knowing he could trust someone . . . He tried to remember the last time he'd been sure of that. For the life of him, he couldn't. He squeezed Sosia tighter. Maybe this *was* love. He still wasn't sure. How could he be, when he had no standard of comparison?

Avornis' green banners fluttering all around him, Grus rode out of the city of Avornis at the head of his army. When he looked back over his shoulder, he saw Queen Estrilda, Queen Sosia, and King Lanius on the battlements waving to him and the soldiers. A maidservant beside Sosia held Prince Crex. Grus waved to all of them. The adults waved back, even Lanius. Grus smiled. They were getting along better. That made everything easier.

Prince Ortalis wasn't there. Under other circumstances, that might have angered Grus. But he knew his son was out hunting. He knew both his sons were out hunting, as a matter of fact. He didn't care one way or the other about whether Anser hunted. His bastard was a good-natured youngster with or without the chase. But Ortalis . . .

Grus aimed what might have been a prayer of thanks heavenward. Since starting to hunt, Ortalis hadn't outraged any maidservants. He'd had a long, fairly friendly affair with one of them, which was, for him, an all-time first. He was much easier to be around—*much less obnoxious,* Grus thought, coming closer to the real truth. He still took no interest in matters of state, but Grus was happy enough with the changes he had seen in his son to fret less about those he hadn't.

General Hirundo, who rode beside him, said something. Grus realized that, but had no idea what Hirundo had told him or asked. "I'm sorry," he said. "Try again, please? I was woolgathering."

"Happens to everybody, Your Majesty," Hirundo said with one of his ready smiles. "There are days I'm glad my head's stuck on good and tight, because I'd lose it if it weren't. What I said was, here's hoping the Thervings don't give us too much trouble this year."

"That would be nice," Grus agreed. "I'm not going to count on it, but it would be very nice indeed."

"How much longer can Dagipert live, do you suppose?" Hirundo wondered.

"He might drop dead tomorrow, or he might last another fifteen years," Grus said with a shrug. "He's still strong, worse luck. When the two of us fought a couple of years ago, he came closer to killing me than I did to killing him." He looked around and lowered his voice before adding, "I'm just glad the Menteshe haven't raised up a prince like him, or we'd have more trouble in the south than we do."

He couldn't help wondering if the Banished One was listening to him. That shouldn't have been possible. He knew as much. After Alca's sorcery, though, he also knew in his belly that no humanly recognizable limits applied to the Banished One.

If the great enemy of Avornis *was* listening, he gave no sign. Grus knew a certain amount of relief, but only a certain amount; the Banished One might be listening and saving up resentment for revenge years later. His scale of time also lay far beyond merely mortal ken.

Meanwhile, Grus enjoyed the fine spring day. Green waxed glorious on the meadows and fields and farms around the city of Avornis. Birds newly returned from the south sang from housetops, twittered in hedgerows, and snatched insects on the wing. Grus wondered why the birds chose to go down to the Banished One's domain for winter, but then realized they'd been flying south long before the gods cast the Banished One from the heavens. The birds weren't to blame.

Hirundo kept his mind more firmly fixed on the task ahead. "Seeing as we will have to face old Dagipert before too long, what do you suppose he'll be up to this campaigning season?"

"No good," Grus replied, which made the general laugh. Grus chuckled, too, but he hadn't been joking. He went on, "He'll do whatever he can to hurt Avornis. He's been doing it for years. Why should he change?"

"He's been doing it altogether too well, too," Hirundo said.

"I'm not the one to tell you you're wrong," Grus said, "but I'm sure

Dagipert would say he hasn't done it well enough. If he had his way, after all, he'd be calling the shots in Avornis these days, and Lanius' children would be his grandchildren, not mine."

Not even the burgeoning growth of spring could mask all the depredations the Thervings had wrought over the past few years. Isolated farmhouses and barns still stood in gaunt, charred ruins. A hawk perched on a chimney that remained upright while the house of which it had been a part was only a memory. It stared at Grus and the oncoming soldiers out of great yellow eyes, then flew away. Weeds smothered what would have been—should have been—fields of wheat or barley or rye.

And country farmhouses weren't all that suffered. Whole villages and even fortified towns had vanished off the face of the earth. "We'll be years rebuilding this," Grus said, a gloomy thought that had occurred to him before.

Even before the army reached the Tuola River, Grus sent scouts out ahead of it and to either side. Unlike Count Corvus, he didn't intend to be taken by surprise.

But whether King Grus intended for it to happen or not, Dagipert did surprise him. The bridges over the Tuola remained down. Only ferryboats connected the western province with the rest of Avornis. That didn't keep Avornans from the west from fleeing over the river with news—the Thervings had marched into the western province as Grus was marching out of the city of Avornis.

One of the refugees said, "That's not our chief news, Your Majesty—that the Thervings are over the border, I mean." Another man standing behind him nodded. "I'm carrying a message from King Dagipert."

"Well, you'd better tell me what is, then," Grus answered. "Don't waste time, either."

The man from the far bank of the Tuola said, "Maybe you won't have to fight. Dagipert wants to talk to you face-to-face."

"Oh, he does, does he?" Grus said. "Someplace near a forest, I'd bet, where he can spring an ambush the first chance he sees."

"No, sir." The man shook his head. "He wants both sides to bridge out from the banks of the Tuola till their spans almost meet in the middle. He says they should stop just too far apart to let a murderer jump from one to the other. He swears by Olor and Quelea he'll go back to Thervingia in peace once you've met."

Grus felt men's eyes on him. He knew it might be a trap. Dagipert might want nothing more than time to solidify his position in the province west of the Tuola. Time would do him only so much good, though.

The Avornans still controlled the river itself. They could use their ships to put an army across almost where they chose—near its headwaters, the Tuola did get too shallow for such games.

After half a minute's thought, Grus decided the chance to win a summer without war—it would be the first of his reign—was too good to pass up. "Will you go back to Dagipert?" he asked the man who'd spoken to him. When the fellow nodded, Grus said, "All right, then. Tell him I agree. We'll build where his ambassadors usually cross the river—he'll know the place."

He led his own army to the remains of the bridge that had stood in happier times. He didn't lead all of it there, though. He sent detachments to cover a couple of other likely crossings, in case Dagipert had some elaborate treachery in mind. But the King of Thervingia certainly seemed to have brought most if not all of his army to the other side of the crossing. Their tents, some of wool, others of leather, formed a sprawling, disorderly town there.

"I wonder how long they can stay in one spot before hunger and disease get loose among 'em," Hirundo said in speculative tones.

"Yes." But Grus' agreement was halfhearted. He knew he could feed his own men for a long time. Disease, though . . . Disease could break out any moment, as the gods willed. Fluxes of the bowels and smallpox sometimes did more to break up a campaign than anything the warriors on the other side might manage.

Avornan engineers built an elegant wooden span halfway across the Tuola. The Thervings' bridge was nowhere near as handsome. Grus doubted it would have held as much weight as the Avornan effort. But, for Dagipert and a few guardsmen, it served perfectly well. And it advanced at least as fast as the bridge the Avornans built.

In a couple of days, Avornans and Thervings who spoke Avornan were shouting back and forth across the narrowing stretch of river that separated them. They agreed Grus and Dagipert would meet at dawn the next morning.

Grus wore royal robes as he stepped out onto the bridge. Under them, he wore a mail shirt. His crown was a helmet with a gold circlet of rank. Several guardsmen with large shields accompanied him, to make sure the Thervings didn't shoot arrows at him while he was within easy range.

On the other side of the Tuola, King Dagipert's preparations looked similar. His royal robes were even gaudier than the Avornan ones they imitated. He wore a real crown over what looked like a brimless, close-fitting iron cap. His guards were enormous and burly men. They carried shields slightly smaller than those the Avornans used, but only slightly.

Dagipert himself had a bushy white beard and a long white braid that hung halfway down his back. His shoulders were stooped, perhaps from years, perhaps from the weight of a mail shirt of his own. As he got closer, Grus saw he had an engagingly ugly face. If he was going to die soon, he didn't know it. Remembering his father, Grus knew that didn't mean anything, but he wished Dagipert would have looked feebler.

Dagipert was studying him, too. In fluent Avornan, the King of Thervingia said, "I should have killed you when we met on the field a couple of years ago."

"And a good day to you, too, Your Majesty," Grus replied. That made Dagipert laugh. Grus went on, "I wouldn't have been sorry to stretch you out in the dirt, either, you know."

"Not the way you handle a horse," Dagipert said. "My grandmother had a better seat when she was eighty-five."

That stung. Grus didn't even think Dagipert was lying, which made it sting all the more. "Did you ask for this meeting so you could insult me?"

"Among other things," Dagipert answered. "You yoked your daughter to Lanius when he should have married mine. Arch-Hallow Bucco made the betrothal agreement."

"He didn't have the authority to do it. And he's dead. You may as well quit complaining about that, Dagipert, especially since Lanius' son"—*and my grandson,* Grus thought, though he didn't say that out loud—"will be one before long."

"Yes, Lanius has a son. You have a grandson," Dagipert said heavily. The King of Thervingia scowled from under bushy eyebrows, reminding Grus of a very old, very sly, very dangerous bear. "And, by the gods, I've made you pay for your thievery."

"Are you telling me you wouldn't have ravished Avornis if I weren't king, if Lanius hadn't wed Sosia?" Grus asked. "I don't believe it for a minute."

"Believe what you please," King Dagipert growled. "I'm telling you that you Avornans robbed me of what should have been mine." He drew himself up with touchy, affronted pride.

"You worship the same gods we do," Grus answered. "People say you give Olor and Quelea and the rest great respect, but you don't act like it. A godless man, a man who'd sooner follow the Banished One, is the sort who kills and plunders innocents."

"Don't you say I have anything to do with the Banished One," Dagipert said hotly. "That's a foul lie!"

No one in Avornis had ever been sure. But aloud Grus replied, "I didn't say you did. I said you *acted* like a man who would sooner follow the Banished One."

"I'm no oath breaker," Dagipert snarled. "You Avornans are the ones who lie through your teeth."

"When have I ever lied to you?" Grus asked. "I had nothing to do with whatever Arch-Hallow Bucco did or didn't say. I'm not bound by it. No Avornan except Bucco ever thought we were bound by it."

"By King Olor's beard, *I* thought you were bound by it," Dagipert said.

I'll bet you did, because it suited you so well. Grus went on with what he'd planned to say before Dagipert sidetracked him with talk of Bucco. "If you *do* honor the gods—and I think you do—stop unjustly plundering and killing the innocent. Make peace with us; we follow the same gods you do. Why should you stain your hands with the blood of those who believe as you do? You're a mortal, like any other man. When you die, the gods will judge you."

"They'll judge you, too," Dagipert said.

"I know." Grus tried not to worry about what would happen after he died. With King Dagipert's white hairs, the Therving had to think about what would come next. Grus went on, "Today you live; tomorrow you're dust. One fever will quench any man's pride. What will you say about all your murders in Avornis when you come before the gods?"

"I'll say they had it coming." The King of Thervingia was a tough customer. But he couldn't keep a small wobble from his voice.

"How will you face those terrible and just judges?" Grus continued. "Will you tell them you did it for wealth? Haven't you stolen enough to satisfy you? Isn't it about time to welcome peace? Live a bloodless and untroubled life from now on, so neither side slaughters fellow believers anymore. What could be worse than that?"

Dagipert glared at him across the gap between the two incomplete spans. "Oh, you're a serpent, you are, and you slay with your tongue," the Therving said.

Grus shrugged. "You were the one who wanted this talk. Can you listen, too?"

"How can I do anything else, the way you blather on?" Dagipert said. "I ought to start the war up again."

"Go ahead," Grus answered. "You haven't had everything your own way these past few years. You won't this time, either."

"Another lie," Dagipert jeered.

"You know better," Grus told him. "Besides, how much harm are you doing to Thervingia with these endless campaigns of yours? You can see what you do to us, but what about to your own people? How many men don't come home? How many smiths and potters and carpenters don't ply their trades? How many crippled men do you try to care for?"

"As though you care for what happens to Thervingia," King Dagipert said.

"I care about Avornis," Grus replied. "I expect you care about Thervingia the same way. Can't you see you're not going to win this war? What point to fighting over and over again across the same stretch of ground?"

Dagipert's face twisted. "What point? To make sure you gods-cursed Avornans don't think you can take my kingdom and me lightly, that's what."

"You've made that point," Grus said. And yet, in another sense, Dagipert hadn't, couldn't, and never would. Avornis was an old, old land—a land with a long, proud past. Other tribes had crossed over the Bantian Mountains from the plains to the west and set up their kingdoms on her borders before the Thervings. After Thervingia fell in ruins, others likely would again. And Avornis? Avornis would endure. When Grus had spoken to Dagipert of passing to dust, he hadn't just meant the King of Thervingia. He'd meant his kingdom, too, and Dagipert knew it.

"You sneery, scoffing, scornful, snooty . . . Avornan," King Dagipert said bitterly. He turned on his heel and walked back toward the west bank of the Tuola. His guards fell in behind him, protecting him with their bodies as well as their shields.

Grus also withdrew. His men started knocking down his segment of bridge. The Thervings did the same. Grus wondered if the talks had accomplished anything or simply infuriated Dagipert even more. He sent his army on the way southeast, to a place where he could cross the Tuola with protections from archers aboard Avornan river galleys.

Before he reached the crossing place, though, word came that the Thervings were moving back, away from the river. Soon it became clear they were going back to Thervingia.

CHAPTER TWENTY-TWO

Two messengers came into the city of Avornis only hours apart. The first was from the plains of the south—an announcement that a baron named Pandion had rebelled against King Grus and announced that *he* was King Lanius' rightful protector. "How can he say that?" Lanius asked the messenger, a cavalry captain who'd stayed loyal to Grus. "I've never met him. I wouldn't take oath I've ever even heard of him."

"How much sleep do you suppose he'll lose about that, Your Majesty?" the captain replied. "With King Grus busy against the Thervings, Pandion figures he'll make hay while the sun shines—get as strong as he can before Grus is able to do much about it. That's how it looks to me, anyhow."

It looked that way to Lanius, too. He praised the officer and dismissed him. He couldn't do anything about Pandion's revolt. Not a soldier outside the royal bodyguard would obey his orders. The uprising was Grus' worry, not his.

The second messenger announced that the Thervings were withdrawing from Avornan soil and Grus was on his way back to the city of Avornis.

Lanius laughed till he cried. "I don't think it's *that* funny," Sosia said.

"No?" Lanius answered. "*I* do, by the gods. Baron Pandion may have started the worst-timed rebellion in all the history of Avornis."

His wife thought about that. Then she smiled, too. "Oh," she said. "I see." A bird flew by their bedroom window. Sosia went on, "You ought to send the man who brought word from the south to my father. He should know what's happened there as soon as he can."

Now it was Lanius' turn to think. He didn't need long before he nodded. "You're right. I wouldn't want your father thinking I tried to conceal anything like that from him."

"I didn't mean that," Sosia said. "He trusts you more than you think."

Was that praise or faint praise? Lanius wasn't sure. He wasn't sure he wanted to find out, either. He said, "I'll attend to it." And he did.

King Grus came back to the city of Avornis a few days later. He met Lanius outside the palace and said, "So this Pandion bastard thinks he can play games with me, does he? I'm going to teach him he hasn't even started to figure out the rules."

"Speaking of games and rules, how did you make Dagipert withdraw so very quickly?" Lanius asked.

"That's the funny thing, Your Majesty—I didn't," Grus answered. "He did it himself." He explained how he and the King of Thervingia had met in the middle of the Tuola, and how Dagipert had pulled back from Avornan soil not long afterward.

"You made him think about what he was doing," Lanius said admiringly. "You *must* tell a scribe exactly what you said to him. That's something future Kings of Avornis need to know."

"When I get a chance." Grus sounded indifferent. Seeing the disappointment Lanius didn't try to hide, the older man went on, "I'm sorry, but that's how it's got to be. I want to move against Pandion as fast as I can. With any luck at all, I'll hit him before he even knows I'm not fighting the Thervings anymore. The faster the better. If he's not ready to fight, I'll roll him up like a rug."

"But you rolled Dagipert up without fighting, don't you see?" Lanius said. "Isn't it important to set down how you did it?"

Grus said, "I didn't roll him up without fighting. We bought him off until we were ready, and then we spent years fighting Thervingia. I just convinced him he couldn't get anything out of one more year of war. See the difference?"

Reluctantly, Lanius nodded. "Yes, I think I do." He was the one who'd read all the histories. That Grus had a deeper view of what had happened than he'd seen himself was embarrassing.

As swiftly as Grus came into the capital, he left again. Very likely a good many of his men marched out of the city with hangovers from a brief carouse. Lanius wouldn't have wanted to tramp off with an aching head, and wouldn't have been happy if he'd had to. When he said as much to Grus, though, his fellow king only smiled. "They may not be happy to march," he said, "but I'll tell you one thing—they're plenty happy they don't have to fight the Thervings this year."

"But they will have to fight Pandion," Lanius said.

Grus smiled again. "If I had a choice between fighting Dagipert's wild men and a baron who'd grown too big for his breeches, Your Majesty, I know which one *I'd* pick, I'll tell you that. Especially when they think they're taking him by surprise."

"Oh," Lanius said. "Yes, that does make sense, doesn't it?"

"I try." As it often did, Grus' voice came dry as the southern plains after a long season without rain.

Lanius' ears burned, as though that dryness had set them afire. "Er, yes," he mumbled, wishing he could escape his father-in-law.

He got his wish, though not quite in the way he'd meant. With a nod, Grus said, "Well, I'll be off soon. Can't keep Pandion waiting, now can we?" He turned to go, then checked himself, adding, "I thank you for sending word of his revolt to me so quick."

"Uh, you're welcome." Lanius too hesitated. Then *he* added, "Uh, it was Sosia's idea." Better Grus should hear that from him than from her.

But by the way Grus nodded, he already knew. He said, "You still had to do it, though. And who knows? You might have wanted Pandion as protector instead of me."

"I don't want *anyone* as protector!" Lanius all but screamed it. Not having anyone as protector, though, wasn't one of the choices life offered him. It never had been. He wondered if it ever would be.

King Grus savored the feel of a pitching deck under his feet, the breeze in his face, the countryside smoothly flowing by as he led his fleet along the Halycus River toward Pandion's estates. "This is the life," he said to Nicator, who stood beside him. "This is more fun than staying cooped up in the palace all the time, gods curse me if it isn't."

"What's that, Your Majesty?" Nicator cupped a hand behind his ear. Patiently, Grus repeated himself. He had to do it yet again before Nicator nodded and said, "You're welcome to the crown, far as I'm concerned. I wouldn't take it on a bet."

I'm certainly lucky, Grus thought. *Every king needs a man like you— someone he can trust at his back, someone who's not ambitious, or not too ambitious, on his own. Not every king finds a man like that.* The king turned away just in time to watch a couple of mergansers take alarm at the river galley and spring into the air. He wished he could enjoy freedom like that.

Nicator spied the saw-billed ducks, too; nothing wrong with his eyes. His thoughts ran in a different direction. "Those miserable birds taste too much like the fish they eat."

"I know," Grus answered.

Farmers tending fields and flocks looked up in surprise as the war galleys glided down the Halycus. A royal war fleet hadn't been seen in the heartland of Avornis for many years. Nobles in their castles were probably every bit as amazed, and a good deal more alarmed. Grus wanted them alarmed. If they were thinking of joining Pandion's revolt, or of starting one of their own, they needed to consider the risks of the game as well as the rewards.

Two days later, Nicator pointed ahead. "That should be Pandion's stronghold."

Grus shaded his eyes with the palm of his hand. "Yes, I think so," he agreed. The keep, of yellow limestone, seemed not so very strong, not so very well sited. Grus peered again. "Are those tents, there all around the moat?"

"Look at all the tents underneath the castle," replied Nicator, who hadn't heard him. He called, "Up the stroke," to the oarmaster. To the trumpeters, he said, "Signal the other ships to speed up, too. The sooner we get there, the less time they'll have to get ready for us." His ears might be—were—bad, but his wits, like his eyes, still worked just fine. Grus wondered if Nicator caught the blaring horn calls or simply assumed they went forth because he'd ordered it.

The fleet had almost come abreast of the castle, which lay about half a mile from the Halycus, before Pandion's encampment began to stir. "Here's an interesting question," Grus shouted into Nicator's ear. "Will he try to fight us, or will he pull back into the castle and let us lay siege to him?"

Once Nicator understood, he said, "He'll fight, if you ask me. He can't pack that many men into the keep. Even if he could, he can't feed 'em long—and the more the place holds, the less time he'll be able to keep 'em fed. If he beats us in a battle, he doesn't have to worry about that—or he doesn't think he does."

"We'll see," Grus bawled. Nicator was likely right. If he'd been in Pandion's shoes, he would have fought. The river galley's keel scraped against the gently sloping bank. Marines and most of the rowers jumped or scrambled off the ship to form the beginning of a battle line ashore. The rest of the rowers stayed behind. They would guard the galley if Pandion's men somehow broke past Grus' army.

Men spilled out of other river galleys, too, and off the barges accompanying them. Horses came off some of the barges, too, already saddled. Soldiers swung up onto them. A horse waited for Grus. He mounted reluctantly—but then, he always mounted reluctantly. More horns blared. The battle line swiftly lengthened. From the horse—a docile gelding—Grus waved. His army advanced on the castle.

Pandion's force was slower forming. These were peasants, most of them, not veterans of years of war against Thervingia and the Menteshe. They followed their overlord's orders, probably because they hadn't thought to do anything else. On they came, their line shorter than Grus' and more ragged. Grus looked to see if the rebel baron made himself obvious. He hadn't.

Arrows began to fly. On both sides, men began to fall. Some never made a sound, but lay still. More thrashed and screamed and cursed and wailed. As the sides drew closer, spears joined arrows. More and more men went down. A spear darted over Grus' left shoulder and buried itself in the ground behind him. Had it been a foot lower . . . He shuddered and did his best not to think of that.

The two lines collided, both yelling and calling on the gods and taking their names in vain. That fight was sword- and pikework. It was very warm work for a little while, too, for the men Pandion led were fierce enough and to spare at the start. But bravery could do only so much against superior numbers and superior skill. Grus' line lapped around the rebels' flanks. Pandion's army had to give ground or face attack from sides and rear. Even when the rebels did give ground, they still had horsemen on their flanks.

After half an hour or so, their spirit began to fail. Grus was surprised they'd held out even that long, being both outnumbered and outfought—not in terms of courage, but in terms of strategy. A few at a time, Pandion's men started slipping out of the line of battle and trying to get away. Some of them made it. Grus' riders cut down more from behind.

And then, all at once, the whole rebel line gave way. Pandion's soldiers scattered, throwing away weapons and helmets to flee the faster. The castle opened its gates. Many of the fugitives made for that shelter, but Grus' men came hard on their heels. Grus wondered if enough of his men would get in along with Pandion's to let them seize the fortress from the inside. He vastly preferred that to besieging it.

But he hadn't even ridden up to inspect the castle at close range before a shout rose from his horsemen. "Pandion!" they cried. For a moment, he feared some few of them, or maybe more than some few, had gone over to the baron. Then he realized they'd captured Pandion.

The fortress kept Grus' soldiers out by slamming the gates shut on many of the rebels. The men who couldn't get in threw down swords and spears—those who hadn't already—threw their hands up, and surrendered in droves.

Grus waited till Pandion was hauled before him. The baron was block-ily built, with a fuzzy gray beard. Several different kinds of fear warred on his face as he stared at Grus. "You wizard!" he burst out. "How did you get here so fast, with so gods-cursed many men? You're supposed to be fight-ing the Thervings!"

"Life is full of surprises, isn't it?" Grus plucked at his own beard. "Now, what am I going to do with you?"

"Take my head—what else?" Pandion owned a certain bleak courage, or perhaps just knew he had nothing to lose.

"Maybe not," Grus said. Watching hope fight not to come back to the baron's face was like watching a youth trying not to look at a girl with whom he was desperately, hopelessly, in love. The king went on, "If you order your stronghold to open its gates and yield to me, I'll send you to the Maze instead. You can keep Corvus company. Of course, if they don't listen to you in there . . . Well, that would be too bad. For you."

"I'll persuade them," Pandion said quickly.

He did, too. Grus had expected that he could. His men wouldn't have followed him into rebellion if they weren't in the habit of obeying him. The sun was still an hour above the western horizon when Grus' men marched into the fortress. They disarmed the soldiers who'd fought for the baron and sent them back to their farms. The peasants were almost wild with relief; they'd been sure they would be massacred if they lost.

"That's how kings does things," one of them said in Grus' hearing. But this wasn't Grus' first round of civil war. He'd seen how Avornis was wounded no matter which side won the fighting. Being as moderate as he could helped.

"Will you let me bring my wives along?" Pandion asked after the cas-tle yielded.

"They can go to the Maze with you, if they want," Grus answered. "They'll go to convents, as you're off to be a cleric. Or they can stay in the world and find new husbands. I won't tell them what to do."

Neither of Pandion's wives seemed the least interested in abandoning the world for his sake. That left the baron affronted and gloomy. He got even gloomier when Grus ordered his two eldest sons—youths not far from Ortalis and Lanius' age—into the Maze with him. So did the youngsters. Grus was unyielding.

"You all have another choice, if you really want one," he told Pandion and his sons.

"What's that?" the baron asked. Grus folded his arms across his chest and waited. Pandion didn't need long to figure out why. "Uh, Your Majesty?" he added.

"Your heads can go up over the gate of your castle here," Grus said. "That's as much of a choice as you get. This is not a friendly chat we're having here, remember. You tried to rise up against me. You lost. Now you're going to pay the price." He gestured to the soldiers who had charge of the baron and his sons. "Take them away. I think they've made up their minds."

Pandion didn't tell him he was wrong.

Nicator said, "Well, Your Majesty, that was a very pretty little campaign. Very pretty indeed, matter of fact."

Grus surveyed the field. Ravens and crows hopped from one corpse to the next, pecking at eyes and tongues and other such dainties. Vultures spiraled down out of the sky to join them at the bounteous feast people had laid out. The wounded from both sides has been gathered up, but they still moaned or sometimes screamed as surgeons and wizards tried to repair what edged and pointed metal had done to them. The odors of blood and dung hung in the air.

"Yes, very pretty," Grus said tonelessly, "and may we never see an ugly one."

Sosia said, "I'm going to have another baby."

"I thought so," Lanius answered. "Your courses didn't come, and you've been sleepy all the time lately. . . ." He chuckled. "I know the signs now."

"You'd better," his wife said. "If you'd forgotten, I'd be angry."

He gave her a kiss. "I wouldn't do that."

"No, I know you wouldn't," Sosia agreed. "I could say this, that, or the other thing about you, but you don't forget much. Once you notice something, it's yours forevermore. Getting you to notice . . . Sometimes that's a different story."

"What do you mean?" Lanius asked, more than a little indignantly. He didn't like to think of himself as missing anything.

"Never mind," Sosia said, which was not at all what he wanted to hear.

Quarreling with his wife over a trifle would have been foolish, though, especially when she'd given him news like that. He kissed her again. In a pear tree outside the bedroom window, a cuckoo called. The day was breathlessly hot, with not a breeze stirring. The bird called again, then fell silent, as though even song were too much effort.

After a few more minutes, the cuckoo did call once more. Lanius laughed as a new thought crossed his mind. "I wonder what the moncats are doing right now," he said.

Sosia laughed, too. "Why do you wonder? They're trying to get the bird. If one of them can find a way out through a window, he'll do it, too."

"I know," Lanius said. "We've made sure the bars are too narrow to let them get out, but the moncats keep working away anyhow."

"They're stubborner than ordinary cats," Sosia said.

"I don't know whether they're stubborner or just wilder," Lanius said. "They do keep working at it, as you say." He put a hand on his wife's shoulder. "And so do we."

"Yes, we do." She smiled. "I wonder if we don't get along better than my father ever thought we would."

"That had occurred to me, too," Lanius said slowly. "I didn't want to say anything, for fear of making you angry—and maybe making him angry, too—but it had crossed my mind. I won't try to tell you any differently."

"It doesn't really matter, you know," Sosia said.

"Oh, yes. Whether you're on your father's side or mine, what King Grus wants is what Avornis is going to get. I know that. I'd better know it. He's rubbed my nose in it often enough."

He bred moncats and helped the mothers raise the kittens. He went into the archives almost every day, soaking up more lore from the ancient days of Avornis. Without false modesty, he knew he'd learned as much about the past of the city and the kingdom as any man living.

And so what? he asked himself. *What good does that do you? What good does it do Avornis?* He found no good answers, none at all. As long as he played with things that had no possible consequences, he made King Grus happy. If ever he didn't, if ever he tried to do anything substantial . . . He didn't know exactly what would happen, but he had a good idea of the range of possibilities. He might end up in the Maze. On the other hand, he might end up dead. And whether Sosia was on his side or not wouldn't matter a bit.

When Grus came back from beating Pandion, Lanius congratulated him in front of the whole city of Avornis. He felt the irony as he mouthed the words. It wasn't that he'd wanted Pandion to overthrow Grus. He hadn't. Lanius had wanted Pandion no more than he wanted Grus—less, in fact.

What Lanius wanted, as he'd once told Grus, was no protector at all. Though he was King of Avornis, that seemed to be one thing he couldn't have.

He retreated into the archives. There, at least, he was master of his world, even if that world was a small one. He pored over some of the oldest records there, trying to learn all he could of the Banished One. But there seemed to be less to learn than he would have hoped. As far as the royal chronicles told the story, the Banished One had simply appeared in the south one day. The power he showed was far beyond any merely earthly—any merely mortal—power. And the exile hadn't aged, either. That became obvious after a generation, and still seemed true today, all these centuries later. Generations meant nothing to the Banished One. By anything the records showed, centuries meant nothing to him, either.

What would the world be like if Olor hadn't cast him out? Lanius wondered. He had no way of answering that. Neither did anyone else. He couldn't even prove the world would be better. Maybe the long struggle against the Banished One had strengthened, steeled, Avornis. Maybe. He couldn't prove it hadn't. But he doubted it.

He kept hoping his reading would give him some clue or another about the Banished One's weaknesses. The more he read, the more he doubted that, too. As far as he could tell, the Banished One *had* no weaknesses—not in the humanly recognizable sense of the word. He wasn't as strong as a god, not while his self, his essence, rested in the material world rather than in the heavens beyond. Had he been that strong, he would have ruled the world from the moment he found himself cast down into it.

Suddenly, Lanius had a new thought, one that he didn't believe had occurred to any Avornan for many long years before his time. Before being cast down from the heavens, the Banished One had surely been a god himself. Which god had he been? Over what heavenly province or attribute had he ruled? The king had never seen the question, let alone the answer, in the royal archives.

I might be able to find out, Lanius realized. Not many records survived from the days before the Banished One came down to earth, but a few did. If they mentioned a god who was no longer worshiped . . .

That thought led to another—*I wish Bucco weren't dead.* The old archhallow had been a conniver, a serpent, but he'd also been a learned man.

He might have known the answer to Lanius' question, or at least how to go about finding the answer. The clerics had records of their own, records that went back at least as far as those in the royal archives.

Anser wouldn't know. Anser wouldn't care, either. Lanius snapped his fingers. "A secretary will know," he said aloud. "Secretaries always know." Top officials came and went. Secretaries went on forever. They were the memory of Avornis. "When I get around to it, I'll ask one of the arch-hallow's secretaries. He may not know the answer, but he'll know where to find out."

He knew it wasn't anything he had to do in a hurry. The answer, if indeed it existed in the clerics' archives, had been sitting there for centuries. A few days one way or the other weren't going to matter.

And then a messenger came riding into the city of Avornis from out of the west. He'd almost killed his horse; it was lathered and blowing under him. And the news he brought to the royal palace drove any thoughts of the Banished One and the clerics' archives right out of Lanius' head.

"King Dagipert is dead!" the messenger cried. "Dagipert of Thervingia is dead at last!"

King Grus sat on the royal throne. "Give me all you know about what happened in Thervingia."

"I only know it was sudden," the man replied. "One day he was ruling the kingdom, the next he was dead. The gods finally got tired of him tormenting us."

"Well, he's in their hands now," Grus said. "I'm going to—" He stopped.

"Going to what, Your Majesty?" the messenger asked.

"Nothing. Never mind." Grus had started to say he was going to order the cathedrals to offer up prayers of thanksgiving for Dagipert's death. But the Thervings worshiped the same gods Avornis did. Publicly thanking those gods for ridding the world of King Dagipert would have insulted Thervingia. Better for Grus to offer his own private thanksgiving. Remembering the niceties, he said, "I'll have to send Prince Berto—King Berto, now—my condolences."

Lanius had said Berto was a man more interested in cathedrals and prayer than in coming over the border at the head of a long column of warriors in chain mail carrying axes. *I'll send some fine Avornan architects to Thervingia to build him there the fanciest cathedral his heart desires.* Making Berto happy that way had to be cheaper than fighting a war.

"It's the end of an era," the messenger said.

King Grus nodded. "It certainly is. King Dagipert was a strong man and a nasty foe." He added, "You'll have your reward, of course, for bringing the news here so quickly. There's not much that could be more important."

The messenger bowed. Grus caught a distinct whiff of horse from him; he'd ridden hard indeed. "Thank you for your kindness, Your Majesty," he said.

"You're welcome. You've earned it. That's the point."

Another bow. "Thank you again. I was thinking, the only thing bigger than Dagipert dying'd be the gods-cursed Menteshe invading us again. Thank the gods they've been quiet lately."

"Yes." Grus had no idea how much the gods did, or could do, to stop the Menteshe—and the Banished One, their patron—from acting as they pleased. They'd cast the Banished One into the material world and then turned their backs on him . . . hadn't they?

He couldn't be sure. He needed to remind himself of that every now and again. If he couldn't fully understand the Banished One, who dwelt in this world with him, how could he hope to understand the gods still up in the heavens?

Stick to affairs of this world, then, he told himself. To a junior courtier, he said, "Fetch General Hirundo, if you'd be so kind."

The man went off at a run. A polite request from the king counted as an order, and he knew it.

Hirundo came to the throne room in a hurry, too. Grus smiled, if only to himself. He'd discovered people paid much more attention to his commands now that he was king than they ever had when he was a mere commodore of river galleys. "You'll have heard the news?" he asked the general.

"You mean about Dagipert? Oh, yes, Your Majesty." Hirundo nodded. "That's all over the palace by now. It's probably all over the city. I wouldn't be surprised if Corvus and Pandion were gossiping about it in the Maze. Rumor has more legs than a millipede, and runs faster, too."

"Now there's a pretty picture," Grus said. "Rumor happens to be true here, which isn't always so. Prince Berto—King Berto, I should say—is supposed to have less fire in his belly than old Dagipert did."

"He could hardly have more," Hirundo remarked. "But that's just rumor, too, eh?"

"Not entirely," Grus replied. "King Lanius met Berto once, when he came here with his father while Dagipert was laying siege to the city. Still, that was a while ago. In case Berto's changed . . ." He took it no further. He didn't want to say Lanius didn't know what he was talking about. He did want to say Avornis couldn't be sure Lanius had everything right, though.

Fortunately, Hirundo understood the fine line he was walking. "You'll want to send soldiers out to the west, just in case Berto turns out to be friskier than we expect."

"That's just what I'll want," Grus agreed. "You'll take care of it for me, I hope? We don't want to look as though we're invading Thervingia, now. We do want to be sure the Thervings won't invade Avornis."

"I understand, Your Majesty," Hirundo said. "I won't go anywhere near the border. But I'll make it very plain I can put up a good fight on the far side of the Tuola."

"That's what I want from you," Grus said. "King Berto will probably send his own ambassador here to announce his accession. That's what the custom is, I think. If he does, I want that ambassador to see your men on the move so he'll know we're ready for whatever happens."

"I'll take care of it," Hirundo promised. Grus dismissed him after that. The king had come to know his general, and to know he could count on a promise of that sort.

And, indeed, Hirundo left for the Tuola and the province beyond it three days before an embassy from Thervingia reached the city of Avornis. At the head of the embassy was Zangrulf, serving Berto as he'd served Dagipert for so many years. He bowed low before King Grus in the throne room. "I gather you will have heard our sad news?" he said in his fluent but gutturally accented Avornan.

"Yes," Grus replied. "Please pass on to King Berto my personal sympathies. I lost my own father a few years ago. It's never easy."

"Thank you, Your Majesty." Zangrulf bowed again. "That is . . . gracious of you. I am sure the king will appreciate it." His tone sharpened. "I am sure he will appreciate it more than the sight of armed Avornans marching toward Thervingia."

Grus shrugged. "They're marching through Avornis, Your Excellency. They have no intention of starting any trouble between our two kingdoms. But at the start of a new reign, it's hard to know what will happen next."

"May I take your assurance back to King Berto?" Zangrulf asked.

"Certainly," Grus answered. "Tell him that as long as you Thervings stay on your side of the border, we'll stay on ours. I don't want any trouble with Thervingia. I never have."

"Really?" Zangrulf raised a sly eyebrow. "If it weren't for Avornis' trouble with Thervingia, you wouldn't be king today."

That was probably true. As a matter of fact, that was bound to be true. Even so, Grus only shrugged again. "I meant what I said, Your Excellency. It's possible to buy some things too dearly. Didn't King Dagipert finally realize that when he was fighting us?"

"Maybe," the Therving ambassador said. "But maybe not, too."

"By the gods, you're not giving me any great secrets," Grus exclaimed. "Dagipert's dead. He won't be attacking us again, come what may."

"He was my master for many years," Zangrulf said. "I keep looking over my shoulder, expecting him to give me some new order. It doesn't happen. It won't happen. I know that. Most of me knows that, anyhow. But there's still that part. . . . He was a strong king."

"So he was." Grus couldn't disagree. No one who'd ever had to deal with Dagipert could have disagreed with that. Grus persisted, "But didn't he finally figure out he couldn't hope to beat us, no matter how strong he was?"

"Maybe. Maybe not," Zangrulf said again. "I'm not going to say any more than that, Your Majesty. There's still that part that thinks he may be listening. And if he is, he's saying, 'Whatever I thought is none of your business, Avornan.'"

Grus laughed. "Have it your way, then, Your Excellency. And would you say King Berto is as strong as King Dagipert was?"

"King Berto is as strong in prayer as King Dagipert was with the sword." Zangrulf picked his words with obvious care.

"May the gods love him, then," Grus said—as safe an answer as he could find. Zangrulf confirmed what Lanius had said about Dagipert's son. Grus added, "May he bring peace, and may the gods love that, as well."

"I hope it will be so. I think it will be so," Zangrulf said. He didn't say whether he thought that would be good. By his tone, he had his doubts. The Thervings were an iron-bellied folk, most of them. Would Berto be able to hold them to peace, even if that was what he intended? Grus shrugged—a shrug so small he could hope his robes hid it from Zangrulf.

"I will give gifts," the king said. "Some to you, for bringing King Berto's greetings, and some to him, in the hope of a long reign for him and peace between our two kingdoms."

Zangrulf bowed. His eyes gleamed. He seemed no more immune to gifts than anyone else. Grus resolved to make them generous, in the hope of getting some use from the man. "Thank you very much, Your Majesty.

Your openhandedness is famous throughout the world," the Therving said.

That made Grus smile. He was no more openhanded than he had to be, and everyone who knew him knew as much. Maybe Zangrulf was wangling for fancier presents. If he was, he'd probably get them. Here, Grus could see he did have to be openhanded, and so he would be.

CHAPTER TWENTY-THREE

King Lanius was picking fleas off Topaz, one of Snitch's kittens, when King Grus came into the chamber where the moncats dwelt. "Don't mean to bother you, Your Majesty," Grus said, by which Lanius was sure he meant to do exactly that, "but there's something I'd like you to take care of for me."

"Oh? What's that?" Lanius caught a flea and crushed it between his thumbnails, the only sure way he'd found to be rid of them.

"King Berto has sent a couple of his yellow-robed clerics to the city of Avornis," Grus answered. "They're touring cathedrals—looks like Berto *is* a pious fellow, just the way you said. Would you be kind enough to show them around a bit?"

"Why me?" As soon as Lanius stopped paying attention to Topaz, the moncat, which didn't like him picking through its fur, fled. The grab he made for it proved futile. Muttering, he went on, "Wouldn't showing cathedrals to the Thervings be Arch-Hallow Anser's job, not mine?"

As he hoped, he succeeded in embarrassing his father-in-law. Reddening, Grus said, "Well, it might be, but Anser's still learning about what he's doing, and you know more of the history about such places than he does right now."

Aside from doing what Grus wanted, Anser didn't seem very interested in learning an arch-hallow's duties. Hunting, with or without Ortalis, excited him far more. Grus had to know that at least as well as Lanius did. Lanius just folded his arms across his chest and looked back at his fellow king.

He was hoping he could make Grus turn red. He didn't; Grus owned more than his share of self-possession. The older man went on, "Besides, having a King of Avornis escort the Thervings would be a privilege for them. It would make Berto feel we were giving him special honors, honors other sovereigns wouldn't expect."

"What other sovereigns?" Lanius asked. "The chiefs of the Chernagor city-states? They wouldn't get honors to match Thervingia's anyhow. Savages like the Heruls? They don't worship our gods at all. Neither do the princes of the Menteshe—they bow down to the Banished One, instead."

King Grus let out a sigh of exaggerated patience. "*Please,* Your Majesty," he said. "I've already told them you'd do it."

"Oh." Lanius drummed his fingers on his thigh. "That means I'm stuck with the job, doesn't it? All right. But I'll thank you not to make any more plans for me without telling me you're doing it."

"I expect that's fair enough, Your Majesty." After a few heartbeats, Grus seemed to realize something more was called for, for he went on, "I won't do it again." That was better, but not good enough. Lanius waited without a word. Again, Grus paused. Again, he found words, this time saying, "I'm sorry."

"You should be," Lanius said, but that was what he'd been waiting to hear. He sighed. "Let's get it over with."

The clerics' names were Grasulf and Berich. Grasulf was tall and fuzzily bearded, while Berich was squat and fuzzily bearded. They both spoke good Avornan, and they both seemed honored that Lanius was taking them around the cathedrals of the city of Avornis. Grasulf said, "King Berto will be so jealous when we go home and tell him all that we have done in your kingdom."

Voice dry, Lanius answered, "King Berto's father did quite a lot in our kingdom, too."

To his amazement, both Therving clerics looked embarrassed. Berich said, "That is too bad, Your Majesty. Many of us thought so even while the war was going on. This is where the worship of the true gods centers. To fight against Avornis is to fight against the gods."

"King Dagipert didn't think so," Lanius said.

"Dagipert was a very strong king," Grasulf said. "While he lived, we had to do what he said. But there is not a cleric in Thervingia who is not glad to have peace with Avornis at last. And the same holds for our soldiers. We fought against your kingdom year after year, and what did we get because of it? Nothing anybody can see. So says King Berto, and we think he is right."

Of course you do, or say you do, Lanius thought. *He is your new king, and you have to obey him. You had better think he is right.* He couldn't say that to Grasulf and Berich, not when what they thought—what Berto thought—was exactly what he wanted Thervingians to think. He did say, "I am glad to hear you speak so. As long as you do, the Banished One will never gain a foothold in Thervingia."

He made the gesture that was supposed to ward off the Banished One (how much good it really did, or whether it did any good at all, he couldn't have said). The two yellow-robed clerics used the same gesture. Berich said, "May his followers never come into our land."

"Yes, may that be so," Lanius agreed.

Grasulf looked over his shoulder, as though afraid Dagipert might still somehow hear what he said. When he spoke, it was in a low voice. "They do say the Banished One sent minions to him who was our king. They say it, though I do not know if it was true."

"I have heard it," Lanius said. "I do not know if it was true, either."

"I believe it," Berich said. "Gods curse me if I do not believe it. Dagipert was always one to trust in his own strength. He would dare hear the Banished One's envoys. He would be sure he could use the Banished One for his own purposes, and not the other way around."

"He would be sure, yes," Grasulf said solemnly. "But would he be right?"

"Who can say?" Berich replied. "That he was confident in his own strength does not mean he was right to be confident."

"True," Lanius said. Such rumors had floated around Dagipert for years, though he always denied them. Lanius had hoped to learn the truth after the formidable King of Thervingia was dead. But maybe Dagipert had been the only one who knew what the truth was, and had taken it onto his pyre with him.

Lanius shook his head. *The Banished One knows,* he reminded himself. *The Banished One knows, and he dies not.* Thinking so vividly of Avornis' great foe made him wonder if he would dream of him that night. He didn't, and wondered why. *Maybe,* he thought, *I worried enough about him that he doesn't need to visit me in dreams. I've already done his work for him.*

That worried him even more than dreaming of the Banished One might have done.

King Grus watched Avornis go through much of a quiet summer. The Thervings left his kingdom alone. So did the Menteshe. No irate baron rose up against him. The first thing he wondered—and it was an amazement that lasted through that easy season—was what had gone wrong; what the gods were planning to make him sorry for those warm, lazy, peaceful months.

Estrilda laughed at him when he said as much to her in the quiet of their bedchamber. "Don't you think you're entitled to take it easy for a little while?" she asked.

"No!" His own vehemence surprised even him, and plainly alarmed his wife. He went on, "When have I ever taken it easy? When have I ever had the chance to take it easy? When, in all the years since I first went aboard a river galley? Why should I start doing it now?"

"You always worked hard," Estrilda said, nodding. "You worked hard so you could get someplace you'd never gone before. But, sweetheart"— she took his hands in hers—"you're King of Avornis. You can't rise any higher than this, can you? Since you can't, you've earned the right to relax."

Grus thought about that. Had he done all he'd done for the sake of getting ahead? Some of it, maybe, but all? He doubted that. The more he thought about it, the more he doubted it, too. He'd worked hard because he liked working hard, because he was good at it. Claiming anything else would be a lie.

And he certainly could rise or fall even though he was King of Avornis. He could be a good king or a bad one, remembered with a smile, remembered with a shudder—or, perhaps worst of all, not remembered. He dreaded that. Women had children to let them know they were immortal. What did men have? Only their names, in the minds and in the mouths of others after they were gone.

If I could be the king who reclaimed the Scepter of Mercy from the Banished One . . . They'd remember me forever, then, and cheer my name whenever they heard it. Grus laughed at himself. When he thought about getting the Scepter of Mercy back, he wasn't just measuring himself against every King of Avornis who'd reigned over the past four hundred years. He was also, in effect, standing back to back with the Banished One himself. If that wasn't mad and overweening pride, what would be?

He didn't presume to mention his ambition to Estrilda. He knew what she would say. He knew she would be right, too.

All he did say was, "I want to be as good a king as I can."

"Well, all right," Estrilda said reasonably. "When things are going on, you should deal with them. And you do—you landed on Pandion like a falling tree last year. But why should you run around and wave your arms and get all excited when nothing's happening that you need to worry about?"

"Because something may be going on behind the scenes," Grus replied. "If I deal with little troubles now, they won't turn into big ones later."

"If you get all upset over nothing, you may make what was a little problem get bigger in a hurry," his wife pointed out, which was also more reasonable than Grus wished it were. "Besides, you said it yourself—there aren't any problems right now."

"There aren't any I can see," Grus said. "That doesn't mean there aren't any at all."

"How do you know it doesn't?" Estrilda asked. "Everything *I* know about seems fine, anyhow." By the way she said it, that proved her point.

Sometimes—far more often than not—a man who grumbled about the way things were was stuck with them, because they wouldn't change. And when they did, he often found himself wishing they hadn't. Knowing when to be content with what you had was something Grus had never mastered.

Only a couple of weeks after he complained to Estrilda about how quiet everything was, a messenger came up from the south—from the Stura River, the border between Avornis and the lands of the Menteshe. "Something strange is afoot, Your Majesty," he said.

"Something strange is always afoot along the border," Grus answered. "I ought to know—I put in enough time down there in my younger days. What is it now?"

"Your Majesty, I'll tell you exactly what's afoot," the messenger answered. "The nomads' thralls are afoot, that's what. They're coming over the Stura into our lands down there by the hundreds, more of 'em every day."

"What?" Grus scratched his head. "But that's crazy. Thralls don't do things like that." Being content with their lot—or perhaps just unable to imagine anything different—was a big part of what made the thralls of the Menteshe so terrifying to ordinary men, to whole men. Grus went on, "When one thrall wakes up and gets away, that's unusual." It was so very unusual, it often meant the "awakened" thrall was in fact not awakened at all, but a spy for the Menteshe and the Banished One. "Hundreds?" Grus said. "That hardly seems possible."

"It's true, though," the messenger said. "What are we going to do with them if they keep coming? How are we going to feed them?"

Grus had a more basic worry. "Why are they doing it?" he asked.

"No one knows, Your Majesty," the man from the south replied. "Some of them are thralls still, even on our side of the river. The rest have no memory of who they were or why they came over the border."

"Isn't that interesting?" Grus whistled tunelessly. He asked the messenger a few more questions, then sent him away to a barracks from which he could be summoned in a hurry at need.

The first thing he did after that was give Lanius the news. "How very peculiar," his son-in-law said when he'd finished.

"Then you've never heard of anything like this?" Grus knew he sounded disappointed; he expected Lanius to know about such things.

But the younger king shook his head. "No, never," he answered in a low, troubled voice. "We'd better try to find out about it, don't you think?"

"Yes, I think that would be a good idea," Grus said. "It's sorcery from the Banished One that makes thralls, and also sorcery from him that lets some of them seem to break free and come into Avornis to spy on us."

"This doesn't sound like either of those things," Lanius observed.

"It has to be sorcery of some sort, don't you think?" Grus said. "What else could make thralls change their ways? They don't do that by accident."

"They never have, anyhow," Lanius said.

"I'll summon Alca the witch," Grus said. "She's seen the Banished One face-to-face in dreams, the same as we have. If anybody can get to the bottom of it, she's the one." Lanius raised an eyebrow. Grus looked back at him, waiting to see if he would say anything. He didn't. Grus added, "I think I'd better go down to the south myself, to see with my own eyes what's going on. This is far enough out of the ordinary that I don't want to rely on secondhand reports."

Lanius raised both eyebrows this time. He said, "It's . . . unusual for the King of Avornis to leave the capital when not on campaign."

"Maybe it shouldn't be." Grus eyed his son-in-law. Could Lanius organize a coup while he was out of the city? That would be reason enough to keep him from going. He shook his head. Lanius might not—surely did not—like him. But his son-in-law didn't have nearly enough backing among the soldiers to overthrow him. Grus made it his business to know such things. He glanced over to Lanius again. He was quite sure the other king knew it, too.

By the way Lanius looked back at him, the younger man was making the same calculation and, to his own dismay, coming to the same conclusions. "Perhaps you're right," Lanius said at last. "Some things do indeed need to be seen at first hand. And you'll be be a grandfather again by the time you get back."

"Yes." Grus nodded. "I don't want my grandchildren to have to worry about being made into thralls themselves. That's why I'm going." He waited for Lanius to tell him he was being foolish or was exaggerating the problem. Lanius said nothing of the sort. That made Grus wonder whether, instead of exaggerating, he was underestimating whatever was going on in the south.

Well, he thought, *I'll find out.*

King Lanius watched King Grus and Alca sail south on a river galley. Grus' retinue of guards and secretaries and servants crowded not only that galley but the one that sailed with it. A king couldn't go anywhere without an appropriate retinue. Lanius took that for granted. It sometimes seemed to chafe Grus.

As his river galley sailed away, Grus stood at the stern by the steersman—the position of command. Anyone looking at him would have guessed he'd been a river-galley skipper before taking the throne. Alca stood at the bow, with one hand on the stempost, looking ahead to the mystery of the south. Though the galley was crowded, no one seemed to think it wise to come near the witch. She had a little space all her own.

Beside Lanius, Sosia said, "I do wonder what's going on down there. I hope it isn't a trap to lure Father into danger."

"With all the men he's taking, he could smash just about any trap," Lanius said.

"Yes, that's so." Sosia looked relieved.

Lanius knew there was something he hadn't said. He thought Grus and the soldiers with him could defeat a Menteshe ambush. Whether Grus and Alca could defeat a sorcerous onslaught from the Banished One, though, might be a different question. The king and the witch had paid each other next to no notice as they went aboard the river galley and took their separate places. Lanius scratched his head. He knew he wasn't understanding something. He wasn't sure what he was missing, which only made him the more curious.

But then Sosia said, "I want to go back to the palace." She set both hands on her swollen belly.

"All right." Lanius was getting tired of seeing Grus off, but preferred staying home himself.

As they returned, they found Anser and Ortalis arguing in a hallway just inside the entrance. Grus' bastard was shaking his head and saying, "No, we can't do that. That isn't hunting, by the gods!"

"What would you call it, then?" Ortalis seemed genuinely amazed his half brother didn't care for what he thought of as fine sport.

"Murder is the word that springs to mind," the young Arch-Hallow of Avornis answered.

That was enough—more than enough—to draw Lanius' attention. Hunting interested him not at all. Something that might be murder was a different story. "What's going on here?" he asked, as casually as he could.

"Nothing," Ortalis said quickly. "Nothing at all."

"It didn't sound like nothing to me," Lanius said.

"It didn't sound like nothing to me, either," Anser added.

Sosia nodded. "Come on, Ortalis—out with it," she said.

Prince Ortalis gave his sister a harried look. "Oh, all right," he muttered. "Regular hunting's all very well, but after a while it gets . . . boring, you know what I mean? I was looking for a way to spice it up. That's all I was doing. Olor's beard, everyone makes such a fuss about every little thing I say."

"What exactly *did* you say?" Lanius asked.

Ortalis pinched his lips together and didn't reply. "If you don't tell him, I will," Anser said.

That drew another glare from King Grus' legitimate son. "Oh, all right," he said again. "I got tired of chasing boar and deer and rabbits, that's all. I was wondering what it would be like to hunt some worthless man."

"And *kill* him?" Lanius said in rising horror. Hunting might have sated Ortalis' bloodlust for a while. Clearly, it hadn't gotten rid of that taste for cruelty altogether.

"Well, if he deserved it," Ortalis answered. "If he was a condemned criminal, say. He'd have it coming to him then."

"I don't think anybody deserves being hunted to death," Lanius said.

"I don't, either," Sosia said. "And I'm sure Father wouldn't. You know that, too, don't you?"

By Ortalis' fierce scowl, he knew it all too well. "Nobody wants me to have any fun!" he shouted.

"That isn't the only kind of *fun* you were talking about," Anser said.

"I was joking!" Ortalis said. "Can't anybody tell when I'm joking?"

"Hunting men was one thing, you said," Anser went on, "but hunting women—"

"I was joking!" Ortalis screamed. Servants stared at him. All through the palace, far out of sight, heads must have whipped around at that cry. Lanius was as sure of it as of his own name. He'd heard some things about Ortalis and serving girls. He didn't know whether he believed them, but he'd heard them. He didn't *want* to believe them—he did know that.

Sosia said, "If Father ever finds out about this, Ortalis—"

"He won't, if you can keep your big fat mouth shut," her brother whispered furiously. "And you'd better, because I *was* just joking."

"We'll make a bargain with you," Lanius said. Beside him, Sosia stirred, but she kept silent. Anser just nodded, waiting to hear what Lanius would propose. He went on, "Here—this is it. We won't tell Grus anything about this, as long as you promise never even to talk about hunting people again, men or women, joking or not. Is that a deal?"

Ortalis looked as though he'd bitten into something nasty. "Everybody gets so excited about every stupid little thing," he muttered.

"Is it a deal?" Lanius asked again.

"Oh, all right." His brother-in-law still looked and sounded disgusted at the world.

"Promise, then," Lanius said.

"Promise in the holy names of King Olor and Queen Quelea and all the other gods in the heavens," Anser added. To Lanius' surprise, King Grus' bastard son could sound like a proper, holy Arch-Hallow of Avornis after all.

Ortalis blinked. Evidently, he hadn't thought Anser could sound like a proper, holy arch-hallow, either. He coughed a couple of times, but finally nodded. "By Olor and Quelea and the other gods, I promise," he choked out.

"The gods hold your words," Anser said. "If you break your promise, they will make you pay. It may not be soon, it may not be the way you expect, but they will make you pay." He nodded to Ortalis, then to Lanius and Sosia, and walked out of the palace, his crimson robes flapping around him.

"I don't know why he started having kittens. I was only joking," Ortalis said. Neither his sister nor his brother-in-law answered. He said something else, something pungent, under his breath and went off in a hurry, his shoulders hunched, his face pinched with the fury he had to hold in for once and couldn't loose on the world around him.

Quietly, Sosia said, "You did well there."

"Did I?" Lanius shrugged. "I don't know. He can't hunt people. I do know that. The rest?" He shrugged again. "Maybe we should tell your father. But maybe Ortalis really was joking. Who can say?"

His wife sighed. "He wasn't joking. You know it as well as I do. He'll do whatever he thinks he can get away with. If he decides he can't get away with hunting people for sport, he won't do it. I hope to the heavens he won't do it, anyhow."

"He won't do it with Anser, that's certain," Lanius said. "More to him than I thought there was. I'm glad to see it." He'd been scandalized when Grus named his illegitimate son Arch-Hallow of Avornis. But if Anser could sound like a proper arch-hallow, maybe he could do everything else a proper arch-hallow needed to do, too. Lanius dared hope.

By the way Sosia sounded, so did she. "I thought I'd despise Anser—after all, I don't like to think about Father running around on Mother, any more than I'd care to think of you running around on me. But I don't. The more I see him, the better I like him."

"Yes, the same with me," Lanius answered. He didn't say anything about running around on Sosia. He hadn't, not yet. But he had noticed a serving woman or two casting glances his way. He could do something about that if he ever decided he wanted to. Even if the palace held a new royal bastard afterward, Grus would hardly be in a position to criticize him.

Lanius laughed, though it wasn't really funny. If Grus wanted to criticize him—or to do worse than that to him—he would. That was what being King of Avornis—being the King of Avornis with the real power in the land—meant. Grus wouldn't need reason or right on his side, only strength. And strength, without a doubt, he had. If anyone in the kingdom was in the position to appreciate the difference between rank and strength, Lanius knew all too well he was the man.

"I don't much care for this country," Alca said as the river galley drew up to a pier in Cumanus. "It's warmer than it ought to be at this season of the year. The soil's the wrong color. People have funny accents, too. And they go around looking nervous all the time."

King Grus smiled at her. "I lived down here in the south for years and years. It seems like home to me, at least as much as the city of Avornis does. Red dirt's as good as brown. If you manure it well, it yields fine crops. I can talk this way as well as the way I usually do." For a sentence, he put on a nasal southern accent.

Alca made a face. "Maybe you can, but I don't see why you'd bother."

"And if you had the Menteshe right across the river from you," Grus went on, "don't you think you'd have an excuse for looking nervous, too?"

The witch couldn't very well argue with that. She didn't even try. "Something must be wrong, badly wrong, on the other side of the Stura," she said. "If it's stirred up the thralls"—she shuddered—"it must be truly dreadful."

"Maybe," Grus said.

"How could it be otherwise?" Alca asked.

"That's what you've come to find out—how it could be otherwise, I mean," Grus answered. "Or if it is otherwise."

"What else could it be but some upheaval?" Alca said.

"I don't know," Grus said. "The point is, you don't know, either."

Thralls worked their fields, took mates—they could hardly be said to marry—and endured whatever their Menteshe overlords chose to dish out to them, year after year after year, till they died. They wore clothes. They spoke—a little. Otherwise, they weren't much different from the beasts they tended. Most of what made men men was burned out of them. So it had been for centuries, in lands where the Menteshe ruled. So the Banished One wished it were all over Avornis.

Every so often, as the Avornans had seen, a thrall would by some accident shake off the dark spell that clouded his life. Then, if he could, he would flee north to Avornis.

But why would a still spellbound thrall suddenly flee over the Stura? Why would hundreds of such thralls come north into Avornis? Grus hoped Alca would be able to tell him. No answer he'd imagined for himself came close to satisfying him.

The witch said, "They'll have thralls here waiting for me to examine?"

"They'd better," Grus answered. "If they don't, someone's going to be very unhappy."

He looked across the Stura into the lands the Menteshe held. They looked no different from Avornan soil on this side of the river. Back before the Menteshe swarmed out of the south, they were Avornan soil, as the thralls' ancestors were Avornan farmers.

Local officials hurried up to the river galley. "Your Majesty," they murmured, bowing low to Grus. "Such an honor that you're here."

"It's good to be back in the south," Grus said. "I wish it hadn't been a problem that brought me here. Now, then—this is Alca the witch, one of the finest sorcerers in the city of Avornis."

"Thank you, Your Majesty," Alca said.

"For what? For the truth? You're welcome." The king turned back to the dignitaries from Cumanus. "You have some of these thralls where the witch can look them over? I'll want to see them, too. I didn't come all this way to twiddle my thumbs."

"Oh, yes, Your Majesty," said the garrison commander, a colonel named Tetrax. "We've got 'em in the amphitheater. It holds a lot of them, and we don't have much trouble guarding 'em there, either."

"That's fine." Grus knew Cumanus' amphitheater well. It was a large semicircular pit scooped out of the ground, with a stage at the bottom and benches along the ground sloping up to the level of the surrounding streets. Tetrax was right; a handful of guards could keep captives there from getting away. "Suppose you take us to them, then. The sooner we understand what's going on here, or start to, the better off everyone will be."

Tetrax nodded. "Come along then, Your Majesty. And you, too, of course, Mistress Alca."

Soldiers from the other river galley formed a guard force around the king and the witch as they made their way through the streets of the city. Shopkeepers and housewives and drunks stared at the procession. A few people cheered. Most just gaped.

When someone shouted that Grus was coming, the guards around the amphitheater stiffened to attention. Even so, their eyes never left the thralls down at the bottom of the excavation. Grus came up to the edge and, Alca at his side, peered down into the pit. He'd never seen so many thralls on this side of the Stura. He hoped he never would again.

They ambled around down there, altogether unconcerned about the guards and the King of Avornis above them. Loaves of bread and pitchers of water (or would it be beer, to keep them from coming down with a flux of the bowels?) stood on a table in the middle of the stage. It might have been a scene from a play, most likely a farce.

The resemblance was heightened when two men seized the same loaf at the same time. They both tugged on it, shouting what might or might not have been words. They clenched their fists. They looked to be on the very point of fighting. Then the loaf tore in two. The thralls, each content with what he had, relaxed and began to eat.

Alca watched them intently. "Bring them both up to me," she said. "Do they speak Avornan or the language of the Menteshe?"

"Avornan, ma'am, after a fashion," Tetrax answered. He nodded to some of the guards. "Go get 'em, boys. The lady's a witch, come to try and figure out what those nasty thralls are doing swimming the Stura."

That got the guards moving. One of them said, "I hope she'll figure out how to send the buggers back, too."

When they took the thralls by the elbows, they were careful not even to seem to be trying to take the bread away from them. The thralls' hair and beards were long and unkempt. By the ripe stench wafting from them, Grus wondered if they'd ever bathed.

"I've never seen them close-up before." By the way Alca said it, she would have been just as happy never to see them again.

"Can you tell anything about them?" Grus asked.

"They're hungry and filthy," Alca answered. "If you mean sorcerously, no. The spell that makes them thralls lies at the very root of their minds and spirits. If it didn't—if it were further up, you might say, where a wizard could sense it more easily—it would be easier to fight, easier to get rid of." She spoke to one of the thralls. "You! Why are you here in Avornis?"

He stared at her. He scratched, caught something, and popped it into his mouth. Alca gulped. The thrall looked her up and down. "Pretty," he said. He wore a shirt and trousers as grimy as he was. The bulge at his crotch said he found Alca more than just pretty.

If the witch noticed that, she gave no sign. She turned to another thrall. "Why did you come to Avornis?"

"Afraid," he answered, and cowered away from her as though she were about to start beating him.

"Afraid of what?" she asked. The thrall didn't answer. "Afraid of what?" Alca repeated, this time more to Grus than to the scrawny, dirty man from across the Stura. "Is he afraid of me? Is that what he means? Or did he come to Avornis because he was afraid of what was happening on the other side of the river?"

"*I* don't know," Grus said. "How do you aim to find out?"

"Questions won't do it—that's plain enough. I'll have to use wizardry." Alca looked unhappy. "I don't like using wizardry to investigate spells the Banished One uses. You saw why, back in the city of Avornis."

"Well, yes," Grus said. "But sometimes these things are important. Don't you think this is?"

Alca sighed. "I wish I could tell you no. But you're right, Your Majesty. This *is* important. I'll do the best I can."

"Thank you," Grus told her.

"I'm not at all sure you're welcome," she answered.

At her command, the guards hauled one of the thralls a few steps farther out of the amphitheater. He stood there, looking around Cumanus with the same dull-eyed lack of curiosity an ox might have shown. *How can she hope to learn anything from him?* Grus wondered. *And even if she does, how can she hope to cure him?* Come to think of it, maybe she couldn't. She'd said, and Grus knew, making men out of thralls was anything but easy.

The witch took a crystal from the sack of sorcerous gear she'd brought. "Is that the one that makes rainbows?" Grus asked. "The one you used on the bowls of snow back in the capital?"

She nodded. "That's right. Now maybe we'll see something interesting. Maybe, mind you, Your Majesty."

Holding the crystal high so it caught a sunbeam, she drew a rainbow from it once again. Grus wondered how the crystal did that; Alca had made it plain the doing there wasn't hers. She twisted the crystal this way and that, and the rainbow moved with it. At last, she made the rainbow fall on the thrall's eyes.

Those eyes got very wide. The man grunted in astonishment. "Do you understand me?" Alca asked him.

"Understand!" he said. Alca nodded. So did Grus. He could hear something new in the thrall's voice. Though the fellow still used only one word, he sounded more like a real man, a full man, and less like a beast of burden that happened to walk on two legs.

"Why did you come here?" Alca asked him, keeping the rainbow shining on his face.

"Had to," the thrall answered.

He seemed to think that was all the reply he needed. "May I ask him something?" Grus said softly. The witch nodded once more. Grus turned to the thrall. "Why did you have to? Why couldn't you just stay where you were?"

This time, the thrall didn't answer right away. He frowned, his face a mask of intense concentration. How much effort did he need, even with Alca's wizardry aiding him, to use words in something close to the way a free man might? "Had to," he repeated. "Had to go. Had to . . . leave." Sweat ran down his face, leaving little clean rills in the filth. "Had to leave. Orders."

"Whose orders?" Grus and Alca said it together.

"Orders." The thrall seemed to have to say things more than once, perhaps to keep them straight in his own mind, such as it was. After a moment, sweating harder than ever, he got out: "*His* orders."

"Whose?" Alca asked. But then the rainbow on the thrall's face began to redden, as had happened with the sorcery back in the capital. The man who'd fled over the Stura groaned. He clutched at his forehead. Alca dropped the crystal. The rainbow vanished. But the thrall crumpled to the ground. A guard felt his wrist, then shook his head. The thrall was dead. He'd given no answer. But Alca and Grus had gotten one even so.

CHAPTER TWENTY-FOUR

The baby yowled. Lanius stared fondly down at her in her mother's arms. Had she been someone else's, the noise would have driven him crazy. He was sure of that. But, since Pitta was his, he didn't mind . . . too much.

Sosia said, "I wish she would have been another boy. Babies don't always stay healthy." That was a careful way of saying they died all too easily.

"I do know that," Lanius said. "I was sickly myself. I think one of the reasons my uncle, Scolopax, never did anything to me was that he thought I wouldn't live to grow up anyhow. But I did, and he died not too long after my father. Crex is healthier than I ever was."

"King Olor and Queen Quelea keep him that way," Sosia said. "And the gods watch over you, too, Pitta."

"Yes," Lanius agreed. Pitta kept right on crying. Raising his voice, the king went on, "We should hear from your father soon."

"He's staying down in the south longer than I thought he would," Sosia said.

"We have a real problem down there," Lanius said. "What are we supposed to do with so many thralls?"

"I'm sure I don't know," Sosia answered.

"Nobody else does, either," Lanius said.

A wet nurse took Pitta from Sosia and bared her breast. The baby settled down to suck. The wet nurse was stolid and plain. Lanius realized all Pitta's wet nurses were stolid and plain. Come to think of it, Crex's had been, too. He laughed. He couldn't help seeing their uncovered breasts. Sosia evidently didn't want him getting any ideas on account of that.

"What's funny?" his wife asked.

"You are," Lanius answered. She gave him an odd look. He didn't explain, not while the wet nurse could hear. She might have known she was stolid, but probably didn't think of herself as plain. Who did, woman or man?

A messenger came into the royal bedchamber. Bowing to Lanius, he said, "Beg pardon, Your Majesty, but I have a letter here from King Grus." He held out a sealed roll of parchment.

Lanius took it. "Thank you," he said. The messenger bowed again and went out. Lanius broke the seal on the letter and unrolled it.

"What does he say?" Sosia asked.

" 'Congratulations, Your Majesties, on the birth of your daughter. I hope the girl is well, and I hope you are well, too, my dear Sosia. Hearing that both these things are so will make my stay down here much more pleasant than it is now. We know little, disappointingly little, and the Banished One is doing his best to keep us from learning more. His best, as you know, is all too good. Still, when Alca can keep him from noticing what she is about, she does learn by bits and pieces. One day before too long, she hopes she can fit the pieces together. May she prove right, for I wish I were back in the city of Avornis with my new granddaughter, my grandson, and the two of you. With fond regards, King Grus.' "

Even in a letter to his daughter, he called himself the king. He knew Lanius would be reading it, too, and wanted to remind him who he was, who had power. Lanius understand that very well indeed.

The wet nurse's nipple slid out of Pitta's mouth. The woman hoisted the sleepy baby to her shoulder and patted her on the back. Pitta gave forth with a resounding belch. "That should keep her happy," the wet nurse said.

It would keep me happy, Lanius thought. A belch like that among his bodyguards would provoke loud laughter. The wet nurse rocked the little princess in her arms for a few minutes, then laid her in the cradle. Pitta didn't start howling again, which proved how tired she was.

Lanius and Sosia yawned, too, both of them at the same time. They were also tired. Sosia was still getting over childbirth. Lanius had no such excuse. But a new baby disrupted the lives of all the people most intimately concerned with it. Even if, being king, he didn't have to take care of Pitta, she kept him up at night. He suspected she kept half the palace up on bad nights.

Bobbing a curtsy, the wet nurse left the chamber. Sosia yawned again, even wider than before. "Sleep if you want to," Lanius told her. "By the gods, you've earned the right."

"If I sleep now, I won't sleep tonight," Sosia answered. "Then I'll be just as sleepy tomorrow."

"I wonder how people ever catch up on sleep till a baby starts sleeping through the night—especially people without servants," Lanius said.

"If you really want to know, you could ask my mother," Sosia said.

"I did that when Crex was born," Lanius answered. "What she said was, 'Mostly, you don't sleep.'"

Sosia yawned one more time. "She's right."

River galleys patrolled the Stura, gliding up and down the river. Standing at the stern of one of them, King Grus felt years slide from his age. He felt as though he were commanding a flotilla again, on the lookout for an invasion from the south. He'd spent a lot of time doing that, and thought he'd done it well. It was certainly a simpler job than King of Avornis.

Having Alca up at the river galley's bow reminded him he still wore those years. The invasion he was looking for wasn't of hard-riding Menteshe horsemen. He wanted to keep more thralls from crossing the Stura and coming up into Avornis. He didn't know what to do with the ones he had. He knew he didn't want to have to deal with any more of them.

"Boat!" shouted a lookout standing not far from the witch. "Boat in the river!" He pointed toward the southern bank of the Stura.

Grus saw the boat, too. He nodded to the oarmaster and the helmsman. "We're going to sink it."

"Aye, aye, sir." The oarmaster upped the stroke.

"Yes, Your Majesty." The helmsman tugged at the steering oar, guiding the galley at the little rowboat ahead. Even as he did so, though, he asked, "Do we really have to do this? He's just trying to get away from the godscursed Menteshe."

"I know." Grus wasn't happy about it, either. "If the thralls were ordinary men, I'd be glad to have them. Even if every third one spied for the Banished One, I'd be glad to have them. We can always use peasants who'll settle down and work. I'd take them up near the border with Thervingia, where we've lost so many farmers of our own. But what can we do with thralls?"

"I don't know, sir," the helmsman admitted.

"Neither do I," Grus said. "I wish I did. They're the Banished One's creatures. If we use them, so are we."

The rowboat drew close as the river galley bore down on it. The thrall in the boat had wit enough to use the oars. But he was so intent on crossing the Stura and getting to the north bank, he never paid the least attention to the galley. Any normal man would have noticed the long, lean, deadly craft speeding toward his boat. Any normal man would have tried to get away, or at least would have cursed the sweating, grunting oarsmen who propelled the galley at him. The thrall just kept on rowing.

A river galley was built to ram another ship of its own kind without coming to grief. It made quick work of the flimsy little rowboat. Grus hardly staggered when the warship rolled over the boat. He got a brief glimpse of the thrall struggling in the Stura. Then the river galley was past.

"Well, there's one of the bastards we don't have to worry about anymore," the oarmaster said as his drum let the rowers ease back.

"Yes," Grus replied, but that was only partially true. He didn't have to worry that that thrall would splash up onto Avornan soil. He looked back over his shoulder. No, that thrall would never come up again. But the reason he'd set out to escape the Menteshe remained a mystery.

Grus knew that, for all his vigilance, he couldn't keep all the thralls who wanted to from crossing the Stura. More and more of them began trying it at night, when the galleys couldn't patrol. Soldiers and farmers who found them brought them to Cumanus, where they went into the amphitheater, and to other towns along the Stura.

"How do they know?" Grus asked Alca one evening.

"How does who know what, Your Majesty?" the witch said.

"How do the thralls know they have a better chance of crossing the Stura at night?" King Grus replied.

"It only stands to reason that . . ." Alca stopped, looking foolish. "Oh. I see what you mean. What do thralls know about reason?"

Grus nodded. "Yes, that's what I was thinking."

"A couple of things occur to me," the witch said. "One is that thralls do use words—after a fashion. That has to mean they're able to think after a fashion, too."

"Maybe," Grus said, but he didn't believe it. "And?"

"The Banished One may be telling them what to do, either directly or through the Menteshe."

King Grus contemplated that. "Well, you're right," he said. "I don't like it a bit. How can you tell whether it's so?"

"I can ask some of the thralls who've crossed the Stura at night whether the Menteshe told them to cross then," Alca said.

"And if they say no, or if you can't tell? How can you find out whether the Banished One gave them a direct order?"

The witch sighed. "I could ask them that, too, I suppose. I don't want to try to use magic to find out. I've been lucky enough to live through that sort of magic twice. The thrall the second time wasn't so lucky, though. And next time it might be me."

"Yes, I understand that," Grus said. "I won't ask you to try anything that might hurt you. I would like to know, though." He paused in thought. "Can you use a truth spell to see if what you're getting out of them is worth having?"

"I can try," Alca answered. "That shouldn't make me run directly up against the Banished One's wizardry, which is what I want *not* to do."

Accompanied by Grus' guards, the witch and the king went back to the amphitheater the next morning. Guardsmen brought another thrall out of the excavated pit. The woman stared at Alca with mild, incurious eyes. She brushed at her filthy, scraggly hair—an absentminded gesture.

Absentminded is right, Grus thought. *If so much of her mind weren't absent, we wouldn't be doing this now.* Alca asked, as she had before, "Why did you cross the Stura? Why did you come into Avornis?"

The thrall stared at her. A frown spread over the woman's dirty, sun-wrinkled face. "Had to," she said at last, her voice rusty from disuse.

"I see." Alca nodded briskly, as though speaking to someone in full possession of her wits. "And why did you have to?"

Another frown from the thrall. She might have been thinking over her answer. She might have been, but she probably wasn't. "Told me," she said at last. Her Avornan was an old-fashioned dialect, with a hissing accent surely taken from the Menteshe who ruled on the southern bank of the river.

"Ah." Alca turned to King Grus. "Now, with a little luck, we begin to learn something. I have the spell ready to go."

"Good," Grus said.

"I hope it's for the good," Alca said. "Remember what happened to that other thrall." She began to make passes in the air in front of her as she asked the woman thrall, "Who told you you had to come here?"

"He did," the woman replied at once.

Alca muttered something under her breath that was more fitting of a longshoreman than a witch. "Let's try again," she said, and repeated the series of passes. "Who was he?" she asked when they were done.

"Him who told me," the thrall said.

The witch muttered some more, louder this time. The thrall ignored that. She looked down at her hands, which were worn and scarred from a lifetime's carelessness and toil. Alca gathered herself. To Grus, she said, "So far, the woman is telling the truth. The only trouble is, it's not a useful truth."

"Is she talking that way on purpose?" Grus asked.

"I don't know," Alca told him. "I hope not. If she—or rather, if the wizardry inside her—is having sport with me . . ." She muttered yet again. "I can't think of a worse insult."

"What can you do about it?" the king asked.

"I don't know. I don't know whether I can do anything," Alca answered. "That's part of what makes it such an insult." She turned back to the thrall. "Did a mortal man tell you to come here?" The woman shook her head. Alca brightened. "Did one who isn't mortal tell you to come here?"

The woman shook her head again.

"Has to be one or the other," Grus said.

"With the Banished One, who knows?" Alca replied. She turned back to the female thrall, took a deep breath, and asked, "Did the Banished One tell you to leave your home and come into Avornis?"

Alca visibly braced herself, waiting for the woman's answer. Grus could hardly blame her, remembering the magic back at the royal palace and remembering the thrall falling over dead here at the amphitheater in Cumanus. The woman grinned—not an expression of mirth, but one that made her look uncommonly like a skull with glittering eyes. "I know," she whispered, and nodded. "Yes, I know."

"Then tell me," the witch commanded. But the woman only kept staring, that—mocking?—grin showing snaggled teeth, several of them broken. Alca's lips thinned in anger at being defied. "In the names of the gods—in the holy names of King Olor and Queen Quelea—tell me!"

The thrall woman's grin vanished, to be replaced by a snarl of hate. "Those names mean nothing to me here. Nothing! Less than nothing!" The voice with which she spoke was not her own, but a resonant baritone. For a moment, it put Grus in mind of the late Arch-Hallow Bucco's golden tones. Then, involuntarily, the king shook his head. Bucco would have killed to claim the sounds coming from this woman's mouth. She—or that which spoke through her—went on, "They cast me down from my rightful place. They sent me hither. That place, they say, is theirs. This place, then, is mine. They trifle with me here at their peril. And one day, I shall see them again in their own habitation, which is mine as well. Then shall they learn even there that they trifled with me at their peril."

After that outburst, the thrall went limp in the guards' arms. Her eyes sagged shut. She still breathed, though, and when Grus felt for a pulse he found one. "Are you answered?" he asked Alca. His voice wobbled. He knew more than a little pride that he'd managed to speak at all.

"I don't know," she answered, and her voice shook, too. "That the Banished One spoke through her there—who could doubt it? But did he himself set upon her the impulse to flee north? Did he himself, or some part of his essence, dwell within her all this while? Did he know we were questioning her? I don't know. How can I tell?"

"What of your truth spell?" Grus asked.

"What of it?" Alca returned. "She—or the Banished One through her—spoke the truth, I think. But he never answered the question I asked."

"Mph." Grus grunted, thinking back. "Yes, you're right. But the woman—or the Banished One—spoke the truth?"

"As far as I could tell. And that spell is a good one," Alca said.

"Does that mean the gods truly mean nothing to the Banished One?" Grus asked. If it *did* mean that, if the Banished One *was* supreme in this world as the gods were in the heavens . . . If that was so, what point to any of his struggles? None he could see, none at all.

But the witch shook her head. "He said their *names* meant nothing to him. That, I think, is true. But he is ever one to twist truth and turn it, so that we see it in mirrors within mirrors within mirrors. Take care with him and his words, Your Majesty. Always take care. That their names mean nothing to him does not mean their essence means nothing."

Grus shivered. "I hope you're right. If you're wrong . . . If you're wrong, we can never hope to beat him, can we?"

Alca shrugged. "What difference does it make? If the Banished One ever swallows Avornis, all of us will be made into thralls. You can look at things however you please. Me, I'd rather be dead. Dead, I know I'm out of his grasp."

"Something to that." Grus looked down into the amphitheater. The thralls in there were indifferent to his presence. They were mostly indifferent to one another, too, though a couple of them sat side by side, picking lice and fleas from each other's shaggy hair and ragged clothes. The sight didn't reassure Grus. Lanius' moncats might have done the same.

"I wish we could free them," Alca said. "Free all of them, I mean, not just the few here where we have at least a chance of eventually lifting the spells that cloud their minds." She looked south, toward the Stura and beyond. In a whisper, she went on, "So many of them under the Banished One's hand. And yet their ancestors were Avornans, just as ours were. It isn't right that they should be made into beasts."

"No, it isn't," Grus agreed. "Winning a war against the Menteshe—and against the Banished One—won't be easy, though. Crossing the Stura to win wars against them would be even harder than beating them back from our own land."

He thought about Lanius again. Lanius knew more Avornan history than Grus cared to contemplate. He knew how many efforts to push the border south of the Stura once more had come to grief. He would undoubtedly be able to give plenty of good reasons why one more would come to grief, too.

One of those good reasons also seemed only too obvious to Grus. "How can we possibly hope to beat the Banished One?" he asked. "Every time Avornis has tried to cross the Stura since the Menteshe took the Scepter of Mercy from us, we've had disasters." He'd known that much before Lanius gave him the gruesome details, though he hadn't known how gruesome they were.

"Mostly, he works through men," Alca insisted. "We can beat the Menteshe taken by themselves, can't we? If we can't do that, all else fails."

"True." Grus made a sour face. "Some of the princes who rule the Menteshe aren't anything much. Prince Ulash, though, who holds the lands right across the river from where we are now . . . He's a cunning old fox, Ulash is. He'd be no bargain even if the Banished One didn't back him."

"Why worry about him, then? Why not go after some of the others—some of the easier ones?"

"For one thing, if we get tied up in a war somewhere else along the river, what's he likely to do? Jump on us with both feet, that's what. And, for another"—King Grus lowered his voice, not that that was likely to do him much good—"Ulash's capital is Yozgat."

"Oh," Alca said in a small voice. Yozgat—where the Scepter of Mercy was held. She bobbed her head to Grus. "Those are good points. Plainly, I would never make a general."

"Well, I would never make a wizard, and that's even plainer." Grus stared down into the amphitheater again. It was alarmingly like watching animals in a cage. It didn't feel like watching people at all. Realizing that hurt.

Alca didn't disagree with him. She went back to the problem he'd been worrying at, too, and asked, "If we got into a fight with any one of the Menteshe princes, won't all of them rush to his aid?"

"I don't think so," Grus answered. "It hasn't worked that way up till now, anyhow. The Menteshe have a lot more—freedom of will, I guess you'd call it—than thralls do. They wouldn't be much use to the Banished One if they acted like . . . that." He pointed into the amphitheater. "He needs them able to think and to fight. And they *do* fight—among themselves, too, sometimes. They won't come to each other's aid unless that looks like a good idea to them."

"I see." Alca frowned as she worked through what that was likely to mean. "Then . . . even if the Banished One disappeared tomorrow—"

"Gods grant that he would!" Grus exclaimed, and then, "Excuse me for interrupting."

"It's all right, Your Majesty." The witch went back to her own train of thought. "Even if the Banished One disappeared tomorrow, the Menteshe would still be just as dangerous to us as ever."

"Not quite," Grus answered. "They wouldn't have his magic, his might, backing them. But they would still be dangerous, the same way the Thervings are dangerous. They're on our border, they're tough fighters, and they wouldn't mind taking our land away from us."

"I see," Alca said again. Now she looked down at the thralls. After a minute or so, biting her lip, she turned away from the amphitheater. "That is a monstrous sorcery, robbing them of so much of what it means to be human."

"Yes." Grus went on, "I wonder if the Banished One feels the same way about Olor and Quelea and the rest of the gods. When they cast him out of the heavens, didn't they rob him of most of what it means to be divine?"

Alca started to answer, then checked herself. "I never thought of that," she said slowly. "I wonder if anyone has ever thought of it. You should talk it over with a high-ranking cleric, not with me. If we understand the Banished One, perhaps we'll have a better chance of doing something about him. How clever you are, Your Majesty! That would never have occurred to me."

Grus didn't feel particularly clever, and he had his doubts about whether understanding the Banished One would do much to hold him back. The problem with trying to oppose him was his divine, or nearly divine, strength. How much would understanding him let the Avornans, or anyone else, undercut that? Not much—not as far as Grus could see.

But he could see other possibilities if Alca happened to be impressed with him. "Will you have supper with me tonight?" he asked, as casually as he could.

The smile Alca gave back wasn't one of eager assent. It was a woman's amused smile. "Remember what happened the last time you asked me that, Your Majesty?"

"Yes," he said. "I don't think that will happen again."

"How do you mean that?" she asked. "Do you mean you won't try feeling me up, or do you mean you think I'll enjoy it more this time?"

He muttered under his breath. He thought he'd phrased that so slyly. He didn't seem as clever as he thought he was, let alone as she thought he was. "I mean whatever you want me to mean," he said at last.

"Do you?" Alca said. Grus gave back a nod that challenged her to call him a liar. For a moment, he thought she would. But then she smiled again, the same mostly wry smile she'd used before. "All right, Your Majesty. How could I possibly doubt you?" The words said she couldn't. Her tone said something else altogether.

Well, Grus thought with an inward sigh, *no seduction tonight.* He still looked forward to the supper. Alca was good company, regardless of whether she cared to let him take her to bed.

Here in Cumanus, the supper would be better than with an army on campaign. The cook had the leisure to do things right, and could buy the best in the marketplace instead of depending on whatever foraging soldiers brought in. The leg of mutton he made was a masterpiece of its kind.

"So much wine?" Alca asked as Grus poured his cup full again.

"If I get drunk, I won't have to think about thralls for a while," he answered. "The less I have to think about thralls, the happier I'll be."

The witch nodded. "Well, I can certainly understand *that,*" she said, and filled her own mug from the jar on the table. After drinking, she asked, "What *will* you do about them, Your Majesty?"

"I don't know. I wish I did." Admitting he didn't have all the answers was something of a relief. Grus could do that with Alca, for she already knew it. He could even ask, "What would you do if you were in my place?"

"I would never want to be queen," Alca said. "How can you go through life never trusting anyone?"

"I don't," Grus answered. "But I'm careful about the people I do trust.

That's one of the reasons I wanted you with me when I came down here to the south."

"One of the reasons." Alca's eyebrows rose. "What were some of the other ones?"

She didn't mind mocking him, whether he was king or not. He smiled his blandest smile. "Funny you should ask. I'm afraid I don't remember." He wondered if she was trying to tease him into making advances so she could slap them down. He hoped not—he'd thought better of her than that—but it struck him as anything but impossible.

"No, eh?" Alca wagged a finger at him. "Do you expect me to believe that?"

"Believe what you please," Grus said. "You will anyhow."

"And what would you have me believe?" Alca asked.

"That I'm doing what I promised earlier today," Grus answered.

"You think so, do you?" The witch filled her wine cup yet again.

What was that supposed to mean? Grus almost asked the question aloud, but checked himself. He said, "I do thank you for all the help you've given me."

"You're welcome, Your Majesty," Alca said gravely. "You're very welcome." She raised the cup. "Your good health."

"And yours," Grus said. He would have a headache in the morning, but morning seemed a long way away.

"Thank you." Alca drank. So did Grus. She eyed him. "Have you decided why so many thralls are coming over the river and into Avornis?"

"My best guess is, the Banished One wants to make trouble and to see what we can do about it," he replied. "We have to take anything seriously if it's got anything to do with the Banished One."

"Yes!" The witch's agreement startled him with its vehemence.

He said, "If only we could strike at him as easily as he strikes at us."

"Yes." Alca sipped again. "I wish . . ."

"What?" Grus asked.

"Nothing. Never mind. I didn't say anything."

"You started to." Grus got to his feet and walked—carefully—toward her.

"If you can't see for yourself, you've got no business knowing."

"Can't see what for myself?"

"Whatever it is you're not seeing, of course."

"You're no help. All I see is you."

"Well, then," Alca said, as though that explained everything.

Grus reached for her like a drowning man reaching for a floating plank. Her arms tightened around him. When their lips met, she kissed him as he was kissing her.

"I didn't think—" Now he was the one who had trouble going on.

"It's all right," Alca answered. "You said you wouldn't do anything I didn't want. You aren't."

"Gods be praised!" Grus said. He kissed her again. He held her tight, tight enough that she couldn't possibly doubt kissing her wasn't the only thing he had in mind. She didn't pull away. His hands began to wander. Alca purred, down deep in her throat.

The bedchamber wasn't far. She hurried toward the bed. Later, he wondered if she went ahead to keep from giving herself time enough for second thoughts. That was later.

They lay down together. It was everything Grus had dreamt it would be, which said a great deal. Alca clutched him with arms and legs. He drove deep into her, and she clutched him inside herself, too. They both groaned together.

No sooner had they spent themselves than Alca pushed him away, saying, "We shouldn't have done that. No good will come of it."

Grus set the palm of his hand on her left breast. Her heart still thudded. When he teased her nipple between thumb and forefinger, her heartbeat sped up again.

She twisted away even so. "We shouldn't have," she said. "It's not what we came here for."

Grus just said, "All we can do is make the best of it now."

"What sort of best is there to make?" she said. "I betrayed my husband, you your wife. No good anywhere there."

"What we did was good by itself, and you can't tell me you didn't think so, too, not while it was going on."

"While it was going on, I didn't think at all, and neither did you." That was true, but it didn't make what Grus had said any less true. With a sigh, the witch went on, "Yes, you pleased me."

"I should hope so," Grus said. "You, ah, pleased me, too, you know. I'll tell you exactly how much when I'm able to see again."

She snorted, not altogether a happy sound. "You know, your hand could please you, too, and you wouldn't talk nonsense to it afterward."

Grus' ears heated; that was bawdier talk than he was used to hearing from a woman. Alca sat up at the edge of the bed and started dressing. Grus almost told her to stop. But he was leery of pushing too hard and antagonizing a witch. And he wasn't sure of his own second round. In his younger days, making love twice in a row would have been nothing. Now, *nothing* was what was more likely to happen the second time.

He said, "You mean a lot to me, you know."

That she noticed—noticed and took seriously. "You mean a lot to me, too, Your Majesty. I wouldn't have done this if you didn't, no matter how much wine I drank. But that doesn't mean I wasn't foolish—or that you weren't foolish. Suppose I bear your bastard. Will you make *him* arch-hallow one of these days?"

"I thought you could . . . know if you'd caught," Grus said. He hadn't thought about a baby at all.

"I'll know if I catch . . . when the times comes, in the usual way. Meanwhile . . . Meanwhile, good night, Your Majesty. I was foolish. We were foolish. We'd best not be again." She left the bedchamber before he could reply, which was probably just as well.

CHAPTER TWENTY-FIVE

I n charge of the royal treasury was a man named Petrosus. Grus had appointed him after the previous treasury minister, a graybeard, retired
to a monastery. As far as Lanius knew, that retirement was voluntary;
Grus hadn't required or even suggested it. Petrosus was a sharp-nosed fellow with a nearsighted squint. Lanius didn't much like him. He had trouble imagining how anyone, including Petrosus' wife, could like him very
much. But that wasn't to say the fellow didn't know his business.

At the moment, his business seemed to consist of driving Lanius out of
his mind. "I'm sorry, Your Majesty, but there's nothing I can do," he said.
Even his voice was irritatingly scratchy.

"What do you mean, there's nothing you can do?" Lanius demanded.
"My household needs more money. You're the man in charge of the money.
I know it's in the treasury; tax receipts have been up lately. So kindly give
me what I need. I'll have to let some servants go unless you do."

"I'm sorry, Your Majesty," Petrosus repeated, sounding not the least bit
sorry. "There's no allocation for any further funding for that purpose."

"What do you mean, there's no allocation?" Lanius was repeating himself, too. "Why in the name of the gods do you need an allocation, anyway? Am I the King of Avornis, or aren't I? If I need money, do I get it or
don't I?"

Petrosus scratched the end of his pointy noise. His fingers were stained with ink. "Well, Your Majesty, it's like this. You're *a* King of Avornis, sure enough. But are you *the* King of Avornis? As a matter of fact, since you're the one that's asking, I have to tell you the answer is no."

Lanius knew exactly what that meant. He'd had his not so pointy nose rubbed in it, the past few years. Grus was the one who gave the orders. Lanius understood that, no matter how little he liked it. But even so . . . "This is money for my household!" Yes, he was repeating himself.

So was the treasury minister. "You already told me that, Your Majesty. And I'm telling you there's no allocation for any more money than you're already getting."

Voice dangerously calm, Lanius asked, "Are you saying King Grus doesn't want his own daughter getting what she needs? Are you saying I can't pay for the servants she has?"

But Petrosus didn't seem to feel the danger. "I'm saying there's no allocation. No allocation, no money. Simple as that, Your Majesty." *Simple as that, you moron,* he might have said.

"Suppose I write to King Grus," Lanius said. "Suppose I tell him how—how obstructive you're being. What do you suppose he will have to say about that?"

"Probably something like, 'Congratulations, Petrosus. Good job. You're not supposed to spend any silver without an allocation,'" the treasury minister said cheerfully. "So if you want to write him, you just go ahead."

That wasn't the answer Lanius had expected or wanted. He stared at Petrosus, who squinted back. After a long pause, Lanius asked, "Are you telling me King Grus doesn't want me to have the money I need?"

"Don't ask me what he wants or doesn't want. I'm telling you I don't spend money without an allocation. That's my job. No allocation, no money. That's all I'm telling you, Your Majesty."

"And how are you supposed to get an allocation?" Lanius asked.

"Why, from King Grus, of course," Petrosus answered. If he'd been asked where light came from, he would have said, *Why, from the sun, of course,* in just that tone of voice.

"Well, if you don't have an allocation from him, suppose you get busy getting one," Lanius said.

"I already know what His Majesty wants me to spend money on—the things I have allocations for," the treasury minister said.

King Lanius was not one who often lost his temper. This time, though, marked one of the exceptions. "You idiot!" he shouted. "You lazy, miserable, worthless, good-for-nothing bastard!"

"Takes one to know one, eh?" Petrosus said. That was the surest proof any man could give that he thought Lanius altogether powerless. Lanius proved him wrong—he punched him in his pointy nose, and blunted it considerably. Petrosus left the chamber dripping blood.

That done, Lanius also wrote to King Grus, explaining in great detail Petrosus' incompetence and insolence. He was amazed his pen didn't scorch the parchment as it raced along. His letter sped south by courier.

In due course, an answer came back. *Petrosus, from all I have heard, is doing a good job on the whole,* Grus wrote. *I have no doubt he is attending to things the same way I would if I were back in the city of Avornis. I am sure you will be able to get along with him once you work a little harder.* Without another word, Grus signed his name.

"By the gods," Lanius muttered. "He really doesn't want me to have the money I need."

Up till then, he hadn't believed that. He'd been sure Grus didn't know what Petrosus was up to. He'd been sure—and he'd been wrong. Grus had known perfectly well. A rival king with less money posed a smaller danger than one with more money. It all seemed very obvious, when you looked at it the right way.

"I'll make money by myself, then," Lanius declared. He was most determined. That he hadn't the faintest idea how to go about making money by himself or for himself worried him only a little.

Lanius' annoyance didn't worry King Grus. He had more important things on his mind. Whenever he looked over the Stura, he imagined Yozgat in his mind's eye. He wanted the Scepter of Mercy so badly, he knew he wasn't even close to being rational about it.

"How can you hope to get it, Your Majesty?" Alca asked one evening. "Whenever Avornans have tried, it's always been a disaster. Why should it be any different now?"

"I don't know," Grus answered. "I truly don't know. But I do know I'm going to see what I can do one of these days."

"How many thralls were made from Avornan armies?" the witch said.

"Too many," Grus admitted. "But there are plenty of other thralls on the far side of the border. If we can cure them—"

"It will be a miracle," Alca said. "You know that as well as I do. We can't even cure the ones who've fled over the river to us. Well, we can cure some of them, maybe, but how reliable is the cure? Not very, you ask me."

"We have to get better at that," he said. "If we're ever going to reconquer the lands south of the Stura, we've got to be able to turn thralls into ordinary farmers again."

Alca nodded. "That's what we need, all right," she agreed. "Whether we can get it is a different question."

"Well," Grus said, "there are plenty of thralls for you to practice on."

"I wondered if you were going to tell me that," she said. "For someone who claims to care about me—"

"I do more than care about you," Grus broke in. "If you don't know that—"

She interrupted in turn, saying, "For someone who claims to care about me, you keep doing your best to get me killed."

"I want to be able to fight the Banished One," Grus said. "I want to take back the lands the Menteshe stole from us."

"If you try to fight the Banished One, strength against strength, you'll lose, Your Majesty," Alca said bluntly. "You have the strength of a man. He has the strength of an exiled god. If he puts it forth, you *will* lose. That's all there is to it."

She spoke with as much certainty as of tomorrow's sunrise. King Grus said, "Then any hope of taking land back from the Banished One is nothing but a foolish dream?"

"I didn't say that," the witch replied. "But if you do it, you have to do it so that he *doesn't* put forth all his strength."

"How?" Grus asked.

"Your Majesty, I don't know," she said. "This is the riddle Avornis has been trying to solve since the Banished One was cast down from the heavens."

"Well, one step at a time," Grus said. "I think the Banished One has been trying to see how strong and clever we are. Otherwise, why would he make all these thralls come over the river and into Avornis?" He didn't wait for an answer, but went on, "Maybe we can make him pay for that. Wouldn't it be poetic justice if we used the thralls to learn how to free people from thralldom?"

"It would be, if we could do that," Alca said. "Whether we can or not, I don't know." She eyed him. "Or are you just looking for reasons to keep me down here in the south and not go back to the city of Avornis?"

"You know what my reasons are," he answered. "And I hope you have some of those reasons, too." He thought he had the right to hope; in spite of what she'd said after they joined the first time, she'd come to his bed several times since. Even so, he went on, "If you think you can do a better job curing thralls in the capital, say the word and we'll go back there. Would having more wizards here help?"

The witch sighed. "I don't think so. I'm not sure where I try will make any difference at all. I'm not sure it can be done. We haven't got many wizards who could help."

"If it can't be . . ." Grus didn't want to think about that, but made himself. "If it can't be, I don't see what chance Avornis has of ever taking any land back from the Menteshe. Do you?"

"No, Your Majesty." Alca sighed again. "All right. You've convinced me the work is important. Now if you'd only convinced me I had any real chance of doing it."

"How do you know until you try?" Grus asked. "It may be easier than you think."

"It almost certainly is easier than I think," Alca said, "for I doubt it can be done at all."

Having gotten the last word, though, the witch did decide to make the effort. Grus smiled to himself and said not a word. In some ways, Alca and Estrilda weren't so very different after all. If he'd said as much to either one of them, she would have made him sorry for it. That being so, he knew he was smart to say nothing.

His guardsmen brought another thrall up from the floor of the amphitheater in Cumanus. An ordinary man might have complained or struggled at such treatment. The thrall just stared around in dull, incurious incomprehension. He didn't know what was going to happen to him, and he didn't care, either.

Alca sighed. "This is foolishness, and nothing but foolishness."

"You've come this far," Grus said. "Why not go a little further?"

"Because of what the Banished One may do if I try?" she suggested. But they'd already seen samples of that. "All right, Your Majesty. I am your fool, sure enough—in more ways than one."

That made Grus wince. Alca turned away from him and began to cast a spell on the thrall. The fellow knew what magic meant. He bawled wordlessly and tried to twist free of the guards, as a beast of burden might have kicked up its heels when it saw a man with a whip in his hand. Grus wondered what sort of wizards the thrall had been unlucky enough to meet in his unhappy life south of the Stura.

The thrall's struggles did him no more good than an ox's might have done it. The guards had no trouble hanging on to him. Alca continued her spell. King Grus winced again. Seeing a man—or someone who still looked like a man, at any rate—reduced to such impotence was hard to bear.

When Alca made a sudden, sharp pass, the thrall stopped struggling as abruptly as he'd started. His mouth fell open, showing teeth that had probably never had any care in all his days. "What's your name?" Alca asked him, her voice quiet and interested.

"Do thralls have names?" Grus asked.

"I don't know," she whispered back. "But *men* have names—I do know that. Now hush."

Grus obeyed. The thrall ignored the byplay between witch and king. His dirty face furrowed. That might have been the hardest question anyone had ever asked him. It might have been the first question anyone had ever asked him. After a long, long pause, he said, "Immer."

That was a name an Avornan might have borne, which surprised Grus. If it also surprised Alca, she gave no sign. Nodding, she said, "All right, Immer, how do we go about setting free the part of you that has a name and knows what it is? How do we bring that part out and leave the rest behind?"

Immer only shrugged. Grus was surprised again, this time that she'd gotten even so much of an answer from him.

And the witch seemed surprised, too. "Isn't that interesting?" she murmured. "There's more of him inside himself than I'd expected. Maybe I'll be able to do this after all."

"Some of our wizards have," Grus said.

"I know," she said. "But some of them thought they had, and then watched their wizardry fail a little at a time. I don't want that to happen. If I can break this spell, I want to break it once and for all."

"Good." Grus nodded. He didn't want to see wizardry done by halves, either.

Immer just stood there, waiting for whatever would come next. Or rather, as far as Grus could tell, he wasn't waiting. He seemed to give no more thought to what might come than a steer would have.

Alca began to chant again. Grus wondered if she would take out her crystal and shine a rainbow onto the thrall's face. She didn't. After a moment's thought, Grus decided he was glad she didn't. The Banished One had caused too much trouble through her magical rainbows. Maybe—no, certainly—he could cause trouble other ways, too. But Grus had seen he could do it that way.

The thrall suddenly stiffened. Grus tensed, wondering if another spell had gone awry. But then Immer blinked. He twisted one arm free of the guard who held it. He brought his hand up to his face and began to weep. "Thank you," he said. "Thank you."

Awe prickled through Grus. "He sounds like . . . like a man," he whispered.

Immer nodded. "Man," he echoed, and pointed at himself with that free hand. "Man!" he said again, proudly this time.

"By the gods, Alca, I think you've done it," Grus said.

"It's a beginning," Alca said. "I don't know how much more than a beginning it is, but it's a beginning."

"Man!" Immer repeated, and nodded once more, so vigorously that locks of his grimy, greasy, matted hair bounced up and down. "Thrall?" This time, he violently shook his head, and his hair flew out around his head. Had he known the word before? Who could guess?

"If he's free of this horrible enchantment, Mistress Alca, why doesn't he talk like a proper man now?" one of the guards asked.

"Because he doesn't know how," the witch replied. "He still knows what he knew when he was a thrall. The spell I used doesn't turn him into a man all by itself. I don't think any spell could do that. It lets him learn the things he needs to become a man, the same way a child would. Before, he couldn't."

"Will he take as long as a child would to learn all those things?" Grus asked in some alarm. If a freed thrall needed fifteen or twenty years to become fully mature, what point to breaking the spell?

But Alca shook her head. "I'm sure he won't," she answered. "In many ways, he already has a man's experience. He'll learn what he needs to know quickly. He *can* learn now, where he couldn't before."

"Learn!" Immer used the word with an avid hunger Grus had never heard attached to it up till that moment. "Learn!"

"You'll have your chance," Grus told him. The thrall—ex-thrall?—frowned in confusion. He didn't understand what Grus meant. "Yes. Learn," Grus said, making it as simple as he could. "You learn." Immer smiled broadly. He understood that. He liked it, too.

"Shall we take him back down with the others, Your Majesty?" one of the guards asked.

Grus shook his head. "No. If he's a man, or on the way to being a man, he shouldn't have to go back in with thralls."

"No thrall!" Immer jabbed a thumb into his own skinny chest. He shook his head, too. "No thrall!"

The guard didn't look convinced. Grus hoped Immer meant it. He glanced at Alca. She gave back a tiny shrug and said, "Whatever he is, I don't think he's a spy for the Banished One."

"All right, then." That made up Grus' mind for him. He told the guards, "Take him to the barracks. Clean him up. Show him what being a man means. If he doesn't learn fast enough to suit you, give him lumps. Don't give him bad ones—that wouldn't be fair. Just enough to keep his attention, you might say."

"Like we would with a little boy?" the guard asked.

"That's right," Grus agreed. "Just like that." *Would Ortalis have turned out better if I'd given him more lumps? Who knows? How can you tell? But how can you keep from wondering, either?* He sighed. Ortalis was what he was. Grus wished he were something else, but he wasn't and never would be. *Too bad,* Grus thought. *Oh, by the gods, too bad!*

At supper that night, Alca said, "I never dreamt it would be so easy. The spell of thralldom really *can* be lifted. And I don't know what the Banished One can do to stop it from being lifted, either. It's not the sort of spell where he can find a handle and turn it against me."

"The way he did with the spell where you used crystals?" Grus asked.

"Yes." The witch shuddered at the memory of those misfortunes. "But this is different. By the gods, it is."

"Good." Grus got up, came around the table, and kissed her. She responded eagerly. When she was pleased with herself, she was pleased with the world around her, too. And the world around her included him.

When morning came, Alca left his bed even before sunrise and hurried to the amphitheater. Grus got there later. The witch didn't look at him. She was intent on the business at hand. The guards brought out another thrall. Alca set to work on the woman, whose name, she learned, was Crecca. Grus watched her conjuration. It seemed to go as smoothly as Immer's unbinding had. That afternoon, Alca broke the ties of darkness that subjected another man.

She might not have had any idea how the Banished One could keep her—and, eventually, other Avornan wizards—from freeing thralls. But he did find a way to stop her. A few days after she started her work, a messenger rode in from the west. "Your Majesty!" he cried.

"What is it?" Grus asked. Whatever it was, he didn't think he would like it.

And he didn't. The messenger said, "Your Majesty, Prince Evren's Menteshe have crossed the Stura! They're burning everything they can reach!"

King Lanius shook his head. Everyone in the royal palace kept asking him the same question. He had no good answer for it. "I don't know much about Prince Evren, Bubulcus," he told the latest questioner.

As several people had before, his servant looked indignant. "You're supposed to know these things, Your Majesty!" Bubulcus exclaimed.

"Why?" Lanius said. "All I know about Evren is that his riders had been quiet lately. Up till now, the Menteshe prince whose men have given us the most trouble is Ulash."

"Well, why isn't Ulash giving us trouble now?" Bubulcus asked. "King Grus is across the river from the land Ulash rules, isn't he?"

"Yes," Lanius admitted. That was a good question, a sensible question. He wouldn't have thought Bubulcus had it in him. He had to answer, "I don't know why Ulash is sitting quiet and Evren isn't, either."

"Hmph!" Bubulcus said. "All I can tell you is, if you don't have the answers when we need them, you've wasted an awful lot of time in the archives." He let out another loud, disdainful sniff.

For reasons Lanius never could fathom afterward, he didn't pick up the nearest blunt instrument and brain the servant with it. He didn't send Bubulcus to the Maze, or even send him out of the palace. All he did was glare, and even his glare was on the sickly side.

Not knowing what a close brush with disaster he'd had, Bubulcus went right on grumbling. Lanius ignored him more and more ostentatiously. At last, the servant stuck his nose in the air and said, "Well, I can take a hint." He flounced off, still muttering under his breath.

"You can take it and . . ." Lanius stopped, shaking his head. Falling to Bubulcus' level—falling below Bubulcus' level—wouldn't do him any good. But the temptation felt almost overwhelming.

So did the temptation to retreat to the archives and find out everything he could about Prince Evren and the principality he ruled. King Lanius wasn't and never had been a man who yielded to many temptations. Wine held no great allure. Neither did women, except for Queen Sosia. Song? He couldn't carry a tune in a bucket. But the prospect of getting dusty in the archives was something else again.

Even in the archives, Avornan writers had more to say about the principality Ulash ruled these days than they did about Evren's. Ulash's domain was larger. It sat along a more important stretch of the Stura. And it had been ruled by a series of strong princes. Evren's predecessors, on the other hand, seemed the most ordinary of men. Some of them seemed a little smarter than average, others a little more foolish. Taken all in all . . . Taken all in all, Evren's predecessors seemed deserving of a long, heartfelt yawn, and nothing more.

Evren himself hadn't attracted much notice, either. He hadn't led many raids over the river into Avornan territory—not until now. He hadn't started any fights with his neighbors, though he hadn't lost any they'd started with him. Maybe that was worth noting. Or—who could be sure?— maybe it wasn't.

Avornan traders who'd gone down into Evren's principality noted that he ran things with a rough justice they liked. One of them had actually prevailed in a quarrel with a Menteshe merchant. The Avornan seemed to regard that as something not far from a miracle. Reading it, so did Lanius.

The more he learned about Prince Evren, the more he wondered why Evren had decided to attack Avornis. Evren never had before—not once in his long reign. His sudden assault left Lanius more puzzled now than he had been before he started digging. Things weren't supposed to work like that.

He wrote down what he had managed to dig up and sent it to Grus in the hope that it would prove useful. He also added a note that said, *Do you have any idea why Evren is fighting us? Everything I can find out here argues that he shouldn't be.*

He wondered if Grus would bother answering. The other King of Avornis often went out of his way not to take him seriously. But Lanius did get a reply, and a very prompt one. *Thanks for giving me this,* Grus wrote. *It tells me more about Evren than I already knew, and I used to patrol the miserable son of a whore's northern border.* Lanius read that several times. It made him proud.

Grus went on, *And yes, Your Majesty, I can tell you just why Prince Evren has gone to war against us just now. He's fighting us because he's the creature of the Banished One. It's exactly that simple.*

Lanius doubted anything was as simple as Grus made it out to be. He wrote back to his father-in-law, asking, *Why would the Banished One set Evren in motion against you when you're across the border from the lands Prince Ulash holds?*

A reply, this time, took much longer coming back than had been true before. But Grus did answer, about when Lanius had begun to give up hope that he would. *Why?* he wrote. *I'll tell you why. To keep me busy.*

That was all Grus said. Lanius stared at the note, trying to tease more sense out of it. After a while, he decided there was no more sense to tease. Muttering to himself, he wrote back, *What do you mean?*

I mean what I said, Grus replied. *What did you think I meant?*

Letters took a couple of weeks to get down to the south. Answers took another couple of weeks to return, plus however long Grus waited before responding. Lanius thought that was much too slow for word games. If Grus happened not to agree with him, though, what could he do about it? Nothing he could see.

No, that wasn't quite right. He could complain. He could, and he did, saying to Sosia, "Why doesn't your father make more sense?"

"Father usually does make sense," she answered. "Why don't you think he does this time?"

Lanius recounted the exchange he'd had with Grus. "If he's making any sense there, I think he's doing his best to hide it," he declared.

His wife frowned. "It seems straightforward enough to me. The Banished One is trying to keep the witch and him too busy with this war to go on with whatever they were doing at Cumanus."

"The witch!" Lanius exclaimed. "That's it! That must be it!"

"Now you're the one who's not making sense," Sosia said.

"Don't you see? It's obvious!" Lanius said. "Alca must be doing something the Banished One doesn't like. That's why the Banished One made the Menteshe start this war. It has to be why."

"Nothing *has* to be anything," Sosia said tartly; maybe she hadn't liked that *It's obvious!* She went on, "If the Banished One was that eager to start trouble, why didn't he have Ulash attack, and not this Prince Evren?"

"Why? Well, because . . ." Lanius' voice trailed away as he realized he had no good answer for that. "I don't know why. I wonder if getting a straight answer to the question would be worth another letter to your father."

In the end, after some hesitation, he did send the letter. If Grus wanted to ignore it, he could. Grus had had a lot of practice ignoring things Lanius said and wrote. But he didn't ignore this. In due course, he wrote, *That is an interesting question if you want to go into detail, isn't it? If you've got any interesting answers, please send them along. One thing I will say is that Evren is a handful all by himself, even without Ulash. I wonder more and more why the foxy old bugger is sitting this one out.* He'd written *bastard* first, but scratched it out almost but not quite to illegibility and replaced it with the other word. Unlike Petrosus, he watched Lanius' feelings, if not quite well enough.

Lanius drummed his fingers on his thigh. He didn't have an answer, whether interesting or otherwise. Only one thing occurred to him—that Ulash had ruled his principality for a very long time, much longer even than Evren had held his. Lanius didn't write that. Grus would know it as well as he did.

When he went in to see how the moncats were doing, Spider laid a present at his feet: the not very neatly disemboweled carcass of a mouse. The moncat stared up at him out of amber eyes. The worst of it was, Spider expected to be praised and made much of for his hunting prowess. Lanius did the job, petting him till he purred and, while purring, tried to nip the King of Avornis' hand.

"Don't you bite me!" Lanius said, and thwapped him on the nose. This time, the stare Spider gave back sent only one message. *If I were big enough,* it said, *I'd eat you.* That stare went a long way toward explaining why people weren't in the habit of making pets of lions and tigers and leopards.

Spider also took a long, thoughtful look at Lanius' leg, as though wondering if he could avenge himself for that thwap. An ordinary cat wouldn't have done that. An ordinary cat would either have run away or tried to bite him again right then. Yaropolk the Chernagor had warned Lanius that moncats were smarter than their everyday cousins. Not for the first time, the king saw that Yaropolk was right.

And Spider very visibly decided he couldn't get away with biting Lanius on the leg. Instead, he picked up the mouse that was to have been a present and carried it away, climbing quickly up toward the roof of the room where he and his relatives lived. There, glowering down at Lanius, he finished dismembering the little animal and ate it.

It's a good thing your kind isn't bigger, Lanius thought. *Otherwise, you might be the ones who kept us for pets.* That was an idea to make a man modest. Then he had another, worse, one. *Or you might keep us so you could treat us the way you treat mice.*

A moment later, the mouse's tail fell from Spider's perch up near the ceiling and landed on the floor. Two moncats sprang forward to pounce on it. They saw each other, and both of them snarled. During that standoff, a third, smaller, moncat sneaked up and made away with the tail. They both chased him, but he escaped with the prize.

"That's what happens," Lanius said. "You weren't paying enough attention, so that other little fellow got a snack."

The two who'd confronted each other both eyed the king. It wasn't—it couldn't have been—that they spoke Avornan. But they gave the impression of listening alertly to whatever he might say. He slowly nodded to himself. He'd seen that before. He wondered if anyone else would believe him. Moncats were much smarter than most people thought they were. Lanius was convinced of that.

How much smarter? he wondered. He didn't know much about monkeys, but what little he did know made him suspect the moncats had wits of similar level. Monkeys, from what little he knew, were social animals. That was much less true of moncats—they differed from monkeys as ordinary cats differed from people.

"Interesting," Lanius murmured. Again, the moncats watched him. They paid close attention when he spoke. What did that mean? How could a mere human being know? With a sigh, Lanius admitted to himself that he couldn't.

He wished he knew more about monkeys. Only old records in the archives spoke of them. Since the days when the Menteshe swarmed out of the south, Avornis hadn't ruled lands where the monkeys lived. *One more reason to wish we could start retaking the lands south of the Stura,* Lanius thought.

He didn't have the chance to go prowling through old parchments after monkeys, not then. A well-founded suspicion that Sosia would clout him if he didn't pay some occasional attention to Crex and Pitta sent him back to his own chamber. He even enjoyed playing with his own children. They loved him without reservation, which was true of no one and nothing else in the world—not Sosia herself, and not the moncats, either. His wife had ties other than the ones that bound her to him; the animals cared for him—to the extent that they did care for him—because he tended them, not because of who he was.

But, being who he was, he didn't forget what he wanted to find out. After a while, Sosia said, "You've got something on your mind—I can tell."

"Monkeys," Lanius answered.

"Monkeys?" Sosia echoed. Whatever she'd expected, that wasn't it. "What about them?"

"Anything you can tell me," Lanius said. "Anything anybody can tell me."

"You've got that look in your eye again," Sosia said, which was undoubtedly true. She went on, "All I know about monkeys is that they live in trees and look like ugly little people with tails and too much hair."

"Except for the tails, you're talking about half the courtiers in the city of Avornis," Lanius said. "More than half."

That startled laughter from his wife, who said, "Well, what do *you* know about monkeys? What do you want to find out?"

"I don't know much," Lanius said. "I want to find out what I don't know—what I don't know and what's true."

"Why do you want to know about monkeys?" Sosia asked. "You never did say."

"I want to find out how they're like moncats and how they're not," Lanius answered.

"Oh, you do?" Sosia sounded tolerantly amused. She'd seen such moods come on her husband before. Even so, she asked, "Why do you want to know that?"

She must have known what Lanius would say before he said it. And, sure enough, he did say it. "I'm just curious."

Queen Sosia laughed again, out loud this time. "Well, Your Majesty," she said, "if you're not entitled to indulge your curiosity, who is?"

"But that's just it," Lanius said. "If the answers aren't in the records, how can I find them? It doesn't matter who I am—without the records, I'm never going to know." He paused. That wasn't necessarily true. "I'm never going to know, I mean, unless I can talk someone into bringing monkeys to the city of Avornis. The Chernagors, maybe, or some Avornan traders."

"Wait a minute. Wait just a minute." His wife no longer sounded amused—or tolerant, either. "Don't you think the palace is enough of a menagerie now, with the moncats? How much mischief would monkeys get into? How much of a mess do monkeys make? How bad does monkey shit stink?"

"I don't know any of those things!" Excitement rose in Lanius' voice. "Wouldn't it be fun to find out?"

"That's not the word I'd use," Sosia answered. "And I'm sure that's not the word my father would use."

She was bound to be right. That didn't make Lanius any less eager—on the contrary. He knew he had to be sly, though. He said, "Well, nobody's brought monkeys here for years and years."

Sosia relaxed. Lanius started laying his plans.

CHAPTER TWENTY-SIX

King Grus was laying his plans as well. He wondered how much good it would do. Turning to Hirundo, who'd come down from the north not long before, he said, "Fighting the Menteshe is like hitting a glob of quicksilver with a hammer. You don't make the glob disappear. You just smash it up into a bunch of little globs."

"Well, then we smash the little globs one at a time," Hirundo answered, cheerful as usual. "You *can* get rid of them for good. It takes work, that's all. You can't do that with a real glob of quicksilver."

"No, you can't," Grus admitted. "But with real quicksilver, the little globs don't go running around trying to turn back into one big one again, either."

"If you're going to worry about *everything* . . ." Hirundo said. Grus laughed, though it wasn't funny. One thing he'd found since becoming king was that he *had* to worry about everything. If he didn't, who would?

The campfire crackled as a stick fell down when the smaller stick supporting it burned through. Off in the distance, an owl hooted mournfully. The Avornan army had extra sentries surrounding the encampment on all sides, and squadrons of horsemen ready to charge into battle at a moment's notice. Grus felt only moderately safe even so.

He said, "The Menteshe are like foxes. They sneak through the night."

"Foxes made of quicksilver," Hirundo said helpfully.

"I didn't order you down here for literary criticism," Grus said. "I wanted you to help me figure out how to beat Prince Evren's men."

"Same way we always beat the nomads—when we do," Hirundo said. "We need a bouncy young chap to drive them down to the river, and a clever captain of river galleys to make sure they don't cross to the south bank."

"Where would we find officers like that?" Grus asked. They both laughed. The days when Hirundo had driven the Menteshe down to the Stura and Grus had kept them from crossing seemed very far away.

As though to prove how distant they were, Grus had to climb onto the back of a horse the next day. He would have given a good deal to have the pitching, rolling deck of a river galley under him instead. He knew how to handle anything that might go wrong there. Even after all these years, his relationship with horses remained wary.

And the relationship between Avornis and the Menteshe remained one of passionate mutual loathing. Hirundo's men managed to surround a band of the nomads, catching them by surprise around their campfires. By the time the Menteshe realized they were in danger, the Avornans had cut off any hope of escape.

For form's sake, King Grus sent in an officer under flag of truce offering to spare the lives of Prince Evren's men if they surrendered. For form's sake, they sent him back alive. Then the killing started.

Grus himself had never made more than an indifferent rider, as he knew to his chagrin. Many Avornans, though, excelled on horseback. To them, horses were friends and comrades, not merely conveniences for getting from here to there faster than a man could walk. Next to the Menteshe, though, they might all have had Grus' attitude and skill. People said the nomads were born in the saddle. After what Grus saw in that fight, he wouldn't have argued for a moment.

The horses they rode were nothing much to look at: plains ponies that hardly reached the shoulders of the Avornans' mounts. But those ponies were fast and strong and seemed never to tire. And what the nomads did from their backs . . . Grus was among the most sincere enemies the Menteshe had, but he knew better than to call them cowards.

When the Avornans came toward them from all sides, they must have known they probably wouldn't escape. Instead of waiting to be slaughtered, though, they galloped forward—straight toward Grus, whether by design or by chance. Although outnumbered eight or ten to one, by the way they came they might have been the ones with numbers on their side.

Then they started shooting, and for a dreadful little while Grus wondered whether they were right to be so confident.

He'd heard things about the archery of the Menteshe. He'd seen some of it in earlier fights here. But this . . . The nomads' bows, backed with horn and sinew, outranged those of the Avornans. And the Menteshe shot faster than merely mortal men had any business doing. People told tales of clouds of arrows darkening the sun as they flew. As the volley from Evren's men hissed through the air toward the Avornans, Grus understood for the first time how such tales were born. He threw his shield up to protect his face.

Had one of those arrows bitten him, the shield probably would have done no good. The nomads' bows gave their shafts not only great range but also great striking power. They pierced shields. They pierced chain mail. And they pierced flesh—the flesh of both men and horses. Men shrieked. Horses screamed and crashed to the ground, throwing or crushing their riders. Other horses tripped over them and went down, too.

An arrow buzzed past Grus' head, so close that the fletching stroked his beard. He didn't even have time to be horrified, for the Menteshe galloped toward him, intent on cutting their way out through the gap they'd shot in the Avornan line. As they neared, they drew their sabers. The blades glittered in the morning sun.

"We have to hold them!" Grus yelled. "We can't let them break through!" Belatedly, he remembered to draw his own sword. He hoped enough men around and behind him remained to hold the Menteshe till the rest of his cavalrymen could close with them and finish them off.

He also hoped, again belatedly, that he would live through the encounter. On the deck of a river galley, he would have had the edge over any nomad ever born. On horseback, though, the tables were turned. Here came one of Evren's men, shouting something in his own language. He cut at Grus. Grus beat the blade aside and slashed at the Menteshe's mount. His sword scored a bleeding line across its croup, not far in front of its tail.

With the terrible cry of a horse in pain, the beast reared. The Menteshe clung to the saddle as burrs clung to the long hair of its tail. Grus cut at him from behind. The nomad wore a shirt of leather boiled in tallow—not as strong as chain mail, but much lighter. It proved strong enough to keep Grus' blade from laying the fellow's back open, though by his grunt of pain the blow still hurt. Grus understood that. He wore padding under his mail to keep swordstrokes from breaking ribs.

The Menteshe twisted, trying to keep his horse under control and fight back at the same time. He turned one more slash from Grus, but the next caught him in the side of the neck, above the boiled-leather shirt and below the iron-plated cap on his head. Blood spurted, improbably red. The Menteshe yammered in pain. Grus struck him again, this time across the face. The nomad's saber slipped from his hands. He slid off his horse and tumbled to the ground.

King Grus had a moment to look around. A few of the Menteshe had managed to break out. Even as he watched, an arrow caught one of them in the back. More were still fighting, trying to get away. And even more were down. He rode forward to help slay the ones yet on their horses.

"Surrender!" he shouted when only four or five Menteshe were left alive. "Surrender and we'll spare your lives."

He didn't really expect them to. More often than not, fights between Avornans and Menteshe were fights to the death. But these nomads surprised him. Deciding they would rather live, they took off their iron-faced caps and hung them on the points of their sabers in token of surrender. "You not make us into thralls?" one of them asked in bad Avornan.

"No, by the gods. We don't do that," Grus replied.

"So you say," the Menteshe said. He spoke to his comrades in their own language. By their tone, they didn't believe Grus, either.

With a sigh compounded of weariness and relief, he turned to his own men. "Take charge of them. And gather up the bows the horses haven't stepped on. We'd be better off if our bowyers could make weapons like those."

They hurried to obey. They also rounded up the horses whose riders had fallen, and put out of their misery the animals too badly hurt to live. Some of them slew Menteshe too badly hurt to live, too, and Grus watched one man quietly cut the throat of an Avornan who'd taken an arrow in the belly and then been trampled. No one said a word to the soldier. By what Grus saw of the hurt man's injuries, the fellow with the dagger had done him a favor.

Hirundo was grinning when he rode up to Grus. "Well, Your Majesty, here's one lump of quicksilver that won't trouble us anymore. And we didn't have to pay too high a price to get rid of it, either."

"That depends," Grus said.

"What do you mean?" Hirundo asked. "They made a nice little charge at us, yes, but we killed a lot more of them than they did of us."

"Well, so we did," Grus said. "When you're talking about the fight just now, you're right, and I can't tell you any different. But how many farmers did those Menteshe kill? How many houses and barns and fields did they burn? How many cows and horses and sheep did they run off or slaughter? Avornis has been paying ever since they crossed the Stura. We got some of our own back now, but is it enough?"

Hirundo gave him a curious look. "You think about all sorts of things, don't you, Your Majesty? If I didn't know better, I'd say I was talking to Lanius."

"He *does* think about all sorts of things, doesn't he?" Grus smiled, but soon grew serious again. "Do you know something, General? The longer I sit on the throne, the more I think that's not such a bad thing to do."

King Lanius was thinking of throwing something at Iron. He was trying to paint a portrait of the moncat, and Iron didn't feel like holding still. Had Lanius wanted Iron to run around, the miserable beast undoubtedly would have frozen in place. As things were, the king couldn't persuade the moncat to assume anything even close to the attitude it had held the day before, when he'd started the picture.

Instead of throwing something, he snapped his fingers. The sound made Iron look his way for a moment, but only for a moment, before scrambling up toward the ceiling. Lanius, for once, didn't much care. "Bribery!" he said, a sudden grin on his face. "What kind of a king am I if I don't think of bribery?"

He left Iron's chamber and hurried to the kitchens. A cook gave him several chunks of mutton and, after some rummaging, a length of twine. "It's something to do with those miserable foreign creatures, isn't it, Your Majesty?" the man said.

"Don't be silly, Colinus," Lanius answered, his voice grave. "I just want to have fun with my food before I eat it." Since the mutton was raw, what he'd said was most unlikely. On the other hand, he'd sounded altogether serious. Leaving the cook scratching his head, Lanius went back to Iron's room.

All of a sudden, the moncat was much friendlier than it had been a few minutes before. The road to its heart definitely ran through its stomach. Lanius tied one of the pieces of mutton to the end of the twine and hung it so that, to reach it, Iron had to stretch into something close to the posture he wanted.

Stretch Iron did. While the moncat stretched, Lanius sketched. Before long, Iron finished the chunk of mutton. The beast turned toward Lanius and meowed pitifully. It was, no doubt, self-pity for not having more mutton; Iron could smell the meat Lanius hadn't yet given.

Lanius doled out the mutton one piece at a time. By the time Iron finished all of it, the king had finished his sketch. He could add color and shading at his leisure, and work on them whenever he wanted. He was doing just that in the bedchamber when Sosia looked over his shoulder. "That's very good," she said.

He would have been happier if she hadn't sounded so surprised, but he didn't show that. "Thanks," he said shortly.

His wife leaned down for a closer look. Her hair tickled his cheek. "That's *very* good," she repeated. "You can practically see him moving."

"Thank you," Lanius said again, this time in warmer tones. "That's what I was trying to show."

"Well, you've done it," Sosia said. "If anyone wants to know what a pouncing moncat is like, all he has to do is look at this picture."

Now Lanius smiled. In fact, he almost purred. "Do you really think it's good?" he asked. He didn't hear praise very often. When he did, he wanted to make the most of it.

"I think it's wonderful," Sosia told him. "Anybody who'd never seen a moncat and wanted to would pay good money for a painting like that."

"Do you really think so?" Lanius knew he was repeating himself again, but couldn't help it.

"I'm sure of it," Sosia said firmly. She gave him a kiss, which somehow seemed to make what she said much more persuasive.

It might have ended as nothing but the sort of friendly praise a good wife would give to a husband she loved. It might have, but it didn't. Lanius suddenly snapped his fingers and exclaimed, "Allocations!"

"What?" Not surprisingly, Sosia had no idea what he was talking about.

"Allocations." And there he went, repeating himself yet again. "Remember when Petrosus wouldn't give us any more money, and we had to let people go? If I can sell paintings, who cares what Petrosus gives us? He may be trying to keep me poor, but that doesn't mean I have to let him."

When he said Petrosus was trying to keep him poor, he meant Grus was trying to keep him poor. He didn't say that, to keep from wounding Sosia's feelings. Petrosus wouldn't have denied him, though, without specific orders from King Grus. Lanius was as sure of that as of his own name.

Sosia said, "*Could* you really sell pictures like that? Has a King of Avornis ever done such a thing?"

"No, I don't think so," Lanius answered. "But then, I don't think a King of Avornis has ever been poor before, either."

He didn't see how a King of Avornis could have been poor. A king, after all, controlled the tax revenues and customs duties his officials collected. He could spend what he wanted on himself. Or most kings could. Grus certainly could now, even if he was moderate in personal habits. Lanius? He laughed. He knew better. He lived on whatever Grus doled out to him.

Or he had. Now . . . Maybe things would be different. Maybe. "If I sell any paintings," he said, "I want to sell them as paintings by an artist, not as paintings by the King of Avornis. Plenty of men would buy them in the hope they would be buying influence along with the canvas."

"You'd get more money if people knew the King of Avornis painted them." Sosia spoke with firm practicality.

"Well, maybe I would," Lanius admitted. "The next question is, how much do I care?"

"I can't answer that—you have to," his wife said. "How much do you want to make What's-his-name—Petrosus—look like a fool?"

That was the right question to ask. *How much* do *I want to make Petrosus look like a fool?* Lanius wondered. He remembered the haughty smile on the treasury minister's face, and how much the fellow had enjoyed telling him no. *How much do I want to make Petrosus look like a fool? Quite a lot, as a matter of fact.*

"All right," he said. "I'll sell them under my own name."

"Them?" Sosia raised an eyebrow. "You'll do more?"

Lanius nodded. "If I'm going to do this, I'm not going to do it halfway. And besides"—he wanted to show he could be practical as well as proud—"we need the money."

King Grus, naturally, made sure he kept up with what went on in the city of Avornis while he campaigned in the south. Lanius might get ideas, or Ortalis, or old Lepturus, or even Anser, or perhaps some other ambitious soul who saw the throne empty and thought his own backside ought to fill it.

When he read in a letter what sort of ambition Lanius was showing, he blinked in bemusement. It must have been a pretty obvious blink, for Hirundo noticed it and asked, "What's interesting, Your Majesty?"

"That's the word, all right," Grus answered. "It seems King Lanius is setting up as an artist."

"An artist?" Hirundo blinked, too. "I didn't know he had it in him. I mean, to say, he's a bright fellow and all, but . . . What kind of artist?"

"A painter. A painter of moncats, of all things," Grus said. "And he's sold three pictures, now, for . . . preposterous prices." He wasn't sure he believed the sums his informant in the city of Avornis claimed. Who would pay that kind of money for a picture of an animal?

Hirundo made him realize he'd asked himself the wrong question. "No price is too preposterous," the general observed, "if you're paying it to the King of Avornis. Well, to *a* King of Avornis, anyhow." He inclined his head to Grus, an oddly courtly gesture when they were sitting in front of a fire roasting chunks of mutton on sticks after another long day chasing Menteshe.

"Yes," Grus said. "That's so, isn't it? I wonder how much influence changes hands with the money. I thought Lanius was above that sort of thing, but maybe I'm wrong."

"How good are the paintings?" Hirundo asked. "That will tell you something."

"Good question." Grus looked down to the letter. "From what it says here, they're quite good. Who *would* have thought it?" He wondered if he ought to order Petrosus to cut back on Lanius' allocation again. After some thought, he decided against it. It would be mean-spirited. If Lanius wanted to supplement what the treasury gave him—and if he'd found a way to do it—he could.

Somewhere off in the distance, a wolf howled. Grus hoped it was a wolf, anyhow. For all he knew, it might have been a Menteshe signal. Or, as Hirundo put it, "There go Evren's men, baying at the moon again."

"If they're sensible, they won't come north over the Stura for quite a while after this," Grus said. "But who knows if they're sensible?"

"Who knows what the Banished One will have them do?" Hirundo said.

Grus sighed. "Yes, there's that, too, of course. They don't always do what they want to do. They do what he wants them to do, or what suits his purposes." He wondered what Alca could have learned about freeing thralls from the dark spells that clouded their lives if Evren's invasion hadn't made her turn her attention to helping protect the kingdom. He wouldn't know for some time, if he ever did.

Hirundo's smile showed sharp teeth. "I hope his purposes include getting lots of them killed, because that's what's happening to them."

"I know," Grus said. "And I don't see how Evren can help knowing, too. What I wonder is why he keeps fighting for the Banished One—why all the Menteshe princes keep fighting for him—when that only brings trouble down on their heads."

With a laugh, Hirundo answered, "Well, if they didn't line up with the

Banished One, they'd have to line up with us instead, and they probably think that's worse."

He might have been joking. No, he *was* joking. Even so, Grus thought he'd hit on an important truth. Like any men, the Menteshe assumed their enemies were wicked just because they were enemies. "They're going to hate us," he said, "but let's make sure they're afraid of us, too. We need to give them something to howl about."

They got their chance the next morning. Scouts came galloping in, reporting a large band of Menteshe not far away. At Grus' shouted orders, horns blared in the Avornan camp. Whooping men flung themselves into the saddle. Before throwing them at the foe, though, Grus sent out more scouts in all directions.

"That's good," Hirundo said. "That's very good. We don't want any nasty surprises."

"We certainly don't," Grus agreed. "Count Corvus was a first-class bastard, but he taught me a good lesson there. If he'd paid attention to what he was doing against the Thervings, odds are he'd be King of Avornis today."

"Good thing he didn't, then," Hirundo said, which made Grus grin.

He grinned again a few minutes later, when a scout came back with news that the Menteshe had hidden a couple of hundred horsemen in an almond grove not far from the plain where most of them camped. "Did they see you?" Grus asked.

"I don't think so, Your Majesty," the scout answered.

"All right," Grus said. "We'll go on with the attack on their main body, just as though we didn't have the slightest idea that outflanking party was around. But when they come out of the trees to give us a surprise, we'll give them one instead. Hirundo!"

"Yes, Your Majesty?" the general said.

"See that our men on that flank know Evren's riders are going to burst out and try to throw them into disorder. I want to make sure that doesn't happen. But I also want to make sure we don't make things too obvious over there. Do you understand me?"

"I think so," Hirundo said. "You want them to try to bring off their ambush, and you want to smash them when they do."

"That's it exactly." King Grus slapped him on the back. "Now let's go see if we're as smart as we think we are."

Grus was starting to feel a little more comfortable on horseback, which he found alarming—it proved he was spending too much time in the saddle. He scarcely noticed the weight of chain mail anymore. As long as he rode a horse that wasn't too spirited—this one was the gelding he'd used while fighting the rebellious baron, Pandion—he did reasonably well.

His men shouted when the Menteshe came into sight. The nomads shouted, too. They were already in a loose line of battle; they must have spotted the dust the Avornan cavalry kicked up. The Menteshe started shooting before the Avornans came close enough for their bows to bite. And then, instead of rushing forward to mix it up with swords, Evren's men rode away, shooting over their shoulders as they went.

That struck Grus as unfair and unsporting. Ineffective? He wished it were. Avornans tumbled out of the saddle one after another. Hardly any Menteshe went down. The nomads weren't doing enough damage to make Grus worry about his army, but they weren't taking any damage at all.

And then, with wild whoops and shouts, the Menteshe who'd hidden in the almond grove burst from cover and thundered after the Avornans. At the same time, the nomads ahead stopped retreating before their foes and charged at them, also shouting in their hissing, incomprehensible language.

If the Avornan scout hadn't spotted the Menteshe lurking in the grove, it might have gone hard for Grus and his men. As things were, Grus shouted, "Forward! Now we have the chance to close with them!" and spurred toward the Menteshe in front of him. He trusted—he bet his life—that the riders at the Avornan left flank and rear would keep the ambushers from throwing his men into chaos.

He knew he would never make a mounted archer. All he could do was draw his sword and wait for the two lines to smash together—if they did; if the Menteshe didn't turn and flee once more.

Evren's men didn't. The nomads in front must have been sure the ambush party from the grove would do its job. By the time they realized the Avornans were neither panic-stricken nor beaten, it was too late for them to break off. Grus and his followers were right on top of them.

"For King Olor and Queen Quelea!" Grus yelled, slashing at a nomad. At closer quarters, the Avornans had the advantage. Their horses were bigger than Menteshe ponies, their chain mail better protection than the treated leather with which Evren's men armored themselves. Now Grus' men, also shouting the names of their gods, hacked Menteshe out of the saddle and took revenge for the long-range punishment their enemies had given them.

A nomad cut at Grus' head. The stroke missed, the Menteshe's blade hissing past less than a hand's breadth in front of Grus' face. The king slashed back. The nomad turned the blow. Sparks flew as his blade and Grus' grated against each other. Before the Menteshe could strike again, another Avornan laid his cheek open with a backhand cut. He howled and sprayed blood and clutched at himself, all else forgotten in his pain. Grus' next stroke made him slide off his horse into the dust.

Grus risked a look back over his shoulder. His men had turned on the warriors who'd burst from the almond grove. He breathed a little easier, seeing that the nomads weren't going to do to him what the Thervings had done to Count Corvus.

All at once, the Menteshe decided they'd had as much of this fight as they wanted. When they galloped off this time, the flight was real, not feigned. One proof the Menteshe truly were running was that they loosed far fewer over-the-shoulder shots at their foes than they had before.

A long pursuit was hopeless. Grus looked around for a trumpeter and, for a wonder, found one. At his order, the fellow blew *Rein in*. Watching the Menteshe run away was one of the most satisfying things an Avornan army could do.

General Hirundo rode up to Grus. "Well, Your Majesty, they're paying for everything they're getting on this side of the river," he said.

"That's true." But Grus had to point out the other side of the coin, as he had before. "They're making us pay, too."

"I know," Hirundo said. "But we can afford it longer than they can."

"Can we? I wonder," Grus said. "This farmland they've ravaged will take years to get back to what it should be. The same for the lands the Thervings plundered again and again. We have to eat, you know. And without farmers to make soldiers and pay taxes, what are we? In trouble, that's what."

Hirundo pointed at him. "So *that's* why you've made such a fuss about nobles who take over small farmers' lands."

"Of course," Grus said, only to realize it wasn't *of course* to Hirundo. "Either I'm King of Avornis, or all these barons and counts get to set up as petty kings inside the kingdom. I don't intend to let that happen." He looked south, toward the cloud of dust that veiled the Menteshe from sight. "I don't intend to let those savages—or their master—ruin Avornis, either."

"You can stop the nomads, especially if you fight as smart a battle as you did here," Hirundo said. "But how do you propose to stop the Banished One?"

Grus started to answer. He stopped without saying a word, though, for he realized he hadn't the least idea.

King Lanius nodded to the green-robed priest who worked out of a tiny room stuck in a back corner of the arch-hallow's residence. Ixoreus had no ecclesiastical rank to speak of. His white beard said he never would, and that he didn't care. Lanius felt more at home with him than with most people, though. The two of them shared a restless, relentless urge to *know*.

The arch-hallow's secretary returned the nod with the air of one equal replying to another. "So you want to go into the archives, do you?" he said.

"That's right." Lanius nodded. "I'm interested in finding out how our prayers and services have changed since earliest times."

Ixoreus blinked at him. Most old men had trouble reading, while they could still see things clearly at a distance. By the way Ixoreus leaned forward, he had trouble with making out things farther away from him—a lucky infirmity in a man who'd devoted his life to books. "Yes, that could be interesting, couldn't it?" he said.

"I think so." Lanius didn't say he was trying to learn what sort of god the Banished One had been before his banishment. He had the feeling that the less he said about the Banished One, the better off he—and Avornis—would be.

"Let's see what we can do, then," Ixoreus said, slowly getting to his feet. His back was stooped; he leaned on a stick. His walk was a shuffle a tortoise might have outsped. Lanius followed without a word, without even a thought, of complaint. The priest, after all, was taking him where he wanted to go. He would have accompanied a willing, pretty girl with hardly more eagerness.

Not far from the altar in the great cathedral was a stairway Lanius had noticed before but never really thought about. He'd assumed it let priests come up more conveniently to attend the altar. And so, no doubt, it did, but that proved to be anything but its main purpose.

Having gone down the stairs, Lanius gaped in wonder. "I never imagined this was here!" he exclaimed.

"You don't understand yet," Ixoreus said, smiling. "This is only the first level."

"How many are there altogether?" Lanius asked.

"Five," the priest answered. "The cathedral's a good deal bigger under the ground than it is on top." He made his halting way toward the stairway down to the next level. As he began to descend, he said, "One of these days I'll fall, and these stairs will be the death of me." Lanius started to shake his head and disagree, but Ixoreus smiled again. "There are plenty of worse ways to go. By now, I've seen most of them."

The archives filled the two lowest levels. Lanius' nostrils twitched at the half musty, half animal smell of old parchment. "No other odor like that in all the world," he said.

His words seemed to reach Ixoreus in a way nothing else had. "Well, none except ink, anyhow," he said. He and Lanius eyed each other in perfect mutual understanding.

Down on the bottommost level, only a few lamps burned. In that dim, flickering light, Lanius felt not only the weight of the centuries but also the weight of everything built and excavated above him. After a moment's fear, he shrugged. If an earthquake made it all collapse, in less than the blink of an eye he would be a red smear thinner than any sheet of parchment. What point to worrying, then?

"Do you want a guide, or would you sooner poke through things on your own?" Ixoreus asked.

"By your leave, most holy sir—" Lanius began.

The priest laughed out loud. "You want me to go away and let you do as you would," he said. "There may be more to you as a searcher than I thought. The run-of-the-mill sort want me to hold their hand. They may find what they're looking for, but somehow they're never looking for anything much. The other kind—well, they often come up empty. When they don't, though . . ."

Lanius hardly heard him. The king looked now here, now there, wondering where to begin. He also wondered why he'd never come here before. True, the royal archives held enough documents to keep a man busy till the end of time. Even so, he should have started going through these records years before.

When he sat down, the stool creaked under him. He wondered if it dated back to the days before the Scepter of Mercy was lost. Then he wondered if it dated back to the days before the Banished One was cast out of the heavens. Anywhere else, he would have laughed at the idea. Down here in the near darkness, it didn't seem so ridiculous anymore.

He almost called Ixoreus back to ask if the records held any order at all. In the end, he didn't—he wanted to find out for himself. He soon discovered there wasn't much. Documents from his father's reign lay beside others dating back before the loss of the Scepter of Mercy. If he wanted something in particular, he was going to need luck and patience.

Luck came from the gods. Patience . . . Lanius shifted on that ancient stool. Patience he had. His lips twisted in a bitter smile. After all, it wasn't as though he would be taking time away from anything vital to Avornis if he came down here and worked his way through the clerical archives one silverfish-nibbled piece of parchment at a time. Grus didn't let him deal with anything vital anyhow.

If he hadn't had practice reading old, old scripts in the royal archives, he would have been altogether at sea here. As things were, that troubled him no more than switching from the hand of one secretary to that of another would have. He felt like shouting when he came upon letters from half a dozen yellow-robed clerics bewailing the irruption of the Menteshe into the lands around their towns. No Avornan clerics had gone to those towns for more than four hundred years.

He felt like cursing when, in the same set of pigeonholes as those letters, he found others about sending consecrated wine to the Chernagor city-states that came from the reign of his great-grandfather. Maybe someone would find those interesting one day, but he didn't.

He shoved them back into their pigeonholes. The next cache of letters also came from the days of his dynasty, which meant they were too recent to be interesting to him. He had to go through them one at a time anyway, because no one except Olor and Quelea could be sure ahead of time what might lie mixed in with them.

As it happened, nothing was mixed in with that batch—nothing Lanius cared about, anyhow. "But if I hadn't looked through them, the parchment I need would be at the bottom of that crate," he muttered. His words vanished without the slightest trace of echo, as though the parchments and the boxes and racks that held them swallowed up sound. They were surely hungry. They wouldn't have had many sounds to swallow down here, not for year upon year upon year.

Lanius went through another crate and another rack. He kept waiting for Ixoreus to come nag him about going back up to the outer world again. But the green-robed priest left him alone. That made him happy. Ixoreus understood, beyond the shadow of a doubt. Lanius had met only a handful of men who did.

And patience and persistence had their reward. Lanius was going through some minutes from a minor ecclesiastical council two hundred fifty years before when he came upon a parchment that didn't belong with the rest. He saw as much at once; the parchment was yellow with age, the writing faded to a pale ghost of itself. He whistled softly. He wasn't sure he'd ever seen anything this old in the royal archives.

He brought three lamps together, to give him the best light he could get down here. Then he bent close to see what he could make out. Not just the script was archaic here; so was the language. He had to puzzle it out a phrase at a time. When he finished, he quietly put the parchment back where he'd found it. He said not a word about it to Ixoreus when they returned to the world of light and air. The priest wouldn't have believed him. Lanius wondered if he believed himself, or wanted to.

CHAPTER TWENTY-SEVEN

lca eyed the Menteshe prisoner with no great warmth. The
Menteshe looked back at her out of narrow dark eyes filled with
fear and suspicion. Grus listened to the rain drumming down on
the roof of his residence in Cumanus. His men and the changing weather
had finally persuaded Prince Evren his attacks were costing him more than
they were worth.

"You speak Avornan?" Alca asked the prisoner.

"I speak some, yes," the nomad answered.

"I chose one for you who did," Grus said.

Alca nodded. She asked the Menteshe, "What is your name?"

"I am Kai-Qubad," he said. If he'd trusted her, he would have given her
his whole genealogy after that; the Menteshe were proud of their ancestors. Grus wondered why. To him, one lizard-eating savage was no different from another. Someone like Lanius, now, had reason to boast about
the family tree. But a Menteshe? Kai-Qubad, though, fell silent after
his own name, not wanting to give Alca more of a hold on him than he
had to.

She didn't press him for more. Instead, she said, "You need to know
that I will know if you lie. Do you understand this? Do you believe it?"

"I understand. I believe. You are . . ." Kai-Qubad said something in his
own tongue.

Grus didn't speak the Menteshe language. He hadn't thought the witch did, either, but she nodded. "All right, then. Tell me why Prince Evren went to war against Avornis."

Kai-Qubad scratched by the side of his mouth. He had a wispy mustache any Avornan man would have been ashamed of, but few Menteshe could have grown a thicker one. After that brief hesitation, he said, "You are there to war on. You should ask, why did we not war on you for so long?"

"When you hadn't warred on us for so long, why did Evren pick that time to start?" Grus asked.

"Am I Evren? Do I know why the prince does what he does?" Kai-Qubad returned.

Sharply, Alca said, "I know when you evade, too. You would do better not to evade. You would do much better, in fact." She waited. Kai-Qubad nodded. So did she. "Answer the king's question," she told him.

"You are the enemy. You will always be the enemy. And our flocks need new grazing lands," the nomad said. "What more reason do we need?"

"I don't know," Grus said. "Did the Banished One order Evren to send men over the Stura? Is that why you chose to fight when you did?"

"The Banished One. So you call him," Kai-Qubad said scornfully. "To us, he is the Fallen Star. He will return to the heavens one day. He will return, and all debts will be paid. Oh, yes—they will be paid."

That prospect—which, unsurprisingly, matched what the Banished One himself had claimed—frightened Grus more than he could say. Kai-Qubad looked forward to it with a gloating anticipation that frightened the king, too. Then Alca said, "You are evading again. Did he order Evren to go over the Stura?"

Kai-Qubad shrugged. He wasn't a very big man, but his movements held a liquid grace. "Do I know the minds of princes?" he asked. A moment later, he let out a sharp yelp of pain.

"I told you not to evade," Alca said. "Now answer."

"No one told me anything," he said, and then yelped again.

"These games get you nowhere," the witch warned. "The more you play them, the sorrier you will be. Tell me what you know. Tell me everything you know, and stop wasting time."

"I don't know what to tell you." Kai-Qubad set his jaw, plainly expecting more pain. He hissed like a snake when it came. This time, it didn't seem to go away at once, but hung on and on.

"That is your own lie tormenting you," Alca said. "If you tell the truth, all will be well once more."

"Ha!" the Menteshe said. But he stood there, huddled in his own misery, for no more than a few minutes before groaning, "Make it stop! I will speak."

"If you speak the truth, it *will* stop," the witch told him.

"Yes, then. Yes! Our lord and master started Evren against you." Kai-Qubad sighed with relief. Evidently Alca had meant what she said.

"How do you know this?" Grus asked the nomad.

"How?" The fellow hesitated. By now, even that pause was plenty to cause him pain. He said, "Make it stop! I'll tell." He hurried on. "I know because my captain's sister is wed to one of Prince Evren's guards. That fellow said the prince had an envoy from the Fallen Star come to court not long before we went over the river against you. When an envoy from him you call the Banished One comes, what can a prince do but obey?"

"We don't," Grus said. "We never have. We never will."

Kai-Qubad looked at him with an emotion he'd never dreamt he would see on any Menteshe's face—pity. "One day, you will bow before the Fallen Star, as we have done. One day, you will know peace, as we do." He meant it. He meant every word of it. That alarmed Grus more than anything.

It didn't alarm Alca. It angered her. "How do you dare talk of peace when you were taken in war?"

"We have peace," the Menteshe insisted. "We have perfect peace. We have yielded to the Fallen Star. He is our master. We accept this. We accept him. We need nothing else. We want nothing else. You are the ones who still struggle. When you accept him, you will have perfect peace, too. We bring him to you."

"You bring plunder and rape and murder," Grus said.

"And you fight among yourselves," Alca added. "What do you have to say about that, if you have perfect peace?"

Kai-Qubad shrugged. "Fighting is our sport." There, for once, Grus believed him completely. He went on, "And some of our enmities go back to ancient days, and do not die at once." Grus believed that, too.

"Our old ways go back even further than yours," Grus said. "Why shouldn't we keep them, if they suit us?"

"Oh, that is very simple," Kai-Qubad answered. "Your ways are wrong, but ours are right." He spoke with complete conviction. He showed no sign of sudden pain, either. As far as he was concerned, he was telling the truth. The spell that would have punished him for lying stayed quiet.

"Do you want to hear anything more from him, Your Majesty?" Alca asked. Grus shook his head. The witch gestured to the guards. They took the Menteshe away. Alca sighed wearily. "What can we do with such people?" she said.

"Beat them," Grus said. "That's the only thing I can see. If we don't beat them, one of these days they'll beat us. And that would be very bad."

He laughed at the understatement. He'd spent these past months either fighting the Menteshe or trying to understand the thralls who'd swarmed over the Stura into Avornis. He imagined the riders carrying destruction and murder all through the kingdom. He also imagined the wizards—or would they be priests, of a particular dark sort?—following in the nomads' wake. He imagined farmers and townsfolk made into thralls. And he imagined the Banished One thriving on their adoration and looking out through their eyes and seeing a world full of slaves to him and thinking it was good. He imagined all that, and the laughter curdled in his throat.

"What are we going to do?" he whispered. "Oh, by the gods, what are we going to do?" He looked at Alca, hoping the witch would have an answer. But she spread her hands, as though to say she didn't know, either. He felt worse than if he hadn't looked her way at all.

Sosia eyed Lanius. "Something is wrong," she said.

"I don't know what you're talking about," he answered, knowing what a liar he was.

His wife knew what a liar he was, too. "I don't believe you, not even for a minute," she said. "Something *is* wrong. When I first realized it, I thought you were having an affair."

"I'm not," Lanius said, which was the truth. There were plenty of pretty serving women in the palace. He enjoyed looking at them. He'd kept his hands to himself, though, ever since he'd married Sosia. He'd thought about taking this one or that one to bed, and he knew some of them had thought about the advantages of bedding him, but nothing of that sort had happened.

"I know you're not," Sosia said now. "I almost wish you were. Almost. Then I'd know *what* was wrong. This way . . ." She shook her head. "This way, I'm guessing, and that's even worse."

"I'm sorry," Lanius said. "You couldn't do anything about it anyway." And *that,* he knew, was also nothing but the truth.

Sosia, who didn't know what he knew, wasn't convinced. "Queen Quelea's tears, how can I believe that when I don't even know what the trouble is?" she demanded.

The oath didn't make things better. The oath, if anything, made them worse. "I'm sorry," Lanius said, and then said no more.

"You shouldn't be sorry. You should tell me whatever it is. If it's not a woman—"

"It's not."

"I know it's not. I already told you that." Sosia sounded impatient. "But since it's not, what's the point to keeping it a secret, whatever it is?"

What's the point to keeping it a secret? Lanius wondered. But he knew the answer to that. He hadn't shown even Ixoreus what he'd found. Maybe the green-robed priest hadn't seen that particular piece of parchment. If he had, he hadn't seen what it meant.

Or maybe he had seen it and had understood it, but didn't know Lanius had and didn't want to discuss it with *him*. Maybe Ixoreus had endured for years the sinking feeling Lanius had known these past few weeks.

Fortunately, Lanius didn't have long to brood over what he'd found. A servant came in and said, "Your Majesty, the envoys from the Chernagor city-states are here. We'll have them in the throne room in a quarter of an hour."

"Oh, very good!" Lanius said. The delay gave him long enough to put on his crown and a pearl-encrusted robe and take his place on the throne before the merchants who doubled as ambassadors entered the chamber.

The Chernagors were big, blocky men with proud noses, dark beards, and hair tied at their napes in neat buns. They wore embroidered shirts and kilts that stopped just above their knees. Lanius had read that the embroidery and the pattern of the kilt varied from one city-state to another. He was willing to believe it, but hadn't seen enough Chernagors to tell one town's distinguishing marks from another's. *They're probably in the archives,* he thought, and wondered where they might lurk.

"Greetings, Your Majesty," a man, evidently their leader, said. His beard showed more gray than black; he wore a massy golden ring on his right finger and even massier gold hoops in his ears. Some Therving men wore earrings, too; Lanius didn't know who'd gotten the custom from whom.

He would have to ask another time, if another time ever came. For now, the tough, sticky web of ceremony held him. "Greetings to you, sir," he replied. "And you are . . . ?"

"I am called Lyashko, Your Majesty." Lyashko's Avornan was fluent, even more so than Yaropolk's had been. "I bring you not only my greetings but also those of my overlord, Prince Bolush of Durdevatz, and also the greetings of all the other princes of the Chernagors."

"I am pleased to accept Prince Bolush's greetings along with your own," Lanius said. The rest of the Chernagor princes undoubtedly had no idea Lyashko existed. Chernagors always tossed in that last bit like cooks adding a sprig of parsley to garnish a supper plate—it had no purpose but decoration.

"Very good. Very good." Lyashko smiled and nodded. The hoops in his ears sparkled as they caught the torchlight.

"I am pleased to give you and your comrades gifts," Lanius said. Out came servants with sacks of coins calculated to the farthing. The gifts Avornis gave to Chernagors rigidly followed the recipients' ranks, and the formulas for presenting them never changed.

Hefting his own sack—larger and heavier than any of the rest—Lyashko nodded again. "And I am pleased to have gifts for you as well, Your Majesty."

Lanius leaned forward in anticipation. So did his courtiers. Gifts from Chernagors to Kings of Avornis could be anything at all. That custom was adhered to just as rigidly.

Lyashko spoke to his men in their own tongue. To Avornan ears, the Chernagor language sounded like a man choking to death. One of the dark-haired men came forward and set a block of fine red wood at the base of Lanius' throne. "It will carve nicely," Lyashko said, returning to Avornan, "and it has a fine odor."

Sure enough, a spicy scent, stronger and sweeter than that of cedar, rose from the block. "Thank you," Lanius said. "Where does this wood come from?"

"An island far out in the Northern Sea," Lyashko answered. His people seldom gave away secrets they didn't have to. Lyashko went back to the Chernagor speech. Another man set a necklace of black pearls on the wood. "For Her Majesty, the Queen."

"In Her Majesty's name, I thank you," Lanius said. Sosia wasn't there to meet the Chernagors; that would have gone flat against custom. Seeing the soft shimmer of light from the pearls, he felt something more was called for. "They're very beautiful," he told Lyashko. "This is a generous gift."

"Why else are we here, but to make you happy?" Lyashko said. The sack of coins he'd just gotten suggested one other reason he might have come to the city of Avornis. Like any other folk, the Chernagors did what was advantageous to them first and worried about other things later. And, like any other folk, they preferred bragging about how generous they were to admitting any such thing.

"Black pearls are rare," Lanius said. Lyashko's big head bobbed up and down in agreement. He spoke in his own language again. A moment later, all the Chernagors were nodding. King Lanius went on, "Where did you find so many?"

"There is, in the Northern Sea, an island where the natives dive deep into the water to take the shellfish the pearls come from," Lyashko replied. "It is hard, dangerous work, and only a very few of the shells have any pearls at all, let alone black ones."

"Whereabouts in the Northern Sea is this island?" Lanius asked.

Lyashko sent him a reproachful look. He wasn't supposed to ask specific questions like that; he was only supposed to marvel. At last, the envoy from Durdevatz answered, "That is not easy to say, Your Majesty, for it lies far from any other land."

King Lanius almost asked the Chernagor what the name of the island was. He started to, but then held back. What point to the question? Lyashko wouldn't give him a straight answer, and he didn't want more evasions. Better just to let it go.

When he didn't ask, Lyashko's broad shoulders shook with a sigh of relief. The envoy spoke in his own language once more. A couple of other Chernagors lugged up a large crate or box covered with a sheet of shining blue silk. Just as Lyashko was about to go into his speech, a series of harsh, shrill screeches came from inside the crate. The Chernagor gave a rather sickly grin. "Knowing your fondness for strange beasts," he said, "we have brought you these, which paid us back by spoiling the surprise."

He brusquely swept aside the silk sheet. Inside the cage—for such it was—was a pair of monkeys. They were mostly black, with white on their bellies, white eyebrows, and great sweeping white mustaches that gave them the look of somber old men. To Lanius' surprise, they were smaller than his moncats. They stared at him from round-black eyes.

As he stared back, he wondered if the pearls Lyashko had brought for Sosia would be enough to reconcile her to the monkeys. He dared hope, anyhow. "Thank you very much," he said. "It's been a long time since anyone here in the city of Avornis has seen animals like these."

"There's a reason for that, too, Your Majesty," Lyashko said. "They're delicate creatures. You have to keep 'em warm all through the winter. If you don't, they'll get a flux of the lungs and die."

"I see," Lanius said. "Tell me everything else I need to know about them, please. Are they a male and a female?"

"They are, but I don't know how much good it'll do you," the Chernagor replied. "I've never heard of 'em breeding while they're caged."

"We'll see," Lanius said, anticipating a new challenge. "What do they eat? That's something else I'd better know."

"In the trees, they eat leaves and fruit and eggs and bugs and anything little they can catch," Lyashko said. "We've been feeding them what we eat, and they've done all right with that. They really like cabbage—they think it's the best stuff in the world."

"Cabbage," Lanius repeated. "I'll remember that." He turned formal. "I thank you again, Lyashko, and again I thank Prince Bolush through you."

"My pleasure, Your Majesty," Lyashko said. "And since you noised it about that you were after monkeys . . ." He got a look at Lanius' face. "Oh, wasn't I supposed to say that out loud? Sorry. Real sorry."

Lanius sighed. Sosia was going to have a thing or two to say to him. Maybe more than a thing or two.

Alca drummed her fingers on the tabletop in Grus' quarters in Cumanus. "Your Majesty, I don't know what more we can learn about thralls here that we can't find out back in the city of Avornis."

Grus sighed. She was right, and he knew it. He sighed again all the same. "I have my reasons for not wanting to go back right away."

"I know you do," the witch answered. "But have those reasons got anything to do with the thralls, or even with the Menteshe?"

"No," Grus admitted. Had he said anything else, she would have known he was lying. Prince Evren's riders had gone back to the south side of the Stura, those who'd escaped Avornan soldiers and river galleys. Grus thought it would take more than even the Banished One's command to get them to move on Avornis again anytime soon. As for the thralls, they'd stopped crossing the river in such large numbers as soon as the war with Evren's men broke out. To put it mildly, Grus doubted that was a coincidence.

Alca said, "Well, then. What's keeping us here, in that case?"

He looked at her. "You know as well as I do."

She reached for the goblet of wine in front of her. After she sipped from it, her tongue flicked out like a cat's to get rid of a deep red drop at a corner of her mouth. Grus watched, fascinated. Alca did her best not to notice him watching. She said, "This has to end. When we go home, we have to be two people who spent a while working together, and nothing more. You see that, don't you?"

"Yes," Grus answered, most reluctantly. It wasn't that he didn't care for Estrilda. It wasn't even that he didn't look forward to taking her to bed again. He supposed Alca was thinking like thoughts about her husband. Even so . . . "I don't want it to end."

"I know that. But it has to, don't you see?" Alca said. "The longer it goes on, the more trouble it will cause when they find out about it back at the capital."

"Who says anyone will find out?" Grus asked.

The look she gave him was not that of a witch foretelling the future. It was the look of a woman who knew how the world worked, and all the more wounding because of that. "Most of the time, ordinary people can't keep their love affairs secret," she said. "You're the King of Avornis. What do you think the odds are?"

He wished she'd put it some other way. "Well, no one will find out from me," he said.

"Or from me," Alca answered. "But what has that got to do with anything? People *will* gossip—about the doings of a king especially."

"We *have* been working together," Grus said. "Everyone knows that. We were friends before we came down to Cumanus. Everyone knows that, too. It will be all right. Nobody will think so much of our seeing a lot of each other." He'd seen as much of her as there was to see. He thought of the little mole she had on the inside of one thigh, and of . . .

But she gave him that worried look again. "Either it will be all right, or it will be all the worse on account of that. I know which way I'd bet. Even so, we should go back to the capital. Otherwise—" She broke off.

"Otherwise what?" Grus asked when she didn't finish the thought.

He didn't think she was going to answer, but she finally did. In a very low voice, she said, "Otherwise I don't think I'll want to go back at all, and we have to. You know we do."

Grus thought about letting the love affair run away with him, about casting Estrilda aside and putting Alca in her place, or about taking Alca as a second wife after she left her husband. He thought about it for perhaps half a minute, and then shook his head.

Alca was watching him. Still very quietly, she said, "You see, Your Majesty."

He wished she hadn't used his title then. It only added to the weight he had to carry. No doubt she'd done it with just that in mind. He sighed. He *was* the king, but even a king had trouble getting away with some things. "We'll go back to the city of Avornis," he said. "Take as many thralls as you think you'll need. Do everything you can to check them first, though. We don't want to take trouble back with us."

"We will be taking trouble back with us," Alca said. "But you're right, of course. We don't want to take that kind of trouble back with us, too."

With another sigh, Grus said, "I'll talk to the river-galley captains and set things moving." Alca smiled happily. That stung.

When Grus did talk to the galley captains, they seemed surprised he was leaving Cumanus. That stung, too. They couldn't have been surprised because of the state of the river—the Stura ran higher in fall than it did in summertime. They couldn't have expected he would find out more about the thralls here anytime soon—Alca hadn't come up with anything new for quite some time. And they probably didn't think the Menteshe would pick this time of year to invade Avornis again.

In that case, they had to be surprised because he was cutting short his affair with Alca. They couldn't be surprised if they didn't know about it. And if they knew about it, they were all too likely to talk once they got back to the city of Avornis.

He didn't tell Alca about that. She might not say, "I told you so," but she would surely think it.

Guarded and urged along by soldiers, half a dozen thralls boarded one of the river galleys bound for the capital. Ordinary peasants would have stared and exclaimed. The thralls took the ship as much in stride as they did everything else. It was only one more incomprehensible thing among the swarm of incomprehensibilities that made up their lives.

Alca, on the other hand, boarded the galley on which she and Grus would travel with every sign of relief. "Wonderful to be going home at last, isn't it?" she said brightly.

"Wonderful," Grus echoed. *What a liar I am,* he thought.

No one required Lanius to come to the piers to greet Grus on his return from the south. Maybe Grus didn't think he'd won enough of a victory to hold a celebration. Maybe it had just slipped his mind to send ahead to the city, and order one. Either way, it didn't bother Lanius. He had his children. He had the archives. He had the moncats. Now he had the monkeys with the ridiculous mustaches, too.

He was with the monkeys when Grus came in. They required a room of their own, not only because they needed to be kept warm whereas the moncats didn't but also because the moncats, larger and fiercer, would have made a meal out of them if they'd lived together.

When the door opened behind Lanius, he turned in some annoyance. By now, the servants knew they weren't supposed to bother him when he was with the animals. Grus, however, was a different story. He did as he pleased. He eyed the monkeys with more than a little curiosity. They stared back at him from their round black eyes with at least as much curiosity. One of them fiddled with its droopy mustache, just as a man might have done.

"Quite a menagerie you're getting," Grus remarked. "I don't think I've ever seen a monkey before."

"I hadn't, either. The Chernagors brought them to me," Lanius answered. More slowly than he should have, he added, "Welcome home."

"Thanks, Your Majesty." Grus' voice was dry. He eyed the monkeys again. "The Chernagors are shrewd. Say what you want about 'em, they're nobody's fools. They must have figured out that you like funny beasts."

"Well . . . yes." Lanius didn't care to admit that he'd given the Chernagors a few hints about what he liked. If he told Grus, it would get back to Sosia. It probably would anyway, sooner or later, because of what Lyashko had said in the throne room. But when it got back to his wife, he knew he would hear about it.

"If you want to see strange creatures, I can show you some I brought back from the south," Grus said.

"Really? What sort of creatures?" Lanius asked eagerly. He knew there were some animals and birds that dwelt in the south but never came up to the capital. He knew which of those he would most like to see, too. Had Grus figured out that the road to his affection ran through his curiosity? Maybe he had. He was nobody's fool, either.

But what he said now—"Thralls"—rocked Lanius back on his heels. Grus went on, "We brought some of them back so we can go on studying them here."

"I see," Lanius said. "But isn't that dangerous?"

"Probably," the older man answered. "We decided *not* bringing 'em back would be even more dangerous, though. I hope we were right." He didn't look altogether contented with the choice he'd made.

For his part, Lanius didn't suppose he could quarrel with that choice till he knew more; whether it proved right or wrong, Grus had obviously made it with care. Lanius said, "Yes, I would like to see the thralls before long."

"Good." Grus nodded in unreserved approval. Lanius cherished that, for he seldom got it. Thoughtfully, Grus went on, "You need to have a notion of just what kind of foe Avornis is up against there."

"Oh." That quite took the urge off Lanius' desire to learn more about thralls. His own voice grim, he said, "As a matter of fact, Your Majesty, so do you."

Grus' eyes widened. Lanius rarely used his title. Then one of the monkeys pulled the other's tail. The victim, screeching, scrambled up the lattice of sticks and boards Lanius had had the carpenters run up to simulate a jungle. Screeching in a different key, the tail-puller pursued. Right over Grus' head, one of them—Lanius didn't see which—did something that monkeys do. People also do those things, but after about the age of two they're more careful about where.

A cloudburst of curses burst from Grus. Then, to Lanius' astonishment, he started to laugh. Pointing an accusing finger at Lanius, he said, "I think you've trained them to do that."

"I have not," Lanius said. "They've gotten me, too. They aren't like moncats—they go where they please. Can I get you a towel?"

"I could use one," his father-in-law answered. "I could use a bath, too, as a matter of fact. And if they can't get the stink out of this robe, the tailors are going to have some very unkind things to say about me—and about your precious pets."

"Here's the towel," Lanius said. "I *am* sorry."

"So am I." Grus scrubbed vigorously at his hair. "Maybe I should have been wearing the crown." After a moment, he shook his head. "No, then more of it would have dripped down onto my face." He threw the towel on the floor. "Thank you kindly, Your Majesty. That helped—some. Now, if you'll excuse me, I'm going off to clean up." He did make sure he latched the door behind him.

And so, Lanius' news didn't get told just then. In fact, he forgot all about it for a while, the first time he'd been able to do that since discovering it. He wagged a finger at the monkeys. "That was naughty," he said. "That was very naughty."

Then, as Grus had before, he started to laugh. His reasons, though, were rather different. He found himself wishing he were much, much smaller. Then he too could have scrambled up into that lattice. He too could have poised himself over the other king's head. And he too could have done just what that little mustachioed monkey had done.

King Grus walked through the royal palace with a curious mix of pleasure and apprehension. He'd never dreamt, when he first boarded a river galley all those years ago, that he would end up here. And he had a firm grip on the throne. Lanius was in no position to challenge him, not really. After what he'd done to the luckless Pandion, none of the nobles seemed inclined to try to take the crown away. Knowing that would have been plenty to please almost any man.

As for the apprehension . . . Like a lot of husbands, Grus feared his wife would find out he hadn't been faithful. Like a good many of those husbands, he feared his wife would find out he hadn't been faithful *again*. He couldn't very well deny he'd slipped once, not when the evidence of his slip was at the moment Arch-Hallow of Avornis. But the difference between once and twice was almost bigger than the difference between never and once. Once could—well, nearly could—be an accident, an aberration. Twice? No, not twice.

Maybe fewer people really knew than Alca thought. Maybe the ones who did know would keep their mouths shut. He was the King of Avornis, after all. If he found out who spread gossip about him, he could make that person sorry for the rest of his days.

If. The trouble with gossip—so he thought, being gossiped about rather than gossiping—was that it was too easy and spread too fast. This one told that one, who told the other one, who told the next one, who . . . Before long, who could say where the chain started?

He sometimes thought he would welcome an invasion from the Thervings. That would let him forget his own troubles and start thinking of Avornis'. But Lanius had known what he was talking about. King Berto, unlike Dagipert, was more interested in praying than fighting. Grus was sure that made Olor and Quelea and the other gods very happy. Most of the time, it would have made him happy, too. Now? That he wondered was a measure of how worried he was.

Not even playing with his grandchildren let him ease his mind. As he tried to keep Pitta from tearing out his beard by handfuls, he wondered whether Lanius was amusing himself outside of Sosia's bed. *If he is, I'll* . . . He stopped, feeling foolish. *I'll what?* Considering what he'd been up to, what *could* he say to his son-in-law? *I can say whatever I want, by the gods, as long as I don't get caught myself.*

Later, he suspected that that blasphemous thought had had something to do with what happened. But, no matter how little he could prove, he knew what he thought.

Once back in the city of Avornis, he didn't watch Alca working with the thralls. That, he thought, would have been asking for trouble. If he spent a lot of time with the witch, one of them or the other might do something or say something to give them away. He could see that plainly, and so he stayed away.

Sometimes, though, whatever you did was wrong. Estrilda said, "Why aren't you paying more attention to those poor people you brought back from the south? Didn't you go down there to try to do more for them?"

Grus was drinking a mug of wine when his wife asked the question. He didn't choke, though he came close. Once he was breathing normally again, he said, "I've been busy. I've had a lot to catch up on since I got back."

"Even so," Estrilda said. "The more the witch finds out, the better off we'll be. And the better off the thralls will be, too. You should keep on eye on what Alca's doing here."

He couldn't even tell her no. If he hadn't taken Alca to bed, he would have been hovering around her, trying to learn as much as he could about what she was up to and what the chances were. If he hung back now, Estrilda would start wondering why. He couldn't have that. Finishing the wine at a gulp, he spoke as casually as he could. "Well, maybe I will."

"I hope you do," Estrilda said. "The thralls are the key to everything, I think."

That, Grus knew, was liable to be true in ways Estrilda hadn't expected. Still, he went off to see Alca with more than a little eagerness.

He found her sooner than he'd thought he would, not in the suite of rooms where she worked with—worked on—the thralls, but wandering through the hallways. He smiled and hurried toward her, but then stopped short. Her face was almost as blank as that of a thrall. She looked as though she'd been through some dreadful disaster and had no idea how she'd come out alive.

"Sweet Quelea's mercy!" Grus exclaimed. "What's wrong?"

Her expression didn't change. Her voice was just as empty as she answered, "He knows."

"Who knows?" Grus asked automatically, though any idiot should have been able to figure that out for himself. Maybe the question was one to which he didn't really want an answer.

Want it or not, he got it. "My husband," Alca said, spelling out the obvious. "He . . . is not pleased with me." By the way she said that, it was as much an understatement as she could make of it.

"How did he find out?" Grus asked.

The witch shrugged. "He did, that's all. He knew enough that I couldn't make it out to be a lie—especially when it was no lie." She paused, then added, "He is going to cast me aside. I don't suppose I can blame him." She stared down at the mosaicwork floor.

Grus knew she loved—or had loved—her husband. He asked, "Do you want me to order him to keep you?"

Alca didn't look up. She simply shook her head. "What good would it do, Your Majesty? The thing is broken. There is no magic to put it back together. I wish there were." She turned away. "I can't even blame him. He has good reason for doing what he does."

"I'll take care of you." Grus set a hand on her shoulder.

She twisted away from him. "We've already taken care of things well enough, wouldn't you say?"

He had no answer for that. Even so, he promised, "You'll not want."

"For money, you mean?" Alca asked, and Grus nodded. Her laugh was bitter as wormwood. "And for love, Your Majesty? Can Petrosus allocate that from the treasury, too?" She held up a hand. "Never mind. It's not your fault alone—it's not as though you forced me. But that doesn't make things easier right now. If you'll excuse me . . ." She walked down the corridor. Grus wanted to follow her, but he knew that would only make matters worse, if they could be any worse.

CHAPTER TWENTY-EIGHT

"S omething's wrong," Sosia said in the quiet of the royal bedchamber.
"Wrong? Where?" The last time she'd said that, it had alarmed Lanius. This time, it only puzzled him. "Everything seems quiet to me.
Thervingia's peaceful. The Chernagors are squabbling amongst themselves
instead of with us. We taught the Menteshe a lesson—I hope we did, anyhow. The moncats are healthy. Even the monkeys are doing well. What
could be wrong?"

His wife sent him an exasperated look. "There are times when I wish
you paid less attention to your beasts and more to the people around you.
Something's wrong with Father."

"Oh." For various reasons he found good, Lanius paid as little attention to Grus as he could get away with. Sometimes, of course, that was like
trying not to pay attention to a natural calamity. A couple of heartbeats
later than he should have, Lanius realized he needed to ask, "What is it?"

"I don't know," Sosia answered. "That's part of what worries me.
Haven't you noticed how he has his mind on something lately, something
that doesn't let him pay attention to things right under his nose?"

"I'm like that all the time," Lanius said.

"Yes, I know." Sosia's tone was quietly devastating. She went on, "But
Father *isn't*. Or he never used to be. If he is now, all of a sudden, it must
be because something isn't the way it ought to be."

"Why don't you ask him what it is?"

Sosia's expression got more exasperated than ever. "Don't you think I have? He just looked at me and said, 'Nothing.' But it *isn't* nothing. If it were nothing, he wouldn't act the way he's acting."

"Maybe he'd tell me if I asked him," Lanius said.

"Maybe he would," Sosia said. "You're a man. Maybe that makes a difference. Would you try, please?"

"All right, when I find the chance." Lanius wondered what he was getting himself into. "The time has to be right. I can't just ask him out of the blue, or he won't tell me anything. I wouldn't tell anybody anything if I got asked out of the blue."

"All right." Sosia didn't complain, which proved how worried she was.

Finding the right time to ask his father-in-law personal questions proved harder than he'd expected. The moment did finally come, though. King Grus was complaining that Evren's Menteshe had done more damage down in the south than he'd thought they would when their invasion started. "Unfortunate," Lanius agreed.

"Worse than unfortunate," Grus said. "Between this and all the losses we had from the civil war and from the Thervings, I just hope the harvest is decent next year. If it's bad, we could see trouble."

"Is that what's been bothering you lately?" Lanius asked, as casually as he could. "Worry about the harvest, I mean?"

Grus gave him a stare as opaque as stone. "Nothing has been bothering me lately," he said tonelessly.

Up until then, Lanius hadn't noticed anything out of the ordinary with Grus. That stare and that unconvincing denial, though, were far out of character—so far out of character, Grus would be bound to prickle up if Lanius called him on it. Instead, Lanius said, "Well, Sosia's been worried that you aren't quite yourself."

"Who else would I be?" Grus' laugh also sounded wrong.

"I'm sure I don't know," Lanius answered. "I'm only telling you what she told me. Women are funny creatures sometimes." He did his best to sound like the man of the world he wasn't.

The effort fell flat. Grus nodded soberly and said, "That they are. You can't live with 'em, and you can't live without 'em." And he told nothing more of whatever was on his mind. A couple of further questions only brought out stares that made the first one seem warm and friendly by comparison. Lanius didn't need long to give up.

That evening, he told Sosia what little her father had said. "Men!" she said, as though writing off half the human race with one scornful word.

"I found out more than you did," Lanius said defensively.

"But you didn't find out enough," Sosia replied.

"Well, if you want to know more, you can ask him yourself," Lanius said. "You didn't see the way he looked at me. Or—" He broke off.

"Or what?" his wife asked.

"Or how he didn't want to talk," Lanius answered. That wasn't what he'd started to say, or anything close to it. But, suddenly, he doubted he ought to suggest that she ask Alca.

"Grus?" Estrilda's voice was soft but determined. "There's something we need to talk about, Grus."

This is what being wounded feels like, Grus thought. *It's been a long time, but I remember. First the shock, then, after a little while, the pain.* As a man sometimes will, he vowed not to show the pain no matter how much it hurt—and no matter how much more it was likely to hurt soon. Nodding to Estrilda, he asked, "What is it?" *Here it comes. Oh, yes, here it comes.*

And then she said, "We ought to find Ortalis a wife. High time he was married. Past time he was married, in fact. If he doesn't get a wife before too long, people will . . . will start to wonder if something's wrong with him."

More than once in the fighting against the Menteshe, arrows had hissed past Grus' head, arrows that would have been deadly if they'd struck home. He'd been in the heat of battle then. He hadn't had time to know relief. He did now. Almost giddy with it, he answered, "You're right, dear. We ought to see what we can do."

This isn't escape. This is only a reprieve. It may not even be a long one. She could find out tomorrow. Olor's beard, she could find out this afternoon. She's bound to find out before too long. So Grus told himself. He still felt as though he'd drunk three cups of strong wine, one right after another.

"We should have started in on this a long time ago," Estrilda said. "It may not be easy, even though you're the king."

Even though you're the king, plenty of fathers may not want to take the chance of marrying any daughter of theirs to your son. That was what she meant. Conversations about Ortalis were always full of things left out, things not spoken, blunt truths turned into euphemisms. Grus wished it were otherwise.

"It's . . . better since he took up hunting," he said. Ortalis was flesh of his flesh, too, and he too talked around his son's troubles.

"Some," Estrilda said. "Have you noticed, though, that he doesn't hunt with Anser anymore? I don't know why, but he doesn't. And there's nothing wrong with Anser . . . now." She couldn't resist tucking on that last word. Grus heard another arrow buzzing by him. Estrilda couldn't help liking Anser. Hardly anyone could help liking him. But she couldn't help remembering he was Grus' bastard, either.

How bad will it be when she finds out about Alca? No sooner had Grus asked himself the question than he decided he didn't want to know the answer. He might, he probably would, find out whether he wanted to or not, but not right now. Back to Ortalis, then. "Have you got anyone particular in mind?"

"Doesn't Marshal Lepturus have a granddaughter who'd be about the right age? That would be a good connection for our family."

"I think he does, yes," Grus answered. "Shall I ask him?"

His wife flashed him an annoyed look. "I wouldn't have mentioned the girl if I didn't want you to, now would I?"

"No, dear," Grus said dutifully.

When he asked Lepturus to dine with him, he made it a private invitation, only the two of them. If Lepturus had some things to say, Grus wanted them to be for his ears alone. The head of the royal bodyguards put him in mind of an old bear—slower than he had been, sometimes almost shambling, but still able to break a man's neck with one swipe of his paw.

They ate. The chef outdid himself with quail stuffed with crayfish gathered from the river outside the city of Avornis. The honey-glazed torte filled with candied fruit that followed the main course was every bit as magnificent in its own way. Grus made sure the wine flowed freely.

Lepturus emptied his goblet—not for the first time—then set it down. "Well, Your Majesty, if I were a pretty girl, you'd have seduced me by now," he rumbled. "But I'm no girl, and I never was pretty. So tell me, what's on your mind?"

Grus told him. Lepturus listened carefully. After the king was done, Lepturus refilled his goblet himself. He sipped. He said not a word. At last, Grus had to ask, "Well?"

"You do me a great honor, Your Majesty, me and my family," Lepturus said. He sipped again. He said not another word.

"Well?" Grus asked again when the silence stretched unbearably tight.

"Well, Your Majesty, as I say, it's a great honor, and mighty generous of you," Lepturus said, and then fell silent once more.

"What else do you have to say about it?" Grus asked.

"Well, Your Majesty . . ." Lepturus punctuated that by draining the goblet yet again. He sighed, then resumed, "Well, Your Majesty, it's a great honor, like I say. It's a great honor, but I'm going to have to turn you down."

Now that Grus had an answer, he wished he didn't. "Why?" he barked.

"Why?" Lepturus echoed, as though he'd never heard the word before. He hesitated, perhaps looking for some polite way to say what he thought needed saying. He must not have found one, for when he went on he was as blunt as before. "It's like this, Your Majesty. My granddaughter's a sweet girl, and—"

"And what?" Grus broke in. "Don't you think she'd be happy with Ortalis?"

"I don't even think she'd be safe with Ortalis," Lepturus said. "Some of the things I've heard about him . . ." He shook his big, heavy-featured head.

"Don't believe everything you hear," Grus said quickly.

"I don't. I don't believe half of it, or even a quarter. What's left is plenty. I want to keep Sponsa happy, and I want to keep her healthy. So thank you very much, Your Majesty, but no thank you."

Whatever Grus had expected, he hadn't expected Lepturus to turn him down flat. He didn't even argue when the guards commander heaved himself to his feet and limped out of the little chamber where they'd dined. He didn't leave himself, not right away. He stayed and got very drunk.

He still remembered everything the next morning. He tried to use more wine to deal with his headache. It didn't work very well. "He said no," he told Estrilda. "Said he didn't want Ortalis marrying her."

His wife's lips thinned. "What are you going to do about that?"

"I don't know," Grus answered, which was itself a confession of sorts. *If I had a marriageable daughter, would I want her wedding Ortalis?* He knew the answer to the question. He knew, but he didn't want to admit it even to himself.

"You need to do *something*," Estrilda said.

"I know," he said.

He summoned Lepturus again the next morning. The guards commander nodded to him. "You decided you're going to take my head because I don't want Sponsa marrying your son?" He sounded more curious than afraid.

"Well, that's up to you," Grus said.

"I'm not going to change my mind, if that's what you want. Do what you want to me, but leave my granddaughter alone."

"That's not what I meant," Grus told him. "How would you like to go into retirement in the Maze?"

"And if I say no, I get the other?" Lepturus tapped a finger against the back of his neck.

"I'm afraid so," Grus said. "I have to do something, you know. You've insulted me and my family. I can't pretend it didn't happen."

"I've got nothing in particular against *you*, Your Majesty," Lepturus said. "You've turned out pretty well—better than I expected, to tell you the truth. But that son of yours . . ." He shook his head. "Anything I say'll just get me in deeper, so I'll shut up now."

"Yes, it probably will," Grus said, though he doubted whether Lepturus could say anything worse about Ortalis than he'd thought himself. He held up a hand. "Wait. Don't shut up yet. You *are* retiring?"

"Oh, yes. I'll do that, if you'll let me. And I thank you for it. I wasn't quite ready to say good-bye to the whole world just yet."

"All right. We'll make the announcement in a day or two, then."

Lepturus nodded and ambled out. He and Grus might have been talking about crops and taxes, not about the choice between exile and execution. *Lepturus understands how the game is played,* Grus thought with relief. *Now I just have to hope Estrilda thinks it's enough.*

King Lanius knew about the royal *we*. He knew about it, but he could never remember using it before. He'd never found a time when he seemed to need it. He did now. Giving Grus his iciest stare, he said, "We are not pleased with you."

"No?" To Lanius' endless frustration, Grus had a thick skin, and a slick one, too. Insult slid off him; it hardly ever pierced. Now he only shrugged and said, "Sorry to hear that, Your Majesty."

"How *dare* you exile Lepturus?" Lanius snarled, letting out the fury he couldn't hold anymore.

"How dare I?" Grus shrugged again. "That's pretty simple—it was either send him to the Maze or kill him. I'm glad I didn't have to do that."

"Why would you even want to?" Lanius asked. "He's guarded me my whole life."

"I know," Grus said patiently. "I'm not happy about it, but he insulted me. It wasn't something I could smile and ignore, either."

"What did he *do?*" Lanius couldn't imagine Lepturus offending the other king.

But Grus answered, "I offered him a match between Ortalis and his granddaughter, Sponsa. He said no. If that's not an insult, what is?"

Good for him, was the first thing that crossed Lanius' mind. He realized he couldn't very well say that to Ortalis' father. What he said instead was, "Oh." He didn't see how "Oh" could get him into trouble.

And it didn't. Grus nodded and said, "That's right. I can't ignore insults, you know."

"No, I suppose not," Lanius said unhappily.

"Lepturus thought I would take his head." Grus sounded proud of his restraint.

Maybe he even had reason to. All the same, Lanius thought, *He was willing to die to keep his granddaughter from marrying Ortalis. Doesn't that tell you something about your son?* He didn't see how he could say that to Grus, either. What he did say was, "I trusted Lepturus to keep me safe. He did the job for my father, and he always did it for me. Who will take his place?"

"We can talk about that later, Your Majesty," Grus answered. "It's not something we have to worry about right away. You *are* safe here in the palace, eh?"

Reluctantly, Lanius nodded. The one thing Lepturus would have done—would have tried to do—was protect him from Grus himself. But that, he had to admit, was a form of protection he didn't need. Grus could have had his head at any time since proclaiming himself king. He'd never shown any interest in taking it.

"I didn't want to do this, Your Majesty," Grus went on. "I didn't ask Lepturus to supper with me intending to send him to the Maze. He hasn't gone yet—you can ask him yourself about that. I asked him intending to make him my daughter-in-law's grandfather. But when he said no . . ." He shrugged.

Even more reluctantly, Lanius nodded again. Grus was doing what he could to solve the problem of Ortalis. He just didn't quite realize how bad a problem he had. Lanius could have told him, but he'd made a bargain with Anser and Ortalis, and Ortalis hadn't actually done what he'd talked about doing. Lanius hoped he hadn't, anyhow.

"So that's how it was," Grus said.

"Oh," Lanius said once more. It still seemed safe. He turned away. Grus let him go. As usual, Grus could have done much worse than he had. As usual, that was small consolation for Lanius. He wished no one else were running Avornis. Having someone relatively mild doing the job was better than having a frightful tyrant doing it, but that wasn't the point.

He doubted Grus would have agreed with him.

As he often did when things went wrong, he shut himself away in the archives. No one would bother him there—or, at least, no one ever had. He wondered what would happen if he disappeared in this part of the palace. How long would it be before anyone came looking for him? Who except for Sosia and his children would even notice he was missing?

For a while, he simply hid there, opening crates of records at random to have something to read under the dusty skylights. Then he began to search more systematically, for he grew curious about what the archives had to say about monkeys. To his disappointment, the answer seemed to be, not much.

But, even though he didn't find what he was looking for that day, the search was enough to calm him down, to ease the fear that had knifed through him when he heard of Lepturus' exile. Life could go on. Life could even go on for Lepturus, if not in the way Lanius would have wanted.

And life could go on for Sponsa. One day, she might marry someone who suited her. She probably had no idea how lucky she was. She wouldn't have to find out, either. Maybe that made her the luckiest one of all.

Sleet coated everything outside with ice. The sky was gray as granite. Grus' mood matched the weather. He'd tried to arrange another match for Ortalis. This time, he'd thought he would try subtlety, hinting to the father of the prospective bride instead of coming right out and asking for her hand. That way, he could get some idea of how the noble felt without putting either one of them on the spot.

He hadn't been subtle enough. Before he could get around to asking the question that needed asking, the noble and his whole family had packed up and left—fled—for the countryside. Grus couldn't very well ask him if he wasn't in the city of Avornis to ask. If he wasn't there to ask, he didn't have to say no, either.

In his bedchamber, Grus drummed his fingers on a bedside table. "I ought to send a letter after him," he growled. "Then he'd have to give me a yes or a no."

"I wouldn't," Estrilda said, "not unless he's someone you really want to get rid of."

She was right. Grus knew as much. That did nothing to improve his temper. "By the gods, the King of Avornis shouldn't have this much trouble finding a wife for his only son."

"Only legitimate son," Estrilda murmured.

"Only legitimate son." Grus accepted the correction. Throwing his hands in the air, he cried, "Is Ortalis that much of a monster?"

Estrilda didn't answer.

Grus felt the silence stretch. He stared at her. "*Is* he?" he demanded. "He's not *that* bad, and he's been getting better."

"Yes, he has been," Estrilda said. "But better isn't the same as good. The stories about what he did with—to—those serving women haven't gotten any smaller in the telling."

"That was a while ago now, and I think I put the fear of Olor's judgment in him—or if not of Olor's, then at least of mine," Grus said. "He hasn't done anything outrageous for a long time." He didn't like listening to his own words. He sounded like someone trying to make a bad case sound good.

"Not so very long ago, he had an argument—a loud argument—with Anser," his wife said. "It was something to do with hunting, and I suppose it was why they stopped going out together. That's all I know. Nobody who knows any more than that seems to want to talk about it."

"I wonder who could tell me," Grus said.

"Either of your sons could," Estrilda said, a small taste of vinegar in her voice.

Grus clicked his tongue between his teeth. "I'm not going to ask Ortalis." He'd just passed judgment on the prince, but he didn't realize it. Thoughtfully, he went on, "Maybe Anser would talk."

"Maybe he would." Estrilda had trouble keeping that same sour edge to her tone. Yes, everyone liked her husband's bastard boy.

"I think I'll find out," Grus said.

But when he paid a call on the arch-hallow a couple of days later, Anser only shrugged and said, "I'm sorry, Your Majesty, but I'm afraid I don't remember."

"I don't believe you," Grus said bluntly.

"That's . . . too bad, isn't it?" his by-blow said. "I don't know what else to tell you." He looked nervous, as though he expected Grus to call for the torturer. And, had he not been flesh of Grus' flesh, the king would have been tempted.

Instead, Grus snapped, "You're not doing anyone a favor by keeping silent." Anser only shrugged—silently. Thwarted, Grus muttered something he never would have said in the presence of any other Arch-Hallow of Avornis. Grus stalked away.

He was still steaming when he returned to the royal palace. Had he run into Ortalis, it might have gone hard for his legitimate son. He didn't, though—he ran into Alca.

He brightened at once. "By the gods, I'm glad to see you!" he said.

"Are you, Your Majesty?" The witch seemed not at all sure she was glad to see him.

"Yes, I am. Can you use your wizardry to figure out what was said in an argument between Ortalis and Anser a while ago?"

"How long is a while?" Alca asked.

"I'm not sure, not to the minute," Grus answered. "Weeks, months—something like that. When we were down in the south."

Alca shook her head. "I'm sorry, but wizardry won't do. What you need is a miracle. The gods give those. You might get one from the Banished One. From me?" She shook her head again. "No."

"A pestilence," Grus said. "I really need to know." He explained why, finishing, "Whatever this is, it's keeping people from wanting to marry their daughters to Ortalis." It probably wasn't the only thing keeping them from wanting to marry their daughters to Ortalis, but Grus preferred not to dwell on that.

Alca's eyebrows came down and together as she thought. "I can't bring back the argument itself, Your Majesty. Maybe I could make your son remember it. Would that do?"

"It might," Grus answered. "Could you make sure he didn't remember remembering it?"

"I think so," the witch said.

"Could you do it here and now, or would you need fancy preparations?"

"Here and now—somewhere off in a quiet room, anyhow—would do. It's not that complicated."

"All right, then. I really need to find out." Grus shouted for the servants. He pointed to several of them in turn. "Bring me Prince Ortalis. If he's in the palace, I want him here as fast as he can get here. Understand me?"

By the way they dashed off, they did. Alca ducked into a chamber close by. Ortalis came up to Grus only moments after the witch left the corridor. "What do you want?" Grus' son asked, adding, "I didn't do anything."

Not lately, anyhow, the king thought. "I want to talk with you," he answered, and pointed to the room into which Alca had just gone. "Let's do it in there."

"What do you think I've done now?" Ortalis asked. "You always think I've done something, and I haven't, not this time. Not lately. I really haven't." He sounded as though he meant it.

"Well, then, everything's fine, isn't it?" Grus said smoothly. "Come on. You'll see."

Ortalis didn't look happy, but he didn't argue anymore, either. To Grus, that proved his son didn't think he'd done anything wrong. Ortalis barely had time to notice Alca and start to turn toward her before the witch said, "Hold, Ortalis son of Grus son of Crex!" And Ortalis *did* hold—his feet might suddenly have frozen to the floor.

His expression froze, too. Grus didn't like that reproachful stare. He was glad his son wouldn't remember this. "May I ask him questions?" he said in a low voice.

"Go ahead," Alca told him. "He will answer truthfully, and he will forget he's done it."

"Thank you." Grus turned to Ortalis. "Do you hear me?"

"I hear you." Ortalis' voice was soft and dull.

"All right, then. What was your quarrel with Anser about?"

"Which quarrel with Anser?"

After some thought, Grus said, "The bad one. The one you don't want anybody to know about."

When the Prince was done, Grus knew much more than he wished he did. Quietly, Alca asked, "And did you truly mean this, or were you only joking?"

Even with the magic driving him, Ortalis was a long time silent. "I don't know," he said at last. "It would have been fun, but"—a shrug—"people don't seem to like that kind of thing."

"'People don't seem to like that kind of thing,'" Grus echoed bitterly. "Well, at least he's noticed. Maybe that's something. Maybe." He gestured to Alca. "Wake him up. He's given me what I wanted to find out."

The witch murmured a charm. She slipped out of the room through a back door before Ortalis stirred, blinked, and nodded to his father. "Well, what do you want to talk about?" he asked.

"Never mind, Son," Grus answered with a sigh. "It's not important."

"See? I told you. I didn't do anything." Ortalis swaggered to the front door and out.

As soon as that front door closed, Alca returned. "Well?" she asked.

"Well," Grus said, "I don't suppose he has to get married right away."

The mustachioed monkeys looked out through the window at the swirling snow. A carefully screened fireplace kept their room warm. They didn't know what the bad weather meant. It interested them just the same.

Their black eyes swung to Lanius, as though asking what he had to do with it.

"Sorry," he told them. "I can't make it go away."

By their expressions—so much more humanlike than those of the moncats—they didn't believe him. He was in charge of their food and water. Why wasn't he in charge of the weather as well?

"I wish I *could* change it," he said. "Believe me, I would."

They didn't believe him. He could tell. One of them turned its back, almost as though it were an affronted courtier. They both retreated closer to the fire. Remembering the warning from the Chernagor who'd given them to him, Lanius hoped he could bring them safely through the cold season of the year.

A knock on the door made the monkeys' ears twitch. "What is it?" Lanius called. Servants had stopped charging into the rooms where his animals lived. He'd persuaded them he was deadly serious about that. Grus might rule Avornis, but in these few chambers, at least, Lanius was king in fact as well as name.

"Come quick, Your Majesty!" That was Bubulcus' voice. If he'd learned his lesson, then surely they all had.

Lanius didn't feel like leaving. "What is it?" he repeated.

"Come quick!" Bubulcus said again—that and no more.

Muttering under his breath, Lanius left the monkeys. The hallway outside was noticeably chillier than their room. His voice was also chilly as he repeated himself once more. "What is it? And why didn't you tell me what it was the first time I asked you?"

"Why? On account of I didn't want to yell it all over everywhere, is why." As usual, Bubulcus was full of invincible self-righteousness. But before Lanius could lose his temper, the servant went on, "Prince Ortalis and Her Majesty the Queen—the queen your wife, I mean, not the queen your mother-in-law—are having a demon of a row. If you can help fix it—"

"Oh, by the gods!" Lanius set off at a dead run. Ortalis hadn't fought with Sosia for a while now, but Ortalis in a temper was dangerous to everyone around him. Of that King Lanius had no doubt at all.

Sosia and her brother were shouting at each other when Lanius hurried into the chamber to which their racket had drawn him. Bubulcus prudently stayed several paces behind the king. To Lanius' relief, it was just shouting; Ortalis didn't seem to have struck out with open hand or fist. "What's going on here?" Lanius demanded.

Grus' son rounded on him. "Maybe she's not the liar after all," he said. "Maybe you are."

"And maybe you're a gods-cursed idiot," Lanius snapped. Ortalis' jaw dropped; Lanius was not in the habit of matching his rudeness. The king continued, "You're certainly acting like one. What is all this senseless commotion about?"

"Somebody blabbed," Ortalis said sullenly. "Somebody told Father what everybody promised nobody would say."

"I keep telling you, I didn't," Sosia said.

"Neither did I," Lanius said. "That leaves Anser."

"He says he didn't, either." Ortalis' eyes flashed furiously. "But *somebody* did, because Father sure knows now. I can tell. He's been giving me these looks, and these little lectures, and I can't stand it anymore. He hardly even knows he's doing it, but he is, and I'm about ready to pop."

"I didn't have anything to do with it," Sosia said.

"I gave my oath I wouldn't, as long as you kept your side of the bargain," Lanius said, and then, "*Have* you kept it?"

"Yes!" Ortalis said—all but howled. "I've kept my mouth shut, and I haven't done—anything. But Father found out. I don't know how. Somebody must have told him. And it had to be one of you three." He glared at Lanius, then at Sosia. Had Anser been there, he would have glared at him, too.

"*We* didn't," Lanius said, pointing first to himself, then to his wife. "And if Anser says he didn't, too, then he probably didn't. He wouldn't lie about something like that."

"Somebody did," Ortalis repeated. "Somebody must have."

"Maybe he found out by magic," Lanius suggested. "He could have done that all by himself."

Some—a little—of the rage faded from Ortalis' eyes. "Maybe," he said grudgingly. "I hadn't thought of that. Maybe it's true. I can try to find out, anyway." Some of the tightness and stiffness seeped from his spine. He no longer seemed on the point of throwing himself at his sister—or at Lanius. In fact, he gave Lanius a nod that seemed almost friendly. "Thanks."

"You're welcome," Lanius answered, but he was talking to Ortalis' back.

"I haven't seen him have a spell like that for a long time," Sosia said once the door had closed behind Grus' son.

"I wouldn't be sorry never to see another one," Lanius said. "You can't tell what he's going to do when he's in a temper." To him, nothing was more damning than lack of predictability.

"If I were Father, I'd try to arrange it so that Ortalis didn't find out about any magic he worked," Sosia said.

"If I were your father, I wouldn't have let Ortalis know I knew anything out of the ordinary," Lanius replied. Then he shrugged. "Something like that, though . . . If you know, how can you help showing you know?"

"I wish we didn't know." Sosia grimaced. "I wish there weren't anything *to* know. I wish—I wish Ortalis were just like everybody else."

"Too much to hope for," Lanius said.

"He *has* been better," Sosia said. Lanius nodded, for that was true. She went on, "Even here, he didn't lose all of his temper. And he calmed down when you gave him an explanation he hadn't thought of." Lanius nodded again. His wife sounded like a woman lavishing praise on a poor child that finally stammered out "Mama" at six or seven. He started to say as much, but then noticed Sosia's eyes were bright with tears.

He kept quiet.

Crex came in a few minutes later. Pitta pattered after him. He was tossing a leather ball stuffed with feathers up into the air and catching it—or, more often, dropping it. When he did, Pitta would grab it. Crex got it back and threw it in Lanius' direction. The king reached for it but missed. Before Crex could run after it and pick it up, Sosia grabbed him and gave him a fierce hug. She didn't seem to want to let him go.

"Put me down!" the little boy squawked.

"In a little while," Sosia told him.

"Now!" Crex said.

Sosia gave him a last squeeze. He twisted free, got the ball away from Pitta, and threw it to his father. Lanius missed it again. The king laughed anyway. Sosia hugged Pitta. Lanius tickled Crex as he went by. Crex squealed. Lanius laughed louder.

CHAPTER TWENTY-NINE

P etrosus didn't look happy. The treasury minister pointed out
through the windows at the drifts of snow surrounding the royal
palace. He said, "Winters like this, Your Majesty, make your legisla-
tion concerning the purchase of smallholders' land by the nobility more
difficult to implement."

"I'm not sure I follow that," said Grus, who was sure he didn't. "What's
the weather got to do with whether laws get followed or not?"

To his surprise, Petrosus had not only an answer but one that made
sense. He said, "Hard winters make smallholders more likely to fail, and
to fall into debt. Because of that, they are more likely to wish to sell their
property. And, when they do sell it, who is more likely to buy than the local nobles?"

"Hmm." Grus plucked at his beard. "Maybe we ought to add to those
laws—something to the effect that they have to try to sell to relatives and
neighbors before they're allowed to take money from nobles."

"That may do some good," Petrosus said judiciously. "I'm not sure
how much it will do, though—their relatives and neighbors are liable to
be looking at the same sort of trouble, don't you think?"

"I wish you made less sense than you do," Grus said. "Draft the revisions anyhow, though, if you'd be so kind. Maybe they won't work so well.
But we'll never know if we don't try, will we?"

"No, Your Majesty," the treasury minister replied. "I do admire your optimism, I must say."

"We have to try," Grus said again. "If things don't work out the way we hope, we'll try something else, that's all." His laugh wasn't in the least self-conscious. "I'm a tinker and a tinkerer, Petrosus. I'll keep fiddling with something till I get it right or till I see it won't work no matter how much tinkering I give it."

"I have noticed that, yes." By the way Petrosus said it, he didn't mean it as praise.

"Draft the revisions," he said once more. "Draft them, and I'll issue them." Petrosus nodded. At Grus' gesture, the treasury minister left the room. He would do as he'd said, and he'd do a good job of making the new laws as likely to be obeyed as he could. He might think Grus a few bricks short of a wall, but he followed the king's commands simply because they *were* the king's commands.

Under a bad king, a man like that would be very dangerous, Grus thought. He hoped he wasn't a bad king. He didn't think he was, but what bad king ever did? Even Scolopax, a bad king if ever there was one, had surely believed he was doing the best job he could.

Having finished his business with Petrosus, Grus went back to the royal chambers. Playing with his grandchildren was more fun than talking about taxation policy with the treasury minister. Or it would have been, if he'd gotten the chance to do it. But the first person he saw there was Estrilda.

They'd been married a long time—long enough for him not even to notice the hard, set expression on her face. That turned out to be a mistake. Without preamble, she said, "I hear—later than I should have, but I do hear—Alca the witch's husband has left her."

"Do you?" Grus said, hoping he could evade disaster.

He couldn't. "I certainly do," Estrilda said. "And I hear why he left her, too."

"Do you?" Grus said again. He wished something—the announcement of an invasion from Thervingia, for instance—would let him escape, but no such luck.

"Yes, I do." Estrilda walked—stalked—up to him. "And I'll tell you exactly what I think about it, too."

"What?" Grus asked. She sounded calm and reasonable, which gave him some cause to hope.

That also proved misplaced. "*This!*" she shouted, and slapped him in the face, a roundhouse blow that snapped his head back. Then—but only then—she burst into tears.

She started to swing on him again. Though his ears were ringing, he caught her wrist. "That's enough," he said. "It was . . . just one of those things."

"Oh, I'll bet it was," Estrilda said. "Let go of me, you—" She called him a few names he wouldn't have expected from Nicator, let alone his own wife.

When he did let her go, she tried to slap him again. He managed to grab her wrist once more. "*Stop* that!"

"Why should I? *You* didn't."

"It wasn't like that," Grus protested.

"Oh, I'm sure it wasn't," Estrilda said. "You were away for a long time, you got lonely, and there she was. . . ."

In another tone of voice, the words might have been sympathetic. As things were, the sarcasm flayed. Grus' face heated. He raised a hand and cautiously touched his cheek. It already felt on fire. "But—" he tried.

"No buts." Estrilda effortlessly overrode him. He might have tried harder to argue back if he hadn't known all too well he was in the wrong. She went on, "I might believe that if I hadn't heard it all before. But I have, gods curse you. That's what you told me after your other little slut went and had Anser. I could believe it once. *Once,* I tell you. If you try to give me the same tired lies twice, you're a fool, and I'd be a bigger one to pay any attention to you."

"But it's true," Grus said—the ancient and useless cry of wandering husbands (and wives) through the ages when they were found out. And he even meant it. *Would I have gone to bed with Alca if we'd stayed here in the city of Avornis?* he asked himself. *Of course not.*

He didn't stop to think that was, not least, because they would have been found out even sooner than they had been. And he didn't stop to think that he would have wanted to take her to bed even if he hadn't done it.

Nor did his excuses help him a bit. "I don't care whether it's true or not," Estrilda snarled. "You did what you told me—what you promised me—you wouldn't do again. That's what I care about."

"I'm sorry," Grus said—another ancient and useless cry.

He had no luck with that one, either. "I'll bet you're sorry," Estrilda said. "You're sorry you got caught. Why else would you be sorry? You were down there in the south having yourself a fine old time. You always have yourself a fine old time down in the south, don't you?"

"It wasn't like that," Grus said.

"Oh, I'm sure. Tell me how it was." His wife shook her head. "No, don't. I don't want to hear it."

"But I love you," Grus said. It was true. He'd never stopped caring for Estrilda. How much good it was likely to do him was a different question.

It did him none at all. "You picked a wonderful way to show it, didn't you?" Estrilda said acidly.

"You don't understand," Grus protested.

"I'm sure you told that to What's-her-name, the witch," Estrilda said with a scornful laugh. "'My wife doesn't understand me.' How many liars have lured women into bed with that one? But I understand you, all right. I understand you just fine." She spat on the floor at Grus' feet. "And that's what I think of you."

"Estrilda—"

She shook her head. "No. I don't want to hear it. Whatever it is, it'll only be another lie." She stabbed out a finger at him; he supposed he should have been glad she didn't have a knife. "What would you say, what would you do, if I'd been screwing one of your handsome bodyguards? Well? What do you have to say about that, *Your Majesty?*" She laced the royal title with revulsion.

"That's different," Grus said. The mere idea filled him with rage.

Estrilda laughed in his face—a vicious laugh, a flaying laugh. "Men say so. Men can afford to say so. They're mostly bigger and stronger than women, and they mostly make the rules. But do you really think I'm any less disgusted with you than the witch's husband is with her?"

Through all of this, Grus had done his best not to think about Alca's husband. He went right on doing his best not to think about him. He said, "How can I show you how sorry I am?"

"Send Alca away," Estrilda said at once. "I don't care where you send her, as long as it's far from the city of Avornis. I never want to see her again. I never want you to see her again, either."

"But she's one of the best sorcerers in the kingdom," Grus protested.

"I'm sure that's what you noticed about her—her sorcery, I mean," his wife said with a glare that could have melted iron.

"If it weren't for her sorcery, I'd be dead," Grus said. "Would that—?" He stopped. If he asked Estrilda, *Would that make you happy?* she was altogether too likely to answer, *Yes.* Instead, he went on, "Her magic was what put an end to Corvus' rebellion, too."

"Huzzah," Estrilda said. "If she's such a wonderful witch, she'll do very well for herself wherever you send her. And if she doesn't, she's always got another trade to fall back on—fall on her back on." She spat again.

"She's no harlot," Grus protested, beginning to get angry himself. Estrilda only laughed another laugh full of daggers. "She isn't," Grus said stubbornly.

"Fine. I don't care what she is, as long as she isn't here," his wife said. "You asked me what you could do, and I told you. That's a start, anyhow. If you don't want to . . ." She didn't say what she would do then. Grus could imagine a good many possibilities, none of them pleasant.

He sighed. He'd put himself in this predicament, and knew it only too well. "Have it your way, then. She'll go."

"All right," Estrilda said. "That's a start. A start, mind you." Another sigh escaped from Grus. He might have known mending fences with his wife would cost him. He *had* known mending fences with his wife would cost him. Now he would have to find out exactly how expensive it was.

Lanius had always chafed at his own obscurity. He'd wanted to be at the heart of great affairs. Once in a while, though, being of no particular importance had its advantages.

King Grus' . . . problems with Queen Estrilda made everyone in the royal palace walk on eggs. The least misstep landed a servant in trouble. Lanius didn't want to think about what sort of trouble a misstep might land him in. But what was he supposed to say when Sosia rounded on him one afternoon and demanded, "You'd never do anything like that, would you?"

As a matter of fact, he knew what he was supposed to say. "Of course not, dear."

"Good," his wife said. "There's nothing worse, nothing lower, than somebody who's unfaithful."

Lanius nodded politely. He was used to keeping his opinions to himself. *Being unfaithful is bad, yes,* he thought. *Getting caught being unfaithful is worse.*

That was one of the things that had kept him from amusing himself with the serving women in the palace, as he'd done before he was married. If he did, Lanius would find himself in the same unpleasant predicament as Grus. Grus was welcome to it.

Besides which, Sosia kept him happy enough. He didn't know whether Estrilda had kept Grus happy. But some men—and, no doubt, some women—fooled around just for the sport of fooling around. He didn't fully understand the impulse.

Sosia went on, "It's hard when you can't trust anybody."

"Yes, it is," Lanius agreed. He'd known about that since he was very small.

"How *could* he?" Sosia demanded.

"If you really want to find out, you'll ask *him*," Lanius answered.

She made a horrible face. "I couldn't do that."

Lanius shrugged. "Well, don't ask me, because I wasn't there and I didn't do it." He wanted her to remember that.

"But you're a man," she said.

"Women go astray, too," he pointed out, which made Sosia scowl again. He added, "The witch here has—had—a husband, too."

"Had," Sosia said. "He threw her out of the house. I wish Mother could throw Father out of her house."

That made Lanius laugh, though it wasn't really funny. "She can't," he said. "Nobody can do anything to your father that he doesn't want done." *Except an assassin,* he thought, but he didn't say that for fear of the evil omen. He didn't want Grus dead, just out of his hair.

Sosia said, "I know nobody can do anything to him. It doesn't seem fair."

"Really?" Lanius laughed again, with even less mirth than before. "I never would have noticed."

His wife turned red. "I know you don't think what's happened is right. I wouldn't be your queen if it hadn't happened, you know."

And would I be happier if you weren't? Lanius didn't know. Most marriages in Avornis were arranged unions, not love matches. This one hadn't worked out badly; by now, the two of them did love each other, perhaps as much from familiarity as for any other reason. As for Grus . . . "Your father isn't that bad a man."

"He's a beast!" Sosia exclaimed.

"No." Lanius shook his head. "If your father were a beast, he would have murdered me. I admit as much. He would have murdered lots of people. He hasn't. He has no taste for blood. Plenty of Kings of Avornis have."

"You know what he did," Sosia said.

"Yes. But he didn't force her—it's very plain he didn't force her. He didn't hurt her. He's not a perfect man. I never said he was. But there's a long way from not being a perfect man to being a beast. And if I can see that in your father, maybe you should, too."

"Maybe," Sosia said, but the look in her eyes might have belonged to a little girl saving up more spit so she could go on with her tantrum.

"He's . . . a good enough king," Lanius said. "I don't want to admit it. But I'm not blind. I can see what he's done. It's . . . good enough, taken all in all."

Could I have done as well? he asked himself. *Could I have gotten people to do as I say, the way Grus does?* He doubted it. He was a man for the archives and for odd animals and for his family and perhaps for a small circle of friends.

Sosia said, "What he did with—with that woman, that wasn't good enough."

"I didn't say it was," Lanius answered. "I suppose he and your mother will eventually straighten it out." Grus wouldn't put Estrilda aside because he was sleeping with another woman, either. Plenty of Kings of Avornis had done things like that, too.

"I hope so," Sosia said. "I don't know how, though."

"Well, it's their worry," Lanius said. *And thank the gods for that,* he thought.

By the way Alca looked at Grus, he might have been something wet and sticky and smelly she'd stepped on in the street. Her expression made *him* feel that way, too. She said, "So it's come to this, has it?"

"I'm afraid it has," he answered miserably.

"You have to send me away?" The witch's gesture held infinite bitterness. "Why not send *her* away?"

With a sigh, he said, "I can't. She's the mother of my children. And—" He stopped again.

Alca finished for him, saying, "And when you get down to it, you'd rather have her around than me."

"I'm sorry," Grus whispered.

"*You're* sorry?" Alca said. "How do you think I feel?"

Grus wished she would have made this easier. She had no reason to, of course. "Go wherever you will, except this city," he said. "Wherever you go, you won't want, I promise."

"I won't want? I'll want for a husband; for a lover; for a *life*. People will whisper behind my back and point fingers at me for the rest of my life. 'She's the one who laid the king, who sucked the king's—'" Alca broke off. "I won't want? Ha!"

"What money can do, I'll make sure money does," Grus said.

"I didn't come to your bed to be your whore."

"I don't want to give you money because you were my whore, gods curse it," Grus said. "I want to give you money because it's all I can give you now."

"You have to save the rest for the mother of your children," Alca said, and Grus winced. She went on, "The mother of your legitimate children, I should say." Grus flinched again. Alca shook her head. "Queen Quelea help me, I *knew* it would come to this."

"Anser and his mother never lacked for anything," Grus said. "I made sure of that."

The witch said, "Ha!" again, even more scornfully than before. "Where was his father? Where was her man?"

"She ended up marrying," Grus said. "Her husband raised the boy as his own."

"He was generous with a cuckoo's egg." Alca's sarcasm flayed. "Do you suppose *I'll* find a man who could cherish something the king used and then discarded? Wouldn't I be lucky?"

"Alca, please—" Grus began.

She shook her head. "I haven't begged you for anything. You have no call to beg me, Your Majesty." Grus' title might have been a curse in her mouth, as it had been in Estrilda's. "Do what you're going to do."

"I told you what I'd do," Grus said. "You know why. Tell me where you'd rather go—"

"I'd *rather* not go anywhere," Alca said.

Grus sighed. "You don't have that choice."

"Send me wherever you please, then," the witch said. "If this is the thanks I get for saving your life and then for thinking . . ." She shook her head again. "No, I never did think that. I was always sure this would end badly."

"I wish things could be different," Grus said.

"You wish you hadn't gotten caught." Yes, Alca sounded very much like Estrilda. "You were a fool, and I was a fool, and . . ." She looked through him, and something in her voice changed. ". . . And you will be a fool again, and your child, your precious child, will make you pay for it."

All of a sudden, Grus wanted her as far away as she could go. She blinked and seemed to come back to herself. Too late, as far as he was concerned. If that wasn't prophecy, what was it? He tried to gather himself, saying, "I'll send you to Pelagonia, then." The town was in the middle of the southern plains, a long way from the capital.

"You can do whatever you want," Alca said. "Whether it's right or fair doesn't matter."

If Grus could do whatever he wanted, why was he doing this? He knew why. Sometimes, even the King of Avornis took orders from a higher authority—and what authority could be higher than an outraged spouse?

People didn't commonly set off on a journey across Avornis in the dead of winter, especially not when the winter in question was a hard one. When Alca left the royal palace, left the city of Avornis, for Pelagonia, no one said a word about what people didn't commonly do. Everyone knew why she was leaving, and everyone knew remarking on it wouldn't be wise.

All Lanius said was, "Maybe we'll have some peace and quiet in the palace now." Even he waited a couple of days before saying anything, and even he made sure only his wife heard him.

"That would be good," Sosia agreed. "We don't need any more scandals of that particular sort." The look she gave him warned he'd better not cause a scandal of that particular sort.

"We don't need any scandals of any sort," he said, being a man who liked things neat and tidy. Having been born as part of a scandal, he particularly deplored them. He knew things weren't always neat and tidy—if they had been, *he* would have ruled Avornis instead of just reigning over it—but he wished they were.

"She's gone. She won't be back," Sosia said, as though that was a very good thing indeed. Lanius had his own views on the subject, had them and made a point of keeping them to himself.

He did need to see King Grus about something else. His father-in-law didn't seem to want to see him—or anyone else, for that matter. Not for the first time, Lanius put it off . . . and then put it off again, and eventually, as he had before, let it slip to the back of his mind. Yes, it was something Grus needed to hear and Lanius needed to tell him, but it wasn't anything Lanius really wanted to talk about or Grus would care to hear. Nobody who carried bad news was eager to blurt it out, especially when the person who got it couldn't do anything about it.

And, before long, Lanius and Grus both had other things to worry about. The winter went on and on and got worse and worse. Lanius suspected the Banished One had more than a little to do with that, as he had before. He didn't know whether Grus suspected the same thing. He didn't feel inclined to ask, either. Grus couldn't very well ask Alca to use her sorcery to help find out, not anymore, and the other king didn't seem to have found a new wizard he could trust.

Whatever or whoever caused the hard winter, it had results neither Lanius nor Grus could ignore. Farmers sent petitions by the score—by the hundred—to their local governors and to the royal capital, asking to be re-lieved of taxes. *How can I pay,* one of them asked, *when all my cows and half my sheeps is dead, and so is my mule?*

Some farmers didn't bother with petitions. They simply abandoned their land and made for the closest town or for the city of Avornis, look-ing for whatever work they could find. Very often, they couldn't find any, and started to starve. "What are you going to do about these fellows?" La-nius asked Grus after a party of half a dozen unlucky men came to the palace to beg.

"I'm not so much worried about them," Grus answered. "I'm worried about their farms."

"Their farms?" Lanius said. "Why do you care about the farms? The men are here, and they're hungry."

"Oh, I know that," his father-in-law said. "But they're here because they're walking away from their farms. Who's going to get that land now? The nobles, probably, in spite of all the laws I've made to keep that from happening."

"Well, yes," Lanius admitted. "Even so . . ." His voice trailed away. Usually, he was the one who thought in abstract terms, while Grus was down-to-earth. Here, though, he saw men and Grus saw agricultural pol-icy. He scratched his head. It made for an odd reversal.

Grus sensed as much, too. "I'm trying to think about the whole king-dom, Your Majesty," he said, his tone edgy. "What's more important than Avornis?"

"Nothing. I'm sure of that," Lanius replied. "But if the Kingdom of Avornis isn't made up of people like these hungry farmers, what is it?"

His father-in-law started to answer, hesitated, started again and again failed, and finally frowned. "You have a point," he said at last. "How are the granaries? *Can* we feed them?"

He expected Lanius to have the answer at his fingertips, and Lanius did. "Oh, yes, we can feed them till spring without too much trouble," he answered. "We've had good harvests the last couple of years, and there's plenty of wheat in the granaries, and even more rye and barley. Oats, too, come to that."

"Oats?" Grus made a face. "A lot of people, especially down in the south, think they're nothing but fodder for horses."

"I never said they were fancy," Lanius answered. "But if it's a choice be-tween boiling oats and making porridge of them on the one hand and go-ing hungry on the other, I know which I'd sooner do."

"I suppose so." Grus still sounded unhappy, but he couldn't very well argue. He drummed his fingers on the side of his thigh. "I wish I knew whether this was just a bad winter of the sort we often get, or a bad winter sent by the Banished One."

"This is a very bad winter, which makes it more likely the Banished One has given us a gift." Lanius paused and then decided to see what happened when he said, "You could use a wizard to help you find out." Grus had given him the opening, after all.

"I haven't got one I can rely on against the Banished One right now," Grus said.

King Lanius eyed him. "And whose fault is that?"

"Oh, it's mine," Grus replied. "Have I ever said any different?" More than a little reluctantly, Lanius shook his head. Grus had never been shy about admitting his own flaws. He wasn't the sort of man to claim he had none, as more than a few kings had been wont to do. Lanius sighed. If only Grus had worked harder to root out those faults . . . Of course, even fewer men tried to do that than admitted they had flaws in the first place. Lanius didn't suppose he could blame Grus too much for failing to root them out. No—not too much, anyhow.

Guards spirited Thraupis into the palace as though he were the most beautiful courtesan in the world. He wasn't. He was a gangling middle-aged man with stooped shoulders, a long, horsy face, and watery gray eyes with a nearsighted squint. King Grus received him in a chamber well separate from his living quarters, and, despite the hunger in the city, gave him roast meat and white bread and sweet wine red as blood.

"Very kind, Your Majesty; very kind," Thraupis said. He started to wipe his mouth on his sleeve, then remembered his manners and used a cloth instead.

"Glad you're pleased," Grus replied. "Now, then—let's see what you've got."

"Happy to oblige, Your Majesty; happy to oblige." Thraupis had a habit of repeating himself. He picked up a wooden case and set it on the table next to his empty platter. A moment later, a servant whisked the platter away. Another servant poured him more wine. "Thank you. Thank you very much," he said, and opened the case.

Grus eyed the contents—cleverly displayed on black velvet—as avidly as he might have eyed a courtesan displayed by the same fabric. The ram-headed spiral gold bracelet with the emeralds for eyes particularly caught his notice. "This is a very fine piece," he said to Thraupis.

By the way the jeweler beamed, Grus knew it was also a very expensive piece. "Glad you like it," Thraupis said. "Mighty glad." He pointed to a pair of elaborate earrings with filigree-work gold disks and boat-shaped pendants and several small golden seeds dangled from each pendant by chains of almost unimaginable fineness. "These'd go well with the bracelet, Your Majesty. They'd go really well."

"I'm sure they would. I'm certain of it." Grus shook his head in bemusement. He was starting to talk like Thraupis. Yes, he was starting to sound just like him. *Stop that,* he told himself sternly. "How much do you want for them? Will the treasury have any money left if I buy them?"

Thraupis named a price. He named it only once. Once was plenty to make Grus yelp. The jeweler clucked. "Can't get much lower, Your Majesty—not much. Gold is gold. Jewels is jewels. My time's worth a little something. Yes, a little something, by the gods."

"You're a thief," Grus said—but weakly. But the King of Avornis couldn't let those pieces go by, not just then he couldn't. He took the bracelet and earrings to Estrilda and gave them to her with as much of a flourish as he could—all things considered, less than he would have wanted. "I hope you like them," he said.

"They're very pretty," Estrilda answered. "Would you have gotten them for me if you hadn't been sleeping with the witch?"

"Dear . . ." Grus said in strained tones.

"Spare me," Estrilda told him. "When you did this the first time, you were easy enough to forgive. You said you wouldn't do it again, and I believed you. The second time? No. I've told you that, too. Fool me once, shame on you. Fool me twice, shame on me."

She eyed him. "And now you're going to say something like, 'Well, if you can't be nice to me, I'll get rid of you and find somebody who can.' Go right ahead—that's all I've got to say to you."

"I wasn't going to say anything at all," Grus said. "I don't want to get rid of you, Estrilda. All I want to do is go back to the way things were before."

"Not likely," Estrilda said. "If you drop a goblet, can you put it back together again?"

"Not easily," Grus answered, "but I'm doing what I can. You'll see cracks on the goblet when I'm done, but I hope it will hold wine again."

"That's a pretty figure of speech," Estrilda said. "Why should I care whether it holds wine or not, though? You're the one who smashed it and spilled the wine it did hold."

"I know," Grus said, "but you wouldn't be so angry at me if you didn't still care at least a little."

Estrilda was silent for a long time. At last, she sighed. "We've been together since before we really finished growing up. How can I help but care? If you think that makes me want to let you touch me now, though, you'd better think again."

"Did I say anything about that?"

"No, and you'd better not," Estrilda told him. "The answer is still no."

"You might want to wait till somebody asks the question before you give the answer," Grus said.

"I might, and then again, I might not," Estrilda said. "Some people, seems to me, need a head start when it comes to getting things straight. And I don't mean getting *that* thing straight. That's what got you into trouble."

"Yes, I know." Grus could hardly disagree with that. "It doesn't happen very often, Estrilda. It's been years." He knew he was pleading. He couldn't help it.

"How can I believe that? How can I be sure of it?" Estrilda asked. "Before, I thought, yes, all right, it happened. Anything can happen once. The world doesn't end with once. Now . . . How can I trust you now? I can't."

"I *am* sorry," Grus said.

"You're sorry you got caught. We've been over that ground before, too." Estrilda poked at the earrings with a forefinger. "And all this jewelry *is* very pretty, but I know why you bought it. You bought it to butter me up."

"I bought it to show you I'm sorry. By the gods, Estrilda, I'm not perfect, but I do love you." Grus took a deep breath, then rolled the dice by asking, "Would I have listened to you when you asked me to send Alca away if I didn't?"

"I didn't ask you to send her away. I *told* you to send her away." But his wife hesitated once more. Then she added, "I should say you're not perfect."

"I already said I wasn't," Grus said. "Every once in a while . . . these things happen. Most of the time, they don't. And I think you know that's true."

Estrilda hesitated again. At last, as grudgingly as she could, she said, "Maybe."

That was as much as she'd yielded since finding out about Grus' affair. He tried for more. "Maybe we can patch things up again, then. We've been together for a long time, after all. You said so yourself. If we can't put up with each other—"

"I can put up with *you*," Estrilda said. "These other women?" She shook her head.

Grus said, "I've done everything I know how to do to make you forgive me. Have I got any chance at all?"

Estrilda turned her back. After a long, long silence, she said, even more grudgingly than before, "Maybe."

CHAPTER THIRTY

Lanius found himself with a pleasant problem—the moncats were having more kittens than he had good names for them. Not only that, keeping track of which moncat owned which name taxed even his formidable memory. He was almost glad the monkeys were unlikely to breed. He would have had to come up with more names yet.

Bronze's belly bulged with what would be two more kittens before much longer. Lanius wasn't sure which younger moncat had sired them. He hoped it was the one he'd named Rusty, a beast even redder than the reddest red tabby. Rusty resembled neither Bronze nor Iron very much; Lanius wondered from which of them, and how, he'd inherited his looks. They had to come down from one of the original pair of moncats or the other—that much, at least, seemed clear.

Rusty, at the moment, seemed to be doing his best to kill himself, swinging about on boards and sticks with what in a human would have been reckless disregard for his life. Even the monkeys might not have been able to match his acrobatics, for he had claws to help him hold on and they didn't. Lanius took out a piece of meat and clucked to him. He had different noises to tell each moncat when a treat was for it—one more thing their burgeoning population threatened to disrupt.

Another moncat, a brownish female, tried to steal the tidbit. "Not for you!" Lanius said, and jerked the meat away. The female gave him a hard look. He was convinced moncats thought and remembered better than ordinary cats. Maybe they were even more clever than his monkeys. He wondered about that, but hadn't found a way to test it.

Down dropped Rusty, fast enough to raise Lanius' hackles. As soon as the moncat came to the floor, it hurried over to Lanius and started trying to climb him. He gave Rusty the piece of meat. The moncat crouched at his feet while it ate. Rusty knew Lanius wouldn't let any of the other animals steal its meat. That made the King of Avornis deserve a little extra affection in the moncat's eyes.

As Lanius often did, he bent down to stroke Rusty. He tried to tame the moncats as much as he could. The Chernagors had warned him the beasts were less affectionate than ordinary cats—a depressing thought if ever there was one—and the sea-rovers hadn't been joking. Every so often, though, a moncat would decide to act like a pet instead of a wild animal.

This was one of those lucky moments. Rusty—again, probably happier than usual because of the treat it had just enjoyed—not only purred but also rolled over and over like a lovable pussycat encouraging its owner to pet it. Rusty even let Lanius rub his stomach, though it and the other moncats usually scratched and bit when the king took such a liberty.

Emboldened, Lanius squatted. He picked Rusty up and put it in his lap. To his delight, the moncat let him get away with that. In fact, Rusty purred louder than ever. Lanius beamed. He hadn't imagined a moncat could act so lovable.

Rusty purred so loud, the King of Avornis didn't notice the knocking on the door for some little while. Even after noticing, he did his best to ignore it. He wanted that moment to last forever. But the knocking went on and on.

"Yes? What is it?" Lanius said when he couldn't ignore it anymore. If some stupid servant was having conniptions about something unimportant, he intended to cut off the fellow's ears and feed them to the moncats.

The door opened. That made Lanius think it was Grus—the servants knew better. Even as Lanius muttered a curse, his hand kept stroking Rusty. The moncat kept purring.

It wasn't Grus. It wasn't any of the servants Lanius recognized, either. After a moment, though, he realized he *did* recognize the man, even if not as a servant. The fellow was one of the thralls Grus and Alca had brought back from Cumanus.

Lanius marveled that he did know him for who—for what—he was. Thralls' faces usually bore the blank stares that could as easily have belonged to barnyard animals. Not here. Not now. Purpose informed this man's features. His eyes glittered as he stared straight at Lanius. The long, sharp knife he held in his right hand glittered, too.

Still eyeing Lanius, the thrall strode into the moncats' room. The animals gaped at him. They weren't used to seeing anybody but the king. The thrall took another slow, deliberate step. Lanius thought he saw the Banished One peering out through the man's eyes.

He's come to kill me, the king thought without undue surprise and—he *was* surprised about this—without undue fear. He wondered whether by that *he* he meant the thrall or the Banished One, who impelled the fellow forward as surely as a merely mortal puppeteer worked his puppet's strings.

Rusty let out a small, questioning mew. Lanius kept hold of the moncat. He came to his feet and took a step back, toward the far wall of the room. Smiling, raising the knife, the thrall came after him.

I'm going to die here, Lanius thought. He didn't know how the thrall had gotten out of the room where Alca had studied him and his fellows— and where they'd stayed, largely ignored, after she left the city of Avornis. How didn't seem to matter at the moment. He was out, and he had a knife, and, smiling, he took another purposeful step toward the king.

Only later did Lanius decide the thrall—and, through him, the Banished One—wanted to watch and savor his fear. Just then, no such elaborate thoughts filled his mind.

He threw Rusty in the thrall's face.

The moncat squalled with fury, and with fear of its own. Up till a moment ago Lanius had been friendly, even loving, and Rusty had returned those feelings as well as an animal could. And now this!

Rusty clung with all four clawed hands—and with tail, as well. The thrall let out a gurgling shriek of pain, surprise, and fury of his own (or of his Master). He grabbed for the moncat to try to tear it loose. Rusty sank needle-sharp teeth into his hand. The thrall shrieked again.

Having had one good idea, Lanius got another one. He fled. Dodging the thrall was no problem. Not even with some part of the Banished One's spirit guiding him could the thrall commit murder with a frenzied, clawing moncat clinging to his head.

Other moncats had already escaped from the chamber. That was one more thing Lanius knew he would have to worry about later. Meanwhile, he burst out into the corridor, crying, "Guards! Guards! An assassination!" He wished the crucial word weren't five syllables long; it took forever to say.

Ordinary servants started shouting, too. Out came the thrall. He'd finally gotten rid of Rusty, but his face looked as though he'd run full speed through a thousand miles of thorn bushes. His left hand bled, too. He kept shaking his head to keep blood from running into his eyes.

Guards pounded up the hallway. "Seize that man!" Lanius shouted. "Take him alive for questioning if you can."

Without a word, the guards rushed at the thrall. He tried to rush at Lanius. Restraining him didn't work. He fought so fiercely, he made them kill him. Lanius cared much less than he'd thought he would. Staring down at the pool of blood spreading across the mosaicwork floor, all he said was, "I hope that was the only mischief afoot here."

A woman's scream rang down the corridor.

A servant said, "You do remember, Your Majesty, that you were going to lunch with Her Majesty?"

"Yes, I remember." Grus didn't look up from the pile of parchments he was wading through.

"You should have gone some little while ago," the servant said.

"I suppose I should," Grus admitted. But he and Estrilda were still so fragile together, even going through petitions for tax relief seemed preferable to eating with her. Still, if he didn't go at all, he'd insult her, and that would only make things between them worse—if they could be worse.

Shaking his head, he rose and went up the hall toward the chambers he still shared with his wife, though much less intimately than he had in the past. "Oh, Your Majesty, aren't you dining with the queen?" asked a servant coming the other way. "A rather strange-seeming fellow was asking after you, and I sent him in that direction."

"Strange-seeming?" Grus frowned. "What do you mean?"

"He sounded like a soldier, though he didn't quite look like one," the man answered. "He looked like . . . I don't know what. A soldier down on his luck, maybe. But he spoke like a lord."

"A soldier down on his luck? What would a soldier down on his luck be doing in . . . ?" Grus started again. "You know, now that I think of it, we put those thralls we brought up from Cumanus in old soldiers' clothes, didn't we?" He pointed at the servant. "When did you see this fellow?"

"Why, just now, Your Majesty," the man answered. "But a thrall wouldn't be able to speak, would he?"

"I wouldn't think so," Grus said. "Not unless—"

Estrilda screamed.

Grus yanked his sword from the scabbard and started to run. The servant pounded after him, though the most obviously lethal thing the man had on his person was a large, shiny brass belt buckle. *I'll have to remember that,* Grus thought. Then Estrilda screamed again, and he stopped thinking about anything but getting to her as fast as he could.

A door slammed. An instant later, a body thudded against it, once, twice, three times. That noise helped guide Grus better than the screams had. So did the sound of the door giving way.

He dashed into the small dining room where he and Estrilda should have been eating. The man who'd just forced the door to the adjoining pantry whirled. A long kitchen knife gleamed in his hand. "Here you are!" he said, and lunged toward Grus.

He *was* a thrall. Grus recognized him, and the old clothes he wore. But his face didn't hold its usual blank look. Hatred blazed from his eyes. If that wasn't the Banished One staring out through them, Grus couldn't imagine ever seeing Avornis' foe face-to-face.

The thrall thrust at him. Grus beat the stroke aside. A long kitchen knife made a fine murder weapon when the victim couldn't fight back. Against a proper sword, it wasn't so much. The thrall tried to stab Grus again. This time, Grus knocked the knife flying. The thrall threw himself at the king bare-handed.

Grus' sword stroke almost separated the man's head from his shoulders. He cursed himself a moment later; he might have been able to wring answers from the would-be assassin. He'd get no answers now. Blood gouted from the thrall. He staggered, still glaring furiously at Grus, and then slowly crumpled to the floor.

Estrilda came out of the little pantry where she'd fled. Her face was white as milk. She looked at the twitching, bleeding corpse and gulped. She seldom got reminded of the sorts of things Grus had done for a living before he donned the crown.

"Are you all right?" he asked.

His wife nodded. "He didn't get a chance to do anything to me," she said, her voice shaky.

Stooping, Grus wiped the sword on the dead thrall's shirt, and jammed it back into the scabbard. Then he went over and took Estrilda in his arms. She clutched him, started to pull away as she remembered she was angry at him, and then seemed to decide this wasn't the right time for that and clutched him after all.

More servants came running up in the wake of the one who'd followed Grus. So did royal bodyguards. Grus jerked a thumb at the thrall's body. "Get that carrion out of here and clean up this mess," he said. "And, by the gods, make sure King Lanius and the rest of my family are all right."

People started leaving as fast as they'd come, and bumped into others coming to see what was happening after it had already happened. Estrilda pointed to a pair of guards. "You men stay," she said. "More of these devils may be loose."

She was right. Grus knew as much. So did the bowing bodyguards. "Yes, Your Majesty," they chorused.

When Grus started to put an arm around his wife again, she did slip away. Her eyes stayed on the dead thrall as a servant dragged the body out by the feet. "You should have let him kill me," she murmured.

"What?" Grus wasn't sure he'd heard right. "What are you talking about?" Before Estrilda could answer, more guards clattered up, their chain-mail shirts jingling. Grus said, "You men—go to the thralls' chamber. You know where that is?" They nodded. "Good," he told them. "See how many are left there, and don't let any more out no matter what." They hurried away. He turned back to Estrilda. "Now what nonsense were you spouting?"

"It isn't nonsense. You should have let him kill me," Estrilda said. "Then you could call your witch back here, and you'd be happy."

Grus stared at her. "Has anyone ever told you you were an idiot?" he asked, his voice harsh. Numbly, she shook her head. He said, "Well, everybody missed a perfect chance, then, because you are. By the gods, Estrilda, I love you. I always have."

"Even when you were with Alca?" she demanded.

"Yes, curse it," Grus said, more or less truthfully. "I never stopped loving you. It was just . . . she was there, and we were working together, and . . ." He shrugged. "One of those things."

Perhaps luckily, a bodyguard chose that moment to announce, "King Lanius is safe, Your Majesty. A thrall *did* come after him, but he got away when he flung a moncat in the son of a whore's face."

"Did he?" Grus said, blinking. "Well, good for him. That's quick thinking." Another guard came in to report that only two thralls were missing, while the rest seemed as passive and animal-like as ever. Grus nodded. "Glad to hear it." But he also had other things on his mind. He turned back to Estrilda. "Will you listen to me, please?"

"It's hard to listen to what you say when I know what you did," she answered. "But I just saw you save me, and so . . ." She gnawed at the inside of her lower lip. "I don't know what to think anymore."

"You know I'm not perfect," Grus said. "But I do try. Could you . . . try to think I'm . . . not quite so bad?" He'd wanted to come out with something ringing. That wasn't it. He had to hope it would do.

Estrilda wasn't looking at him. She was still eyeing the pool and trail of blood the thrall had left behind. Slowly—very slowly—she nodded. "I'll try."

Together, Lanius and Grus eyed the door to the palace chamber that had held the thralls—that still did hold all but two of them. The door was now closed, the bar on the outside back in place. The thralls in there couldn't get outside. Of course, the two murderous thralls who had been in there shouldn't have been able to get outside, either. They shouldn't have been able to, but they had.

Lanius eyed the guards who'd stood in front of the door when the thralls escaped. The guards looked back, a sort of wooden embarrassment on their faces. "But couldn't you hear the bar was coming out of the bracket?" Lanius asked them.

In identical rhythms, they shook their heads. "No, Your Majesty," one of them said.

"Everything looked fine to us," the other added.

"You didn't notice the two thralls sneaking past you?" Grus demanded.

The royal bodyguards shook their heads. "No, Your Majesty," one said.

"We didn't see anything funny," the other agreed.

"I believe them," Lanius said.

"So do I, worse luck," Grus said. Now he shook *his* head, in the manner of a man disgusted with himself. "This whole sorry mess is my fault."

"*Your* fault?" Lanius said in surprise. "How?"

"I should have had a wizard keeping guard on the thralls all the time," Grus answered. "I should have, but I didn't. After Alca . . . left the capital, I just let that go. I didn't have a wizard I particularly trusted—I still don't—and the thralls seemed harmless, so I thought a couple of ordinary soldiers and a door barred on the outside would keep them out of mischief. I turned out to be wrong."

"Underestimating the Banished One doesn't pay." Lanius snapped his fingers.

"What is it?" Grus asked.

"Later." Lanius nodded toward the guards, as though to say, *Not in front of them*. Their wooden expressions never changed. After a moment, he realized terror lay beneath that woodenness. They had to wonder if they would lose their heads for almost letting the two Kings of Avornis be murdered. Lanius nodded toward them again. "It's not their fault. They were ensorcelled."

He waited to see if Grus would hold a grudge. Grus didn't usually, but he didn't usually have a narrow escape from assassination, either. Lanius knew a certain amount of relief when Grus said, "Yes, I know that. The Banished One has a cursed long reach, and we can't always hope to out-guess him." The guards showed their relief, mute but very obvious. Grus went on, "Sometimes I wonder if we can ever hope to outguess him."

"So do I," Lanius said, as fervently as though he were praying in a temple. He wished the comparison weren't so apt.

A messenger hurried up the corridor, calling, "Your Majesty! Your Majesty!"

"Yes?" Lanius and Grus spoke together.

Lanius wondered why he bothered. The messenger, inevitably, wanted to talk to Grus. "Your Majesty, the treasury minister reminds you that you were supposed to meet with him more than an hour ago."

The treasury minister wouldn't let a little thing like an assassination attempt interrupt his schedule. "Tell Petrosus—" Grus began, but then caught himself. "Tell Petrosus I'll be with him soon. The quicker we get back to normal, the better." He nodded to Lanius. "Isn't that right, Your Majesty?"

"Well, yes, but—"

Grus didn't let him finish. "Glad you agree. I'll see you in a bit. Meanwhile, I'd better go find out what's in Petrosus' beady little mind. So if you'll excuse me . . ." He started after the messenger.

"But there was something I needed to tell you," Lanius said. "Something important."

"I'm sure it will keep," Grus said over his shoulder, by which he couldn't mean anything but, *I'm sure that, whatever you have to tell me, it can't possibly be important.*

Before Lanius could shout at Grus and tell him what a blockhead he was, the other king was around the corner and gone. Lanius muttered under his breath. Then he cursed out loud, which did him no more good than the other had. He almost followed Grus. What point, though? Grus wouldn't listen to him now. The palace servants would. He set them to rounding up the moncats that had gotten out of their room after the thrall opened the door.

Later that day, Sosia said, "King Olor be praised you're all right. You and Father both, I mean."

Even her relief was enough to stab at Lanius, almost as though it were the knife the thrall had tried to use against him. "King Olor be praised indeed," he said, and wondered when he'd been so sarcastic before. He couldn't think of a time.

He was glad Sosia didn't notice. She said, "Father's had a lot happen to him lately."

"So he has." But Lanius couldn't help adding, "He did some of it to himself, you know."

Sosia didn't argue. "Of course he did. But not today, not unless you're going to blame him for bringing those thralls north so he could study them."

Grus had already blamed himself for that. But Lanius said, "I'll never blame anybody for trying to learn things. I do wish he'd listened to me when I tried to tell him that—"

But Sosia suddenly wasn't listening to him anymore, either. Crex came in crying and limping on a scraped knee. That had to be washed off—which produced more wails and tears—and he had to be cuddled by both Sosia and Lanius. By the time Crex decided he might possibly be all right after all, the servants were bringing in supper. Lanius drank more wine with the food than he usually did. He went to bed not long after supper and slept like a log—except that logs don't usually wake up the next morning with a headache.

Grus reached for the carafe. "Here," he said to Estrilda. "Let me pour you some more wine."

She pushed her goblet across the table toward him. "Thanks," she said. "Tonight I can use it."

He filled the goblet for her, and poured more for himself, too. As they both sipped, he said, "I should think so." He'd seen a lot of fighting. Nobody had ever tried to kill Estrilda before, even if she'd been an afterthought to the thrall.

She set down the goblet. "Did I say thank you?" she asked.

"You have now." Grus shrugged. "You didn't need to."

"I think I did. I . . . may have been harder on you lately than I should have been."

"It's all right." Grus shrugged again. "I can't say you didn't have your reasons. I can't say I didn't give them to you, either."

"You could have just let . . . whatever was going to happen there, happen." Estrilda took a long pull at the wine. "Then you wouldn't have had to worry about this mess anymore."

"You said that earlier," Grus said. Estrilda nodded. He went on, "I don't think you've ever said anything that made me angrier. It's a sorry business when I have to kill somebody to show you I love you, that's all *I've* got to say."

"Yes." His wife nodded. "It is a sorry business, isn't it?"

Grus started to answer that, then suddenly realized odds were he'd be better off keeping his mouth shut. Since it was already open, he couldn't very well do that. He could pour more wine down his throat—he could, and he did. His cheeks and ears started feeling numb. He wondered just how much wine he'd drunk. Enough, evidently.

Estrilda reached for her goblet, missed, laughed much too loud, and at last succeeded in capturing it. "I'm going to wish I was dead tomorrow morning," she said, "but I don't care right now. I'm going to keep on drinking, because I'm not dead."

"No, and I'm glad you're not," Grus said.

"So am I." She yawned. "I may not be dead, but I *am* sleepy." None too steadily, she got to her feet. "I'm going to bed."

"Wait. I'll come with you." The room spun a little as Grus got up. He thought his walk back to the royal bedchamber was fine, if a little slow. By the way she giggled, Estrilda didn't. Grus thought her swaying strides pretty funny, too, but he didn't giggle. He felt proud of his own restraint.

"Do you need anything, Your Majesties?" a servant asked. Grus shook his head, which made the room spin more. The servant left, closing the door behind him. Grus undressed and got under the covers; even inside the palace, the night was cold. Estrilda got into bed with him. They'd been sleeping in the same bed all along. Usually, since finding out about Alca, she'd built a barricade of pillows to make sure sleeping was the only thing they did together.

Tonight, she didn't. Grus noticed that, but he just lay there, waiting to see what she would do or say. Pushing too hard too soon could only be a mistake. "Good night," he said, and blew out the lamp.

"Good night," Estrilda answered as night swallowed the room. Grus shifted a little. He felt Estrilda shifting, too.

Their knees bumped. It was the first time they'd touched in bed since she found out. Grus said, "Sorry."

"It's all right." His wife shook her head, making the mattress sway a little on the leather lashings that supported it. "No. It's not all right. But I thought it was the end of the world, and it's not that, either. There are pieces left. Maybe we *can* put some of them back together again."

"I hope so," Grus said. "I—" The words wouldn't come. He reached for her instead, there in the darkness. If she pushed him away . . . If she did, she did, that was all.

She didn't. She reached for him, too. "I'm not going to tell you no tonight," she said, "not after . . ." She checked herself. "I'm not going to tell you no."

He caressed her. He knew what pleased her. He'd had years and years to find out. It wasn't the way it had been with Alca, where he'd learned something new every time. Now he shook his head. If she'd try not to be angry tonight, he'd try not to think of Alca. That seemed only fair.

Then, a little later, he wondered if he could do what he wanted to do. He wished he hadn't had so much wine. But he managed. By the way Estrilda quivered beneath him, he managed more than well enough. He gave her a kiss as he slid from on her to beside her. "Good night," he muttered, spent.

"Good night," she answered. He wasn't sure he even heard her. Already he slid into sleep as deep and dark as the blackness filling the bedroom.

Lanius needed a way to get Grus' attention. He didn't like the one he found, but that didn't mean it wouldn't work. With a resigned mental sigh, he said, "Your Majesty?"

Grus always noticed when Lanius admitted he too was King of Avornis, not least because Lanius did it so seldom. "Yes, Your Majesty?"

"We need to talk for a few minutes," Lanius said. "It's important. Seeing what happened yesterday, I think it's very important."

That got through. Grus nodded. "Say what you have to say. I promise I'll listen."

"Let's go someplace quiet, where we can talk by ourselves." Lanius' gaze flicked toward the servants bustling along the corridor.

"Whatever this is, you're serious about it," Grus remarked. Now Lanius nodded. Grus asked, "Is this—whatever it is—is it what you've already started to tell me a couple of times?"

"Yes," Lanius said. "I had to put it off then. After yesterday, I can't put it off anymore."

"All right, Your Majesty." Grus did do him the courtesy of taking him seriously. "Let's go somewhere and talk."

A couple of maidservants were gossiping in the first room whose door the kings opened. The women stared in astonishment. Now they would have something new to gossip about. The next room the kings tried had shelves piled high with bed linen, and only a little space in which to stand while putting things on those shelves or taking them down.

"Will this do?" Lanius asked doubtfully.

"Nobody will bother us in here, that's for sure," his father-in-law answered. "Go on, shut the door." After Lanius had, Grus asked, "Well, what's on your mind?"

"Have you ever heard the name . . . Milvago?" Lanius asked. He'd never said the name aloud before, and looked around nervously as he did. Someone—*something*—might be listening.

To Grus, it was only a name, and an unfamiliar one. "Can't say I have," he replied, indifferent. "Sounds like it ought to be Avornan, but I wouldn't want to guess past that. You're the one who's talking, so tell me about this Milvago."

"I can't tell you much," Lanius said. "I don't know much. Most of what was written has been dust and ashes for hundreds of years, and the priests have made sure all the ceremonies are different nowadays. They tried to get rid of all the records, too, but they couldn't quite manage it. They're only human, after all. Even the peasants have forgotten him, and peasants can have longer memories than anybody."

"Who is he? Or should I say, who was he?" Grus asked. "You're the one who knows history, so I expect you can tell me. Some long-ago heretic? Sounds like it, by the way you talk."

"You might say so." Lanius knew his voice sounded strange. "Yes, you just might say so."

"All right. Fair enough," Grus said. "But please don't get angry at me, Your Majesty, when I ask you why I need to know any of this."

"I won't get angry," Lanius said. "It's a reasonable question. And the answer is, we still hear about him today. The only difference is, we call him the Banished One."

That got Grus' full and complete attention. Lanius had been sure it would. The older man leaned toward him, intent as a hunter on his prey. "Milvago was . . . what? The name he had before he was cast down from the heavens?"

"Yes." Lanius nodded. "The name he had when he was a god. I found it on an ancient parchment in the ecclesiastical archives under the cathedral."

"The name he had when he was a god," Grus echoed. "Do you have any idea how strange that sounds?"

"Believe me, Your Majesty, it sounds at least as strange to me as it does to you," Lanius replied. "I haven't said anything about this to anyone, not till now."

Twice in the space of a few minutes, he'd used Grus' royal title. It had been months, maybe years, since the last two times he'd used it. And Grus noticed. Lanius could see as much. But the other King of Avornis didn't mention it. Instead, he asked the right question. Lanius had noticed his gift for that. "Well," Grus said, "if this Milvago was a god once upon a time, what was he the god *of*? Bad weather, maybe? Or just bad temper generally?"

Those were good, quick, reasonable guesses. Lanius wished with all his heart one of them was right. But he answered with the truth—what he was convinced was the truth—he'd found far under the cathedral. He gave that truth in one word—"Everything."

"What do you mean?" Grus asked. "What was he the god of?"

"Everything," Lanius repeated miserably. "As best I can tell, he was the chief god in the heavens, the god from whom Olor and Quelea and the rest sprang long, long ago."

"You're joking."

"By the gods" —Lanius laughed, though it was anything but funny— "I am not."

"What did they do?" Grus demanded. "Turn on him and cast him down, the way nasty sons will turn on a rich father when they're too impatient to wait for him to die?"

Now he was the one who sounded as though he was joking. But Lanius nodded, saying, "Yes, I believe that's exactly what they did, though Milvago may have been the nasty one. The way he's behaved here on earth would make you think so, anyhow."

Grus' eyes were wide and staring. "And we have to stand against a god like that?"

"We don't *have* to do anything," Lanius answered. "If you don't believe we still have free will, what's the point to anything?"

But the details of philosophical discussion had never interested Grus. He waved Lanius' words away. "How are we supposed to fight against the god who made the ground we're walking on? *How*, by the—" He broke off. Lanius understood that. Why swear by the gods when you were talking of the one who'd sired them?

But, in literal terms, Grus' question had an answer, or Lanius hoped it did. "How? The same way we've been fighting him ever since he was cast down from the heavens. Even if he was all-powerful once upon a time, he isn't anymore. If he were, he couldn't very well have been cast down from the heavens in the first place, could he? And as for creating the world, who knows whether Milvago did that or not? What happened to *his* father, if he had one?"

He waited to see how Grus would take that. He'd always respected his father-in-law's resourcefulness; without it, Grus never would have won his share of the crown. For the moment, it seemed to have abandoned the older man. Lanius didn't suppose he could blame Grus. He himself had had a while to work through, to work past, his shattering discovery. The other king was trying to take it in all at once.

"Don't tell anybody else," Grus said suddenly.

"What?" Lanius asked, taken aback.

"Whatever you do, don't tell anybody else," Grus repeated. "Do you want Avornans worshiping the Banished One, the way the Menteshe do? Some of them would."

He was bound to be right. Lanius hadn't thought of that. Maybe Grus' resourcefulness hadn't deserted him after all. Lanius said, "I haven't even told Sosia or Anser."

"Good," Grus said. "Don't. By Olor's——" He broke off again, shaking his head like a man bedeviled by gnats. "I half wish you hadn't told me. Maybe more than half."

"How do you think *I* felt when I found out?" Lanius exclaimed. "There I was, down in the deepest level of the archives, all alone with a secret no one but the Banished One has known for . . . for a very long time." His sense of chronology, usually so sharp, deserted him.

Grus set a hand on his shoulder. He seldom cared to have anyone but Sosia or his children touch him, but the warmth and solid weight of Grus' hand felt oddly reassuring. Grus said, "We just have to go on, that's all. We've always known he was stronger than we are. If he's . . . even stronger than we thought, what difference does that make, really?"

We just have to go on. That was easy to say, harder to do. "If we had the Scepter of Mercy . . ." Lanius said.

"Yes. If," Grus said.

"The Banished One—Milvago—wants to make sure that we don't have it, that we can't use it." Lanius looked south, in the direction of Yozgat. "So we really have to get it back, don't we?" Grus nodded.